THE
AWAKENED
CITY

ALSO BY VICTORIA STRAUSS

The Burning Land
The Arm of the Stone
The Garden of the Stone

VICTORIA STRAUSS

THE
AWAKENED
CITY

An Imprint of HarperCollins*Publishers*

FIRST EDITION

Eos is a federally registered trademark of HarperCollins Publishers.

Designed by Renato Stanisic
Map by Michael Capobianco

Printed on acid-free paper

Library of Congress Cataloging-in-Publication Data has been applied for.

ISBN-13: 978-0-380-97892-2
ISBN-10: 0-380-97892-X

06 07 08 09 10 JTC/RRD 10 9 8 7 6 5 4 3 2 1

Arsacian Pronunciation

"X" is pronounced "sh"—as in Axane (Ah-SHANE); Caryax (Car-YASH); *Darxasa* (Dar-sha-SA); Santaxma (San-tash-MA).

"iy" is pronounced "y"—as in Vivaniya (Vi-van-YA); Athiya (Ath-YA).

The stress in proper names is generally placed on the last syllable—as in Diasarta (Di-a-sar-TA); Baushpar (Baush-PAR); Sundit (Sun-DIT); Ardashir (Ar-da-SHIR)—except . . .

. . . A circumflex (^) indicates a long "a" sound (as in "father") where stress is placed on that syllable—as in Ârata (AH-ra-ta); Râvar (RAH-var); Ninyâser (Nin-YAH-ser); Dracâriya (Dra-CAHR-ya).

GALEA

The Doctrine of Baushpar

We the Brethren, incarnate Sons and Daughters of the First Messenger of Ârata, leaders of the Âratist faith and guardians of the Way of Ârata, do promulgate these seven principles, which we hold and assert to be the true wisdom of the church:

1. That the capacity for shaping is the gift of Ârata, a reflection of his own power of creation, and therefore divine and precious.
2. That the use of shaping is governed by human will in service to human desire, and therefore fallible and dangerous.
3. That because it is divine and precious, shaping must be honored; that because it is fallible and dangerous, shaping must be guarded.
4. That men and women who have vowed the Way of Ârata, having sworn their lives to Ârata's service and renounced in his name the failings of doubt, ignorance, greed, complacency, pride, and fear, are of all human beings best suited to accomplish both these tasks; and that all shaping, therefore, shall be gathered within the church.
5. That of all uses of shaping, the most proper is the glory and remembrance of Ârata through ceremony and observance.
6. That no practitioner of shaping shall employ it otherwise, lest any come to follow the dark ambition that has lately brought such a plague of death and misery upon Galea.
7. That no practitioner of shaping shall own more power than any other, that there may not come to be rivalry and contention between them; and that this equality shall be accomplished through use of the drug manita.

Thus the god's gift will be employed fittingly and by those fit to its employment, and the conflicts lately ended will never come again.

To this promise we the Brethren set our hands, in the holy city of Baushpar, in the land of Arsace, on the continent of Galea, in this ninety-second year of the second century Post Emergence.

Prologue
The Brethren's Covenant

(A night-story told by Brethren foster parents to their spirit-wards)

Tonight, little one, I will tell you one of the most wondrous tales I know—of how the thirty sons and five daughters of the First Messenger, by Ârata's favor, became the Brethren. It's a tale of the past, for twelve centuries have gone by since that time. It's a tale of the present, for those thirty-five souls are still alive upon the earth. And it is your tale—for it is the story of how you claimed your birthright, and became immortal.

Long ago, so long there are no words for the years that have fled since then, the god Ârata fashioned our world and everything in it out of his own bright substance—Ârata, as tall as the sky, with skin the color of the hottest flame and hair and eyes like new-minted gold. For eons he ruled unchallenged over his creation. All was perfection in that time, the primal age. But Ârata's dark brother Ârdaxcasa coveted Ârata's light-filled world, and on a storm of shadows came to seize it for himself. The gods fought—long they fought, and terribly, till the lands were stripped of life and sank beneath the seas. At last only our own great continent of Galea remained. There, in the southern desert called the Burning Land, Ârata vanquished his Enemy in a cataclysm of holy fire and, grievously wounded, lay down inside the earth to sleep. His golden Blood poured out around him, alight with his divinity. If you had been able to see him, little one, it would have seemed to you he lay within a lake of flame.

As Ârata fell into unconsciousness, the communion between his great mind and the small minds he had created was severed. Our world was abandoned to the emptiness of the cosmos. Time began its cruel flow, and death came into being. This is why we speak of Ârata's slumber as the Age of Exile.

Now, in the violence of Ârdaxcasa's destruction, his flesh was turned to ash and every living creature breathed a portion of it in. The Enemy's cold dark nature took root in us, beside the warm bright nature Ârata had given us. Thus evil was born into the world. From that moment, all was war—each man within himself, every man with every other, the very earth wracked with storm and quake, plague and drought and every kind of ill. At last the chaos grew so terrible that Ârata could no longer rest. In a dream, he summoned to the Burning Land a man named Marduspida, to whom he gave three things: a teaching called the Way of Ârata, with Five Foundations of thought and practice to govern humankind during the time of the god's slumber; a Promise, that one day he would rise to cleanse his Enemy's darkness from the world and usher in a new primal age; and a Sign, a single drop of his fiery Blood, rendered hard as crystal by the passing of the ages. Thus his Messenger would be known.

Marduspida, the First Messenger, returned to Arsace. He wrote down all of Ârata's words in the holy book called *Darxasa*, and set out to bring its wisdom to Galea. We, his thirty sons and five daughters, became his first disciples. Those were years of trial, little one. There were many more kingdoms then than the seven we know now, and in most of them Ârata had been forgotten. The people turned from the teachings of the Way, the cities cast us out with stones and curses—even, sometimes, at the points of swords. But they were also years of joy, as we seeded Ârata's word across the lands, and humbled Ârata's Aspects that had come to be worshiped as separate gods, and founded monasteries and temples in Ârata's name.

The time came when our father, who had not been a young man when he received the god's call, could no longer travel. He retired to Baushpar, the city gifted to our faith by King Fârat of Arsace. Our holy city was not grand then, as it is today. The streets were narrow and the dwellings small; the First Temple of Ârata was not yet complete and as for the Evening City, our beautiful palace with its many rooms and corridors and courts and halls, it had not even been dreamed of. Our father lived in an ordinary house, with an ordinary garden. If you try, little one, you may remember it, for we sons and daughters often visited him there.

At last our father's final illness came upon him. He summoned his children to his side—some of us near, overseeing the rebuilding of Baushpar, others distant, traveling and teaching in far lands. When we were all assembled, he kissed us farewell, each in the order of his or her birth. Then he took from around his neck the great necklace that had been made to hold the crystal of Ârata's Blood, which had not left his body in the thirty years since his emergence from the Burning Land. And he said:

Two things I bequeath to you, my sons and daughters. They are all in the world I have to give, yet no man ever gave so much. The first is this holy Sign, this Blood by which Ârata marked me as his Messenger. It will mark you as my inheritors. The second is the fearful hope, the terrible duty, that Ârata laid upon me: to spread his word and his truth through all the kingdoms of Galea. With my dying breath I charge you—forever and for all your lives, guard his Way. Teach his Promise. Proclaim the certainty of his return.

He spoke no more, and soon after died. We buried him in his garden, as he had wished. Then we gathered to discuss how we might honor his bequests. At once, little one, we were presented with a difficulty. No one can say when Ârata will return—and though the Way must go on for long and long, we human creatures go on for only a little while. How then could we do as our father asked? How could we guard the Way, and teach the Promise, and proclaim the certainty of the god's return, not just for all our lives but forever?

The purpose we Brethren follow makes us one, as if we shared a single heart. Yet we are also thirty-five separate souls, whose qualities and humors are as various as a handful of colored stones. As we often do, we fell into argument. Some proposed the creation of a priesthood, to guard the Way when all of us were gone. Others declared that we should pass leadership to our sons and daughters, as kings and princes do. Still others rejected every plan, but could suggest no scheme of their own. At last, when the dispute had eaten up a week of days, Utamnos rose to speak. He is the eldest and wisest of us all. It is his way to listen rather than to dispute. Till that moment, he had not said a word.

These arguments only circle the truth, he said. *Our father did not say to us "for all our lives and then forever" but "forever and for all our lives." It must be us, do you see, brothers and sisters? It must be we who guard forever.*

But how can we do that? cried Kudrâcari, whose temper it is to challenge all that others say, that they might find a way to say it better. *We are mortal. We cannot go on forever.*

Then, Utamnos replied, *we must ask Ârata to make us immortal.*

Can you imagine the amazement that came over us, little one? None of us had thought of it. Yet it was so clear, so simple.

How may we accomplish such a thing? asked Sundit, her practical mind turning, as ever, to the how and why of what must be done. *Ârata sleeps. How shall we make him hear us?*

We will fast and pray, said Baushtas, whose faith shines like a beacon on a mountaintop, so high and pure is it. *Our reverence will summon him.*

We'll sleep, said Artavâdhi, who is twin to Baushtas, her faith as perfect as his. *We'll entreat him in our dreams.*

A sleeper needs noise to rouse, objected Dâdar, whose impatience drives him always to seek the directest way. *We'll go to the Burning Land with drums and kanshas, and sing him awake.*

Vivaniya, ardent and impulsive, leaped to his feet. *Let us do all these things!* he cried. *We will raise such a storm of entreaty that Ârata cannot help but wake!*

What if we anger the god with so much noise? asked Hysanet, the youngest of us and the most gentle.

Do we know what it is we ask? This from Taxmârata, whose somber spirit turns always toward the darkest question. *The weight of mortal years is almost more than a man can bear. If Ârata grants our request, how will our souls endure the centuries?*

It is too presumptuous, Ariamnes declared. He is the most stubborn of us; his thoughts are like ironwood once they take root. *The god will never grant such a boon.*

Do you speak for Ârata, then, brother? laughed Martyas, who delights in piercing others with the needle of his wit. *Perhaps it's you we should entreat!*

Utamnos held up his hands for silence.

Ârata will hear us, he said. *We are our father's children. But there is a thing you've forgotten, brothers and sisters. In matters of entreaty, there must be exchange. If we ask, we must also give. What gift shall we give to Ârata? What shall we offer him?*

Well, little one, a perfect storm of discussion followed. Some suggested material gifts: images, inscriptions, houses of worship. Some suggested gifts of faith: new ceremonies, fresh hymns, special chants and catechisms. Some suggested gifts of soul: so many hearts brought to the Way, so many lands. *No*, Utamnos said to each as it was proposed. *No*. At last Kudrâcari grew angry.

Who are you to tell us No, and No, and No? she cried. *Is your knowledge greater than ours? If so, why do you keep us in ignorance?*

Here is what my heart tells me, sister, Utamnos replied. *These are gifts of doing. They are things accomplished in the world and thus born of the world. But the world is dark with ash. The gift we give to Ârata must have no ash in it. It must be wholly bright.*

Sundit said, *How can any gift be wholly bright, when we who give it are as stained as the world?*

There was silence, little one, for none of us knew how to answer. Then Utamnos said:

Though we do not know what our gift must be, let us offer it even so. If we are pure and free in this intent, the god will tell us what to do.

So we went apart, each of us to a place that he or she found holy, where

Ârata's bright nature seemed to speak most clearly through the world's veil of ash. For twelve days and nights we meditated, and fasted, and sang, according to our preference. On the thirteenth night the god walked into our dreams, high and terrible as a storm. He was all the colors of flame and gold. On his body gaped the thousand wounds inflicted by his Enemy.

I have heard your call, children of the First Messenger, he said in a voice like the ruin of mountains, like the draining of oceans. *I will grant your entreaty. Your souls shall not sleep with the passing of your mortal flesh, but will remain awake across the centuries, born always into new vessels. Thus will you guide my Way until I rise to cleanse the world and usher in the new primal age. In exchange for this boon I will accept the gift you offer, the bright gift that has no stain in it of my Enemy's ash.*

Great Ârata, we answered, trembling with the god's majesty. *Tell us what the gift shall be.*

And the god said: *When the time of cleansing comes, I shall not burn away your darkness, as I will for others, that their light may shine undimmed in the glory of the new primal age. Instead, whatever brightness remains in you I will take back into myself, who made you. Others will rise, but you will not—the end of the Age of Exile will also be your end. That is your gift, children of the First Messenger, if you choose to give it: your own light.*

Ah, little one, it was a fearful thing to hear. The boon we asked was great, and we had known that what Ârata demanded in return would be great as well. But none of us had imagined anything so great as this. To live forever in the Age of Exile, but never rise into the brilliance of the new primal age. To be immortal in the time of ash, and nothing in the time of light!

Of what came next, I will say only that just as there were those of us who were truly ready, and vowed the gift at once, there were those who struggled and denied. No names need be spoken; each remembers who he or she is. In the end, even the most fearful of us could not turn from duty—to Ârata, to his Way, to our father, the First Messenger. In the end, all gave freely what the god required.

Many weeks later, we gathered in our father's garden. Our bodies were weak with fasting and with trial. Yet already we could feel the change, the separation of our souls from our human shells, which had been indivisible before. We were no longer sons and daughters, but Sons and Daughters: the Brethren. Around our father's grave we joined hands, and swore a Covenant to Ârata and to each other—to guard his Way, to teach his Promise, to proclaim the certainty of his return, for all our lives and forever.

So we have done across the centuries since. So we will do across the centuries yet to come, until the day of Ârata's return. It is a long work, little one. We know now that it is true, what Taxmârata said at the first council: The years weigh heavy on a mortal soul. Even those of us who struggled with the gift no longer fear the giving of it. When the Next Messenger arrives to herald Ârata's awakening, we will be glad, at last, to sleep.

Part I

THE WAKING ROAD

The Messenger

He wore light—shimmering veils and coils of it, moving around him as he walked. It was not the natural radiance of his flesh, which only he could see, but illusion, shaped from the substance of the air. Beneath it he was as he had first come to them, naked but for a breechclout and the cloak of his long black hair. It was cold in the passage—the cold of rock, of deep subterranean places—and his body was tense with chill. A heavy golden chain lay around his neck. From it, cased in gold, hung an amber-colored crystal larger than a man's clenched fist, with a heart of flame.

The passage kinked. He could hear the crowd—a rushing sound that reminded him, briefly, of the hiss of wind across the meadows of his lost home. Ahead, a slash of brightness split the passage's black. He increased his pace, launching himself into the illumination as if into water.

Below, on the tumbled and stalagmited floor of a deep cavern, his faithful massed more than a thousand strong. To his Shaper senses they were not just a throng of men and women, but a roiling play of color and light, stippled here and there with the ordinary flame of torches. At the sight of him, they roared. He stood above them on the ledge he had made, his radiant arms spread wide, their adulation pouring like sunlight into the dark void at his center. He was warm now, warm as the heat patterns the torches printed on the substance of the air. He threw back his head and laughed.

"People!" he shouted. The natural acoustics of the cavern sent his voice pealing out above the clamor. "People of the Promise!"

"Fulfiller of the Promise!" they shouted back. "He who opens the way!"

"People of the new age!"

"Guardian of Interim, who speaks the word of the risen god!"

"People of Ârata!"

"Beloved of Ârata, who sets our feet upon the Waking Road!"

He was not certain when these phrases had become invariable. In the beginning, his calls and their responses had altered with each ceremony. But now the cadences were constant, as if they were part of a true religious rite, and not the basest and most final blasphemy.

He gathered himself and leaped outward into nothingness, focusing his will upon the air below his feet so that it grew slow and thick, allowing him to drift leaflike to the cavern's floor. Unlike the illusory brilliance in which he was clad, this was real shaping, accompanied by the flash and thunder all transformation made; but to his followers, who because of the strange proscriptions of this world had never witnessed unfettered shaping, his descent was not the exercise of a human power, but a miracle. He allowed his shimmering attire to billow as he fell, so they might glimpse his body; he knew that he was beautiful to both men and women, and that for many, faith was most urgent when it was bound to carnal longing.

He alighted gently on the broken rock. Before him, his followers were a scintillating wall—men and women and children, young and middle-aged and elderly, individuals and couples and even families. There were soldiers here, and blacksmiths, and seamstresses, and prostitutes; there were people who had given up their wealth to join him and people who had owned nothing to sacrifice. There were those who had passed all their lives in virtue and those who had followed the most violent of criminal pursuits. Yet in that place, in that moment, they were all alike, for they were all his creatures—stolen souls, every one of them, blackened past any point of cleansing with the blasphemy into which he had enticed them. The wonder and dread and desire in their faces seemed to flow from a single heart.

He stepped toward them. They parted like grass, those closest to him sinking to their knees. Slowly he walked among them, his hands held before him, palms out, so they could see the terrible scars the Blood of Ârata had inflicted when he brought it out of the Burning Land. They were allowed to touch his wounds if they dared, and many did, quick feather brushes of finger on finger, palm on palm—and occasionally a brief warm shock on ankle or hip or shoulder, as those driven by greater courage or greater need sought a more intimate contact. It had taken an act of will in the beginning to endure it, but over time it had become part of the larger thing he had learned to crave: their awe, their adoration, which for a little while filled up the emptiness in him where those same passions once had lived.

"Messenger," they sighed. "Beloved One. Most beautiful."

He made a single circuit of the cavern. Then he left them for the heights above, thickening the air before him to make a kind of invisible stairway he could climb. That was far more difficult than the trick he had performed to descend—beyond the capacity of most Shapers, in fact—but to his huge gift it was nothing. On the overhang again, he turned toward the faithful. They responded—not a roar this time, but a rumble, a mutter, which was somehow more powerful than the greater noise. He imagined he could feel it under his bare feet.

"People of the Promise."

"Beloved One." Many held up their palms, showing him the proof of their faith. "Child of Ârata."

"You who have gathered here in Ârata's name. You who have woken to the truth. You who in understanding have chosen me, and thus become my father's chosen. Look upon the sign my father has given, the sign of his rising, the sign of his will, the sign that his age-old promise soon will be fulfilled."

With his hands he swept aside the wreathing brilliance at his breast, revealing the great crystal in its setting of gold. Not one part of what he said to them was true: not what he claimed to be, not what he urged them to believe, not what he pledged for the time to come. But the crystal was real. He had taken it himself from the Cavern of the Blood, where Ârata had slept the eons away and now slept no more. Its realness was the reason he could lie.

"It is my task to bear this Blood, and my father's will, into a world that does not yet know me." The hugeness of the falsehood shook him, the completeness of the blasphemy. "It is your task also, you citizens of this holy community, this Awakened City. With me, you will open the way for Ârata's return, and bring an end to the Age of Exile."

"Ârata," they chanted. "Ârata who slept. Ârata who has risen. Ârata who will return."

"Abide now with me, in anticipation of the fulfillment of this sacred purpose. Abide in expectation of the sign that will reveal the predestined moment of our emergence. Abide in eagerness for the work that we will do when we march upon the lands beyond these mountains, and to their ignorance and corruption shout the truth we know—that Ârata has risen! That the time of cleansing is at hand, when all will be seared clean in the god's holy fires! That the primal age approaches, and soon will reign anew!"

"In faith we abide! In love we abide! In strength we abide!"

"I give you blessing now, in my name and in my father's name and in the name of the time to come. In my name, in my father's name, in the name of the time to come, I bid you go in light!"

He flung up his glowing arms. A flash, a pulse of sound, and from the air above the crowd burst a rain of gold. They shouted, jumping, shoving one another, snatching at the treasure. He had early realized the importance of providing them with items they could keep and hold, in counterpoint to the intangibles of faith; he gave them something with every ceremony, jewels or crystals or nuggets of precious metal. Many had substantial hoards of these trinkets, which they treated as holy talismans.

Fools, he thought, looking down at them. *I can say anything, and they will believe. I can order anything, and they will obey.* The familiar dark thrill of it ran through him, and he shuddered. With his shaping he controlled the elements, the very framework of reality. With his voice and his person, he commanded souls. Were those not the powers of a god?

He left them, passing once more into the pitchy darkness of the passage. He abandoned the illusion that clothed him, the gaudy trappings of the role he played, and strode through the mountain's heart with only the light of his own life to guide him, and, on his chest, the trembling fire of Ârata's Blood.

In his private domain, a succession of cave rooms that he had shaped and altered in very particular ways, he sought the third chamber, where a circular well was punched into the floor. He had shaped it full of water before the ceremony; now he caused the water's patterns to dance with heat, so that steam billowed toward the ceiling. He removed the chain that held the Blood and laid it on the floor—gently, for in spite of everything he could not quite break himself of the habit of reverence.

He unwound his breechclout and slid into the warmth, sighing. He lay with his eyes closed, his long hair coiling round him like a shadow-memory of the light he had worn. The last of the ceremony's exaltation slipped away, and the residue of his followers, all the hundreds of little touches they had pressed into his skin, leaving him clean, leaving him empty. The hush of his quarters settled around him—the quiet of the deep spaces inside the rock, and, behind it, a greater silence. He could speak or cough or roil the water, and the mountain's quiet would be banished. The other silence was beyond his power to break. The shouting of his followers filled it, but only briefly.

He remained in the water until the balance began to tip, the relief of his aloneness eclipsed by the discomfort of it. He hated being alone. In some ways it was the most difficult part of his charade, to be pulled always between his contempt for the creatures who surrounded him, whose adulation he had grown to crave but could not endure for long, and his horror of solitude. He climbed from his bath and walked dripping to his bedchamber, where he pulled on his clothes, clumsy with his ruined hands. He made as much noise as possible, but he could still sense the silence, waiting underneath.

It will be different soon, he told himself. An end to loneliness. It was a hope, not a certainty. In the old days, he would have prayed. These days he had only himself to rely on, and knew it had always been so, even when he had believed in a listening god.

He tightened his belt and stamped into his boots (nomad-made, their toes shod with silver), and left his quarters, to walk the blind inner spaces of the mountain and fill them with the light and tumult of his power, shattering the silence until he grew tired enough to sleep.

Sundit

Last night I had the dream again.

It began as it always does. I stood between a pair of gilded pillars. In my hands I held a wooden box, its cover closed. Behind me lay a vast dark courtyard; before me, a wide room pulsed with light, though there were no windows, and no lamps burned.

Inside, so far away I almost could not make out their faces, my Brothers and Sisters stood in their present bodies, gathered as if for council—all of them, even those who were reborn into Arsace during Caryaxist times and thus were lost to us. Near each, crowded close as if for comfort, a host of shadow-presences drifted: the many flesh-shells each of us has worn, the changing bodies that have ferried our undying souls across the centuries.

Only I, solitary between my pillars, was absent from that gathering. Only I had no huddled shadows to bind my present form to the blood and bone and sinew that first housed me. I felt small and lonely, unmoored upon the flow of time.

I remembered the box. I fell to my knees and removed the lid. Within lay a heap of beaten-metal discs: mirrors, twenty-nine of them, one for each of my incarnations. Each, when I lifted it and held it close, filled up with my face, but when I lowered it grew blank again. That made me angry. It seemed to me they should reflect me even when I was not before them. Were they not my mirrors? How dare they show me emptiness?

In rage I hurled the box aside. The mirrors spun into the light, flashing, so that for a moment I was blind. When my vision cleared, I saw that my spirit-siblings had turned toward me. Shoulder to shoulder they stood, ranged in the original order of their birth, their shadow-lives lined up behind them. There should have been a place for me, sixteenth in the succession of Marduspida's children. But they had left no gap, no space into which I might insert myself.

Terror seized me. For my shadows were absent and my mirrors were gone, and there was only this one self, this singular Sundit, to challenge them.

Then I was awake, sitting bolt upright in bed.

After a moment I rose and wrapped myself in my stole and went to stand at the window, whose screens I had left open to the chill spring air. It was nearly dawn; gray light filled the little garden in the court outside. I performed breathing exercises, seeking calm. But as sometimes happens the dream was slow to fade, and I was still by my window when the sun crested the tiled roofs of the Evening City and the bells of Baushpar began to ring for Communion services. How many times, I wonder, have I dreamed this dream? Someday I must go back through my journals and tally its recurrences. It seems to me that it has changed since it first came to me in childhood, though I cannot quite remember how.

Perhaps I shouldn't dwell so much on such personal matters, which rise not from my immortal soul but from its present shell of flesh (for my journals do not record this dream in any of my other incarnations). We are meant in these pages only to make a record of the actions of our lives, so that future incarnations may more easily regain the wisdom gathered in other bodies—to memorialize our debates and decisions, not our fears and fancies. Yet I believe that there is value in a fuller portrait. Our souls endure, but our bodies change, and the vessel shapes what it contains. Should I not set down the odd experiences, the rogue thoughts, the unsettling dreams, if only that my future selves may better distinguish what is immortal in them from what is merely body-nature?

Or perhaps it's symmetry that compelled me to start this account as I did. I began the day in dread, and in dread I end it.

Vivaniya dined with me tonight. I did not suggest it; he came to me of his own accord to ask if he might join me. I was pleased, thinking it another sign of Dâdar's loosening hold on him, another step in the campaign he seems to have been waging, since his return from the Burning Land, to mend the rift between us.

He was late, which irritated me. When he arrived he plumped down on his cushion with barely a word, and shoved food into his mouth as if he did not taste it—which irritated me more, since I had taken trouble with the ordering of the meal.

"Where are you, Vanyi?" I asked at last, sharply. "For plainly you are not here with me."

His eyes rose to mine, guilty. "I'm sorry. It's . . . I'm remembering yesterday."

"The council meeting," I said, imagining I understood. "We have all, I'm sure, been preoccupied with that."

He picked up his goblet, set it down again. "This so-called Next Messenger . . . it's obvious he is no ordinary heretic."

"To put it mildly. But we already suspected that, or we wouldn't have sent our agents to spy on him."

"One of whom chose to join him."

"Yes. Clearly he is convincing. And clever." This had struck me very forcefully in yesterday's council, as I listened with growing dismay to the remaining agent's report. "To claim that it was he who brought down Thuxra prison, as the act of destruction foretold in Ârata's Promise, with everything that cursed place meant—there's a kind of genius in that."

"If it is a lie."

I looked at him sharply. "Of course it's a lie. There can no longer be any doubt that he is an apostate Shaper, but no Shaper is that powerful. Even in the days when Shapers went untethered, there's no record of such an act. Thuxra City was destroyed by earthquake."

"Oh, Sunni, Sunni! I am a wretched sinner."

The despair in his voice shocked me. He turned away, pulling his body inward and clasping his hands between his knees—the same pose he used to adopt when he was a child and had something terrible to confess.

"Vanyi." Over the past months I've been careful not to press him; but tonight felt different. "I know things are not right with you. Do you think I haven't seen the change in you since you came back from the Burning Land? Something happened there, didn't it? Something you haven't spoken of. I may no longer be your guardian—we may not be close as we once were. But you can speak to me. You can tell me anything. You know that."

"I came here tonight to tell you. But it's hard."

I waited. I could hear the hissing of the lamp wicks. He sighed, rolled his shoulders.

"We did a terrible thing in the Burning Land." He did not look at me. "Dâdar and I."

Again, I thought I understood. "You mean what happened to the people of Refuge."

He began to shake his head, then changed his mind. "That, too. I dream about it, Sunni. The way the manita made them choke and weep and cough. The way the soldiers walked among them while they were helpless. Dâdar and

I were waiting at a distance, but we saw everything. Every arrow shot. Every sword thrust."

I felt the weight of it—an atrocity none of us intended, not even Kudrâcari and her supporters, for all their bitter hatred of Refuge's heresy. "You aren't to blame," I told him gently. "Your decision was forced by circumstance. You weren't to know that it would turn into a massacre."

"No?" Now he sounded angry. "Would it not have been a massacre, even if they had spared the children and the elders as we asked? Only their Shapers were supposed to die. We were to bring the rest of them back with us alive. I know . . . that the situation had changed. I know there was no other way to make sure of the Shapers, since we had no way to tell the Shapers from the rest. But I can't forget that they were human beings. Human beings. And we spoke a word, Dâdar and I, and on that word more than two hundred people perished."

"We are forced sometimes to do terrible things, in service of the charge our father gave us. It's one of the reasons for our Covenant. So that we may do what we must without fear."

It cannot be comfort. Nor should it be. But it is the truth.

"Yes," he said bitterly. "We whose souls will never feel the agony of Ârata's cleansing fires, and thus need not dread the darkness our actions bring upon us." He raised his swimming gaze to mine. "But Consciousness is the Fourth Foundation of the Way, Sunni. We must also live with what we do."

"It will fade, Vanyi. If not in this body, then in the next."

"Like all the other evil memories I've gathered in my lives, which mean no more to me now than dry words written in the pages of my journal. Perhaps that's why I cannot let this memory go. It stands for all the rest."

It surprised me. Not that he suffered, but that he considered his suffering. Vivaniya is ardent, impetuous, brimming with restless vigor, but he has never been reflective, and even less so in this incarnation than in many of the others.

He turned toward me, striking the table with his knee so that everything on it jumped and clattered. I used to hope he would outgrow his clumsiness, but he is as awkward as a man as he was as a child. "Do you ever think of the apostate Gyalo Amdo Samchen?" he asked. "About how different things might be, if we had never sent him into the Burning Land?"

"Sometimes. But we had to send him, Vanyi. We knew there were refugees in the Land. How could we not try to find them, to bring them home?"

"So much came of it. Not just . . . the massacre. We've always disagreed on the issues of our rule, we Brethren, but now we are in factions. And the rift between us and the King . . . and the King's blasphemy, his mining of the Burning Land . . ."

"You forget," I said with old bitterness. "The mines aren't blasphemous—we Brethren have decreed it so. Vanyi, what's the point of this? Why this dwelling on what cannot be changed?"

"There's something you don't know." He drew a breath.

"What do you mean?"

"When Dâdar and I came back from the Burning Land, we told the council that we found no Cavern of the Blood where Gyalo Amdo Samchen claimed it was. We said we conducted a thorough search to make sure it wasn't located elsewhere, or hidden through some Shaper trick. We said there was no question that Samchen had lied, that the cavern did not exist. Do you remember?"

"Of course I remember."

"Well—it wasn't so."

I felt a prickling of all my skin, as if some huge presence had slipped up behind me. "What are you telling me, Vanyi?"

"We didn't find the Cavern. That's true. But we didn't search. We knew the Shapers might have concealed it, but we agreed to accept the evidence of our senses and turn away without looking further."

I stared at him. I could not speak.

"As we drew near to Refuge, we saw a light rising above the cliffs at night. It was just as Samchen described—a great golden light, not like firelight, not like torchlight, not like any light I've ever seen. And yet I recognized it, Sunni, for it was the same light that burns inside the crystal of the Blood that hangs from our father's necklace."

"Vanyi. Vanyi, what are you saying?" He and Dâdar had spoken no word, last year, about a light.

"It was there the night we marched on Refuge. I saw it even through the smoke of battle, when their Shapers attacked us. But in the morning, when the battle was won and Dâdar and I went up into Refuge, the light was gone and there was no sign of anything that might have made it. Ah, Sunni, I'd dreaded finding the source of that light. I never wanted Samchen's story to be true. I never wanted to find Ârata's empty resting place in Refuge. When we reached the place Samchen had described and saw only a blank cliff, I was relieved. *Relieved.*

"Dâdar said it was the light that had been the trick, an illusion or distraction created to confuse us. The Shapers had fled along with the rest of Refuge, so of course the light was gone. Obviously, he said, there had never been an opening in the cliff. Part of me understood what he was doing—he wanted Samchen to be a liar even more than I did. But the rest of me . . . the rest of me wanted to believe him. So when he declared that we had seen all there was to be seen and need do no more, I agreed. Do you understand, Sunni? I closed my eyes to the truth I knew and embraced the truth I wanted. Because it was easier. And I was afraid."

I said nothing. Even now, hours later, I can scarcely say what it was I felt.

"So we came back, and told the council half the truth. We didn't mention the light—why speak of Shaper tricks? By that time, I understood what I'd done. But I was too cowardly to stand against Dâdar, or to confess myself a liar before you all. I salved my conscience by telling myself that we might have been right. That if we were, our lie didn't matter, because Ârata was still sleeping; and if we were wrong and he had risen, his Messenger would come, lie or no. But after yesterday—" He leaned toward me. "Sunni, I can't stop thinking about it. We don't know what's in those cliffs, not for certain. If Gyalo Amdo Samchen told the truth—if there really is a Cavern of the Blood—then this pretender with his miracles and his act of destruction and his fiery crystal that our agent swore on his life was the true Blood, he may be—he may really be—"

He caught his breath, unable to say it.

For a moment there was silence. I sat like a stone, my mind refusing the implications of what he had just told me.

"Sunni." His voice was quiet. "What shall I do?"

I swallowed. My mouth was like a desert. "You must tell the truth."

"Dâdar will deny it."

"You mustn't involve him. You must go directly to Taxmârata."

"Will you come with me?" he asked, like a child.

"Yes. Yes, I will come with you. We'll go tomorrow morning, as early as we may."

All his features seemed to tremble. "How you must despise me."

"No," I said, though I was not sure what I felt.

"I despise myself."

"Ah, Vanyi."

He pushed to his feet. He came round the table and sank to the floor in front of me and laid his cheek upon my knees, as he used to when he was a boy. For a moment I could not respond, my mind still caught in the awful thing he had told me. Then my love for him rose up, bruised and angry but impossible to resist. I've always loved him best, my first spirit-ward in my present incarnation, who came to me when he was three and I was twenty-two. I bent over him; I kissed his forehead, and stroked his shaven scalp.

At last he drew away, and rose.

"Tomorrow," he said. He was composed again. He looked drawn and weary, older than his thirty-one body-years.

"Tomorrow," I replied. "We'll make it right, Vanyi."

"You are the best of us, Sunni. I don't deserve your love."

He turned before I could answer and left the room.

I don't know how long I sat over the remains of our meal. At last I summoned Ha-tsun to clear the food, then went to look in on Utamnos. He woke at my step, disoriented and fearful, and I stayed until he slept again. How I miss him—Utamnos in his previous body, that is, my confidant, my friend. It is wrong, I know; the flesh-shell comes and goes, and we are not supposed to mourn it. When he is old enough in this shell, he will be my friend again.

I sought my own chambers. There I have been sitting since, thinking, like Vanyi, of the apostate Gyalo Amdo Samchen. It was for his piety that we chose him, five years ago, to go into the Burning Land in search of refugees from Caryaxist persecution. We knew they might have untethered Shapers among them—how else could they have survived the harshness of the sacred desert? But we thought that Gyalo, with his pure faith, his shining devotion to the Doctrine of Baushpar, would resist all temptation.

We were wrong. In the desert he cast aside his manita and broke his Shaper vows, using his shaping to call water from the earth. True, it was an unintended apostasy, born of the disaster that overtook the expedition, and he saved not just his own life but those of his companions. True, he voluntarily resumed the drug and the strictures of his vow on his return to Arsace—something only a handful of apostates have ever had the will to do. True, when he came before us he confessed the whole of his sin, sparing himself no condemnation. But apostasy is apostasy, and apostates, even unwilling ones, cannot be trusted. Even if he had not broken his vow, how could we have accepted his outlandish claim—that the people of Refuge, wandering deep into the Burning Land, had discovered Ârata's empty resting place, this so-called Cavern of the Blood? That Ârata had risen; that the Age of Exile was at an end and the time of the Next Messenger was at hand?

He did offer proof, of a sort: the testimony of Teispas and Diasarta, the two soldiers whose lives he saved; the word of a heretic of Refuge, a woman named Axane, who for reasons we did not entirely trust had chosen to return with him. And a crystal of the Blood—the true Blood, there was never any doubt—which he swore had been taken from the Cavern—where, he said, there were thousands of them, an ocean of them, as indeed there must be in the place where Ârata lay down to sleep. Some few of my spirit-siblings believed him utterly: Baushtas, Artavâdhi, Martyas. Others, Kudrâcari and what is now her faction (Vivaniya is right to name it so), were inflexibly certain that he lied. More—they claimed that because he had brought the Blood out of the Burning Land, as Ârata's Promise says the Next Messenger will do, he had come to believe himself the Messenger, embracing the same blasphemy as the people of Refuge, who, when he arrived among them out of the emptiness of the desert, mistook him for Ârata's herald.

I did not agree. I saw no sign that he believed himself the Messenger. Nor was I one of those who accepted the claims he did make. Even the Blood, which all our lore and scripture tells us exists nowhere but in Ârata's resting place and in our father's necklace, did not convince me. Yet it raised questions, that crystal, too many to be rejected out of hand. And there were other concerns: the need to cleanse the sacred Land of the taint of Refuge's heresy, the threat of Refuge's untethered Shapers, which even at such a distance we could not leave unaddressed. A second expedition was necessary—though had I been Blood Bearer, I would have found a way other than the one we took. I would not have chosen Dâdar to search for signs of Ârata's awakening. I would not have sought Santaxma's help—or if I had, I would not have paid the blasphemous price he demanded for his soldiers. I would never have granted him official sanction to mine the Burning Land, whose riches should be beyond the reach of human greed.

Maybe then the heretics would still be alive. Maybe Vivaniya would not have brought back a lie. Maybe I would not be sitting in my chambers, writing the word "heretic" by long habit, thinking as I shape the letters: What if I should call them something else?

Ah, there is a thought to chill the bones.

We desire the coming of the new primal age, we Brethren. Of course we do. But it means the end of us, the extinguishing of our souls. That is what Gyalo Amdo Samchen told us when he brought the Blood of Ârata out of the Burning Land: that we would end. That's the fear that lives in Vanyi's and Dâdar's lie. We all felt it, even Baushtas and Artavâdhi and Martyas, who believed. Even I, who waited judgment on my Brothers' return, could not deny my relief when they swore the Cavern of the Blood did not exist. Or earlier, when we learned that Gyalo Amdo Samchen had died in imprisonment at Faal . . .

Nothing is certain, I remind myself. As Vanyi said, we don't know what was really in those cliffs. Nor does it necessarily follow from anything he told me tonight that this pretender in the mountains is the true Next Messenger. It's as likely that he is precisely what we decided yesterday, on the evidence our agent gave us: a charlatan, a madman, an apostate Shaper with a cunningly crafted simulacrum.

But . . . nothing is certain. If he is what he claims . . . Ah, I can hardly write it. If he is, what might that mean for us, who turned away from word of Ârata's rising?

Gyalo

How much for a letter, scribe?"

Gyalo looked up from the box into which he was packing his writing materials. "A half karshana for each page for black ink on rough paper," he said, shading his eyes against the late-afternoon sun and the questioner's own lifelight. "A three-quarter if you want a fair copy. If you want colored ink or better paper, I've a stock for you to look at and we can agree on the extra price. For another half, I can see it goes into the temple's mail pouch."

"Does that mean it'll get to Yashri Province?"

"Yes. Or anywhere else in Galea."

"You're pricier than the others."

Gyalo shrugged. "Take it or leave it."

The young man stood a moment, irresolute. "All right," he said abruptly, and sat down on the stool Gyalo kept for customers, fumbling with the wallet on his belt. "There's four quarters." He held out the coins. "One page. No copy. And I want it delivered."

Gyalo put the coins away, then took what he needed from the box and prepared to write. "Just speak as you normally would," he said, when the boy remained silent.

"I'm thinking." The boy shifted on the stool. His coppery lifelight sprang energetically out around him, shading to yellow at its edges. A grubby bandage wrapped his left palm; he cradled that hand in the other, as if it pained him. "All right. Greetings to Mother and Ansi and Soris and— No, wait. Just write . . . just write 'Greetings to my family.'"

Gyalo made the change.

"I'm going away on pilgrimage—wait, don't say that. Just, I'm going away for a while. Ummm . . . I don't know when I can—when I will be back. But I'll be in good company, so you're not to worry. I'll send word when I can. Read that back, scribe."

Gyalo did.

"Ummm . . . This letter is for family, so when you've read it you must burn it. I'm not supposed—" He paused. "We aren't allowed—"

Again he stopped. Gyalo waited, pen poised above the paper. Faintly, from beyond the temple walls, the clamor of the city's streets rose up—the great voice of Ninyâser, which even at midnight was never still. Here in the forecourt it was quiet, with only the murmuring of the scribes and their customers, and the whisper-sound of devotee-priests and worshipers passing to and fro in cloth temple shoes, to stir the air.

The boy looked up. His face was set. "I've changed my mind. Tear it up."

"Are you sure?"

"It's my letter, scribe. Tear it up!"

Gyalo set his pen in its rest and tore the paper in half and in half again. The boy held out his uninjured hand.

"Give me the pieces."

Gyalo handed them over. "I want my money back," the boy said, stuffing the scraps into his wallet. "You wrote, so I figure you earned a quarter, but it wasn't a whole letter and now there's nothing to deliver. So I want a quarter and a half back."

"A page is a page, no matter how many lines are written on it." Gyalo opened his own wallet. "I'll give you back the half for delivery, but that's all."

The boy scowled, then snatched the coin. "You can't tell anyone I was here."

"Who would I tell?"

"It doesn't matter. You have to promise." The belligerence was gone. "Please, scribe. We aren't supposed to tell our families. I'll get in trouble if anyone finds out."

Gyalo shrugged. "Very well." Then, when the boy did not move: "Was there anything else?"

A sly expression had come across the boy's face. "Aren't you curious? About where I'm going?"

"I thought you weren't supposed to say." Gyalo tapped the ink from his pen back into the inkpot, and cleaned the nib on a rag.

"Only to families and friends and suchlike, if they're not coming with us. Our oath's like a knife, it cuts off our old lives, cuts 'em at the root. We can't walk free on the path of faith if we drag our loves and hates and desires after us." He was obviously reciting something that had been told to him. "But we can pass the word to strangers if they want to hear."

Gyalo put the cleaned pen with its fellows in the box, corked the inkpot, and stowed it in its slot. The nature of his business had changed over the past year; he had regular copying commissions now and could often work in comfort at home. But the small documents, the letters and wills and bills of sale, were still the foundation of his income, and at least three days a week he wheeled his cart to the temple of Inriku, Patron of learning and the arts, and took his place among the scribes and notaries who gathered daily under the portico of its forecourt. The people who used his services turned to the written word only in extremity; there was a tale, sometimes a terrible one, behind every document he produced, and they were often all too willing to confide it. It had been his duty to listen, when he was sworn to the Way of Ârata. But he was no longer a vowed Âratist.

"Well, I don't want to hear," he said, shutting the box and starting to close up his portable writing desk. "No offense."

"Not even if I told you"—the boy's voice dropped—"that I was going to meet the Next Messenger?"

The light of late afternoon seemed suddenly to dim. "The Next Messenger?"

"Yes!" The boy leaned eagerly forward. "Because he's come to open the way for Ârata's return, and he's calling all the faithful to his side!"

Gyalo drew a long breath. He latched the lid of his desk and folded his hands atop it, and said, quietly: "Tell me more."

A smile of triumph broke across the boy's face. "I'll tell you the whole story! I'm apprenticed to—well, never mind. A couple of days ago one of the other apprentices was talking about a conjurer he'd heard of. Some of us decided to go, but it turned out it wasn't a conjurer at all, but a holy man. The others got angry and left, but I figured since I'd come all that way I might as well listen for a while. I've heard holy men before, who hasn't? But this one—he had a way of talking. It *made* you listen. It *made* you believe. He said that Ârata had woken, and the Next Messenger had come. He said the fall of Thuxra City was the act of destruction that marks his coming, like it says in Ârata's Promise—"

"Thuxra was destroyed by an earthquake," Gyalo said sharply.

"No, no!" The boy shook his head, his long hair swinging. "That's just what everyone thought. It was the Next Messenger who did it. He stood before it and told it to fall, and down it came. It made a noise so loud it was like the earth itself opened up its mouth and shouted Ârata's name!"

Gyalo felt a heaviness in his chest. Till that moment he had held a slim hope that the boy had only encountered some god-crazed itinerant prophet. Even now, six years after the Caryaxists' defeat, there was no shortage of these. But the boy knew the truth about Thuxra. That made it certain.

Râvar.

"And then he said—the holy man said—that the Next Messenger was summoning the faithful, and anyone who believed could come to the city he had made, the Awakened City, and live in holiness. And it was like . . . like the world turned over underneath me! I don't remember getting up, I was just there, in front of him. He took my face into his hands and kissed me, and told me what I had to do. And that night I did it. I swore myself to the Messenger's service. There was—" He drew his bandaged hand a little closer against his body. "A ritual. Then they told me how to go to him in his stronghold."

"His stronghold? You know where he is?"

"I know how to get there." The boy grinned. "But if *you* want to know, scribe, you'll have to do the ritual. He's at the Red Lantern on Shiriya Street in the western quarter—the holy man, I mean. You'll know him by the scar on his neck, a prison-collar scar. He doesn't try to hide it." His expression grew dreamy. "They say the Messenger is beautiful, more beautiful than any human man. They say he's clothed in light. He made the place where we're going, made it with his power so the faithful could have shelter. They eat the food of the gods there, and every day the Messenger works a miracle."

Gyalo could not restrain himself. "There's nothing miraculous about it."

The boy drew back, affronted. "What do you know about it, scribe?"

"This is a fraud, boy. A cheat. A lie to blacken your soul."

"You don't know what you're talking about!"

"Listen to me." Gyalo willed into his voice the authority of the religious rank he had once held. "You've been deceived. This so-called Messenger is false. There's no holiness at the end of your journey, only suffering and blasphemy."

The boy surged to his feet, oversetting the stool, and spat on the worn flagstones beside him. "*That's* how much I care for what you think, scribe! You're just an ash-cursed unbeliever like all the rest. When I'm living in bliss in the new primal age, you'll still be roasting in Ârata's fires. And I hope you scream so much you tear your throat out!"

He wrenched around, and was gone in a blur of copper light.

For a moment Gyalo sat looking after him. He was aware of the regard of the nearby scribes and their customers, their interest drawn by the boy's raised voice. *Stupid*, he chided himself. Secure as he was in his new life, he still had the habits of a fugitive; he did not like to attract attention.

He returned to the task of packing up, loading his desk and other materials into his pushcart and binding a canvas cover over the whole. He maneuvered the cart across the uneven pavement toward the temple's entrance, where stood a bronze image of Inriku, holding the symbols of his patronage in his hands. The image was modeled in a contemporary style, no doubt to replace an original destroyed by the Caryaxists; its clean sharp contours did not quite fit the time-smoothed stones and columns of its home. Before it, separated by the requisite distance, a smaller image of Ârata Eon Sleeper reclined upon a plinth. This was Inriku's temple, but all who entered it must acknowledge that Inriku was only an Aspect of the greater god, dreamed into being during Ârata's long slumber. On all four sides of the plinth, the Five Foundations of the Way were written out, words that were recognizable even to those who could not read: Faith, Affirmation, Increase, Consciousness, Compassion.

On the temple's broad porch Gyalo paused to exchange his indoor shoes for a pair of high-soled sandals, then bumped his cart down the shallow steps and joined the procession of human and animal traffic. Shops and houses crowded on either side, their roofs tiled red and green and yellow, their fronts festooned with shuttered balconies. An unseasonable heat had settled on the city, and the air was summer-thick with stink: animals, cooking, sewage, the smoke of a thousand braziers. From all directions came the sound of temple bells, announcing evening services. These things Gyalo perceived with his ordinary senses. But he was a free Shaper, and so he also perceived what ordinary senses could not encompass: the gemlike light shed by all living things, the patterns of being and change that composed unliving objects, which a free Shaper could manipulate at will—though to do so openly would be to break ecclesiastical law, which for all intents and purposes was also civil law, and transform himself again into a fugitive.

He reached one of the many bridges that spanned the Year-Canal, the great water thoroughfare that split the city into northern and southern halves, and joined the slow line of traffic across it. On the Canal's south side the streets grew meaner, the buildings more ramshackle; if Gyalo continued on for half a mile he would come upon the Nines, a sprawling slum that clung to the city's southern flank. But the sections nearest the Canal possessed a kind of shabby gentility, and four months ago, on the strength of a new copying commission, he had rented a house on a small enclosed court, with a roof of green-glazed tiles and a tiny garden in back. He and Axane had worked for weeks, cleaning, replastering, painting. Like him, Axane had never lived in a house of her own. He still caught her, sometimes, looking around her as if she could not quite believe it; it made him smile, for he felt the same.

He pushed the cart across the ancient paving of the court, rounding the fountain that bubbled at its center (a rare amenity in that part of the city, and one of the reasons they had taken the house), nodding a greeting to his neighbors. He chained the cart beside the door, which he had painted green to match the roof, and carried his materials inside, leaving his sandals on the mat. The interior was simple—one room and a kitchen downstairs, a single long chamber upstairs where he had a desk, and he and Axane and the baby slept. As yet they owned only the meager furnishings from the apartment where they had lived before. But bare as it was, Gyalo was more content than in any of the finely appointed suites he had commanded in his monastic days, when he had had access to all the luxury of one who served the Brethren.

"I'm home," he called, and went into the kitchen, where Axane, enclosed in the astonishing emerald-sapphire of her lifelight, was slicing onions for the evening meal. She dropped her knife and turned toward him, smiling; he closed her into an embrace, her sea colors filling up his vision. When they were first reunited, he had not been able to stop touching her, as if her body were bound to his by the same force that pulls a dropped object inevitably to the ground; when she was not with him he had felt unbearably restrained, wanting always to fall toward her. They had been together for eight months (and married for all but one day of that time), and the urgency had eased. But there were still no moments in his life as sweet as these, when he held her in his arms.

She pulled away and returned to her preparations. "It'll be a little while, I'm afraid. I was called out this afternoon. It took longer than I expected."

"Was it bad?"

"A little girl bitten by a street dog. She needed stitching. Her father waited two days before he called for me, and it wasn't because he couldn't pay. It made me so angry I charged half again what I normally would have."

Gyalo smiled. When he had first met her, she had not understood the use of currency, for she had grown up in a place that did not employ it. But she had become as sharp with money as anyone he had ever known. "A paying customer. How unusual."

"They all pay, Gyalo, just not always in coin. I know you don't like me helping the poor ones. But the registered healers won't, and all they have is someone like me."

"It's you going down into the Nines that I don't like."

"I never go alone."

It was an old argument. Axane was fiercely devoted to her healing craft, which she had insisted on following into the eighth month of her pregnancy, and had taken up again only a few weeks after Chokyi's birth. She had been angered by the restrictions of Ninyâser's registration requirements, which, being who and what she was, she could not fulfill; but she had found a different mission in her service among the poor. Gyalo was aware that most men of his income and profession would not have permitted their wives to go out as she did, or tolerated the late suppers and dusty corners that resulted. But in the profoundly isolated community into which Axane had been born, everyone had worked, and it had not occurred to her that she should not be a healer in Arsace as well. In truth, Gyalo had as little experience of the world's convention as she. Between them they did what seemed right, rather than what was proper, and thus far it had worked out very well.

From her basket near the stove, Chokyi began to cry. "Would you see to her, love?" Axane said. "My hands are all over onions."

Gyalo went to lift the baby, warm and milky-smelling in her linen wrappings. She quieted at his touch. He carried her to the kitchen door, open against the heat of the room, and settled on the threshold. She gurgled at him, waving tiny fists.

"Little bird," he whispered. "Little bird."

She was not his child. She did not even have similar features, for both her father and Axane were of a different racial stock than he, round-eyed and dark-skinned where he was almond-eyed and pale. But from the beginning he had loved her completely—he, who had never thought to be a father or a husband. They had named her for his mother. Her lifelight, which like Axane's leaped flamelike around her body, was the color of apple jade.

He sat in the doorway, the dozing baby in his arms, as the soft spring twilight descended on the garden and Axane moved about the kitchen. Ordinarily he took deep pleasure in such moments of tranquil domesticity, the heart and essence of the new life he led. But he could not banish the young pilgrim from his mind, and below the peace of the evening the unease the encounter had woken in him stirred like an incipient sickness.

When the meal was ready he put Chokyi in her basket and carried her out to the low table in the other room, and lit the lamps and drew the shutters while Axane set out the food. They sat across from one another on cushions and talked of small things as they ate. All the while his thoughts kept returning to the boy. At last he said, across the end of one of Axane's sentences:

"A customer came to me today for a letter."

She stilled at once, perhaps hearing something in his voice, and listened without interrupting as he told her the boy's story. When he was finished she drew a long breath, and said: "Râvar." ❧

The name lingered on the air. They sat listening to its echoes. Chokyi slept on the floor, plump arms clasped atop her covers. Lamplight trembled on the walls, into whose plaster Gyalo had mixed a yellow tint so they would look sunlit even in shadow.

"How long has it been?" Axane said. "Since his missionaries were ordered out of Ninyâser?"

"Seven months at least."

"And now they're back."

"Or maybe they never left. Maybe they just went underground. Recruiting by word of mouth, rather than by public proselytizing."

It was hard to talk of that. Just after they were reunited, Axane had told Gyalo everything: how, after her escape from Baushpar, she had inserted herself among the camp followers of the Brethren's army so she might get across the Burning Land and warn her people, how she and Râvar escaped Refuge's destruction and the massacre that followed, how Râvar dragged her back across the desert, and, at the end of that harsh journey, brought down the walls of Thuxra City and declared himself Next Messenger before a throng of awestruck prisoners. She and Gyalo had speculated about where Râvar might be hiding, when he might emerge, how much of his planned vengeance he might accomplish—conjectures that contained no *ifs*, but only *whens*. But then Râvar's missionaries, who had begun openly preaching in Ninyâser several weeks before Axane arrived, were ejected by decree of the King. It had felt like a reprieve. For a little while it became possible to ignore the approaching darkness, to immerse themselves in the joys and challenges of their life as if there were no other future. Since the missionaries' departure, neither had spoken Râvar's name aloud.

Gyalo looked at his wife. She sat very still, her face calm, her eyes cast down, her hands folded neatly in her lap. To someone who did not know her, it might have seemed the pose of a quiet woman, at ease within her world, tranquil in her thoughts. But Gyalo did know her, knew the truth of her restless, fierce nature, which for much of her life she had kept hidden. He understood, therefore, that what he saw was not tranquillity, but concealment. It was when she was most still that she was least like herself.

"There's something I need to tell you."

"Ah," he said.

"I've begun dreaming again." Axane was a Dreamer, one whose mind was capable of traveling out across the world in sleep. In the late stages of her pregnancy her Dreams had ceased; he knew that without them she felt blind. This should, therefore, have been good news. But her manner told him it was not, and it seemed to him he had already heard her next words, even as she spoke them: "About Râvar."

It was inevitable, he told himself. *It had to happen.* "For how long?"

"Since just after Chokyi was born."

"What? You've been dreaming about him for four months and you never told me?"

She did not look at him. "I'm telling you now."

"Ârata's wounds, Axane! How many of these Dreams have you had?"

"Nine or ten, maybe. They take me to the place where he lives with his followers." She had begun to turn her rice bowl between her hands, around and around on the glossy surface of the table. "It's a cave, or rather a lot of caves, all interconnected. I think . . . there must be a thousand people living there. Maybe more."

"So many? Are you sure?"

"We knew he planned to build an army, didn't we?" She gave the bowl a savage twist. "It's very organized. There are living areas, places where they make things—clothing, furnishings, tools. There are food stores. It's like a little city."

"The Awakened City," Gyalo said, hearing the boy.

"What?"

"The Awakened City. That's what they call it. Can you tell where it is?"

She shook her head. "I've only seen the caves. Never what's outside them."

"Have you seen anything to tell you what he's planning?"

"I'm only there when people are asleep, Gyalo. I don't hear them talking. Even when I dream of . . . him, he's always alone." She shuddered, a tremor that ran through her from head to foot. "All I know is that there are a lot of them. And they keep coming."

Gyalo sat silent. *A thousand*, he thought. It did not surprise him, not at all. Yet it was one thing to suspect, another to know.

Axane said: "You're angry."

"No." But that was not exactly true. "Axane, you shouldn't have waited so long to tell me."

"I didn't want to worry you."

"*Worry* me? Axane—"

"Do you think I *want* to dream of him?" She pushed her bowl away, sharply, so that it skated across the table. "I'm bound to him by blood, by Chokyi's blood, and . . . and by Refuge—" She dragged in her breath. "As bound to him in a way as I am to you, for all he doesn't know it. You know what that means for me. Some of the time . . . some of the time I can fight it. I can make myself wake up. But I can't stop the dreaming, any more than I could not dream you when we were apart."

"I know that, Axane."

"What would have been the good of telling you? It's not as if it would have changed anything. I knew you'd hate it, I knew you'd just get angry, the way you are now. You think of him, I know you do—I see the way you look at Chokyi sometimes. As if . . . as if you were judging her."

Gyalo felt a stab of guilt, for he did sometimes look into Chokyi's face and search for her father there. "I don't judge her."

"No? She has his eyes! His skin! How can you look into her face and not see him? How can you not think of . . . of . . . of . . ."

"I *don't* think of that. Axane, I don't judge her, and I don't judge you. Why should I, when you judge yourself so harshly?" She drew in her breath, turned her face away. "You know that, just as you know I love Chokyi. As you know I love you."

"Oh, Gyalo." Her voice cracked. "I'm sorry."

"My love, I understand."

"I should have told you about the Dreams. But I didn't want to speak of him. I didn't want to say his name. I'm so happy, with you and Chokyi, but I feel . . . sometimes I feel I must be imagining it all, and any minute I'll look around and none of it will be true. I feel that if I stop paying attention, it'll all turn to smoke and blow away, and I'll be in the Burning Land again, with *him* . . ."

Gyalo pushed himself off his cushion and went to her. She clutched the fabric of his shirt and buried her face in his shoulder. "This is real," he said into her hair. "It can't vanish. Do you believe me?"

Against his shoulder, she nodded.

"No more secrets, Axane. Promise me. When you dream him, you must tell me. This is our burden, both of us together."

"I promise," she whispered.

He tightened his arms around her and closed his eyes against her light, breathing her in. If, when he was still a vowed Âratist, he had been asked whether he regretted renouncing a life like the one he now lived, he would in all honesty have said no. Though he had struggled sometimes with the celibacy his religious service required, he had never felt any great grief, as some of his colleagues did, to be barred from the secular comforts of marriage and family. But that was only because he had not understood. He still did not entirely comprehend how to live this new life of his, which often seemed like a complicated city whose streets he would never fully know, whose turns and junctions could not be anticipated, but only chosen, one by one, as he encountered them. Yet for every blind alley, for every wrong turning, there was this simple wonder: the weight of another's body, the cage of another's arms. Far more precious to him, perhaps, than to someone who had not discovered them so late.

"Do you think," he said softly after a time, "that he may actually have come to believe himself the Next Messenger?"

"No." He felt her voice against his chest. "To blaspheme against the god he rejected. To come as a counterfeit Messenger to Galea, as he thinks you came as a counterfeit Messenger to Refuge. To destroy the Brethren, as they destroyed our people. He must not just be false, but know himself as false. It won't be the proper revenge otherwise."

"It's such a huge deception. Surely at some point he will stumble. Give himself away."

"That's what I've been hoping. Arsace was strange to me when you first brought me here, but I was prepared, because I'd been dreaming it for so long. But all he knew was what I told him while we were traveling. At the end . . . he still spoke as if he thought everything beyond the Burning Land was a realm of demons."

"He cannot think that now."

"I wish I'd lied when he asked me all those questions. Misguided him. You know how I feel about the Brethren. If it were only them he meant to harm, I wouldn't care. But there's everyone else, all the people he's cheated into false belief, everyone who'll suffer when he emerges."

"You didn't know to lie. He never told you what he was planning."

"I could have stopped him, Gyalo. Bashed his head in with a rock while he slept. I thought of doing it, after . . ." She bit off the words. "I think I could have. I hated him enough. But then I would have died, too, all alone in the Burning Land without his shaping to make food and water for me. And I didn't want to die."

There was a painful savagery in her voice. Gyalo knew the shadow that lived in her: her grief for her father and for her people, her guilt for what she believed was her part in Refuge's destruction, her terrible shame and rage at the rape she had suffered at Râvar's hands. It had changed her. There was a hardness in her that had not been present when he first knew her. It was another of the things they never talked about. He could count on the fingers of one hand the number of times she had spoken of the matters they were discussing, or allowed him to speak of them.

"You didn't know," he said again. "Don't blame yourself for what can't be changed."

"But I don't want to change it, Gyalo! If I could go back to the beginning and do it all again, I wouldn't do any of it differently. Because then I wouldn't have you or the life we have together, here in this world where I don't have to hide what I am, where I don't have to pretend to believe in things I know aren't true. And do you know what that means, Gyalo? It means I wish my people dead. It means I wish my *father* dead."

"Oh, love," Gyalo said, stroking her hair. "Why do you torment yourself like this?"

She pulled away from him. "He can't succeed," she said. "Something will go wrong. He'll betray himself. Or maybe the King will act, once he emerges."

She did not sound as if she believed it.

Chokyi woke and began to cry. Axane lifted the baby from the basket and unfastened the pin at the shoulder of her dress so Chokyi could nurse. "There, little bird," she said. Her downturned face smoothed, grew intent. For a little while Gyalo watched, feeling the odd blend of tenderness and exclusion that always gripped him at such times. Then he got to his feet and fetched his box of writing implements from beside the door, and took a lamp from a side table and went upstairs.

His desk was not a real desk, but three wide boards that he had sanded smooth, supported on stacks of scavenged brick. Candles stood in pottery saucers—beeswax, not tallow, for their clear smokeless light. He kindled them from the lamp and set to work on his current copying commission. He had worried, when he first took up scribing, that he would find it insupportably dull after the complex duties he had performed as aide to the Son Utamnos. But though he missed the scholarship of his former life—missed it painfully sometimes, especially access to a library—he had learned to appreciate scribing's lack of challenge: the simplicity of instructions that allowed no latitude, of tasks that required no interpretation, of work that on completion vanished from his life forever. It was even, once he mastered the trick of copying without thinking about the meaning of the words, a little like meditation.

He sank into the rhythm of the work. The sharp edges of the evening smoothed away. He was aware of Axane moving about downstairs, then nearby. The wash of candlelight shaded green. Warm arms went around his shoulders.

"Put out the candles, love," she whispered.

He snuffed the flames and followed her to the bed. She had left the shutters open against the heat; the moon, nearly full, printed dim bars of silver on the floor. She shone much brighter, a jewel held to the sun—emerald, sapphire, lapis, jade. He fell into her embrace as if into water. The shock of her bare skin against his own was always, somehow, like the first time. Her radiance wrapped him like the currents of the sea, slipping along his body, streaming through his eyes and nose and open mouth, as if for a little while they passed together into a different element and swam tides beyond the world.

Gyalo was in his office in the Evening City. Lamps burned in niches on the walls; trays of candles danced with flame, illuminating lacquered cabinets and crowded document cases, a pair of iron braziers, his desk strewn with bound books and folios and scrolls. Before him was a sheet of paper; inscribed on it, in the blocky characters of the Chonggyean language to which he had been born, were the syllables of his name.

He set the brush he held on its stand. He looked down at himself: He wore the loose red gown and trousers of a vowed Âratist, and his arms and shoulders were draped with a golden Shaper stole. His scalp was naked, his chin clean-shaven. He could feel the tether of manita, a tight clenching at his center. His vision was the vision of an ordinary man.

Emotion rose in him, a strange mix of sorrow and relief. "A dream," he whispered. His journey into the Burning Land, his discoveries there, his apostasy . . . Axane. All a dream.

His hand fell to his chest in a gesture of long habit, seeking his simulacrum, the smaller replica of the First Messenger's great necklace that all vowed Âratists wore. But his fingers found only the fabric of his stole. In sudden panic he felt around his neck: It was bare. His simulacrum was gone.

He rose and crossed his office. The copy room beyond was deserted. He paced between the desks, searching for the gleam of gold. Finding nothing, he left the copy room for the labyrinth of the Evening City, traversing halls and passageways, courts and galleries, rooms and suites and reception chambers. His simulacrum was nowhere to be found. In all that vast and magnificent space, there seemed to be no living soul except himself.

He came at last to a passage with walls of rough red stone. The air smelled familiar—of dust, of dryness, of rock cracked by the hammer of the sun. Beneath it, faintly, he caught the aromatic scent of . . . bitterbark? And suddenly a searing wind struck him and he was in the Burning Land, red soil and gray-green scrub spreading out forever beneath a harsh cobalt sky. The sun drilled down like an auger; his shadow was the merest puddle at his feet. The air was almost too hot to breathe.

Ahead he saw a human form, distorted with distance and the metallic tides of heat. He started toward it, his feet catching in the low vegetation. It waited, unmoving; he could see its ragged garments, its tangled black hair. There was something deeply familiar in that straight, square-shouldered stance. All at once he knew; and with that recognition, they were face-to-face.

"Teispas," he said.

The captain smiled. He looked as he had during their ordeal in the Burning Land: dark skin scabbed and peeling with sunburn, hawk face half hidden behind a bush of beard. He held his cupped hands toward Gyalo. Fire flashed upon his palms.

"I've been saving it for you," he said.

It was the lost simulacrum. Gyalo reached to take it. But the sun-heated metal scorched his fingers, and he gasped and dropped it. It fell more slowly than was natural; he could count each link of the gold neck chain, each wire of the golden cage suspended from it, each facet of the glass jewel the cage contained, each swirl of the iridescent metal at the jewel's heart, cunningly crafted to mimic the true Blood's core of living flame. It struck the ground, sending up a little puff of red dust.

"You must pick it up," Teispas said.

An immense weariness swept over Gyalo. The brilliant world around him seemed to dim. "But it's only a copy."

Teispas shook his head, as if in disappointment. The wind lifted his hair and tossed it across his face.

"Teispas—" Gyalo realized he was dreaming. The grief that filled his throat came from his waking self, rising out of sleep. Still he said the words he always said, for dreams were the only place in which Teispas heard them: "I'm sorry. I'm so sorry."

Teispas's face was drawn in lines of agony. He turned. His tunic was torn; Gyalo saw the marks of the lash, weals that opened to the bone.

"Teispas," he called. "Teispas—"

And he was awake.

The scars on his hands throbbed, as they did when he grew agitated. Tears had tracked from the corners of his eyes into his hair. He rubbed them away and sat up. The bars of moonlight on the floor had barely moved. Axane lay huddled on the edge of the bed, wreathed in shifting color.

He pulled on his trousers and checked on Chokyi, and padded down the stairs by his own pale light. In the kitchen he drew a dipper of water from the cask and drank, then unbarred the door and went out into the garden. It was a tiny space, enclosed by walls of the same yellow brick as the house. Axane had dug herb beds, and with typical enterprise had traded healing services to a mason for a stone path with a little paved rectangle at its midpoint, on which sat a wooden bench. The mason had pounded the earth and laid a bed of gravel so the stones would sit firm—to the ordinary eye a neat and pleasing work, but to Gyalo's Shaper senses riven with imperfection, for he could see the stress lines where the stones would eventually crack, the areas of instability where they would rise and shift, and of course the patterns of their being, which told him not simply what kind of stone they were, but how they had been formed and how they would decay and how he might, if he chose, transform them into something else or even banish them entirely. Nothing in the world was static; everything, at every moment, held within itself the whole cycle of its growth and dissolution, every possibility of metamorphosis and destruction.

He sat on the bench and rubbed his palms together, trying to soothe the ache. Nearby the herb plants shed their little lights; the moon looked down, its face almost the exact hue of his own radiance, and the air stirred with the rising heat of stone and brick and tile. Beyond the quiet of the enclosure, he could hear the sporadic night sounds of Ninyâser: shouting, someone tossing liquid out a window, the barking of dogs.

Often when he could not sleep he sought the calm of meditation, one of the few habits he retained from his monastic days. He knew better than to try that now. In the humid city darkness, he could almost catch the arid whiff of stone and dust and bitter herbs that was the odor of the Burning Land. The moment he closed his eyes, he would see Teispas's bloody back again.

He did not know if Teispas had died of the lash. But he did know that the captain had perished in captivity in King Santaxma's dungeons in Ninyâser, long before Râvar came out of the Burning Land. It was Diasarta who discovered this, over the course of many months of patient inquiry and a small fortune paid in bribes.

"You didn't really think we'd find him alive, did you?" Diasarta had said when he came to give the news. "You had to expect this."

Gyalo had. But, sitting stunned with grief and guilt, he found it made little difference.

"It isn't your fault," Diasarta said. "He chose to stay."

"I should have known. I should have done more to make him go."

Diasarta shook his head. "He'd never have left you."

Gyalo knew it was true. In his mind's eye, he saw the series of events he had not witnessed, but had conjured so many times in imagination it almost seemed as if he had: Axane and Diasarta, crawling after Teispas across the

Evening City's maze of interconnected roofs. Teispas, balanced on the ridge-line where the roofs butted up against the outer wall, lowering a rope for the other two to slide down; then, having secretly made up his mind not to accompany them, starting to draw it up again. Diasarta, realizing his intent, leaping instinctively to grab the rope, causing Teispas to slip. The crashing of loosened roof tiles in the court below; the alerted servants, the summoned guards. And, grafted seamlessly to this parade of invention, the moment for which Gyalo had actually been present: Teispas, bound and bruised and on his knees before the leader of the Brethren, declaring that he and Diasarta and Axane had plotted alone to escape Baushpar, and Gyalo was ignorant of their plan. When in fact it had been Gyalo, realizing too late that the Brethren suspected them all of heresy, who had ordered his companions to go.

"It's funny, y'know," Diasarta said. "He was such a bloody arrogant man. There were times in the Burning Land when I hated his guts. Even later on I can't say I ever really got to like him."

Gyalo nodded. He had felt much the same.

"But we were part of something, y'know? What we went through in the desert . . . it binds you, a thing like that. Ârata help me, I grieve for him the same as for my brother. And I loved my brother."

Axane and Diasarta had not been recaptured, though the Brethren had searched for them. Teispas was hauled off for interrogation by the King, who dreaded heresy as much as the Brethren did, if for different reasons. Gyalo was sent into imprisonment, both for his apostasy and (he realized only later) for the sake of the Brethren's fear of him. And the Brethren purchased an army from Santaxma, and dispatched it into the Burning Land to obliterate the people of Refuge. Thus, in grief and bloodshed, ended the task that Gyalo had believed, then, had been given him by Ârata himself: to bring news of the god's rising to the Brethren and prepare them for Ârata's return.

Now, amid the quiet garden, a different memory swept him, its gem-bright immediacy undiminished by the years that divided it from this moment: Teispas, mantled in the cobalt lifelight that had been absent from Gyalo's dream. Teispas's voice, harsh in the inhuman silence of the desert night: *You really don't see it, do you. That you are the Next Messenger.*

Gyalo drew a breath, shuddering. For four years those words had over-looked his life. While he lived, Teispas had not allowed Gyalo to forget them. Dead, he came in dreams, to insert into Gyalo's sleep the reproaches he could no longer utter in waking time.

Gyalo had turned from him that night in horror, hardly able to believe that Teispas, that hard and pragmatic man, could make the same error the people of Refuge had. But though the hubris of it stopped his breath, he could not entirely deny the pattern Teispas saw: the message he bore, the Blood he carried, exactly as foretold in Ârata's Promise. Over time he came, struggling, some way toward belief. But beyond the thought-twisting isolation of the desert, what had seemed terrifyingly possible—or at least, not entirely deniable—became preposterous. Who was he to name himself the god's herald? He carried news of Ârata's rising, yes, but by chance discovery, not divine revelation. The Blood had not been given him by Ârata, but by Axane, who had pilfered it from the Cavern. How could he, a mortal man, accomplish what the Next Messenger must accomplish—open the way, whatever that meant, and bring an end to the Age of Exile? Where were the acts of destruction and generation that were supposed to follow on the Next Messenger's arrival? To understand those things was like waking from an awful dream in which he had forgotten who he was. By the time he reached Baushpar, he had rejected any significance in the manner of his return—though Teispas and Diasarta, for all his efforts to dissuade them, suffered no such change of heart.

He had known the Brethren would imprison him. Even if they had believed him, it was the sentence for apostasy, an inevitable consequence of his return. He had not imagined any possibility of reprieve. But then, incredibly, the chance for escape had come—in the form of Diasarta, who tracked him to Faal, the isolated monastery where he was confined. Teispas's pattern had seemed to flicker again, like lightning along a far horizon: Ârata's hand reaching into his life once more, offering a second chance. In dread and obedience he had embraced freedom, finally and forever renouncing the church and its strictures on his shaping, transforming himself thereby into the thing he had been taught all his life to know as anathema: a true apostate, an unbound Shaper whose liberty had not been forced, but chosen.

Uneasy in his liberty, he waited for a sign, some confirmation that his choice had been correct. *Great Ârata*, he prayed, *am I your Messenger? What is my duty? What must I do?* Ârata awake was as silent as Ârata sleeping; it did not entirely surprise him that no answer came. Yet during the bitter days of his imprisonment he had come to doubt nearly everything he had done or chosen, even whether Ârata had meant him to bring word to the Brethren; and while this made clear to him the risks of human assumption—including doubt—in matters of the divine, it left him little certain ground on which to stand. So much in him had shifted: his altered view of the Sons and Daughters he once had served so faithfully, his changing comprehension of what his time among them had really been meant to accomplish, his stumbling sense that the church's control of shaping—whose necessity he had once accepted as he accepted the rhythm of his own pulse—was in some deep way mistaken. Free for the first time in his life, he found himself unable to move forward, either to take the final step into belief or turn his back upon the question once and for all.

Then Axane dreamed her way back to him—as he had hoped, but not quite dared believe, she would—and in the joy of their reunion he forgot the questions for a while. It had really seemed, in those early days, that they might set the past aside and date their lives from the moment of their marriage—as if that had been the point, as if all the suffering and betrayal and destruction had been meant only to bring the two of them together. At last, Gyalo told himself, he would set duty aside. He would be an ordinary man—a husband, a father, a scribe, rising each day to go to his work, returning nightly to his family. From these simple actions he would build a life. When, at its end, he looked back upon the events that had terminated his Âratist service, he would find them as strange and unlikely as a dream.

But he had never been skilled at self-deception. The silence he and Axane had built across the past did not banish it, but only made a fiction of the present. Since Chokyi's birth he had found it increasingly difficult to ignore the artificiality of his life—which was not, after all, a bright new world he had created for himself, but only a wall desperately thrown up in a vain attempt to exclude what lay outside.

The wall had been breached that evening, by Axane's revelation of her Dreams. Eventually, perhaps, she would learn the location of Râvar's stronghold. Another choice would stand before Gyalo then: he who was also a Shaper, who knew what Râvar was and the havoc he intended.

Fear closed a fist inside Gyalo's chest. Râvar was hugely powerful, freakishly so. Beside the great wind of Râvar's shaping, Gyalo's own ability was a breath, a sigh. Nor had he employed it since his escape from Faal—not once, even in the smallest way. In part this was for fear of discovery. But it was a different fear that really held his ability prisoner—as firmly tethered, in a sense, as it had been when he was still bound by vows and by the Doctrine of Baushpar.

Did he have to choose? Ârata had risen. In these last of days, was it still necessary to stand against atrocity? Did even blasphemy matter, at the close of the Age of Exile? Râvar was hidden now, gathering himself like some malignant sickness, but once he emerged the eye of the world would be upon him. Surely, as Axane had said, the King would not tolerate such disruption. Surely Râvar would stumble or go too far, and tear the veil of his deception. He could not succeed. He could not.

Gyalo's hands still burned. He opened them, looked down at the white welts that crossed his palms and fingers. The scars were a legacy of Refuge, of the Cavern of the Blood; in his wonder, he had fallen to his knees and touched the crystals, forgetting their razor facets, opening up his flesh. The scar tissue was stiff; he could not completely straighten the fingers of either hand, or close them firmly into fists. It made him clumsy sometimes. But he was still adept enough to write, to lift Chokyi, to touch Axane. To do what was important.

For a moment, sharply, he recalled the relief that had filled him in his dream, to think he had only imagined the past five years. There had been grief as well. But the relief had been very powerful.

He bowed his face into his palms. "Ârata," he whispered, "risen god of all the world, forgive my hesitation. Forgive my uncertainty. Forgive me for wishing it were easier. I am and always have been your servant. Only let me know what it is you want me to do. Please, great Ârata. Show me how to choose."

The words flew out into the night. Because he was an honest man, Gyalo also heard the words he did not speak, the prayer that lay behind all the rest: *Let it not be me. Let it not be me.*

Gyalo

The unseasonable heat receded, and the spring rains returned. Gyalo wheeled his cart through wet streets, or worked at home to the sound of water sheeting from the eaves. On a rare day of sun Axane packed a picnic basket and bound Chokyi to her back, and he and she crossed the Year-Canal and spent the day in the grounds of the Hundred-Domed Palace. For centuries the Palace had been the seat of Arsace's monarchs—and also, briefly, of the Voice of Caryax, who, denouncing the private luxuries of rank and wealth, had excluded himself from such proscriptions, and lived in the Palace exactly like the line of kings he had deposed. When Santaxma reclaimed his throne, he found the Palace well cared for. As a symbol of Arsace's liberation, he had thrown a portion of the surrounding parklands open to the public.

Later, Gyalo would recall that afternoon as one of the few bright moments in a troubled time. A tension had come upon Axane since the night she confessed her Dreams, as if the truth had not relieved her of a burden but knotted her up still more. Soon after their picnic, she woke him in the small hours of the night, creeping into his arms and telling him, disjointedly, of dreaming Râvar striding through darkness, preceded by the lightning bursts of shaping and followed by its thunder.

"He looked at me," she said, her whole body shuddering. "He looked at me, as if—as if he knew I dreamed him."

"No, love," Gyalo soothed. "He doesn't even know you're a Dreamer. You never told him. Remember?"

"Oh, Gyalo, I'm so afraid."

"Sshh." Gyalo stroked her hair. Rain pattered softly on the courtyard outside. "It was only a Dream."

"No—no—I'm afraid he's coming for me. Me and Chokyi."

"Sweetheart, how could he? He doesn't know where you are."

"But I told him!" By her own light, he saw the dread that distorted her features. "In the Burning Land. He asked me what I would have done if I'd stayed in Arsace, if I hadn't come back to warn Refuge, and I told him, I told him, I said I would have gone to Ninyâser and become a healer!"

In spite of himself, Gyalo felt a chill. "Axane, even if you said that, he has no way of knowing it's actually what you did."

"But it *is* what I did, Gyalo! He's had a year to think about it, about me and Chokyi, about letting us go. A year to decide he should have kept us. You don't know him—he gets what he wants, he *always* gets what he wants—"

"Axane." Gyalo took her by the shoulders, speaking firmly into her face. "He isn't searching for you. And even if he were—Ninyâser is an enormous city. It'd be like searching for one bean in a barrelful. He couldn't possibly find you. You're safe, my love. Do you hear? Safe with me."

She clutched him. "Promise me you won't do anything foolish."

"What do you mean?"

"Promise me! Swear you won't go in search of him!"

His hands fell from her shoulders. "Why should you think I'd do that?"

"Oh, Gyalo!" Her voice cracked. "Don't pretend! Wasn't I there in the Evening City when you came before the Brethren? When it was obvious the cause was lost, that they weren't going to believe you, but you wouldn't give up, wouldn't save yourself, because you believed it was your duty? You're thinking the same thing now, I know you are—you're thinking that you can learn from my Dreams where he is, and because you're the only one besides me who knows the truth, it's up to you to try to stop him. But you have to promise me, you have to *swear to me* that you won't try. Because you couldn't do it! He's too strong!" Her voice was rising. "Why do you really think I never told you about my Dreams? I knew they'd make you think of this! I knew that if you thought of it, in the end you wouldn't be able to stop yourself from doing it!"

They looked at each other. In her cradle, Chokyi began to cry.

"Go to her," he said.

She held his eyes a moment longer, then slid off the bed and went to get the baby. Returning, she sat on the opposite edge of the mattress and dropped the shoulder of her bed gown so Chokyi could nurse.

"You still believe it," she said into the renewed quiet. "What Teispas believed of you. Don't think I don't know."

He looked at her, bent over the suckling baby, her heavy hair swept across one shoulder, the back of her long neck exposed. He could have denied it. It would have been at least partly true. But such half assurances were not what she wanted. What she wanted, what she truly wanted, was for him to abandon the question.

"Axane, I haven't decided anything."

"But you will." The anger was gone. "I always knew it would be like this. I've been pretending it was possible for you to live a normal life. But I always knew . . ." She sighed. "Promise at least that you'll tell me. When you do make up your mind."

Outside the rain intensified, drumming on the roof. A damp wind breathed through the shutters and died away. Gyalo felt the last vestiges of the happy fiction they had lived these past months go with it. For an instant he was pierced by a terrible grief.

"I promise," he said.

He lay down again. After a little while she joined him, arranging Chokyi between them. The baby slept, but he remained awake, and he thought she did also.

They did not speak of it again—a different sort of silence than the one they had kept before, not of things hidden or avoided but of things too clearly known. He longed sometimes to break it, to talk with her openly, if not for counsel, then at least for comfort. He loved her, loved her as he had not thought it possible to love anyone. But there were matters between them that were untouchable, and one of these was faith—in particular, his faith.

Though she had never actually confessed it, he had realized long ago that she did not believe in very much. Mostly, this was a product of her dreaming, which from childhood she had kept secret, in terror of the fate that Refuge forced upon its Dreamers—to spend all their adult lives in sleep, dreaming the Dream-veil that Refuge had believed protected it from its enemies. Not trained to Dream only of Refuge as the other Dreamers were, her sleeping mind had traveled freely across the earth, coming upon the kingdoms of Galea, which according to the heretical philosophy of her people did not exist. She had described to him how these Dream-discoveries had eroded her faith in her people's teachings, so that by the time he came to Refuge she had rejected nearly every part of their distorted vision of the world. It was this that made it possible for her, alone of all of them, to recognize him not as a Messenger sent by Ârata or a demon sent by Ârdaxcasa, but as what he was, an ordinary man. It was this that had driven her choice to return with him and Teispas and Diasarta, in flight from the lie she had lived among her people, in search of a world in which she would not have to hide her gift.

Her loss of faith in Refuge, he suspected, had damaged her capacity for any kind of belief, just as her long deception had ingrained in her the habit of concealment. But there was also something in her—an obstinacy, an ardent independence, an unwillingness to yield her will to others'—that inclined her more to question than to faith, and compelled her always to go her own way. He could not regret it; those very fierce qualities were part of what had brought him to love her, in defiance of his religious vows. But how then could he talk to her about the questions he could not set aside, the choices he could not find a way to make, his reproachful dreams of Teispas? The anger he had heard in her voice when she accused him of belief, of Teispas's belief, was always there, waiting. He did not want to confront it. He did not want to argue with it.

The weather turned fine again, and Gyalo set up his portable desk in the garden on the days he worked at home, sheltered by an awning he rigged from wooden poles and a sheet. He was there one afternoon when there came a knocking on the door. Axane got up from the herb bed she was tending and went to answer. When she did not return, he followed; he did not like to admit it, but since the night of her Dream he had been edgy.

She was standing in the doorway, one hand on the jamb. The room was dim, the shutters drawn against the heat; against the bright light outside she was a stark silhouette, devoid of detail. "And what makes you think it'll be a breech birth?" she was saying, as he came up behind her.

"It's my wife who thinks it." The man to whom she spoke was small and weathered, with a garnet-colored lifelight. The collar of his shirt was drawn up over his throat; the toes of his boots, in odd contrast with his shabby clothes, were shod with silver. "Her sister died of a breech birth, and ever since she's been afraid the same will come on her."

"Well, if it is a breech, I can try and turn it." Axane had assumed her crisp professional manner. "My fee's ten karshanas."

"I haven't got that much." The man's eyes flicked to Gyalo, then away.

"I see. Well, I don't work free."

"I understand." He bobbed a bow. "Thanks anyway, mistress."

He walked away across the sun-bright court. Axane stood looking after him; not until he had passed into the shadow of the alley did she close the door.

"You don't work free?" Gyalo said, meaning to tease her. "Since when?"

There was an odd expression on her face. "I didn't like him."

"Nor did I. I'll wager there was a prison scar under that collar."

"When I opened the door he stared at me, as if he were, I don't know, comparing me to something." She shook her head. "If he comes back, I won't go. Not even for ten karshanas."

"For that price, I don't think you need to worry he'll be back."

They returned to the garden, where Chokyi lay in her basket in the shade, gurgling and grabbing at her toes. "Little bird!" Gyalo said, and picked her up and swooped her high over his head in the way she loved. She shrieked with laughter, and Axane laughed, too, and they forgot about the visitor.

Two days later, Gyalo took his cart to the temple of Inriku. He returned near sunset, tired and thinking of his supper. He knew at once that Axane had gone out, for the shutters were drawn, and the door was locked. Inside, the front room was dim, but there was light beyond, in the kitchen—the garden door, hanging open.

He put down his scribing materials. The clay stove was cold. A pottery dish sat on the table, the bread dough inside it flaccid with overrising. The basket Axane took on healing calls was gone, along with Chokyi's carrying cradle; the neat array of boxes and bowls and paper packets in which she kept her healing supplies was disordered and pushed about, as if she had rummaged quickly through them. *An urgent call*, he thought. The open door was strange, though—it was not like her to be careless.

He closed the door and latched it, then took his scribing materials upstairs. The long room was neat, his desk just as he had left it: nothing out of order. *Why should I think that, as if there were a reason something should be?* He dropped what he carried on his desk, then ran down the stairs and out into the court again, and knocked at the door of Ciri, the neighbor woman who sometimes kept Chokyi when Axane went out.

"Did my wife leave word for me?" he asked when Ciri answered, wiping her hands on her apron.

"No, master scribe. But I saw her go out, just before noon, with the baby on her back and her basket on her arm. I was sweeping my step. I called hello, but she didn't hear. She was in an awful rush, or at least the men who came to fetch her were."

"Men?"

She nodded. "Two of them."

"What did they look like?"

"I couldn't say. Oh—but one of them had silver on his boots."

"Silver." Gyalo felt as if a hand had clutched him round the heart.

"Yes, I noticed it special. Not a thing you often see round here." She gave him a sharp look. "Is something wrong?"

"No," he said, trying to believe it. "No, I just wasn't expecting her to be out today."

He returned to the house. For something to do, he prepared a meal, then sat before it without eating. He thought of the expression on Axane's face when the man with the silver-shod boots had come to the door, remembered the determination with which she had said, *I won't go with him.* Why had she changed her mind? Might she have been coerced? Could that be the meaning of the open door—a sign to him, a signal that she had been taken against her will?

You're being ridiculous, he told himself. *Why shouldn't she forget to close the door if it was an urgent call?*

Abandoning the food, he went upstairs and tried to work. But every noise from outside compelled him over to the window, to see if it were she. Finally, he put away his pens and blew out his candles and, drawing a stool to the sill, gave himself up to waiting.

The hours passed. The moon rose. One by one, the lights that showed through chinked shutters across the way winked out. It was no longer possible to pretend that something was not wrong. She would never stay away so long without sending word. Had she and Chokyi been taken for ransom? It was not inconceivable; scribes could earn a good income, and one of her less reputable customers might have thought to make a profit. Or perhaps there was some darker reason, something that would not produce a ransom note. Or maybe it had nothing to do with the man with the silver-shod boots at all. Maybe she had met with misadventure on the streets, run afoul of some feud or battle in the Nines.

Behind these realistic, reasonable speculations, he seemed to hear her voice, urgent in the darkness: *I'm so afraid he's looking for me. . . .*

No, he thought. *It's not possible.*

But as the night wore on, it began to seem very possible indeed. Why should Râvar not have changed his mind about letting her go—or if not her, the child? Why should he not have remembered what she had told him about Ninyâser? Why should he, or his people, not succeed in finding her, even in the city's anonymous hugeness—by questioning herb sellers in the markets, for instance, or the craftsmen who made the knives and other instruments healers used? Especially since it had never occurred to either of them that there was any need for her to conceal herself?

At last he found the courage to rise and go to the chest where she kept her things and Chokyi's. Inside he found what he had expected, and dreaded, to see: most of her gowns and chemises gone, together with her boots and all

of Chokyi's linens—things that would hardly be required for a healing call
or bothered with in a hasty kidnapping, but certainly would be needed for
a journey to the mountains. He thought of the disorder of her healing supplies; she must have emptied out her healer's basket and packed the clothing
into it. Her kidnappers had been clever, forcing her to make it seem that she
had gone out on a call, so when she failed to return he would assume she was
delayed somewhere in the city. But not clever enough to order her to close
the kitchen door.

Or to notice what she had left behind, glinting amid the tumbled clothing that remained at the bottom of the chest: the silver bracelet he had given
her on their wedding day, which she never took off, even when she scrubbed
the floors. And something else, a pair of hairpins carved from the silky, ash-
colored wood of a tree that grew nowhere in Galea except the Burning Land.
They were from Refuge, the only mementos she possessed of her vanished
people. She wore them daily.

She had done all she could to tell him what had happened.

He lowered his face, resting his forehead on the smooth edge of the
chest, digging his fingers into the unyielding wood. He had been careful for
himself—changing his appearance, changing his name. But he had not been
careful for her or Chokyi. Until the night she confessed her fear, he had not
once thought that Râvar might try to get them back.

He returned to his chair. All night he sat by the open window, the bracelet
in one hand, the hairpins in the other. When dawn arrived, he got to his feet
and went in search of Diasarta.

"I don't know," Diasarta said in his deliberate way. "Seems pretty thin to me."

"No!" Gyalo drew a breath, trying to quell his blazing impatience. "No,"
he repeated more quietly. "This is what's happened. I'm sure of it."

"But how many healers are there in Ninyâser?" Diasarta had only just
returned from his job as a guard in an all-hours gambling house; he smelled of
beer and smoke, and within the wan green nimbus of his lifelight his homely
face was weary. They had not seen each other for weeks, yet there had been no
flicker of surprise when he found Gyalo waiting for him in the street. "I mean,
what are the odds that he could find her?"

"All it would take is time and questions. How many healers could there be
called Axane, with an infant, come to the city only recently?"

"You really think he wants her back that much?"

"He was in love with her when they lived in Refuge. Obsessed with her. It never faded, even after she left. It was part of why he . . . mistreated her, when they were alone in the Burning Land."

"No offense, Brother, but he got what he wanted of her then. There's nothing like getting what you want to cure you of wanting it."

"But that *wasn't* what he wanted. He wanted her to love him." A sudden vision unfolded inside his mind: Axane under Râvar's hands. He willed it away. "And there's Chokyi. His blood, all that's left of Refuge. Maybe it's her he wants."

Diasarta was silent, fingering the scar that bisected his right cheek, as he always did when he was thinking. A sluggish breeze stirred the air, drawing up a potent whiff of night soil from the alley below the narrow balcony on which they sat. Diasarta's room was neat and clean, but the rooming house itself, which was much closer to the Nines than Gyalo's home, was truly squalid—to Gyalo's Shaper senses even more than to ordinary eyes, for he could see the patterns of rot and shift that had weakened the balcony's structure, and identify the exact spots where plaster would next crack off the brick. He had urged Diasarta to look for better accommodations; he had even offered to pay for them. But the ex-soldier had refused, just as he had refused Gyalo's other offers of assistance: clothing, furnishing, the rent on a vendor's stall when he had briefly tried to set himself up in business as a knife sharpener.

"You're sure of this, then," Diasarta said.

"Yes. Yes, I'm sure."

"All right." Diasarta let his hand fall. "I believe you. What do you want to do?"

"Go after them."

"And how d'you plan on that, seeing as you don't know where he is?"

"I know where one of his missionaries is. I can pretend to be a convert. Converts are told how to get to him."

"And once you do get to him? What then?"

"I don't know. I'll think of something. Ârata, Dasa, what should I do? Give up? Let him have her? Sit here in Ninyâser doing nothing while he— while he—"

"Keep your skin on, Brother." Diasarta had never been able to break himself of the habit of using Gyalo's former title. "I'm only trying to get a feel for how I'm going to be spending my time these next few months." He gave a wry smile. "You do mean me to go with you, don't you?"

"Yes," Gyalo admitted.

"You needn't look like you just told me to cut my finger off." There was an edge to Diasarta's voice. "You know well I'll follow you anywhere. All you've got to do is ask."

Gyalo glanced away, at the scabrous wall beside him. It was true. Coming here, he had not expected to be refused.

"So where is this missionary?"

"At the Red Lantern Inn, on Shiriya Street in the western quarter."

"Bloody ashes, that's nearly two hours from here. Well." Diasarta braced his hands on his knees and got up from his mat, favoring the leg he had broken in the Burning Land, which had healed slightly shorter than the other. "We'd better get started."

But the missionary was not at the Red Lantern, when they finally found it in the breathless heat of noon. And both the innkeeper and the stable master swore they had never heard of such a person.

"A holy man?" the innkeeper repeated, as if Gyalo had asked whether he were harboring lepers. "This is an inn, not a temple. That's the sort of thing puts customers off. I wouldn't give space to a holy man if he offered me money for it." He guffawed. "And how likely is that?"

Gyalo knew he should have expected failure—it was, after all, more than a month since his encounter with the young pilgrim. But the disappointment he felt was crushing. Outside the inn he paused, steadying himself against one of the red-painted columns that flanked the gateway, closing his eyes against the sudden dizziness that gripped him.

"You all right, Brother?"

"Yes." Gyalo straightened. On the column by his hand, a sign to ward off spirits was crudely marked in yellow paint: a hexagon with a squiggle inside it. "Yes, I'm all right."

"They may have been telling the truth in there, and they may not. Either way, there's more to be learned. I'll poke around and see what I can find out."

"There are other inns. We can go street by street—"

"Brother." Diasarta wore a determined expression. "I think you should let me do this. By myself."

Gyalo felt a flash of anger. Diasarta, who had cared for him like a child during the ordeal of manita withdrawal that followed his escape from Faal, had never quite stopped trying to treat him like someone who needed special care. "I'm as capable as you of asking questions."

"That may be. But in a place like this"—Diasarta made a gesture that encompassed the dilapidated neighborhood—not quite a slum but rough enough, the sort of place where canal workers and porters and day laborers lived—"a man like me fits in, and a man like you doesn't. People will talk to me. They may not to you."

It made sense, but in his frustration Gyalo could not admit it. "And what am I supposed to do? Sit at home and bite my nails?"

"Do your work. Earn your fees. We'll need money for the journey." Diasarta laid his hand on Gyalo's arm. "You go home now, Brother. I'll come to you tonight and we'll talk."

They parted. Gyalo set out for home, but on impulse turned east along the boulevard that flanked the north side of the Year-Canal. Pedestrians crowded it, and vendors' stalls, and, at the numerous debarkation points, trains of porters loading or unloading boats.

He reached the Âratist religious complex, a walled compound of monasteries and nunneries and guesthouses and charity houses the size of a small town, and entered the enormous domed bulk of the temple of Ârata, following the circular outer gallery into the temple's cylindrical core. The core was dim and cool and smelled of incense and ancient stone. A wave of nostalgia swept him, a vivid sense-memory of the thousands of hours he had spent in temples like it. The secular population was only expected to attend religious services once a week, but daily attendance was required of vowed Âratists: Communion in the morning, joyous in anticipation of Ârata's return, the Banishing in the evening, doleful in remembrance of his absence. But the rites and observances, devised for the time of the god's slumber, held little meaning for one who knew Ârata awake. During his time as a fugitive, Gyalo had come to understand a truth that he once would absolutely have denied: that faith was a thing distinct and separate from the formal apparatus of its expression. It was a long time since he had attended a ceremony, and he owned no devotional objects, not even a string of Communion beads. So much in him had changed these past two years, so many understandings lost and gained; this, which struck at the foundation of the life he had once lived, was neither the greatest nor the most subversive.

He dropped a coin into the donation box, lit a cone of incense, and settled himself cross-legged on one of the contemplation mats laid out before the colossal image of Ârata Creator. Hundreds of candles were set in banks about the god's feet and in trays along the wall behind him; their light shimmered on the gilded pleats of his robes and the golden tresses of his hair, struck sparks from the gems on his brow and the golden sun he held between his great red hands.

Ârata, Gyalo thought, gazing into the god's jeweled eyes, which were trained not on him but on eternity. *Ârata*. But his mind would go no further into prayer. Here in the god's sanctuary, the thought he had struggled all night not to think rose up in him like nausea. Should he perceive more than Râvar's hand in Axane's and Chokyi's abduction? Was it a punishment for his doubt? A spur to the choices he could not bring himself to make?

He had prayed for a sign. Had it been given at last?

As usual, he could only guess. No godly intervention was needed to explain the chain of circumstance, rooted as it was in human character and action and entirely human tragedy. All matters of the divine were fraught with this duality—was it the mundane logic of the event that was illusory, or the greater purpose glimpsed shadowy within it?

Sometimes, though, the imperative was clear. His wife and child had been stolen. They must be rescued. That was the purpose he was following. It was his own purpose; if it were also the god's, he would trust to time to show it.

What will come of it, he said silently into Ârata's serene and distant face, *will come.*

Ciri was sitting at her front door when Gyalo returned home, stringing beans and keeping an eye on her two youngest children, who were tumbling about the court.

"Is all well with your wife?" she called when she saw him.

Gyalo had prepared a lie. "I got word last night. She's gone to visit her sister."

"I never knew she had a sister."

"Didn't you?"

A small pause. "Well," Ciri said, "I'm glad to know it. I could see you were worried."

"Yes," Gyalo said. He knew her curiosity contained some measure of real concern. "Thank you."

He went into his house. The emptiness received him, the horrible silence. He set his back against the door, slid down it to the floor. *In the dark of a night that has not yet passed, I reach for you / So I may see your face in the light of a day that is yet to come.* It was a verse from the devotional poet Ansi, returning to him as such things sometimes did, remnants of his former life, relics of the scholarship that had once been so important to him. Axane's face hung before his inner eye, shining as Ârata's had, in the temple. All night, Ansi's lines sang relentlessly through his head.

In the days that followed, he did as Diasarta had suggested, and devoted himself to work. The monotony absorbed his attention, giving him some respite from the dread, the savage impatience, that otherwise consumed him.

Each evening Diasarta came to report. They had not seen each other so often since they had come together to Ninyâser. He had found a stableboy at the Red Lantern who was willing to admit to the missionary's presence, though the boy said the man had moved on three weeks earlier, where he did not know. Since then Diasarta had been going from inn to market to hostel, on the assumption that the missionary had moved to a new venue within Ninyâser, or if not, that there were others like him to be found.

After Diasarta departed, the emptiness of the house fell on Gyalo like a punishment. That unbearable feeling of restraint, which once had afflicted him when Axane left his side even for a moment, was always with him now; he could hardly breathe for wanting to fall toward her, for knowing he could not. Wherever she was, he knew she dreamed him. Her visions were involuntary, but the bond of love commanded them, like the bond of blood, and just as she had not been able to prevent her sleeping mind from traveling to Râvar, he knew she must be nightly drawn back to him. He sat up past midnight, so her Dream-self would find him wakeful; by his hand he set a sheet of paper, on which he had written in large letters: *I know Râvar has taken you. I will follow.* He said it aloud, too, the words falling strangely on the quiet air: *I will follow.*

On the seventh morning of their absence, Diasarta arrived as Gyalo was loading his cart for the day's work. Gyalo needed only to look at the ex-soldier's face to know.

"You found him."

"Yes." Diasarta was heavy-eyed and unshaven; he must have come direct from work. "I could do with some breakfast."

Gyalo brought him to the garden, then returned to the kitchen and with unsteady hands set out cheese and fruit and what was left of last night's rice on a tray. He went back out.

"Tell me," he commanded, setting the tray down with a thump.

"Food first, if you don't mind." Diasarta's obvious exhaustion rebuked Gyalo's impatience. He held up his left hand, which was wrapped in a blood-stained bandage. "Cut the cheese, would you?"

"What happened to your hand?"

"A keepsake from last night."

Gyalo did not question it; the gambling house was a rough place. Unable to keep still, he paced around the garden as Diasarta ate. At last the ex-soldier sighed and pushed away the tray.

"Come sit down," he said, "before you wear out those stones."

Gyalo did. Diasarta had taken his injured hand in his good one and drawn it close against his body, a gesture Gyalo found oddly familiar. In the bright morning sun, his parched-grass lifelight looked more faded than ever.

"Yesterday afternoon, a boy came up to me and said that he could take me to the holy man. Naturally I was suspicious, but he led me to the missionary right enough. He was waiting in the basement of one of the hostels. Big, he was, and ugly, with knife scars on his arms and the marks of the prison collar at his neck. He wanted to know why I was looking for him. I said what we agreed. He questioned me a bit, and then he must have decided I was all right, because he began to preach heresy at me."

"What did he say?"

"Oh . . . that Ârata had risen at last from his resting place, which was at the heart of the Burning Land in a great cave inside high red cliffs, above a mighty river flowing to the sea—"

"Refuge," Gyalo said. "He's put Refuge into his story."

"Sounds that way, doesn't it. So Ârata walked the world for a while to see what had become of it while he was asleep. Then he went back into the Land and made the Next Messenger out of flesh, and set divine fire beating in his breast, and gave him a crystal of the Blood and sent him back to the world. Now the Messenger is calling all the faithful, and when there are enough they'll march on Baushpar and the Messenger will be acknowledged by the Brethren and he'll lead the Way of Ârata during the time of Interim."

"The time of Interim? What's that?"

"Your guess is as good as mine. I'd had about as much as I could stand at that point, so I interrupted him—he wasn't too pleased about that—and asked where I could find the Next Messenger, because I just couldn't live another minute without knowing how to go to him. He said I should come back at midnight, and if I proved my faith, the way would be given to me. So I did."

"You went back? Alone?"

"I wasn't sure it wasn't a trap. Didn't make sense to set us both at risk."

"But, Dasa, we agreed we'd go together!"

"It seemed best," Diasarta repeated, "to go alone."

With an effort, Gyalo held his temper. "Go on."

"There were about twenty there besides me—men mostly, a few women. All ages—all classes, too. He said we'd shown our faith by coming that far, but now we had to prove it. To be worthy to come to the Next Messenger's side we must agree to take his mark, as a sign of our belief in him."

"His mark?"

"A slash on the hand. To make a scar, like the ones they say he got from carrying the Blood."

Gyalo looked at Diasarta's hand, cradled in his lap, and realized why the gesture had seemed familiar: the pilgrim boy, who had also worn a bandage across his palm, had held his hands just so. He closed his fingers, feeling the sting of his own scars. "You let them cut you?"

"It was either that or leave."

"Dasa, you should have waited. You should have let me do it."

"And what if we never found the man again, Brother?"

It was true enough. "Go on."

"A few left. Most stayed. He had us go up and kneel, one by one. He gave us an oath to speak, and then his man held us down and he cut us. Then he told us the first leg of the journey. At the end of each leg is a way station, where they tell us what the next part of the trip will be. No one knows more than one part at a time, and only those who've got to the end of it know it all."

"So we don't actually know where we're going?" said Gyalo, feeling the familiar frustration.

"South. For now, anyhow. They call it the Waking Road, the way we'll be traveling, because we believers are supposed to have woken up. Like Ârata." His voice was heavy with disgust. "Here." He fumbled in his wallet, pulled out a scrap of paper. "There are signs we're to look for. They mark the turning points, and also the places where pilgrims can get food and shelter."

A series of pictograms was scrawled on the paper: a circle with an open eye, a coiled spiral, a crude rendering of a hand slashed by a diagonal line—and one Gyalo recognized, a hexagon with a squiggle inside it, like a flame.

"Look." He showed Diasarta the hexagon. "This was painted on the column of the Red Lantern. I thought it was a sign against spirits. It's really quite clever—the symbols are distinctive, yet they look enough like warding signs that they wouldn't attract special notice."

"It's bloody ridiculous, if you ask me. All this secret mystery nonsense."

Gyalo set the paper aside. "Let me see your hand."

Diasarta extended it. Carefully Gyalo unwound the bandage. As in the pictogram, the cut had been made diagonally across Diasarta's palm. Its edges gaped, still oozing blood. A dark substance had been smeared into it.

"What's this black stuff?"

"An ointment, so it'll be sure to leave a scar. A sign anyone can see—yet easy to hide as closing your hand. So the missionary said."

"And those who accept the sign do a thing they can't take back. They're bound to him beyond any oath that can be spoken—transformed, set apart from others."

A tremor, or a shiver, passed through Diasarta's body. "I'm just glad it wasn't something worse."

But if it had been, you'd have endured it, wouldn't you? Gyalo looked down at the hand he held in his. It was Diasarta who had engineered his escape from Faal. It was Diasarta who had cared for him afterward, as he weaned himself off manita. It was Diasarta who had come with him to Ninyâser, and helped him learn the ways of secular life—as alien, to a man vowed from childhood to the Way of Ârata, as the language of a foreign land. Diasarta had given more than Gyalo could ever hope to repay, even if he had a lifetime to do it. And what he gave most was what Gyalo wanted least: faith.

They never spoke of it, of what Gyalo knew Diasarta still believed: that he, Gyalo, was the Next Messenger. Yet it lay behind every word that passed between them. Gyalo hated it—hated it for the obligation it laid on him, for the rebuke it gave to his own inaction. Once he had grown comfortable in his secular life, he began to find excuses to avoid Diasarta. After Axane arrived, the distance between them became greater still; in the months since Chokyi's birth, he had seen the ex-soldier only twice. Diasarta, who was more sensitive than he seemed, had not tested that distance. Yet seven days ago, when he found Gyalo waiting on his doorstep, there had been no surprise—as if Diasarta had been waiting for something like this, for Gyalo to have need of him again. Now, in the other man's face, Gyalo saw the same faith that had been present four months ago, a year ago, two years ago—undiminished by absence, untarnished by neglect.

"I'm sorry, Dasa."

"Don't feel too bad, Brother," Diasarta said drily. "You'll have to have one of these as well. We've got to show it when we get there, or they won't let us in."

Gyalo got up and went into the kitchen, where he dipped water into a bowl and selected from Axane's healing supplies some rags, a roll of bandages, and the astringent-smelling salve she used for cuts and burns. Diasarta sat still while Gyalo cleaned away the blood, but snatched his hand back when Gyalo reached for the salve.

"It's got to scar. Burn it, Brother, d'you want me to have gone through this for nothing?"

Gyalo sighed. "Let me give you a fresh bandage at least."

That Diasarta allowed.

"Well," Gyalo said when he was done, "I suppose there's no reason to delay."

"Brother."

"Yes?"

"Are you sure about this?"

"What do you mean?"

"I could go alone. I already have the mark." He lifted his hand. "There's no need for you to put yourself at risk."

"What? No, absolutely not. Dasa, I can't believe you'd even suggest such a thing."

"All right, all right. I had to ask." Diasarta got to his feet. "I'll go home and get my pack. I'll meet you in two hours at the King's Gate." He pointed to the slip of paper he had paid such a price to obtain, lying discarded on the path. "Don't forget that."

Gyalo had already assembled his travel kit; it remained only to set the house in order. He got rid of the perishable food, swept out the kitchen, emptied the water cask, latched the shutters, stowed away the pens and ink stones and paper that normally sat on his desk. His last commission had been finished and delivered two days ago. Finally, he took the box that held his and Axane's savings from its hiding place under the floorboards of the upstairs room and emptied the coins into a pouch. There was less than he would have liked. A few days earlier he had gone to the rental agent and paid the rent on the house for the next year. A foolish thing to do, perhaps, but it had seemed important, as a pledge of hope.

He tied the pouch around his waist under his shirt, and heaved his pack onto his back. He glanced around the room, dim with its shutters closed. Already it looked abandoned. *How long before I stand here again?* he thought. And then: *Will I stand here again?*

He shook the questions away. He would not allow Diasarta's misgivings to affect him.

At Ciri's house, he knocked.

"I'm going away for a while," he told her when she answered. "To join my wife. Will you keep an eye on the house for us?"

"Of course," she said. "When will you be back?"

"I can't say. Not for a long time, perhaps. The rent's paid up until next year."

Her eyes widened, but all she said was, "We'll miss you, you and your wife. You've been good neighbors."

"As have you," he said, meaning it. He held out the spare key. "I'd like you to keep this. For when we return." *In case she comes back, and I don't.*

"Ârata's blessing to you," she said, taking it. "And safe journey, wherever it is you're going."

"Thank you, Ciri. Go in light."

"Great is Ârata. Great is his Way. Go in light, master scribe."

He left the court. The city, with its vivid noise and jostle and stink that normally commanded his senses, seemed pale and distant; he could feel it dropping away from him, like a room into which he might never go again. Beneath his clothing, strung on a cord, was Axane's bracelet; it lay against his heart as his simulacrum once had, the emblem of his new service. He felt the tidal force that bound him to her—fainter than it had been, stretched thin across the miles separating them, but hooked as firmly as ever into his heart. He was falling toward her at last.

Part II

THE BLACKENED MEN

5

Sundit

We stop this night in a village whose name I cannot at the moment call to mind. Reanu has commandeered for us the house of the headman; it's crude in its appointments but comfortable enough. The others are asleep; I sit up by candlelight, bringing my journal entries up to date, which I have not done since before we left Baushpar. I must not allow myself, on this most important of journeys, to grow lax.

The day before departure was consumed by a predictable whirlwind of preparation: meetings with my aides, a final consultation with Drolma on the books and other items to pack and bring along, farewell visits to certain of my Brothers and Sisters. Of course there were also those I did not intend to visit. But the Evening City, labyrinthine as it is, can sometimes be a very small place. Midway through the afternoon, crossing the Butterfly Court on my way to call on Hysanet, I encountered Kudrâcari, with Okhsa scurrying along beside her like the weasel he resembles.

"Great is Ârata." Okhsa showed his pointed teeth. Kudrâcari's smile was equally unconvincing. "Great is his Way."

"Go in light," I replied.

"Okhsa and I have been intending to visit you," Kudrâcari said, "to offer blessings for your safe journey."

"Thank you." I knew they intended no such thing. "Blessings are always welcome."

"The preparations go well, I hope? If there is anything you need, please, don't hesitate to call on us."

"That's kind," I said, imagining how they would react if I actually asked for their assistance. "But I have things well in hand. In fact, I was just on my way to see to some final matters."

I made to move around them. Kudrâcari stepped forward and put her hand on my arm.

"Sister. We are alone here. Will you not admit, just once, what it is that you believe?"

I pulled away. "You've heard me speak in council."

"Yes, I've heard you." Her small eyes were narrow. "But you are not like Magabyras or Hysanet, Sister, pulled always between one view and another, never able to make up your mind. You have an opinion on everything. You affect impartiality, but I think you have come to a conclusion on this blasphemer, this pretender in the mountains, and I fear I know what that conclusion is. I can't forget that you supported the apostate Gyalo Amdo Samchen, when he made his blasphemous claims."

"I did not support him, Sister. I simply did not agree with you and your supporters."

"Will you answer me, Sundit?"

"I *have* answered, Kudrâcari. Many times. If you won't believe me, there's nothing I can do."

"Taxmârata is a fool," she hissed. All her pretense of pleasantness was gone. She wore her true face, mouth as tight as a sithra string, eyes alight with the anger that burns so hot in her in this incarnation. "And this is a fool's mission. But if two of us must go, it should be two whose minds are not already made up!"

"What, like yours? Kudrâ, do you think I don't see what's really at issue here? You didn't vote against this mission because you have any rational reason to be certain of the claimant's falsity, but for the sake of your own pride. If you were to admit the necessity of investigating this so-called Next Messenger's claims, you'd also have to admit you might have been wrong two and a half years ago when you condemned Gyalo Amdo Samchen as a heretic and a liar. And that, despite all evidence to the contrary, you cannot do!"

I should not have said it. Kudrâ is not her own master in such things; she is ridden by her rage, which may aggrandize and exalt her, but cannot make her happy. But my temper was well and truly lost. She was too astonished to reply. Okhsa had edged behind her, as if for protection. I pushed past them both and left the court.

I took the evening meal with Utamnos, who is greatly distressed at the prospect of my absence. At bedtime he did not want to let me go. But at last he succumbed to sleep, and I wrapped myself in a cloak and drew the hood down to hide my tattoo and left the Evening City, crossing the great square that opens at Baushpar's center like a rivet fastening the city to the earth and entering the incense-scented dimness of the First Temple of Ârata. There I sat for some time, unremarked in my cloak, in contemplation of Ârata Eon Sleeper. Usually I am satisfied to perform my devotions in my personal chapel, but that night I needed more: the First Temple's vastness, its silence, its ancient majesty. Its reminder of the glory and the permanence of the church.

On my way out I paused, as most worshipers do, to brush my fingers across the words of Ârata's Promise, incised beneath the painting of the Next Messenger. One of the council's few unanimous decisions of recent years was to leave this image as we found it on our return to Baushpar, as a reminder of Arsace's eight decades of suffering under the heel of the Caryaxist regime. The Messenger is obscured by Caryaxist graffiti: his face, his near-naked body, his hands, bleeding from the wounds inflicted by the Blood. But his dark eyes look through, clear and extraordinarily real. In the flickering lamplight, they almost seem to move to meet one's own.

As a meditation and a reminder, I write the words of the Promise here. For the Promise travels with me on this journey, as surely as do any of my human companions.

> *You are only the first. Watch always for the next. He will be born out of a dark time. He will come among you ravaged from the burning lands, bearing my blood with him. One act of destruction will follow on his coming, and one of generation. Thus shall you know him. He will bring news of me, and he will open the way, so that my children may be brought out of exile.*

When I returned, Ha-tsun told me that Taxmârata had come, and was waiting for me in the moon garden. I needn't say how much this surprised me; I confess that for a moment I was tempted not to go. I found him in the gallery, pacing in his restless way.

"Brother," I said.

He turned. I was reminded of what a big man he is: broad of shoulder and deep of chest, his shadow wide enough to engulf me, had I been standing in it. The Blood of Ârata pulsed on his chest, an ember in the dimness.

"Sister." He gestured toward the garden. "Shall we walk?"

We stepped onto the path. Around us the night-blooming flowers glimmered, shedding the fragrances called forth by darkness. By a shrub planted in a pottery urn Taxmârata paused, bringing his face close to the pale trumpets that hung among its leaves.

"It's called queen-of-the-night," I said.

" 'Beautiful is her face in the night / Shining on dark pillows,' " he said, and then, in answer to my look of inquiry, "A poem about the moon. I can't remember the poet, but I have always loved that line."

"Moon gardens are an Isaran custom," I said. "In Rimpang it was too dry and hot for most of these plants, but Baushpar's climate is perfect."

"You've made a paradoxical beauty here, Sundit. In the dark, it's easy to see Ârata's light."

For some reason it did not please me that he saw the truth of my moon garden—that it is not simply a gathering of leaves and flowers and stone and water, but a devotion, like the beauties of my apartments, like the magnificence of the Evening City, like the glory of Baushpar. Like all the splendor and luxury with which we Brethren so lavishly surround ourselves, often forgetting that such impermanent things are not to be cherished for themselves but for the way they speak to us of Ârata's bright substance, shining still through the world's veil of ash.

"Brother," I said sharply, "have you something to say to me?"

"I haven't properly thanked you for your part in all of this, Sundit. For the help and counsel you've offered me. It has reminded me a little . . . of old times."

I did not think I owed him any response to that.

"I know you have misgivings about Vivaniya," he said.

"You didn't ask for my opinion when you chose him to go with me. I'm surprised you would raise the matter now."

"I'm aware of the rift between the two of you. But I was under the impression it was mended."

"That is not the source of my concern."

"Is it that you think as Kudrâcari and her supporters do, that he cannot be trusted to speak the truth?"

"You should know me better than to imagine I'd ever share a thought with Kudrâcari."

Taxmârata turned abruptly, with that restlessness that will never allow him to stop too long in any single place, and began to pace again. "Vanyi is truly repentant. I believe he will work all the harder in service of the truth—harder perhaps than one who had not chosen falsehood, and learned the consequences of doing so."

"He certainly worked hard to persuade you of it."

"Do you mistrust his motives, then?"

"No." I sighed, annoyed at my own pettishness. "It's his judgment that concerns me. I think his guilt has already more than half convinced him that this claimant is truly the Next Messenger."

Taxmârata nodded. "I see that, too. But how many among us can claim an open mind on this matter? Not Kudrâcari or Ariamnes or Okhsa, who not only voted against this journey but did all they could to persuade others to oppose it also. Not Dâdar, who even now will not admit he did wrong in withholding such a crucial part of the truth. Not Artavâdhi or Baushtas, who believed the word of the apostate Gyalo Amdo Samchen, and have been waiting for the Next Messenger ever since. Vimâta and Hysanet are too untried to go; Martyas and Haminâser are too infirm. Magabyras is too indecisive—the only one of us who withheld his vote. Clearly, I cannot abandon my duties here. That leaves Vivaniya—who, if he is not an ideal choice, is at least a better choice than the rest."

"Concerns aside, I cannot disagree."

"And, of course, you. From the beginning it was obvious that you should be the one to go. You're the only one of us who truly *does* possess an open mind. I know that when you reach this so-called Next Messenger, you will look on him with unclouded eyes."

"Kudrâcari doesn't think so," I said, remembering the afternoon.

"Kudrâcari is blinded by her own bias. I only wish it were not so perilous. But risk or no, we have no choice. We must see this man, or whatever he is, for ourselves. We must know."

In this, at least, he and I have been of a mind from the start.

We walked on. Now and then he reached to touch a blossom or a spray of leaves, or to run his fingers along the coping of a fountain. At last the circuit of the path delivered us back to the columned gallery where we had begun. Before its steps he paused, as if reluctant to move back into shadow. The Blood burned on his chest. The whites of his eyes, and his ivory stole, gleamed like the faces of the flowers.

"These are dark times, Sister," he said softly.

I was silent.

"Five years ago the future seemed so glorious. We stood ready to redress the Caryaxists' persecution, to restore the Way of Ârata to Arsace, the god's first kingdom. It was to be a new beginning—I and Santaxma, he with his Lords' Assembly rebuilding the land, I with the Brethren rebuilding the church, both of us together bringing a new age of peace and tolerance to birth." He shook his head. "And now look at us. The Arsacian people love the Way of Ârata, but we never knew till we returned to Baushpar how many no longer love the Brethren and condemn us for fleeing to Rimpang when the Caryaxists came. Santaxma has revealed himself as my foe, as the church's foe, an impious man who has denied us the political voice he swore we should have, and commits daily blasphemy with his mining of the Burning Land. And we Brethren are divided, perhaps more than in all our centuries of rule, by word brought by an apostate Shaper out of the Burning Land and by the actions we have taken in response."

I was sorely tempted to respond—to remind him that it was his over-weening political ambition that first alienated Santaxma, and that Santaxma would not be defiling the Burning Land if we had not allowed it. More—that by our sanction of the King's mining we have opened the door to the private prospecting of the Land by individuals and cartels that no longer fear a charge of blasphemy. Even before our demon's bargain with Santaxma, our censure meant little in the world beyond the church—the Lords' Assembly certainly did not heed it, when the issue of mining first arose. Now it means absolutely nothing. But what would have been the point? Taxmârata knows these things as well as I.

"Do not mistake me," Taxmârata continued. "I do not say we could have acted differently. We have no military capacity—we needed Santaxma's sol-diers to march on Refuge, to round up its heretics and destroy its apostate Shapers. We needed shaping power of our own, so the army could survive the Land. So we paid Santaxma the price he demanded for his aid, trusting that Ârata would understand our need, and we released twenty-five Shapers from the tether of manita. Darknesses, yes—but necessary, unavoidable. Yet from them, what unintended darkness flowed! Not just Refuge's Shapers slain, but all its people killed. Dâdar's and Vivaniya's deception—as terrible a thing as any of us has ever done." He took a step toward me. "I sense that this burdens you, Sundit, as it burdens me. I haven't forgotten that we were, once, much of a mind."

This time my anger would not allow me to keep silent. "It does burden me, Brother. But my regret is not like yours, for I would not have made the choices you made. I would not have bargained with Santaxma. I would not have paid his blasphemous price. I would never have chosen Dâdar to go into the Burning Land! This I tell you—if I had been Bearer when Gyalo Amdo Samchen returned, we would not now be in this plight!"

A thousand times I've thought this. Not once have I ever said it. I vowed long ago that I would not remind him of the sacrifice I made for his sake, and I've kept that vow, until tonight. It struck him, for a moment, entirely to still-ness. The moonlight falling on his face made it seem carved from stone.

"Other things might have been different," he said finally. "But not the mission on which we sent Gyalo Amdo Samchen, or the news he brought back, or the dissension it seeded among us. And even if you'd found another way to raise the army, Sunni, you'd still have had to free the Shapers. You'd still have had to incur that darkness."

I said nothing, for I knew he was right.

"We sent Gyalo Amdo Samchen into the wilderness." He looked away from me, at the ghostly reaches of my garden. "But I have begun to wonder whether . . . whether another's hand might have sent him back. Whether Ârata intended him to test us." He drew in his breath. "Whether we failed that test, by turning from his words."

I stared at him. I could not speak. He turned toward me again. I saw, with astonishment, that his eyes were full of tears.

"The past can't be undone," he said. "But I've been wrong to distance myself from you. I would change that, when you come back. If you will allow it."

The turmoil of emotion that gripped me is impossible to describe. Anger, yes. Bitterness. But also my love for him, which has not been destroyed, but only buried, by all that has gone wrong between us in this life.

"We shall see." I wanted to reach out to him, but my pride would not allow it. "When I come back."

A pause. Then he nodded. "Safe journey, Sunni." He made the sign of Ârata. "Great is Ârata. Great is his Way."

"Go in light, Mâra."

It slipped out without my willing it, the pet name I haven't used in . . . how long? Years. The corners of his mouth curved into the smallest of smiles. He mounted the steps and passed into shadow. I saw the pale glimmer of his stole as he moved along the gallery.

I returned to my chamber. Ha-tsun had already completed my packing; there was nothing left for me to do but write in this journal, which I was too weary and unsettled even to contemplate. I got into bed and tried to sleep. I was still awake when Utamnos came pattering in and crept beneath my covers.

"Did you have a bad dream, little mouse?"

"No." He huddled into my arms. "I don't want you to go away, Sister Sunni."

"I don't want to go either, little mouse. But I have to."

"Why?"

"Our spirit-brother Taxmârata has given me an errand. And we must all obey the Blood Bearer, mustn't we?"

He wriggled in a way that conveyed his disagreement. "Tell Sister Hysa to go."

"Hysa has to stay here and take care of you. You'll like staying with her and Rukhsane."

"Don't *want* to stay with her. Want to stay with you." He began to sob. "I want my mother! I want to go home!"

"This is your home now, little mouse. This is your family."

"No," he wept. "No."

I held him as he cried himself to sleep. My heart ached for him—the fear and homesickness of my own first months in the Evening City are still very vivid to me. Of course, I was five when I was identified in this incarnation; it's much harder for the older ones. Utamnos is only two and a half. In a year he will not remember any other life.

Hysanet came at dawn to take him. We departed without incident—Vivaniya and I in our separate coaches, with one aide and one body servant each, our guards riding alongside—twenty of them, ten from my guard and ten from Vivaniya's, with my Reanu in command. The agent who returned last month from the claimant's stronghold is also with us; he will serve as our guide. We do not move by easy stages, but hasten forward with all the speed we can—already we have nearly reached Ninyâser, a journey that normally takes closer to two weeks than one. Fearing for our safety south of Darna, where many of the bandit bands that harass the Great South Way are former Caryaxists, Reanu has caused the insignia on our carriages to be painted over. From the presence of the Tapati, whose face and arm tattoos proclaim them the legendary guardians of the church, it is apparent that we are high-ranking Âratists. But it will not be guessed that we are Brethren.

Taxmârata's words travel with me. *I have begun to wonder whether Gyalo Amdo Samchen was sent to test us* . . . How much his heart must have changed, to say such a thing! I have been remembering our friendship—how, at thirteen, he sought me out and became my protégé, despite the displeasure of his spirit-guardian Ariamnes, that pompous pedant. How I taught him to share my passion for reform: the abolishment of taxation to support the church, the reversal of the Way's long indifference to the scientific and mechanical arts, the promulgation of new doctrines to address the perennial affliction of greed and graft within our monasteries and nunneries. How I stood aside when the office of Blood Bearer became vacant, supporting his candidacy instead for the sake of his bond with Santaxma. How after he was elected, political ambition seized him, driving him to the errors and miscalculations that have so divided us from the King, who now pays the barest lip service to the church without which he could not have gained his throne. Thus died the dream I had thought Mâra and I shared, of a Golden Age for the church in a newly liberated Arsace.

Do I want to be his ally again? I don't imagine he intends to recommit himself to those bold reforms. It's too late, in any case: Even had Santaxma not turned against the Way, reform could only have been accomplished had we pursued it from the start, when Arsace still stood between the travesty of governance imposed by the Caryaxists and the inevitable reassertion of the ways of life and rule that gave rise to the rebellion. Also, these past years have greatly changed my view of him. In all his incarnations he is a formidable man—a powerful personality, an incisive intellect. But in this body he is also vain and excessively ambitious. And there is brittleness to his will. With the weight of twelve hundred years of life behind him, he could not stand against Santaxma. Though in truth, not many could.

I cannot read in the jouncing coach, for it makes me ill, and neither Hatsun nor Drolma have much gift for conversation. So I am alone with my thoughts. I pick at them, turn them round and about inside my head. Even as I do, I'm aware of their fragility. For under them, like bedrock beneath a scattering of topsoil, lies the purpose of this journey, and the truths—or falsehoods—we will discover at its end. Will I be able, afterward, to return to these musings of mine? Will I want to?

Vivaniya and I don't speak of this. We see one another only in the evening, when we are weary, and in the morning, when we are half-awake. When we talk, it is of practical matters. But I can see his eagerness. I can feel his impatience.

Twice now I've dreamed of a desert, red and empty like the Burning Land. At the horizon a light rises up, as if a fire were raging somewhere far below. My dream-self walks toward it, walks and walks, but the light never nears. When I wake, I feel a pressure in my chest, as if a great hand were closing there. It's always a moment before I can breathe again.

Râvar

She arrived at night.

Râvar was just rising from his bath. When he heard the sound of summons, a rhythmic booming from a stretched-hide drum at the entrance to his quarters, he almost did not go out. But there had been clashes recently between his hunting bands and the nomad tribes that roamed the great grass steppes below the caverns, and it was possible that the matter was urgent. He wrung out his hair, then crossed swiftly to his bedchamber and pulled a long tunic over his nakedness. Settling the Blood of Ârata around his neck, he went to see what was wanted of him.

In the first of the four rooms of his private domain, beyond which none of his followers were allowed to go, Ardashir stood waiting. At his side was a weathered man with a garnet-colored lifelight. Râvar felt his heart stop, then leap forward at twice the speed. The man was Zabrades, one of four who had been sent to Ninyâser, months earlier, to search for Axane. Both men bowed.

"Well?" Râvar said.

"Beloved One." Ardashir's bandaged hands were clasped before him. A complex and forceful man, he owned one of the weakest lifelights Râvar had ever seen, no more than a shadowy blue flickering at the margins of his body. In bright illumination, it was barely visible. "The woman and her child have arrived."

It was not possible, for a moment, to speak. Râvar put his hands behind his back and paced to the dais at the center of the room, where a massive chair of translucent quartz thrust seamlessly out of the red-orange sandstone. He seated himself and shook back his wet hair. "Why have you not brought them?"

"Zabrades begged leave to speak with you first, Beloved One."

"Oh?" Râvar turned his eyes upon the other man.

"Beloved One." Zabrades bowed again. He was one of the First Faithful, part of the band of prisoners who had seen Râvar bring down the walls of Thuxra City. He wore nomad clothing, one of several things that distinguished the First Faithful from Râvar's other followers; at the base of his throat was a puckered band of scar tissue, the mark of the prison collar he had worn for seventeen years before Râvar set him free. "The woman is well. The child is well. But I wanted to prepare you."

"Prepare me for what?"

"Beloved One, we didn't have any trouble at first. When Sariya and I showed up to take her, she didn't even act surprised. It was almost like she was expecting us."

Râvar closed his ruined hands on the arms of the chair. As she had possessed his thoughts this past year, he had owned hers. As he had come to realize he had been wrong to let her go, she had grown to understand that he would reach out and take her back. He had hoped it would be so.

"But once we got on the road, she did all she could to delay us. She said she was sick, said the baby was sick, pretended she'd turned her ankle. Every chance she got she tried to give us the slip, and she didn't take kindly to being caught—she nearly broke Sariya's nose one time, for all she had the baby on her back. We had to do something, for her safety and the child's. We couldn't tie her hands, since she needed them for the babe, so what we did—well, what we did, we put a leash around her neck. We padded it as best we could. But it left a mark, Beloved One."

"A leash," Râvar repeated. How she must have hated that.

"Yes, Beloved One." Zabrades drew a breath. "It was me made the decision. If there's punishment coming, it's mine."

"No, Zabrades. I'm not angry. You did what you had to do to fulfill the task I gave you. There's no blame to that."

"Beloved One." Relief was clear on Zabrades's face.

"Did she speak to you as I said she might?"

"She cursed us, Beloved One, especially at the start. Apart from that she hardly opened her mouth at all, except to eat."

Râvar had struggled with what to tell them when he sent them out for her. His first thought was to concoct some sort of mythic tale on the order of the stories he had already invented. As Ârata had created him to be the Next Messenger, the god had created Axane to be his wife and companion during his sojourn upon the earth. During their wanderings in the desert they had conceived a child. But in the aftermath of Thuxra they were separated, and she, fearful and confused, wandered off and vanished—lost forever, he feared, until merciful Ârata granted him a dream of her, so he might send his followers to find her and return her to his side.

Such a story had no place in the legend of the Next Messenger. But he had already considerably altered the legend, and had little fear of his followers' doubt—for he knew that they were drawn to him not simply by belief, but by the desire to believe, and that this gave them an almost infinite capacity for acceptance, as long as he was careful not to contradict his own inventions. In the end, though, he decided on something less elaborate. If things went wrong—and he knew they might go very badly wrong indeed—fewer details would mean less need for justification. He had informed Ardashir simply that there was a woman and a child in Ninyâser whom he wanted found and brought to him, and ordered the First Disciple to arrange it. Hoping she would come willingly, aware she might not, he had told Zabrades and the others that her mind was disordered, that she might try and tempt them from their faith with lies. He saw the curiosity in their faces, but, obedient, they did not ask. It was not their place.

Ardashir, of course, believed his place was different. He accepted the unexplained instructions without comment, but Râvar felt his jealousy, and, a few days after the First Faithful departed, he came to ask the questions Râvar had been expecting: Who were the woman and her child? What were they to the Messenger? Râvar stared at the First Disciple until he dropped his eyes, then told him, gently, that he must wait to learn, and that all would be made clear in time. Ardashir had not quite been able to conceal his frustration, but since then had said nothing more.

"Was it difficult to find her?" Râvar asked.

"Not so much, Beloved One. Healers in Ninyâser aren't supposed to work unless they're registered, and they can't register unless they've done a full apprenticeship and have papers. We knew she couldn't have come by those the proper way, seeing as how you told us she was new to Arsace, so we figured she'd either have gotten the papers forged, or she'd be working unregistered. Plenty do. Merchants don't like the unregistered ones, and there's only so many places they can get the herbs and other things they need—all we had to do was ask around. Took less than a week. We watched the house and waited till her husband went out, then we came back for her and the child—"

"Her *husband*?"

Zabrades faltered. "Yes, Beloved One. She's married. A foreigner from Chonggye, a scribe. His name's Gyalo Timpurin Chok."

Râvar sat motionless. Gyalo. It was what the false Messenger had been called. He, too, had been from the kingdom of Chonggye . . . No. No, it was not possible. Besides, the false Messenger's other names had been different. It had to be coincidence, that first name.

But a husband . . .

"Beloved One?"

Râvar forced his attention back to the men before him. "You've done well, Zabrades. I'm pleased. Come, I'll give you blessing."

Râvar held out his hands. Zabrades came forward, and knelt to kiss the scarred palms.

"Child of Ârata. For your duty, gratitude. For your labor, rest. For your soul, light." Râvar touched the forefinger of his right hand to Zabrades's forehead. A small point of brilliance blossomed there. "In my father's name and mine, in the name of the time to come, I give you blessing."

Zabrades shuddered. Blinking rapidly, he rose and bowed. "Beloved One."

"Ardashir, bring them to me. See I am not disturbed again."

"Beloved One." Ardashir bowed also, though not quite so low—one of the privileges he claimed as First Disciple. He took Zabrades's arm, guiding him from the chamber.

Râvar left the reception chamber for the chamber beyond. A fire burned in a bowl-shaped depression he had shaped into the floor. Around it, six curved benches made a circle. He sat down on one of them, his hands clasped between his knees. Irrationally, in the fulfillment of the moment for which he had waited so long, he found himself wishing it either past or yet to come. *A husband*, he thought. He breathed deeply, striving for calm.

There was no sound. But he sensed a change and looked up. She stood in the chamber's entrance—a small woman, enclosed in an astonishing cloud of emerald and sapphire light. The sight of her struck him like a fist. Emotion flooded him. It felt like anger, like regret, like desire, like grief, like guilt, like need—like all those things, and none of them. For a moment, he could not breathe.

Carefully, he got to his feet. She stood motionless as he approached, but he saw the tensile quality of her stillness, like an animal about to bolt. She was slim, as he remembered, but her face and breasts were fuller. *The pregnancy*, he thought. She was trembling—or perhaps only shivering, for the caverns were chilly. He had prepared a speech, but could not recall a single word.

"Axane," he said.

Her nostrils flared. Every muscle in her body seemed to leap.

"Don't be afraid of me."

She stared at him. It was unexpectedly uncomfortable to be enclosed in such a gaze: the gaze of a person who knew exactly who he was. Not since he let her go had anyone looked at him that way. His eyes fell from hers, to her neck, where bruises lay dark on the dark skin.

"I'm sorry." He resisted the impulse to reach out and touch the injured spot. "That they had to bind you."

"I gave them no choice," she said in a low voice. Then: "Why have you brought me here?"

How can you ask? "I want you with me. I want our child."

She took a step back, her hands rising to the straps of the pack she wore—which he saw now was not a pack, but an infant's carrying cradle. "I thought you hated me," she said. "I thought you were glad to be rid of me."

"No. Never." He knew what had to be said, and forced himself to say it. "I wronged you. In the Burning Land. Whatever else—whatever else there was between us, I shouldn't have done to you what I did." He closed his eyes, convulsively, remembering. "I never knew I had such baseness in me, Axane, before that night. I'm sorry. I am so sorry."

She watched him. He could read nothing in her expression.

"I wish I could undo it. I wish that with all my heart. But I can't. I can only ask for your forgiveness. I love you, Axane, I've always loved you. You and I are the last of Refuge. We are all who remember it, all who grieve for it. There are terrible things between us, but we have both come so far, we've both lost so much. We share things we can never share with others. How can we be apart?" He willed into the words all the force of which he was capable, all the art of persuasion he had honed and perfected during the time of his deception. "However it was conceived, this is my child. My flesh, my blood, the only kin I have left in all the world. How can we not become a family, the three of us, you and I and our child?"

"A family," she repeated.

"If you ask it, I'll swear never to lay my hands on you again. But I want you with me, you and our child. It's hard . . . it is very hard . . . to be alone."

"But you're not alone. You have all this." She made a gesture, encompassing his chambers and everything that lay beyond them. "All these people who believe in you."

"But they're not *my* people! I share no history with them, no memories, no blood. You know what that means, I know you do. Haven't you longed for your own kin, your own kind? I know you can't be happy, all alone in this world you weren't born to—"

But she had not been alone. In the shock of seeing her, he had forgotten.

"What does it matter?" she said, out of her frozen face. "When has what I wanted ever mattered to you?"

In more than a year, not one person had dared speak to him so. Anger flared, the anger that had done so much damage between them. He breathed it away. *It's her fear,* he told himself; then, deliberately, probing the wound: *To which she is entitled.*

He had known her, growing up, as everyone in Refuge knew everyone else: the daughter of Refuge's leader, the child of her father's heart, a quiet girl who seemed somehow to be alone even in the company of other people. She was not pretty—slim as a reed, dark-skinned, her black hair too heavy and her brown eyes too large and her nose and mouth too proud. But then his shaping manifested, and he saw suddenly that she was beautiful—beautiful in a way only a Shaper could understand, beautiful in her jewel-colored light. The contrast between her lifelight's rich abandon and her own tight self-containment entranced him. How could so much light boil from so drab a woman? Surely she must hide some great secret, some seething passion, at the center of her soul.

Of course, as he was to learn, the qualities of lifelights were random, and reflected people's natures no better than their faces or their bodies did. Yet that first fascination never waned, and as he watched her going quietly about her business he grew convinced that the bland face she showed the world was a mask across a very different self. As soon as he was old enough, he began to woo her. He did not care that she was four years his elder, or that his friends thought her dull and ugly. He did not care that she rejected him, over and over, with a stubbornness that only proved what he already knew: She was more than she seemed. Concealed inside this yielding woman was a will of iron. He knew that he would win her. He was strong, and beautiful, and would one day be Refuge's Principal Shaper. It needed only time.

In the end his patience had run out. He turned to her father, who was only too pleased to order his stubborn daughter to accept such a prestigious match. It had not seemed to matter that her consent had been coerced—he had been that certain, once she was in his arms, that he could make her love him. But then the false Messenger, Gyalo Amdo Samchen, arrived in Refuge, and when he fled, she fled with him—a double betrayal, not just of Râvar and the love he had laid at her feet, but of Refuge, which he loved even more. He had not known it was possible to feel such pain. It enraged him that he could not cut her from his heart; it incensed him that he could not keep from dreaming her, and from desiring her in his dreams. He had punished her for that, in the aftermath of Refuge's destruction, as they traveled back across the Burning Land—punished her also for the truth he finally understood: that she had never believed in Refuge. *That* was the secret hidden inside her light: She had no faith. By then, of course, he had no faith either. He punished her for that as well, for his own unbearable grief and guilt, plumbing as he did the depths of a baseness he had not known was in him.

It was why he had set her free, just before he destroyed Thuxra City—as atonement, and also to ensure the survival of some piece of himself, through the child he knew she bore. But in the time that followed, in the loneliness of his sojourn among strangers, he had come to regret that decision. The ugliness between them grew dim. All that seemed to matter was the heritage they shared, and his own blood flowing in the child. She had betrayed him. He had wronged her. But they had both lost everything, and in that, perhaps, the rest of it might balance, and allow them to begin anew.

Now she stood before him, as unyielding as ever. He had forgotten that— how hard she was. *But you knew she wouldn't easily forgive*, he told himself. *You knew you'd have to work to win her.*

He turned away. "Come."

He seated himself again on the alabaster bench. After a hesitation she followed, and perched gingerly opposite him.

"This is a strange place," she said. "So much stranger than I—" She seemed to stop herself. "Expected."

He looked at the chamber, for a moment seeing it fresh. The pattern of the rock into which the cavern complex wormed its way was unfamiliar to him, as so much in this world was. So he had banished it from the interlocking chambers of his quarters, altering the rooms' proportions and overlaying them with a veneer of sandstone, banded orange and cream and gold like the sandstone of Refuge. For furnishing, he had made benches of jade and moonstone and hematite and onyx, tables of opal and chrysolite, and in his night chamber a fantastic bed of malachite, creating them by shaping blocks of gemstone, then unmaking the stone selectively into the form he desired—a technique he had developed in Refuge to amuse himself, and had never thought to put to any practical purpose. For illumination, he scooped niches into the walls and set flames inside them. The floor-fires were natural, fed with the pressed-grass bricks the pilgrims used, but the wall-flames were an artifice of his own invention, designed to eat the substance of the air and thus to burn without any visible source of fuel. It was a feat never dreamed of, even by the skilled and powerful Shapers of Refuge. He had taught himself many things in the past year that his teachers would have called impossible.

She was watching him. That frozen quality had relaxed; she seemed softer, more hesitant. "Did you remember what I told you in the Burning Land, about where I meant to go?" she asked. "Is that how you knew where to look for me?"

"Yes. My men said you barely spoke to them. I thought you might have tried to tell them something about me, to get them to let you go."

She shook her head. "I could see they wouldn't listen. Anyway, they wouldn't have been surprised to hear about Refuge. You've put it into your stories."

"Yes."

"Why do you call it the Awakened City? This place?"

"Because Ârata is awake. Because my followers are awake, or so they think."

She looked at him.

"I was sick after Thuxra," he said. "I almost died. When I woke I was surrounded by strangers—evildoers, all of them, blackened men. I was too weak to shape. They might have killed me, they might have torn me into pieces, and I couldn't have done a thing to stop them. Instead, I took those blackened men and made them mine. I changed the legend of the Next Messenger to suit myself. I made a plan and put it into motion. I have more than a thousand followers now, Axane. My missionaries are everywhere. Almost every day, new pilgrims arrive." The harsh pride of it rose in him. "I built this. I built it all out of nothing."

"It's a lie."

He felt as if she had slapped him. Once more he had to breathe away his anger.

"They told me about you, the men who took me. What you teach. What you plan. It's—" She paused. "Different from what you told me in the Burning Land. You said you meant to destroy the world. To destroy the Brethren."

"I was wrong to think I could destroy the world," he admitted. "But I do mean to destroy the Brethren."

"Your men said—"

"I know what they said. I couldn't tell them the truth, could I? I told them what I thought they would accept. I said I'd command the Brethren to bow down to me, and yield to me the leadership of the Âratist faith. And I do mean to make them do that. But I won't send them peacefully into retirement. Once they've acknowledged me, once their souls are black with blasphemy past any point of cleansing, I'll open the earth and close them all inside, and bring their ash-cursed city down upon them." A rush of indescribable elation gripped him. It was the first time he had ever uttered his intent aloud. Not until that moment had there been anyone he could speak it to. "And because none of them will survive, there will be no one to recognize their reborn souls, and they'll live out the rest of their incarnations in ignorance of what they are. If indeed they are immortal, as they claim."

"What will you tell your followers?"

He shrugged. "Whatever I need to."

"You think they will believe you?"

"They believe anything I say." It was the simple truth.

Complex emotion moved in her face. "Do you think our people would want this? Do you think your family would? Do you think my father would?"

Anger sparked again. "It's what *I* want."

"Don't you fear Ârata's judgment?"

"You know well what I think of Ârata and his judgment. Why should you ask me such a thing, anyway? You have no faith. Do you think I've forgotten?"

She looked down at her hands. Within the blue-green currents of her light, her face seemed pinched. "Râvar . . ." She hesitated, then continued in a rush. "Râvar, you must know you can't succeed. The people of this world will oppose you. Or you'll make a mistake, and your followers will turn on you. You've told so many lies—how long can you keep it up? How long can it go on?"

"For as long as I need it to go on."

"How long do *you* want to go on, then? Suppose you do destroy the Brethren. Will you still pretend to be the Next Messenger?" She raised her eyes to his. "Râvar, what you said, about wanting family . . . I understand that, I do. I know how hard it is to live in a world where you have no kin. Every day, every night I feel the hole in the world where my father used to be, where Refuge used to be. Maybe . . . if you had a family . . . you wouldn't need all this."

"Oh?" He raised his brows. "Are you saying you will be my family? You and the child?"

"Yes."

"And once I have you I should stop. Abandon the Awakened City. Steal away."

"You could do that," she said evenly. "If you wanted to."

He saw what she was trying to do, saw it as clearly as the room around him. He felt no anger this time, only weariness and disappointment.

"Show me my child."

For an instant she went completely still. Then she reached up to the straps of the carrying cradle and carefully slid them off her shoulders, rising to lay the cradle flat on the bench. She unlaced its ties and lifted out the child. It was swaddled in a blanket; its light was nearly as turbulent as its mother's, the color of apple jade. It woke at her touch and began to whimper.

"Give it to me." Râvar held out his hands.

The baby started to cry in earnest. With visible effort Axane stepped toward him, close enough that the margins of her lifelight brushed him. Something happened in her face, a paroxysm of dread.

"You won't . . . hurt her, will you?"

Her question shocked him. "Give her to me," he said roughly.

She dropped her eyes. Bending, she placed the yelling infant in his arms. The warm, struggling bundle was unexpectedly heavy. He held the baby to his chest, clumsy with his crippled hands. Her sobs diminished, then ceased. She gazed up at him with green eyes that were almost the same color as her lifelight.

My child, he thought, astonished. *From my body. From the ugly thing Axane and I did.*

"How old is she?"

"Nearly seven months." He heard the strain in Axane's voice. "Her name is Chokyi."

"Chokyi." The baby hiccuped. "What sort of name is that?"

"It's just a name."

"Was it your *husband* who chose it?"

She looked at him. Her eyes were large with dread.

"Oh yes, I know all about him. My men told me. I even know his name. *Gyalo.* Like the false Messenger."

An indescribable expression flickered across her features. And, that simply, he knew.

For a moment all he could do was sit. Then, slowly, he rose to his feet. She fell back—one step, two.

"Not *like* the false Messenger," he said. His voice seemed to come from a great distance. "He *is* the false Messenger."

Her silence admitted everything.

"You lived with." He could not get his breath. "You *married.* The creature who destroyed. Our people."

"No—"

"*No?* Do you deny it?"

"No—no—but it isn't what you think—I can explain—"

Râvar felt the room closing on him. The baby had begun to cry again;

he was surprised to realize he still held her. He stooped and laid her on the bench, losing hold of her a little so that she made a thump upon the stone. Axane gasped.

"Râvar, don't put her there—she'll fall—"

"Even you," he said. "Even you." Meaning: *I did not think even you were capable of such betrayal. I did not think even you could be so base.* But the words ran together in his head, and he could not force his tongue to form them. Blood roared behind his eyes. Behind him, the baby howled.

"Please." Axane was weeping now. "Let me have her."

He covered the space between them in a single stride. She flinched, a convulsion of her entire body, her hands coming up before her face.

"Don't hurt me. I'm her mother, she needs me—"

Her fear disgusted him. He gripped her arm with his good hand and began to walk, pulling her after him.

"Râvar, please. Let me have her. Please, please. Don't separate us." She was weeping so hard she could barely speak. "I'll do anything, anything. Don't take me from my child!"

She began to struggle. In the end he had to grab her around the waist; his hands were crippled, but his arms were still strong. She twisted against his grip, screaming, kicking out with her heavy boots, beating at him with her fists. Reaching his bedchamber, he hurled her into it; she went sprawling, but was up almost at once, flinging herself toward him even as he shaped stone across the entrance. He could almost feel the impact as she struck it.

He stood a moment, his ears ringing from the thunder of shaping in the enclosed space, half his vision stolen by its light. Then, turning, he set his body against the new-formed rock and slid slowly to the floor. He drew up his knees and set his elbows on them, digging the heels of his hands into his eyes. He was sick with disillusion and disgust. Her soul was alien to him. How could he have deceived himself so? How could he have forgotten? How could he have permitted himself to slip back into the old madness, the old fallacy—that if he tried hard enough, if he strove long enough, he could win her love? That he could change her? That she was worth changing? His own stupidity stunned him.

He could still hear her, distantly, screaming from behind the rock. At last it dawned on him that it was not Axane at all, but the baby, abandoned in the empty chamber.

He pushed himself wearily to his feet and trudged back the way he had come. The baby lay on the bench, shrieking like a little bellows. He went to her, thinking only to stop the noise. Slipping his nearly useless left hand beneath her body and gripping her with his right, he managed to heave her up and settle her against his shoulder. In Refuge, his brothers and sisters had had infants, and he knew what to do; he held her, pacing back and forth, jogging her gently. She was hot and damp, and smelled of sour milk and dirty linen. But there was a surprising pleasure in the feel of her, this tiny creature in his arms.

She quieted at last, hiccuping into his neck. He sat on one of the benches, letting her slip down so that she lay in the crook of his arm. He pulled his sleeve over his right hand and wiped her cheeks and nose. She had a cap of wispy black hair, stuck to her scalp now with sweat, and had inherited his fine-grained amber skin. She stared up at him with her green eyes, her gaze grave and fearless. There was no knowledge in it, no judgment, no desire, no need. She did not see him as a savior. She did not see him as a rapist. She simply saw him.

My child, he thought, this time with wonder.

She squirmed, her limbs pushing against the constriction of her blanket. He drew back its folds, freeing her little arms. She gave a small crowing cry, and reached up to grab a strand of his hair. Gently he detached it, giving her a crooked finger to hold instead. She clutched it with surprising strength and chuckled, her plump cheeks creasing. He felt a softening within himself, as if a sharp edge had fallen away. Warmth unfolded in the region of his heart. At first he did not recognize it.

Love.

Sometime later she began to howl, and nothing he could do would soothe her. He returned to his bedchamber and unblocked it. Axane was crouched against the bed; she sprang to her feet at once. There was a spreading bruise on one cheek. She had eyes only for the child.

He stood a moment, prolonging her suffering. But the baby's cries were becoming desperate, and at last he stepped forward and offered her to her mother. Axane gasped and clutched her shrieking daughter to her breast, burying her face in the baby's shoulder.

"Thank you," she said. "Oh, thank you, thank you."

"I could find a woman from among my followers to nurse her." He had to raise his voice to be heard above the baby's yells. "It wouldn't be difficult."

Axane raised her head. "Please don't. I won't give you any trouble, I swear."

"I was wrong to bring you here." The admission of his failure was like lead upon his tongue. "It could never have worked. I see that now."

In her face he saw a despair beyond fear. "What will you do with us?"

What, indeed? He turned away. "You can have this room. For now."

He closed them in again. He made his way through his empty apartment, to the bench where he had sat a few moments ago with his daughter in his arms. He sank down on it, his hands hanging between his knees, and did not move for a long time.

7

Râvar

He was entombed within the rock, and cold, so cold. To his left was light, a golden ocean of it, pulsing like a living thing. To his right lay the darkness of the passage he had blocked off. Beyond the passage an army waited, demons in the form of men. They had come to Refuge to extinguish the light—to destroy the Cavern of the Blood, where Ârata had slept away the eons but slept no more. But he was the Cavern's protector, by duty and desire. He had sealed it from the demons' sight with a shaping so perfect that even another Shaper would not be able to detect it. And he had closed himself inside, to defend it.

He had done what was needed, and done it well. What then was the dread that possessed him, the sense of something left terribly unfinished? *Wasn't there something else . . . something else I should have saved—*

A jolt. Time paused, stuttering, then leaped forward at dizzying speed. He was no longer in the Cavern, but on the ledge beneath it. Below, the river Revelation sang its joyous song, rushing down to Refuge. The demons had gone. *Safe*, he thought. But the cold was still inside him, and the dread, the certainty of some horrible oversight—

Another jolt. He stood in Refuge. But where the Temple had been, and Labyrinth and the Treasury and the House of Dreams, there was only rubble. The demons had destroyed his home, defacing the carvings and smashing the equipment and pulling down the walls and ceilings of the caves where his people had lived and worked. "Why?" he shouted. "Why?" The ruin of Refuge drank his words like water, giving nothing back, not even an echo. And the voice inside his head, frantic now, screamed: *Run! There may still be time—*

Another jolt. He was at the mouth of the cleft. He could see the trail the demons had left beside the river. He was following it, running—

Another jolt. The cleft was far behind; he was among the bitterbark trees that grew on Revelation's banks. He understood now that he was dreaming. He fought to pull away, for he knew where the dream would take him. He could already hear the sound, the awful whining—

Another jolt. And the bluff was there, ahead, with Revelation rolling past and the roaring of the flies and the sprawling darkness on the banks—

He screamed—aloud? It hardly mattered, for in reality, as in his dream, there was no one to hear him—and twisted like a fish on a hook. The dream broke. He bolted upright. He sat gasping, eyes open on the dimness of his chamber, afraid even to blink for fear that sleep would seize him back and force him to complete the journey.

At last, certain he was fully awake, Râvar drew up his knees and laid his forehead on them, drawing long breaths, willing his knotted muscles to relax. At least this time he had been able to interrupt it. He could not always manage that. What waited at the dream's end was cobbled and distorted out of his real memories, yet even the hideous pictures inside his head were not as terrible as what the dreams forced him to witness. Sometimes he saw his family die, his mother thrust through with a lance, his sisters and their children pierced by arrows, his cousins cut down with swords, while he stood rooted to the spot, unable even to cry out. Sometimes he arrived after the massacre was done, and was compelled to crawl among the corpses like one of the carrion-eaters that had been at them when he found them. Worst was when they spoke to him. *Become like us,* they murmured. *Be nothing, no one. Let no living soul remember you.* Or they reproached him: *What is faith beside the ties of blood? How could you choose Ârata over us?* Or, horribly and for that very thing, they praised him. *You made the bravest choice,* they sighed. *Ârata is eternal. We are whispers, blades of grass.*

It did not matter what they said. He knew the truth, knew it waking and sleeping: He was guilty of their deaths—he, the last of Refuge's ordained Shapers. There had been only him, after the failure of the resistance he and his fellow Shapers had mounted against the Brethren's army, to defend his people. Instead, he had chosen to defend the Cavern of the Blood. Never mind that it was the charge laid on him by Refuge's leader. Never mind that he had not imagined that Ârata would allow Refuge to be destroyed: He and his people were Ârata's chosen, whom the god might test but would not abandon. The truth, the bare truth, was that he had been afraid—afraid of the demon soldiers with their manita that could kill a Shaper's power, afraid to stand against them alone. And because of his fear, Refuge had died.

They had taught him this, his people—or their corpses had, when he found them. They had taught him other things as well, a learning begun and completed in the two days he spent upon the riverbank, watching them rot. Either Ârata was a capricious god, who cruelly turned his face away from suffering and injustice, or the founders of Refuge had been mistaken and Ârata had never chosen Refuge at all. His faith left him as he sat there, the faith that had sometimes filled him up so hugely he thought his skin must split to let it out. He had felt it burning out of him, as if it were water and his murdered people were the sun.

I choose you, he had sworn to them at the end of his vigil, the flame of new intent flickering in the void where faith had been—a very tiny flame, but still a light against the nothingness that had nearly consumed him. *Not Ârata. Never Ârata, never again.* He had buried them, opening up the riverbank and closing them beneath it, smoothing the ground so no trace of their agony remained. Then he had turned his back and taken the first step on the long, long journey that had brought him to this world.

Do you think it's what they would have wanted? The question Axane had asked on the night of her arrival spoke inside his mind. *It's what I want,* he had told her. Thinking of that reply, he felt ashamed. It *was* what he wanted. But the Awakened City was not for him. It was for Refuge. All of it, all of it for Refuge.

His face was wet with tears. He rubbed them away with the heels of his hands, then wadded up his pillows and leaned back, drawing up the coverings of his bed—not the elaborate malachite affair in the room he had given to Axane and the baby, but a simple platform he had shaped against one wall of his bathing chamber. He had extinguished the sourceless flames so he could sleep, but they still burned in the room beyond, and by their warm light he could see the wall opposite, where stone plugged the entrance to his night chamber. Behind it, Axane slept. He was uncomfortably aware of her closeness, as he had been for each of the six days and nights since her arrival—an awareness that, depending on his mood and the direction of his thoughts, was angry, painful, bitter, or, with profound unwillingness, desirous. It had always been a thing apart, his desire for her, entirely separate from his intellect, from anything he knew or understood, a drive as indifferent to will and logic as the currents of the river Revelation. He was troubled by thoughts of how he had forced her in the Burning Land—of how it had felt not just to expend his lust but to humble her. It was not what he had wanted with her; it was never what he had wanted. But it was what he had done, and he could not prevent himself from remembering, or from being stirred.

In the aftermath of the dream, it was not lust he felt, nor anger or disgust or any of those raw emotions, but something more like longing. To wake from nightmares to the warmth of another's body, the comfort of another's arms. To speak his dreams aloud, to drag those dark things out of the cage of his mind and expose them to the light—where, perhaps, they might begin to wither, to loosen their grip.

No, he thought, bracing himself against his weakness. *Don't think of it.* He turned on his side so he would not see the wall, and waited open-eyed for morning.

Above the bathing pool, he had shaped a wide channel through the rock, all the way to the top of the ridge within which the caverns ran. He had grown up in caves, but never beyond easy sight of the world outside, and in this deep place it had oppressed him not to be able to gauge the passage of time. Rain fell through the opening, and sometimes things less pleasant—but it was worth it, to follow the exchange of day and night.

The light that stole down the channel was still spectral when the announcement drum sounded. He rose and went out to the reception room, where the guard on duty had left his morning meal: two dishes of the wheat-and-rice porridge that was the community's staple, two cups of metallic-tasting water. It was what his followers ate; apart from his private living space and the gifts they gave him, he made it a point to have nothing the faithful could not share. This was less noble than it seemed, given that he could shape food for himself. He did so now: honey to sweeten the bland grain, a handful of the tart red berries that the people of Refuge had called bloodglobes, which did not grow in the world beyond the Burning Land. It was one of the things that bolstered his followers' belief in the miraculousness of his powers, that he was able to shape things completely foreign to them.

With his right hand, which still worked more or less as a hand should, he lifted one of the cups, and, holding it to his chest with his crippled left hand, took up one of the bowls. He returned to his night chamber and put forth his will. A flash, a cracking percussion; and the plug that blocked the entrance was gone.

Axane was nursing the baby. She turned away, but not quickly enough to spare him the sight of her bare shoulder and naked breast. It went through him like a knife; for a moment he could not move.

"She'll be finished soon." Her voice was dull. The child's jade green light trembled within the storm of her mother's darker colors.

"I'll come back later." It had become his habit to take the baby in the mornings; that day, though, he had other obligations. He set the food on the floor and closed them in again.

He ate his own breakfast, then shaped water in a basin and shaved his face with a razor that had been a gift from one of his followers. He dressed in garments bartered from the nomads: a quilted undertunic, a bright-dyed overtunic, quilted leggings, leather boots shod with silver. He was to go among his followers, but he would not wear his cloak of light; on ritual occasions he went to them as a god, but at other times he appeared in a more ordinary guise, to remind them that part of him was human. He combed the tangles from his hair, leaving it loose down his back since he no longer possessed the dexterity to braid or bind it. Once he had taken pleasure in his good looks and devoted much attention to dressing and grooming himself. It had been a long time since that was so. But the faithful expected him to be beautiful for them, and though they belonged to him soul and body, there was a sense in which they owned him, too, or at least the semblance of him that was the object of their faith.

He retrieved the necklace from beneath the overturned bowl where he kept it at night, so the restless fire of the Blood would not disturb his sleep. He had shaped the gold of which it was made; one of the First Faithful, a jeweler before his imprisonment, had crafted it, with a heavy chain and a thick casing to hold the crystal, as big as a man's clenched fist. At night when he removed it, he could trace the grooves the links had printed in the skin of his neck. He lowered it over his head—carefully, for the casing left the Blood's razor facets uncovered at the front. He could read the lattice structure of the crystal, common to any gem; but the fire at its heart resisted understanding, for though it was not alive, it resembled the light of life, which Shaper senses could perceive but not comprehend.

The announcement drum sounded again, and he left his chambers. The passage beyond ran between the huge cavern at the front, where the citizens of the Awakened City lived, and the smaller, deeper cave where daily ceremonies were conducted. Originally it had been little more than a rough fissure, but for the comfort of his followers Râvar had widened and smoothed it, and shaped a stairway into the sharp drop that led down to the ceremonial cave. Ardashir was waiting with two members of the Band of Twenty, the specially chosen group of men who served the First Disciple as aides and assistants and, sometimes, enforcers. The Twentymen wore plaited grass armbands to mark their status; they carried staves of pale bitterbark wood, shaped by Râvar, and held smoky torches made of twisted grass soaked in animal fat.

"Beloved One." All three bowed low. The Twentymen turned and led the way along the passage's uphill slope. Râvar and Ardashir fell in behind.

A squared opening at the passage's end gave onto the twilit reaches of the main cavern. Its floor was crowded with the encampments of the faithful, marked out and made crudely private with dividers improvised from draped fabric or woven grass or stacked stones. In each, a carefully tended cook fire burned. Despite their cobbled and primitive air, the little living areas were neat—Ardashir, who supervised every aspect of life and work in the Awakened City, decreed it should be so. Natural fissures dispelled most of the smoke, but the atmosphere was acrid, pungent with the smell of crowded humanity. Far away, the perfect arch of the entrance framed blank blue sky. The ridge that held the cavern complex rose at the margin of the foothills of the Range of Clouds; below lay only a descending slope and the flatness of the steppe.

A broad aisle between the encampments served as a kind of thoroughfare. At this hour of the day most of Râvar's followers were elsewhere, performing their allotted labor, but there were always a few who remained—the sick, the injured, those who had just arrived and had not yet been assigned a work group. Men and women propped themselves up in their blankets to watch Râvar pass, or hitched to their knees in attitudes of prayer, or scurried forward to get a closer look.

"Messenger!" Their whispers followed him. Their lifelights glinted in the dimness. "Beautiful One! Beloved of Ârata!"

Râvar spread his hands in benediction, but, according to the custom of these excursions, did not pause.

Near the entrance, another passage opened in the left-hand wall. This passage was entirely artificial, punched by Râvar through the solid stone to give access to the otherwise inaccessible cave adjacent to the main cavern. Walls, floor, and ceiling displayed the precise proportions, the water-smooth planes and rounded angles that were the hallmark of Shaper stonework. By the standards of Refuge, it was an unremarkable making; but in this world that feared and hated shaping and knew nothing of its uses, it was a great wonder.

The Twentymen quickened their pace as they neared the passage's end. "The Next Messenger comes!" they called. "Prepare for the Next Messenger!" By the time Râvar emerged into the cave, all the workers were on their knees.

"Messenger," they murmured. "Beloved One."

"Rise, children. Return to your work."

They obeyed. This cave, lower-ceilinged than the main cavern but nearly as large, held the community's food stores—the grain and salt and fruit Râvar replenished weekly, the meat and other edibles brought back by the hunting and foraging parties—and also much of the work that maintained the

Awakened City. Here as elsewhere, Ardashir's genius for organization was apparent. The workers were grouped by activity—the pounding and spinning of steppe grass into coarse thread, the weaving of fabric on crude standing looms, the sewing of blankets and simple garments (for many of the faithful arrived in rags), the pressing of the grass bricks that fueled the pilgrims' cook fires, the knapping of flint blades and arrowheads for hunting, the preparation of bows and arrow shafts and knife hafts. Though there was no opening to the outside, the atmosphere was fresh; all the caverns were riddled with fissures, invisible to the naked eye but apparent to Râvar's patternsense, and he had enhanced them here so that the great space breathed, drawing in new air, expelling old.

By each area of activity, he paused to allow the workers to demonstrate work in progress and show off work completed. He gave them praise; he let them kiss the scars upon his palms; he touched their foreheads and left little sparks of blessing, causing some to fall swooning to the ground. The bolder ones reached out to stroke his clothing or his hair, kissing their fingers afterward. He despised them, his sheeplike faithful; but it was impossible to be indifferent to their adoration, impossible not to be thrilled by his power, by their surrender, by the way those things fed back and forth between them, a brilliant tension that sparked in his belly and drew tight within his chest.

When the tour was done he returned to the cavern's entrance and extended his hands, calling illusion above his palms so that flames seemed to leap there—an intentional echo of Ârata in his guise of Risen Judge, ruler of the time of cleansing.

"Children, your industry pleases me. I thank you for your endeavor, which sustains our community of the faithful. You do this labor now, that you may labor no more in the time to come. Blessings be on you."

"Messenger," they chorused. "Blessings be on you."

He closed his fingers, quenching the false flames, and left them.

Supplicants still waited at the edges of the encampments. This time, he paused to speak to them and dispense blessings. As he turned from one of these groups, there was a sudden flurry of motion. A woman came thrusting forward and flung herself to her knees in front of him, clutching at the hem of his tunic.

"Beloved One," she gasped. With her free arm she held a dirty bundle to her breast. "Please. My little girl."

The Twentymen stepped toward her, ready to drive her back, but Râvar held up his hand.

"Release me, child." She obeyed. "What do you want of me?"

"My baby, Beloved One." She had that starved, stunned look all new arrivals seemed to wear at first; her lifelight was a pale and lovely amethyst. "She's sick. Beloved One, please heal her!"

There was a murmur from the pilgrims. Healing was an issue Râvar had been forced to confront early on, for many of his followers had expected him to display powers he did not possess. It still cropped up from time to time, fueled in part by his missionaries, who told those they recruited that the Next Messenger could do miracles and let the pilgrims draw their own conclusions.

"I cannot do that, child," he told her. "The power to heal the sick is the power of life. Only gods possess it."

"But you *are* a god."

"Only partly, child. Half of me is human. My power is beyond any mortal's, but I cannot shape life. Even to me, my father did not give that ability."

She gasped, and sobbed. "You cannot heal her?"

"No, child."

"Will you bless her, then, Beloved One?"

"If you wish it."

With tender hands she laid the bundle down and pulled aside the cloth. The child stared up at Râvar with the unnatural apathy of prolonged illness or starvation. Her lifelight, grass green, stabbed him unbidden with the thought of his own little girl.

"Her name is Vikrit, Beloved One." The woman wiped her wet cheeks with the backs of her hands.

Râvar stooped and touched his fingers to the small hot forehead. "I call Ârata's blessing on you, Vikrit, in hope that he will make you well and strong again. Abide in my father's love and in the promise of the age to come."

He began to draw away. Before he could prevent it the mother seized his hand and pressed it to her lips.

"Thank you, Beloved One. Thank you."

Her tears fell on his skin. He pulled away, repulsed. "Don't thank me, child. Ârata is the god of love and light, but sometimes he demands our suffering. Your daughter may yet die."

"But she will rise into the light of the new primal age. And I'll rise, too, when the way is opened. I'll be with her again."

He saw the hope in her face, the blind faith. It was impossible even to be cruel to these people. Whatever he said to her, she would only blame her own unworthiness, and search for signs of Ârata's will in the Next Messenger's harsh judgment.

"Yes," he said. "You'll rise." He got to his feet, beckoning Ardashir. "See she gets a healer."

"Yes, Beloved One."

Râvar strode down the thoroughfare, ignoring the faithful who humbly waited for his attention. He plunged into the ancient darkness of the passage, charting his steps by his lifelight and by the torches burning beside the opening to his rooms. He mounted the short flight of steps, the Twentyman on guard bowing low as he passed, and entered with deep relief into the warm colors and soothing patterns of his own domain.

He flung himself down on a bench in the second chamber, leaning toward the warmth of the floor-fire. In pausing for the woman and her child he had meant to demonstrate the compassion his followers believed he possessed, but he wished now that he had allowed the Twentymen to remove her. He did not often pity his followers, these souls he had stolen from Ârata by blackening them with false belief; if they were fools enough to embrace the fraud he offered them, they had only themselves to blame. But that small green lifelight would not leave his mind. He could still feel the dying child's papery skin under his fingers. He rubbed his hands together, trying to banish it.

A tapping on the announcement drum let him know he had been followed. Sighing, for he knew who it must be, he returned to the reception chamber.

"Beloved One." Ardashir clasped his hands—one of which he had left unbandaged that day, as he did sometimes so the pilgrims could see his wounds—and bowed. He was a blocky, dark-skinned man, with bulbous features that seemed somehow unfinished, like a sculpture that had been abandoned just short of completion. Râvar guessed him to be somewhere in his fifties, but his hair, which he wore cropped close to his scalp, showed no gray, and he carried himself like a man at least a decade younger. He was faultlessly controlled, rarely smiling or frowning or raising his voice—a master of the telling stare, the speaking silence. Râvar had seen him bend men to his will simply by looking at them.

"I sent the healer, Beloved One." In contrast to his unhandsome face, Ardashir's voice was remarkably beautiful, a resonant baritone, an orator's voice. "Though I think the child will die. You mustn't grieve too much. You cannot save them all."

Râvar turned away, and seated himself in the pink quartz chair. "Have you come to make your report?"

"With your permission, Beloved One."

Ardashir took up his reporting stance—hands behind his back, body punctiliously straight, feet placed with precision—and began, as he did each day, to speak of the affairs of the Awakened City. The population had been swelled by a party of new arrivals, nine in all. The task schedules, intricate plans of Ardashir's devising that rotated workers between cavern duty and the hunting-and-gathering bands, were running smoothly. There were the usual petty disputes between the pilgrims, none needing immediate resolution. More seriously, there had been another confrontation between a hunting group and a nomad band. The nomads, who had had the steppes to themselves for uncounted centuries, were alarmed by the influx of new inhabitants, whom they suspected of plotting to poach their horse herds.

"It's time we sent gifts again, Beloved One. Gold, some gems—I will draw up a list for you."

"See to it," Râvar said. These administrative matters bored him. Long ago, in Refuge, he had resented the customs that bound Shapers solely to religious duty, for in his impetuous ambition he had wanted not just the office of Principal Shaper, but Refuge's secular leadership as well. When, by a series of chances he could never have anticipated, that leadership actually fell to him, he had discovered that the pleasure of being able to give orders was outweighed by the tedium of the endless details involved in overseeing a community.

He recognized how fortunate he was to have found a man like Ardashir, who took satisfaction in both. Ardashir's skills had been honed on one of the immense communal plantations the Caryaxists had created in Arsace's heartland, as part of their effort to abolish the evils of private property. Born into a family of field hands, his brilliance and his implacable will had lifted him first to work leader, then to section chief, and finally to headman. For nearly ten years he had been the ruler of his own small kingdom, managing the plantings and the harvests, governing every aspect of his workers' lives. Those skills and qualities had served him also after he was sent to Thuxra City, for even in that bleak environment amenities could be bargained, favors traded, life made a little less wretched. Ardashir's facility for such maneuverings had won him first respect, then power. In time, in a strange mirror of his former life, he had become a leader among the imprisoned men.

"Do you have any instruction for me, Beloved One?" Ardashir had finished his recital.

"No. You've everything perfectly in hand, as usual."

Ardashir inclined his head; the praise was his due, and he knew it. "How fares the woman, Beloved One? And the child? Do they require anything for their comfort?"

Râvar suppressed his annoyance. Ardashir had asked this question almost daily since Axane and the baby had arrived. "You need not worry about their comfort, Ardashir."

There was a pause. Râvar waited. Eventually, he knew, Ardashir would not be able to resist his need to probe; his sense of entitlement would get the better of him, his driving desire to be admitted into every aspect of the life of the Messenger he served so passionately. If Râvar had allowed it, Ardashir would have waited on him hand and foot, as he had done in the beginning. It was a constant, unspoken tension between them: Ardashir's compulsion to draw close, Râvar's aversion to such closeness—which he must always balance with the need not to test Ardashir too far.

"Beloved One . . ." Ardashir hesitated, and Râvar knew the moment had come. "I know there are things that must remain closed to me. But I cannot deny the question in my heart, and I would not dishonor my service to you by concealing it. Will you not tell me why you shelter them, the woman and the child?"

"I've already answered that question, Ardashir."

"Yes, Beloved One. But I ask not just for myself, but for your faithful. They will wonder—" Ardashir's gaze dropped. "If you've taken a consort."

"And what if I have?"

"Beloved One, you are human, and human flesh has needs . . . Ârata knows, there are many here who would tempt those needs if they could. But if she is your consort, should you not reveal it?"

Râvar shifted on the hard quartz seat. If things had turned out as he had hoped, he might indeed have introduced Axane as his consort. He had even half planned the ceremony with which he would present her. Obviously that was no longer possible. The day after her arrival he had ordered Ardashir to dispatch Zabrades and the other kidnappers back into the world at once as missionaries; the fewer people who knew of her, the better. But that was as far as he had gone in deciding what to do. Frustration twisted in him at the complication of it.

"She's not my consort," he said. "If such a person exists, I have not yet found her. But she and the child are souls my father in his compassion desires me to protect. If I do not tell you more, Ardashir, it's not because I wish to keep his purpose hidden from you, whom I trust beyond any of my followers, beyond any mortal on this earth. It's because the moment is not yet right. I ask for your patience. I promise that in time all will be made clear."

A beat of silence. Then Ardashir bowed his head. "Thank you, Beloved One."

"Is there anything else?"

"One last matter, Beloved One, if I may beg your indulgence."

Râvar resisted the impulse to sigh. "Go on."

"You know how eagerly your faithful look forward to the Awakened City's emergence. They are aware that there must first be a time of waiting, of gathering. But they can't help wondering when the great work we have pledged to undertake will commence."

"I've told them. When I receive the sign my father promised."

"Yes, Beloved One. But time, for mortals, is a heavy burden." Ardashir, who believed that Râvar was still learning to be human, never lost the chance to provide instruction. "They find the waiting difficult. Could you not tell them when the sign will arrive? Or let them know what it will be?"

Râvar frowned. "Is there question about this?"

"Yes, Beloved One, growing question. Growing impatience. The Awakened City has become very large, and in large populations such feelings take greater hold, have greater impact. Also, there are certain citizens . . ." Ardashir paused, selecting his words. "Who are more inclined than others to discontent. Beloved One, you've decreed that the Awakened City must be open to all who seek it. *My love is a palace without walls, an empire without borders,* Ârata says in the *Darxasa,* and so it is for you. But this has drawn to you not just good and honest men and women, but those whose lives, whose pursuits have not been so clean—"

"I'm well aware of that," Râvar said with some irritation. It was an old disagreement. Ardashir had long urged that pilgrims of questionable character should be excluded from the body of the faithful—counsel Râvar had no intention of following, for it suited his purpose to populate his pilgrim army with such people. Given that almost all the First Faithful, and of course Ardashir himself, had been prisoners at Thuxra, Ardashir's insistence might have seemed hypocritical; but Râvar knew it was not, or not entirely. Blackened man that Ardashir was, blackened men that all the First Faithful were, they had been exalted by their witness of Râvar's emergence from the Burning Land, by the fact that they were the first to acknowledge him—or so Ardashir believed. Their sin had not been removed, but they had been given a means to transcend it that other sinners, arriving later, could not possess. In his own way, Ardashir adhered to as rigid a moral code as any priest. "Just as you're aware that I'll deny no one who wants to follow me."

"Beloved One, I must be blunt. I don't say these people are not faithful. No one could take the mark and make the journey otherwise. But a thief who believes is still a thief. A prostitute who believes is still a whore. Such people are fertile soil for the seeds of rumor and discontent, and if those weeds are not pulled out, they will overrun the garden we have planted here. *Give only for the grace of giving*, the *Darxasa* tells us of the Foundation of Compassion, but it is also written, *Poverty of the flesh may be relieved, but poverty of the soul is a well that is never filled.* This may seem strange to you, Beloved One, who in your innocence are not familiar with the depth of human baseness. Nor should you be—that is what I am for, to shield you from such things. I beg you, therefore, accept my advice. Speak to the questions. Let your faithful know their waiting will have an end. Give them something to hold, to look toward! Only thus can you ensure that question does not grow into something more troublesome."

He held Râvar's gaze. Ardashir could be deferent to the point of obsequiousness (though there was not the least insincerity in it), but he took with fierce literalness his role as adviser, and never hesitated to put forth his opinions or to argue in support of them, even where they contradicted Râvar's.

"Very well." Experience had taught Râvar that in matters of this sort Ardashir was usually correct. "I'll speak to it."

"Thank you, Beloved One. You are wise."

"Are you finished? I'd like to be alone."

"Yes, Beloved One. Remember, there are audiences this afternoon."

Enemy take the audiences, Râvar thought. "I haven't forgotten."

He stretched out his hands. Ardashir came forward and knelt to press a kiss into each scarred palm. He closed his eyes, like someone receiving Communion marks, brushing the backs of Râvar's hands with his own fingers. Râvar glimpsed the swollen scabs and weeping cuts crisscrossing Ardashir's right palm, the stains on the bandages that wrapped the left. Ardashir was fastidious to the point of mania; even in the first days of the Awakened City he had been less dirty than the rest, less wild. The bandages were the sole exception. After Thuxra's destruction, he had been the first of the prisoner-witnesses to reach Râvar's side; he had caught the Blood of Ârata as, drained nearly to death by that enormous act of shaping, Râvar collapsed into unconsciousness. The crystal's facets had sliced him to the bone. In the time since, the injuries somehow had never healed. It was assumed by Râvar's followers that human flesh could not bear the touch of the divine Blood; Râvar, who had grown up with the Blood, knew very well this was not so, and guessed that Ardashir opened the cuts himself—whether as penance for his sins or as an incomprehensible act of devotion, Râvar did not care to guess. Or maybe Ardashir had a shrewder reason. He had been a powerful man among the prisoners even before Râvar came, but his wounds conferred on him an echo of divinity. His right to call himself the First Disciple, to function as the de facto ruler of the Awakened City, had never been questioned.

Ardashir departed. Râvar rose and went into his bathing room, where the sun admitted by the roof opening plunged a shaft of gold into the pool. He had intended to take his daughter for a little while. But as he approached the wall behind which Axane and the baby were confined, an image of the dying child's green lifelight returned to him, and he was abruptly possessed by the need to escape the caverns, to breathe open air. He removed the Blood and prisoned it beneath its bowl, then caught up a blanket from his bed and left his quarters—not by the exit in his reception room, but through the passage that led off the bathing chamber, which ended on the precipice where he began the daily ceremonies. Branching off this corridor was another, winding a circuitous upward route through, and ultimately beyond, the caverns.

He passed through perfect darkness without stumbling, for he carried his own illumination with him. It was cold in the inner caves, a chill that did not change no matter what the season; the air smelled wet, metallic, and very, very old. He traversed passages that were level and others that rose like stairs, edged through fissures barely wide enough to admit him and jumped crevasses that seemed to have no bottom, crossed galleries filled with fantastical formations: pillars glistening with minerals, ceilings fanged with sharp stone daggers, walls where the rock seemed to have melted and flowed down. Even in these deep places there was life, thriving in the clammy dark, throwing off the light all living things possessed—pale molds and mosses, sticklike insects, and in the pools, strange eyeless water creatures.

A slash of sunlight announced the caverns' end. He emerged on a ledge above the steppe, into a whipping gale and the brilliant glare of noon. He had discovered this high place soon after the First Faithful claimed the cavern complex, driven to exploration by his horror of idle time. It reminded him a little of the Plains of Blessing, which had swept just as hugely out beneath the red cliffs of Refuge. The steppe grasses were short and tawny, not tall and silver, and the air did not carry the sharp smell of bitterbark. But if he half closed his eyes and stilled his mind, he could sometimes recapture a little of the feeling of home.

In a fold of rock that gave some shelter from the wind, he folded the blanket into a pad and sat down. He raised his face to the midsummer sun, trying to lose himself in its warmth, in the bright clarity of the air. Instead, he found himself thinking about Ardashir's admonition.

The sign. What am I going to do about the ash-cursed sign?

There was no sign, of course. It was something he had made up, to inspire his followers and lend glamour to their waiting. It would be easy enough, he had thought, to invent some portent when the time was right. But when would the time be right? His followers numbered well over a thousand. His missionaries had been spreading word, in Arsace and elsewhere, for more than a year. Was it enough? How could he know? The search for Axane had allowed him to postpone the question, for no decision could be made until she was found or his men returned empty-handed. But she had come; and he found himself no closer to an answer than he had ever been.

I'll think of something, he told himself. *I always do.*

The wind gusted, harrying the clouds. He pushed his tangled hair back from his face. He had made the Awakened City, shaped it as much as any of the creations of his power; it was his possession, like the necklace that held the Blood, and though it was heavy, he was well capable of standing straight beneath its weight. Still, he was conscious sometimes not of leading but of being swept, as if he had jumped into a turbulent river. The jump he had chosen. But the journey, in many ways, chose itself.

If all this had been described to me a year ago, would I have believed it?

No. The Awakened City had not been his plan at all.

He remembered the acts with which he had claimed his false title—a chain of disconnected images, as brilliant and static as the religious paintings on the gallery walls of Refuge's lost Temple. Striding among the mines of Thuxra City, the Blood held before him on bleeding palms. The prisoner-workers, falling to the ground in awe, dropping their tools and stumbling after him. Standing before the walls of the prison, hurling against them the power that had shaken them apart—a power that in memory hardly seemed to be his own, but some vaster, stranger force summoned by his rage and grief out of the very substance of the world. He had named himself Next Messenger and unmade the prisoners' chains. And then he had let go—of his body, of consciousness. After that, all was dark.

He opened his eyes on fire. It seemed to him that he was pierced by shafts of flame. He bolted upright, gasping, certain he had died, and Ârata had wakened him to be judged. But then he realized he was in a room, made of stones so badly fitted that sunlight, solid with dust, lanced in everywhere through the chinks. Beside him knelt a barrel-chested man, his face half-hidden in a forest of black beard. Gently, the man pressed Râvar down again.

"Rest, Messenger," he murmured. His lifelight was the merest blue shimmer around his body.

Râvar's mind spun. Who was this man? Where was he? But the intensity of his panic had taken all his strength. He closed his eyes and sank again into blackness.

When he woke again, it was to the consciousness of being lifted. Someone's arm supported him; someone's hands held a cup to his lips. He drank—water, warm and sulfurous—and was lowered again. His helper pulled away. It was the same man who had been by him before, the one with the dim lifelight.

"What . . ." Râvar coughed, tried again. "What's happened to me?"

"You've been ill, Messenger," the man said. "For near two weeks. We've brought you here to abide while you replenish yourself."

Messenger, Râvar thought. And then: *Two weeks?* There was a weight above his heart; he raised a curiously clumsy hand and touched something hard.

"The Blood, Messenger," the man said. "I wrapped it up and hung it around your neck. You were separated from it for no more than an hour."

Râvar felt the lightness of his body, the looseness of his limbs. He knew, without testing the knowledge, that he would not be able to summon any shaping. He was at this man's mercy.

"Where is this place?" His heart raced; it was difficult to breathe. "Who are you?"

The man leaned close, like someone craning over the edge of a precipice. He smelled of sweat and dirty clothing. His eyes were silvery dark, the color of the sheen on a pounded nail head. "My name is Ardashir dar Adrax, Messenger. I am an evil man, blackened utterly with sin. But when you fell unconscious I was the first to reach your side, and when the Blood of Ârata slipped from your hands, I caught it. See how it scored my flesh." He lifted his own hands, the palms wrapped in bandages. "The pain of these wounds is the greatest joy I've ever known, for in them I see Ârata's mercy, which I believed was lost to me. I am your First Disciple. I lead the others, but I belong to you. Anything you desire, anything you require—only speak. *Only whisper,* and I will accomplish it."

The man's gaze seemed to burn Râvar's flesh. Râvar gasped and clenched his eyes closed.

"Messenger." The air moved. There was a sound of water. Something wet pressed against Râvar's cheeks, his forehead. "Sleep now," Ardashir whispered, as if to a child. "Rest."

Râvar made his breathing deep. Eventually he sensed that Ardashir had gone. *A demon,* he thought with shuddering horror. *A demon laid his hands on me*. He no longer really believed that the people of this realm were demons; but it was a new learning, and in his weakness it was less powerful than the old instincts, the teachings of his childhood. The remembered feel of Ardashir's fingers made him want to crawl out of his skin.

I'm alone. The knowledge pierced him, terrifying. He had been alone as he crossed the Burning Land, his people dead, his faith lost—but there had still been Axane. He thought it would be a relief to be rid of her. They had hated each other; toward the end, when he realized she was pregnant, he could hardly stand to look at her. But she had been the only remnant of his old life, the only person left in the world who remembered the things he remembered. Now, helpless in this alien place, he longed for her as he had never longed for anyone. Tears leaked from his eyes; he was too weak to sob. At last, mercifully, he slipped once more into sleep.

In the time that followed, Ardashir cared for him like a baby, heedless of his own injuries. The older man showed neither reticence nor embarrassment, as if spooning food into Râvar's mouth and emptying his slop basin and sponging his soiled body were honors no less divine than taking custody of the Blood of Ârata. Râvar loathed it, found it sordid and humiliating; but he had no choice, for even if he had been strong enough to care for himself, the bandages that wrapped his hands would not allow it. How could Ardashir do these disgusting human things and still believe him the divine Messenger? Daily he expected Ardashir to guess the truth, knowing that when it happened there was nothing he could do to defend himself. But the tenderness of Ardashir's ministrations never faltered. The only emotion Râvar saw in those pounded-metal eyes was reverence.

"We could not stay at the prison, Messenger, for you destroyed it utterly," Ardashir told him when he asked about the aftermath of Thuxra. "Nor did we dare go over the Notch while you were so ill. So we brought you farther out into the desert, to the barracks where the mine workers lived during the days of the Caryaxists. The pressure wells still flow, and there's abundant food not far away, for in your wisdom you did not destroy Thuxra's gardens. We have been waiting for you to wake and tell us what to do."

"We," Râvar repeated.

"I and your followers. You've many of them, Messenger."

Râvar knew there were others here; he could hear them, talking and moving beyond the dusty cloth that had been cobbled into a curtain to close off the space where he lay. Occasionally one or another of them helped with food or water or new bedding, though Ardashir never allowed them to remain for long. *Followers*, he thought. Creatures of the outside world, waiting on his direction . . . He had not thought of followers. He had not really thought of very much at all, beyond Thuxra City's destruction.

"The decisions were mine, Messenger," Ardashir said. "I hope they don't displease you."

"No. Umm . . . How many of these . . . followers do I have?"

"There were near five hundred prisoners working the mines when you came out of the Burning Land, Messenger. Many had no stomach for miracles—when you unmade their chains all they saw was the chance of freedom, and they took it. Others left to bring word of you to the kingdoms of Galea, as you bid them. But many wanted to remain at your side. I am . . . I was . . . something of a leader among them. I took charge of them and brought them here. Altogether, we are a little less than two hundred."

Two hundred! It was almost as many as had been left in Refuge, just before the Brethren's army came.

"They're eager to see you, Messenger, impatient for the day you will come out to them again. But I've explained your need. They know they must wait till you are ready."

"Ready," Râvar repeated.

"Yes, replenished and in balance, as when you first came to us, before you worked the first of the acts of Ârata's Promise and forced your human flesh to bear the weight of so much power."

Râvar felt a pressure in his chest. "My . . . *human* . . . flesh."

"Messenger, if I've presumed too much—" For the first time Ardashir seemed to falter. "It was only because they questioned. Only because some of them were frightened at your illness. *How could he have done a miracle*, they said, *and yet be so frail? How can the Messenger feel pain, how can he sweat and bleed and suffer as we do?* The truth seemed clear to me, and so I spoke it, that Ârata clothed his divine Messenger in a human body, made him god and man at once, a paradox, so that in enduring the frailties we do, in suffering as we do, he might more truly know and love and lead us, and we more truly know and love and follow him." His face, what was visible of it above the beard, was full of apprehension. "Messenger, my pride has ever been my failing. If I've done wrong, it's my offense—no one else's. Punish me, but spare the others."

"Leave me." It was all Râvar trusted himself to say. He rolled over, turning his back. A pause; then he felt Ardashir depart.

Human *and* divine. Such a thing would never have occurred to him. According to the lore of Refuge, there was no humanity in the Next Messenger at all; he was a spark of Ârata's own divinity, molded in the shape of a man so that those he was sent to lead would not fear him too much to follow. Râvar had never thought to present himself as other than a god, though he had had no clear idea how he could maintain such a pretense. But if the Messenger could be human, too . . .

Conceiving his great act of blasphemy, he had given only hazy consideration to what would come after his claim of Messengerhood. For all his dark resolve, he had not been sure he would succeed. That his shaping gift was extraordinary he knew; but nothing he had ever done approached the magnitude of what he must achieve at Thuxra City. More to the point—would Ârata allow it? Why should he tolerate such blasphemy? All across the Burning Land, Râvar had waited to be struck down. Even as he stood before Thuxra's walls, he had been prepared for the god's fires to engulf him. It was hard to believe, afterward, that he was still alive and breathing.

Nor did he understand the outside world. He knew its past; though the people of Refuge had believed it utterly destroyed, they had also believed it was their destiny to re-create it, and every child was taught its history. He knew something of its present, for Axane had told him a great deal as they traveled. But her stories were full of gaps, for there was also much she did not know, and he was aware that the little he had learned was far outweighed by his ignorance. It was impossible, therefore, to imagine in any but the vaguest terms what his course should be. Some sort of swift progress across Arsace . . . some strategy for tempting the populace to belief . . . the storming of Baushpar, where the Brethren would be brought to account . . . and then . . . what? He had no idea. He knew he might not even get so far: At some point the forces of the outside world would surely be arrayed against him. Or perhaps, tardily, the god would decide to make an end.

With each day of his convalescence, he grew more aware of how his lack of strategy threatened him. He knew now why Ardashir could minister to him so intimately and still believe, why the others could accept him despite his weakness—but whatever faith they had in him would surely be forfeit soon if he could not find a way to take up his expected role. The thought made him cold with dread. It was not leadership that frightened him. He had led others all his life: From earliest childhood, he had been first among his friends and siblings and cousins, admired, imitated, beloved. But he had never led strangers. He had never led by deception. He had never imagined *followers*—people who might protect him (for even a Shaper could not guard against an arrow in the back, and of course the people of this world had that accursed drug, manita), but whom he would have to deceive, without fault or flaw, every moment he spent among them. What were the great deeds he had already accomplished, compared to that?

I can't do it, he thought, when Ardashir leaned over him with suffocating solicitude, or when he heard the coarse laughter of the men beyond the curtain, or when he woke gasping in the middle of the night, struggling to remember where he was. *It's too much. It's too hard.* But then came memories of the riverbank, of ruined Refuge. He feared the men beyond the curtain. He feared this alien world. He feared his own aloneness. But far more, he feared admitting to the ghosts that stalked his dreams: *I did not try.*

In the end, that was what it came to. He had no choice.

One thing he did not fear at all: the consequences of his blasphemy. He knew that after death he would suffer horribly in Ârata's fires. He knew that nothing of him would survive. But he had rejected Ârata's paradise. Better, a thousand times better, to be burned to ash at the end of time than to spend eternity under the light of the god he despised.

"Ardashir," he said one day, "do all the people of Galea believe as you do? About my . . . nature?"

Ardashir set down the water he had brought and stepped back. As soon Râvar had been able to grip a bowl between his swollen palms and hitch himself across the floor, he had insisted on tending to himself; Ardashir knew now to keep his distance, though it was clear he would have preferred otherwise. He settled on his knees, back straight, his hands placed precisely on his thighs. Râvar was beginning to know that air of dignified self-containment.

"They believe many things, Messenger. Some think you must be entirely a god. Others say you must be wholly mortal, like the First Messenger. But I've always thought that Ârata would do as he chose, and we human creatures could never say what that would be. When you revealed yourself, I followed the understanding of my heart. If I was wrong . . . Messenger, I know I am more fallible than other men. I'm ready for instruction."

Râvar shook his head. "You are correct."

Ardashir drew in his breath, let it out again. "Ah."

"I am . . . god and man at once, just as you said." Râvar felt a cold prickling across his body. Even with all he had already done, it took an act of will to say the words aloud. "Ârata shaped me out of flesh and blood and bone, and breathed the fire of his own . . . spirit into me to give me life. I am more than the . . . the bearer of his word. I am a bridge . . . between the old age and the new. Between the human Age of Exile and the divinity of the primal age to come." He drew a breath. "I'm grateful, Ardashir, for your understanding of these things, and for your care of my . . . human flesh during my sickness."

"Ârata set me in your path." Ardashir wore the inward, revelatory expression of a man whose deepest certainties had been vindicated. "I knew it. I knew it."

"But I need more than your care now. Ârata, my . . . father, gave me this human body that I might know human suffering." Râvar spread his wounded hands. "As you see. But I am new-made in my flesh. I know much of . . . divinity, but it has been left to me to discover the ways of humanness, just as, just as you humans do when you grow from childhood." Part of him still stood apart, marveling. But he was beginning to discover a giddy thrill in spinning such a web of blasphemy, in the way Ardashir hung upon each word. "You're a man of wisdom, that's clear. I ask a boon of you, which will serve my . . . father as well as me. Be my guide. Help me learn how to be human."

All the joy went out of Ardashir's face. Râvar realized, with a chill that snuffed his rash confidence like a pinched flame, that he had misstepped.

"You want a better guide than me, Messenger. I told you when you woke that I'm an evil man. I'm not worthy to advise you."

Carefully, Râvar said: "What is your sin, Ardashir?"

"Can you not look into my face, Messenger, and see it there?"

Râvar's mind raced. "Of course. But you must name it. I ask again, what is your sin?"

"To tell you, Messenger, I must first tell you of my life."

"Then do so."

Ardashir glanced down at his hands, at rest upon his knees. Spears of sun slanted around him, whirling with dust, their brilliance almost canceling the dim glimmer of his lifelight.

"I was born in Arsace, in Isriya Province, on one of the great Caryaxist plantations. My father and mother were field-workers, as were their fathers and mothers before them . . ." He described his childhood, his adolescence, his ambition to be more than his parents were, his pursuit of power and his success in grasping it. He spoke of the Âratist faith he had been raised to follow, in defiance of the official atheism of the Caryaxists—the secret congregation of Âratist believers to which he and his family had belonged, the vows he had taken at the age of twenty so he could lead the truncated Communion ceremonies that were all that could be performed in the absence of ordained Shapers.

"So you were a priest," Râvar said.

"As much of one as I could be, Messenger, in those evil times. If I'd been born in a different age, I would have vowed the Way. It may be arrogant to say, but I think that what I did, what men like me did, was perhaps a greater service—not just leading my congregation, not just honoring Ârata, but guarding faith during the time of oppression. Holding the flame of the god's word against the darkness." He paused, memory moving in his face. "It was the joy of my heart, that service. I strove to carry that joy into my secular life as well, to put the Five Foundations daily into practice, to stand like one of those Foundations within my community, a pillar and an example for the rest. *In a well-lived life lies the seed of a thousand others,* the *Darxasa* says, and I thought my life well lived indeed. The only change I imagined could overtake me was the Caryaxists' fall and Arsace's liberation." He drew a breath, and said, without any change of inflection: "And then I murdered my wife."

Râvar felt everything in him go still. Of course he had known that Ardashir was an evil man, and not just because Ardashir had told him so. Axane had explained to him what Thuxra City was—a place created to hold the worst of the worst, men whom even the creatures of this dark realm could not tolerate free among them. But in Refuge's more than seven decades of existence, there had been just one deliberate killing. It was an unspeakable, almost an inconceivable, crime.

Ardashir was watching him, his face expressionless and yet alight, like a door closed on a burning room. "How," Râvar made himself say, "did you come to do such a thing?"

And Ardashir told him, efficiently, in the barest minimum of words. How he had wished for celibacy, like the priest he could never truly be, and had married only to satisfy convention. How he had persuaded his wife, a devout member of his congregation, to swear an oath to renounce the union of the body. How his wife grew dissatisfied, and began to beg him for a child. How he began to suspect that she was seeking elsewhere what he would not give her. How one morning he feigned departure, then returned to spy on her, tracking her to the worker's hut where she had gone to keep her tryst. Rage had overwhelmed him when he saw her with her lover; the world had gone dark. When he came to himself, her neck was broken and her lover lay dying on the floor.

He paused then, his eyes fixed on the packed-earth floor as if the images of his deed repeated themselves there. Râvar waited. This was the world into which he had come, he told himself: a world in which such people existed.

"I always suspected I was capable of such a thing." Feeling had come into Ardashir's voice, a depth of self-disgust so profound it seemed to press against Râvar's skin. "But I never knew for certain till that night. It wasn't for love that I killed her. Even then I understood that. We'd been ugly with one another for a long time. If she'd asked me to divorce her, I might have agreed.

Instead, she broke the oath we made together, our marriage vows. I had a position in the world, a duty. I had respect. She betrayed those things, all the things I built up out of nothing. She made a mockery of me—" He bit off the words, his mouth twisting. For a moment he sat silent, breathing deeply. "Still I should have borne my anger. I swore an oath as I sat by them, swore it to the god, though I knew I was damned beyond any hope of cleansing. *I will never do such a thing again.*"

The whole cold strength of his will rang in his voice.

"I don't know how long I stayed there. When I left, I let the door stand open so they would be quickly found. I went to my office and put my files in order, and wrote out instructions for my successor. My wife's blood was on me—there wasn't any question who was responsible, once the authorities came.

"I was sentenced to twenty years at labor in the mines of Thuxra. Eight years later the Caryaxists fell, and King Santaxma's Exile Army came to occupy the prison. It was supposed to be emptied and torn down, but no one knew what to do with us real criminals once the political prisoners were freed, so the prison was left standing and we were kept working, defiling the Burning Land just as we had before, but for a different master. Yet I was glad they kept us. For I knew that you were soon to come and hoped I might see you when you did."

"You knew this?"

"All the faithful knew it, Messenger. During the time of the Caryaxists, the people of Arsace sent up such a storm of prayer, such a tempest of entreaty! Ârata could not sleep through so much noise. He woke and saw our suffering, and in his wrath he wrought the Caryaxists' destruction, using Santaxma as his instrument. Who later turned to blasphemy, curse his name."

"So you were actually expecting the Next Messenger," Râvar said, marveling. "Expecting me. Even before I came."

"Yes." Ardashir raised his face. "I've long known paradise was lost to me, that I would burn to nothing at the end of time. But I have hope now, the first hope in years. Ârata has placed me in your path—he has given me to you for your own—" He stopped, struggling for composure. "Perhaps he means to let me scour some of my darkness away. Or maybe he's only given me to you because a man who has done what I've done need not fear to do anything else. All I know is that I am yours, that I serve you to death and beyond." He looked down again at the littered floor. "I also know that I am not fit to offer more."

Râvar's heart raced with exhilaration. He had intended only to flatter

Ardashir's desire for privilege and status, which was obvious not just in his self-bestowed title but in the jealous way he claimed custody of Râvar's care. Yet the role he had offered Ardashir notched so precisely into the spaces of the First Disciple's own character and need that it might have been constructed just for Ardashir, or Ardashir for it.

A murderer, he thought. A blackened man, whom even the worst blasphemy could not further stain. A dangerous man, whose violence might one day turn upon the one he served. Yet Râvar's shaping regained strength each day; soon he would have nothing to fear from any of these creatures. And what better guide, in a killing world, than a killer?

"I do not have the power to absolve you of your crime," he said. "Nor to promise that you will not suffer when the time of cleansing comes. But the service I offer you will lead you back to light, and something in you will survive to rise into brilliance of the new primal age. It is as you said: My father put you in my path. You will be my right hand and my guide. You'll teach me, and you will teach the others also—everything I've said to you this day, everything I say in the days to come, you will tell them. That is my wish, Ardashir. It is my father's wish. Will you accept it?"

Ardashir's rough features trembled. Tears overspilled his eyes. "Yes," he said. "Yes."

"Then I am satisfied."

"I cursed my life," Ardashir said. "But now I bless it." Before Râvar could pull away, he leaned forward and caught Râvar's hands, and pressed a kiss into each lacerated palm. "Messenger. Beloved of Ârata." He smiled, for the first time Râvar could remember, showing gapped teeth. "I swear I will not fail you."

When he was gone Râvar clasped his hands, which still felt the pressure of that unexpected, unwelcome contact, and sank back into his bedding. The air was thick with heat. He was utterly exhausted. He thought of the words Ardashir, that blackened man, was spreading even now among the other blackened men who were his followers. Something harsh caught at his throat.

See, Ârata. See how I defy you.

As usual, there was only silence.

Ardashir seemed never to have doubted that Râvar would recover, but in his weakness Râvar knew he had come close to dying. Three weeks after returning to consciousness he was still gaunt, and spent more time sleeping than awake. His skin, scarified by the sun, had peeled off in sheets, frightening him with the thought that it might never heal, and his palms and fingers were still painfully webbed with scabs. But the infection was gone, and he had put on a little flesh. More important, he was now strong enough to shape. He knew he could no longer put off the necessity of going before his followers.

On the morning he had chosen, he ordered Ardashir to return to him at noon. Then he took out the razor and the comb he had requested some days earlier, shaped water to fill a bowl, and used it as a mirror to shave off his filthy, matted beard. It was a slow process, with his clumsy hands; in the past week he had begun to stretch them, tearing the scabs, but even so he feared they were healing twisted. With a rag he swabbed his body, then rubbed scented ointment from a little alabaster pot into the sore skin of his face. His followers regularly scavenged the wreckage of Thuxra's custodians' quarters, whose shocked and injured survivors were too preoccupied with their plight to care about strangers wandering among the ruins; they brought back many offerings for their Messenger: jewelry, clothing, small items such as the pot of ointment. Râvar sometimes looked at these things and thought about the people who had owned them, most or all of whom now lay buried under a mountain of fallen stone. He had done that. It was, and remained, a curiously abstract concept.

He spent an interminable time teasing out the tangles of his hair, which was not only wretchedly dirty but knotted with sand, twigs, even pebbles. At last it lay smooth over his shoulders, sleeked with more ointment, falling past his waist. He unmade the noisome mess his grooming had produced, and from a pile of garments, neatly folded by Ardashir, selected a knee-length tunic and loose leg coverings of some sliding, lustrous fabric whose patterns his Shaper senses did not recognize. Last, carefully, he withdrew from beneath his bedding the product of several days of painstaking labor: the Blood, wrapped with silver wire he had untwisted from a necklace, padded on one side with Ardashir's pouch, the whole strung on the pouch's leather thong. He slipped it over his head. The huge crystal lay heavy on his chest, the fire at its heart pulsing at the bottom of his vision.

He emptied the water in the bowl and shaped fresh, then bent over it, holding back his hair. Was he still good to look at? Throughout his life he had been matter-of-factly conscious of his beauty, and of others' response to it—not just desire or envy, but the awe evoked by any truly rare thing. He had deliberately abused himself in the Burning Land to become the desert-ravaged Messenger Ârata's Promise demanded; he had not thought to need his looks again. But it seemed to him now that to bind his followers to him he must use every tool at his disposal, including the perfection of his face and body, if any trace of that remained. The Blood's light sparked on the water. Of himself he could see only planes and shadows, for the incorporeal fires of his lifelight could not be reflected. They were recognizably his features, if not exactly as he remembered them. Still, his face seemed the face of a stranger.

He sat cross-legged on the ground, his back to the curtain that closed off his private space. When the rods of sun stood straight between floor and ceiling, he heard Ardashir enter. Gathering himself, he rose and turned. Ardashir stopped short. For an instant he stood motionless; then he sank to his knees.

"Beloved One." His eyes moved on Râvar's face. "I should have known Ârata would make you beautiful."

"I will go out, Ardashir. To my followers."

"Now?"

"Yes."

"But . . . shall I not announce you? Prepare your way?"

"I will go this moment, as I am."

Ardashir got to his feet. "Let me help you."

"I don't need help. But stay by me."

Râvar stepped forward. It required an effort of will. *I don't need to fear these men,* he told himself as Ardashir held the curtain for him. *They are just men. I am a Shaper.*

The barracks was a long building, with wide entranceways at the midpoint of each lengthwise wall. The prisoners had improvised beds for themselves with materials scavenged from the desert and from Thuxra, setting them out in two long rows with a narrow aisle between, a makeshift arrangement that was surprisingly neat and tidy. A few men sat or lay on their pallets, their lifelights glinting amid the golden shafts of sun that pierced the gapped roof slabs. As Râvar emerged, those who faced the curtain fell still. Their transfixed attention communicated itself to the rest. By the time Râvar had taken ten steps they were all immobile, staring.

One of the closest, a starved-looking man with graying hair and a garnet-colored lifelight, hitched himself to his knees, crossing his arms before his face. "Great is Ârata," he said in a strangled voice. "Great is his Way."

The rest scrambled to follow his example. "Great is Ârata. Great is his Way," they chorused raggedly.

"Go in light," Râvar said. His heart pounded like a hammer. "First faithful of this new age, I, Ârata's Messenger, greet you."

"Beloved of Ârata," said the man with the garnet lifelight.

"Beloved One." The whisper swept the gathering. The crowd was growing; men slipped through the entranceways to join the kneeling congregation, adding their colors to the rest. The patterns of the air broke and shimmered with their motion. Râvar saw the awe in their faces. A sudden excitement seized him.

"Children of Ârata!" His voice rang strong and true. On impulse he called illusion, a white brilliance that burst around him like the sun on polished metal. As one, they gasped. "Heed me!"

It was his first sermon. Some of it he had worked out in advance, but much of it came to him as he spoke. He told them how he had woken up to fire, as Ârata breathed the life-spark of divinity into his shell of flesh. He described his travels through the Burning Land. He spoke of Thuxra City's destruction, the first of the two great acts described in Ârata's Promise. He told them how he had felt their faith in the darkness that had fallen on him afterward, drawing him back to consciousness, to light. The words fell from his lips as if there were some flowing spring of them inside him. His followers were rapt. Even in Refuge, after he had become Principal Shaper, he had not been the focus of such intense attention. He could say anything to them, anything at all, and they would believe. He knew it with an instinct beyond question.

"The time of cleansing nears, children." At some point he had sunk to his knees, though he did not remember moving. "When Ârata with his holy fires will burn all living creatures clean of the ash that is their birth-burden, and of the darkness they have gathered in their lives. I know you dread those fires, blackened men that you are. But I have come to give you hope. In following me, you will gather light again. When you stand before Ârata, his judgment will be harsh—but that light will be in you, and it will survive. This I tell you—not one of you who believes in me will fail to rise into the brilliance of the new primal age. That is my promise, by the power of the Promise I have been sent among you to fulfill."

He was finished. But the hush that held the gathering did not acknowledge ending. Two hundred faces held him, two hundred pairs of eyes. Something more was needed. Into his mind came an image of Ardashir, reaching for his hands.

"See the marks of my service, the injury set by my father's holy Blood into the flesh he made to clothe me." He held out his hands, showing them the scabs, the distorted fingers. "This was done so you might always remember how I came to you. Now come to me and kiss these marks as a sign of your faith, and I will give you blessing."

For a moment no one moved. Then the man with the garnet lifelight pushed to his feet. He stepped forward and knelt again. Hesitantly, he bent toward Râvar's proffered hands and touched his lips to them, first the right, then the left. He smelled of sweat and of the desert, dry and hot. His bony shoulders trembled.

"Go in light, child of Ârata," Râvar said softly. "May my father's brightness burn in you, as it burns in me, as it burns in all living things. In Ârata's name I give you blessing."

He set the tips of his fingers on the man's forehead, calling illusion so that his touch seemed to leave a little point of radiance behind. The man's eyes rolled; Râvar thought he might faint, but he mastered himself and rose. As he turned a whisper rolled through the gathering, soft invocations of the god's name. The man stumbled to his pallet like someone dreaming.

The rest flocked forward. Râvar gave them his hands to kiss, and blessed them, and set light upon their skins. Some cried out when he touched them; some wept. Many had to be helped to their feet. Râvar felt outside himself; he seemed to be acting from some great remove. At last they all sat in their places again. They were still waiting. But for what? He had used up all his invention and nearly all his strength. His mind was blank.

And all at once, as if a cord had been cut, the earth seemed to roll over and everything became its opposite. He was aware of himself, one man before two hundred, clad in the thinnest veil of deception. He was aware of them, not worshipful but predatory, not awed but avid. Their belief was not the warm malleable thing he had thought, but as brittle as crystal. One wrong word, one mistaken act, and it would shatter. He was afraid to move, to breathe, lest he betray himself.

With enormous effort, he said: "Go in light. The ceremony is ended."

He did not care if it was wrong; he wanted only to make an end. But it was exactly, and simply, what they wanted: dismissal. The tension broke. They lay back on their pallets, or rose to go about their business. Ardashir, who all this time had stood tensely by his side, stooped. Râvar let the other man assist him to his feet and guide him through the curtain, into his own space.

"Leave me," he whispered.

Ardashir obeyed. Râvar stumbled to his bed. He was deliriously thirsty. He seized the bowl of water he had shaped to look at himself, spilling half of it in his haste, and gulped it dry. He let the bowl slip from his hands and sank down on the ground.

For a time he remained there, folded in on himself. Terror shook him like a fever. His lies rose up like the Range of Clouds: vast, unscalable. The rough faces of the waiting men, their devouring gaze, spun behind his eyes. *Demons*, the old instinct whispered. He could almost feel their hands, ripping him to pieces.

Gradually, he calmed. *They're just men,* he told himself. Why should he fear creatures he could seal into the earth, or destroy with storm and fire? He was no longer helpless; he was strong, and would grow stronger. He had held them in his hand today, played like a musician upon their awe and faith, made them tremble to his will. He could do so again. And if he did misstep, if he lost their belief . . . why, he would make others believe in him. He knew how to do it now. He knew something else: He had a talent for it.

I will do this thing. Like a plague he would sweep down upon the world beyond the mountains, bringing to it what it had sent on Refuge: a false Messenger, a blasphemous faith, as much destruction as he could make. He would steal the souls of its people, blackening them with blasphemy past any point of cleansing. He would bring justice on the Brethren. And when he died and came before Ârata at last, he would laugh as the flames enclosed him, and shout into the god's great face: *I would do it all again!*

He lay down in his blankets, and fell asleep. He woke to touch: gentle fingers, brushing the tumbled hair back from his face. For a moment, still half-unconscious, he thought it was Axane. It was Ardashir. The older man drew away when Râvar opened his eyes, his dark face unreadable. He had, Râvar realized, shaved off his own beard.

"I've brought you food, Beloved One."

Râvar found that he was hungry. He sat up and ate.

After that he went out to his followers every day. Sometimes, in a parody of the Communion ceremonies he had conducted in Refuge, he gave them thoughts for meditation and led them in the Communion litany. Sometimes he preached, expanding his message, refining his falsehoods, elaborating his invented doctrine. Sometimes he sat and answered questions, for they were eager to know the details of his creation, the wonders he had seen in the Burning Land. He began to wind Refuge into his stories—the Cavern of the Blood where he told them he had woken, the red sandstone cliffs that had been his first shelter, the bitterbark-shaded banks of the river Revelation, from which, new in his flesh, he had drunk. It was a way of anchoring his fictions in something real, but it also pleased him to seal Refuge at the heart of his deception, so they would know in some form the lost world that was the cause of their destruction.

To set his power on display, he shaped for them. He made fire for warmth in the desert night. He parted the earth to release an underground spring, and formed a large sandstone basin so they had a place to bathe and wash their clothes. He shaped wheat and rice, for the prison's storehouses had been destroyed in the collapse and the irrigated gardens of Thuxra City grew no grain. For his own pleasure he shaped the fruits and nuts he had known in Refuge; when he realized they were unfamiliar to his followers, he said they were the food of paradise, which he had eaten in the time after his creation. These were minor shapings, none requiring more than a fraction of his power. But to the men, who had lived their preprison lives under Caryaxist rule and had never witnessed even the manita-crippled abilities of the Shapers of the Âratist church, they were wonders, further proof of his divinity.

They begged audiences with him, at which, like Ardashir, they wanted to acknowledge their misdeeds. Many had been thieves, or lived by cheating others—bad men, but not incomprehensibly so. But some had done things that eclipsed even Ardashir's horrible crime, and their confessions opened a window on a degeneracy Râvar could not have imagined, even when he still believed the outside world a realm of demons. It made him feel soiled to hear these tales. Still he listened, for he understood that the men's surrender of their secrets was an act of faith more compelling than any oath.

The panic he had suffered after his first sermon never visited him again. Each time he went out to them it was easier. Each time he spoke, he grew more confident of his ability to seize them with his words. He had always known he spoke well; from childhood, he had delighted in outtalking his cousins and his friends, and later his fellow Shaper trainees. But this was more. To weave nets with words and entrap those who listened. To *change* his listeners, as if his speech were a power as potent as his shaping. He was beginning also to recognize the self-sustaining nature of the role he played, the backward justification their belief forced on them. If his actions seemed strange, it was not him they doubted, but their own understanding. If his words seemed out of place, they found a way to make them fit. Even the reactions he sometimes could not suppress—his horror at their crimes, his distaste for their coarse ways—served him, for they believed him innocent in his new flesh, pure as a child. They did their best to check their rough talk in his presence. They began to keep their clothes and bodies clean, to trim their beards and braid their hair.

Some weeks after he began to go out, one of Ardashir's scavenging parties encountered a band of travelers, exhausted and hungry from the journey over Thuxra Notch. A holy man had passed through their village, they said, with word of the Next Messenger; they had come to see for themselves if it were true. They were brought to Râvar, trembling with awe. When he blessed them, two fell down in fits.

It was these travelers, these pilgrims who had abandoned their homes and families on word from a wandering ex-criminal (for the so-called holy man was certainly one of the prisoners who had witnessed Thuxra's fall), who sparked in Râvar the idea of the Awakened City. Even as he cemented his followers' belief, he had not been certain of exactly what he would do next. Now he thought he saw a way to build not just a mass of followers but an army of them—and at the same time to prepare his path, to sow seeds of belief that could be harvested as he marched upon Baushpar. It was far more ambitious than anything he had previously imagined. It went against his impatient nature, for it meant waiting, perhaps for a considerable time. Could he bear to spend so long among these alien people, playing Messenger for them, giving them his power, taking on their sins? But if he could not, why had he come?

He sought Ardashir's advice, gladder than ever that he had enlisted this man as his teacher, for he was able to present his ignorance as part of his effort to become proficient in the ways of humanity. Ardashir was an eager adviser, offering counsel drawn from his experience as the leader of a large and complex community. When at last the plan was firm, Râvar went out to address his followers.

He had ordered Ardashir to assemble them outside the barracks. The sun was just beginning to set. He had wrapped himself in light, a dozen different jewel colors that coiled about his body and flowed out upon the ground. His heart raced, as it had the first time he had ever spoken to them.

"Children of Ârata," he began.

"Messenger," they responded. "Beloved of Ârata."

"Children of the Promise."

"Fulfiller of the Promise. He who opens the way."

"You've been patient during the time of my healing, and I am grateful. But now I am replenished, in balance again, and the time has come to take up once more the task my father gave me—to bring light into the world's darkness, to herald the dawning of the new age, to open the way for Ârata's return."

"Praise Ârata's name!"

"One of the signs of Ârata's Promise has been given, the act of destruction that brought down Thuxra City. The second sign, the act of generation, will raise a city: the Awakened City, a City you and I will build together." He described this perfect community of the faithful, which would be seeded in some sheltered place yet to be discovered, and nurtured there to strength. He told them how its citizens would be washed in light—the darkness they possessed already, the ash of their birth-burden and the stain of their sins, could not be purged, but no further deed would mark them. He told them how, at the proper time, the City would emerge and march upon Baushpar, where the

Brethren would surrender to the Messenger the leadership of the church—a church remade, a new faith for the time of Interim that lay between Ârata's rising and his return, a Way of Ârata awake. Afterward, they would march upon the rest of Galea, bearing word of the risen god. Thus Ârata's children would be led out of exile. Thus the way would be opened for Ârata's return.

As always, he had prepared what he would say. As always the words seized him, pouring from him as they would. His followers stood enthralled, their lifelights shimmering against the deepening darkness.

"Will you follow me, children of Ârata?" he called at last. "Will you join me in this act of generation? Will you abide with me in this holy time of Interim? Will you embrace this new Way of Ârata, the Way of Ârata awake?"

"Yes!" they cried. "We will follow!"

"I do not promise you ease, children. I do not promise you rest. Many will turn away from the word we speak. Many will reject us. But more will follow. And though there will be struggle, and suffering, and sorrow, there will also be joy. There will be light—light such as has not been seen in this corrupted world since my father lay down to sleep. We will set Galea ablaze! Is it enough, children? Will you stand with me? Will you make this journey?"

"Beloved of Ârata! We will stand! Lead us! Lead us!"

Their faith embraced him. He could no longer feel the boundaries of his body. He was part of the night, as vast and vaporous as a god.

"Ârata!" He flung out his light-wreathed arms. "Risen god of all the world! Look down on your children, look down on these souls I have taken for my own, and *know what I do in your name!*"

The stars spun. His followers roared.

They departed the next morning, bringing with them nothing but the clothes they wore and their sleeping pallets. All else, Râvar assured them, he would provide. They passed the ruins of Thuxra City, recently emptied of its remaining survivors. Râvar had destroyed it from a distance; not till that day had he seen it close. He remembered that great act of power; he relived it sometimes in his dreams. Still it shocked him to realize the weight and breadth of what he had brought down.

I did that. I.

He led them over Thuxra Notch, along an artificial river of flat stones that they told him was called a road. He provided for them as he had promised, making water flow when there was none, shaping food twice daily, kindling fires for them to huddle over at night. Each evening he blessed them with light before they slept. The weather was kind. Some of the men grumbled and fell behind, and the pilgrims from the village kept apart in fear of the ex-prisoners, but there was little conflict or mishap. By the time they reached the steppe, the journey was already sliding into legend. Ardashir had made a name for it: the First Pilgrimage. He had named the journeyers as well: the First Faithful.

They left the road, turning west into the trackless grasslands, searching for a place to establish a permanent camp. A band of nomads led them to the cavern complex. The moment he perceived its patterns, Râvar knew it was the proper place: large enough to hold an army, obscure enough to let it gather in secret, accessible enough that those who sought it could easily reach it. He announced to his weary followers that the First Pilgrimage was done; here they would stop, and build their City. Summoning the strength he had not fully tested since his recovery, he made a miracle for them, vaporizing the rock of the ridge in six blinding explosions so that the narrow fissure of the caverns' entrance became a perfect half circle, its lip as smooth and glossy as polished metal.

He allowed the faithful a few days of rest and exploration, then ordered Ardashir to call them all together. He had kindled a fire, and made food; the great cold spaces of the cave pressed around them as they ate, and the entrance's new arch was filled with stars. After they had eaten, a leather pouch was passed among them. It held two hundred and seven stalks of grass, one hundred of them short. Those who drew short would go into the world as missionaries, proclaiming Râvar's coming and recruiting pilgrims to send back, according to a plan devised by Ardashir. The rest would remain to begin the building of the new community.

When all the stalks were drawn, Râvar addressed them—not passionately, as when he preached, but quietly, intimately.

"The ceremony I give you tonight will never be repeated. I intend to ask a pledge of you, a sacrifice. You all know the marks I bear upon my hands"— he extended them, ridged with scar tissue, crippled and twisted—"the injury taken in my flesh as the sign of my service to my father. Now I ask the same of you. Wear my mark, as a sign of your faith in me. Those you call to our Awakened City will also bear the mark, but of all my followers, only you will bear it on both your hands. For you are my First Faithful, whom I love above all others who will ever follow me."

Ardashir had protested. The marks, he said, would make the missionaries and the pilgrims too identifiable. But to Râvar, it seemed important that his followers be set apart—not in others' perception, but in their own. Talismans or amulets could be lost or set aside. But scars they would always carry with them.

"Approach me now, and accept the marks."

One by one they came forward, and in the leaping firelight knelt so that a man chosen by Ardashir, who was skilled with a knife, could score a shallow cut across their palms and smear soot into the wounds. No one hesitated, not even the village pilgrims. The man marked his own hands last, the second one with difficulty. Râvar set a point of light upon his forehead, as he had on the foreheads of the others.

"You are sealed now," he told them, "sealed to my father and to me. In the history of this world, there has not been another moment like this one. Great is Ârata. Great is his awakened Way."

"Go in light," they chorused, making the god's sign with their newly wounded hands.

The missionaries departed the following day, and the rest of the First Faithful set about the labor of preparation. Ardashir dispatched scouting parties to survey the terrain and began to plan the organization of the community, a task Râvar was content to leave entirely to him. The steppes and the surrounding hills provided some sustenance; what could not be hunted or gathered, Râvar shaped. He altered and improved the caverns, and created his own domain. He preached sermons, heard confessions, gave blessings. He spent hours on the ridge above the steppe, scanning the horizon for approaching pilgrims. He began to fear that his gamble was a failure. But two months after the missionaries' departure, converts began to arrive, by ones and twos and dozens, with his mark on their hands and his faith in their hearts. He welcomed and blessed them. When their numbers grew too large for him to dispense individual blessings, he began to conduct the mass rituals in the smaller cavern.

It was some time since he had been conscious of walking the razor's edge. He had grown confident in his role, like a rope dancer so accustomed to the rope that he had forgotten both the difficulty and the unnaturalness of his performance. His duties, ably directed by Ardashir, occupied much of his time; his idle moments he filled compulsively with activity, exploring the distant reaches of the caverns, inventing new tricks of shaping to amuse himself and astonish his followers. But as his attention turned from the necessities of survival, as his blasphemy hardened into dogma and the pretense that had required constant vigilance became instinctive, he began to be aware again, as in the raw aftermath of Refuge, of the void of loss—of the emptiness where once had lived all that had been stolen from him, all he had repudiated. Like a dwelling built above a pit, his new life straddled the void but did not fill it. Vengeance would fill it. The Brethren's death would fill it. But those things still lay far ahead.

Sometimes he woke in the deep hours of the night and could hardly breathe for loneliness. In Refuge he had not known what loneliness was. There had barely been a moment when he was not surrounded by his loving kin, his admiring friends, his fellow Shapers. And always there had been Ârata, a vast living presence, an enormous warm attention turned upon his own small self. In prayer and meditation he had felt the weight of Ârata's love like hands pressing on his shoulders. All his people were Ârata's chosen. But he had always, secretly, felt more chosen than the rest.

He was no one's chosen. The faith in which he had grown up was as base a delusion as the one he forced upon his followers. The void had always been there. Only now he knew it.

Ârata was silent. He could not even sense the god's anger. Sometimes this enraged him: How could the god ignore his blasphemy? Sometimes he felt contempt: Was Ârata really so indifferent? Sometimes he would have given anything to feel the agony of Ârata's fires, just to fill the emptiness.

He had rarely thought about Axane since the early days of his convalescence, other than to wonder if she had indeed gone to Ninyâser as she had planned, and, occasionally, to calculate where she was in her pregnancy. Now she and the child were always in his mind. It made less and less sense that they should be apart from him, the last of Refuge, the last of his blood, adrift in this alien world. In the night he longed for Axane, whom he had loved so terribly and hated so wretchedly, who had betrayed him and whom he had betrayed. He longed for his child. One morning he woke knowing beyond doubt that it had been the worst mistake of his life to let them go. So he had reached out his hand, and fetched them back.

And now he had them. And what was he to do with them?

He rose at last and left the windswept ridge. He returned to his rooms and unshaped the stone that blocked his night chamber. Axane was sitting on the bed. Beside her the baby, disturbed by the crack of power, began to cry.

The room was transformed. Lengths of linen lay spread on the floor to dry, and the receptacles Axane had requested for washing—tight-woven grass baskets whose water Râvar replaced daily—sat seeping against one wall. Her own clothes hung across the fanciful malachite ornamentation of the bed. In this room as in others, Râvar had used the natural patterns of the stone to create fissures for air exchange, and sunk a small shaft in one corner for the emptying of his chamber pot. Still the air smelled foul.

"I'll take her now." Impatiently, he beckoned.

Axane obeyed, docile as any of his followers, and helped him settle the child against his chest, his left arm under her little rump, his right hand on her back. She felt natural in his embrace; he might have been holding her since her birth. His touch quieted her, as it nearly always did. She gripped a fold of his tunic and turned her face against his shoulder, making sleepy sounds. Growing up, he had never taken any special interest in children. No doubt this would have changed in the normal run of things—but he did not think he could have cared for any child of his the way he cared for this one.

"The baskets need new water," Axane said.

"When I come back."

"Râvar." She stood before him, small and dark at the center of her storm of light, like a hard kernel in a luscious fruit. "I'm going mad in this room. Please, won't you let me out?"

"So you can try to run away?"

"No, I swear I wouldn't do that. I could . . . I could leave the baby with you. You know I'd never leave without her."

"Ah. So you don't fear anymore that I might harm her."

She dropped her eyes. "I shouldn't have said that. I can see you love her."

"How kind of you to acknowledge it."

"Râvar, I have skills. I could be useful. Surely you need a healer here."

"We have many healers. We don't need another."

"Râvar . . ." She sounded close to tears. "I was afraid when we came here, because . . . I didn't know what you wanted of me. But I've had time to think about it, and I see how you are with Chokyi—"

"Don't use that ugly name! You know she's called Parvâti now!"

She caught her breath. "I'm sorry. I forgot. I know I've offended you. You may not believe it, but I understand—" Her voice shook. "I understand your anger, and I'm sorry, I'm truly sorry. If you'd just let me explain, if you'd just let me tell you why things turned out the way they did—"

Râvar felt the clutch of rage. Against his shoulder the baby stirred and whimpered. "No." He breathed in through his nose, mastering himself. "No."

She stared at him, her hands dragging at her stole. Tears stood in her eyes. He turned away.

"I won't block you in this time. I don't want to disturb Parvâti. But I'll be nearby. Don't try to leave this room."

He went into the second chamber and sat down. He cradled his sleeping daughter, trying to take comfort in the feel of her. Still he saw Axane's small tense body; still he heard her pleading voice.

Ârata! he thought, for perhaps the hundredth time. *What am I to do with her?*

He did not want to give Parvâti up. He had understood that on the first night. The love that had risen in him as he held her was absolute: the purest thing, apart from his grief, that he had ever felt. She was the only thing in the world that truly belonged to him; as long as he had her, he would never be alone. But Axane's presence was an unbearable reminder of his own stupidity. And how would he deal with her once the time came to march upon Baushpar, and he could no longer keep her caged in stone?

He could send her away, of course. It would be easy to do as he had threatened on the night she arrived, and find a woman to care for Parvâti. But he knew very well that Axane's apparent meekness was pretense; he had not forgotten her stubbornness, her iron will. She would not go quietly. Nor would she stay away. She would strive until she got Parvâti back, or perished trying.

That, of course, was the other solution.

He did not want to think it. He despised her. Yes: despised her. But he did not want her dead.

He closed his eyes, turning his face against the baby's floss-soft hair. "Parvâti," he whispered. Her little heart beat against his hand; he heard the flutter of her breathing. He sat listening, until the tapping of the announcement drum told him that Ardashir had come to fetch him to the afternoon audiences.

8

Râvar

Parvâti clutched Râvar's leggings and tried to hoist herself upright.

"Clever girl," he told her. "Clever girl."

She gurgled, delighted, then lost her grip and plumped down on the floor. Getting her legs under her, she crawled off after one of the toys he had shaped for her, a ring of bitterbark wood like the one he had had when he was a child. He watched her go, ready to jump up and deflect her if she showed signs of heading for the bathing pool; she was fascinated by the shaft of light that plunged into the water, and had several times attempted to slide into the pool in pursuit of it. She grabbed the ring and began chewing on it, her eyes as round as a bird's. He laughed aloud.

Except when he slept, he no longer bothered to close up his night chamber when he was in his rooms, and from where he sat he could see a slice of the chamber's interior, bright with the ruddy light of the niche-flames. Axane waited out of sight, enduring the moments until he returned Parvâti to her. Yesterday, again, she had asked if she could come out; again he had refused. He glanced away, not wanting to spoil his pleasure with thoughts of her.

The announcement drum sounded. He scooped up a wriggling Parvâti and carried her in to her mother, then settled the Blood around his neck and went out to the reception room. Ardashir was waiting, pacing back and forth, picking with one bandaged hand at the wrappings of the other. This was so untypical of his usual control that Râvar knew instantly something was amiss.

"What is it, Ardashir?"

"Beloved One." Ardashir let his hands fall, bowed. "There is news. I . . . hardly know how to say it."

"Tell me."

"Travelers have arrived. Not pilgrims." He drew a breath. "A Son and Daughter of the Brethren."

Râvar felt as if someone had struck him in the chest. *"What?"*

"It is so, Beloved One. When the news was brought to me I doubted it, and went myself to investigate. Of course I have never seen the Brethren, so I took with me a man who made pilgrimage last year to Baushpar. He confirms it. They have the sun tattoos of the Brethren, and they are escorted by armed guards who also wear tattoos, in the manner of the Âratist ordinates from Kanu-Tapa who are the Brethren's traditional guardians. They say they are the Son Vivaniya and the Daughter Sundit."

Râvar struggled to compose himself. *The spy,* he thought. It had be the spy; who else could have guided them here? Actually, there had been two spies; one had converted and betrayed the other, but not quickly enough to prevent the other from fleeing back to his masters in Baushpar. Râvar had not been pleased, though he knew it was inevitable that the Brethren discover him. He had anticipated other spies, or some action against his proselytizers. But never, not once, had he imagined that the Brethren would come to him.

"Beloved One, they . . . *demand* . . . an audience with you." Ardashir's tone conveyed his outrage at such temerity. "I informed them that only Ârata has the power to demand anything of the Next Messenger, and told them that I would ask your will."

"I will see them, Ardashir. At once."

"Beloved One, if I may offer counsel . . . make them wait a day or two. Remind them they have no authority here."

"No." Râvar shook his head. Excitement sparked in his belly. "I want to hear what they've come to say to me. Have the torches lit in the audience cave and conduct them there immediately. How many of these guards are there?"

"Twenty, Beloved One. All armed."

"They have permission to bring six. But no weapons. This is a place of peace. We will not have swords here."

"Knives, Beloved One. The Brethren's guardians carry knives."

"Knives, then."

"And if they refuse, Beloved One?"

"If they refuse, they shall have no audience. Ardashir—"

"Yes, Beloved One?"

"I confess I am as surprised by this as you. I had thought the Brethren would wait for me in Baushpar; I did not imagine they would come all this long way. In this, it seems my father did not see fit to share his will with me."

A rare smile, as faint as his lifelight, curved Ardashir's lips. "I shall tell them you've been expecting them all along, Beloved One. We'll see how arrogant they are then."

"Go, Ardashir. See it done."

Ardashir departed. Râvar returned to the bathing room. Excitement sat in his throat, and something else, a pressure he could not swallow down. *The Brethren. Here.* A feeling of dream overwhelmed him. For just a moment, he was tempted to call Ardashir back and tell him to make them wait after all.

How should he receive them? In his god guise, nearly naked and wreathed in light? No doubt they had heard about that from their spy. But the caves were cold, and he did not want them to see him do so ordinary a thing as shiver. No. He would go before them as a human Messenger, like the one they believed had fathered them centuries ago. The god-face he would save for later.

He rummaged through the clothing strewn around his bed, searching for the embroidered overrobe he sometimes wore. His hands trembled, making him even more clumsy than usual. He found the robe and dragged it on, then took a comb and yanked it through his hair. Shaking the heavy tresses back over his shoulders, he crossed to his night chamber. Axane sat on a cushion, Parvâti crawling near her on the floor. She looked up as he appeared.

"The two Brethren who traveled with the army to Refuge," he said. "One of them was named Vivaniya, yes?"

He could see how much she wanted to ask why. "Yes. And the other—"

"Was called Dâdar. I remember." He had been sure, but he wanted to be certain. It was not something he knew about firsthand, for he had been shut up in the Cavern when the Brethren's army came into Refuge. Axane had told him—and also what she had overheard the two Sons say to one another, after the battle.

"Shall I help you with that?"

She pointed. He realized he still held the comb. Lately she had begun offering him assistance—mending his clothes, cleaning his rooms, or as now, dressing his hair.

"No."

He closed them in, then went out into the passage, where a pair of Twentymen stood waiting with their staves and smoky torches. Near the main cavern, another passage branched to the right, opening, after a short distance, into the cave where Râvar held his audiences. It was little more than an oversized fissure, narrow at the front, bellying at its midpoint, with a drop-off into blackness at its back. Its walls were frosted with crystalline deposits that caught and magnified the light of a dozen torches, fixed to crystal rods that Râvar had planted in the floor. To one side, a slumping moon white pillar joined floor to ceiling. Râvar had shaped a seat into it and smoothed the rock around it to form a kind of dais.

He arranged himself on the pillar seat. The Twentymen positioned themselves to either side. His pulse beat fast and high. Drafts roiled the substance of the air; the torch flames danced in counterpoint, sending up long tails of smoke.

Light fell across the entrance. Ardashir appeared, a torch raised in one bandaged hand. After him came three large men in loose red gowns and trousers, with white stoles wound around their chests and shoulders. Sinuous tattoos disfigured their faces and their muscled right arms, left bare by the draping of their stoles. Behind them walked a man and woman, side by side. They, too, were shaven-headed, dressed in garments identical in cut and color to their attendants', but, Râvar's patternsense informed him, made of richer fabrics. On their foreheads a stylized rendering of the sun, Ârata's symbol, was tattooed in red. The man checked when he saw Râvar, falling still all in an instant, like a startled animal; the woman took hold of his arm, urging him into motion again. Three more attendants followed, and, bringing up the rear, several Twentymen. The cave was barely large enough to hold them all.

"Beloved One," said Ardashir. "I present to you the Son Vivaniya and the Daughter Sundit." He turned on the two Brethren. "Kneel," he said harshly. "Kneel to Ârata's Messenger."

"No." Râvar held up his hand. "I do not command it."

He regarded them, letting the silence stretch. The Son looked to be in his early thirties, a narrow man with a pale complexion and eyes that swept upward at the outer corners. His lifelight was the color of a dying coal. His eyes were riveted on Râvar's face; the folds of his elaborately draped white stole trembled with his rapid breathing. The Daughter seemed far more self-possessed. Her skin was pale like her companion's, but she had the round eyes and high-bridged nose of an Arsacian. She was small, rising only to the Son's shoulder, and sturdily built. Râvar guessed her to be somewhere in her fifth decade. Her lifelight was pure clear blue, with surges of darker color.

These are my enemies, Râvar thought. *This woman decreed Refuge's destruction. This man walked among its ruins.* Hatred shook him. He held himself motionless, letting it quake through him and away.

"Children of the First Messenger." His voice rang across the silence of the cave. "Be welcome in the Awakened City."

The Daughter Sundit inclined her head. "We thank you."

"You've traveled the Waking Road, as my faithful do. Yet I see you do not come to me in belief."

"We are here neither in belief nor disbelief." Within her cool light, the Daughter's face revealed nothing. "We are here to learn the truth."

Ardashir's glare might have cracked stone. Râvar smiled.

"I understand," he said. "You are guardians of the Way of Ârata. You cannot simply embrace faith, as others do, for it is not only your own souls that are at issue. If you believe, the Way believes. The church believes. Is that not so?"

He could see he had surprised her. "It is exactly so."

"Tell me, then." He held her eyes. "How may I convince you?"

"Show us what you have built in this place, this . . . Awakened City. Let us learn of you, and from you."

"Should I tell you of myself, then? How my father shaped me out of flesh and breathed into me the fire of his own divinity? Or shall I tell you of my father, mighty Ârata, of his beauty and his majesty, of his stern judgment and his infinite compassion? Shall I describe his resting place, where I first opened my eyes upon the world, the crystal ocean of his Blood blazing around me like the sun? Or perhaps I should speak of my wanderings in the Burning Land, of the terror and the ecstasy I endured in that sacred place." He shifted his gaze abruptly to the Son Vivaniya. "You know of what I speak, Vivaniya of the Brethren. For you, too, have wandered there."

The Son's eyes stretched. His mouth came a little open. The Daughter glanced at him, a small frown between her brows.

"Or perhaps I won't give you words at all. Perhaps it would be better simply . . . to show you."

A burst of blue-white light. A shuddering crack deep within the stone. The rock at the Brethren's feet split like the rind of a fruit, opening a chasm as black as blindness. The Son shouted and staggered back; he might have fallen had not one of his guards caught him beneath the arms. The Daughter backtracked also, though she made no sound. The guards closed around them both, their tattooed faces like something out of nightmare.

Once more Râvar extended his shaping will. The rock regenerated with an impact that shook the floor. The guards and the Son looked wildly round the cavern as if they expected it to collapse upon their heads. Râvar laughed; he could not help it.

"You are all quite safe," he said. "That was but a small demonstration of the power that accomplished the first act of Ârata's Promise, and brought the walls of Thuxra prison down."

The Daughter said something too soft to hear. The guards moved back. Deliberately she paced forward, halting exactly where the chasm had been. Râvar felt reluctant admiration. She was formidable.

"I see your eyes upon my necklace, Sundit of the Brethren." Carefully he lifted it from around his neck. "Ardashir. Show the Blood to our guests. Let them see it close."

Ardashir's face was like a mask. He brought the necklace to the Brethren, resting the crystal on one bandaged palm so they could inspect it. The Son simply stared, but the Daughter bent over it, peering into its fiery heart.

"You may touch it," Râvar said. "If you wish."

She glanced at him, then back at the great stone. She reached out, stroked it lightly with one finger. For a moment she stared at her fingertip. Then she closed her hand into a fist and straightened.

"Thank you." For the first time, she seemed uncertain. "I . . . this is . . ." She paused. "You understand. We must be sure."

He inclined his head, acknowledging.

"What is your intent?"

He heard the change in her voice. She was speaking not for the others' benefit, but for her own. He leaned toward her, his eyes capturing hers.

"I am the Next Messenger, Sundit of the Brethren. I have come to fulfill Ârata's Promise, to bring word of his rising and open the way for his return." He summoned illusion as he spoke, allowing light to bleed out around him, brightening briefly, flickering out at the final word. She blinked, uncertain of what she had seen. "I know the impediment of the authority you bear, which will not easily allow you to accept me. I do not fault you for this. I ask only that you watch, that you listen, that you learn. That you keep an open heart." He raised his right hand and placed it on his breast. "I promise, if you do, you will find the truth."

She stared at him, her small fingers still folded into a fist.

"Ardashir."

Ardashir returned the necklace. Râvar put it on again, feeling the links settle back into the grooves upon his neck.

"Sundit and Vivaniya of the Brethren, you are welcome among us for as long as you choose to remain. Ardashir, see to their accommodations. See that they are conducted around the Awakened City, that all their questions are answered. Nothing is to be closed to them, do you understand?"

"Yes, Beloved One." Ardashir was as stiff as stone.

"In the evenings I speak to my followers. We would welcome both of you among us."

The Daughter had moved to take her speechless companion's arm. "Thank you. We will attend."

"Great is Ârata. Great is his wakened Way." Râvar saw her register the alteration in the traditional phrase. "We'll talk again soon."

He sat watching from his throne as Ardashir ushered them away.

He returned to his chambers. Triumph blazed in his belly, and he felt as if his blood had turned to light.

He could not think of being still. He left his quarters by the passage that opened off the bathing room and plunged into the darkness of the caverns. He paid no heed to where he went, for the pattern of the caves was as clear to him as the sense of his own body. He swept his will across a gallery fanged with stalactites, bringing them all crashing down. He hurled a bridge of crystal across a crevasse, shaping its arch all in an instant. He transmuted the rough gray rock to opal and lapis and moonstone, veined it with copper and gold. He abandoned all restraint, mixing the patterns of one thing with the patterns of another, skewing patterns as he called them into being, shaping things not known in nature or imagination. The rock groaned with his thunder, and depths that had never known the smallest spark of brightness cowered beneath his light.

The Brethren had come to him. To *him*. And he had spoken to them and shown them his power, silenced one with awe and the other with uncertainty. He would own them both before they left the Awakened City—by Ârata, they would be his, as completely as any of his followers. And he would send them back to speak their faith to the rest, and by the time he reached Baushpar they would all belong to him. He would stand before them and they would fall at his feet and pledge themselves to him finally and forever, and when they had done that, when their souls were black with blasphemy, he would tell them the truth: Who he was. Why he had come. What their fate would be. They would know him then. He would watch the faith burn out of them, as it had burned out of him on the banks of Revelation. And then he would open the ground and seal them beneath it, and bring their holy city down. And he would laugh as it fell—laugh as he laughed now, in the pitchy passages of the underworld.

Do you hear me, Ârata? Do you hear me laughing?

At last, exhausted, he returned to his quarters. He cast the Blood aside and fell on his bed, sinking instantly into sleep. There were no nightmares this time. The dream that came to him was kind. He was with his cousin Kâruvisya, strolling along the banks of Revelation where it flowed beyond the cleft. The fallen leaves of the bitterbark trees crackled underfoot. The sun struck sparks from the river as it whispered past, and the air was full of birdsong. Kâruvisya had his slingshot; he launched pebbles at the ripe heads of rushes, causing them to explode into clouds of downy seed heads, shouting each time he made a hit . . .

Râvar woke. He lay with his eyes closed, holding for as long as he could to the feeling of the dream. Beneath him the bed seemed to sway, like the water of the river. The silence of his chambers held him like a hand.

At last he sat up. It seemed an age must have passed since the morning, but the shaft of light above the bathing pool told him it was only midafternoon. His body ached as if with hard use, which he supposed it had had.

He rose and unblocked the entrance to his night chamber. Its sour smell greeted him. Axane sat on the edge of the bed, combing her hair. Parvâti, folded into a nest of blankets beside her, woke at the sound of shaping and began to wail, but after only a few breaths subsided into silence.

"She just got off to sleep." Axane put down the comb.

Râvar went to stand over his child. Her dark lashes fluttered; one small fist was thrust underneath her chin. He reached out and gently drew a crooked finger down her cheek, feeling the impossible softness of her skin. Aware of Axane's observation, he stepped back and folded both hands inside the sleeves of his robe.

"Râvar." Axane's tone was tentative. "Would you let me look at your hands?"

It was her boldest offer yet. But to his surprise, he found he was not angry. "What for?"

"I'm a skilled healer. I might be able to help."

No. He heard himself saying it, saw himself turning away. Instead, he took his hands from his sleeves and held them out.

"Well?" he said when she sat motionless. It gave him a little amusement to see how taken aback she was.

She reached out, tentative, and took his hands in hers. She turned them over, inspecting them, pressing at the scar tissue. Her touch was cool. Her lifelight, surging out around her, swallowed his arms to the elbow; it did not eclipse his own golden aura, which was much brighter, but transformed it, like the sun seen through water. Close to her that way, he could see that her hair was greasy and her dress stained. She smelled unclean.

"Ah," he hissed, as she pulled at his frozen thumb.

Her eyes flew to his. "I'm sorry."

She released him. He stepped back, beyond reach of her surging colors.

"Most of the trouble is the scarring," she said. "If you'd had proper care when the injuries were fresh, your fingers might have healed straighter, and you'd have better use of them. There's nothing to be done for that now. You may be able to get more strength in your right hand, if you work at it—the muscles have withered, but you could build them up again with exercise. Even so, I think you'll probably only ever have limited use of it. As for your left hand, it's possible that cutting the scars might give you some flexibility in the thumb, but I couldn't say for certain. And it would be painful." She paused, and said again: "I'm sorry."

She had, he realized, given him an honest assessment. It surprised him. False hope, counterfeit optimism—that was what he had expected. On the other hand, to promise what she knew she could not accomplish would be foolish. And she was not foolish.

She sat quietly beneath his gaze. This was the face she had shown in Refuge: yielding, obedient, self-effacing. He knew it was not her real face, but the mask she wore to hide her secrets—whose mystery once had drawn him irresistibly to her, and now warned him to keep away. She was not to be trusted.

"Do you ever think of Refuge?" The words were out before he knew he meant to speak them. "As it was?"

Her mouth tightened. "Yes."

"What do you remember most?"

She did not answer at once. "In the dry season," she said at last, "I liked to go to the summit of the cleft and watch the Shapers calling storms. I remember how the clouds gathered . . . how the rain would come sweeping over the Plains like a silver curtain . . . and then the clouds would pass and the sun would come back, and the smell of the earth would rise up. Even from so high, you could smell it. And the scent of the bitterbark trees, when the wind shifted . . . It was always so hot under those trees, do you remember? And the way the leaves crackled underfoot, the way the wind fell at noon, and everything went quiet . . ."

The images bloomed in his mind as she evoked them. For an instant he was in his dream again, with Kâruvisya and his slingshot. This was not wise. He knew it was not wise. But who else in the world could remember how the bitterbarks had smelled?

"I'm afraid I'm starting to forget it," she said. "I walk through it in my mind, along the ledge, through the spaces—Labyrinth, the Temple, the Treasury. I lean out over Revelation and listen to its song. I go up the summit and look down on the Plains of Blessing. But sometimes I can't remember exactly how the columns along the face of the Treasury looked, or the sequence of the paintings in the Temple gallery. I try to hold it, but it's fading, and I can't stop it."

The grief in her voice sounded real. That was one loss, at least, he did not have to bear. He had a Shaper's memory, trained to pattern. If he wished, he could walk through Refuge in his mind and see it entire, down to the last detail.

"But you wanted to forget it," he said. "You ran away."

"I came back, Râvar. *I came back.*"

"Yes, with destruction following at your heels!" He felt the writhing of his own guilt. If she had tried to defend herself, if she had said a single word, he might have struck her to the floor. But she only bowed her head. The mantle of her hair followed the motion, sliding over her shoulders and across her breast.

"Was it everything you hoped?" he demanded harshly. "Living in Ninyâser? Pretending to be a citizen of this world?"

"No."

"*No?*"

"I didn't know . . . I had no idea what it would be like."

"But you were there before. When you ran away from Refuge. How could you not know what it was like?"

"I didn't understand." She drew a ragged breath. "The first time . . . the first time it terrified me, but still I thought I could find a way to live in it, to make a home in that city and use my skills to support myself. But I wasn't there long enough. I didn't understand how hard it would be to survive alone."

"You weren't," Râvar said viciously, "*alone.*"

"But I was!" Her head came up. He saw, with a strange stutter of his heart, that her mask had slipped. Tears filled her eyes. Pain was naked in her face. "In my heart. In my soul. The night I got here, you asked me if I hadn't longed for my own kin, my own kind. You asked how I could find comfort in a world I wasn't born to. I was afraid, and I pretended not to understand. But I did understand, I did. Oh, Râvar, I've been so unhappy!"

The words turned in him like an edge of crystal. He could not speak.

"I stayed on at Thuxra City," she said after a moment.

"What? After—after—?"

"Yes. There were survivors. They needed help. But then the relief party came, and there was no more use for me." She lifted her hands to wipe her wet cheeks, folded them in her lap again. "I went to Ninyâser, because it was the only place I knew to go. I tried to find work as a healer. But healers in Ninyâser have to be registered, and I couldn't register because I didn't have the proper training. It's hard to get work if you don't have a registration, and the pregnancy was proceeding . . . Oh, Râvar, they are selfish in this world, they give nothing away. There is so little kindness. I thought I might starve to death. I thought I might lose our child. I didn't know what to do. And then . . ." She paused. "I met *him*."

"The false Messenger."

"It was chance. He saw me in the street. I didn't recognize him, but he knew me. He'd left the Brethren's service and was working as a scribe. There are terrible penalties in this world for Shapers who . . . who slip away, who stop taking manita and let their shaping free. He was living in hiding, under a different name—"

"Gyalo Timpurin Chok."

She nodded. "He offered me a place in his home. He offered me marriage. Râvar, what was I to do? It was shelter. It was food." She swallowed. The knuckles of her clasped hands were white. "So I said yes. He . . . he was in love with me. I'd realized that before, the first time, when he brought me to Arsace. He knew I didn't feel the same. He said it didn't matter. I thought I would be able to bear it, for the baby's sake. But every time I looked at him I saw my father's face, my father who would still be alive if he'd never come to Refuge. And then, after the baby was born . . . she has your eyes, Râvar, your green eyes. I saw him looking at her, thinking she was another man's child."

"Did he know she was my child?"

She shook her head, her hair sliding on her shoulders. "We never spoke of it. Of you."

"So he knows nothing of me? You expect me to believe that?"

"It's the truth. He doesn't even know I went back to Refuge. I never told him, and he never asked."

"Was he your lover?" he said convulsively.

Her gaze was unflinching. "I was his wife. It was what he expected of me, after the baby was born. The barter for my shelter."

"Did you find it an easy trade?"

"No!" She gasped. "No. I knew I had to find a way to leave, to get free. I'd learned more about how to live. I'd found some custom as a healer. I had some coins. I was gathering up the courage to try. But then your men came. Oh, I was angry—angry at you for taking me, angry still for . . . for what happened in the Burning Land. But I've been thinking about what you said to me the day I got here . . ." Her eyes beseeched his. "That you and I and our child are the last of Refuge. That we should be a family—"

"You've already tried to bribe me with that. Do you think I've forgotten?"

"No, and you're right, I didn't mean it then, but I've had time to think, to see how you are with her, with our little girl, and I mean it now, I swear I do. Oh, Râvar, I am ashamed. I'm so ashamed of what I've done."

Was there any chance she was not lying? Yet if she were not, what difference would it make? What would it change?

"You should have died," he said, speaking each word as if it were a stone. "Before you went to him."

"Sometimes I wish I had. But then our child would be dead too."

She bowed her face into her hands and sat motionless, a little hunched dark statue. The tresses of her hair still trailed over her breast. It was her one physical beauty, her hair—thick and waving, black without a trace of brown or red. The desire to touch it, to reach out and loop it back over her shoulders, was suddenly overwhelming.

She did not call after him as he turned away. He went into the bathing chamber, and then, because that was not far enough, into the second chamber, where he sat down on the floor next to the fire, his hands—which still felt the press of her fingers—loose upon his knees. His weakness angered and shamed him. He told himself he had been weary, off guard from the dream of Kâruvisya. He would not make such a mistake again.

How strange that she had been at Thuxra while he lay healing among his followers. What would he have done, if he had known she was so close?

Gyalo Amdo Samchen. That hated name. Did he grieve to lose Axane, his willing or unwilling wife? Did it torment him not to know where she had gone, to think she had abandoned him? Almost, Râvar regretted that ignorance. It would have been satisfying to think he knew the truth, for the truth was much more painful.

Once, he had wished death on Gyalo Amdo Samchen. But he had come to desire a more subtle punishment. He wanted the man who had been the ruin of Refuge to recognize the true nature of the ruin that Râvar meant to bring on his people, and how that ruin was sourced in his own actions. He wanted the false Messenger who had corrupted Refuge through its faith to watch as another false Messenger drew the kingdoms of Galea into blasphemy, and understand why. He wanted Gyalo Amdo Samchen to stand amid the wreckage of his world, with no company but his grief, and know that he was guilty. Oh yes. That was worse than death. Râvar knew.

Maybe I'll search him out when I reach Ninyâser. Maybe I'll tell him then.

His masters came to me today. The Brethren came to me.

The fierce joy of it seized him, banishing the sour sense of failure. He rose and fetched the Blood. He settled the familiar weight of it around his neck, not looking at the entrance to his night chamber, and went to sit in his pink quartz chair, waiting for the drum to call him to the evening ceremony.

Gyalo

Look, Brother," Diasarta said. "Up there. Think that might be it?"

Gyalo halted, shading his eyes against the sizzling glare of the midday sun. To the south, close enough to make out contour but too far to read pattern, a ridge stretched like a dozing giant across the flatness of the steppe. Heat haze distorted the air, but halfway up the tawny slope he could see a patch of darkness.

"The location's right," he said. "Let's keep to the track a little longer. It'll be a while yet before we're close enough for anyone to spot us."

They set off again along the narrow trail, one of hundreds printed on the steppe by the migrations of countless generations of nomads, whose travels had beaten the ground as bare and hard as iron. The wind, whipping constantly across the grasses, was like the breath of an oven; Gyalo's hair was plastered to his scalp under his hat, and his clothes were soaked with sweat. Beyond the ridge, a line of bluffs marked the first of the great series of foldings and upthrustings that culminated in the mighty snow-wrapped peaks of the Range of Clouds; in all other directions there was nothing but steppe, a vastness of amber grass broken now and then by stands of scrub and, more rarely, an improbable splash of violet, where colonies of steppe gentian lifted their faces to the punishing sun. White clouds sailed overhead, their shadows pacing them like phantom armies, a constant interchange of light and shade.

They had been traveling for nearly three months—a journey that would have been shorter had they been able to go by a direct route. The general trend was south, toward the Range of Clouds, but whether as a test of the pilgrims' resolve or from concern for secrecy, the pilgrim way stations were in odd, out-of-the-way locations, which often took the companions far to the east or west. Almost at once Gyalo saw that they would not overtake Axane and Chokyi; the kidnappers, who—unlike the pilgrims—knew their destination, certainly would not bother with these diversions and byways. It was infuriating, but there was nothing to be done. He resigned himself to the tedious process of the journey, expending his frustration by setting a grueling pace.

Diasarta, bitterly contemptuous of everything to do with Râvar and the Awakened City, was less patient, and cursed the travel and the pilgrims until Gyalo grew weary of hearing him. He could not contain his fury when the map to the final way station revealed that it was near the village of Fashir, which lay right beside the Great South Way, the thoroughfare built by the Caryaxists to shuttle prisoners and treasure between Ninyâser and Thuxra City.

"Ash of the Enemy! If we'd known, we could have gone straight down the Way, without all these ash-cursed detours!"

"What if the way station keepers are making a record of who passes through, Dasa? What if they're told to turn away anyone who hasn't stopped at the previous station?"

"Even so. What a foul *bloody* waste of time."

The Fashir station was a goat herder's holding some distance beyond the village. A pilgrim band was resting there when the companions arrived. It was a typically motley group: a retired soldier, a number of peasant youths, a middle-aged woman who might have been a widow or a whore, a well-dressed merchant with his servant, and an entire family of husband, wife, two children, and a baby. The companions could not avoid taking the evening meal with the pilgrims, or kneeling with them afterward in meditation; but they refused the merchant's invitation to travel on in company, as they had refused similar offers along the way. At first light they moved on, equipped by the station keeper with a pair of straw hats and the final map, crudely drawn on a square of linen, with water sources marked in red.

The regions around Fashir, wracked by the struggles between local warlords in the chaotic final years of the Caryaxist regime, were plagued by bandits, but Gyalo and Diasarta were not accosted, and saw few travelers besides themselves. Once they reached the steppe they met no one at all—except, on the third day, a band of horsemen that overtook them from behind. Gyalo assumed at first it was a convoy heading for Thuxra. But well before the riders drew close enough for Gyalo to make out their tattoos, he recognized them, for with their red-and-white clothing they could only be vowed Âratists, and only one kind of vowed Âratist went mounted.

He and Diasarta stepped off the road to let the procession pass: ten Tapati ordinates riding in pairs, their shaven heads and ink-marked faces bare to the punishing sun; two carriages without insignia, window covers laced shut, driven by tattooless monks; ten more Tapati bringing up the rear.

Diasarta stared after them. "Where d'you think they're going?"

"To Thuxra, maybe. To observe the mines."

It did not make a lot of sense. But the other possibility, that the procession's destination was the same as theirs, made even less.

They set off again. Ahead, the convoy dwindled into the distance. Its light, the gathered brightness of the many lives that composed it, was the last thing to disappear.

Three days later they reached the point where they were to turn west: one of the snaking nomad tracks, marked by a cairn of stones with a pictogram of an open eye painted in red upon the topmost rock. They had been following the track for four days when the patch of darkness came in sight.

When the darkness had grown to the size of Gyalo's palm, he halted again. He could read enough probability in the ridge's contours to be certain that it was indeed a cave. The knot of tension beneath his breastbone, which with each day upon the steppe seemed to draw a little tighter, twisted tighter still.

"The Awakened City," he said.

"Time to turn off, then."

"Yes."

They had decided not to approach the Awakened City at once, but to camp nearby and spend a day or two reconnoitering. They left the track, striking southeast. The ridge rose slowly larger, eating up the horizon. By dusk the Range of Clouds, which for most of the past two weeks had hung like a jagged gray dream across the southern sky, had sunk entirely out of sight behind it. The moon was up when they reached the place that Gyalo, surveying the patterns of the terrain, had picked for their camp: a relatively level spot halfway up the ridge, with a little stream springing out over a lip of rock. They laid out their bedrolls and set some of the dried meat and hard biscuit the Fashir station keeper had given them in a pannier of water to soften. They ate in weary silence, then rolled themselves into their blankets to sleep.

Diasarta quickly began snoring, but Gyalo lay awake, listening to the breathing of the wind, staring out at the life-glimmering expanses of the steppe, where the patterns of the day's departing heat breathed like smoke toward the luminous hemisphere of the sky. After a time he freed his arm from the folds of his blanket and reached up through the watery substance of the air, as if to grasp a hand held down to him. The wind dragged cloud across the waxing moon and chased it away again, filling his palm with silver.

"Are you here?" he whispered. "Can you see me?"

He had never prayed for Axane's and Chokyi's safety. Whether or not their abduction was Ârata's will, he knew the god was indifferent to his desires; what would be would be, prayers or no. But one of the things that had made the journey bearable was to know that the distance between them meant nothing to Axane's dreaming. It had become a kind of devotion to speak this way, to reach up this way. He did it every night. On the edge of sleep it almost seemed sometimes that he sensed her—her breath upon his cheek, her scent upon the air.

So little divided them now: an hour's walk, a few thicknesses of rock. As he lay waiting in the dark, so, somewhere, did she. He had disciplined himself, over the past weeks, to think only of the waiting. In the rest of it—in Râvar's possession of her body, in the enormity of Râvar's power—lay madness. It was not always possible to confine his thoughts so narrowly, of course, and in sleep he was defenseless. But he owned a lifetime's rigorous meditation training, and it was more possible for him than it might have been for another man to fix himself in the present moment, to leash back his thoughts when they tried to rush down terrible paths of speculation.

One thing he had sworn: When they were together again, he would never ask her to speak of her ordeal. He would never ask her to tell him what she had had to suffer or do. They would put it behind them, as they had before. They would go forward from that moment, as if it were the first.

The grasses hissed. The water plashed. Clouds stole the moon and gave it back again. At last he turned on his side and, slipping his hand under his shirt, laced his fingers through her silver bracelet. He closed his eyes and slept.

Diasarta left at dawn to scout the Awakened City. Gyalo waited, forcing himself to a patience he was very far from feeling. He tried to meditate. He paced back and forth along the ridge side. He scoured the pots they had used the night before, unpacked and repacked his travel kit, shook out his and Diasarta's blankets and spread them to air. He simply sat, watching the cloud shadow race across the grasses, trying to open himself to the beauty of the sight. The world was veiled with the ash of Ârdaxcasa's destruction, but its substance was Ârata's own, and it was important—no, essential—to remember that.

He also inspected the supplies and shaped a variety of foods to supplement them. He had begun to use his shaping as soon as they left Ninyâser, knowing he would need it for what was to come. During his first apostasy, he had not had time to gain any true mastery of his gift; during his second, he had not shaped at all. He had expected, therefore, to be clumsy and inexpert. Yet almost at once he achieved a versatility and control beyond anything he had ever managed before. Initially he attempted only small shapings; in Arsace's heavily populated central regions it seemed unwise to risk more. But when he and Diasarta reached the steppe and he began to try his hand at greater feats, he realized that not only was he much stronger than he recalled, but he was able to accomplish things he could not remember learning. It was as if the process of exploration he had haltingly begun during his first apostasy had been continuing all this time, somewhere invisible within himself.

He knew he should be glad. Instead, for reasons he understood too well, he found his unbidden mastery deeply discomforting. In the Burning Land he had believed his apostasy a sin—a necessary sin, the god's will, for only by his shaping could he survive to reach the Brethren, but a sin nonetheless. Still he had embraced discovery, avidly pursuing the limits of his competence, snatching at knowledge like a man who had only just realized he was starving. Now he knew, or thought he knew, that apostasy was not a sin at all, that a free Shaper was not inevitably driven mad or corrupt by his unleashed ability, as he had been taught during his Âratist training. Yet he searched himself daily for signs of change. If he felt himself drawn to any particular act of power, he chose to perform another. He did not prolong his practice sessions—nor did he, who once had loved the exercise of his gift with urgent and consuming passion, take any joy in them.

Diasarta returned near dark. He had spent the day watching the Awakened City from various angles—not an easy task, for the ridge with its sparse vegetation did not afford much cover. There was little traffic in or out, he reported: Some women going down to the steppe to cut grass, a band of hunters with bows and arrows, a few people tossing rubbish down the hill, were all he had seen all day. On the crest of the path leading to the cavern was a constantly staffed checkpoint; it was some distance from the cavern's entrance, but anyone trying to avoid the checkpoint by coming at the entrance from a different angle would likely be seen.

"During the day, anyway. At night you could probably do it."

Gyalo shrugged. They had discussed the merits of entering the Awakened City secretly as opposed to coming to it openly as pilgrims, and had agreed that it made more sense to have official sanction for their presence, since it might take several days to learn all they needed to know.

"There's something else, Brother. Remember those coaches that passed us on the road? Well, both of 'em are sitting at the bottom of the ridge, with the horses staked out and fourteen of those tattooed monks camped alongside."

"The same coaches? Are you sure?"

"There's nothing wrong with my eyes, Brother. D'you think they've sent someone to parley with him? The Brethren, I mean?"

"I don't know." The Brethren surely knew about Râvar, with his proselytizers and his pilgrims. If they believed the stories of his power, they would assume he was an apostate Shaper; that, and his heresy, demanded action. But sending high-ranking Âratists to meet with him? Coaches or no coaches, Gyalo found it hard to conceive. "Well. Whatever it means, it's nothing to do with us. Anything else?"

"No. I think I've learned as much as I can from outside. We may as well go in tomorrow."

Gyalo braced himself. "Not us. Just me."

"Ah, no, Brother, not this again."

"My mind's made up."

"Brother, we've talked about this! We've agreed!"

"No. I just stopped disagreeing. Dasa, it only makes sense. If we go in together, we risk being caught together. This way, if I—" He could not bring himself to say the word *fail*. "If I don't come back, you'll be here to try in my place."

"I could try in the first place. You could be the one to stay."

"Can you open stone? Can you read patterns? I've got the best chance of succeeding."

"Burn it, Brother! You dragged me all this ash-cursed way, and now you won't let me help you? What's the point of me even being here?"

"If they're walled up somewhere and only shaping can free them, you won't be able to do anything anyway. You can help me most by waiting on the outside. I need to know there'll be someone else to try if I don't come back. I need to know . . . that I'm not their last hope. Please, Dasa, try and understand."

"Maybe you think I'm stupid, Brother, but I've seen more of the world than you have, and I've done more, too. D'you think I don't know what's behind this? Ash of the Enemy, I've seen it from the first. This isn't just about Axane and the baby. You think that because you know what he is, because you're a Shaper, too, you've got to be the one to confront him, to stop him, just you by yourself—the same way you thought you had to stand up to the bloody Brethren and make them believe in Ârata's awakening. We tried to stand with you then, but you wouldn't let us. You had to do it all yourself. It's the same now, so don't try and deny it."

Gyalo had done little all day long but wait, but all at once he felt profoundly weary. "Dasa, I am going in there to rescue Axane and Chokyi. That's all. If there is more . . ." Dread tried to rise in him; he pressed it back. "Then there will be more, as Ârata wills. But that's not why I'm going in alone."

The sky was clear; the wind had chased all the clouds into the east. In the mingled light of the moon and his own green aura, the anger in Diasarta's face was clear—and behind it, the injury. Gyalo suspected that Diasarta was aware of the fact that his stubborn insistence on offering faith to a man who did not want it was not so very different from Gyalo's equally stubborn rejection of that faith—both of them refusing to yield to the wishes of the other. But occasionally, he could not quite conceal how much the rejection wounded him.

"Did you ever think," Diasarta said, "that maybe you don't have the right to risk yourself this way?"

Anger struck Gyalo like an open hand. "Don't tell me what I have the right to do. Don't hold me to the standards of your faith."

"It should be *your* faith, Brother."

"My faith is not your concern."

"Yes, and that's the bloody problem, isn't it?"

"This discussion," Gyalo said tightly, "is pointless."

"Don't I know it?" Diasarta cried. "Don't I watch you day after day, turning from the truth of what you are?" He hurled his water cup aside; it struck a rock, making a pinging sound. "Burn me, I don't know why I bother. You've never walked the path that Ârata gave you. Not once, since we came out of the Burning Land."

It silenced them both.

"I'm not going to change my mind," Gyalo said at last. "Will you honor my decision?"

"What if I say no?"

But it was not a serious threat. Diasarta knew very well the consequences of refusing a man who could bend the natural world to his will.

"All right, Brother. You win. You bloody win."

He got roughly to his feet and stamped over to the stream. Gyalo got into his bedroll and pulled his blankets over his head. After a time he heard Diasarta's returning footsteps, then the rustle of bedding. Silence fell. Neither of them slept.

*　　*　　*

Gyalo departed at moonset. He rolled up his blankets and attached them to his pack, which he had prepared the day before. Diasarta lay unmoving through these preparations.

"Good-bye, Dasa."

"Three days, Brother." Diasarta did not stir. "Three days I'm giving you. You don't come out by then, I'm coming in after you." Then, softly: "Go in light."

Gyalo walked northwest, watching for the subtle shifts of pattern that marked the track. He found it just as dawn began to break. The watchers at the checkpoint would see him on it as the light rose, as if he had been following it all along. He made a mark so he would find the spot again, twisting several stalks of grass together and bending them toward the ground—then checked a moment, on the edge of the end of his long journey. The world around him, the grass and the wind and the clouds and the fading stars, seemed extraordinarily clear. *Ârata*, he thought. Not a prayer: an acknowledgment. An announcement of intent. He no longer felt any apprehension, only readiness.

The sun was well above the horizon by the time he reached the bottom of the ridge. For some distance the grass had been hacked to the ground, like a harvested wheatfield, a jarring man-made break in the smooth natural patterns of the steppe. The coaches sat in this cleared area, squat and black against the pale stubble. Several of the Tapati were training, repeating a series of steps and turns in dancelike sequence; another squatted by the cook fire, his lifelight the same color as the flames. The rest tended the horses. The dancers paid no attention to Gyalo as he trudged past, but the cook and the horse tenders looked up, their tattooed faces masklike in the morning sun. Gyalo stared back at them, feigning the awe that an ordinary man would surely feel, confronted by the church's legendary guardians.

The checkpoint was four poles driven into the stony soil, with a plaited-grass awning stretched atop. Beyond it the track tipped downward to the cavern's entrance, perhaps two hundred paces distant; it was even more gigantic than it had appeared from below, and obviously artificial, a smoothly regular arch. Two men lounged on grass mats in the awning's shade. One got to his feet as Gyalo approached.

"At whose call do you come?" he asked—the routine challenge made to all pilgrims, according to the station keeper in Fashir.

"I come at the Next Messenger's call," Gyalo replied. "I've followed the Waking Road. I claim citizenship in the Awakened City."

"Have you accepted the mark?"

"I have."

"Show me."

Gyalo extended his left hand, disfigured by a diagonal black scar. Diasarta had cut him the night after they left Ninyâser, and rubbed soot from their campfire into the wound. The man wet his finger and rubbed at the scar, presumably to test that Gyalo had not simply marked himself with charcoal, then tilted Gyalo's hand to the light.

"Let's see the other one." He scrutinized it. "Cina." He spoke over his shoulder to his companion. "Have a look."

The second man came to peer at Gyalo's palms. "Where'd you get the other marks?" he said. "Those white ones?"

"I got into some trouble a few years back," Gyalo said.

"You didn't make them yourself?"

"Why would I do that?"

"Wait here," the second man said. He started toward the cavern. The first sentry dropped Gyalo's hands and folded his arms.

"What's going on?" Gyalo asked.

"You heard him. Wait."

Gyalo stood, trying to conceal his rising apprehension. He had done what he could to alter his appearance, growing out his beard and letting his hair hang down over his face; he could not change his lifelight, but pearl was a common color, and Râvar had only seen him briefly, years ago. But he had not considered his scars. In Refuge, Râvar had seen him cut his hands on the Blood—could he have told his men to watch for a pilgrim with hand scars? Surely not. Râvar might or might not recognize Gyalo if he saw him again, but given the trouble Râvar's men had taken to make Axane's kidnapping look like a simple disappearance, there was no reason Râvar should be expecting him.

The sentry returned, accompanied by an ugly man with cropped black hair and an unmistakable air of authority. There was something peculiar about him as he approached; with a small shock, Gyalo realized that he did not seem to have a lifelight.

"Show me your hands, pilgrim."

Gyalo obeyed. The man took Gyalo's hands and examined them—the palms, then the backs, then the palms again. His own palms were bandaged, the cloth stained pinkish brown, as if with the seepage of some sort of skin disease. Otherwise, he was fastidiously neat and clean; Gyalo could not smell even the tang of sweat. Close to, it was apparent that he did have a lifelight, but a dimmer one than Gyalo had ever seen, the merest night blue shadow around his body.

"How did you get these scars?" He had a beautiful voice, a rich baritone that contrasted oddly with his lumpy features.

"It's not a tale that does me credit, sir." Gyalo had concocted this story soon after he began scribing, for his customers sometimes asked about his hands. "I borrowed money a few years ago to set up my business. It was more than I could afford. When the time came, I couldn't pay it all. The man I owed had my hands cut with a razor."

"A razor, eh." The man's dark eyes had an odd metallic sheen. "That must have been painful."

"It hurt like fire, sir. I couldn't work for two weeks."

"What is your work?"

"I am—I was—a scribe, sir."

"A scribe. Hmmm." He dropped Gyalo's hands and stepped back, folding his own bandaged hands at his waist. "You know of the Next Messenger's scars, do you not?"

"Yes, sir. The scars made by the Blood of Ârata—" And all at once Gyalo understood.

"When he carried it out of the Burning Land, yes. A reminder of his Messengerhood to all who see him, and also of the fact that Ârata chose to clothe the divine Messenger in human flesh. There are pilgrims who arrive not simply with the mark we require of the faithful, but with other scars, in imitation of the Messenger's own. We prize devotion, even sacrifice. But to mimic the Messenger is blasphemy. Those who show such marks are turned away. But I do believe you came by your scars as you say, for it's clear they are old. Be welcome in the Awakened City . . . what's your name, pilgrim?"

"Timpurin, sir."

"Be welcome in the Awakened City, Timpurin. I am Ardashir, the First Disciple. The Messenger is the ruler of our souls, but in this place and by his will I command all else."

It seemed to demand a bow, so Gyalo gave him one.

"Cina." Ardashir flicked a glance at the sentry who had fetched him. "Escort our new citizen inside and find him a place."

"Thank you, sir." Gyalo bowed again.

Ardashir departed, striding swiftly back the way he had come. The other sentry sat down on his mat again.

"Come along, citizen," said Cina. "I haven't got all day."

Gyalo hurried to catch him up. Below, Ardashir was already passing inside the cave, whose interior, viewed from the sunlit path, seemed as black as the night sky. Like the sky, it was strewn with light: the spectral hues of lifelights, the red glint of fire. The perspective expanded as they descended, rolling back into the ridge as if the cavern had no end.

"Why do they call him the First Disciple?" Gyalo asked.

"Because that's what he is." Cina was a leathery man with a yellow life-light and manacle marks at his neck and wrists—perhaps one of Râvar's original prisoner-followers. "After the Next Messenger brought down the walls of Thuxra City he fell unconscious, and the Blood of Ârata slipped from his hands. Ardashir caught it before it could touch the ground. It cut him deep. The cuts have never closed. You saw the bandages. It's a great suffering for him."

"Why have the cuts not closed?"

"Because human flesh can't bear the touch of the divine Blood. The Messenger's flesh is also human, but he's filled with Ârata's divinity just like the Blood is, so his wounds healed. They scarred, though, they scarred terribly. You'll see for yourself."

The cavern's chill came out to meet them. They passed through its great mouth; looking up at that perfect curve, gleaming with the distinctive gloss of Shaper stoneworking, Gyalo could not suppress a tremor of awe at the power that could shape such a thing. The cave's interior was even more enormous than the view from outside had suggested—at least five or six times the width of the entrance, and so long that Gyalo could discern its far end only as a point where there were no more lights. The ceiling seemed to rise much of the height of the ridge. Other than a broad clear space at the approximate midpoint, which ran like a roadway toward the rear, every inch of floor was occupied by pilgrim encampments. Axane's Dreams had prepared Gyalo for the vastness of this place, but still the reality was stunning. How many people were here? Fifteen hundred? Two thousand? More?

"You must have heard stories." Beside him, Cina was grinning at his amazement. "But I'll wager you never imagined anything like this."

"No," Gyalo said. "Not like this."

Cina led him into the dim regions beyond the sun-bright entrance. The air grew colder, the odor of smoke and unwashed humanity stronger. Gyalo's Shaper senses read the patterns of the rock—its structure, which he recognized as limestone, the subtler configurations that spoke of the proliferating complex of caves beyond this one, thrusting back and down within the ridge. How many others were inhabited? The perimeters of the pilgrim settlements were neatly marked with stones or mats or bundles of grass; they were sparse but very tidy, blankets folded, bags and boxes stacked, cooking and eating utensils carefully stowed. Many were empty, but lifelights glinted here and there, and heads turned as Gyalo and Cina passed, though without much interest. New pilgrims must be a common sight.

Cina delivered Gyalo to a spot near the cavern's eastern wall, where the arrangement of two settlements had left a gap.

"You can set up your own cook fire here," he said, "or find a fire to share, whatever suits you. Ask someone to show you where to go for food—the Messenger provides for us, praise his name, but his bounty isn't endless, so there's a daily ration. In a day or two you'll be assigned to a work group. I hope you're ready to work. Everyone in the Awakened City does."

"I'm ready."

"The First Disciple likes to give a talk to new citizens, just to let them know what's what, and then the Next Messenger receives and blesses them. He usually waits till there's a group. You're the first to get here in a week, so you won't have your blessing right away."

That was a stroke of luck. Gyalo thought of the pilgrim band in Fashir, several days behind by now. Maybe he would be gone by the time they arrived. *Axane*, he thought.

"Don't worry, though," Cina was saying. "You won't have to wait long. So. Any questions?"

"No," Gyalo said. "Thank you."

"Be welcome in the Awakened City . . ." Cina searched his memory. "Timpurin."

He departed. Gyalo swung his pack off his back and set it down. He was close to the cavern's rear, deep within its perpetual dusk. The distant arch of the entrance was blindingly bright by contrast. Around him spread the settlements, angled together like the chips of a mosaic. The noise of human activity barely challenged the innate silence of the vast space. *I'm here*, he thought. He felt a surge of exhilaration. He was not happy about the attention his arrival had drawn. But the first obstacle had been conquered: He was inside.

Several settlements along, a man with a rippling topaz lifelight crouched over the embers of his fire, coaxing it to a blaze. Gyalo picked up his pack and approached. "Great is Ârata, great is his Way," he said. "Greetings, citizen."

The man looked around. "His wakened Way."

"What?"

"We use a different form of the greeting here. Great is Ârata. Great is his wakened Way."

"I'm sorry. I've only just arrived."

"Yes, I saw you come in."

"My name is Timpurin. I was wondering if perhaps I could share your fire."

The man regarded him. He looked to be in his fifties, his face lined, his gray hair cropped short. "You're from one of the other kingdoms," he said. "Not Arsace."

"I was born in Chonggye, but Ninyâser is my home. Was my home."

The man nodded. "There are others like you here. We're from all the kingdoms of Galea, we citizens of the Awakened City, and from none of them. We make our own kingdom, a new kingdom for a new age. Fourteen hundred and seventy-six at last census, praise Ârata." He made the god's sign, then smiled, his cheeks creasing. "Well, why not? As long as the others don't mind. There's five of us. We stick together, and share what we've got. My name's Gaubanita."

"Thanks, Gaubanita. I've got something to share." Gyalo dug into his pack for the provisions he had packed yesterday for authenticity's sake. "It's the last of what I brought with me."

"Meat!" Gaubanita took it eagerly. "That's welcome. Mostly we eat wheat and rice." He indicated a bag that sat nearby, amid an orderly array of containers and utensils. "It's filling, but after four months that's all the good I can say of it. Still, I shouldn't complain. How many people can say they eat divine food every day?"

"Divine food?"

"Made by the Messenger himself." Again Gaubanita made the sign of Ârata. "Praise his beloved name. He provides for us, like a father for his children. He makes the grain, and the salt, and the fruit that keeps us from the mouthrot sickness, a different kind every week. He eats it, same as us. He could dwell in a palace and have servants to set him out a feast every morning, noon, and night, but he lives like we do, and he works like we do. You'll see, Timpurin. Whatever you've heard while you were journeying here, it's nothing to the truth."

"Ârata be praised."

Gyalo sat down on his bedroll. Gaubanita tossed handfuls of grain into the pot he had set to boil, adding salt from another bag and tearing apart and incorporating Gyalo's strips of dried meat. The others who shared the settlement returned, and Gaubanita made introductions. They were the usual odd assortment: a pair of brothers from a farm in northern Arsace, a shoemaker from Ninyâser, a temple artist from one of the expatriate Arsacian communities in Haruko. Like their little encampment, they were neat and clean, their hair combed and their beards trimmed. The shoemaker seemed put out by Gyalo's presence, but the others were friendly.

They settled around the fire to eat. The pilgrims wanted to know about Gyalo's conversion, and he obliged with the tale he had told others, borrowed from the boy who had come to him for the letter. They offered their own stories. The brothers, taking goods to market, had heard one of Râvar's missionaries proselytizing in the town square; they made their minds up there and then to seek the Awakened City, and set out without ever returning home. The artist had been brought by a friend to a secret assembly of faithful; he had dismissed their message but was drawn to return again and again, until he could no longer deny the belief that had awoken in him. Gaubanita, sole survivor of the fire that destroyed his cookshop and killed his family, had encountered a missionary at the end of a long quest for spiritual relief. "My soul was still burning," he said simply, "and his words were water."

Gyalo heard also what they did not say: the brothers' desire to escape the grinding labor and poverty of their family farm, Gaubanita's flight from grief, the artist's thwarted dreams of greatness, which Râvar's promises of glory in the afterlife allowed him to shape anew. Such shadow-motives stood behind nearly every pilgrim tale he had ever heard—something hidden or unexpressed, something they could not confess or were desperate to deny. Only the shoemaker, a scowling man with a shimmering plum-colored lifelight, appeared to have no deeper motive. "I always knew their evil would wake Ârata up," he said of the Caryaxists. "I've been waiting for the Next Messenger ever since those bastards fell."

They were eager to answer Gyalo's questions about the Awakened City, of which they were obviously very proud, and even more eager to speak about Râvar: his compassion and his beauty, the stirring ceremonies he conducted, the many wonders he had worked in the caverns and elsewhere. They talked of his arrival from the Burning Land as if they had actually witnessed it, and told the tale of Thuxra City's destruction in words that had the formality of scripture, trading the phrases back and forth between them. Râvar was no legend to these men: They saw him daily in the flesh. Yet they displayed the same half-tranced, almost childish wonder as the pilgrims along the Waking Road, to whom he was still only a dream, a promise.

"When he looks at you, you can feel it," one of the brothers said, describing the audience he had recently been granted. "When he blesses you it's like fire shooting through you. He puts light on your skin." He touched a spot between his eyes. "Just here."

"He gives us gifts." The other brother rummaged in his pocket and pulled out a palmful of colored stones. "At every ceremony he lifts his arms, and there's a sort of thunderclap, and they just come raining down. There's rubies here. Real rubies!" Gyalo leaned to look, but the boy snatched his hand away. "If you want some, you'll have to get your own."

"Does the Messenger have a companion?" Gyalo asked. "Does he consort with women?"

The artist drew back, affronted, but the brothers sniggered and Gaubanita smiled. "The Next Messenger is human," he said. "As well as divine. He hungers and sleeps and even can be wounded, just like us. But that need he doesn't seem to have."

"Or else he hasn't found the proper one to answer it," the shoemaker said.

"So there's no woman who accompanies him? No woman he keeps for himself?"

"Oh, so it's that way with you, is it?" The shoemaker laughed unpleasantly. "Well, you won't be the first. Half those who ask for audiences have that in mind, and half of them are men."

"Even though his seed is fire," said the younger brother, nodding. "They'd let themselves be burned up, just to lie with him."

"Don't be stupid," his sibling said. "He's made like we are, bones and flesh and blood, and seed as well."

"It's foolish to argue about such things," Gaubanita said. "None of us will ever know, and that's a fact."

"I was wondering," Gyalo said. "Down on the steppe, I saw a pair of coaches, and vowed Âratists with tattoos."

"Ah yes," Gaubanita said. "The guardians of the Brethren."

"I was wondering why they're here."

"Why, because the Brethren are here."

Gyalo nearly dropped his bowl. *"What?"*

"They arrived four days ago. The Son Vivaniya and the Daughter Sundit. They are the Messenger's guests."

"The Brethren," Gyalo said, trying to get his mind around it. "Are *here?*"

"Didn't he just say so?" the artist demanded.

"You shouldn't be so surprised," Gaubanita said gently. "Doesn't the Messenger teach that the Brethren will bow down to him and yield to him the leadership of the church during the holy time of Interim? Why shouldn't they seek him out, even before he begins his glorious march upon Baushpar?"

The Brethren. Not their representatives—*the Brethren themselves.*

Vivaniya, who had been present at Refuge's destruction. Sundit, who had been one of the few to speak for Gyalo when he returned from the Burning Land.

"You don't look well, citizen," the artist said. "Anyone would think you'd had bad news."

The brothers, too, were staring at him. But the shoemaker, who all this time had not relaxed his hostile scowl, was grinning.

"I know what his problem is," he said. "He's like me. That's it, isn't it, Timpurin?"

"I—"

"Go on, you can admit it. We're free men here. You can say you hate their ash-cursed guts. You can say you'd rather the Messenger had sealed the Awakened City up than let their cowardly betraying carcasses inside."

"Burn it, Obâna, we're sick of that kind of talk," said the artist with some heat. "You know the rest of us don't feel the same."

"Well, Timpurin does. Don't you, Timpurin?" Obâna clapped him on the shoulder. "Excellent. A man who sees things the way I do."

"The Messenger does as he wills," said Gaubanita quietly. "We only follow."

The artist got to his feet. "I'm going back to work."

Gaubanita rose also. "Since you'll be staying here, Timpurin, you can watch the fire and clean the dishes."

They departed. Gyalo stacked the bowls and spoons into the empty cooking pot and made his way to the cavern's western wall, where a fall of water splashed from somewhere overhead into a series of stair-stepped pools, their rims glittering with mineral deposits. He waited while a woman with a rose-colored lifelight filled a jug; she smiled at him as she turned to go, and made the sign of Ârata.

By the time he had washed the utensils and brought them back to the settlement and stacked them neatly by the food supplies, he was calmer. There was a mystery, certainly. But it was not his concern. He had not come to worry about the Brethren.

He took a grass brick from the stack at the settlement's edge and put it on the fire. From Gaubanita and the others, he had learned that Râvar did indeed live apart, in a series of chambers opening off a passage at the cavern's rear. The same passage led down to the smaller cave where the daily ceremonies were conducted. Might he conceal himself before the ceremony and steal into Râvar's quarters when everyone had gone? But there would surely be a guard upon the entrance. Perhaps it would be possible to use his patternsense to find a way through the labyrinth of caves and passages, and come at Râvar's quarters from a different angle.

Yes. He got to his feet. It was time to go exploring.

"You. Timpurin."

That rich voice was unmistakable. Ardashir, he of the shadow light and bandaged hands, stood at the perimeter of the settlement. He had two men with him, each with a staff and an armband of plaited grass.

"I've a job for you," Ardashir said, and beckoned.

Like the obedient servant Ardashir thought him, Gyalo stepped forward. There were swift footsteps behind him. He began to turn. But he was not fast enough to duck the blow.

Gyalo

He did not quite lose consciousness, though the world grew gray and foggy. He was aware of being borne up under the arms and legs, carried through some long dark place. Then suddenly there was light, and he discovered that he was lying on his belly, his cheek turned against cold stone. There were voices, too soft to understand. The air moved. He felt himself pulled over on his back. Fingers pushed the hair off his face, gripped his chin, turned his head from side to side. It had grown dark again—no, his eyes had fallen closed. He struggled to open them. He saw a face above him, a blur outlined in sharp golden light. It hurt to look at it. He shut his eyes again.

Perhaps that time he did fall unconscious. When he became aware once more, he was still on his back. His head ached abominably, but his vision had cleared. He was no longer in the cavern. The ceiling above him was low and washed in ruddy light; its patterns were not those of limestone, but of sandstone, polished to water-soft smoothness. There was something very familiar about that glossy surface, those sinuous bands of red and rust and rose. He struggled to remember . . . Refuge, that was it. It looked like the sandstone of Refuge, like the Shaper-made living spaces he had seen there.

A flood of icy water seemed to spill inside his chest.

He rolled his head painfully to the side. He lay before a shallow dais, smooth and gleaming like the ceiling. From it, without any visible seam, rose a massive chair of translucent pink quartz. In the chair sat a young man in a long robe, his lustrous black hair pulled forward across one shoulder and the honey-shaded fire of the Blood of Ârata pulsing on his chest. His piercing golden aura outlined his body, like the sun blazing around the edges of an eclipse.

Râvar.

The world went away for a moment, then returned in a burst of agony that made Gyalo gasp. He lay as it subsided, then, dizzily, struggled to a sitting position, supporting himself with one hand on the floor. Râvar watched. His fine-cut features—older and harder than Gyalo remembered, but no less perfect—were devoid of feeling, but his green eyes never left Gyalo's face. His hands were buried in the wide sleeves of his robe.

"Do you recognize me?" It was said so softly that the quiet hardly seemed to break.

"Yes."

"You don't seem surprised."

"Why . . ." Gyalo's tongue felt thick. "Why should I be surprised?"

Râvar regarded him. The silence stretched. Despite his peril, Gyalo was distracted by the rosy illumination of the chamber, which had a strange, fixed quality entirely unlike the unstable living patterns of fire- or candlelight. He raised his eyes to the niches that ran around the walls, and realized with an odd cold shock that what he had thought were lamps were in fact just flames, burning without any apparent source of combustion. He stared, not quite believing it. Any Shaper could call fire, but to keep it alight without fuel . . . ?

Râvar said, "Would you like to how I knew it was you?"

"Yes."

"I don't expect I would have recognized you if you'd come before me in the ordinary way. I remember your face from Refuge—oh yes, I do remember it. But you have a common lifelight. And the beard and the hair make you seem quite different. When I look closely I can see it's you, but I doubt I would have found any reason to look closely."

He paused, possibly waiting for a response. When Gyalo gave him none, he continued.

"Ardashir came to me before the noon meal, as he does each day, to report on the happenings of my City. He told me of a new arrival, a scribe, who he thought might be useful. He said he'd been called out to inspect this new arrival on suspicion of blasphemy—a man with a Chonggyean name, Timpurin, with thick scars across his palms and fingers. Now, I happen to know that you were working as a scribe in Ninyâser, and that Timpurin is one of the false names you took for yourself. And I remember how you cut your hands in Refuge. I knew you would have scars. I hardly thought it could actually be you, even with so many coincidences, but I don't leave such things to chance. I sent Ardashir to fetch you. The knock on the head was a precaution." He shifted his posture, withdrawing his hands from his sleeves—the fingers, Gyalo saw, cruelly bent and twisted—and laying them on the arms of the chair. "And a good thing, too."

Gyalo saw that he had been a fool. He had feared Râvar's power; even so, he had thought he understood it. Had he not seen the works of the unbound Shapers of Refuge? Was he not familiar, from Axane's eyewitness account, with every detail of the destruction of Thuxra City? Was he not a Shaper himself—a very poor kind of Shaper, but a Shaper nonetheless? But here in Râvar's presence, with Râvar's quiet words in his ears and Râvar's piercing aura in his eyes and around him the great sum of Râvar's creation, from the slick sandstone of the chambers to the sourceless flames in their wall-niches to the mighty City of enslaved souls beyond, he realized that he had not understood at all. Râvar's was power beyond any dream of it. He had never had a chance.

Diasarta spoke inside his head: *Did you ever think that maybe you don't have the right to risk yourself this way?*

Oh, Axane, he thought in anguish. And all at once he realized that she must be here, right now, perhaps only on the other side of the wall. He turned involuntarily to his left, where a square opening gave onto a second artificially sleek, unnaturally illuminated room, and beyond that a third, into which a shaft of daylight seemed improbably to fall. An insane impulse swept him—to leap to his feet, to dash into those gleaming spaces, though he knew he would not get three steps before Râvar struck him down.

"Tell me," Râvar said. "Why have you come to my City?"

Gyalo cleared his throat. His heart was pounding. "You know why."

"Some of my followers fear that I can see inside their heads and read their thoughts. I know you know it isn't true. Tell me why you've come."

"For Axane. For the child."

Râvar went absolutely still. "Why should you imagine they are here?"

"She was sure you were looking for her. When I found her gone, it was the first thing I thought of."

"Ah." Râvar's voice was strange, the first obvious emotion he had shown, though Gyalo could not read exactly what that emotion was. "So she did tell you about me."

Ârata, Gyalo thought, *what mistake did I just make?*

"Do you know the child is mine?"

"What does it matter?"

Râvar raised perfect brows. "It doesn't matter very much at all. But I'd like to know if you're aware of my intent. If you know the reason—the real reason"—he swept out an arm in a gesture that encompassed the whole of the Awakened City—"for all this."

"I've heard what your followers say."

"My followers are fools." Râvar slid his hands along the arms of his chair, leaning forward. "What were you planning to do? Were you going to challenge me? I know you're free of the tether of manita, but even free, you are not my equal. No Shaper in the world is my equal." It was said without pride: simply as a fact. "Or maybe you thought you could steal her back through some kind of trickery. Is that it?"

"What does it matter?" Gyalo said again.

"I wonder how far you would have gotten, if it hadn't been for Ardashir. Do you know why we watch for hand scars? It's not because of me. I care nothing if they are stupid enough to copy my scars. It's Ardashir. He doesn't want rivals. Did anyone tell you about his wounds?"

"Yes."

"Look. Look what the Blood did to me." Râvar thrust out his hands, and Gyalo saw how maimed they really were: the clawed fingers, the welted scars. His own palms burned in sympathy. "Can you imagine what it's like to live with hands like these? You're lucky you touched the Blood so lightly when we brought you to the Cavern."

His face was suddenly alight with rage. Gyalo was certain the moment had come: a blast of fire, the rock suddenly vanishing from beneath him. But Râvar sat back, folding his arms, hiding his hands again. He regarded Gyalo with slow-blinking eyes. At his throat, the Blood pulsed flame. The crystal was huge—nearly twice as large as the one the Bearer wore.

"Do you know that your masters the Brethren have come to me? Two of them, anyway."

"Yes."

"They've already all but acknowledged me. They'll be mine by the time they leave. What do you think of that?"

Gyalo was silent.

"Ah, but I forget. You forswore your vows and renounced your church. So perhaps you think it's fitting that I should claim their souls."

"I won't play this game with you."

"Game?"

"We both know you're going to kill me."

"Kill you? Is that what you think?" The rage was there again, like a fault opening in the earth. "Oh no. That is not my plan at all. I have a better punishment in mind. I want you to know me. I want you to watch me as I march upon Baushpar, as I force the Brethren to bow down and worship me, then bury them beneath the rubble of their city and their temple. I want you to watch as I corrupt your people, as I steal their souls from Ârata and bind them to myself, so there will be no light left in them to rise into the new primal age. I want you to watch me bring ruin upon your world—you, who brought ruin on mine! I want you to know that you are helpless to prevent it. I want you to grieve, to weep as if there were no end to weeping. I want you to *wish* for death." He sat back in his chair, out of which, again, his passion had half pulled him. "But I will not give it to you."

There was a long, frozen pause. Gyalo did not dare even to blink. Then Râvar sighed, as if letting something go.

"What you've come for isn't here."

"What?"

"They're dead."

". . . What?"

"They. Are. Dead. Axane and the child."

"You're lying."

"No."

"What—what—how?"

"It happened while they were on their way to me. An accident. She kept trying to escape. She fell down a hill, struck her head on a rock. The baby was on her back. The child was killed at once. She died a few days later."

He said it coolly, as if he were speaking of one of his pathetic followers, not a woman he had loved with an obsessive passion, not a child he had gone to enormous effort to steal. Gyalo closed his eyes. Against the darkness of his lids, he saw them: Axane, clothed in the storm of her great light; Chokyi, laughing, small fists waving. The floor under him seemed to tip. He felt himself beginning to slide off the edge of the world.

"So now you know." Râvar's voice seemed to come from very far off. "You came for nothing." A pause. "Have you nothing to say to me?" Another pause. "Very well."

A rustling. The air moved. The sound of footsteps, then silence. The steps returned.

"Open your eyes," said Râvar. "Look at me."

Gyalo obeyed. Râvar stood before him, his ruined hands hanging by his sides.

"My men are coming to take you. You are not to try to return. I won't spare your life a second time. Do you understand?"

Gyalo stared at him. Râvar crouched down, spoke directly into his face.

"I know what it means to be a free Shaper in your world. I don't think there's much chance that you'll go to your former masters to warn them about me. But in case I'm mistaken, know this. They *will* be mine, the two that are here, and I will send them back to the others to announce my divinity. Against that, your words will mean nothing. When I arrive they will be waiting to embrace me. All of them."

Less than an arm's length separated them. Gyalo knew he had no hope against Râvar's shaping, but against Râvar's crippled hands . . . but even as he gathered himself, one of those hands flashed out and struck his chest, with more strength than he would have expected.

"Don't think it," Râvar said softly. "I have skills you can't imagine. I can harden the air to imprison you. I can make a void around you so you suffocate. I can do any of these things more quickly than you can blink, and without the least effect upon myself. You cannot harm me." He seized Gyalo's chin with his twisted fingers, dragging Gyalo's face within inches of his own. "All the blame is yours," he whispered. "Remember that, as you watch me pass through your world."

He let go. Gyalo tipped forward, catching himself with his hands. Râvar rose and turned. Ardashir stood in the chamber's entrance, with several men behind him.

"This man," Râvar said, "told you his name was Timpurin. That was a lie. His true name is Gyalo Amdo Samchen. He is a Shaper who has abandoned his vows. He sought to conceal his crime in order to join our City, but I perceived the truth. I do not turn away the faithful, no matter how they have sinned against one another; but this man has sinned against my father, whose will it is that Shapers be bound. I therefore repudiate him, and banish him from my presence. You will take him from here alive, but if ever he tries to return, he is to be killed on sight. Is that clear?"

"Yes, Beloved One," Ardashir replied.

"Ardashir, strike him unconscious."

Ardashir made a gesture. One of the Twentymen stepped forward, raising his staff. Gyalo turned his face away.

He returned to awareness by degrees. The pain in his head was so intense it did not really seem like pain at all, but like something separate from himself, a howling tempest of which he was the single focus. His memory was disordered. Where was he? What had happened? It seemed to him he had been dreaming, a terrible dream in which Axane and Chokyi were dead . . .

He groaned. Nearby he sensed motion. Something prodded him in the side.

"Gyalo Amdo Samchen. Are you awake?"

He knew that voice. With enormous effort he opened his eyes. The face leaning over him was also familiar, dark against the sky. What was the man's name? He tried to think, but the moving clouds distracted him. How had he gotten outside?

"Can you hear me?" The man leaned closer.

Ardashir. That was it. And all at once Gyalo remembered everything, a flood of understanding that made the storm inside his head seem gentle by comparison. "Ârata," he whispered, anguished. "Ah, Ârata."

"It will do you no good to call upon the god," Ardashir said. "In his mercy, the Messenger has spared your life. I would not have been so kind."

Gyalo closed his eyes again. Hands seized the front of his shirt and shook him. He gasped.

"I heard the last thing he said to you," Ardashir hissed. "Why should he speak to you so? What have you done?" Another shake. "Who are you?"

"No one," Gyalo whispered.

"What does he blame you for? How have you troubled my Messenger?"

"Your Messenger . . . is a fraud."

"Blasphemer!"

"He has . . . stolen your soul. He'll burn you . . . to ashes in the end."

Ardashir growled and yanked Gyalo upright. The pain in Gyalo's head crested; a cold wave of nausea broke across his body. He gagged and vomited, incapable even of turning aside. Ardashir shouted in disgust and leaped away. Gyalo collapsed back onto the ground. A gray veil swam across his vision.

"Blasphemer. Filthy dog." The voice seemed to come from a long distance off, as did the kick that accompanied it. Then there was stillness.

Gyalo's pain pinned him to the earth. Far more agonizing was the weight of understanding. He lay staring at the sky, longing for unconsciousness, but this time it did not come.

Râvar

Râvar was still sitting on his quartz throne when Ardashir returned. The First Disciple had changed his clothes; the bandages on his hands were fresh.

"He's gone, Beloved One," he said. "I took him down to the steppe as you ordered and left him well along the track."

"Good."

"I had my men look at his face. They will know him if he comes again."

Râvar nodded.

"Beloved One—" Ardashir hesitated.

"What is it, Ardashir?"

"He will not trouble you again. By Ârata I swear it." His face and voice were fierce, as if this were an oath of great significance. "I and my men will keep watch. If he comes near the Awakened City, he will die."

"I know you will do your duty."

Ardashir departed, and still Râvar sat. The blazing triumph he had felt to have his enemy before him, to taunt him with the truth and torment him with lies, had dwindled. Had he been wrong to let Gyalo Amdo Samchen go? Would it have been better to kill him after all? Or rather, to have him killed—for Râvar, who had killed invisible thousands from a distance, was not sure he had the stomach to take a life face-to-face. Yet this was what he had wanted. It was what, only a few days ago, he had explicitly imagined, without ever really thinking it could actually come to pass. What threat was this man, this enemy, now that he believed Axane was dead? Râvar summoned up the memory of how his enemy's face had changed when he spoke those words, the eyes closing, all the muscles going slack. He felt an echo of the cruel pleasure it had given him.

When he emerged onto the precipice above the ceremonial cave that evening, he saw the Brethren at once, standing at the edge of the bright gathering of the faithful, squinting up at him like mice looking at the sun. The Son and Daughter were arm in arm; at their sides were the two aides they had requested be brought up from the steppe (Shapers, both of them, crippled with manita in the manner of this world). At their backs the six guards formed a tense half circle. As he had each night since their arrival, Râvar directed his progress through the crowd so that it brought him last to where they waited. He paused a moment, testing them with his gaze, which the Daughter could not break and the Son and the two aides could not hold; then, satisfied, he whirled around, his garment of illusion billowing, and flung himself upward through the air. When he turned, his bare toes even with the precipice's lip, the roaring of the faithful seemed enough to crack the rock.

His sleep that night was disturbed by dreams, not all of them, mercifully, nightmares. He woke with an aching head and heavy limbs. He fetched Axane's bowl and cup and unblocked the night chamber. She was nursing Parvâti, turned from the entrance with a stole draped across her back to hide her bare skin. He set the food on the floor and stood watching, thinking of what she had told him five days ago. He knew for certain that she had lied, for Gyalo Amdo Samchen had not, as she claimed, been ignorant of him. Had she been trying to protect the husband she had sworn she despised?

"There's water in the pool," he said abruptly, surprising himself. "You can use it if you like."

She did not turn. "Thank you."

"Call when you're ready, and I'll take the baby."

He carried Parvâti, sleepy after her feeding, into the second room and sat down against the wall, out of any possible sight of the bathing chamber, listening to the faint sound of splashing and trying not to think of Axane, naked in the pool. At last she called that she was finished. He returned Parvâti to her, and unmade the water that had touched her body.

A little while later the announcement drum sounded. It was Ardashir. Outwardly he seemed composed, but to one who knew him his fury was apparent. In the beginning Râvar had often looked at his First Disciple—this upright, contained, fastidious man—and wondered where in him lived the violence that had ended the lives of his wife and her lover. Over time, though, he had come to see that Ardashir's formidable control was like a stone over a fire pit. The fire did not shift the stone, but sometimes, when it burned high enough, the heat seeped out around the edges.

"For five days, Beloved One," Ardashir said, "I have tended to the Brethren as you bid me. From the living quarters to the work spaces, there is not a corner of the Awakened City they have not seen. There is not one of their questions I have not answered. But it is not enough for them, Beloved One. This morning I discovered them preparing to go unescorted among the faithful. When I instructed them to halt so I could summon my men, they refused and went forth without me."

"I have no objection to that."

"Beloved One, I do not trust their intentions. You must be aware of where they go and what they say. They should not be allowed to meet with the faithful outside your sight."

"What do you think they will do, Ardashir? Speak against me? I think you are wrong. Besides, do you suppose our faith here is so frail that it can be weakened at a word?"

"Not just any word, Beloved One. They are the leaders of the Way of Ârata."

"Of the *old* Way of Ârata. Of the Way of Ârata sleeping. Which my faithful have left behind."

"Beloved One." Frustration snapped in Ardashir's voice. "Faith is all very well, but caution sometimes is an equal virtue. You cannot simply let them go about alone!"

"*Cannot*, Ardashir?"

Even through his fury, Ardashir realized he had gone too far. "Forgive me, Beloved One. I misspoke."

"Indeed you did."

"It is only that I cannot bear their arrogance, Beloved One. This is *your* domain. They have no authority here. Yet they behave as if they can command us!"

Râvar suspected that it was the challenge to Ardashir's own authority that rankled most. Ardashir's loathing of the Brethren went deep—like many of Râvar's followers, he believed that the Sons and Daughters had grown corrupt over the centuries of their reincarnation, their flight from the Caryaxists being the final demonstration of that failing, proof that they were unfit to lead the church. When, still imprisoned, he had learned that the Brethren ruled again in Baushpar, he had been incensed. Of the many items of faith Râvar had given him, one of the most difficult for him to accept had been that the Messenger would come to the Brethren in love rather than in punishment. Râvar was sometimes tempted to tell him the truth—though always, at the last moment, he drew back.

"I know the cause of your anger, Ardashir. It clouds your judgment. In this, you must trust that I am wiser than you."

A painful flush rose into Ardashir's dark cheeks. "Beloved One, your wisdom is Ârata's own—I never meant to imply—"

Râvar held up his hand. "I acknowledge, however, that caution is never unwarranted. If the Son and Daughter don't want an escort, they do not have to have one, but you may assign some of your men to follow them and question the pilgrims they approach."

"Beloved One." Ardashir bowed low. "Thank you."

Râvar went to take Parvâti back from her mother, and sat with the baby on the floor of his bathing room, coaxing her to play. But for once his mind was not on his daughter. Was he really so confident of the Brethren's hearts? For nearly a week they and their people had been in the Awakened City, and as yet there was no indication that any of them were turning to belief—not even the Son, who had seemed so awestruck at the initial meeting. No doubt he was influenced by his hard-faced Sister, whose apparent softening on that first day had been illusion, for she had shown no sign of it since. *They will be wholly mine*, he had told Gyalo Amdo Samchen, believing it utterly; but as he searched for that certainty, he could not find it.

At last, unable to bear his restlessness, he gave Parvâti to Axane—whose hair, clean now, rippled like a black river down her back—and climbed up through the dark of the ridge to his high ledge, where he sat for the rest of the afternoon, gazing across the sweep of the steppe and wondering where Gyalo Amdo Samchen was at this very moment.

The next morning, the Brethren requested an interview. Counting the audience on the day of their arrival, it would be the third. Râvar ordered them brought to his audience chamber and went to them alone, without Ardashir. They stood like supplicants before his pillar throne, their aides kneeling at their sides, industriously taking notes. The guards waited at the chamber's rear, tattooed faces fierce, arms clasped beneath their stoles.

As before, Vivaniya was silent, staring sometimes at Râvar and sometimes at his hands, which played continuously with the tassels of his stole. Sundit did all the talking. There was not the least humility in her questions, or in the crisp directness of her manner. During the previous interview, she had asked about Râvar's emergence from the Burning Land, about Ârata's Promise and the destruction of Thuxra (not troubling to hide her skepticism), about the building of the Awakened City. Today she wanted to speak about doctrine. He answered her openly and fully, smiling as beguilingly as he could, willing toward her the power of his charm and beauty. She might be a religious leader, and elderly, but she was still a woman. It had no discernible effect.

"You say that the Next Messenger will lead the church during this time of Interim," she said. "That it will be a new church, a new Way of Ârata."

"In fulfillment of the second portion of my father's Promise, yes."

"But in the *Darxasa*, Ârata said to Marduspida, *Cast all else aside, for it is ash: This is the one path, the one foundation, the one Way*. One Way. Only one."

"And there will be only one. The Way of Ârata awake."

"Still, that is a second Way. Is the *Darxasa* in error?"

Râvar met her narrow brown gaze, reminded oddly of his teacher Gâvarti, who had interrogated him on theological matters with equal sharpness. "In elision, perhaps. The *Darxasa* is Ârata's word, but it was given to a mortal man. There is much that might be lost in such translation."

She pounced. "Do you not teach that you are mortal? So cannot the same be said of you?"

"I am *half*-mortal, Sundit of the Brethren." He forced himself, again, to smile. "Half of me is divine fire. In that fire Ârata's word is contained, received by me infallibly and entire."

"So you yourself are the proof of what you teach."

"What can be proven, Sundit of the Brethren?" Râvar spread his hands. "That is why we have faith."

"An interestingly circular argument. Even so, I find it curious that there is no mention whatever in the *Darxasa* of this doctrine of Interim, on which you place such weight."

"The words of the *Darxasa* were given to the First Messenger. I am the Next Messenger. I speak the word that was given to me."

Frowning, she began another question, but Râvar had had enough.

"I have duties to attend to," he said, getting to his feet. "If you wish it, we will speak again."

He returned to his rooms, where Ardashir was waiting to fetch him for an afternoon of personal audiences. These were held every other day, with pilgrims chosen according to a lottery system that ensured each citizen a turn alone with the Next Messenger at least once every three months. Unlike the rituals or his periodic progresses among the faithful, Râvar found the audiences actively unpleasant—for while many of the petitioners simply wished to receive his blessing and kiss his hands, others wanted, as the First Faithful had, to confess their sins and wrongs and evil thoughts, while still others tried to offer him their bodies. If he had wished, he could have had a different lover every night, sired a legion of children to carry his blood into this alien world.

But even if he had been willing to pollute himself by such congress—and he had sometimes been tempted, not just out of body-need but because it would have been so easy—he recognized the danger that lay in that particular form of self-indulgence. So he ignored the gestures and the hints, and gently turned aside the bolder propositions—an abstinence that, far from discouraging his followers' attempts, seemed only to make them more persistent.

After the evening ceremony he drifted for a time in the bathing pool, then fetched food for his captives and ate his own meal. When the announcement drum sounded he assumed it must be Ardashir, come to report on the activities of the Brethren. He donned the Blood and went out, barefoot, his damp hair hanging down his back.

But it was not Ardashir. It was the Twentyman on guard.

"Beloved One," he said, bowing low. "The Son Vivaniya is outside your chambers with two of his men. He asks urgently to see you. In fact, Beloved One, he would hardly be restrained. It was all I could do to stop him from coming in unannounced."

Râvar felt his pulse leap with premonition. "I'll see him. Without his guards."

"Yes, Beloved One."

Râvar crossed to the quartz chair and sat, feeling the chill of the stone along his back and legs, aware of the beating of his heart. Beneath the humming quiet of the room, he heard the low sound of voices. Then silence.

Vivaniya appeared in the chamber's entrance. He paused as if struck, falling utterly still, as he had the first time Râvar had ever seen him.

"It's late, child of the First Messenger," Râvar said. "What is so important that it could not keep till morning?"

The Son took a step into the room, then checked again. His ember-colored lifelight was a perfect oval, its edge as sharp as flint. "I had to speak with you."

"I'm listening."

"You said . . . the first day . . . that you knew I had wandered in the Burning Land." His voice was not quite under his control. "Tell me how you knew."

Râvar smiled. "I know because it is so."

"The river cleft. The red cliffs below the Cavern of the Blood where you were—where you say you were born. You speak of them as if they are . . . only cliffs."

Râvar felt a fierce thrill. "Is there another way I should describe them?"

"If there were . . . something in them. Something . . . not naturally formed."

"Ah. Now I see. You mean the city carved in stone."

The Son audibly caught his breath.

"I did not speak of the city," Râvar said, "because it no longer exists. It was destroyed." He let the smile fall from his face. He leaned toward the Son, pinning him with his gaze. "But you know that, don't you, Vivaniya of the Brethren? You saw it happen."

"Tell me. Tell me what you know."

"Are you testing me, child of the First Messenger?"

The Son shook his head. "Please understand. I must be sure."

"I think you are already sure. But you cannot yet accept your certainty, and so you ask for proof, as if proof meant anything to faith. You ask me to prove *myself*, as if Ârata's divinity, as if this"—Râvar gestured to the Blood around his neck—"needed to be proven. But I am not angry, Vivaniya of the Brethren. I've hoped you would come to me like this."

The air hummed. In the shadowless light of the wall-flames, the Son's face looked utterly bloodless.

"A little over two years ago, you and your Brother Dâdar set out across the Burning Land with an army that included twenty-five Shapers, secretly unbound by the Brethren's order from the tether of manita."

The Son's mouth opened, though no sound emerged.

"You marched in search of a secret known, so you thought, to none but you—a hidden city at the heart of the Land, a city cut into the walls of a river cleft. A city its people called *Refuge*." Râvar paused, letting it sink in. "You feared Refuge and its people, for they had among them Shapers not bound to the strictures of your church, and you and your kind detest free shaping above all else. So you destroyed the city and slaughtered all who lived in it. *And then you did worse.* You and your Brother Dâdar stood before the truth Refuge had been made to guard, the Cavern of the Blood, Ârata's empty resting place, and you denied it."

The Son looked as if he were about to collapse under the weight of this apparently godlike knowledge of a secret only he and his Brother should know.

"The Cavern was hidden, protected by the last of Refuge's Shapers. You knew this. You knew the rock that concealed it was not the truth, for you'd seen the Cavern's light, the light shed by the Blood inside it, rising up at night as you and your army approached. Even so, you chose to accept the rock as truth. With your Brother Dâdar you undertook to persuade your Brothers and Sisters to accept it also, so that they, like you, would turn from the truth of Ârata's rising."

"How is this possible?" the Son whispered. "How can you know this?"

"That is a foolish question, Vivaniya of the Brethren. Have I not told you that I know what my father knows? What, then, can you imagine is hidden from me?"

Then the Son did collapse, falling to his knees. The neat oval of his life-light halved, like an egg sliced in two.

"Ârata forgive me." His eyes were closed. He swayed, as if he might faint. "It's true, it's all true. We feared Ârata's rising, Dâdar and I. We feared what it meant for the Brethren. So we deceived ourselves, deceived our spirit-siblings. I knew I sinned. But I did not understand how I would grow to hate my sin. How it would eat at me, like a cancer. Ah, I am sick with it." He caught his breath in a sob. "Sick with it."

Râvar was astonished. Guilt. He would never have suspected it.

"I cannot free you of your sin, Vivaniya of the Brethren." He schooled his voice to a gentleness he could never feel toward this evil and perfidious being. "Only my father has such power. But I can give you something to set against it. Something that may balance it."

"Yes. Yes."

"In your fear you chose to turn from the truth. Now, in repentance, turn toward it. Acknowledge me. Speak my name."

"I knew," the Son whispered. "Even before we reached this place, I knew who you must be. I was afraid, but I am afraid no longer. Ârata has risen. You are the Next Messenger."

The words took Râvar by the throat. Briefly he seemed to lose himself, returning with a shock that was like falling. He clutched the arms of his chair. Across the room, Vivaniya waited on his knees, his face slack with surrender.

"Come to me, child of the First Messenger."

Clumsily the Son got to his feet. He stumbled to the dais and sank down again.

"Look at my hands." Râvar leaned forward, extending them. "They are ugly, yes? Crippled. Yet I love my scars, and so must you, for they are the marks left by my father's Blood. Kiss them now, as my followers do, to pledge your faith."

The Son pressed his lips to Râvar's palms. His slanted eyes were closed. Tears crept from between his lids.

"Abide in light, child of the First Messenger," Râvar said softly, "first of the Brethren to acknowledge me. You will not be the last."

He touched the Son between the eyes, leaving behind a point of ember-orange light.

"Beloved One," the Son breathed. "I can hardly bear my joy."

"You must do more than bear it, Vivaniya of the Brethren. You must share it. This is the task I give you: Return to your Brothers and Sisters. Prepare them for my arrival. You came to me as their emissary. You will go back as mine."

"Yes." The Son nodded eagerly, tears shining on his cheeks, the little blessing mark glinting on his forehead. "I will go at once. I will teach the truth. I will speak your word night and day! I will bring you not just my spirit-siblings, but all Baushpar!"

"Bring only your spirit-siblings, and I will be satisfied. But tell me—what of your Sister Sundit? I think her heart is not as open as yours."

"My Sister does not give herself lightly to any understanding. That's how she is made. But I will speak to her. I will persuade her."

Râvar thought of the Daughter's steady brown gaze, her forceful questions, and was not so certain. "Let it be the first service you perform for me. Tomorrow, at the evening ceremony, I'll present you to the faithful, so they may rejoice as I do."

"I will stand before them in joy."

"Go now, with my blessing."

The Son rose. "Beloved One," he said. He hesitated, then bowed low, holding the pose a moment. Râvar understood the significance of the gesture. To whom, in the world they ruled, had the Brethren ever bowed?

The Son departed. Râvar summoned the Twentyman and instructed him to fetch Ardashir, then returned to his chair to wait. Everything around him— the patterns of the sandstone walls, the flames in their wall-niches, the substance of the air—seemed preternaturally vivid and distinct. His body pulsed with excitement; his mind raced with plans. This was the sign, the sign he had promised to his faithful. It had come to him as naturally as if it really were a sign. At last, at last, the Awakened City would march.

We will march.

And all at once the amazement of it swept him and he began to laugh, a helpless laughter that shook his body and curled his ruined hands into fists. It burned his throat, scoured his chest.

Ârata, are you watching? Do you see? DO YOU SEE?

He had control of himself by the time Ardashir arrived. If the First Disciple had been roused from sleep, there was no sign; he was as faultlessly dressed and groomed as always—except for his bandages, stiff with the day's seepage from his wounds.

"Beloved One." He bowed.

"I have news, Ardashir. Such news! The Son Vivaniya has acknowledged me."

A beat of silence. Ardashir said: "That is news indeed, Beloved One."

"This is the sign, Ardashir, the sign my father promised! I will announce
it tomorrow at the evening ceremony. Afterward, the Son will leave to carry
word of me back to Baushpar, and you and I will ready the Awakened City for
departure. Ardashir, be glad! Our great work is about to begin!"

Ardashir regarded him with silver-dark eyes that held no trace of glad-
ness. "This is . . . sudden, Beloved One."

"What do you mean, Ardashir? Wasn't it you, two weeks ago, who begged
me to soothe the faithful's impatience? Well, now they need be impatient no
longer. We will march!"

"Beloved One, I beg you, do not trust this Son's conversion. We do
not truly know why these two came to us. It may have been exactly for this
purpose—to touch your heart, to beguile you with false faith, and then betray
you."

Râvar sighed. "Ardashir, your suspicion wearies me."

"Beloved One, I have controlled my personal feelings less well than I
would have liked these past days, to my shame. But it's not my hatred of the
Brethren that speaks now. It is your nature to see what is best and purest in
the world, but it is my task, blackened man that I am, to see what's worst. It is
written, *What stands in sun is dark behind, and he who forgets this may be surprised
by his own shadow.* Allow me at least to send some of the First Faithful with
the Son when he departs. They will be able to add their voices to his when he
reaches Baushpar and testify to your truth and to your doctrine. In the meantime, they will help make sure his heart remains turned toward you."

Even in his anger, Râvar could see that this was a reasonable suggestion.
"His heart is mine and will always be. But very well."

"Beloved One, if I may ask, what of the Daughter Sundit?"

"She doesn't yet share her Brother's faith. He has said he will persuade
her."

"What if he does not, Beloved One? Will you allow her to speak against
you in Baushpar?"

Râvar did not want to think about the Daughter Sundit. "Let me worry
about that. How long will it take to ready the Awakened City for departure?"

"Two weeks, Beloved One. Perhaps a little less."

"Make it less. Begin immediately."

"Yes, Beloved One." Ardashir hesitated. "And the woman and her child?
Are they to travel with us?"

He could not have asked a more unwelcome question. "Why should that be your concern?"

"I only wish to know what arrangements I should make, Beloved One. How I should introduce them to your faithful—"

"It is not your task to introduce them to the faithful! By the Blood, you try me with these objections. You should be on your knees, giving thanks for the news I've just given you!"

"Beloved One—"

"No. I'm done with you. Go."

Ardashir bowed, stone-faced, and left the chamber. Râvar paced his rooms, trying to subdue his anger, but the very fact that he was angry only made him angrier—all his triumph, ruined by Ardashir with his questions and suspicions. He halted at last beside the bathing pool, before the wall behind which his captives were confined for the night. Against his will, he knew that Ardashir was right—he would have to make up his mind, once and for all, about Axane.

For some reason a memory came to him, of himself and her, in the moments before he went forth to destroy Thuxra City. He had asked her to bear witness to that act, to the beginning of his deception: the one person in the world who knew the truth of who he was and why he had come. She had refused. Yet afterward, just before he fell into unconsciousness, he had glimpsed her—a small dark figure within her tumult of ocean colors, watching after all.

He put forth his power. The wall before him vanished in a shout of sound and light. Parvâti, roused, began to cry. Axane was sitting up in bed. She turned on him a face wet with tears.

"Why are you weeping?"

"I was . . ." She caught her breath. "Dreaming." She dragged her hands across her face, then turned to lift the howling child. "Hush." She held Parvâti to her shoulder, stroking the baby's stiff little back. "Hush, little bird."

"The Son Vivaniya acknowledged me tonight," Râvar said, above Parvâti's dwindling cries.

Axane's brimming eyes rose to his.

"It's true. He got down on his knees and named me the Next Messenger. You didn't think I could do it, did you. You thought I'd fail."

"No," she whispered. Parvâti was hiccuping.

"He's going back to the others as my emissary. He'll give them word of me, just as he gave them the lie about the Cavern, and teach them to believe it. When I get to Baushpar, they'll all be waiting."

She nodded, docile as a doll. Tears still welled from her eyes. What had he expected? That she would rejoice? The bitter anger rose again—cheated a second time of his triumph, all his jubilation turned to ash.

"You'll see it," he said, viciously. "I'll bring you with me. I'll make you watch it all, every moment, all the way to Baushpar. I won't let you close your eyes. Do you understand?"

"Yes," she whispered.

The despair in her face gave him an ugly jolt of pleasure. His eyes moved on her slender throat, her bare brown arms. The thin fabric of her chemise was pulled tight across her breasts. In imagination he bridged the gap between them; he felt her under his ruined hands. Desire shook him as his anger had—or perhaps they were the same—and something else, the nameless thing that, all his life, had impelled him to try and turn the world around him to his will, whether or not the world was willing.

For just an instant, he felt the naked truth of his aloneness.

He turned away. He closed her in, slamming the stone into place as if he were striking her. He strode toward the passage that opened on the underworld, to spend himself amid the depths, where only he would ever see the light he made, or hear the cataclysms of his unleashed power.

12

Sundit

I can hardly believe what I must write. I can hardly bear to record it.

Vivaniya went out last night after we had all retired, taking Mur and Karamsuu with him. I wondered at it but was not alarmed, assuming that in the morning he would explain. I did not hear him return; when I woke, he was still asleep. He did not rise for the Communion ceremony, or for breakfast. Not until the morning was well advanced did he call Yailin to attend him. He emerged soon after from his tent, stumbling in his clumsy way, and crossed to where Drolma and I were sorting her notes from yesterday.

"Sister, I need to speak with you." He looked flushed and feverish, as if he were beginning to grow sick.

"Brother, are you unwell?" I reached to set my hand on his forehead, but he leaned away.

"Please, Sundit."

I led him to my tent. He looped the flaps down behind us, hiding us from the others' sight, then knelt before me on the matting, not bothering with a cushion.

"I went to see him," he said without preamble. "Last night."

I did not have to ask whom he meant. It surprised me (though perhaps it should not have)—but again, did not alarm me. So there was nothing more than irritation in my response. "Vanyi, we're here to make a *mutual* determination. You should have waited."

"I had a question. I needed an answer."

"Right at that moment? You could not let it keep till morning?"

"Sunni." His gaze captured mine, and I realized that the fire in him was not fever. I felt the breath of disaster even as he spoke. "He is the Next Messenger."

It was a moment before I could find my voice. "Vanyi. There is not yet sufficient evidence to conclude such a thing."

"He knows." He leaned toward me. I could feel the heat coming off him. "He knows everything. Not just that I'd traveled in the Burning Land. About Refuge. About what happened there. About . . . me and Dâdar, our lie. He told me my own story as I stood listening, as if he'd witnessed it. How could he have such knowledge unless Ârata gave it to him?"

"Did he tell you that?" I'd opened my eyes that morning in the same state of uncertainty in which I had closed them the night before—halfway between believing and not believing, between the Blood the claimant bears, his beauty and his power and his perception, and his strange divergent doctrines, which have no precedent in the *Darxasa* or any of the teachings of our father. While the real Messenger might indeed possess god-given understanding of Vanyi's deed, it seemed to me that a false Messenger might have come by the information also, in a less miraculous way. On the day of our arrival, Vanyi demonstrated his awe and dread as clearly as if he had shouted them aloud. A clever pretender—who, to build a deception as elaborate as this Awakened City must certainly be capable of extraordinary feats of spiritual and emotional manipulation—might well have exploited that, drawing Vivaniya to confess the secrets that burden him so terribly, then feigning prior knowledge. "Did he say his knowledge comes from the god?"

"What other possibility is there? Sunni, I've been fighting the truth since we arrived, since I first saw him on his throne. Last night I could no longer fight. I could no longer deny the truth that is in my heart. I surrendered, and all my burden slipped away." He smiled, an expression of terrible joy. "I knelt to him. I declared my faith. I looked into his face, and saw forgiveness there. Oh, Sunni, what that means . . ."

"Brother." I tried to remain calm. "This certainly demands investigation. But it's too soon to make a final determination. There are too many unanswered questions. There is still too much we do not know. We have discussed this—"

"No, *you* have discussed. I have only listened. You say that he is too arrogant, that he is too beautiful, that he glories too much in the display of his power—but should the Next Messenger be humble, and ugly, and hide his divinity? Where is it written he must be like that, or indeed, like anything at all? Will not Ârata make his Messenger as he chooses?"

"Of course. That is why we must take care."

"Must everything be so closely proven, Sunni? What of faith?"

"It is for the sake of faith that I hesitate."

"He wears the true Blood around his neck. You held it in your hands. You cut your finger on its facets. How can that not move you? You say you stand between belief and disbelief—let me guide you from that barren place, let me help you to the truth. Let me take you to him. He'll speak to you as he did to me. He will know your secrets, too."

I felt an entirely irrational chill. "I have no desire to hear my secrets spoken, even supposing he could do such a thing."

"You disguise it as deliberation, Sunni, but I see the truth. You are afraid—afraid as I was afraid when I denied the Cavern of the Blood, afraid as we all are afraid, all us Brethren. Do you remember, in the beginning, how we longed for the fulfillment of Ârata's Promise? How we said to each other *May it be soon*, as the Shapers do in their Communion services? How we said *Let sleep come*? How long has it been since any of us truly wished for sleep? We have lived too long, and now we can't let go of life, even though that is what our Covenant requires. It is as the people say. We have grown weak. We are unfit to lead the church. The Messenger is right to demand we step aside and yield rule of Ârata's Way to him."

A horror had fallen on me as he spoke. To hear such things from him—my straightforward unreflective Vanyi, who in his lives has rarely spoken against the majority, or questioned the ways of tradition . . . I looked into the handsome face he wears in this incarnation, a face that I have known in youth and adolescence, in sickness and in vigor, in joy and anger and despair, and knew with falling certainty that he was lost to me, that no word of mine could turn him from this disastrous course. Still I tried.

"Vanyi, I beg you, withhold conclusion for a little while. That's all I ask—just that you hold back. Let us finish our investigation here and return with our findings to our spirit-siblings. Let us all decide together."

"It's too late. I've already promised."

Cold fear stabbed me. "Promised? Promised what?"

"To be his emissary. To carry his word to Baushpar and to our spirit-siblings."

"Vanyi, no! You cannot promise such a thing! You must go to him, you must go to him at once and tell him you cannot do it!"

He surged to his feet, knocking his head against a strut of the collapsible tent frame and setting the whole structure shuddering. "Sunni, I love you. But your heart is closed. I can't listen to you any longer."

"Vanyi, wait!"

But he was already gone, blundering through the tent flaps. I heard him call to Mur and Karamsuu. I did not try to pursue him—I did not want to set our disagreement on public display, and sensed anyway that it would do no good. My dismay was already passing into anger. I cursed Vivaniya for his guilt, cursed myself for my inattention. I knew the conflict in him. I saw how his dread and eagerness grew as we approached this place, though he made efforts to conceal it. I should have watched him more closely once we arrived. I should have made more effort to pierce his silence. But I've been preoccupied with the things we have seen, with the questions they have raised. And in honesty, with my own discomfort in those questions.

I left my tent and summoned Reanu and Apui. We swept out into the main cavern, with its dark, toothed ceiling and its glimmering cook fires, its stench of smoke and unclean people and stale cooking and ordure. Heads turned as we passed, but no hard-faced functionary came hurrying to halt us, and we reached the passageway at the cavern's back wall unmolested. By the low, unnaturally regular stairway that leads to the claimant's quarters, one of the so-called Twentymen who serve as aides to that odious creature, Ardashir, stood guard.

"Tell him I am here to see him." I could not bring myself to speak the title. "Now!"

All my fury flew from me in that word. The man flinched and hurried to obey. As in the rest of Arsace, some here despise us, but many still hold us in reverence.

I heard a thrumming sound—a drum? Then silence. The guard reappeared. "The Next Messenger will see you, Old One."

He bowed and stepped aside. I mounted the steps, Reanu and Apui behind me. A short corridor lay slantwise beyond the entrance, ending on a sizable space filled with rosy light. It was not another cavern: It was, or seemed to be, a real room, with four flat walls and a smooth regular ceiling and a level floor, formed not of the gray limestone that makes up the rest of this place but of some rock striated in glowing shades of red and russet and orange and cream. Little niches marched around the walls, each with a small flame inside it. At the room's center, raised on a shallow dais, stood a massive chair hewn from quartz.

I had no time to wonder at these things, strange as they were, for beside the chair the claimant stood waiting, and like a torch in a darkened room he immediately captured all my attention. I've described him as I saw him first, robed and throned, and as I saw him later, wrapped miraculously in light. Now he appeared in a third guise, clad in a rough dun-colored tunic, his feet bare and his long black hair pulled untidily over one shoulder. In his disarray he was no less charismatic, no less beautiful. The Blood of Ârata (which, as Vanyi said, I know beyond any doubt is the true Blood) burned like a coal upon his chest.

"Welcome," he said in his light quick voice, and smiled. He has an odd accent, flat in the vowels and soft on some of the consonants, as if Arsacian were not his native language.

At my back, I felt Reanu's and Apui's tension. I did not want to thank him for receiving me, so I simply nodded. His smile deepened, as if he perceived what I was thinking. Turning, he stepped gracefully up onto the dais, and seated himself in the enormous chair. The pink stone gleamed, as smooth as water. Every surface in the room showed that same slick gloss, those same softly rounded contours, as if an army of jewelers had gone through it with polishing cloths. The chamber next door was also faced with gleaming banded stone, a collection of stone benches sprouting from its floor as if they had grown there. Beyond lay a third chamber, empty but for a shaft of light spearing down from above—for all the world like sunlight, though I am sure that cannot be—and a shadowy fourth, whose details I could not make out.

"What do you want of me, child of the First Messenger?"

He looked down on me, as regal as a king. I had gone to him in towering anger. But, beneath his gaze, the signs of his power all around me, it struck me with renewed force that *I did not know the truth*. This dazzling young man might be an imposter, an unbound Shaper of huge ability. Or he might be exactly what he claimed: Ârata's herald, harbinger of the god's return.

For the first time it occurred to me that by rushing so impetuously to confront him, I might have put my men and me in danger.

"Perhaps you're testing me," he said into my silence. "As your Brother did. Perhaps you want me to reveal the truth that is in your heart. But I don't need any special powers of perception to guess that you are here because your Brother has spoken with you."

"Yes," I said.

"I am listening." He cocked his head, conveying interest. His twisted hands lay along the arms of the chair.

All my anger had left me. I called upon my pride instead. "You know that we have come here in question. By your words when you first received us, I believe you understand our concerns. The Brethren's concerns."

He nodded, his eyes—which from a distance seem dark but in fact are cloudy green—steady on my face.

"You realize, then, that we are only ambassadors, my Brother and I. It is not our task to decide. We are here only to observe, to gather facts and carry them back to our spirit-siblings."

"Do your hearts not come into it at all?" he inquired.

"It is not our hearts that are at issue."

"No?" He watched me as if he knew exactly what was going on inside my mind. It's one of the most disconcerting things about him, his air of *knowing*. "I think, Sundit of the Brethren, that you speak only for yourself."

"I am not here to discuss myself. My Brother tells me that he has acknowledged you."

"It is true."

"Apart from the fact that it's premature, I must tell you that this is not a considered choice. My Brother labors under a burden of guilt for an action undertaken in his present body-life." I had to force myself to say it. Stringently as we Brethren chide one another for our failings, never, never do we confess them to outsiders. "He is . . . preoccupied with the desire to expiate it. Understand that I make no judgments, on you or on your claim—I say only that the allegiance he has given you rises not from deliberation or doctrinal study, not from the store of wisdom he carries in his soul, but from his own individual need and desire."

The claimant raised perfect eyebrows. "Is faith not wisdom? The wisdom of the heart?"

"My Brother has not given you faith," I said. "He has given you remorse."

"Remorse." He shifted on his throne, crossing one leg over the other, flexing his bare foot. Like all of him but his hands, they are flawless—slender, high-arched, the bones fanning elegantly beneath smooth skin. "One would think that twelve hundred years of living would have cured the Brethren of such frailties."

"If you are willing to accept the gift of my Brother's human heart, you can hardly dismiss the weight of his human guilt."

He smiled his enchanting smile. "I suppose I cannot argue that."

"Will you help me, then?"

The smile vanished. "What are you asking, Sundit of the Brethren?"

"Release my Brother. Tell him you cannot accept his pledge."

"No. In my father's sight he acknowledged me. It is not for me to undo such a thing."

"But I've told you it's not a true pledge. Surely you cannot want that."

"He spoke his faith. He spoke my name. Those things are their own truth."

"Then free him of the promise he made you. Tell him you do not need an . . . an emissary."

"I do not choose to free him."

His voice was flat. His face had hardened. I saw, as certainly as if I had already lived these moments, that no further word of mine would move him.

Within such a weight of rock, silence is a profound thing. I could hear nothing at all in the pause that followed except, behind me, the whisper of my guards' breathing. Perhaps it was the utter quiet that made the sound, when it came, so startling—a rising wail, unmistakably a baby's cry. All my muscles jumped. My eyes followed the direction of the cry, which seemed to be coming from beyond the shaft of brightness, from that shadowy fourth room.

The wailing stopped. I turned back to the claimant. He was sitting straight in his chair, both feet on the floor. Nothing else had changed, but somehow, indefinably, he seemed less like a king and more like a young man.

"Is that all?" he said, and his voice, too, had lost some of that exalted quality.

"I shall speak to my Brother," I said. "I shall remind him of his duty."

I thought then that something flared in his face, some intense dark emotion; but it was gone almost as I perceived it. "Do as you choose," he said. Then: "I'll send Ardashir to bring you to the ceremony this evening. I don't want you to miss it."

I did not trust myself to respond. I turned. As I did, I saw a thing I somehow had not perceived before: The little flames in the wall-niches sprang not from lamps or from candles, but from . . . nothing. They burned directly on the stone, without oil or wick to sustain them. I don't know why this should have struck me so, with all the strangeness I've seen in this place. A freezing shaft of dread went through me. I might have stumbled if Reanu had not reached out and smoothly caught my arm.

We returned to our little cave. Vivaniya was still absent. Drolma was at her writing desk; she rose when I entered, but I waved her back to work and went to my tent, where Ha-tsun plumped a cushion for me and brought me tea. I had her tie back the tent flap so I would be sure to see Vanyi when he arrived. I would talk to him, I told myself. I would present him with his duty. I would exert my authority as his elder, not just in this body but in the original order of our births. I would accomplish what the claimant had refused to do. I would turn him from his oath.

He never returned. And at some point during the long afternoon, I realized that a pair of Ardashir's staff-carrying aides had come to stand before the entrance to our cave. I glanced toward the Tapati, who were sitting together and playing one of the portable board games of which they are so fond. Any of them, unaided, could have overcome the two Twentymen. But that was not the point. The claimant had decided that we—that I—needed to be watched.

Did I suspect then what was to come? I think I did. But I could not allow myself to admit it.

At last our sentinels stepped aside. My heart leaped, but it was only Ardashir, followed by two more of his Twentymen. I came out of my tent to meet him.

"Sundit of the Brethren." He did not bow, but stared insolently into my face. He has quite a stare, this so-called First Disciple—I imagine the people here quail before it. But in my lives I have matched gazes with worse men than he. If he thought to discompose me, he was mistaken. "I've come to escort you to the evening ceremony."

What would he have done if I had refused? Did he know that his thuggish aides had no chance against my Tapati? But I had no intention of refusing. I knew that something awful waited for me in that ceremony. I also knew I had to see it.

I stepped firmly toward him, so that he either had to allow me to collide with him or give way. He chose to give way, his mouth like a knife cut.

"Reanu," I called. "Omarau. Lopalo. Drolma. You will accompany me. Apui—you will remain here, with Ha-tsun and Yailin."

Ardashir turned, flanked by his aides, and stalked off. We followed. In the main cavern, the little settlements were deserted, their inhabitants already gathered for the ritual. Two more Twentymen were waiting by the passage, torches in their hands; one went ahead to light the way, while the other fell in behind my guards. Down the passage we went, past the claimant's quarters. As the incline sharpened, I began to hear the noise of the crowd. We reached the steeply plunging stairs, emerging abruptly from beneath the hood of the passage's ceiling. The dim spaces of the cavern sprang out before us. Below, the faithful formed a shifting insectile mantle across the floor, studded with the flare of torches. The sense of entrapment that has seized me each time I've entered here took me again, closing up my throat. I could feel the leaning pressure of the ridge above me. I could feel the fragility of this little space, a bubble in the rock.

We descended. Ardashir did not chivvy us to the side, as on previous days, but led us to the cavern's midpoint, positioning us directly below the ledge on which the claimant makes his appearance at these ceremonies. The pilgrims pressed away from us. Reanu and his companions closed tensely around Drolma and me. I took Drolma's arm—for my comfort as much as hers.

The claimant's light preceded him, a sudden luster on the darkness of the ledge. Abruptly, he appeared above us—a man of inhuman beauty clad in light, the Blood of Ârata blazing a different sort of fire at his chest. The faithful shouted, a cry that seemed to rise from a single massive throat.

"People!" He spread wide his shimmering arms. His voice was like a bell; it is hard to believe such a sound can come from a human mouth. "People of the Promise!"

"Fulfiller of the Promise!" the crowd howled back. "He who opens the Way!"

"People of the new age!"

"Guardian of the Interim, who speaks the word of the risen god!"

"People of Ârata!"

"Beloved of Ârata, who sets our feet upon the Waking Road!"

I cannot deny the power of the calls and responses. I cannot deny the strength of the faith written on all those upturned faces. I cannot deny that if Ârata were to send a divine Messenger into this world, he might look, and sound, exactly thus.

The claimant stepped to the precipice's edge. I expected him to launch himself into empty air and drift like a burning leaf to the cavern's floor, as he had before. Instead, he raised his hands for silence, and waited while it fell.

"People of the Promise." His glowing garment writhed like a living thing, here flashing prismatic color, there parting to reveal an expanse of naked skin. "Tonight I offer you a different ritual."

A murmur of surprise.

"I have long promised that Ârata will send a portent, a sign to mark the proper moment of our emergence. You have been patient in your waiting, my people, patient in your faith. I am grateful."

All around us, his followers sighed. "Messenger. Beautiful One. Beloved of Ârata."

"Tonight, my people, my faithful, your patience is rewarded. Tonight, the sign my father promised will be given! Tonight, tonight, you all shall know it!"

The thunder of jubilation that followed seemed to shake the ridge; I swear I felt it in my bones. He let it continue for a time, then signaled again for quiet.

"The sign comes to us in the form of a pledge and a promise—a pledge and a promise unlike any that has been made since the First Messenger came out of the Burning Land." He turned toward the darkness behind him and extended a blazing arm. "Come forward!"

I already knew. I knew the moment he spoke of a pledge. And there was

Vivaniya, for whom I had waited in vain all the afternoon, advancing toward the edge of the precipice. His face was . . . how can I describe his face? He looked as if he were dreaming with his eyes open. He moved like a dreamer, stiffly, stumbling as he came to the claimant's side.

The gathered faithful did not know what to make of it. They stirred and muttered. They looked toward me and Drolma and our guards—wondering, no doubt, why we were not up on the ledge with Vivaniya.

"People of the Promise," the claimant called. "Last night the Son Vivaniya came to me in my chambers. This is what he said to me: 'Beloved One, I arrived in uncertainty, but in you and in the joyous faith of those who follow you, I have seen the truth. I name you the Next Messenger, herald of Ârata's awakening, and yield to you my place as guardian of the Way of Ârata. The Age of Exile has ended. The time of Interim has begun.' People of the new age, when I heard those words I knew them for the sign my father promised. The time has come at last for us to leave our sanctuary, to take the Awakened City to the world. The time has come to set our great work in motion!"

The faithful erupted, throwing up their arms, leaping in exultation. They bellowed triumph at the daggered ceiling. Drolma clutched me in terror; Reanu and Omarau and Lopalo linked their arms, making a wall of their bodies against the chaos that surrounded us. Firelight and shadow swept the cavern's fissured walls; so dizzy was I with dread and horror that it seemed to me the stone itself was moving, swinging in and out of the light.

The claimant gestured. The throng stilled. He turned toward my Brother, who all this time had been gazing at him, rapt as any pilgrim.

"Child of the First Messenger." The claimant's voice had dropped. His light trembled, coalesced, parted. "In sight of the faithful, kneel to me now and repeat your pledge. Swear as you did when you came to me. Let those who follow me see, as I have seen, the absoluteness of your surrender."

Did Vanyi know this would be asked of him? Perhaps not—I thought I saw him hesitate, and for a moment, wildly, I thought he might refuse. But he obeyed, dropping to his knees so awkwardly that he overbalanced and had to fling out a hand to catch himself, his fingers curling over the precipice's very lip. My heart seemed to stop. For the space of a breath he remained in that pose, his body tilted out above the drop; then he straightened and sat back on his heels.

The crowd appeared to understand the significance of what it was witnessing. Utter silence fell.

"Ârata is risen." Vivaniya's voice shook, but he could be clearly heard. "You are the Next Messenger. The Age of Exile is ended. I pledge my faith to you, and yield to you the guardianship of the Way of Ârata. I shall go as your emissary to my Brothers and Sisters. I shall speak your word to them, and prepare them for your arrival."

"Your promise is accepted," the claimant said. "Now kiss my hands, as a seal upon your word."

He held out his scarred palms. Vanyi leaned forward and pressed them with his lips—the right, then the left. The claimant bent, the Blood of Ârata swinging forward, his black hair sliding over his shoulders, and set his own lingering kiss on my Brother's forehead. The radiance that wrapped him tore from heel to shoulder; for a moment the whole of his near-naked body could be seen.

He stepped away, shaking back his hair. Looking down on my kneeling Brother, he smiled. I had not been sure, earlier, that I had really seen the harsh dark emotion that had seemed to flare in his face just before I left him. But I was certain then. It was there, that same darkness, fully present in his smile. And I understood, beyond any possibility of question, that he is false. It was such a wholly human smile. It held such triumph, such cruelty. No god could smile thus, nor any man who did a god's purpose.

"Rise, Vivaniya of the Brethren," the false Messenger said. "Rise, and take your place at my side."

Vivaniya obeyed. The pretender gripped Vivaniya by the wrist and raised both their arms high. The faithful roared.

"We will march!" Even over the incredible tumult, his voice somehow carried clear. "In Ârata's name! To Ârata's glory! To the dawning of the new primal age!"

"Ârata!" the crowd howled, surging around us like the ocean. "Ârata!"

I turned to Reanu. It's difficult to read expression behind his branching tattoos, but I thought he looked afraid. "Get us out of here," I mouthed. "Now."

He signaled to the others in the sign language of their order. He and Lo-palo took my arms; Omarau took Drolma's. Swiftly they bore us toward the stairs. Ardashir and his men did not appear to note our departure—or at least, they did not try to stop us.

At our camp, Apui waited with Ha-tsun and Yailin.

"We'll leave at once," I said. "Don't bother with the tents or any of the rest of it. All I want is my books and papers."

"The Son . . . ?" Reanu said.

"For the moment, my Brother and I walk different paths."

He nodded. "They have our weapons, Old One."

"It can't be helped. Now go, get ready. Drolma, gather the papers. Ha-tsun, fetch my journal and my writing desk. Yailin, I wish I could take you, but I cannot. You must wait for your master."

There was fear in his face, and his eyes spoke a thousand questions. But he is a good servant. He bowed, and returned to his mat.

Already I could hear noise from the cavern beyond: the faithful, returning to their settlements. Drolma and Reanu and the others made haste, yet they seemed impossibly slow. At last they were done. Reanu organized us: himself and Omarau in front, then me, then Drolma and Ha-tsun with my paper cases in their arms, and Lopalo and Apui at the rear with the bags of books bound to their backs. The Tapati had redraped their stoles to leave both arms bare.

"Stay close," Reanu instructed. "Don't pause, no matter what. Just walk."

They stopped us halfway to the entrance—all twenty of Ardashir's aides, and Ardashir. I knew it was hopeless. Even so, I stepped forward.

"Let us pass."

Ardashir fixed me with his metallic gaze. "Surely you are not leaving us so soon."

"Let us pass," I repeated.

"I cannot." Ardashir shook his head, as if in regret. "The Next Messenger has invited you to remain in our City as his guest. He has sent me to make sure his invitation is received."

I looked past him, at the men who followed him. "You know who I am. In Ârata's name, stand aside."

They held their ground, though some of them could not meet my eyes.

"Come." Ardashir gestured with one bandaged hand toward the cavern from which we had come. "I will see you back to your quarters."

"Old One, what shall I do?" Reanu said to me, low.

Well, what could we do? The Tapati are trained to be deadly, even weaponless, but we were too greatly outnumbered. So I obeyed, and took my people back to the cavern, now explicitly our prison.

"If there is anything you require for your comfort, you have only to ask." Ardashir was all silky courtesy once he had the upper hand. "My men will remain, just outside. It's my Messenger's wish that you be comfortable."

"Get out," I said. "Begone, you odious man!"

A beat; then, very slowly, he smiled. It was one of the most malignant smiles I have ever seen. His eyes are dark, but in that instant I swear that they flared red.

"As you wish, *Old One*."

The way he spoke my title was a blasphemy. I heard Reanu draw in his breath. I reached out and closed my fingers on his wrist; I don't know, otherwise, what he might have done.

Ardashir turned on his heel and departed. Ten of the men he had brought with him ranged themselves across the entrance.

"The dog," Reanu said quietly.

"Yes. He is loathsome."

"What are your orders, Old One?"

"I don't know, Reanu. I must think."

I sat in my tent with Drolma and Ha-tsun. Ha-tsun brewed tea over our little brazier and we drank it in silence. I felt their fear, but could not gather myself to soothe it. This cave is not so deep within the ridge as the ceremonial cavern, and I had not previously been troubled by a sense of oppression. But I felt it then—I feel it now. Those walls, close around us. Those men outside, impassable as rock.

Some time later there were footsteps. It was Vivaniya, with Amchila and Mur and Karamsuu.

"Pack my things," he ordered Yailin. "Amchila, see to my papers. You two"—to the Tapati—"take down the tent."

"Brother," I said, approaching him. "What is this?"

But I already knew. Of course I knew.

"I'm leaving." He stooped to roll up a mat. He could not look at me. "It has to be this way. I cannot have you speaking against me when I reach Baushpar."

I could hardly breathe for sadness and rage. "You have given me up to be his hostage."

The blood rushed into his downturned face. "You will be his *guest*, Sister! When they leave the Awakened City, you'll be free to go."

"Ah, Brother. Did he promise you that?"

"I'll leave you Reanu and Omarau and Lopalo and Apui, and six of the Tapati who wait beyond the checkpoint, and your carriage and horses, so you may travel in safety when you leave."

"Vanyi." I knew it was pointless, but once again I could not help myself. "You came to me for guidance in Baushpar. Please, be guided by me now. This man is false—a charlatan, an apostate Shaper. I saw it tonight, as clear as I see you. Turn away from him. I beg you, turn away."

He pushed the mat aside. He got to his feet. He turned his back. "Goodbye, Sundit."

I said no more and went back to my tent. Drolma and Ha-tsun, who of course had heard everything, looked at me in fearful silence. We sat listening to the noise of preparation outside, then to the sound of retreating footsteps. I admit I wept, when silence returned. Drolma sat rigid, horrified at my lapse of dignity, my display of raw humanity. They do not wonder at our anger, our mortal servants; why should they wonder at our grief? But Ha-tsun, Ârata bless her, came and put her arms around me.

"Shhh," she whispered, as she used to when I was a child in this body. "Shhh."

They are asleep, as are the Tapati, except for Reanu who stands watch. It comforts me to know he is with me, wakeful and faithful. I know he would give his life for me. I pray he will not have to. I do not fear for myself—I cannot believe that even this mad, arrogant boy would dare harm one of the Brethren. But I fear for my people.

Ah, Vivaniya. All this, from the guilt of a single deed. In a life span of twelve centuries, how can one deed loom so large? Why is it, as the pretender said to me today, that twelve hundred years of living is sometimes not enough to make us wise? Of course, we live those centuries one life at a time. We live them through the medium of the human vessels that bear us through the ages, whose nature it is constantly to distract us with their physicality, with the experience of our senses. Our human guises limit us. They drive us into shame and error. So with Vivaniya, whose actions in this matter have been so wholly human—the measured wisdom that I know is in him, which should have tempered the storms of his mortal heart, apparently entirely blotted out. All of us have fallen in this way, some of us more than once—though few with such disastrous consequences.

Yet even as I condemn him I am aware that it could not be otherwise. The very humanity that clouds our judgment, that tyrannizes our understanding, is the source of our enduring strength. Without it, we could not bear the years. We would grow weary and jaded and uncaring, distant from the human world it is our charge to guide. From the earliest days of our Covenant, we have cherished our humanity. We have never tried to diminish or disguise it, to abandon or transcend it, even to tame it through physical and mental discipline—though periodically one or another of us will argue that we should. Instead, we strive to strike a balance between our humanness and our immortality, between the fiery needs of a single life and the cool certainties of a perpetual one.

And if we sometimes fail . . .

I cannot deny that we seem to fail more often of late. The bitter struggle two hundred years ago between Karuva and Vimâta for the Bearer's necklace.

Our flight from Baushpar when the Voice of Caryax took Ninyâser—like the others, I believed we had no choice, but in light of the anger born of our abandonment I am no longer so sure. The disagreements and betrayals of our time in Rimpang . . . Taxmârata's election, which seemed to offer so much hope, but in fact has led to such dissension . . . the way we fell into factions after Gyalo Amdo Samchen came. Though of course that could not have occurred if the divisions were not already there—which, in a way, is even worse.

We must do better in the time to come. If there *is* a time to come. This is the insight I have gained, at the end of this terrible day. I know he is no Messenger, this beautiful, cruel boy who names himself so. Yet if I can now dismiss the question that dispatched us here, I can't dismiss the one that preceded it. I can't dismiss Vivaniya's and Dâdar's lie.

And if Gyalo Amdo Samchen told the truth . . . if Ârata is awake . . . if this boy is not the Next Messenger . . . who is?

Part III

THE BLASPHEMER KING

Gyalo

Gyalo woke from a sleep that for once contained no dreams. He lay a moment, looking up at the sky, which was the perfect, gilded blue that comes just after sunrise. Then he kicked out of his blankets and went over to Diasarta, who was leaning against one of the boulders that concealed their campsite.

"Morning, Brother."

"Anything new?" Gyalo yawned and ran his hands through his hair, wincing as his fingers caught the knot at the back of his head, still hard and painful even after so many days.

"Yes, for once. Some men came down last night and took those monks up to the caves."

"Really?" Gyalo peered over the boulder, down at the tawny expanse of stubble that spread below the Awakened City. Sure enough, the Tapati were gone. The horses were staked out as usual, and beside the coach—only one coach now; the other had been gone when the companions arrived—the Tapatis' bedrolls lay around their cook fire, whose embers still emitted heat. Gyalo could just see the patterns from that distance. "The other Brethren must be leaving."

"Well, wake me if anything happens," Diasarta said. "I'm going to get some sleep."

He headed for the blankets, which they shared now, one sleeping while the other watched, Gyalo's pack and equipment having been left behind in the Awakened City.

He had lain through the night after Ardashir departed, passing in and out of consciousness. Every time he woke, the terrible weight of understanding fell on him anew. Day came; the sun rose, burning down on his exposed skin. He could not summon the will even to lift his arm to cover his eyes.

At some point there was the sound of voices. The air moved; fingers touched his throat. "He's alive."

"Isn't that the pilgrim who passed through before we left Fashir?"

"Yes—yes, I think you're right." A hand gripped his shoulder. "Pilgrim. Pilgrim, what's happened to you? Where's your companion?"

Gyalo turned his face away. "Leave me alone," he whispered.

"You need help. Let us—"

"Leave me alone."

The hand withdrew. "Suit yourself."

They moved on. Gyalo tried to return to his half-conscious state. But his body demanded his attention: His bladder was full, and he was terribly thirsty. Slowly, pausing to allow fits of dizziness to pass, he got to his knees and dealt with the first, then shaped his cupped hands full of water to satisfy the second. His mouth tasted foul; dried blood and vomit crusted his beard. He shaped more water, cleaning himself as best he could. Gingerly, he felt his scalp. There was an enormous welt, and more dried blood. His ribs were bruised where Ardashir had kicked him.

The pain in his head and side made it difficult to breathe, and the dizziness and blurred vision made it hard to walk. Still he was able, by an act of will, to put one foot before the other. Ardashir had left him only a little way from the point where he had joined the track the day before, but in his confused state he missed the mark he had made, and blundered on for some distance before he realized he needed to turn back. It was near dark when he reached the camp. Diasarta came limping down the slope to meet him, glinting green against the dusk.

"Ârata's Blood! What happened?"

Gyalo sank down on the ground and told him, in flat, exhausted phrases.

"Dead?" Diasarta said, appalled, when Gyalo reached that part of the story.

"I think . . . I hope . . . he was lying." That hope had come to him over the course of the long day, as he labored through the grass. "To keep me from coming back, or maybe just to torment me. He knew I worked as a scribe, and that I used the name Timpurin. The men he sent to steal her might have discovered her husband's name and work, but why should he connect those things with me, unless she told him? So she can't have died along the way, as he said. She must have gotten to the Awakened City. She may still be alive. Chokyi may still be alive."

"Pray Ârata it's so."

"But I don't know, Dasa. I don't *know*."

"It's a hope, at least. Something to hold on to." Diasarta frowned. "Why would he let you go, though? Why wouldn't he just kill you?"

"I'm no threat to him. Besides, he wants to punish me. He wants me to watch him march across Arsace, he wants me to understand what he's doing and why he's doing it. He wants me to be a witness."

He heard Râvar's voice, speaking the words that Ardashir had overheard: *All the blame is yours.* In a way it was true. Grief spasmed in his chest, far more solid than the small hope that had woken in him this afternoon.

"You can say it now, Dasa."

"What?"

" 'I told you so.' What I saw in that place . . . the power I felt in him . . . You were right. I never had a chance."

For a long moment Diasarta was silent, fingering his scar as he did when he was thinking. Full night had fallen; stars massed the blackness of the sky, and the moon tipped low above the shimmering steppe. "You weren't to know about the scars," he said finally. "Neither of us thought of those."

"I have to stay. If there's any chance they're still alive—"

"I know, Brother. I know."

Diasarta assisted Gyalo up to their campsite. By the little stream, he removed Gyalo's filthy shirt and washed Gyalo's face and chest. Gently, he cleaned the knot at the back of Gyalo's head. Gyalo sat like a child under these ministrations; will, not strength, had carried him there, and he could hardly keep upright. At last Diasarta laid out his own bedding and helped Gyalo to lie down.

"You sleep now, Brother." He drew the blankets up under Gyalo's chin. "I'll keep watch."

Pain accompanied Gyalo into sleep, but also the sight of Diasarta's broad back, haloed in his familiar lifelight. The whole world was dizzily in motion—the wind, the grasses, the circling stars—but Diasarta was still, like a stake fixed in the earth. Gyalo found his immobility deeply comforting.

They remained where they were for two days, to allow Gyalo to recover some of his strength, then moved west along the ridge, in search of a place from which they could spy upon the Awakened City. Amid an area of tumbled boulders they made camp and settled in to watch. Apart from the sweep of night and day across the steppe, there was not much to see—the small, moving figures of the horses and the Tapati, bands of pilgrims cutting grass, occasional groups of gatherers and hunters. Diasarta bore the tedium with his usual equanimity; the anger he had released on the night Gyalo left him seemed to have gone back into its hiding place. Gyalo coped much less well. With his head he knew he would not see anything to tell him whether Axane and Chokyi still lived; with his heart, he waited constantly for a sign. Sometimes hope blazed up in him, so strong he could not doubt that Râvar had lied; sometimes despair possessed him utterly, and he was certain he would never see them again in this life. In his lowest moments he prayed for their lives as he had not for their safety, desperate pleas launched into silence—useless pleas, for if they lived, no prayers were needed, and if they were dead, no prayers would help.

The companions had been watching for nine days.

The caverns lay beneath and to the right of Gyalo's high vantage point. The entrance and the checkpoint were hidden by the configurations of the ridge, but he had a good view of the empty track. The hours wore on. The wind breathed in Gyalo's ears and plucked at his clothes. His eyes burned from the glare, and from the immensity below, whose vast and not-quite-graspable patterns he found difficult to contemplate for very long. He closed them for a moment, resting.

When he looked down again, a group of men had appeared midway along the track. They reached the bottom of the ridge and headed for the coach. They untethered the horses, leading two to the coach for harnessing, saddling and bridling the rest. Whoever they were, they were not Tapati; it was too far to see whether they were tattooed, but their heads were not shaven, and none wore Âratist red.

One man opened the coach's door and unfolded the steps, then climbed to the driver's platform. The rest stood to the side, holding the horses. Above, there was movement on the track: another group of men, led by one whom Gyalo recognized by his lack of luster as Ardashir. They descended to the steppe, and mounted the prepared horses. Ardashir raised his arm in some sort of signal.

For a moment nothing happened. Then a company of pilgrims walked out from behind the ridge fold, ranked four abreast, as ordered as a column of Exile soldiers. They carried bags and bundles in their arms and on their backs; some held infants, or led children by the hand, or supported the elderly and infirm. Their voices rose: They were singing, a song with solemn cadences like a hymn, though it was not any hymn Gyalo knew.

He felt as if his entire body had come alight. "Dasa," he called urgently. "Dasa! Come here!"

Diasarta roused at once. There was a scatter of small rocks as the ex-soldier hurried to stand beside him.

"Ârata! They're leaving."

"Yes."

The last rank of pilgrims reached the foot of the ridge. Another company emerged, as ordered as the first, and then another. Company by company, the Awakened City marched down to the steppe and tramped away across the grasses. It seemed to take an enormously long time. Gyalo counted: ten companies, fifteen, eighteen. The sound of their singing rose and fell, rose and fell, as the wind snatched it away and gave it back.

The twenty-first company descended. No more appeared. The singing died as the procession drew away, leaving only the voice of the wind. Still Ardashir sat his horse, his companions at his side.

"They're waiting for *him*," Diasarta said.

"Yes." Gyalo could hardly speak, his heart was racing so.

Moment followed moment. The track remained empty. Then all at once, between one blink and the next, Râvar was there, mantled in his unmistakable golden aura, and by his side—

"Ârata!"

Diasarta caught Gyalo's arm. "What is it? Brother, do you see them?"

"Yes. It's Axane." He could not make out her face. But that storm of jade and cobalt could not be mistaken. "I see her colors, Dasa. She's alive."

"Brother." Diasarta gripped his shoulder. "Ah, Brother. That's good."

Gyalo bowed his face into his hands. A brief, uncontrollable spasm of weeping shook him: joy for the hope that had been fulfilled, grief for the one that had not. For he had seen Axane's light, but not Chokyi's.

"He's heading for the coach," Diasarta said.

Gyalo raised his head. Râvar mounted the steps, vanished inside. Axane followed, carefully, as if she bore something fragile. Gyalo felt hope stir again: Perhaps she was simply too far away for the baby's paler colors to show within her own.

The driver left his perch to stow the steps and slam the door. He climbed up again and gathered the reins. The coach lumbered off in the wake of the departing pilgrims. Ardashir and his men fell in behind, riding two by two like the Tapati guards whose place they had usurped.

"What now, Brother?"

Gyalo drew an unsteady breath. "We'll follow. Now they're out in the open it should be easier to slip in among them, as long as we stay clear of the coach. We can try tonight, when they camp."

Diasarta nodded. "What d'you suppose happened to the second Brethren?"

"Râvar commandeered the coach. Perhaps they left together in the other one."

"Without their attendants?"

"I don't know." Nor did he care. "We'll wait a couple of hours, then get started, yes?"

"Good." Diasarta yawned. "I could use some more sleep."

Gyalo stared down at the Awakened City, a line of jeweled brilliance against the paler luminance of the grass—far in the distance now, trailed by the black blot of the coach and its little group of outriders. The force of the procession's passage roiled the air, drawing behind it a pattern of turbulence that to his Shaper senses resembled the wake of a boat, but slower to resolve back to calm. Soon he and Diasarta, or perhaps just Diasarta, would be part of it. And then? Follow. Watch. Wait for some chance, some opening.

Chokyi, he thought, trying to hold the hope that had returned as he watched Axane climb into the carriage. Instead, the sourceless flames in Râvar's chambers rose before his inner eye—each one, tiny as it was, holding in itself the full measure of Râvar's terrifying power. He was seized suddenly by a perverse desire—to explore those chambers, to discover where Axane, and perhaps Chokyi, had been imprisoned.

"I'm going down. To the caverns."

Diasarta paused in midstretch. "What? Why?"

"They may have left things behind. I could use a travel kit."

"But Brother, we don't know for sure that they've all gone."

"If we meet anyone, we can pass ourselves off as stragglers. You don't have to come with me, Dasa."

"Ârata's wounds. You know I won't let you go alone."

They went slantwise down the slope, the wind like a hand at their backs. They reached the fold of ridge that had hidden the track from view and started upward again. Beyond the short downward incline at the track's crest, the cavern's great mouth gaped—purely dark now, its counterfeit galaxy of lifelight and firelight extinguished by the City's departure.

Inside, Gyalo moved along the wall, searching for the torches he remembered had been fixed there. The first was too charred, but the second was usable. He wove heat patterns, making it burst into flame, then found another and lit it as well.

They began to walk along the central thoroughfare. The settlements' precisely marked borders were intact, but apart from stray bricks of grass and the ash of cook fires and a scattering of things too broken or ragged to be worth carrying, they had been stripped. There was something eerie about the emptiness; moving ever deeper into inky blackness, able to see no farther than the trembling double ring of illumination cast by the torches, Gyalo was seized by the sense that he passed through a place not newly deserted, but forsaken for hundreds of years. Only the odor of smoke and the lingering stench of overcrowded living conditions attested to the City's recent occupancy.

"Doesn't look like they've left anything useful," said Diasarta.

"No."

"You seen enough yet, Brother?"

Gyalo hesitated, glancing back toward the brightness of the entrance. In the pause, something that for a little while had been tugging at his attention came abruptly into focus.

"Do you hear that?" he said.

"Hear what, Brother?"

It came again: a thudding, barely audible, as of stone pounding against stone.

"Bloody ashes. I told you they mightn't all be gone."

A bizarre suspicion was growing in Gyalo's mind. "What if it's not by choice?"

"What, you think he left people shut up inside the rock?" Even as he said it, Gyalo saw the comprehension on Diasarta's face.

"It's coming from the back."

Gyalo strode forward. The sound of pounding rose. They were closer to the cavern's rear than he had realized; it materialized before them at the margins of the torchlight, punctured by another smooth symmetrical Shaper-made opening, with more blackness beyond.

They found themselves in a downward-sloping passage. Another passage forked off to the left; it was from there that the pounding came. Within a few steps they reached its source: a great plaque of banded sandstone, sunk like a plug into the gray limestone of the cavern wall. The torchlight slid across the gleaming rock.

"There was an opening here," Gyalo said. "He blocked it off."

"Ârata! You think maybe it's the other Brethren in there?"

Thud. Thud. Thud. The blows continued, not fast and panicked, but measured, steady. Did they understand they could not break through? The patterns of the plaque did not indicate great thickness, but the stone was dense; without tools, they could work for days and only chip it. And they did not have days. If, as seemed plain, Râvar had shut them up in there to die, he would not have left them food or water.

"Take my torch, Dasa, and stand back."

Diasarta obeyed. Gyalo put his mouth close to the plaque and cupped his hands around his lips. "Hey!" he yelled, into a pause between the blows. "Hey!"

The thudding ceased. A voice came, very faint: "Is someone there?"

"Yes. Can you hear me?"

"We hear you! We're trapped. Can you help us?"

"Stand back and cover your eyes. There will be a light. Do you understand? Stand back and cover your eyes."

There was a hesitation. "We understand."

By the guttering torchlight Gyalo surveyed the structure of the plaque, searching for the best point on which to focus his shaping will. It was, by several orders of magnitude, the largest work he had attempted since his return to practice—and the most exacting, for if he were to unmake more than the plaque, he might compromise the structure of the passage. Yet he was confident of his skill. By the uncanny unconscious process that had deepened his understanding of his power even as he kept it prisoner, he knew exactly what to do.

He breathed, gathering himself, then thrust his will forth like a pair of grasping hands, seizing the structure of the sandstone, forcing it apart, banishing it into the void of pre-being. Thunder rolled through the darkness; a flare of blue-white brilliance canceled for an instant the cavern's artificial night. Gyalo shook his head, blinking away the afterimages. The sandstone was gone. Where it had been, the pitchy blackness was broken by the gleam of lifelights: several Tapati guards, gathered in a tight group, their stance suggesting shock or fear—and why not? Shaping had imprisoned them, but they could not possibly have expected it to release them.

A figure in red-and-white clothing pushed through the knot of guards. One, a large man with a wheat-colored lifelight, reached out a hand, as if to restrain her. "Old One—"

"It's all right, Reanu."

She halted in front of her men: the Daughter Sundit. She was exactly as Gyalo remembered her from Baushpar—small and sturdy, with a square, intelligent face. Her lifelight (which he had not known before, for he had never before seen her without the tether of manita), was a clear lapis blue, shot with darker currents. She squinted against the brightness of Diasarta's torches, her hand raised to shield her eyes from what, after so long in darkness, must seem unbearable illumination. She showed no trace of her guards' astonishment. She was as self-possessed as if she stood in her own domain.

"That was shaping you used to free us." Her voice held the arrogant command that Gyalo remembered so well—not peculiar to her but common to all the Brethren, who were trained to it over scores of lifetimes. Though when last he stood before her and her spirit-siblings, he had not thought it arrogance at all, but right—the right of the First Messenger's children, immortal beings to whom he owed unquestioning allegiance.

"Yes." Discarded habit stirred in him, his tongue wanting to add her title: *Old One.*

"You are apostate, then."

He was acutely aware of the nakedness of his face. He had shaved his beard a few days ago, tired of the itch; his hair was pulled back and braided. But why should she know him? It had been a long time. He was greatly changed. She believed him dead. "Yes."

"Who are you? Answer me."

He thought of Ardashir, who had made the same demand. "I am no one."

She stepped closer. Her tattooed brow creased. And suddenly there it was: the change, the shift. Recognition.

"It can't be." It was a whisper. "Are you—can you be Gyalo Amdo Samchen?"

He said nothing.

"You are. I see you are. But we were told you were dead, fallen from your window in Faal. How did you get free?" Her shock was ebbing, giving way to anger. "Why are you here? Have you joined the army of the pretender? Do you believe his ugly blasphemy, you who thought that Ârata was awake?"

"He has nothing to do with that ash-cursed blasphemer." It was Diasarta, coming to stand at Gyalo's elbow. Anger roughened his voice. "Ârata, Brother! Don't let her talk to you like that!"

Sundit's gaze raked Diasarta's face. "I remember you, too."

"And well you should, after what you and your kin put me through. You've done enough for these people, Brother. Let's go."

"Apostate!" Sundit commanded. "You are not dismissed!"

"You are hardly in a position to give me orders," Gyalo said. "I could seal you in again as easily as I released you."

"You do not dare."

"Are you so sure?"

"Why *did* you release us?" She frowned. "Did you know who you would find behind the stone?"

"I suspected."

"Why, then? It's hardly in your interest. And after—you could have turned away, but you did not. You let me recognize you."

Gyalo was aware of the Tapati at her back. He could open up the stone beneath their feet, but could he unmake a thrown knife before it struck him?

"If you do not follow the pretender," she said, "why are you in his City?"

"He stole something from me. I came to get it back. Why did he imprison you?"

An indescribable bitterness came across her face. "Because I would not bow down to him. Because my Brother did."

"What?"

"Oh yes. It's true. Vivaniya of the Brethren swore his faith to a blasphemer. He knelt before that evil boy and acknowledged him the Messenger. And it is even worse than that. Do you know who he is, this pretender?"

"I do. Do you?"

"He told me before he shut me in." Her mouth twisted. "The last of Refuge's Shapers. I would not have credited it, except how else could he know of Refuge? And it explains . . ." She broke off. "Did you recognize him from Refuge?"

"I knew who he was before I got here."

"How?"

"Not all of Refuge died at your soldiers' hands. There was another survivor. Axane, who is now my wife."

"The same Axane . . . ?" Her eyes widened.

"Yes. After she fled Baushpar, she hid herself among the hangers-on of your army so she could return and warn her people. He and she escaped the massacre. He brought her back with him across the desert. He told her everything he intended. She saw him destroy Thuxra City."

Sundit was shaking her head. "Surely not. It's part of his pretense, the destruction of the prison. Obviously he is powerful, but no Shaper is capable of such a thing. There's no record of any act so great, even from the time before the Shaper War."

"Axane witnessed it, I tell you. Set aside your prejudices, the things you think you know. Râvar is no mere apostate. He is a Shaper unbound all his life, trained to skills our world has long forgotten—skills perhaps it never owned. He is immensely powerful—*immensely* powerful, perhaps more powerful than any Shaper who has ever lived. He is capable of all he threatens, and more."

She looked at him. He saw her struggling with her disbelief. "Râvar?" she said at last. "That's his name?"

"Yes."

"He told me . . . before he shut me in . . . what he meant to do." She seemed to be speaking to herself. "How he will bring suffering on Arsace.

How he means to revenge himself upon the Brethren. I asked him if he did not know that the Brethren's souls are immortal, and cannot be destroyed as our bodies can be, and he said, *With your bodies dead and Baushpar gone, who will there be to seek you out when you are reborn?* I said to him, *You will never destroy Baushpar,* and he looked at me . . . he looked at me and laughed. *One of my enemies gone,* he said, and closed us into the rock. I didn't think . . . but if he could do it . . . if he could . . ."

The words trailed off. For a moment she stood, her face intense with thought. Then, abruptly, she turned to her guards.

"Reanu. Take one of the torches and ready us for departure."

So firm was this command that Diasarta did not protest when the large guard stepped forward, but willingly yielded up the torch.

"He took your coach," Gyalo said. "The horses, too."

"No matter. We'll walk. We'll go overland to Darna, which, if I'm not mistaken, lies due north of here. Even on foot, we will move more quickly than he, with that mass of followers. At Darna we will get horses, and continue along the Great South Way. We should be weeks ahead of him by the time we reach Ninyâser."

"Ninyâser?"

"I will go to the King. I've been planning it, sitting in the dark, even though I knew I would not get free. Whatever the truth of his power, this creature, this . . . Râvar . . . must be stopped. We Brethren do not have the resources, but Santaxma does, and though he may not care for Baushpar or the Brethren, he will not tolerate a threat to Arsace." She took a step forward. "And you, apostate, will come with me."

Diasarta sucked in his breath. Gyalo laughed.

"You think I am jesting?" Sundit snapped.

"You can't seriously imagine I would subject myself to the church, after all this time."

"No, no!" She made an impatient gesture. "It is your help I need. There was just one obstacle I could not see my way around—that my word alone might not be enough. But now I have you. You will stand with me, and confirm with the authority of firsthand experience who this Râvar is. You will speak of his intent, and of this great power he wields. You will help me persuade the King to act."

"Let me understand," Gyalo said. "You want *my* help—a free Shaper, corrupt and possibly insane, not to mention an escaped prisoner and a man you once suspected of the basest heresy?"

Her gaze did not flinch. "Things are not well between the Brethren and the King, as I believe you know. I fear he will not heed me."

"And you think he will heed *me*? More likely he'll order me killed the moment he learns who I am."

"No. He is faithless. As long as he does not believe you dangerous, your apostasy won't concern him. I'll tell him you've submitted to my authority, that you have repented and revowed yourself to the church. I'll even say you are retethered. The risk you take in facing him will speak as clearly as your words of the urgency of this matter."

"He won't believe you," Gyalo said tightly. "What free Shaper would willingly retether himself?"

"You." She held his eyes. "You did it once before. He knows that. If it can be believed of anyone, it can be believed of you."

"And am I to suppose that at the end of it you wouldn't try to hold me? That you'd simply let me go?"

"How could I prevent it?" She stepped toward him. He could almost feel the force of her will, pressing on the air between them. "Listen to me. There is more at stake here than the Doctrine of Baushpar. I would not have thought I could say such a thing, but it is so, and in the name of survival we sometimes have no choice but to set aside our principles and our enmities. This must be true now for you as well as me. I know you've renounced the church. For all I know, you may have renounced Ârata himself. But I remember you, Gyalo Amdo Samchen, I remember the man you were, and I cannot believe you are indifferent to Arsace's fate, to the suffering of its people. I cannot believe you do not see the duty here, you who did so much for what you believed to be your duty. You knew it was I behind the stone, yet you did not turn away. Don't turn from this."

"Ârata! This is madness. Come, Diasarta."

He turned to leave. Sundit's voice rang after him.

"Gyalo Amdo Samchen! By the oaths you once followed, in the name of the god to whom you were once vowed, by the reverence you once bore me and my kin, I command you to accompany me!"

Fury seized Gyalo, a rage such as he had rarely felt. It swung him around; it propelled him toward her, one step, two, before he was able to stop himself. Her face changed. Reanu surged forward, clasping his ink-marked arms around her waist, lifting her off her feet and swinging her around, placing his broad body between her and Gyalo.

This time, when Gyalo turned away, only silence followed him.

After so much darkness, daylight was a blessing. He left the track and began to climb the ridge. On a jut of rock above the caverns, he sat down. Diasarta, slowed by his shortened leg, caught up and sat nearby, panting.

"She had no right," he said between breaths. "No right."

Gyalo closed his eyes. His scars were throbbing; he pressed his hands together, trying to quell the ache. Anger still turned in him, but the white-hot rage had gone. He saw again how Sundit's face had changed, the arrogance erased by fear, and felt the strangeness of it—that she, the woman whose presence two and a half years ago would have drawn him reflexively to his knees, whose eyes he would not have dared engage directly in dread he might glimpse within them the arctic alienness of a soul twelve centuries old, should be afraid of him. But she had not seen a man stepping toward her. It was a monster she had seen, the monster of the apostate tales Gyalo had been taught during his Shaper training—mad, corrupt, uncontrollable. *This is what it is to be a free Shaper,* he thought: to make even the mighty afraid.

He opened his eyes on the immensity before him—the pale ocean of the steppe, the sun-seared vault of the sky, the braided currents of the wind. He thought of her, the Daughter Sundit—one of the most tolerant of the Brethren in this incarnation, an advocate of advancement and reform. He had known her when he served the Son Utamnos, whose close ally she had been. Unlike some of her spirit-siblings, for whom all mortals, even Shapers, were servants, she had treated him with respect; after he returned from the Burning Land she had seemed to look past his apostasy, as many of her spirit-siblings did not, and hear what he had to say—though he had never had any sense that she was tempted to believe it. In the end, of course, she had chosen with the others to silence him, to send him into exile.

And now she wanted him to stand with her before the King—he, the apostate, the monster, whose terrible sin threatened to pass its taint to any who drew too close, whose very existence was anathema. *There is more at stake here than the Doctrine of Baushpar*—she had actually said that, words he would have sworn no Son or Daughter, even the most enlightened, could ever speak.

She was right, of course. She was right about Santaxma, too. In the King lay the best hope that Râvar and his pilgrim army might be stopped. Could it really be that things had grown so bad between the Brethren and the King that her word alone would not be sufficient to convince him? If Santaxma chose not to act, and Râvar proceeded unopposed, the danger would at some point become apparent. But by then it might be too late.

He heard her voice: *I cannot believe you are indifferent to the fate of the land you live in* . . . Renewed anger clutched him. He was not indifferent. Why else had he let her recognize him; why else had he given warning? She understood Râvar's power now, knew what was really coming for her and her spirit-siblings, what was really coming for Arsace. He had no further obligation. Especially, he had no obligation to risk his life. If Santaxma would not believe her warning, why would he believe her claim that Gyalo had resubmitted himself to the church?

Still, she spoke inside his head. *The risk you take in facing him will speak more clearly than your words of the urgency of this matter.*

"Ârata!" he said aloud, making Diasarta jump. Could he actually be thinking of doing as she asked? It was insanity. More than that, it meant abandoning Axane. Abandoning Chokyi, if she lived. Yet all hope aside, what could he do for them if he stayed? Râvar's golden lifelight rose before his inner eye; he saw Axane climbing after Râvar into the coach, saw the door slamming closed behind her. What chance did he have of breaching that containment? Helplessness swept him. He could follow like a beggar. He could watch from afar. He could die trying to get near them. But that was all. That was all he could do.

Râvar's defeat would free them. Santaxma's victory would free them. Of course, those things might also kill them.

He bowed his face into his aching hands. The images he tried never to admit into his thoughts overwhelmed him: Axane's body under Râvar's. Râvar's hands on Axane's dark skin. Chokyi in her true father's arms. Beneath his clothes, her bracelet seemed to sear his chest. He heard Sundit again: *I cannot believe you do not see the duty here, you who did so much for what you believed to be your duty.* He heard himself, telling Diasarta: *If there is more, then there will be more, as Ârata wills.*

Would Axane despair when she dreamed him leaving? Would she curse him?

Some time later, Diasarta said, "Brother. They're going."

Gyalo raised his head. A little procession had appeared below: ten Tapati, Sundit, a woman with a white stole who must be her servant, another with a golden stole—a Shaper, her aide. All had bundles on their backs and containers of various sorts clasped in their arms, even Sundit. How long, Gyalo wondered, had it been since she had had to carry anything for herself?

At the margin of the stubbled area, she paused and looked back—at the cavern, Gyalo thought, but then her face lifted to the ridge. Her eyes found Gyalo and Diasarta, perched in plain view. Even from that distance Gyalo felt the power of her gaze—not her own power, which he no longer acknowledged even in the hidden corners of his being, but the power of what she had asked of him.

She turned away. The group resumed its progress. When they were no more than a knot of light upon the grasses, Gyalo rose.

"You're going with her," Diasarta said.

"I have to."

"You don't owe her anything." Diasarta's face was all straight lines: the slash of his mouth, the incision of his scar, the slits of his eyes, narrowed against the sun. "You don't owe the bloody Brethren anything."

"It isn't for her. If Râvar succeeds . . ." Gyalo drew a breath. "Santaxma is the only possibility of stopping him."

"Suppose the King thinks you need stopping, too?"

"She said she would tell him I was tethered."

"You believe her?"

"As a matter of fact, I do."

"Think the King will?"

"Do you think this is an easy choice for me? I feel I'm abandoning them. I'm afraid I'm putting them in greater danger. I'm afraid—" He stopped, unable for a moment to go on. "But I couldn't get them free. Even if I tried. This—this could be their only chance."

"It could also get you killed."

"Ârata, Diasarta! What do you want me to do?"

"I don't know, Brother. It's not my job to know those things."

"What is your job, then? To argue every decision I make?"

Diasarta met his gaze. "Maybe."

The anger went out of Gyalo all at once. He sank down on his heels and put his head in his hands. "For good or ill, this is what I have to do." He let his hands fall. "I wish I didn't. But I can't see any alternative."

Diasarta's jaw was tight. "All right, Brother. You make your choice. I'll make mine. I'll do as we planned. I'll join the blasphemer's army."

"No, Dasa! There's no need for that now."

"What'll I do, come to Ninyâser with you to see the King? I'm a deserter, Brother, remember? No. I'll follow the blasphemer. He'll be watching out for you, but not for me. Maybe there'll be something I can do."

Gyalo sighed. "I can't pretend I won't be glad to know you're there."

"I'm not doing it for you, Brother. I'm doing it for her. She was my companion, too."

They returned to their campsite so Diasarta could gather his things, then set off along the track. Where the track curved east, a pattern of disturbance marked the point where Sundit and her party had continued north.

"This is where we part," Gyalo said.

Diasarta nodded. The sun was sinking toward the end of the long summer afternoon, pulling their shadows out beside them.

"Be careful, Dasa. Don't take any unnecessary risks."

"I'd say the same to you, Brother, except I know it's useless."

"I'll come back. Once I'm done in Ninyâser, I will come back."

"Brother—" Diasarta drew a breath. "What you said about arguing. You were right."

Gyalo shook his head. "I was angry."

"Yes. But it's not my place to tell you how to act, or to pass judgment on you either. I've never known when to close my mouth. Why should you do what I think is right? What do I know of such things?"

"You owe me no apologies."

"You brought Ârata's Blood out of the Burning Land." Diasarta's gaze was steady. "You carried his word out of the wilderness. *You* did those things. No other. Even so, you never asked me to believe. You've never really wanted me— you may think I don't know that, but I do. I understand well enough why you stopped coming round to see me in Ninyâser. No, Brother—don't look away. I'm not reproaching you. I'm just telling you I understand. You've a way to travel, and you travel it how you need. But I have a way as well. You'll not change that by turning from me, any more than I'll change you by arguing. D'you see?"

"Yes."

"So you do what you must, and I'll do the same, and maybe we can find a way not to vex each other so much."

In spite of everything, Gyalo could not help laughing.

"Will you give me your blessing, Brother?"

"Gladly."

Diasarta knelt by the track, where the Awakened City's passage had broken the grass. Gyalo set his hand on the ex-soldier's head.

"Go in light, child of Ârata," he said, his tongue falling easily back into the forms of Âratist blessing. "May the god grant the blessing of his love. May he hold you in his hand. You are his true servant, a man of purer faith than any I have known. Go in light, child of Ârata."

He began to draw away. Diasarta reached up and seized his hand, and pressed his lips to the scarred palm. "Messenger," he murmured. And though Gyalo felt the old flinch, the deep instinctive dread, he was able for the first time simply to accept what Diasarta gave him, as a gift.

Diasarta rose. He gripped Gyalo's shoulders and pulled him into a rough embrace. Turning, he struck off along the track, limping on his shortened leg. He did not look back.

14

Sundit

I thought the astonishments of this day were done, but it seems I must take up my pen to write of more.

As I was settling to sleep, I heard the sentry's challenge. A few moments later, Reanu spoke outside my tent.

"Old One. The apostate has followed us."

I wrapped my stole around me and went out into the windy night. The Tapati were all on their feet. The apostate stood at the edge of the area of grass we had flattened for our camp, apparently at ease despite my men's concentrated attention. He was alone.

"Well?" I said. Reanu stood by me, tense and ready.

"I'll come with you," he said. "On one condition."

Such arrogance! "And what is that?"

"Your oath as a Daughter of the Brethren that after we've spoken with the King, you won't try to prevent me from leaving."

I looked at him. He looked back. Well, what choice did I have? I need him, and he knows it.

"You have my oath," I said. "What of your companion?"

"He did not choose to accompany me."

I turned to my people. "This man will travel with us to Ninyâser, and assist me in bearing warning to the King." I looked at each of them as I spoke, including Drolma, peering fearfully from behind the tent. "He has surrendered to my authority. Though he is apostate, you need not fear him."

It occurred to me as I said it that he might dispute me; I know very well that I have no authority over him at all. Yet he is an intelligent man. He said nothing.

A little later, Reanu came to me.

"I've placed him at the margin of the camp, Old One, and redeployed the men to circle you and Sister Drolma and Sister Ha-tsun. I myself will keep watch tonight."

"Thank you, Reanu."

He hesitated. "Forgive my presumption, Old One. But in duty I must ask—is this wise?"

Into my mind came the image I knew must be in his: the apostate, incandescent with fury, turning on me in the caverns. "I need him, Reanu. I need his testimony."

"Old One, we don't know how he came to be in that place, or what his purpose was, or even why he changed his mind. Do you not wonder what scheme of his own he serves by coming with us?"

"You may be right. Still I believe this is necessary."

"I was by you, Old One, when you spoke with him. I know as well as you that he did not surrender to you."

"You express yourself very frankly, Reanu."

"Old One, in Baushpar, in Ninyâser, in the world you rule, it's my duty only to obey. But this is a different world. In it, my duty also is different. So I do speak to you frankly, Old One, and hope that you will suffer it."

I looked at him in the uncertain light of my candle, sitting back on his heels, his hands braced on his knees in his habitual pose. The crisp calligraphy of his tattoos is blurred by the dark stubble beginning to show on his scalp and face. He smells, like all of us, of old sweat. I thought of how, when the pretender trapped us, he refused to surrender to the inevitability of death, and in pitch-darkness organized his men to pound upon the rock. I thought of how greatly, during this ordeal, I have grown to rely upon his courage and his strength.

"I acknowledge your concern, Reanu. But he, too, risks much in accompanying us. It makes a balance of sorts. Besides, he set us free. He could have left us, but he set us free."

"Old One, he is *apostate*. A blasphemer. Corrupt, perhaps mad. My men fear him."

"I know." I sighed. "Still, he will come with us. That's my decision, and it is final."

Warrior that he is, he knows when a battle is lost. He bowed and left me.

Gyalo Amdo Samchen, the apostate. Gyalo Amdo Samchen, who I thought was dead. I remember him well from the time he served Utamnos, for he was my dear spirit-brother's favorite: brilliant, diligent, and always so *correct.* Most Shapers, when their manita dose becomes inadequate, either do not perceive it or profess they do not, leaving it to the manita masters in their yearly examinations to decide. But he himself approached Utamnos when he sensed his need had changed. He was no self-righteous prig, however, no narrow-minded zealot—he was intelligent and generous in his faith, and his love of his vocation was shiningly apparent. It shocked me no less than it did Utamnos to learn he had turned apostate in the Burning Land.

Now here he is, apostate for the second time, proving yet again one of the truths that lie behind the Doctrine of Baushpar: No Shaper, having tasted the freedom of his gift, can ever again be trusted. Nor can I ignore the implications of his honesty with Utamnos. How many Shapers still require adjustment of their manita dosage past their ordination? He must have been near thirty the last time his dose was changed. What does that say about the magnitude of the power he has unbound? I know, as Reanu cannot, that it was only human anger he turned on me in the caverns, not any corruption or insanity. But human anger in an untethered Shaper is no small thing. In that moment, I was terrified.

And yet . . . he saved us all from certain body-death. He gave me truths he did not have to give me. He has chosen to follow me.

Reanu may be right. He may serve some mysterious purpose of his own. Still, I need him with me. I can force Santaxma to receive me, I can force him to hear me, but I cannot force him to heed me. And I greatly fear he will not heed me, not only in his displeasure with the Brethren but also in his particular dislike of me.

Râvar's face hangs in my mind. The hatred in it when he told me who he is. His smile as he shut us in that little place to die, ugly on his beautiful mouth. "My first enemy," he said. I can still hear it.

He marches now. But so do we. And we are faster.

I was too angry last night to make this entry. Anger boiled in me most of this day as well. But now, as I prepare to write, I find my rage has gone, and all I feel is worn, and drained, and very, very tired.

Supplies have been an anxious concern. The guards who waited with my coach had some food, as did we, and we were able to scavenge grain and other edibles from the Awakened City's leavings. But it is a very meager store, requiring strict rationing. Even worse is the situation with the water. To our own waterskins we added vessels left behind by the pilgrims, as many as we could find and carry—but nowhere near enough to get us across the steppe.

We've been trusting that we will find a water source; in the meantime, water is also rationed.

The apostate approached me on the second evening. "Let me help," he said. "You need water and food. I can create both."

It took me aback—not just that he would offer, but that in worrying about the possible dangers of his power I had not once considered its possible uses. He mistook my silence, I think, for judgment. His expression hardened.

"I know your opinion of me and what you suppose to be my corruption," he said. "But be practical. Even if the food you carry is enough to take you across the steppe, the water will be gone in a few days."

"I don't fear corruption. But my staff do. I don't even know if they would be willing to partake of what you made."

"They will if they are thirsty enough."

"Be that as it may, I shall continue to hope for a natural source of water."

"Well, I've no desire to starve. I'll shape my own supplies."

I spoke with an authority I did not feel. "Go apart to do it."

To my surprise he heeded me, stalking off into the grass. He returned with an array of fruit and nuts, which he consumed with (I thought) unnecessary ostentation. The Tapati cast glances and muttered among themselves. Drolma vanished behind my tent. It occurred to me that by refusing his offer I had put myself in the position of having to beg his help if no water source appeared.

On the fourth evening, the water nearly gone and no stream or well reported by Reanu's scouts, I swallowed my pride. I thought he might toy with me, or gloat, or even refuse. But he only nodded, and told me tersely what he meant to do. We stood by, like spectators at a play, as he created quantities of the same foods he had made for himself, causing them to appear in piles on a cloth Reanu had laid out. It has been centuries since I've seen the practice of unfettered shaping, but it seemed to me that the noise and light of what he did was not really very different from what one sees at a Communion ceremony. What came next, though, was entirely unfamiliar. He paused, his eyes moving on the ground, as if searching for something. Then there was a burst of brilliance, as if lightning had leaped out of the grass; a deep roll of thunder pulsed below our feet. Ha-tsun, beside me, gasped. For a moment nothing happened. I stood, blinking at the spots before my eyes. Then a spray of water rose up, sparkling in the light of sunset.

There was a murmur from the men. The apostate stepped back. The expression on his face was odd; he seemed to look on us with contempt, we mortals who feared his ability so, but I'm sure I also saw defiance, as though against his will our judgment touched him.

"That's all," he said. "I'm finished."

My people stood like stones. With all the authority I could muster I stepped forward and filled my cup with water. Turning to my staring staff, I drank a long draught. I know what I know; I spoke the truth when I told him I feared no corruption. Still, something primitive in me was relieved to find that the water tasted like . . . water. Cold, faintly metallic, delicious.

"Gyalo Amdo Samchen has shaped these things for our necessity," I said, pitching my voice much louder than was needed, as if I stood not in the middle of a wilderness but within the shadowy precincts of the First Temple. "On my authority as a Daughter of the Brethren, I declare them free of taint. You may eat and drink without fear for your souls."

They came forward then—some matter-of-factly, piling their bowls as if these were any rations, some hesitant, making the sign of Ârata before picking among the apricots and apples and cherries, the almonds and cashews and walnuts, the green onions and radishes. Drolma, who had turned pale when I told her what was to occur, had once again retreated behind my tent. When I took a bowl and cup to her, she refused them.

"I have what I need, Old One." She indicated a jar with perhaps a finger length of water in it and a bowl in which she was soaking grain and dried meat to soften it enough to chew.

"Drolma, there may be enough natural food to last you across the steppe, but even if I gather all the remaining water from the caverns, it won't last long. What he has shaped can't harm you, I swear it."

"Old One," she said with perfect calm, "if you order me to eat and drink, I will obey. Yet of my own will I cannot put these things into my mouth. I'm a Shaper, bound by Shaper vows. By refusing, I affirm those vows, which you and your Brothers and Sisters in your wisdom created to protect us all. I repudiate the choice *he* has made."

I looked at her. Like all of us, she is dirty, her face and scalp peeling painfully with sunburn. I've always thought her dry and pedantic—excellent qualities in an aide, dull qualities in a companion, and one of the principal reasons I selected her for this journey, in hopes she would be less likely to succumb in the manner of our first spy. In that moment, I found a new respect for her.

"I will honor your choice, Drolma. I will also excuse you from your ceremonial duties for as long as he is with us."

"Thank you, Old One." I saw the relief in her face, that she would not have to conduct Communion or Banishing in the presence of an apostate.

I went to my tent. Elderly as she is, Ha-tsun fares poorly on this journey; to spare her strength I have forbidden her to tend me, but as usual she had disobeyed, lighting my lamp and preparing my bedding. I eyed this journal and thought of writing. Instead another impulse gripped me. I got up and ducked outside again.

"Reanu, I am going to speak with the apostate."

I saw him struggle with his desire to challenge me. "I will be watching, Old One."

The moon seems to shine more brightly in this vast and empty place than elsewhere in the world. I could see every detail of the flattened grasses at my feet as I made my way toward the camp's edge, where the apostate had laid out the blanket Reanu had given him (for he came to us with nothing but the ragged clothes he wore). He sat facing south. As I drew near I heard him whispering, like someone telling Communion beads.

He heard me and turned. One hand rested on his chest, closed around some object under his shirt, for all the world as if he still wore an Âratist simulacrum. For a moment we regarded one another. He looks very different than he did in Baushpar, with his hair grown out; if I had passed him in the street, I might not have given him a second glance. Yet the long, tilted eyes are the same, the level brows, the broad cheekbones and full mouth; and there is the way he holds one's gaze, a stillness, an intensity, the whole of him present in a single look. That really is how I knew him when we stood face-to-face again: by the way he looked at me.

"Your captain doesn't seem happy."

I glanced back. Reanu had risen to his feet. His arms were folded under his stole; no doubt his knives were half-unsheathed. "It is his duty to be mistrustful," I said.

"So he has given me to understand, in no uncertain terms."

"Has he threatened you?"

"Only if I don't behave." He smiled a small tight smile. "I appreciate his position. After all, I'm a mad apostate."

"Whatever else you are, Gyalo Amdo Samchen, it's clear you are not mad. Even though you sit whispering to nothing in the night."

He removed his hand from his chest and placed it on his knee. "Perhaps I was telling my beads."

"I thought you had rejected the church."

"I have *left* the church."

"Is there a difference?"

"Yes." He sighed. "I was talking to my wife."

"Your wife?"

"She's a Dreamer. At night I speak into her Dreams, so she'll know what has happened to me during the day."

"I don't recall that about her. That she was a Dreamer."

"She didn't confess it. I'm the only one who has ever known."

It did not surprise me to learn she had held something back. I remember her from Baushpar, a small dark woman, unexceptionable but for her lustrous wealth of hair, quiet and yielding in her manner—yet in the core of herself as hard as iron, as basalt. I never thought, as some of my Brothers and Sisters did, that the apostate had broken his celibate vow with her. Yet there must have been something between them, for now she is his wife.

I pulled my stole closer. Hot as it is in the day, at night the steppe is cold. "It must comfort you to know she sees you."

"In a way." He sighed again. "She's the reason I came to the Awakened City. Râvar has her. Her and our child. He kidnapped them."

I remembered he had spoken of something being stolen. "Why?"

"In the Burning Land, while they were traveling, he . . . forced himself on her. Got a child on her. He let her go at Thuxra, and she found her way to me by dreaming. But he had . . . time, I suppose, to realize he wanted her back. He sent his people to Ninyâser, where he knew she meant to go, and took her and the child. I came after them. He caught me. He recognized me, just as you did."

"He remembered you from Refuge?"

"Yes. I thought he'd kill me, but he let me go. It pleased him to think I would be watching, helpless, as he made his way across Arsace. He told me Axane and Chokyi were dead. He lied about Axane—I saw her when they marched away. But Chokyi—" He stopped. "I still don't know."

My mind flashed back to the caverns. "I heard a child crying in his chambers."

"What? When?"

"Before he imprisoned me. I went to see him unannounced."

"She's alive, then." The apostate put his hand to his eyes.

"You care for her," I said. "Even though she's not yours."

"I love her." He drew a long breath. "It's not her fault who her natural father is."

"Not every man would see it that way."

"I haven't abandoned them," he said, as if I had accused him of doing so. "It's just that I could never get to them on my own. I have some power, but it's a spark compared to his. A mote. And even if that weren't so, he knows my lifelight. I can disguise my face, but my lifelight I can't hide. The only way to free them is to stop him. Only the King has any chance of that."

"So you don't accompany me for Arsace's sake after all."

"You should be glad. Self-interest is a more reliable motive."

All this time I had been standing. Now I knelt on the springy, broken grass. He watched me with that steady gaze of his. No doubt he found it strange that I should approach him. Yet even now, after the terrible things he said to me, I cannot deny the mystery of him, and how it eats at me: Gyalo Amdo Samchen, risen from the dead.

"Tell me how you escaped from Faal."

"Diasarta tracked me there. He hired on as a laborer and found out where I was being kept. One night he picked the lock of my room and took me away."

"Did you expect him to try to rescue you?"

He plucked a grass stem and turned it between his fingers, watching the heavy seed head bob. "No. I didn't even know till I saw him whether he was alive or dead."

"There was a body on the rocks below your window."

"He arranged it. He wouldn't tell me how."

"And then the manita sickness. As I recall, you were sentenced to four-teen measures. That's a massive dose. I'm surprised you survived."

"Diasarta stole manita from Faal's stores. I was able to wean myself off it gradually. It was bad." He swallowed, as if revisited by a memory of that ter-rible nausea. We did not know, when we promulgated the Doctrine of Baush-par, how manita binds those who use it; but we have had much reason since to be glad, human nature being what it is. "But not as bad as stopping all at once. Diasarta took care of me."

"He has been a good friend to you."

He nodded once, forcefully. "Better than I deserve."

"Yet he is not with you now."

"He's following the Awakened City. Waiting for me to come back. And I do mean to go back. Whatever the King chooses to do, I don't expect he'll take special measures for my wife and child."

It angered me, his matter-of-fact assumption of his continued freedom, though I have given my oath that he shall have it.

"Diasarta's loyalty to you was clear in Baushpar," I said. "He made no at-tempt to hide it, even though he must have realized it would damn him. It was the same with the Exile captain, Teispas. I've always wondered—did they be-lieve you the Next Messenger, as some of my Brothers and Sisters thought?"

"Does that really matter now?"

"I am curious."

He tossed the grass stem aside. His mouth was tight. "I don't have to answer such questions. I no longer acknowledge your authority."

"Yet I do have that authority, whether you acknowledge it or not. I am the guardian of Ârata's Way. I am the shepherd of all souls upon this earth."

"So you teach the faithful to believe. Yet the *Darxasa* says nothing of the Brethren or their Covenant."

"How could it? The *Darxasa* predates the Brethren."

"Yes, and is that not convenient for you all?"

For a moment I was speechless. "Do you deny the Covenant?"

"You say that Ârata granted you immortality on the First Messenger's death, thus sanctifying your Covenant and legitimizing your rule. But the second point rests upon assumption of the first. Deny that, and the logic fails. What is there, really, to prove that your souls are reborn? Do you regain your memories, or merely learn them through study of your journals?"

I could hardly believe I had heard aright. It was not just the shocking heresy of what he said; it was the absolutely fearless way he said it, as if it were not an assault upon twelve hundred years of doctrine, but merely a question of interpretation. I should have condemned him. I should have cursed him. I should have gotten to my feet and left him. I did none of those things, though I cannot now say why.

"In Baushpar," he said, "when Kudrâcari and her supporters invoked the similarities between the manner of my emergence from the Burning Land and the events foretold in Ârata's Promise, they intended only that the Brethren consider the possibility that I had heretically come to believe myself the Next Messenger. But what resulted from their efforts was not what they expected, for in forcing you to examine the question of my falsity, they also forced you to confront the possibility that I might not be false at all. It terrified you so much that you packed me off to Faal without allowing me to speak, even in denial. Time, you must have thought, would prove it one way or the other. I'm sure you all rejoiced when you learned I was dead. Final confirmation that I was just an apostate after all, and not the Messenger, herald of the end of the Age of Exile. Which is also your end."

"You do not dare say such things," I whispered, stupidly, as if I could deny the evidence of my own ears.

"You asked the question." He leaned toward me. His long clear eyes held mine. "Now you will hear my answer. Yes, Diasarta and Teispas believed me the Next Messenger, though I tried to persuade them to abandon their belief.

I saw the same signs they did, I could not help but question—but long before I stood before you in Baushpar, question led me to denial. I would have said so to you all, had you permitted it. But then Diasarta came to me in Faal, offering a freedom I had not dared imagine, and I saw Ârata's hand in that, giving me a second chance. I chose to take it—*chose* to take it, and though you might think it was an easy choice, it was not, for I still believed what you had taught me, I still feared my Shaper self, and to *choose* apostasy, not to have it thrust on me but to *choose* it of my own considered will— No. It was not easy. I'm no closer now than I was that night to understanding what I am meant to do with my freedom. Ârata is silent, and though I see his hand in all that has occurred, I can't tell what it is he wants of me. What is it to fulfill his Promise? What is it to open the way? What if I name myself the Messenger, and am false without knowing it? What if I refuse, and the falsity lies there? What if, fearing to choose, I stand upon the razor's edge all my life?"

He caught his breath, as if taken unawares by his own words. The look on his face was almost of exaltation, but there was dread there too, as of a man who gives wild tongue to the deepest and most hidden of his secrets.

"But there's one thing I do know. When you condemned me to Faal I thought I had failed the task Ârata gave me in the Burning Land, for I had not made you, the Brethren, believe in his rising. But I know now—I am certain now—that this was not what he intended me to do. I was sent to try you. To test you. To prove your faith. It was not I who failed. It was you."

Such a cold came over me then. The night seemed to dim, as if clouds had suddenly surged across the moon. But above us the moon shone clear.

"You are worse even than apostate." My voice seemed hardly louder than the wind. "You are anathema."

Having released such a torrent of evil words, he apparently had no more to say. He only looked at me, his eyes like glass.

I gathered myself to do what I should have done before, and got to my feet. I was aware of him at every step, watching as I walked away. Reanu watched, too, tense and still. As I drew level with him he asked, softly, "Do you need me, Old One?"

I shook my head. I did not trust myself to speak.

I thought that to write this record might ease me. It has not. I can still hear the last words the apostate said to me, with their uncanny echo of the words Taxmârata spoke the night I left Baushpar . . . To hear them from his mouth, the mouth of this man whose apparent death seemed to prove something that now is unproven . . . ah, merciful Ârata! I am filled with the awful hollow understanding that rises on realization of a mistake one should not have made. With all my heart I long to turn back time, to undo my foolish impulse to go out to him.

Yet what would that change, but knowledge?

I have considered banishing him. But what if he did not obey me? What of my mission to Santaxma? More to the point, what would we do for food and water? We are dependent on him now. Perhaps that was his intent when he offered his assistance.

I will endure his presence, because I must. Once we are finished in Ninyâser I will let him free—not because I wish it but because I have no choice. And I will hope, with all the power of hope I have left in me, never to hear of him again.

Today the apostate found water.

We have been walking for six days. Each day Reanu has dispatched scouts, but they have found no trace of any natural water source. This is no longer important for us, for we drink what the apostate provides quite naturally now. Drolma, however, has suffered. As I promised, I ordered the remaining water from the caverns gathered for her exclusive use; but though she has been thrifty, by this morning it was nearly gone.

In the middle of the afternoon we stopped to rest. Reanu set four of his men to hold a blanket by its corners so Drolma and Ha-tsun and I might have shade. I and Ha-tsun drank the water the apostate had made the night before. Drolma sipped from her own small cache, then lay back and closed her eyes. Her face ran with sweat. I eyed her, knowing she would allow herself to perish rather than drink the apostate's water, dreading the moment when I would have to order her to partake.

"Old One." Reanu came to crouch outside the square of shade cast by the blanket. "The apostate says there is a stream."

"A stream? Where?"

"To the east. We can see nothing, but he claims there are *patterns*"—his mouth curled with disgust—"in the air that tell him of water. Shall I investigate?"

I looked past him, to where the apostate sat a little apart from the rest, his knees drawn up and his arms draped loosely over them. "Yes. If you find it, we'll make our camp there."

He chose two of his men and sent them off. I bent over Drolma, using the end of my filthy stole to blot the sweat from her cheeks.

"I'm sorry to be so weak, Old One," she whispered.

"Hush," I told her. "Rest."

The men returned to report that there was indeed a stream. We began to walk again. At last we crested a rise and saw the stream below, its course fringed with brush and low bushes. The heat of summer had reduced it to a shallow flow across the tumbled rocks at the center of its bed, but the current was brisk and the water sweet. What a luxury it was to bathe! Drolma and Ha-tsun and I took turns holding up a screen of blankets, and the Tapati went downstream in groups. Reanu escorted the apostate separately. Reanu must know—of course he knows—that this guard-and-prisoner behavior is mostly a charade; the apostate is no more immune to a punch knife than anyone else, but apart from that there's little Reanu can do to prevent him from behaving exactly as he pleases. Still Reanu maintains the appearance of control, setting watches at night, ensuring that the apostate is flanked during the day by at least two men. What's interesting is that the apostate consents to this, behaving exactly as a prisoner would.

He created food for us and we ate, sitting by the water in the twilight. Drolma as usual drew on her own supplies. Then she and Ha-tsun retired to their bedrolls, as did the Tapati. And I . . .

I went to the apostate.

I truly intended, at the close of my last entry, never to go near him again, never to allow him another chance to pour ugly words into my ear. But over the past two days I've grown to realize (or perhaps only to admit I realize) that I cannot be done with him so easily, much as I might wish it. He is a question, this man. He demands an answer. I cannot explain it more clearly than that.

Reanu was on guard before my tent, as usual. I told him what I meant to do. He said nothing, but I felt his eyes on me as I walked to where the apostate had spread his blanket. He sat cross-legged—whispering, perhaps, to his Dreamer wife. Like the rest of us, he had washed his clothes and put them on again wet; his long hair, which he normally keeps tightly braided, hung loose down his back. He seemed neither surprised nor dismayed to see me. Our confrontation might never have occurred. I was already angry at myself for the need, or curiosity, or whatever it was, that had drawn me to him; I felt myself grow angrier. I had meant to thank him for finding water, but the words stuck in my throat.

"How is your aide?" he asked. "I was afraid she would allow herself to die of thirst."

"I'm surprised you would feel any sympathy for her."

"Why? Because as an apostate, I must wish to tempt all Shapers from their vows?" He shook his head. "I haven't forgotten that I was once as she is. In her situation, I would have felt the same."

"Well," I said. "She is better now." Still, I could not bring myself to thank him. "Reanu told me you saw signs in the air that spoke of water."

"Yes."

"That is part of an apostate's skill?"

"It's part of a free gift of shaping. There are signs . . . patterns . . . in everything that exists. But you know this. Surely you remember, from before the Shaper War."

"Ah, but you don't believe in my immortality. Isn't that what you told me the other night?"

"I've speculated about many things," he said quietly. "It's not the same as certainty."

The night was clear and full of moonlight, the sound of water just audible below the hiss of the wind. On the body of the steppe the dominant grasses are tall and tough, with nodding heads like wheat or rye, but a different strain grows by the stream, short and threadlike. I stared at it, wondering in the front of my mind how a place of such apparent monotony can in fact be so infinitely varied, while with a deeper part of myself I considered the apostate. The deadly power he had used to help us. His feigning of the ways of prisonerhood—so that our fear of him might be eased? So that Reanu, before his men, might not lose face? For his own amusement? How, in the caverns, he stood and let me recognize him. I thought of the impossible fact of his survival, of the even more impossible chance that the two of us should ever meet. I thought of the accusations he had flung at me the other night—of the horrible cold shock I felt, not of anger, but of recognition. A voice seemed to speak inside my head: *Here he is. Here I am.* For just an instant I felt—seemed to feel—the presence of something huge, leaning up out of the night.

I sank to my knees across from him, hugging my damp stole around me against the chilly air. "Centuries ago," I said, "before the Shaper War, we Brethren had Shapers to guard us. Did you know that?"

I saw his surprise. "No."

"Those are old, old memories. It has been long since I was face-to-face with an untethered Shaper, longer still since I spoke with one. Tell me of these patterns you perceive."

His brow creased into a frown. "Why?"

"Because I am here." I spoke my thought. "Because you are."

"I'm not a book, Sundit of the Brethren. You won't be able to close me if I say things you don't want to hear."

"But I can rise and walk away."

He watched me, troubled. I began to think he might refuse. "What do you want to know?"

Thus began one of the strangest conversations I believe I have ever had—not simply for the sake of what I am and what he is, but because I had not, till then, realized how much I had allowed myself to forget—beyond the basics, I mean, the narrow knowledge necessary to administer the Doctrine of Baushpar: the signs of shaping's manifestation in girls and boys at the time of puberty, the art of manita preparation and dosage, the training by which young Shapers are habituated to their tethers and prepared for priestly service. With utter frankness he spoke of the patterns he sees in all things, as integral to his perception as form and color to a non-Shaper—the patterns of unliving things, which he can grasp and manipulate, and the patterns of living things, whose light he can perceive but whose structure he can neither understand nor re-create. "What color is my light?" I asked, and he told me it is lapis blue with darker currents, and that his is the color of a pearl, and that Drolma's is pale rose, and that Reanu's is the exact hue of ripe wheat. He described how the steppe appears to him: the wind roiling the substance of the air like currents in clear water, the grasses breathing the pale light of their life, the birds and insects and small ground-dwelling creatures glinting like sparks or stars. Of the stars themselves, which whisper a design too vast even for a Shaper to comprehend.

"The ability I knew while I served the church," he said, "was like peering through a half-open door. The freedom I have now is like knocking down not just the door, but the wall into which it was set."

He claims he is still pursuing the limits of his gift. There are restrictions: He can infinitely re-create the natural, insensate world, but he cannot make what is artificial or what is living. The clay he can shape, but not the brick; he can shape oranges or almonds or roses, which are dead in the instant of their plucking, but not the growing tree or the rooted plant. He described, a little, the process by which he has passed beyond the narrow boundaries of Âratist training: his experiments in the Burning Land during his first apostasy, his more recent preparation for his arrival in the Awakened City. Apart from this, he claims, he has not used his gift at all since his escape from Faal—never, not once. I found that very difficult to believe, and said so. He shrugged.

"It's true, whether you believe it or not. For one thing, it wasn't safe. Shaping can't be practiced discreetly—that's obvious even from small uses of it. Even inside my own house, I would have risked discovery." He paused. "I also feared how it might change me, if I used it freely."

"Madness and corruption, you mean, like the tales of the apostates of old?"

"No." He shook his head. "I haven't believed that for a long time, that a free ability inevitably drives a Shaper to such things. I feel no madness in myself, and never have. I saw no madness in the Shapers of Refuge, who were free all their lives. Hubris, perhaps—but hubris is not madness. Yet shaping is the very power Ârata used at creation—born into us in miniature, it's true, but far greater than any human ability. If you are capable of anything, what's to stop you from *doing* anything, apart from your own will, your own sense of right and wrong? Which in each man or woman is a different thing, and in some is barely a sense at all. Such power tempts the failings of our ash-natures, the pride and greed and cruelty we all possess. The danger of shaping is not that Shapers *must* misuse their gifts. It is that they might."

"Does it really make a difference? Whether it's shaping that corrupts the soul or the soul that corrupts shaping, the result is the same."

"No. For if you can yield, you can also resist."

"Did you fear yourself incapable of resisting, then?"

He did not reply at once. He had taken up the hem of his shirt and was smoothing it between his fingers. "It seems to me that there must be a middle way, a way between total freedom and absolute restriction. Unfettered shaping is perilous. But the Doctrine of Baushpar belittles the god's gift, makes a ghost of it. I think the Shapers of Refuge came close to a middle way, their shaping free and yet bound by oaths of service—"

"But there is Râvar. Who alone justifies every restriction of the Doctrine."

"But who's to say, if I'd never discovered Refuge, that Râvar would have lived anything but a blameless life? Of course, the danger is always there. I am not like Râvar . . . I am not . . . proud. Or cruel. But I have failings, many of them. What if the temptation were so subtle that I could not see it? What if I were to change, and not know? So I imagined the possibility of a middle way, but I didn't try to pursue it. You're right. I was afraid. I *am* afraid."

That raw honesty again. In spite of myself, it moved me. "It can't be easy to have such a thing within you and never set it free."

"But it *is* free. I see as a Shaper. I think as a Shaper. I experience the world as a Shaper. That's always been what I loved most about the gift, even when I was bound—the beauty it shows me. The beauty the god himself must have seen, when he made the world. The beauty that lives in all things, untouched by the Enemy's ash."

"Will that be enough, when all of this is over?"

"Do you mean, having finally begun to use my power, will I stop? No," he said. "I don't think I will."

Something in his voice suggested that he had only just that moment understood it. His words might have been a challenge, but they were not, nor did I hear them so. It seems strange now to remember. Yet as we spoke we had somehow passed beyond the ordinary world, in which he is a base and wretched sinner, and I am the implacable prosecutor of that sin.

He dropped his shirt hem and clasped his hands—which, I have only lately noticed, are scarred across the palms and fingers like Râvar's, though he is not perceptibly crippled. "You've never said why you and your Brother were in the Awakened City."

"We came to investigate Râvar's claim."

"There have been other claims like his. How many of them have the Brethren investigated—themselves, I mean, in person?"

"Not like his. It was a heresy more organized and consistent than any we have encountered in some time, with a leader who appeared to be an apostate Shaper." Of course I did not tell him the whole truth. I was not—am not—ready to confront the ramifications of that. "Even so, we did not expect what we found."

"How is it that your Brother fell to belief?"

"Vivaniya in this incarnation is . . . vulnerable to persuasion. As you know, Râvar is persuasive. I tried to intervene. I was not successful."

"And so your Brother left you there."

"Yes." I sighed. "Perhaps I should have feigned belief. But I could not force myself to such pretense, even in self-protection. Besides, I didn't yet know Râvar's true intent. I thought I was only to be a hostage—it never occurred to me he would dare to harm me. Although apparently he did not dare do so openly. He came alone to fetch us to the cave where you found us, after his City had departed. Even that creature Ardashir, who would have looked on my body-death and smiled, doesn't know what he did."

"Will any of your spirit-siblings heed your Brother?"

"One or two may. Most will not. Râvar is a clever boy, but not as clever as he imagines. He supposes we are all the same. He supposes the word of any of us will sway the rest. It isn't so. The harm he has done is all to my Brother."

I became aware that I was winding the tassels of my stole around my fingers; I let them fall.

"How did Utamnos die?" the apostate asked.

I told him some of it—how, soon after he was dispatched to Faal, my dear Brother took to his bed, how I sat by him as his spirit's hold upon its flesh-shell weakened. I did not speak of the fear he conceived before he left his body: that we had been mistaken in turning from news of Ârata's rising.

I used to wish he had clung to his shell long enough to know of Dâdar's and Vivaniya's return. Now I am glad, for it would have been false relief.

"I'd just come to Ninyâser when it happened," the apostate said. "I made an offering for him in the temple of Inriku." I nodded, remembering my Brother's devotion to that Aspect. "It always seemed appropriate that I should follow my new trade there."

"I'm fostering him," I said. "His new incarnation."

"I'm glad it's you."

That surprised me.

We had been talking for a long time. The moon had moved some distance in its circuit. The ever-present wind plucked at my stole; behind us the stream sang to itself. Before my tent, Reanu watched.

What I said next rose naturally out of what had already passed between us. Or so it seemed to me then. Now, writing it, I am not so sure.

"You have discovered in yourself a truth of history, Gyalo Amdo Samchen. Or, more accurately, a truth that history has lost."

He raised his eyes, which had been fixed on his clasped hands. "What truth?"

"That it is the soul that corrupts shaping, and not shaping that corrupts the soul. The free Shapers before the Shaper War, and the pagan Shapers who fought it, were not mad. But the horrors of the War gave rise to rumors of corruption and insanity, and it served our purpose, the Brethren's purpose, to let those rumors stand. The more the common people feared free shaping, the more possible it was to bring shaping into the keeping of the church. The more Shapers feared their own ability, the less likely it was that they would stray. We did not yet know, you see, how manita binds those who use it. Unfortunately, memories fade, and even immortal beings are vulnerable to prejudice. Many of my Brothers and Sisters have come to believe genuinely in the corrupting power of an untethered gift."

He sat silent in the flooding moonlight. His face, his hands, every part of him was completely still. I did not have the sense that he was shocked or angry or even particularly surprised. Yet there was something in the way he looked at me that made me—me, Sundit of the Brethren—want to look away.

"So Shapers are taught a lie," he said at last. "So that they may fear and hate the power in themselves. The power that was the god's own gift to humankind."

"One untruth, to uphold a far greater good. The danger of shaping is not a lie. The damage it did during the War was not a lie. The need to contain it is not a lie."

"Did you reveal the truth to the Shapers you freed to march on Refuge?"

"No," I said.

"That was not the first time, was it. Refuge was not the first time you released Shapers to do your will."

I think from the beginning I had known that it was more than curiosity that had drawn me out to him. But I cannot say how or when the balance between us had changed so greatly—to make what he asked seem judgment, and my answer, my honest answer, confession.

"No. It was not the first time."

"How many other times?"

"Seven," I said. "Only seven."

"*Only* seven? So you who made the law do not consider yourselves bound by it."

"In extremity, the law must sometimes be stretched."

"Stretched! Is that what you call it? Did you execute them, too, when you were done with them, those other Shapers?"

Of course we did. They knew what he knows: that there is a hidden world, not merely of their gift but of the Brethren's counsel. Mere apostates can be confined and dosed with manita, but there is no drug that can undo that other knowledge. I did not say this, however. I did not say anything at all.

He watched me. Once again, I felt judged. And here is the strange thing, perhaps the strangest thing about this strange evening (and perhaps I should not even write it down, but in these journals where I set the whole of my soul upon the page, I cannot lie, as I so often do in speech and action): His judgment did not anger me. Instead, it weighed on me, pressed on me, so that my muscles tensed and my breath came short. As if he somehow had the *right* to judge. As if I was required to bear his judgment.

He turned his face away, a dismissal as clear as words. I got to my feet without a word and returned to my tent. Reanu's watchful attention reached out like hands to draw me home. Beside him, I paused and glanced back. The apostate sat in profile, his back straight, his loose hair stirring in the wind. For an instant I almost thought I saw his lifelight, the pearly aura he described to me.

Of course it was only the moon, the moon and my own exhaustion. There's much I am not certain of. But I'm absolutely sure of that.

Gyalo

It took them ten days to cross the steppe, and another four to get to Darna. The Shaper administrator of the Âratist monastery there was stunned by the unannounced arrival of a Daughter of the Brethren, exhausted and on foot, accompanied by so small an entourage; but he assembled the horses and supplies Sundit demanded with admirable dispatch. Ha-tsun, who had fallen sick, remained in the infirmary, with one of the Tapati to see her home once she recovered; the rest of the party rode hard for Ninyâser. They made good speed along the Great South Way, commandeering new mounts as they needed them. When the coin the Darna administrator had given them ran out, Sundit left notes of value sealed with her signet. If, as was occasionally apparent, those they encountered were not friendly to the church, they still did not dare refuse her.

They reached Ninyâser in just over three weeks, a little over half the normal travel time. They entered the city as Gyalo had departed it more than five months earlier, by the King's Gate—which was not really a gate at all, for Ninyâser was not a walled city, but a triumphal arch built by King Vandapâya IV to commemorate the twentieth year of his reign. Only a few months after its completion he had been deposed by the Caryaxists, who, aware perhaps of the irony, had allowed the Gate to stand, with its heroic reliefs of Vandapâya's deeds and florid words of dedication inlaid in bronze on the entablature. Passing into its shadow, tipped hugely across the road by the late-afternoon sun, Gyalo felt as if he were dreaming, or waking from a dream; for a moment he was certain that if he turned aside at the Year-Canal and rode to his own house, Axane and Chokyi would be waiting there.

Sundit's tattoo was concealed by a wide-brimmed peasant hat, and the

Tapati were swathed in cloaks and hoods. Only Drolma and Gyalo—the fugitive, the renegade—had no need to hide their faces. Traffic was heavy, and it was near sunset by the time they crossed the Canal by the Golden Bridge, which led directly to the Âratist complex. The residence of the administrator was located at the compound's rear, a graceful stucco building with a tiered roof of yellow tile. Reanu flung back his hood and dismounted, and beat on the door with the flat of his hand. The startled servant girl who answered went running for her master, who also came running, falling to his knees when he saw Sundit.

"Great is Ârata," he gasped. "Great is his Way."

"Go in light," Sundit said wearily.

The administrator scrambled to his feet. "Old One, I did not expect you for several weeks! The Son Vivaniya said you had been delayed."

"My Brother was here?" Sundit's voice was suddenly sharp.

"Not three days ago, Old One. He stayed the night and traveled on in haste."

"I see. Well, I will be remaining for longer than that. I have business in Ninyâser. I hope I may impose upon your hospitality."

"I am honored, Old One! Please, come in!"

The next morning, Sundit composed a letter to Santaxma requesting audience on a matter of vital importance, sealed it with her signet, and gave it to Reanu to deliver to the King's chamberlain. The Tapati captain departed bareheaded and uncloaked, in all the glorious complication of his tattoos. Like their arrival incognito, this was strategy: That Sundit would enter the city in secret attested to the urgency of her errand, but her use of Reanu as her messenger ensured that important people were aware both of her presence and of her approach to the King. "He thus cannot refuse to receive me," she had told Gyalo, "as might be his first impulse, things being as they are. And though he will make me wait, for he won't want it to seem I can command him, he cannot afford to delay too long."

She did not send word to her spirit-siblings, either of her presence in Ninyâser or her mission to the King. A summons to Baushpar would surely follow, and time was too short, either to debate her actions or refuse to debate them. "Sometimes," she said wryly, "it's easier to explain a thing after you have done it."

In the afternoon she sent for Gyalo. She was sitting on a granite bench in the administrator's private garden, a small space carefully engineered to seem artless and natural, as if it had sprung into being unassisted by human craft, though to Gyalo's Shaper senses its man-made artifice was glaringly apparent.

One of the Tapati watched discreetly from a little distance. Sundit's scalp was smoothly shaven and she was freshly dressed, but the rigors of the journey were apparent in the pallor of her face, the bruised skin beneath her eyes.

"It's done," she said. "It took Reanu all the day and almost an entire purse. Once his face alone would have been enough." She smiled a wry smile. "But the letter is delivered into the chamberlain's hands."

"Good."

She patted the bench. "Keep me company."

It was a request, not a command—she had long ago stopped trying to command him. Gyalo sat, feeling the coolness of the stone through the coarse fabric of his trousers. He wore a servant's castoffs, having refused the Âratist garments he had been offered the night before.

"Are you prepared?" Sundit asked.

"Yes."

"Are you afraid?"

"Not for myself."

"You can still change your mind, you know. I'm still willing to tell him you are tethered."

"We've already settled this." Weeks ago, in fact, before they left the steppe.

"Yes, but I have been thinking about it since."

"No. There's too great a risk he won't believe you. It's true I voluntarily retethered myself after the Burning Land, but I was still a vowed Âratist then. What reason would I have to do it now? And if you present me as captured and forcibly retethered, a prisoner facing a lifetime of arrest, how plausible is it that I would have shared my knowledge with you? The whole of my credibility rests on the truth of who I am and the fact that I make no attempt to hide it. That means I must go before him as I am, a free Shaper with no intention of becoming otherwise."

"What if he thinks I have brought you to do him harm?"

She had never raised that possibility before. It gave him pause. "Have things really come to such a pass?"

She raised one shoulder in a not-quite shrug. "He's a clever, watchful man, who might do such a thing himself if he had the opportunity."

"No. If that were your intent, why would you reveal me? You'd present me as an ordinary man, a disaffected citizen of the Awakened City perhaps. The truth testifies to the honesty of your intent as much as it does to mine."

"This is beyond perilous for you."

"It's a little late to worry about that." He did not try to disguise the sharpness of his voice. "Besides, I can protect myself."

"That I know."

Sundit watched the gazing pool before them, where the backs of carp flashed gold and black and orange in the water. The sky was overcast; in the pearly light her lapis aura seemed especially intense. Her sun tattoo was blood-dark on her forehead.

"These arguments of yours are sensible enough," she said. "But the reality, I think, is that you simply cannot bear to lie."

"I can lie when I have to."

"Can you? I've always wondered, in Baushpar, why you told the truth about your apostasy. You'd retethered yourself. Your companions would never have betrayed you. If you hadn't confessed, we never would have known."

He was silent in surprise.

"It could have been so different for you, Gyalo, if you had only lied."

"But you would have questioned. If I'd told you we survived the desert on luck and skill alone, a Shaper and his companions cast on the direst circumstances in the most hostile environment in Galea, would you have believed me? No. And those doubts would have brought you to the same point the truth did."

"Perhaps." A dove winged down to rest on the far side of the gazing pool. Her eyes followed its descent. "Do you know the tyranny of a long life like mine?"

"No."

"The inflexible straightness of time. It is a rod at whose end one always stands, unable to reach back."

She turned to look into his face. He had known her a little when he still served the Brethren. He knew her far better now—from the hardships of the journey, which had both tested and revealed her steadfast, stubborn character, and from the conversations in which she had nightly engaged him as they traveled. She told him of politics, of the rifts and conflicts between her Brothers and Sisters; he described the world of his Shaper senses, about which she possessed an inexhaustible curiosity. None of what he said to her was cathartic, as on the night he had condemned her and her spirit-siblings. None of what she shared with him was revelatory, as on the night she had admitted the Brethren's long pattern of secret rule. Yet there was an honesty to these discussions, an engagement, such as he had not shared with anyone except Axane. Sundit had handed him the truth like a gift—a truth he had long suspected, but had never thought to know for certain. He had told her things about himself that he had never admitted aloud to another human being—that no other human being, perhaps, could fully comprehend. In that there was a kind of balance;

and also, strangely, in their mutual rejection, he the apostate she condemned, she the ruler he repudiated. A peculiar bond had grown between them, less kind than friendship, more intimate than companionship.

His view of her had altered in another way as well. His interrogation in Baushpar after he returned from the Burning Land had revealed the Brethren in all the rivalry and prejudice and pettiness and spite they normally concealed from their mortal servants—an absolute and utter *humanness* that had seemed to him, then, profoundly at odds with the wisdom and experience that should inform such ancient souls. It had been that, as much as the failure of faith that caused them to turn from the truth he gave them, that brought him to doubt their immortality. But in his daily association with Sundit, in his experience of her human will and human anger and human weakness and human courage, he found himself urged paradoxically toward belief. He had begun to think that what he had seen in Baushpar was not contradiction, but contrast—a disjunction that only threw the truth into sharper relief.

It was not something he would ever have expected. It was not something he welcomed. But these days he was often conscious of the immortal Daughter behind the flesh-mask of the aging woman. She was there now, in Sundit's level gaze—ancient, unfathomable, the long shadow of her dark deeds stretched out behind her, the many atrocities and betrayals of the Brethren—who had also, it could not be denied, ruled across the centuries with great wisdom.

It was she, at last, who broke the gaze.

He took the evening meal with the Tapati, then returned to his little chamber under the eaves. He had been allowed to occupy it alone; over the course of the journey Reanu and the others had more or less stopped keeping watch on him. The room's owner, a maidservant, had been turned out to accommodate him, leaving behind one of her sashes and a small shrine to the Aspect Tane, Patron of crops and the moon. Tane was the Aspect his own long-dead mother had favored; for her sake, he had brought a little offering to place in Tane's brass bowl, a perfect green plum selected from a platter of them in the kitchen.

He went to lean on the sill of the single window, whose screen he had pushed back to admit the breeze. The days were still hot, but summer was nearly at an end, and the nights were growing cool. Outside in the deepening dusk, the windows of the monasteries and guesthouses glowed with lamp- and candlelight. The first stars spangled the vault of the sky.

His mind returned to Sundit. He had told her the truth that afternoon: All his dread was bound to others, to Axane and Chokyi and Diasarta, and to a lesser extent, to the hundreds or thousands or tens of thousands who would suffer if Râvar were not halted. For himself he was not afraid, or not very much.

South of Darna, the party had come under bandit attack. A dozen horsemen had swept down from the crags that rose beyond the track, shouting like demons, sunlight flashing from their swords and knives. Apui and Lopalo and Omarau drew their own knives and prepared to stand; Reanu seized Sundit and bore her back along the track, shouting for Gyalo to follow. But Gyalo, gripped by an instinct that partook of no conscious intent, strode forward and struck the earth before the horsemen with his shaping will, breaking the ground and sending men and horses tumbling, then setting them to terrified flight with fusillades of lightning and volleys of thunder. As the last of them vanished over the crest of the hills from which they had come, he hurled a final sizzling bolt, sending a great explosion of grass and earth and stones high into the air.

In the sudden silence he turned to the others. The Tapati stood frozen, their faces stark with shock. When he stepped toward them, Apui and Omarau actually fell back. Down the track, still clasped in Reanu's arms, Sundit squinted at him, as if she were seeing something very bright or very far away.

He had thought, in her fascination with his shaping, that she would speak of it. She never did. He had dismissed his first thought, that she was afraid; since then, he had wondered.

It marked the beginning of a change in the Tapatis' attitude toward him. He had awed them; more, he had defended them, and if that were not enough to make them trust him, it was at least enough to convince them he was neither mad nor malign. More important, it marked a shift within himself. For nearly three years he had held his shaping captive. If not for Râvar, it seemed quite possible he might never have returned to practice; and the practice to which he did return was small and joyless, crippled by his fear. In the hills he found the joy again. He drew his shaping like a bow, set it free with exquisite precision and control. He did not hesitate or hold back; in instinctive response he tapped the well of his power as he had never, in conscious practice, given himself leave to do. It was revelatory. It was ecstatic.

Afterward, for the sake of the temptation he knew was there, he asked Ârata for forgiveness, if his actions or his delight in them were wrong. But in his heart he could not believe they were. The first time he had ever released his unfettered gift, dying of thirst in the Burning Land, he had experienced that same epiphanic recognition, the same sense of knowing himself entire. In his dread of misusing his power, he had forgotten. He had set his fear above the truth that above all should have guided him: that what lived in him was sacred. Surely that, too, was a sin.

Whatever came of it, one thing was irrevocably changed: He could never fear physical risk again. He knew in his body, in his bones, what he had before known only with his intellect: No rope or chain could hold him. No prison could confine him. He could shatter the sword as it left the scabbard, unmake the spear as it flew from the hand.

I am a man of power.

The awareness of it filled him like an indrawn breath.

When it was full dark he left the window, sat cross-legged on the floor, and meditated for the space of two thousand breaths. Then he stripped off his clothes and lay down on the bed. Closing his hand around Axane's bracelet, he began his nightly devotions to her dreaming, whispering to her all that had passed that day. At last he stretched his free hand up through the transparent substance of the air, his pearl-lit palm cupping emptiness, imagining her Dream-fingers brushing his.

"I love you."

The summons came at noon two days later, in the form of a courier with a mounted escort and several curtained palanquins borne by servants in royal livery. Sundit dismissed all but one of the palanquins, which she occupied with Gyalo, while the Tapati came behind on foot, their tattoos unconcealed. The courier was dismayed, but did not dare to argue.

They scythed through the busy streets, the horsemen riding ahead to part the traffic. Sundit had looped the curtains up so she could be seen; she wore new Âratist garments of heavy silk and her simulacrum, normally hidden beneath her stole, lay on her breast, its glass replica of the Blood flashing fire when the light caught it. Ninyâser was a large city, used to processions; many people barely paused to note their passage. But others, recognizing the Tapati or Sundit's tattoo or even her face, from one of the little portraits of the Sons and Daughters that were popular devotional items, knelt and made the sign of Ârata, or ran beside the palanquin begging blessings, which Sundit dispensed with regal grace.

The towering brick walls that enclosed the grounds of the Hundred-Domed Palace were broken by seven massive gates, each named for a different gem. The procession entered through the Ruby Gate, which gave onto the private portion of the great estate. Its glades and paths and lawns were much like those in the public preserve, where Gyalo and Axane and Chokyi had wandered one sunny afternoon before Râvar reached out and tore their lives apart. Gyalo felt the memory touch him with fleeting sweetness as the exquisite prospects flowed past the palanquin's open sides.

They halted amid a spike-leaved stand of bamboo. Reanu came to offer Sundit his arm. Gyalo followed, adjusting the long tassels of his sash and feeling the pinch of badly fitted shoes. His garments, too, were new, bought for him by Sundit so the King would not be insulted by his appearance.

"Old One." The courier bowed. "The King waits."

Beyond the bamboo's filigree shade, a slope led down to a moss-banked stream, sweeping in a graceful arc toward a copse of birches that breathed a light as pale as their blanched trunks. Embraced within the stream's curve stood a circular wooden summerhouse, with gilded pillars and a conical roof of amethyst-glazed tile. A quarter company of the King's Guard waited before it.

Sundit led the way across a little bridge, passing into the shadow of the ancient bo tree that fanned its branches high above the summerhouse. Moss lay green and springy underfoot, ridged with massive roots. The Guard captain, a barrel-chested man with a milky lifelight much like Gyalo's own, came forward and knelt.

"Great is Ârata. Great is his Way."

"Go in light," Sundit replied.

The captain rose. "Old One, it is the King's pleasure to receive with you not only this man"—he nodded toward Gyalo—"as you have requested, but also one of your guards. He bids me ask that any weapons they carry be given into my keeping."

Reanu reached beneath his flawlessly draped stole and withdrew his knives, which he tossed in the air and caught by the blades and offered to the captain hilt first, his eyes never leaving the other man's face. The captain received them, matching him gaze for gaze, and handed them to a subordinate. He turned to Gyalo.

"I carry no weapon," Gyalo said. The thought came to him, irresistible: *Except myself.*

"You will forgive me," said the captain, "but I must be sure." He ran his hands efficiently along Gyalo's body, then stood back and bowed. "Please, Old One. Proceed."

Sundit stepped forward. Reanu followed, and Gyalo. In a few moments, for the first time since his release, he would voluntarily admit the truth of his apostasy to one who did not already know it. The inhibition of a fugitive tensed along his jaw. Anticipation coiled beneath his breastbone like hot wire.

He closed his fingers against the throbbing of his palms, and to the silent god sent a silent prayer: *Ârata, grant me eloquence.*

The summerhouse's golden pillars gleamed against the dimness within; the ceiling was gilded also, hung with tasseled wind bells. At the precise center of the floor stood a massive carven chair, with two guards standing to attention behind it, amber and azure lifelights overlapping in an oily wash of green. In the chair, Santaxma sat waiting—Santaxma, who had conquered the Caryaxists, who had restored the Brethren to Baushpar, then turned their need against them, bending the immortal leaders of the church of Ârata to his will. Santaxma, the blasphemer King.

Sundit halted. As was her right as a ruler of the church, she made no obeisance. Gyalo and Reanu sank to their knees and bowed their heads to the floor. There was a pause, underscored rather than broken by the chiming of the bells. Gyalo smelled the honey scent of the wax that glossed the floorboards; his eyes traced its patterns, layer upon layer, and beneath them the dense, grained structure of the wood.

"Great is Ârata," the King said. "Great is his Way."

It was a victory for Sundit: She had forced him to speak first. "Go in light, Majesty."

"Your men may rise."

They obeyed. Santaxma's eyes, close-set and dark, assessed Reanu, then, more lingeringly, Gyalo. Gyalo's skin prickled, but no recognition dawned in the King's face.

"You are welcome in Ninyâser, Old One." Like most Arsacian nobles Santaxma was light-skinned, with handsome, fleshy features. He wore flowing clothes of sky-blue silk; gold clips held back his long, waxed curls, and jewels glinted at his wrists and neck and hung heavy from his ears. His lifelight was a silver cloud, shimmering like falling water. "And in my home. As you see, but for my guards and your men we are alone, as you requested."

"Your graciousness delights me, Majesty."

"Old One, you have indicated that this is a matter of some urgency. I suggest, therefore, that we dispense with the customary etiquette, with tedious pleasantries about your journey and my household, with time spent in the exchange of gifts and the consumption of refreshment, and come directly to the issue at hand. Will you agree?"

Since there was no sign of servants, or any furnishing in the summerhouse but his chair, it was obvious that this was not a suggestion at all. Sundit chose to ignore the insult. "Majesty, the matter is urgent indeed, and greater haste profits us all."

Santaxma smiled a small tight smile. A breeze swept through the summerhouse; the bells sang a silvery crescendo. "Speak, then."

"Are you aware, Majesty, that a man has lately arisen who calls himself the Next Messenger?"

"There were rabble-rousers in the city a year ago who claimed to speak of such a man. On my order, they were expelled."

"Where those departed, Majesty, others returned, more circumspect in their proselytizing. We Brethren were concerned by the reports we received . . ."

She described her and Vivaniya's embassy to the Awakened City, Vivaniya's conversion, and what had happened after, omitting only the details of how she and her men had escaped the cave in which Râvar prisoned them. Santaxma listened without interrupting. He had disposed himself with elaborate casualness, one leg stretched before him, his left elbow resting upon the arm of his chair and his chin supported on that hand—a pose that was as much a show of ease as ease itself, for there was nothing casual about his direct black gaze.

"So this so-called Next Messenger is not a god-crazed madman, but a deliberate pretender," he said when Sundit paused, crisply summing up. "An apostate Shaper, now traveling with his followers through Arsace, seeking to convert others to heretical belief and to depose the Brethren." He nodded. "I am aware of his advance. My Dreamers have been tracking a large train of people moving up the Great South Way. At present it is some days short of Darna."

One of Santaxma's great advantages during the war he had waged on the failing Caryaxist regime had been his corps of Dreamers—not Âratist-style Dreamers, whose duties were chiefly mystical and who were trained to Dream in signs and symbols impenetrable to those not experienced in interpreting them, but Dreamers like Axane, who saw the world simply and directly through their sleep. In peacetime he continued to employ them, in the tradition of his royal ancestors, to keep watch over the land he ruled.

"That he is apostate I suspected from all the reports I have received, but my Dreamers have not been able positively to confirm it. I thank you for the warning, Old One. I shall tell my commanders to be prepared."

"Majesty, do you plan some action?"

"Of course. We cannot have a rabble of pilgrims overrunning Arsace, or a false Messenger stirring the people to heresy. The garrison at Darna will arrest him and disperse his followers. I trust the monastery there will oblige us with a supply of manita."

"Majesty, I wish it were so easy. This is no ordinary apostate. He is extremely skilled, extremely powerful. A conventional offensive, even with manita, may not be enough. And you cannot risk failure. It is not his intent merely to play out this charade of Messengerhood. He means to lay your kingdom waste."

"Lay it waste?" The King smiled, in the manner of a not-very-patient nephew humoring an eccentric aunt. "Forgive me, Old One, these are ecclesiastical matters, which you of course understand better than I. But a single apostate surely does not pose so great a threat, no matter how robust his strength or malign his ambition. Why in any case should he embrace so dark an objective? What has Arsace done to him, that he should detest it so?"

"Majesty," Sundit said, with a sharpness no ordinary mortal would have dared to show, "you have not heard the entire tale. This man I've brought before you has firsthand knowledge of the pretender, his power and his intent, and will confirm all I have said."

Even from where he stood, Gyalo saw the flare in the King's eyes. "Indeed," he said tightly. "Why is he standing silent, then?"

"Majesty, this man freed my people and me from our confinement in the pretender's stronghold, in which otherwise we surely would have died. Along the way of our journey he saved our lives again—"

"Can he not tell me these things himself?" The King did not trouble to conceal his impatience.

"Majesty, it is important that you know the precise circumstances that have brought him before you."

Her words were more strategy. She would praise Gyalo, speak of the services he had done her and her people, hoping by this catalogue of virtues to soften Santaxma's shock when he discovered a free Shaper standing not twenty paces from him. But to Gyalo it was already apparent that things were going wrong. In Santaxma's subtle slights of etiquette, in his patronizing manner, in his narrowed eyes and tightened mouth, Gyalo read a pattern, clear as the world-patterns revealed by his Shaper senses: the King's dislike of Sundit, his resentment at being manipulated into receiving her, his growing annoyance with her warnings of peril, which he clearly thought he understood better than she—all of which might turn, in the moment of revelation, not to shock but to rage. Instinct filled Gyalo; as on the track south of Darna, he let it carry him.

"Majesty," he said across Sundit's words. He took a step forward and fell to his knees. "I beg a boon of you."

The King's head snapped toward him. The guards tensed like puppets whose strings had suddenly jerked taut. Sundit pivoted, her lips still parted, her face a mask of surprise. For a moment there was no sound but the soft chiming of the wind bells.

"It was my impression," the King said, "that you were here to grant a boon to me. Namely, this information that the Daughter Sundit judges so very vital."

"Majesty, I will gladly give you that information—"

"What you are doing?" Sundit hissed.

"And I will tell you who I am to give it." He raised his voice. "But first, order one of your guards to come to me, to draw his sword and set it at my back and stand ready to run me through without a second's hesitation."

Santaxma's plucked black brows rose. "That is your boon?"

"Majesty, it is."

"I confess myself intrigued." The King lifted one ringed hand. "Roas. Do it."

The azure guard strode forward, his sword whispering from his sash. He came up behind Gyalo; Gyalo felt the sword point come to rest between his shoulder blades, a pressure just short of pain.

"Is that satisfactory?" A smile pulled at the corners of the King's mouth. "Perhaps you should tell me under what circumstances he is to kill you."

"If at any point I take any action that imperils you or anyone in this room. As I speak to you, Majesty, I will know my life is forfeit if I do harm. As you hear me, you will know the same."

The smile widened. "Are you really such a dangerous fellow?"

"You may judge for yourself, Majesty. You've not shown that you remember my face, but you have seen me before—two and a half years ago, to be exact, in the Pavilion of the Sun in Baushpar. My name is Gyalo Amdo Samchen. I am the Shaper the Brethren sent into the Burning Land. I am—"

"The apostate." Santaxma's amusement had vanished. "The heretic. I remember. You were imprisoned." He frowned. "You have been released?"

"No, Majesty. I escaped my imprisonment and have been living free ever since." The King's face seemed frozen. "I am apostate once more, fully so. I kneel before you a free Shaper."

The guard behind him audibly drew in his breath. The pressure of the sword vanished for an instant, then returned, a deeper bite this time, on the edge of thrust. "Majesty?" the man said softly.

"Not yet." The King had abandoned his nonchalant pose; both hands rested on the chair arms now, and his feet were square on the floor. There was tension in his voice, but no apparent fear. "Do you mean me harm, Gyalo Amdo Samchen?"

"No, Majesty. On the Blood of Ârata I swear it."

Santaxma's eyes flicked to Sundit. "You know of this." It was not a question. "It was the reason for your tedious introduction."

"Yes, Majesty. I have known it since he unmade the stone that imprisoned me and my servants."

"Perhaps I should perceive a mortal insult here, that you would bring an untethered apostate before me."

"Majesty, perceive instead the urgency of my warning. Think on what it means for me to ally with such a man."

"Indeed." The King nodded. "I am aware of the anathema he represents to you and your kin. Though that can cut many ways. Yet if need explains your tolerance of him, what explains his of you? Tell me, Gyalo Amdo Samchen, why would an untethered Shaper keep company with a Daughter of the Brethren? Do you plan to submit yourself to the church again?"

"No, Majesty." The sword point had penetrated Gyalo's skin; he could feel blood trickling down his back. "I am free, and mean to remain so. But the Daughter and I share a common cause. Like her, I have come to give you warning."

"Against your own kind. Against an apostate."

"Majesty, he is a Shaper, but he is not my kind. Nor is he apostate, as I will explain if you allow it. Majesty, the risk I take in revealing myself demands your belief. This is why I asked that your man set his sword at my back—to make that risk explicit."

"Not so explicit if you could shatter the sword before it pierces you."

"I don't know if I could, Majesty. I've never before tried to unmake a thing I could not see."

It was the truth. The King regarded him with unblinking obsidian eyes. Gyalo's heart drummed; the edges of his vision shimmered. His scarred palms burned.

"If this is a ruse," Santaxma said, "it's too complex for credibility. I will hear what you have to say." He pointed a gold-heavy finger at Gyalo's chest. "But don't think I do not take you at your word. If you try to rise, if you so much as lift your hand to wipe the sweat from your face, your life *will* be forfeit. Roas is admirably skilled. He can run you through twice in the time it takes to blink." The sword point dug deeper; Gyalo clenched his teeth. Santaxma leaned back in his chair. "Very well. Proceed."

"Majesty, if you recall, I discovered a settlement in the Burning Land, a settlement called Refuge."

"I remember. What has that to do with this?"

"It will become apparent, Majesty. The people of Refuge followed a heresy. They believed that Ârdaxcasa had risen and Ârata had woken to oppose him, and their renewed battle had destroyed the world beyond the Range of Clouds. Like true Âratists, they waited for the Next Messenger—not for news of Ârata's rising, but rather for word of his victory over the Enemy. This Messenger then would lead them back to the outside world, where they would remake the human race. When I arrived, many of them mistook me for that Messenger. Others thought me one of Ârdaxcasa's demons—including one very powerful young Shaper called Râvar."

The King's eyes flickered with comprehension. "Are you saying that the heretic on the Great South Way is one of the untethered Shapers of Refuge?"

"Yes, Majesty. Râvar survived Refuge's destruction, along with a woman named Axane."

The King's eyes shifted to Sundit. "It would seem you and your spirit-siblings were not so successful as you thought."

"We did not know," Sundit said quietly. "We had no way of knowing."

He watched her a moment, his face like stone. Then he turned back to Gyalo. "Continue."

"In his rage, in the arrogance of his power, Râvar swore vengeance for his people. He would come upon Arsace as a false Messenger, as he believed I had been sent to Refuge as a false Messenger. He would wreak havoc upon Arsace, as Arsace had wreaked havoc on Refuge. And especially, he would punish the Brethren, whom he blamed for his people's death. He and Axane traveled back across the Burning Land. When they reached Thuxra City, he used his shaping to destroy it, claiming it as the act of destruction in Ârata's Promise."

"You expect me to believe that? A single Shaper?"

"Free all his life, Majesty, trained from adolescence in techniques devised by Refuge's original Shapers to enable them to survive a hostile land. With my own eyes I saw their strength—and felt it, too, for it was a storm called by a Shaper that destroyed the expedition of which I was a part. It was no ordinary gift that brought Thuxra down—Râvar's ability is very great, far greater than any of his fellows'. But it was his power, and his alone. I know this is so. Axane, who is now my wife, witnessed it."

"This woman Axane is your wife?" For the first time, the King seemed taken aback.

"Yes, Majesty." Gyalo described how she had found him in Ninyâser, how Râvar had stolen her and Chokyi, how he had tried and failed to save them. How Râvar had captured him and taunted him and set him free. All the while he felt the pressure of Roas's sword, the slow crawl of blood down his back. "Until I stood before him, I did not truly believe he could succeed. I believe it now, Majesty. I believe it utterly."

"Do his followers know this?"

"His second may. Ardashir, the man they call the First Disciple. The rest know nothing."

"He will surely lose them when they learn."

"Majesty, they think he is half a god. What can a god do wrong? Whatever he tells them, they will believe it."

"He commands not just their awe, Majesty, but their love." Sundit spoke again. "I saw it clearly while I was in his City. There is a fire in him. I felt it, my Brother felt it—yes, and fell to it, just as his mortal followers did. If he can win a soul twelve centuries old, what soul is safe from him? Majesty, you know the truth now. This is what you face—an extraordinary shaping gift wielded by a mind and heart steeped in rage and hate, by a soul so black there is no deed dark enough for it to fear. For the safety of your realm, you must stand against this man. You cannot let him pass."

The King sat silent. His chin was on his palm again, his eyes narrow. His lifelight flowed around him like rain on beaten silver. At the roof, the bells dropped clear notes into the air.

"I should not be surprised," Santaxma said at last. "The Caryaxists in their zeal sought to starve the Way of Ârata, as one might starve a fire by covering it with earth. Instead, it burned downward, into bedrock, and when the earth was dug away it blazed up again, twice as high as before. You and your kin"—his black gaze flicked to Sundit—"were supposed to contain it, this fever of released faith. You swore to put an end to the visions in the temples, to the false miracles and the mad holy men, to this damnable tide of apocalypteering. You swore you would eradicate this heretical rumor that it was not my skill and perseverance that wrought the Caryaxists' fall, but the god working through me, using me as his instrument. But it has been more than five years, and still the miracles fester and the rumors boil, and a wild-eyed prophet rises every week to stir the people in the marketplace. You have failed your trust. No." He leveled a jeweled finger at Sundit's face. "Say nothing. And this is the culmination of your failure: this pretender, who survived your bloody desert massacre, whose followers are the very exemplars of the Caryaxist-bred fanaticism against which you and your kin have shown yourself helpless. And now you come to me, and expect me to set right what you have made wrong, and for the sake of my people, my poor beleaguered people, I have no choice but to agree."

An echoing silence followed on this bitter speech.

"Well." The King's face was hard, remote. "I will think on what I have heard, and consider how to proceed. Roas, put up your sword and see these people out."

The sword point withdrew, leaving behind a burning echo of itself. Gyalo prostrated himself; beside him, Reanu did the same. Sundit turned, straight as a spear; she spoke no word of farewell, not even the invocation of the god.

They paused outside the summerhouse so that Reanu could receive his knives back. In the palanquin, Sundit leaned back her head and closed her eyes, allowing herself at last to show her desperate weariness. Gyalo's wound throbbed; he sat bent forward, so his blood-wet tunic would not touch the palanquin's silk padding. He, too, was exhausted, light-headed with the release of tension. Reanu had looped the curtains down, isolating them in a stifling red box.

"He's partly right, you know." Sundit spoke without opening her eyes. "The Caryaxists did more than merely suppress the Way of Ârata. A plant that grows and seeds in secret for eighty years does not breed true. We did know that. We expected change. We expected damage. But we didn't expect the extent of it, or how we would be blamed." She sighed. "He, whom many revile as a blasphemer, should understand how difficult it is to make peace when you first must win back the hearts of those you need to pacify."

They turned a corner. The palanquin jolted. Gyalo grasped at the curtains to steady himself.

"I used to tutor him in Rimpang, when we were all in exile. He could not sit still for more than a quarter of an hour at a time . . . I called him my little lightning bolt. I used to tell him of our father Marduspida, who hated his lessons, too. 'But I'm not going to be a prophet, Sister Sunni,' he'd say, 'I'm going to be a soldier. A soldier doesn't need to read books.'" Again she sighed. "I never understood how he came to dislike me so." She opened her eyes. "Was it planned, what you did today?"

"No." It was an effort to speak. "I saw his impatience. His anger. It seemed to me his interest must be seized a different way, or he would become too angry to hear us out."

"*Could* you have unmade that sword?"

Gyalo shook his head. "I told him the truth."

"So you were prepared to let yourself be killed."

"I had to offer something real."

She regarded him. The sun shone through the curtains, casting a red gloom across her face, darkening her tattoo. At last she closed her eyes again.

"Remind me to get someone to tend your back."

Gyalo

Gyalo dreamed that night of Teispas. The captain was unwounded; he wore the dress uniform of the Exile Army and his black hair was smoothly combed and braided. Gyalo stood beside him in the moonlight, on the second-floor balcony of the dwelling of Thuxra City's military administrator, where he and the exploration party had stopped before their departure into the Burning Land. *Did you remember?* Teispas said, staring out at the shadows of the administrator's garden, and Gyalo, puzzled, asked, *Remember what?* And Teispas replied, angry: *You don't ask the proper questions,* then turned and walked away and would not pause, no matter how Gyalo called after him. His red coat shredded as he went, revealing the lash marks on his back.

Gyalo woke uneasy in the first gray light of dawn, his scars aching. Just a dream, he reassured himself. He had not forgotten anything. Everything had been said.

That afternoon a palanquin arrived to fetch Sundit to the King. She remained for several hours. Since she did not summon Gyalo afterward to tell him what had transpired, he sought out Reanu, who had accompanied her.

"He asked questions," the big Tapati said. "About the pretender. Also about you. He's very interested in you."

"What did he want to know?"

"What do you think? About your shaping."

"What did she say?"

"She told him about the cave. About the bandits. He questioned me, too."

"And what did you say?"

"What she did. More or less."

"I see."

Reanu regarded Gyalo. With his gravity and bulk he gave the impression of an older man, but Gyalo guessed he was probably no more than twenty-five. He was handsome beneath his tattoos, with a well-shaped mouth and large, heavy-lidded eyes. At his throat he wore the amulet of the Aspect Skambys, the soldiers' Aspect, Patron of war and weather; it and the thong that tied it were the exact blue-black of his tattoos, and it had been some time before Gyalo realized they were not a permanent part of his anatomy.

"It took some grit to do what you did yesterday."

Gyalo shrugged.

"Was it true about the sword? Were you really not sure you could shatter it?"

"It was true."

Reanu nodded, thoughtfully.

Two more days passed. There was no reason, really, to remain, and Gyalo urgently desired to be on his way. Yet he could not bring himself to leave without being certain that he and Sundit had been successful. "I'm sorry," he whispered to Axane, at night before he slept. "Just a little longer."

On the fourth day another palanquin arrived, with a summons not for Sundit but for Gyalo. Word was brought to him in the garden; he sent the servant away, then spent some minutes considering what to do. Did the King simply wish to question him, as he had Sundit and Reanu? Was this something more? A dozen scenarios chased through his mind, from an arrest with manita to something more permanent. Yet if he refused to go, what impact would that have on his and Sundit's embassy? At last he rose and went out to the palanquin just as he was, in his coarse servant's clothing, his hair loose over his shoulders.

He was borne not to the gardens but to the palace itself. In an elaborately columned inner courtyard, a liveried functionary was waiting to conduct him through a magnificent maze of halls and corridors; the functionary's disapproval of Gyalo's uncourtly appearance was clear, but he gave no sign of realizing that he was in the presence of an apostate. They came at last to a pair of lacquered doors with ornate silver hinges. The functionary pushed them open and bowed low, and spoke Gyalo's name. Then he stepped aside, gesturing for Gyalo to go in.

The chamber was large, its ivory-paneled walls painted with a series of life-size hunting scenes—of which, but for their varicolored auras, the guards positioned in each corner might have been a part. Sun fell through a long row of windows; the air was faintly hazed with the smoke of the incense that burned on a small brazier. There was no furnishing but a large table at the room's center, and a smaller table nearby. Santaxma stood waiting, the rain cloud of his lifelight shimmering around him, his hair hidden beneath a golden turban and his silken garments glowing several shades of crimson.

Gyalo prostrated himself, every sense alert.

"Rise," the King said, pleasantly. He gestured to the smaller table, which held an enameled jug, a pair of matching goblets, and several plates of small edibles. "May I offer you refreshment? Perhaps some wine?"

"Wine would be welcome, Majesty."

Santaxma crossed briskly to the table, his gold-embroidered indoor shoes silent on the tile, and poured both goblets full. He held one toward Gyalo, who came forward to take it. Their eyes met. Santaxma's were knowing, entirely unafraid.

"Come." Santaxma returned to the larger table. "See what I have here."

It was an enormous, exquisitely detailed map of Arsace, drawn with colored inks on heavy parchment. The King set his goblet on the table's edge and leaned over the map in a whisper of red silks, his pear-shaped ruby earrings swinging.

"According to my Dreamers," he said, "the pretender and his band are approximately here." His manicured forefinger came to rest on a point just north of Darna, on the black-ink ribbon of the Great South Way.

"You let him pass Darna, Majesty?"

Santaxma smiled. "I did. Thus far they are advancing peacefully, moving at a rate of less than ten miles a day—not surprising for such a large train. Now, I believe he will hold this route all the way to Ninyâser." His finger stroked up the road's great length, more than half the length of Arsace itself. "It's the easiest and most obvious way for a large party heading for Baushpar—also, as the Daughter Sundit has pointed out to me, the towns and cities where his missionaries have been sighted all lie along the Great South Way—Darna, Orimene, Sardis, Hâras, Abaxtra, and of course Ninyâser—" He tapped each, lightly, as he named it. "She surmises, and I think it is a reasonable supposition, that their purpose was not simply to send him believers, but to prepare his way in those cities, so he will gather yet more followers as he passes through."

Gyalo held his goblet, whose contents he had not yet sampled, trying to divine in the King's words and manner some inkling of his intent. The guards were armed with crossbows; ranged as they were at the corners of the room, there was always at least one who was out of his sight. *Clever,* he thought.

"About halfway between Darna and Ninyâser, the Way passes through the Dracâriya region." Santaxma touched the map again, at a spot where the road's thick black line ran through an area of hills, carefully drawn and shaded in green ink. "You know the place I mean, yes?"

"I do, Majesty." The Dracâriya hills were barren moorland, not natural but man-made, created centuries ago by overtimbering and erosion. The Way twisted between them, so deep that at times it was like traveling through a gorge.

"It's there, I believe, that we have the best chance of coming on him un-awares. Assuming he continues to move at his current pace, we should have no difficulty intercepting him. Now, since he does not know you found your way to the Daughter, or that she found her way to me, he has no reason to assume that anyone apart from you knows who and what he really is." San-taxma raised his hard black gaze from the map, his finger still planted atop the Dracâriya hills. "Would you agree?"

"Yes, Majesty."

"Nevertheless"—his eyes fell again—"if he is shrewd, and from what you have told me it seems abundantly clear that he is, he will anticipate opposi-tion, especially once he begins his campaign of destruction. I think it is wise to assume he will scout the way ahead. So I cannot approach before an army. Nor is there need. He himself is dangerous, but his followers are only rabble. Is that not so?"

"Ordinary men and women, Majesty. Yes."

"What I'll do, therefore, is separately to dispatch several half companies of horse and foot to the Dracâriya hills. They will take up positions above and beyond the chosen ambush point. At the same time, I myself will advance openly along the Great South Way, with a sizable, but unremarkable, reti-nue."

Gyalo said: "You intend to lead this force yourself, Majesty?"

"You would suggest someone else?"

"Forgive me, Majesty, it is only that it is a grave risk."

"As you may recall, I am no stranger to risk. Thus far, I seem to have managed rather well." Santaxma smiled one of his tight smiles. "I'll dispatch an embassy with much pomp and honor, to say that the King has heard of the man who calls himself the Next Messenger, and has come to parley with him. I will propose we meet somewhere here." He tapped a spot where the hills drew especially close to the road. "I will wait for him with certain of my staff and a guard, as is appropriate. Meanwhile, men will have been placed in concealment above the road, equipped with glass vessels of manita, which at the proper moment they will drop before and behind him, entirely enveloping him in the drug." He brought his closed fist down upon the parchment. "Any attendants he has brought with him will be killed, and he will be seized and bound. The men stationed in the hills will surround and contain his followers, so they will not riot when they discover their Messenger has been taken from them."

"Ârata," Gyalo said, forgetting himself in his dismay. "You still intend to capture him alive."

"Certainly I do. Dangerous as this man may be for his Shaper strength, the power of his call is far more perilous. If he dies, his shaping dies—but what of the legend he has built around himself, which echoes so ruinously in the hearts of my people? He may become a saint, a martyr, like the seditionist Caryax, whose execution did not destroy his ideas but ensured their survival, so they might later be embraced by those who brought so much misery on Arsace. And will I not then be blamed for murdering a Messenger? No. It is the myth I want to kill, and for that he must be alive. I will bring him back to Ninyâser, where I will expose him as the heretic he is. The people will know me not only as the liberator of Arsace, but as a defender of the faith, vanquisher of a great and terrible blasphemy." A different sort of smile curved his lips, inward, anticipatory. "They will not be so ready, then, to call *me* blasphemer."

"Majesty, forgive me, but this is the man who *brought down the walls of Thuxra City!* There is only one way to be sure of him, and that is to kill him!"

"And so I shall, I promise you. Once his charlatanry has been revealed, I will provide him with a most public execution."

"What if you fail to subdue him, Majesty? Even if you succeed, how will you hold him? How will you keep him powerless?"

"How does the church keep its captured apostates powerless, when they refuse to take their prescribed manita doses? I have already consulted with the most renowned manita masters in Ninyâser, one of whom will be accompanying me to tend to him after he is taken. I am to be provided with a specially concentrated formula—more powerful, I am assured, even than the manita with which King Vantyas won the Battle of Clay, and capable in sufficient quantity of subduing the most mighty Shaper. Now, there is always the chance he will see through the ruse, or for some other reason refuse my embassy. In that case, I will have to employ a more direct approach, for which my men will also be prepared—though I pray it does not come to that, for then it may not be possible to avoid killing large numbers of his followers. But I don't think he will refuse. I will send him gifts, as to a fellow prince, and a proclamation that my ambassadors will read, to make it seem I am considering whether to acknowledge him. Did you not say it is his ambition to steal souls from Ârata? How could he resist the opportunity to steal Arsace's King?"

He spoke with easy confidence. Plainly, in his own mind at least, he had already answered every objection. With a terrible falling understanding, Gyalo saw that he and Sundit had succeeded—but not on their terms. They had tried to invoke the specter of the Shaper War, the terror of Râvar's extraordinary gift; but what Santaxma had seen was the threat of more religiously inspired unrest, for that was what he himself feared most. His scheme might indeed succeed in luring Râvar into ambush; Gyalo thought the King was probably correct about the temptation his soul would pose. But after that . . . Gyalo saw, flickering in his mind, the sourceless flames in Râvar's chambers, a feat of power he, another Shaper, could not begin to comprehend.

"So." Santaxma brought his ringed hands lightly together, the gesture of a man who has made his case and is ready to move on. "I trust your concerns are addressed?"

It was not really a question. Gyalo's back prickled with awareness of the guards he could not see. "Yes, Majesty."

"Excellent." The King smiled. "You haven't tried your wine."

Gyalo raised the goblet and sipped. The wine was sweetened, fiery with spices.

"As you may already have surmised," Santaxma said, "I haven't called you here merely to discuss strategy. I have a proposition to put to you. I am a man accustomed to using every resource at my disposal. When I march against the pretender, I want you with me. A Shaper to oppose a Shaper."

Gyalo was dumbfounded. With all the possibilities he had anxiously considered as the palanquin carried him through the streets of Ninyâser, this one had never crossed his mind.

"Majesty . . ." He groped for words, conscious of the thinness of the edge he walked. "I have but a fraction of his strength or skill. I don't think I would be any use to you."

"I suspect you underestimate yourself. The Daughter Sundit has told me of your deeds."

"Majesty . . . to associate yourself with someone like me . . . if people impute blasphemy to you now, what will be said if it becomes known that you employed an apostate?"

"Ah, but by the side of my mining of the Land, it is a very small transgression, wouldn't you agree? I am certain, in any case, that I can gain the Brethren's pardon—given that they would not wish it known that in the matter of untethered Shapers, they have sinned much worse than I." Again the King smiled. "Now, I am a pragmatic man. For all I am your sovereign, to whom by law you owe duty, I do not expect you to undertake this of your own goodwill. I realize you have no need to bow to any authority, or take any actions but those that please you. Even an offer of payment presents a dilemma, for what is gold to one who can create it for himself? But I have put my mind to it, and here is what I propose. I have no doubt you fear greatly for your wife and child. When my men ride down on the pretender's train, there will be those whose sole instruction is to find your family and bear them to safety. Further, I will deed to you a house and land, so you and your family may live in comfort. And I will undertake, when all of this is finished, to convince the Brethren you are dead—truly dead this time—so you need never fear their interference."

The interview had taken on a surreal quality. "You would tolerate a free Shaper loose in your kingdom, Majesty?"

"Just one. With—if I judge right, and I usually do—no wish to live other than a peaceful life. Ah, do not look so amazed!" The King laughed with what seemed genuine amusement. "I have long had reason to doubt the Brethren's pronouncements on a variety of issues, so is it surprising that I should also doubt their dire warnings about free Shapers? In the days before the Doctrine of Baushpar, kings had Shaper servants—yes, and Shaper guards and generals, too. I shall be like the kings of old! And you shall be like the Shapers of old." His smile sharpened. "Make no mistake. I am a careful man. Though I am not often wrong, I am always prepared for the possibility of error." He gestured with one gold-heavy hand to the guards in their corners. "As you see. So. What do you say?"

Within the watery currents of his lifelight, his face was both expectant and intent. The guards watched impassively, their crossbows held at easy angles. With what he hoped was convincing deference, Gyalo bowed in the formal Arsacian manner, putting his fingers to his lips and extending his hands toward the King.

"It is a generous offer, Majesty. I accept, with gratitude."

"Excellent!" The King's face broke into a smile—a real smile this time, and Gyalo perceived the warmth this man could bestow on those who pleased him. He raised his wine. "A toast. To cooperation."

"To cooperation." Gyalo touched his lips to the rim of his goblet. The King drank deeply from his.

"Tell me something. Apostate that you are, do you still believe?"

"I do, Majesty."

"You set aside your vows, then, but not your faith. And the claim you made when you returned from the Burning Land, that the god has risen. Do you still hold to that?"

Gyalo hesitated. "Yes, Majesty."

"So you are a heretic as well." Santaxma nodded. "We've something in common, you and I. I, too, stand outside the laws of the church, with my mining of the Burning Land. Yet I, too, believe. It is only that I do not believe in a stupid god, a cruel god, a god who would capriciously deny the riches of his sacred resting place to the first and most beloved of his kingdoms, when its need is so profound." Beneath the smooth mask of power, Gyalo glimpsed again the bitter, serious man who had spoken in the summerhouse of fanaticism and suffering. "Perhaps your god, too, is more forbearing. A god who tolerates unbound Shapers."

"I don't know, Majesty. I can only act as I feel is right, and trust I am not wrong."

"And is that not the very meaning of faith? Not to know, and yet to trust."

Gyalo sipped his wine.

"Before you go," the King said, "I wonder if you might favor me with a demonstration."

"A demonstration, Majesty?"

"Of your ability. Your shaping."

Once again Gyalo was silenced—this time not only by surprise but also, sharply, by distaste.

"Come now, don't tell me you are reluctant. Or perhaps you fear to alarm me? I assure you, I am not easily alarmed."

"It's your guards I fear, Majesty. You will forgive me, but I'd like to hear you tell them they are not to kill me."

Santaxma laughed. He raised his voice. "You heard him. No matter what you see, you are not to kill him!" He looked at Gyalo, still smiling. "Will that do?"

Once again, Gyalo could see no wise way to refuse. He set aside his goblet. "What would you have me shape, Majesty?"

"Surprise me."

Gyalo extended his hands and conjured flame upon his palms—illusion, not real shaping, but impressive to look at. He closed his fingers, quenching the blaze, then opened them again and with a puff of light, a sound like cracking twigs, filled his hands with cherries. He spilled the fruit across the map, then shaped a dozen rubies, reproducing the pattern of the stones in the King's earrings so that they glinted an identical shade of crimson. These, too, he cast across the map. In quick succession he called into being a rose, a hill of grain, a chunk of spicewood, a knob of gold. With a sweep of his arm he unmade it all, except the rubies, which he scooped up and proffered to the King—a cheap gesture, he thought as he did it, like a street performer.

The King shook his head. "This is only a little different from what I've witnessed every day of my life in Communion and Banishing ceremonies. Show me something greater. Astonish me."

Anger shook Gyalo, unbidden and intense. Turning, he flung his shaping will at the small table that held the food and drink, finding the patterns of its being, wrenching them apart. A burst of brilliance, a hollow boom, and the table was gone, its substance banished into the wider world, the items it had supported spinning to the floor.

"Ârata!" Santaxma's face was avid; there was no fear in it at all. Beyond him the two guards Gyalo could see maintained their stiff positions. "More," the King said softly. "Show me more."

Already Gyalo regretted his loss of self-control. "Majesty, I fear to endanger you in this confined space."

"We will go outside, then."

"Majesty, if I may suggest . . . perhaps it would not be wise to allow my nature to become widely known."

The King's reluctance was obvious. But he was a shrewd man. "It's reasonable advice. Once we are on our way, however, there will be no such concerns." He fixed Gyalo with obsidian eyes. "When I make this request again, I shall not expect you to refuse."

"I understand, Majesty."

"We'll depart within the week. I will send for you as soon as preparations are complete."

The functionary was waiting in the hall to conduct Gyalo back to the palanquin. In its hot, curtained confinement, Gyalo breathed on his palms, which stung as if the illusion of fire he had conjured had been real. Understanding sat in him like ice: He and Sundit had failed. The plan Santaxma had conceived was doomed. He felt the weight of all the nights he had woken in a sweat of horror to think he had abandoned Axane and Chokyi, all the times he had painfully reconvinced himself that his choice had been the right one. How could he have been such a fool? So much time wasted on a pointless mission—all of which, every moment of which, could have been used instead to search for a way to set Axane and Chokyi free. He saw himself, standing on the ridge above the Awakened City as Sundit and her people walked away, struggling to decide whether to follow or remain. None of the reasons that had moved him so strongly then made any sense to him now.

By the time he reached the Âratist complex he was in such a fever of remorse and urgency that he could hardly bear not to depart there and then. He forced himself to be sensible. He would wait until nightfall, when he could slip away unnoticed.

In his attic room, he took the blanket and the quilt from the bed and rolled them around the clothes Sundit had bought for him, tying the bundle with the sash the maidservant had left behind, then sat by the window as darkness came, with only his pearly colors for illumination. The throbbing in his hands would not abate. He thought, with dull humiliation, of the tricks he had performed at Santaxma's request. If he had accepted the King's offer in truth, and if they all survived, it would have been he, ultimately, who paid the price—for what were the odds that Santaxma, that self-described pragmatic man, would have used him only once? He imagined himself, the King's pet apostate, held in reserve for urgent crises and looming disasters—or perhaps the King's private treasury, creating gold to order. It came to him, in a burst of understanding, that he had not held his shaping captive for so long only in dread of what, employing it, he might become. He had feared also what that employment might make of it—that he would cheapen it, trivialize it, use it as a means to small and selfish ends. That he might, like the King, come to view the power in him, the god's sacred and transcendent gift, as no more than an instrument, a tool. *A resource*, as the King had said.

At last it was late enough. With his bundle he slipped out of his room and descended to the second floor. Reanu reclined on a pallet before Sundit's door, his lifelight flaring wheat gold in the dimness of the hall. Perhaps he was sleeping and perhaps not; but he was on his feet before Gyalo had closed more than half the distance, his hands ready on his knives.

"I need to see her." Gyalo had struggled with this. What he really wanted was just to go, without explanations or farewells. But something in him would not quite allow it.

"It's late." Reanu had relaxed when he recognized Gyalo, but he did not remove his hands from beneath his stole.

"I know. Please."

Reanu's eyes fell to the bundle, rose again to Gyalo's face. Turning, he rapped at Sundit's door. A pause; then footsteps, and the sound of a latch. "Yes?" Sundit said.

"The apostate wants to see you."

Sundit pulled the door a little wider. Her eyes made the same journey Reanu's had. "Come in."

Gyalo slipped into the room. Sundit closed the door and returned to the window, where, like him, she had been sitting. She wore a sumptuous night robe of golden silk and her feet were bare, but lamps still burned on tables and in the corners of the room, and the bed, with its high carved head- and footboard and rich quilts, was undisturbed.

"You're leaving," she said.

"Yes."

She seated herself, tucking her feet under her gown, folding her hands on her lap. Her lapis lifelight, alive with darker currents, shone half against the darkness of the unscreened window, half against the illumination of her chamber. "You refused the King's offer, then. I thought you would."

"He told you about that?"

"Yes. I could see he wanted me to call on my authority, to condemn him, so he could inform me how little he cares for the Brethren's censure. I didn't give him the satisfaction." She shook her head. "Childish."

"Actually, I accepted. It didn't seem wise to refuse. But I have no intention of doing what he asks."

"He'll be very angry."

"Yes."

"Do you think you can save them? Your wife and child?"

"I'm not Râvar's equal. But I know myself better than I did when I left them."

She nodded. Did she understand he owed some of that to her? He had not needed her to tell him that an unbound gift of shaping did not breed corruption. But he had only known it in himself, *for* himself. She had brought the knowledge outside him, made it general. It made more difference than he would have guessed—more, really, than he liked to admit. He was honest enough to suspect that it had played a part in the way he had responded south of Darna—not in the instinct to oppose the bandits' attack, perhaps, but in his ability to answer it. He could not say that to her, of course. He could not inform one of the architects of the Doctrine of Baushpar that she had helped seal him to his power.

"Will you return to Baushpar?" he asked.

"Not yet. I'll accompany Santaxma to Dracâriya. I'll see it done."

"No!" Gyalo stepped toward her. "It's too dangerous. The King's plan can't succeed."

"Why? Whatever his flaws, Santaxma is an excellent tactician."

"He wants to take Râvar alive. It's madness. Even if the ambush doesn't fail, I don't know if any quantity of the drug is enough to keep him powerless."

She shook her head. "The preparation Santaxma will be using is specially concentrated. Far more so than the ordinary drug. I've spoken with the manita master myself."

He saw that in her way she was as blind as Santaxma, unable to look beyond the world she knew, in which manita was an infallible defense against Shapers. "For safety, then," he said, "when Râvar comes, keep well away from the King."

"Of course. Râvar thinks me dead." Her eyes fell to his bundle. "Is that all you're taking with you?"

"I'd also planned to take a horse."

"Call Reanu in, if you would."

Gyalo summoned the Tapati captain. Sundit instructed him to escort Gyalo to the stables, and respond with her authority if challenged. He was also to give Gyalo thirty silver karshanas from her purse, which the temple treasury had replenished. "Come in to me after," she said, "to tell me it is done."

"Yes, Old One." Reanu was as impassive as a pillar.

"Well, Gyalo Amdo Samchen. I wish you fortune."

Surely she was conscious of the strangeness of it—a Daughter of the Brethren wishing fortune to an apostate. Yet no stranger than that she should freely let him go, knowing that if he survived he would remain unbound. No stranger than that he should bow to her, as formally as he had earlier bowed to the King.

"Great is Ârata. Great is his Way. Thank you for your generosity . . ." Her title, which he had not once used in all the time they had traveled together, rose naturally to his lips. ". . . Old One."

He was at the door when she called after him.

"Wait." The word was raw, as if torn from her against her will. He turned. She had gotten to her feet again. "There's something more . . . something else I need to tell you. Reanu, leave us."

Gyalo stepped back into the room. Reanu pulled the door closed, the latch clicking softly. Across the lamplit space between them, Sundit held Gyalo's eyes. Her hands were clasped at her waist; her face held an expression he could not read.

"I told you that Vivaniya and I were sent to the Awakened City for the sake of the Brethren's concern for heresy." Her voice was low, so low he had to strain to hear. "That was not the truth, or not entirely. In the Burning Land . . . Vivaniya and Dâdar conspired in a lie. As they neared Refuge and its river cleft, they saw a . . . a light, a golden light, rising up at night above it. After the battle the light was gone, and when they came into Refuge and sought the place where you said the Cavern of the Blood would be, they saw no trace of it. They chose to ignore the earlier evidence of their senses, to accept that apparently solid cliff as the truth. They returned to Baushpar and told us they had found nothing, that there was nothing to find—that you had lied, and plotted with your companions to support your lie. They did not speak of the light. They made a pact between themselves to keep it secret."

"I know," Gyalo said.

It struck her speechless for a moment. She put one hand to her throat. "How? How can you know?"

"From Axane. She was caught in Refuge after the battle. When the army came up to destroy it, she hid. She heard the Sons conspiring. She heard every word they spoke."

"Ârata." Sundit closed her eyes, opened them again. "Did she tell him, too? Did she tell Râvar?"

"Yes."

"So that's how he knew. Oh, Vanyi." She shook her head. She sounded as if she might weep. "Vanyi, you fool."

"They wouldn't have found the Cavern even if they had searched for it. Râvar concealed it. He shut himself inside. If your Shapers had tried to open the stone, he would have held it closed. Lie or truth, what your Brothers told you would have been the same."

"But they would not have lied about the light. We would have known about the light."

"Would it have made a difference?"

"Perhaps." She accepted his condemnation without a flicker. "Perhaps not. We believed what Dâdar and Vanyi told us. There was no reason not to. Word had already come that you had thrown yourself from your window in Faal. The last question seemed to be answered. Ah, Gyalo, you were right in so much of what you said to me the night you and I first talked—it *was* relief, blessed relief, to think those questions were finally behind us. And if Vivaniya had been as conscienceless as Dâdar, we might have rested secure in our false understanding. My Brother is not strong, in this life especially, but there is honor in his soul, and the guilt of what he did ate at him. Not just the lie, but . . . the rest of it, the possibility behind the lie. When we received the first eyewitness report of the Awakened City, he could bear it no longer. He came to me and confessed everything. Together we informed the others. That's why he and I were sent—for the sake of the lie, which meant we did not after all know the truth about the Cavern of the Blood, which meant—"

"That Râvar might have been real." Incredulous, Gyalo laughed. "You feared he might truly be the Messenger."

Sundit raised her hands, as if in supplication. "Understand. It was like an earthquake, the discovery of my Brothers' lie. That whole abyss of question, yawning out before us again . . . It threw us into utter turmoil. Some few of us maintained their rejection—I think you can probably guess which ones. But the rest of us, the majority, agreed that the question had to be addressed. And so Vivaniya and I were sent. I myself . . . made every effort to keep an open mind. But Vivaniya was consumed by guilt, by guilt and the desire to atone. I saw it, but I never thought . . . and how was I to know that Râvar had the means to turn his lie against him? That's how Râvar won him, by demonstrating knowledge of his darkest secret. A charlatan's trick, but my Brother fell, he fell as Râvar's followers fall—a soul twelve centuries old, undone by a single lifetime's burden of remorse."

"While for you, the abyss of question is closed again." Gyalo could not keep the bitterness from his voice. Much as had changed between them, this still lay at the root. "Since you now know Râvar false."

"No." Sundit took a step forward. "You mistake me. Râvar is false, that is certain. But my Brothers' lie remains, and the light they saw, the golden light. And you, the news you brought us. I've spent much time, these past weeks, thinking about what it may mean."

Gyalo's palms were burning again. "Are you saying . . . that you've come to believe me? To believe that Ârata has risen?"

"I do not know what else to think."

"*Now!*" He had to strain against the constriction in his throat. "You believe me *now*! When it does no good! When it's so much too late!"

Once again she did not try to defend herself. She stood silent, her body braced as if against a wind: a small, sturdy woman enclosed in a shell of sapphire light, who bore within her fragile flesh twelve hundred years of memory, of knowledge and benevolence and ruthlessness and cruelty. In that moment she did not seem the arrogant vessel of those years, but bowed beneath their weight. It came to him, in a burst of recognition that turned his rage to ash, that she was afraid. Not of what was to come, or of anything outside that room. Of what was there.

Of him.

Their eyes held. Understanding passed between them in the singing silence.

He broke the gaze, turning without a word, and left her. This time, she did not call after him.

Reanu led the way to the stables, his broad body like a shield. A sleepy ostler challenged them, but was happy enough, when he recognized Reanu's tattoos, to return to his bed. Reanu stood by, holding a lantern, while Gyalo led out the mare he had ridden into Ninyâser and saddled her. She stamped and nickered, puzzled to be out of her warm stall in the middle of the night. Her solid presence, the familiar motions of readying her, calmed him, allowed him to dismiss Sundit and what he had seen in her face, to shut her from his mind. To turn his thoughts instead to what lay ahead.

He tightened the girth a second time and swung into the saddle. Reanu held up a leather wallet.

"The silver."

Gyalo took it and stowed it in one of his saddlebags. "Thanks."

"You're going back, aren't you. For your wife and child."

"Yes."

"Good luck."

"Thanks."

"You'll need it." Reanu regarded Gyalo from behind the inked ferocity of his tattoos. "You're not what I thought, apostate. Not what I thought at all."

"I'm glad to have confounded your prejudice."

Reanu nodded slowly, though it was not clear what he was acknowledging.

"Great is Ârata." Gyalo looked the big man in the eye. "Great is his Way."

"Go in light." A pause. "Gyalo."

Gyalo

He drove the mare as hard as he dared along the Great South Way. When she went lame south of the town of Hâras, he unsaddled and unbridled her and let her free, and continued on foot, with the saddlebags over his shoulder and his bedroll tied to his back. He was grateful for Sundit's coins, which were easier to exchange than the raw gold or silver he would have shaped for himself; with it he purchased shelter in stables or outbuildings when it rained and he could not sleep by the roadside, and bought hot meals when he tired of foods of his own creation.

An overpowering urgency filled him, an agonizing awareness of lost and wasted time. He walked from before dawn until after dark, barely conscious of fatigue, pausing for rest only because he knew his body needed it. The landscape passed as if in a dream: the rich agricultural plains of Arsace's center, the forested regions to the south, the desolate moorland of the Dracâriya hills. Once again he did not pray, not even for strength. But he imagined the god's attention turned on him as he traveled, incomprehensible, implacable. For the first time in his life, he did not care.

He whispered promises into Axane's sleep: *I'm coming for you. I'll be with you soon.* He dreamed of her and of Chokyi, sometimes gentle dreams drawn from their life together, sometimes violent dreams he preferred not to recall. Once she was with Teispas, walking far ahead of him, deaf to all his shouts and pleas. He woke sweating, breathless with the guilt of having failed her. Failed them.

The road's heaviest traffic ran between Ninyâser and the town of Sardis, which lay on the banks of the river Hatane. Since Râvar and his pilgrim army were still below the river, only a few of the travelers Gyalo encountered had word of him: a long-haul carter on his way to the capital, a group of itinerant musicians, a military courier from Darna who had been in that city when the pilgrims stopped outside it and had overtaken them on his way north. "There's well over two thousand, I'd guess," he said, in answer to Gyalo's question. "They took near a hundred of the townspeople with them when they stopped in Darna. You'd think they'd strip the land like locusts, but I saw no sign of that." Nor had he seen Râvar, either at Darna or on the road, though he had heard tales. "Some say he's a Shaper, a vow-breaker, but if that was true, you wouldn't think he'd still be free. What times we live in, eh?" He touched his eyes in the sign of Ârata.

In Sardis there was word, and worry. Pausing at a cookshop, Gyalo listened as a group of men traded speculation and rumor.

". . . five thousand of 'em, so the peddler said, strung out along the road for a mile and more." The speaker, a portly man with a silver lifelight, hunched forward over his meal. "It took him half the day to get past."

"Five thousand!" scoffed his neighbor.

"He swore it was the god's truth."

"The oath of a peddler. There's something to rely on."

"I've heard the stories, too," said a third tablemate, a quiet man who wore the sash of the city guard. "There's been many travelers through the gates these past two weeks who talk of these pilgrims."

"Heretics, you mean." The scoffer made the sign of Ârata.

"Remember those madmen who got chased out of town a few months ago?" asked a fourth man, younger than the rest. "The ones who said the Next Messenger was calling the faithful to his side? D'you think this is the same one? The same Messenger, I mean?"

"What I think," the scoffer said, "is if I had a karshana for every villain who's come down the road talking about miracles and wonders, I'd not have to worry about my old age."

"What do they want, these marchers?" asked a fifth man, by his muddy clothes one of the brickmakers who mined the clay beds of the Hatane. "Where are they going?"

"To Ninyâser, to see the King," said Silver-light.

"Baushpar's what I heard," the guardsman said.

"The peddler said he's half again as tall as a regular man, the one who leads them," Silver-light said. "With a voice like a trumpet and a face too bright to look at for more than a minute at a time. He's got a cloak made out of light."

"Cloak of light, my arse." The scoffer was getting angry.

"If he's got even half the followers these travelers say he does," said the quiet guardsman, "they'll put a sore burden on Sardis when they come."

"Then you fellows had better do your bloody job for once, and turn 'em away," snapped the scoffer.

"Yes, but . . ." The young man paused.

"But what?"

"What if it's true? What if—"

"Ash of the Enemy," the scoffer said. "You need a drink. Or a knock on the head."

"I heard he does things," Silver-light said. "Wonders. Storms out of clear air. Gold from the sky."

"Maybe he turns water into beer. That'd be useful."

"He had some, the peddler."

"What, beer?"

"Gold. A nugget big as the end of my thumb."

"And I'll wager he gave you a peek at it, and told you he'd part with it for half its worth." Silver-light hunched into himself and did not reply. "Burn me! You fell for it, didn't you, you soft fool!"

"Well, we'll see for ourselves soon enough," the guardsman said, wrapping both hands around his cup as if to anchor himself in the world of familiar things. "For one thing's sure, they're moving up the Great South Way and will soon be here."

Gyalo moved on, but the conversation remained with him. In each of the habitations he had passed through—the cities or larger towns whose names had been written in black ink on Santaxma's map, the villages that were too small for the map to note, the farmsteads and the roadside inns—he had looked into the faces of the people and wondered which of them would welcome Râvar when he came. The men gave flesh to his uneasy speculations: the credulity of Silver-light, the uncertainty of the younger man, the apprehension of the guardsman and the brickmaker, the anger of the scoffer.

There had been no bridge at Sardis until the Caryaxists built one to carry the Great South Way over the Hatane, in one of the great feats of engineering that had marked the regime's early years. It strode across the river on pilings like giants' legs, more than a mile long, the water weaving complex patterns of flow and force around it. On the far side spread rolling tracts of grazing land, through which the Way ran as straight as a carpenter's rule. A late spell of fine weather made the air almost as warm as midsummer; the shimmering meadows baked beneath a cobalt sky, and the nights were clear and filled with stars. Across that dreaming landscape, the shadow of Râvar's imminence lay.

There was talk of him in the inns and in the villages. Northbound travelers called warnings to those headed south: *A train of pilgrims, big as an army. Go another way if you can.*

Four days beyond the Hatane, in the fragile light of dawn, a dirty blot appeared on the southern sky. Gyalo halted, feeling a sudden pressure in his chest. The patterns were too far to read, but even so he knew that what he saw was not a thundercloud or a meadow fire, but the gathered smoke of hundreds of campsites.

The Awakened City.

He continued until the sun stood directly overhead, then left the road. Behind a stand of brush, its growth dense enough to conceal his body and its pale lifeglow enough like his pearly human colors to disguise them, he settled to wait. The afternoon crept by. Except for an occasional cart or traveler, the road lay empty. But at last, when the sun had sunk low and shadows stretched long across the grass, Râvar's army came in sight.

A pair of horsemen rode in the vanguard; by his lightlessness, Gyalo recognized one of them as Ardashir. Next came Sundit's coach, plodding at the slowest of paces. Another pair of riders followed, then, like a long, long plume of dust, the citizens of the Awakened City. Apart from the riders who flanked the line—all with staves and armbands, members of Ardashir's Band of Twenty—there was no trace of the near-military order of the pilgrims' exit from the caverns. Nor were they singing. They were just a crowd—massed and shapeless, tramping along in the dull manner of people for whom walking had become an activity as unthinking as breathing, and were propelled less by their own will than by the grinding momentum of the whole. The shuffling of their passage overwhelmed the air. Their gathered lifelights made a dazzling show; Gyalo had thought to watch for Diasarta's parched-grass green, but in such a mass of people it was impossible to pick one light from the rest. A few went mounted, and there were a number of oxcarts and mule carts—the new converts the military courier had mentioned, perhaps. Faithful must also have been lost along the way, culled by sickness or injury or the constant labor of the journey. Even so, it seemed to Gyalo that the City, while nowhere near the size suggested by the men in the Sardis cookshop, was considerably larger than when he and Diasarta had watched it march away.

The sun had set by the time the main body of the train was past. Gyalo abandoned his concealment and returned to the road, falling in among the stragglers. Dirty and travel-worn as he was, no one questioned his presence. As full dark descended the horsemen came riding back, shouting for a halt. Wearily, the pilgrims left the road and made camp alongside. Some had shelter, tents or lean-tos rigged with poles and cloth or steppe-grass mats, but for many there was nothing but the ground and the air—no hardship, in the mild false summer, but what would become of them when the winter rains arrived?

Gyalo struck off into the meadow again, making his way up the line. To his right, across the width of the road, the City lay like a gathering of stars, little constellations of cook fires and lifelights burning bright against the paler luster of the land. He heard the sound of voices, and now and again of song; when the breeze shifted he smelled dust and woodsmoke and the miasmic whiff of too many people crowded too close together. Several times he encountered groups foraging for brush to feed their fires. They assumed him on the same errand and saluted him as a fellow convert, holding up their black-marked palms. "Great is Ârata," they said. "Great is his wakened Way." "Go in light," he replied, showing them his own mark.

Near the procession's head he dropped to his hands and knees, crawling forward under cover of the vegetation. The encampments of the pilgrims terminated as abruptly as if they had come up against a fence. Across a small empty distance lay Râvar's camp: a large tent, a cluster of smaller ones. The coach had been unharnessed and drawn alongside, the horses staked out to graze. A fire burned, tended by a pair of lifelights, crimson and green. Two men with silvery colors flanked the opening of the large tent, and other lifelights moved nearby, including the shadow-glint, just visible against the dark, of Ardashir.

Gyalo crouched, his eyes fixed on Râvar's tent. He could read its patterns like a written page—the grass cloth that composed it, the stresses of the poles and ropes that held it up. Useless information, for what mattered was what he could not see—Axane and Chokyi, imprisoned within.

Light flared abruptly inside the tent. The men on guard by the opening turned to draw back the flaps. A storm of brilliance erupted into the night. In its gemlike intensity it was a little like the radiance of life, but far larger; and it was not a single aura, or one with varied shadings, but a gathering of more than a dozen different colors, coiling and rippling like a nest of serpents. At its center a more piercing illumination, a harsh sharp gold, burned in the shape of a human figure.

Râvar.

The star trail of the procession stirred, as those who could not see their own true brightness glimpsed Râvar's false refulgence. Pilgrims began to crowd forward, though they did not advance beyond the margin that separated Râvar's camp from theirs. Close to them, but not too close, Râvar halted.

His arms rose, parting his garment of illusion. He spoke; Gyalo could hear his voice, but could not make out the words. The air shook. Lightning catapulted from the earth. And again, and again. Shaping.

The echoes died. Râvar spoke once more, gesturing. A cry rose from the pilgrims. He stood a moment, arms spread, head tipped back; then he dropped the pose and strode back toward his tent. The guards pulled the flaps aside again. For a moment his light could still be seen, sliding across the fabric. Then, like a blown flame, it vanished.

Gyalo watched from his hiding place as Ardashir and his men settled round the fire, as food was prepared and brought to Râvar's tent. In the pilgrim encampment, lifelights drifted in steady procession toward and away from the place where Râvar had done his shaping. At last both camps were still. Gyalo crept forward then through the wan moonlight, through the grass and underbrush whose milky glow was so much like his own, halting just short of the curbed margin of the road. He was barely aware of the breathing night around him, barely heard the stamping of the horses or the crackle of the fire, barely felt the grass against his face or the sharp throbbing in his hands. The world had contracted; it was no larger than Râvar's tent, and the distance between it and the place where Gyalo lay watching. In the Burning Land, Râvar had forced Axane every night; he might be forcing her right then, behind the tent's obscuring fabric. By an act of will Gyalo had excluded such thoughts as he traveled, but he was powerless against them now. Wild impulses shook him. He would circle around, creep beneath the canvas, spirit Axane and Chokyi away while Râvar slept. He would shape fire on the grasses to draw Râvar out, and free them while Râvar was absent. He would shape lightning, as he had south of Darna, and strike Râvar to ash. *If I whisper it aloud she'll hear me, she'll hear me in her Dreams, she'll be ready . . .*

He knew better than to try. All night he lay, wracked with futile hatred—of Râvar, of his own helplessness. At last, when dawn cracked the eastern sky, he stole silently back to a safer distance.

The City rose with the sun. The riders trotted along the encampment, rousing the pilgrims. Food was prepared over Râvar's fire; Ardashir supervised the harnessing of the coach, drawing it around so its open door faced the tent's entrance. Râvar emerged, naked of illusion, enclosed only in his own painful light. Gyalo had no time to feel more than the smallest shock of loathing—for close on his heels followed Axane. She was uncloaked. Chokyi was clearly visible, clasped in her mother's arms.

The sight of them pierced Gyalo like a javelin, fixed him to the ground. If Râvar himself had come striding toward him, he could not have moved.

She knew he was there, certainly she knew it. But she never faltered, never glanced in his direction. Ten steps brought her to the coach. Balancing Chokyi in one arm, she grasped the strap beside the door and pulled herself inside. Briefly her light was visible through the opening. Then Ardashir slammed the door, and it was gone.

Gyalo bowed his head into his burning palms. He heard the sounds of preparation: thuds and thumps, shouts. When at last he was able to look up, the tents had been struck and the coach loaded, and the driver was pulling the horses around. As yesterday, Ardashir led the way. The other horsemen trotted down the line of the encampment, chivvying the pilgrims into motion. Slowly, with many fits and starts, the Awakened City began to move.

Gyalo rose from his hiding place and joined the stragglers again. Passing the spot where Râvar had shaped the night before, he saw a litter of grain and an area of trampled mud where water must have flowed. Sustenance for the faithful. Food of the gods.

During the days that followed Gyalo walked in the City's wake, improvising the sash Sundit had bought him into a head covering that he could also wrap around his mouth and nose, should Ardashir ride back that far. At night he stole the length of the procession and settled opposite Râvar's camp, watching for any chance to act, but mostly waiting for the morning and the brief moment of Axane's and Chokyi's passage between tent and coach. Each evening Râvar emerged, clad in his cloak of light, to provide for his faithful. Sometimes he gave a sermon or address. Gyalo could not always make out what he said, but the crowd's responses were audible: *Fulfiller of the Promise, he who opens the way! Beloved of Ârata, who sets our feet upon the Waking Road! Beloved One, child of Ârata!* When he had finished speaking Râvar flung up his arms, causing a brief tempest of shaping to burst above the crowd; the pilgrims shouted and grabbed at the rain of small objects that followed. Gyalo thought of the man in Sardis who had bought a nugget of gold from a peddler, and the boy in the caverns with his handful of precious stones. It was longer than usual on those nights before the camp was still.

On the other side of the Hatane, the mayor of Sardis and his staff were waiting with ten wagons piled with provisions, which they offered to Râvar in exchange for leading his pilgrims past the town. Râvar agreed, on condition that he might address those citizens of Sardis who wished to hear him. When the Awakened City departed, its numbers had swelled by more than a hundred converts. Gyalo, at the City's rear, did not witness this, but he spoke with one of the new recruits, an older man who had abandoned his home and a large extended family to follow the Messenger. All his life, the man said, he had dreamed of making pilgrimage to Baushpar, but when the blockade was removed after the Caryaxists' fall, he had believed himself too old. The Messenger, with his glorious news of Ârata's rising, had made him see otherwise. "Ârata be praised," he said, and made the god's sign, his face alight with the fever Gyalo had seen in the caverns, in the faces of Gaubanita and his companions.

The City moved on into the increasingly barren and elevated landscape of the Dracâriya region. Axane and Chokyi were never in the open except for brief moments at morning and evening, and they were out of Râvar's immediate company only when he showed himself to the faithful, which never took him more than a few dozen paces away from the tent. Just once, two days north of Sardis, did he deviate from that pattern. He shaped the evening's grain and water, then, accompanied by Ardashir and five of Ardashir's staff-carrying Twentymen, moved down the margin of the encampment, pausing to greet and bless the pilgrims who crowded eagerly toward him. Hidden on a hillside, Gyalo knelt in an agony of indecision. It would take Râvar some time to walk the length of the camp and back. But Axane and Chokyi were certainly restrained in some way—otherwise what was to prevent Axane from simply slipping under the back of the tent?—and if freeing them required shaping, a hue and cry would be raised. How far would they get before Râvar came flying back? Unlike Gyalo's modest light, Axane's boiling radiance could not be hidden behind a boulder or a stand of brush. Could he defend them? Though he knew well he was not Râvar's equal, he might not have hesitated for himself. But for Axane and Chokyi . . .

Ultimately his indecision made the decision for him. Râvar's cloak of light, which had vanished beyond a bend in the road, reappeared. Gyalo watched Râvar return, feeling a terrible sense of failure, even though he was certain he could not have succeeded. "I'm sorry," he whispered later into Axane's Dreams, trying not to think that he had sentenced her to another night of pain and terror. "I'm sorry."

More and more, it seemed likely that he would have to wait for what he had hoped would be a last chance, but now looked to be the only one: Santaxma's embassy. If successful, it would draw Râvar away from the Awakened City. If not, Santaxma would attack, and in the attendant panic and confusion Gyalo could act. He detested waiting; the thought that there might be one chance, and no more, terrified him. But he could think of nothing else to do.

He watched constantly for Diasarta's green light, but never saw it. This was not really surprising in a gathering of such size, especially given Gyalo's confinement to the rear and to the margins. He hoped for Diasarta's safety and tried not to think the ex-soldier might have come to harm.

Sundit, too, was often in his mind. After their final meeting, he had been angry; but once his feeling cooled, he was surprised to discover how little her confession of faith moved him. Once, the Brethren's belief had been what he most desired: hers, Utamnos's, all of them. It had been a long time since that was so, a long time since he had blamed himself for their rejection of Ârata's rising. That she had come to believe it now, years late, changed nothing.

On the night he left Ninyâser he had ridden past the temple of Ârata, hulking at the front of the Âratist complex. He had not been tempted to go in, yet something had drawn him to rein in his horse and stand before it for a while, his eyes roaming over its domes and arches, its columns and galleries, its Aspect-sculptures and its intricate friezes depicting the deeds of Ârata during the primal age. Yellow lamplight spilled from the gallery's entrance. In imagination, he traversed the gallery's perfect circle; he entered the dim cylinder of the core and gazed up at the image of Ârata Creator, smiling in eternal bliss. He felt the press of some powerful emotion, yet he could not have said what it was.

When at last he rode on, it was with a sense of finality—as if, rather than departing from a place he expected to see again, he was leaving a land to which he knew he would not return. It seemed, then, an awareness born of the possibility of death, of the dangers ahead. But in the time since, he had come to feel that the abandoned land was the temple, the temple and all it represented. Somehow, the last of his bonds to the church had dropped away—more than the vows he had renounced, more than the rituals and affirmations that had lost their meaning now that Ârata was awake: his acceptance of the very purpose and structure of the church, its very place upon the earth. Like the rituals, like the affirmations, the church had been built for the time of Ârata's slumber, a temporary edifice never meant to last—just as the Brethren, who thought themselves immortal, had never been meant to live forever. Somewhere within himself, he had known this for a long time. But it was only now he fully comprehended it.

It was another transition he owed to Sundit. In confessing her belief, she had made him see its irrelevance, and therefore the true irrelevance of the Brethren. Before, he had repudiated their authority; now he saw that they owned no authority to repudiate, not simply because Ârata's rising had ended their time on earth, but because, by their failures of faith, they had forfeited their right to rule. Did she have any inkling, when she let him go, how fully she had cut him free? He remembered the dread he had seen in her face, the dread of a soul standing before oblivion—a familiar enough horror to a mortal, but to her an unknown country. Looking into his eyes, she had acknowledged her own ending.

And more, perhaps. In the shiver of understanding that had passed between them, much lay contained. The part of him that feared choice shrank from it, recoiled from the recognition she had seemed to offer him. But at some point during their journey—he did not know exactly when—a new desire had been born in him: for resolution, no matter what the resolution was. He was tired of living under the shadow of question. He was tired of his own dread. He wanted to move forward—to confront, like Sundit, the unknown country. Though he knew that when he did, he might be forced to admit that her belief meant something to him after all.

Not yet, though. Not until Axane and Chokyi were safe. Even Ârata must wait on that.

Six days into the Dracâriya region, in a portion of the Way that cut through a narrow valley, the horsemen who governed the pilgrims' starting and stopping called a halt in the middle of the afternoon. To those who questioned, they said only: "The Next Messenger commands it."

Gyalo, tramping as usual among the stragglers, felt everything in him spring to alertness. He left the City and climbed the heights above the road, paralleling it along the broken ridgeline. Near the head of the procession he angled downward, dropping to his hands and knees among the boulders and the bushes and the tussocky grass. Behind a stand of scrub bamboo, he halted.

He had been right. Santaxma's embassy had arrived.

Râvar stood before his coach, the wind molding his garments to his body and tossing his long hair out behind him like a flag. He wore no illusion. Ardashir waited nearby, with a contingent of his men. Facing this group across a distance of several paces were the King's emissaries, a small man with a yellow aura and a taller man with an ivory one. They were accompanied by six armored and mounted guards and three attendants, one of whom held the emissaries' horses. The other two supported between them a large wooden chest. So late in the day, the road lay fully in the hills' shadow. Even Ardashir's weak lifelight seemed bright, and the great crystal on Râvar's breast shone like a torch.

The small emissary was apparently just finishing a speech. He beckoned to the attendants with the chest. Ardashir raised his hand, clearly uttering some sort of prohibition; the attendants stopped short and set the chest upon the ground. Ardashir tipped back its lid and glanced inside, then spoke a command to two of his aides, who lifted the chest and took it to Râvar. Râvar gazed at its contents for a moment. Looking up, he said something to the emissaries, finishing with a spreading gesture of his hands.

The emissaries bowed with every appearance of respect and returned to their horses. The party departed, riding north, vanishing around a curve in the road.

Gyalo seethed with frustration. Had Râvar refused the embassy? Was he taking time to consider it? There was no answer below; but for the earlier-than-usual hour, things were proceeding as always, the horses unharnessed and staked out to graze, the tents unstrapped and pitched, the bundles carried inside. Ardashir knocked on the coach's door, where Râvar had retreated to wait; he emerged, Axane behind him in a billow of jade and cobalt, Chokyi in her arms. Gyalo watched them hungrily. Three breaths, and they were gone.

Night fell. Râvar came out and shaped and went in again. The pilgrims availed themselves of what he provided. When the camp slept, Gyalo crept down the hill to a closer vantage point. The tent had been pitched on the opposite side of the road, in a natural indentation in the hillside. If he could manage to get behind it without being spotted, he would be hidden as he crawled beneath the fabric.

If Râvar went to Santaxma.

Gyalo whispered what he meant to do, repeating it several times so Axane's Dream-self would be sure to hear him. At last he retreated to the windswept emptiness of the ridge. In past days he had wondered if he might glimpse Santaxma's men, moving into position above the road, but so far he had seen no one on the heights but a shepherd with his flock. He settled among some rocks and tried to sleep, without much success.

At dawn Ardashir's men rode along the encampment, calling the pilgrims to wake. They did not gather up their bags and bundles and douse their fires and dismantle their makeshift shelters; as the sun rose, they remained in place. In Râvar's camp, food was brought to Râvar's tent, but the horses were not saddled, nor the coach harnessed.

The morning wore on. The hill shadow retreated. The camp simmered under the full weight of the sun. At last, near noon, a party came in sight from the north: the emissaries of yesterday with their guard. They halted at the roadside. Ardashir, fetched from elsewhere in the camp, came to receive them, then went to Râvar's tent, evidently announcing their arrival.

There was a pause—not a long one, but to Gyalo, watching tensely from above, it seemed to last forever. Then the tent flaps parted and Râvar emerged. He was clad in a flowing, many-colored robe, his black hair loose down his back. The usual cloud of illusion was absent. Instead, he seemed somehow to gather light, like a piece of polished metal. The tall emissary put up his hand to shield his eyes, while the other controlled his nervous horse.

Râvar paused. Ardashir came to stand behind him, with six of his men, ranged in pairs and carrying their staves. Still Râvar stood, watching the emissaries. Gyalo could almost feel the contest of wills. At last the small emissary dismounted and approached. There was an exchange of words. By the emissary's reaction, he was considerably taken aback. More discussion; then the emissary turned, with an abruptness that spoke of anger imperfectly suppressed, and called to the others. They swung off their mounts. Serenely, Râvar inclined his head: the nod of a king. Already, he had the upper hand.

Followed by his escort, Râvar began to walk. The emissaries and their guards fell in behind, leading their mounts. The party dwindled northward. It reached the curve in the road and fell from sight. Except for the two men on guard before the tent, Râvar's camp was deserted.

Gyalo felt his body come alight.

Now.

He scrambled to the top of the ridge and ran toward the Awakened City, intending to cross the road under cover of the pilgrim throng, a sufficient distance from the tent and its watchful guards. He descended, forcing himself to slow as he neared the encampment, his body taut with the frustration of holding a normal pace. He threaded his way through the crowd, stray perceptions catching at his senses: the smell of woodsmoke and unwashed bodies, the slipperiness of a patch of mud, snatches of conversation: "Ori, watch your sister . . ." " . . . over there, curse you!" " . . . no, turn it that way . . ." " . . . swear, if you don't believe me . . ." " . . . Brother! Hey, Brother!" None of it touched him. There was room in him only for intent.

At last he was past the City. He began to run again. The hills were less steep than on the other side, but their slope was longer; he labored upward, feeling he would never get high enough. He reached the crest, a scrubby plateau broken by upthrusting rock, and turned back toward the tent. His heart was beating strangely; he had to pause once to get his breath, his hands braced on his knees and his head hanging. Even then his pulse would not slow.

Below he saw the tent, snug in its indentation. Only a few more moments, and he would be there—

And then it came: a great double percussion that rolled like thunder but was not. The ground jumped under his feet—once, twice, like an enormous beast twitching its hide. A deep rumbling shook the air, a building roar that filled Gyalo's head, seized his bones, and vibrated in his flesh. It was like nothing he had ever heard, nothing he had ever experienced; and yet he knew it, knew it in the core of his Shaper soul, knew precisely what had happened, what was happening.

Silence shuddered down at last. Gyalo found himself on his hands and knees, without any awareness of having fallen. The stillness held him. He could not make himself rise, could not compel his body to his will. His heart no longer raced. It felt as if it did not beat at all.

Into the enormous quiet came a noise. It was a moment before Gyalo recognized it: the sound of approaching horsemen. The riders rounded a stand of tumbled rock, sunlight flashing on their helms and hauberks. For days Gyalo had watched for Santaxma's men, and seen nothing. Now, suddenly, they were here.

A shout. They had spotted him. He forced himself to his feet. His mind was strangely disordered—without even thinking about it, he turned to run. He heard a whining sound. Something struck him a terrific blow on his left shoulder, flinging him forward on his face.

What . . . ? His shoulder was numb, but there was a profound wrongness to the sensation that told him something terrible had occurred. He craned his neck, trying to see. A stick—no, a shaft. An arrow shaft. He thought, astonished: *I've been shot.*

More sounds. Shadows fell on him. "Burn it, Orasa. We're not supposed to harm them unless they engage us."

"He was running, Captain. He might've warned the others."

"Captain, he's still alive. Should I finish him?"

"No. Leave him, poor bastard."

"We should've heard the signal by now. Something's wrong."

"I've told you once already, Orasa, no more of that kind of talk."

"But it was close, Captain. That . . . sound. Maybe we should go back."

"This day is cursed—"

"The next man to talk of curses will regret it. We have our orders. We'll wait for the signal, then we'll do the job we came to do. Now move on. Move on, I say!"

The hoofbeats receded. Gyalo lay staring at the tussock of grass by his face. Though it was not near evening, the air seemed to be dimming. The numbness was yielding to an enormous, pulsing pain.

Get up. There's still time. He tried to get his arms under him, but his left arm would not obey. He reached with his right to grab at the grass, but his muscles had no strength. He could feel the warmth of his own blood, running over his shoulder and down his back, pooling underneath him.

Oh, Axane.

But for some reason it was Sundit's face that came into his mind, as he had last seen it, alive with fear and recognition.

I'll never know now. I'll never have the chance to choose.

It was a regret as sharp as the knowledge of his unrescued family in the tent below.

Another breath. Then nothing.

Part IV

THE TIME OF ASH

Sundit

The sun is setting, the darkness just closing in. We did not get far today. I am sick with horror; as the afternoon drew toward a close I began to feel so ill that I was forced to call a halt. Reanu made a bed for me with leaves and bracken, and he and Lopalo and Apui and Omarau unwound their stoles to cover me. I'm a little better now, though the ground still seems to sway underneath me, and there's a roaring in my ears, as if I were still hearing that terrible collapse. I know I should sleep. But I want to write—now, at once, in the rawness of my shock.

It required more than four weeks to reach the Dracâriya region—a three-week journey, really, but stretched by the protocols of royal traveling, though we were not a large group by royal standards. I had with me just Reanu and Apui and Omarau and Lopalo; Drolma and the rest of the Tapati remained behind in Ninyâser. Santaxma was accompanied by two secretaries, body servants and attendants, several of his ministers, a majordomo to oversee their entourages and his own, a fleet of grooms and cooks, a train of packhorses and wagons, and fifty soldiers of the King's Guard, under command of the captain who had received Gyalo and me in the gardens of the Hundred-Domed Palace. There was also a pair of Dreamers to keep track of Râvar's progress—strong and vigorous, both of them, nothing like the church's Dreamers, who sleep away their lives and can barely rise from their beds unassisted. Their straightforward reports made me think, with some bitterness, of my unsuccessful struggles to persuade my spirit-siblings that some of our Dreamers should be trained in a less arcane manner, so they could more easily serve this sort of practical duty.

A portion of the Great South Way follows the dry bed of a river that in ancient times cleaved its way through the Dracâriya hills. Rocky slopes draw in on either side, not high but in some areas quite sheer, and there are many turns and switchbacks. It was here that Santaxma laid his ambush, along a relatively straight stretch of road above which men could lie hidden, some with glass globes of manita to drop as Râvar passed beneath, others with crossbows to deal with anyone who might escape the initial assault. Once Râvar had been captured, a trumpet signal would be given, and the cavalry companies waiting in the hills above the encamped pilgrims would sweep down and round them up.

That was Santaxma's plan. And it was a good plan, or so it seemed to me then. Gyalo's warning had troubled me, but I believed him mistaken in his fears. I could not imagine that Râvar, no matter how great his gift, could possibly withstand the massive dose of specially prepared manita Santaxma planned to hurl down on him. He might refuse the trap, in which case Santaxma had other plans—but if he walked into it, he would be caught, and he would be held. There were ten globes of manita. Ten. They could not miss.

They did not. But I'm outpacing myself.

The slow travel taxed my patience sorely, but appeared to disturb Santaxma not at all—although in truth I saw him too rarely to draw any firm conclusions about his state of mind. Mindful of observers, he could not entirely ignore me, but he paid me the barest minimum of courtesy he could. He did not want me along at all, of course; he told me so before we left, and I told him I did not care, and there we left it, the most open display of hostility we have ever had. He blames me for Gyalo's defection, or at least for his escape. Another way, no doubt, in which he believes the Brethren have failed him.

Râvar, with his great train, was moving even more slowly than we; according to the Dreamers, he and his pilgrims were still two days off when we reached the chosen ambush point. We made camp some distance back, on the road itself. A few miles behind us a contingent of the King's Guard set up a blockade to bar traffic. Santaxma and the Guard captain and their aides surveyed the terrain, choosing the points where men would be hidden, designating the place where the King himself would wait. The grooms set up an elaborate pavilion, suitable for a royal parley. With typical thoroughness, Santaxma wished to create the perfect illusion.

When Râvar drew close, Santaxma dispatched his embassy. Expecting that Râvar might come at once, he ordered his soldiers to take up their positions. Obviously I could not remain as part of his entourage—nor, I imagine, would Reanu have allowed it, for it is his duty always to be prepared for the worst. So I and my guards climbed to the top of the cliffs to a place that satisfied Reanu's caution, where we could conceal ourselves among rocky folds yet observe what passed below. The King ordered his second secretary, Cas, to accompany us, so events could be recorded from a different angle. He is as diligent a record-keeper as we Brethren—except that, being a king, he does not have to write the words himself.

We waited in the silence of utter tension. After what seemed an interminable amount of time the lookouts jogged back; a few minutes later the emissaries came in sight, alone. I and my company clambered down. Râvar, we learned, intended to consider the King's invitation. The emissaries were to return before noon tomorrow to receive his answer.

For caution's sake Santaxma kept the lookouts at their posts. We passed an anxious night. The next day—that is to say, this morning—the emissaries went off again, and Reanu and Omarau and Lopalo and Apui and Cas and I climbed up to our perch to wait. It was noon and there was no shade; the sun beat directly on our heads. Now and then I noticed that all my muscles had gone rigid and forced them to relax, only to realize a little later that they had knotted up again. I ache in all my limbs now from that unnatural tension.

Then down the road a man came flying: one of the lookouts. My pulse leaped. I could tell just by the way he ran: Râvar was coming.

It seemed an eternity before he came in sight along the Way's uneven course, though it could not have been more than a quarter of an hour. He wore the flowing overrobe in which he had received Vivaniya and me in the caverns, and also some sort of glamour or illusion that made him almost too bright to look upon. The nearest I can come to describing it is to say that he seemed to be encased in a shell of fluid crystal. It was an astonishing sight. Even knowing what I know about him, I could not help but feel a chill of awe. Beside me Cas drew in his breath, forgetting to scribble.

Ardashir walked at Râvar's back. After him came an escort of six men, by their staves members of Ardashir's Band of Twenty. The emissaries brought up the rear—on foot, oddly, leading their horses. Well away on the other side, Santaxma waited by the pavilion with his standard-bearers and his ministers, all of them resplendently clad and jeweled—a rich sight, but nothing to the marvel that approached them. On Râvar came, ever closer to the ambush point. At every moment it seemed that he must guess and turn aside, or guess and attack, or, not guessing, simply take an action that the plan could not accommodate. Beside me Reanu and the others were as still as the rocks among which we crouched; Cas's pen hung motionless in his fingers. And I . . . I don't remember breathing.

Râvar and his attendants reached the point where the emissaries were to halt and bid him and his people go on alone. Since they were behind him, they simply halted. Ardashir glanced back, but Râvar never paused. *Walk*, I willed him. *Walk*. Santaxma, too, had begun to move forward—part of the charade of embassy, the better to persuade Râvar that there was nothing to fear from the empty stretch of road between them.

I come now to the most difficult part of this account—not only for the horror of what happened, but because it happened so fast. I cannot be entirely certain of the accuracy of my memory. But I've spent a good deal of time thinking about it, piecing it together . . . this is what I think I saw.

Râvar passed the boundary of the trap, the spot above which the first of the hidden soldiers crouched. Perhaps twenty paces on lay the signal point, where the actual attack would commence. Râvar reached it, stepped beyond it . . . and the ambushers rose up from their concealment and hurled down their globes. The glass flashed as it fell, catching the sun—I remember it clearly—and I think Ardashir may have looked up. Then the globes struck, behind Râvar, before him, alongside. There was a tremendous sound of shattering. Manita flew up, spreading to form a sparkling cloud, fully enveloping Râvar and his people.

It was perfectly done. Perfectly. And at first it seemed to have succeeded. Ardashir and his men fell to the ground. Râvar also stumbled to his knees, throwing up his arms as if to shield himself. But there was a wrongness to the tableau, and in the next instant it came to me: They were *still*. They were not choking, coughing, clawing for breath, as those not habituated to the drug do when they breathe it in. And Râvar . . . Râvar was still encased in light. In power.

"Ârata!" It was Reanu, understanding even as I did.

Down the road, Santaxma had halted, not yet recognizing what he saw. Even when Râvar rose to his feet the King did not seem to comprehend; he remained where he was, his ministers behind him. Râvar stood straight as a spear, his shell of crystal brilliance blurred by the dancing haze of manita. My memory—true or false—tells me there was rage on his face, that his ruined hands were fisted at his sides.

It was then that the archers in the rocks, realizing the manita had failed, loosed a volley of arrows. Râvar should have been pierced, and Ardashir, who was on his feet now also, and Ardashir's men, most of whom still cowered on the ground. But the shafts fell short—all of them at once, as if they had struck a wall. Ardashir leaped in shock. Râvar did not even flinch.

I think I saw him lift his hand, though by this time his brilliance was so piercing that it was not easy to tell that there was anything human at its heart.

The King had turned to flee, but it was too late—it had always been too late. The air above him rippled like hot oil. On the cliff, or perhaps before it, arced a great and terrible light. There was a concussion that seemed to come from inside my own head, so huge was it. The ground jumped. Then there was a different kind of roaring. I saw the cliff begin to fall.

I was transfixed. I had utterly forgotten myself; it would not have occurred to me to move. Dimly I heard shouting. I felt myself seized, lifted like a child. My vision blurred; I was being carried. The world lit up behind me. Thunder cracked again, and the earth rose to slam me in the face. A primal terror seized me, like nothing I have ever felt in this life. Beside me someone reached down—Reanu. He grabbed my arm, dragged me to my feet. Hand in hand, we ran.

At some point I fell again. The noise had stopped. Everything was quiet, a huge and spreading silence, as if all creation held its breath. Reanu and I knelt together, trembling. Reanu's tattoos were stark against his ashy skin. There seemed to be a veil between us. Dust, I realized—the dust of that huge collapse.

"Is it over?" I asked. My ears were ringing; I could hardly hear my own words.

"I don't know."

"The others—"

"They ran, too."

"Where?"

I tried to rise. He gripped my arms. "Wait here. I'll go."

I obeyed him. We had come to rest in a grassy hollow, with ridges of stone jutting up beyond; I had no idea where we were or how far we had run. My thoughts were too disordered, anyway, for me to do more than wait for Reanu to return. At last he did. He had found the others: Apui and Lopalo and Omarau, their faces so grimed that their tattoos showed only as shadows, and Cas, his lap desk clutched tight against his chest as if it were the only stability in the world.

Something possessed me, a kind of desperation. I struggled to my feet.

"Old One," Reanu said, stepping to intercept me. "It's dangerous."

"I have to see."

He shook his head. "There's nothing to see. Nothing but dust."

"I have to see."

I pushed past him, stumbling down the slopes we had raced up a little while before. My throat burned; my eyes streamed. The dust grew even thicker. It was hardly past noon, but it might have been twilight. Before me, the ground dipped.

Iron fingers closed around my arm. I felt myself yanked backward.

"No farther, Old One," Reanu said, his voice muffled by the ringing in my ears and the folds of stole he had wound about his nose and mouth. "There's no more ground. Look."

It was true. Beyond what I had thought was an indentation in the slope, there was nothing at all. Dust hung solid there, filling up the emptiness. The place where we had waited was gone. Somewhere below, under all that rock, Santaxma and his people lay crushed.

I sank to my knees. I could not move or speak. I did not resist when Reanu picked me up again. He carried me back to the little hollow where the others waited. I was too shattered even to think, much less give orders; it was he who got the others on their feet, who got them moving. He carried me on his back. When he tired Omarau took me, then Lopalo.

The air is clear where we've camped. I have placed myself so that I cannot see the dust plume, which is still visible behind us, lit luridly by the last light of sunset. We have not returned to the Great South Way, but are traveling overland; there is a monastery to the east, not too far off if I am correct, where we can obtain supplies and horses. The Tapati have built a fire; they sit round it, silent but for occasional coughing. Cas is curled nearby. We have nothing but the clothes on our backs—and Cas's writing desk, which has furnished the paper and ink to write this account. I'm grateful. It has eased me, a little, to set it down, to pour my horror and my shock out upon the page.

Santaxma is dead. I am certain that Râvar is not. He held away the manita, he blocked the arrows; if the hills did fall where he was, I have no doubt he was able to shield himself. He will continue now, and there will be no one to stop him. What will become of Arsace? But I cannot think of that. There is only one thing left for me to do, and that is to return home and persuade my spirit-siblings to flee. Baushpar will fall—our beautiful city, so recently regained. But we will endure, for long enough, at least, to discover if there is any purpose in our survival.

I wonder if Gyalo saved his family.

I am not given, as some of my spirit-siblings are, to quoting passages of scripture. But a line from the *Book of the Messenger* has been running through my mind, the words my father Marduspida cried in awe and terror when Ârata first appeared to him in the Burning Land: *Before I only knew; now I see, and it is terrible, terrible!*

Gyalo told me of Râvar's power. Most explicitly he told me. So I knew, even though I did not really believe. But today I saw, and it is terrible indeed.

Râvar

Râvar dreamed of collapse. He heard the thunder of it, cascading waves of sound that beat sickeningly inside his head.

Slowly he became aware that the thunder was indeed inside his head, a pounding ache that gripped him like a metal cap, tightening and releasing with each surge of his pulse. He groaned. Wet cloth moved against his skin. He reached out, thrust it away.

"Beloved One."

He opened his eyes. Ardashir leaned over him, flickering shadow blue.

"Beloved One, you're safe." The beautiful voice was cracked and rough. "You're in your tent."

My tent. Over Ardashir's shoulder he saw the familiar fabric at which he lay staring each night before sleep, and to which he woke each morning—the spiky patterns of the grass thread, the rough patterns of its weaving, the dull patterns of the dust and grime accumulated over weeks of travel. The air was dim, hazed with the smoke of the brazier that smoldered nearby. He remembered . . . He put a hand to his throbbing head. Collapse. The King of this land had tried to kill him. And he . . . and he . . .

"Give me water," he croaked.

Ardashir produced a cup and leaned in again, ready to slip an arm beneath Râvar's shoulders, but Râvar said sharply, "No," and raised himself, his head surging with new tides of pain. He took the cup and sipped. At the first touch of water his stomach turned; he had to sit motionless, eyes closed, willing himself not to vomit.

"Tell me what happened," he said when he could, his eyes still shut. "After."

"You fell unconscious, Beloved One, as you did after Thuxra. The protection you placed over us was broken then. The dust was so thick we could barely breathe. It was all we could do to carry you away. You've been sleeping since. Such a thing you did, Beloved One. Such judgment you brought down. You crushed the hills! You destroyed them utterly!"

Râvar opened his eyes. Ardashir's ugly face wore a revelatory expression.

"How long . . . have I been sleeping?"

"It's just after sunset now. Beloved One, I would spare you if I could, but there's something you must know. The King, curse his blaspheming soul, did not confine his treachery to you. While we were absent, Exile cavalry came upon the rear of the Awakened City. Our people rallied and the Exiles were routed. But many were wounded. And some are dead."

"Dead." Râvar set down the water cup.

"Forty-three, Beloved One, at last report."

Râvar closed his eyes again. He felt out of step, off-balance, as if he had gone to sleep in one skin and woken in another.

"Beloved One?"

"Summon a citizen who saw this attack. I want to hear of it firsthand. And then . . . I'll visit the wounded."

"They will be glad, Beloved One. They are in need of comfort."

"Go now. I'll follow you in a little while."

He felt the air move, heard the sound of the tent flap falling. For a moment he was alone with his pain. Then a voice spoke out of the darkness.

"What have you done?"

He opened his eyes. Axane crouched on the far side of the tent, a wreathing cloud of sapphire and emerald, cobalt and viridian. Beside her Parvâti lay asleep. Around them both rose the rodlike patterns of the cage of air he had shaped to confine them, invisible to anyone but a Shaper.

"Râvar." More urgent this time. "What have you done?"

"I killed their King."

Her mouth came open.

"Be quiet now. I need to think."

He rested his elbows on his drawn-up knees and clasped his hands around his pounding head, feeling in his hair the grit of the fallen hills. In the blackness behind his eyes he could see his pain, a spidering network of red lines.

I killed their King. It had been instinctive, split seconds of action and reaction. The sun flashing from the vessels they had hurled at him. The heart-stopping sound of shattering. The billowing cloud of manita, whose patterns he had seen once before, in Refuge—a million million deadly particles of it, the only weapon of this world he feared. His defense had held; none of the drug had gotten through, nor had the buzzing flight of arrows that followed. Incandescent rage had seized him then—not just that they would try to murder him, but that he had allowed himself, even momentarily, to be beguiled. He had punched his shaping will into the rock and brought the hillside thundering down. After that, as after Thuxra, all was darkness.

Ardashir had not been beguiled. His rigid prejudice would not allow it. "He is a blasphemer!" he spat, after the King's emissaries had come and gone. "You cannot trust him. It's a trick." But he had said much the same about the Son Vivaniya. And if Vivaniya of the Brethren could acknowledge Râvar, why not the King of all Arsace? If it were true, it was too good a chance to miss. Râvar did not abandon caution—he had agreed that sentries should be posted along the length of the encampment. He had encased himself and his people in a box of stiffened air similar to the one in which he confined Axane. Still, when the attack came, for just an instant he had been surprised.

You knew the forces of this world would be arrayed against you. You knew it.

Judgment, Ardashir had said. Of course he, who hated the King for his desecration of the Burning Land, would see it so. But would Râvar's faithful agree? Might this be the error, the act that would undo his followers' belief? It had been a long time since Râvar had feared such a thing. Or even thought of it.

He picked up the cup and took another cautious sip. This time the water tasted good, and he downed the rest. Then, carefully, he got to his feet. If he did not move too sharply, the pain was bearable. Dust shook from his clothes. He was not just weary, but drained; he could feel the hollow his great release of power had made in him, not the utter depletion that had crippled him after Thuxra, but deep enough that he knew it would require effort even to summon a garment of light. The Blood of Ârata, burning on his chest, would have to do.

He stooped through the opening of the tent, past the two Twentymen on guard. The air was chilly, alive with breeze currents. Above the hills the sky still flamed with sunset, but beneath them it was already twilight. The radiance of grass and brush spread pale on either side of the black river of the road; to the south, both the lightless stone and the glimmering vegetation were obscured by the massed brightness of the Awakened City. Ardashir stood waiting, with two more Twentymen, and a dirty boy with tangled hair and his arm tied in a sling. They bowed low as Râvar appeared.

"Beloved One," Ardashir said. "This is Narser, who helped drive off the Exile soldiers."

"Beloved One," Narser bowed again. Within his throbbing topaz aura, his face was pinched with exhaustion. "I praise Ârata for your safety."

"Tell me what happened, Narser," Râvar said.

Narser cleared his throat. "My fire mates and me have a camp near the end of the line. A bit past noon, we heard . . . a noise, a big booming, like thunder. The ground shook. We thought it was an earthquake, and got up out of our shelters. That's when we heard the horses. Riders, coming up from the rear—thirty of 'em, more or less, armed and armored."

"The King's men," Râvar said. The fresh air was helping; the pounding in his head had eased.

"Yes, Beloved One. They had Exile colors. We saw you'd been betrayed. We grabbed up our sticks to fight 'em off. Some of us had bows or knives, but some just used tent poles, iron pots, whatever they could find. We shouted your name as we fought, Beloved One. You'd've been proud."

"There were two other companies, Beloved One," Ardashir said. "Also toward the rear. Part of a larger force, possibly, meant to come on us if the attack on you had succeeded. Perhaps those horsemen did not realize it failed."

"Don't fear, Beloved One," Narser said. "If any return, we'll send 'em running."

"I've doubled the number of sentries, Beloved One," Ardashir said. "We will not be surprised again."

"Treachery," Râvar said softly.

"Treachery," Ardashir repeated, in firm tones.

"Treachery." Narser nodded.

"You fought valiantly, Narser, you and your fellows. Come, I will give you blessing."

The boy approached and fell to his knees, turning his face up like a child. Râvar spoke a few words; then, gathering himself, he set a point of light on Narser's forehead. It was not as difficult as he had feared. He gave Narser his hands to kiss, then turned to Ardashir.

"I'll go among my faithful now."

Night had fully fallen. The fires and the lifelights blazed against the darkness. The pilgrims flocked to him, sinking to their knees or falling on their faces, plucking at his clothes, entreating his attention. He dispensed blessings, bestowed sparks of light. The City was much larger than it had been; he knew that not only from his own observation but from the census Ardashir contrived to keep even amid the confusion of the journey, recording new arrivals, noting those who deserted or fell by the wayside. The new recruits believed as fiercely as the older ones, plunged as eagerly down the slope of their own damnation. Yet their devotion was not quite the same. Their fervor was bolder. They crowded closer, begged more brazenly for favor. Râvar was glad of the Twentymen, who used their staves to thrust away those who grew too persistent—something that had never been necessary in the caverns.

Toward the encampment's end, he began to come on pilgrims who had participated in the fighting. Many of the fire bands, the families and pseudo-families into which the faithful had gathered themselves in the caverns, had endured along the journey; each group built its own encampment at night, sharing food and blankets and such shelter as they had. Now each group tended its own fallen. There were arrow wounds and sword cuts and limbs crushed by the Exiles' horses. Ardashir, with his usual extraordinary prepared-ness, knew where they all were, and guided Râvar from fire to fire. Every wound had a story; where the injured man or woman was unconscious, their fire mates told it for them. Râvar listened. He praised. He laid his crooked hands upon the hurts and entreated Ârata for healing. When they asked him why such a terrible thing had happened, he told them, sorrowful, that the edge of the world's doubt had at last been turned upon them. It was the first of the trials he had warned them they would face.

The dead were past the final fires, ranged in rows, as void of light as the inanimate stones on which they lay. Here Râvar paused. How long had he been walking? His limbs felt porous with fatigue. His headache pulsed behind his eyes.

"This is a sore sight, Beloved One." Ardashir laid a bandaged hand on Râvar's arm. "You need not go farther."

But the First Disciple was wrong. At Râvar's back the faithful massed. Many had risen from their fires and followed him through the camp. He could hear their muttering; he could feel their expectation. His progress would not be complete until he blessed the dead.

He started forward. There was no moon. The radiance of the pilgrims and their fires was behind him, and the light shed by the living hills did not illuminate the road. Where the corpses lay it was so dark that he and the Twentymen burned like stars, and even Ardashir's dim colors seemed bright. Someone, Ardashir no doubt, had caused the dead to be decorously arrayed, legs together, hands folded, eyes weighted closed with small stones. Many seemed almost to be sleeping. Others showed dreadful hurts. There was the stench of blood and bowel, and there were flies—not veils of them, as in Râvar's nightmares, yet horrible enough.

He walked among the bodies, murmuring blessings, stooping to bestow beads of light. Rising from the last slain pilgrim, he saw that there were more dead, lying just off the road, stripped and tossed together like sticks.

"Beloved One," Ardashir said. "Those are the dogs that attacked your people."

Râvar halted before the tangle of limbs. He was so far past exhaustion he could no longer feel it; it hardly seemed to be his own will that moved him. He raised his hands, realizing as he did that he was encased in light—illusion, though he could not remember summoning it. From somewhere, words came to him.

"See now," he called. "See what waits for those who harm my children."

He thrust the harsh fingers of his shaping into the soil, into the rock below. Pattern surrendered to his will. The earth groaned at its roots; blue-white lightning turned night to day. Then the light was gone, and so were the Exile dead. A crevasse gaped where they had been, black as an inkblot at the side of the road. In the chill of the night, it exhaled a deeper cold.

Judgment.

Râvar turned, trailing brilliance, and strode back toward the waiting pilgrims. Instinct filled him, pure and certain, as it had the first time he had ever preached to the First Faithful. Before the Awakened City, the living City, he stopped. His attendants hurried up behind him.

"People of the Promise." The faithful were a scintillating wall across the road. Many were on their knees. Others reached toward him, or made the sign of Ârata. He felt the wind of their desire: *Lift us. Transform us. Give us certainty.* "I told you before this journey began that you would march not just in joy but in sorrow. Today that sorrow has come. Today you felt the scourge of the world's ignorance. Today you grieve, and I grieve with you."

They murmured. They wiped their cheeks of tears.

"Today, my children, my people, I, too, felt the harsh sting of betrayal."

They swayed in shock. They hissed in denial.

"Not far from here the hills lie broken. And under them . . . under them lies Santaxma, who was the King of this great land. It was I who broke the hills. It was I who made his death."

Confusion now. Bewilderment. He felt the change, like a shifting of the wind. Still they waited on his words. *Tell us this has meaning,* their attention begged. *Make us understand.* He felt the edge on which he danced—on which he always danced, though he rarely tested his balance so severely.

"Yesterday the King sent emissaries to our City, begging me to come to him and speak of Ârata's rising. Now, this King was a blasphemer, for like those who came before him, those men and women who called themselves Caryaxists, he defiled the sacred ground of my father's resting place, dug copper from its soft red skin, wrenched gold and jewels from its secret depths. Yet any sinner may repent and turn toward the light. How could I, the bearer of my father's word, refuse even a blasphemer's call?"

They listened, wide-eyed, openmouthed, rapt.

"So I went to this King, this Santaxma. In joy I went to him, with my father's word upon my lips. In love I went to him, with my father's mercy in my heart. But he did not give such treasures back to me. No, children—it was murder he intended. In his faithlessness, he desired to destroy this flesh I wear, to disperse the fire of my spirit and silence the truth that I have come to give the world."

Gasps. Cries of horror.

"You see me before you, children! His betrayal could not touch me! It was he who felt the sting of it, his own foul act turned back against him. I stood amid the poison meant to overcome me, I stood before the arrows meant to pierce me, and I brought my father's judgment down. Like a fist I brought it down! The hills split. The rock fell. The very air shattered with the thunder of it! You heard it, children. You heard the thunder. You felt the ground shake beneath your feet."

"Yes!" they cried. "Yes!"

"Judgment is a fearful thing, children. I grieve for what I was forced to do this day, in answer to Santaxma's treachery. But I am my father's instrument. I am his word, and his word must prevail. This I say to you—whoever turns on me, whoever turns upon my faithful, shall reap that same judgment!"

Such a shout they raised, as if to bring down the hills a second time. He flung wide his arms, sweeping light across the night.

"You are the people of the Promise! You are the righteous, the faithful, the first of the new age! You came to me as pilgrims, but now you are summoned to be warriors. There will be more days like this one. You will be called again to defend the truth. That truth must be given as it will be understood—what the world turns on you, you must turn back on it, measure for measure. For kindness give kindness, for mercy offer mercy, but for betrayal, for cruelty, mete out the same! This is my word, children! This is my father's will and mine!"

They were falling to their knees, reaching toward the sky. He saw the ecstasy in their faces: they, who knew what the world did not and so were better than the world. Their adoration seized him, tossed him beyond himself, so that he seemed to see the gathering from on high, a river of light upon the glowing land, himself a white-hot star. But even as he achieved that transcendent vision he was falling, collapsing back into his own exhausted body. He sensed the emptiness that waited for him there; as often happened when he spoke with such power, the torrent of inspiration had dried up as suddenly as it had come.

"Return to your fires, children. I will rest, too, then we will march on. In my father's name I give you blessing. Go in light!"

"Great is Ârata!" they thundered. "Great is his wakened Way!"

"Ardashir," he said softly to the First Disciple. "Help me."

Ardashir slipped a bandaged hand beneath Râvar's elbow, gripping him in a way that disguised Râvar's need for the support. If it were painful to his wounded palms, he did not complain. Slowly, too slowly, they made their way up the line. Not all the faithful had followed Râvar through the camp; there were many who had not heard him speak. But those who had would tell the rest. By morning, every pilgrim would know what he had said. It would become scripture, too, written by Ardashir's scribes from Ardashir's dictation.

At the tent Ardashir reached for the flaps, intending to assist Râvar inside. The Twentymen who guarded the tent were not permitted to enter; only Ardashir had ever seen its interior, where Axane and Chokyi waited in their prison—though of course he did not recognize their confinement, for it was not visible to ordinary eyes. But Râvar kept these incursions as infrequent as he could. Now he pulled away.

"Thank you, Ardashir. I can manage."

"Beloved One, is there anything you need? Anything I may fetch for you?"

"No. I just want to sleep."

Râvar stooped toward the entrance, but his unsteady legs betrayed him, and he stumbled. Ardashir sprang to grip his arm again.

"Beloved One, let me sit by you this night, as I did in the desert. You need care."

"I have care."

"The woman?" Something that was not exactly anger came into Ardashir's face. "When I carried you into your tent unconscious, Beloved One, she sat in the corner and did not stir to help me."

"She saw that you were with me. She did not wish to usurp your place." Again Râvar freed himself, more gently this time. "Thank you, my faithful Disciple. Good night."

Inside the tent he fell to his knees. Axane and Parvâti lay in their corner, asleep. Tipping forward onto his crippled hands, he crawled to his bedding. He fumbled off the heavy necklace and pushed it beneath a fold of blanket. Lying down made his headache worse. Even as he was thinking it would be impossible to sleep, he slid into unconsciousness.

*   *   *

He woke with a gasp. He had been dreaming, images that vanished in the instant of waking.

He lay on his back, his bedding tangled around him. The pounding in his head had diminished. He felt voided, as if after a violent sickness, utterly hollowed out. It was fearful in a way to be so empty, yet at the same time strangely restful.

Outside his tent, the Awakened City slept. He imagined he could sense its breathing—the gathered breath of all those souls, a heaving and subsidence that seemed to stir the earth itself. Often, when he lay awake at night—which he did with growing frequency, for since leaving the caverns he had been much afflicted by sleeplessness—he was aware of it this way: not as a dense throng of individuals, but as a single entity, a huge hunched beast. He had never suffered from such fancies in the caverns. But in the caverns, he had been separated from his faithful by great thicknesses of rock, and had been able to escape them whenever he chose. On the journey he was concealed by nothing but a stretch of fabric—or, in daylight, by the thin wooden walls of the coach. And he was never away from them, not for a single moment of a single day.

On the morning the Awakened City marched out across the steppes, he had felt the most exalted, blazing certainty—the long months of waiting over, the great work begun at last. He was not a fool; he had not expected such euphoria to last. He had known the travel would be difficult and unpleasant; he had understood that to lead upon the road would not be like ruling in the caverns, where all was circumscribed and controlled. Still he had not expected to find it so tedious—the endless hours in the jolting coach, the nightly provision for the faithful, the monotony of the administrative and logistical details that Ardashir insisted on bringing to his attention. Nor had he thought to be so oppressed by the unfamiliar patterns of this world. It had been very difficult during the first days to bear the confinement of the coach, and in the towns they had entered, which were not like anything he had ever known or even imagined, it required all his self-control to hide his confusion and distress. Refuge, like any city, had been fabricated by human hands; but it had existed within the natural matrix of the sandstone cleft that contained it, and because of the nature of Shaper stoneworking, everything had been curved, arched, rounded, flowing. In this world, the habitations were all sharp edges and harsh angles, cramped spaces and incomprehensible structures—so painfully alien sometimes that they actually made him feel ill.

It won't be like this forever, he told himself. *Every day we get a little closer.* Closer to Baushpar. Closer to judgment. Closer to vengeance. Yet the progress was so slow, and the days so similar, that sometimes it was difficult to believe. Sometimes he felt he was simply drifting, without plan or purpose. Sometimes he imagined that the dead river of the road secretly and malignly rolled itself forward every night, so that every day he traveled the same stretch of it.

But this day had been different. Till then, he had simply passed through the world; this day, he had laid his hand upon the world in change. He had brought down a mountain. He had killed a king. And he had seized that act, which might have undone him, and turned it to his purpose. He had made anger part of the pilgrimage, and retribution—just as he had wished, just as he had planned. The punishment, the true punishment, had begun.

He heard again the thunder of destruction, saw again the hills' slow collapse. The memory filled him—even him—with a kind of wonder. The annihilation of Thuxra City, a shaping so great that he had not been able fully to conceive it except in the doing, was almost like a dream; it had seemed possible that it was a singular act, born of grief and desire, unrepeatable. He knew now that was not so. No force of this world could touch him. Even the poison drug manita he could turn aside.

See how constant I am, Ârata. See how faithful.

Had his enemy, Gyalo Amdo Samchen, been watching when the hills came down? If not, he would hear of it. He would hear of it, and know. It gave Râvar a fierce satisfaction to imagine it.

There was a rustling in Axane's corner of the tent, then a low cry. Râvar turned in time to see Axane bolt upright amid her bedding. For a moment she stared at the night—blindly, her mouth open as if in horror. Then she began to weep, great soundless sobs that shook her like invisible hands. She bowed her face, clutched at her hair.

Parvâti, woken by her mother's distress, began to wail. When Axane made no move to tend her, Râvar got up. With far more effort than he had needed earlier to entomb the Exile dead, he unmade their cage. Its walls, less than the thickness of a hair, produced only the smallest puff of sound and light as they disappeared. He lifted the screaming baby, the adeptness of habit compensating for the clumsiness of his hands, and positioned her against his shoulder in the way she liked. She howled and struggled for a moment, then hiccuped abruptly to silence.

"Axane," he said. "Axane!"

She was rocking back and forth, her hands still wound into her hair. He hesitated, then reached to touch her shoulder. She jumped as if arrow-shot, and turned on him a face so contorted he barely recognized it.

"Axane." It shocked him. "What is it?"

"I dreamed—I dreamed—" She gave a great gasp. "Of Refuge."

It was always Refuge when she woke weeping in the night, or so she claimed. Once, wincing with the memory of his own dreams, he had said harshly: *Are you sure it's not your soft life in Ninyâser that you dream of?* She had looked away from him and said, with such sadness that he found, suddenly, that he did believe her: *I wish it were that.*

"I'm sorry to wake you." She hitched a breath.

"Go back to sleep. I'll take Parvâti."

She nodded. She had begun to shiver, long shudders that shook her from head to toe.

He returned to his bed. Against his shoulder, Parvâti was already dozing again. Carefully he lowered her to the pallet. She grew heavier by the day—he would not be able to manage holding her for much longer. He lay down next to her, his back turned on Axane, propping his head on his outstretched arm. Gently he touched the soft skin of her neck, brushed the curling hair from her forehead. Her lashes made dark crescents on her cheeks. Her jade green light flared emerald-bright where it intersected his.

My flesh, he thought, with the amazement that never seemed to dim. *Mine.*

Parvâti stirred, made a small sound. He rested one hand gently on her little chest, feeling her pulse under his fingers. He brought his breathing into time with hers. Outside in the night, the beast breathed, too, a vast susurrus driven by the beating of two thousand hearts. But he was lost in the rhythm of just one, and did not hear it.

Sundit

It has been more than four weeks since I last wrote in this journal. Since I recorded what I saw in the Dracâriya hills, I have lacked the heart. Of our journey to Baushpar there is little to tell, in any case; and though the days since our arrival have been eventful, I've found myself reluctant to relive them by committing them to paper.

The monastery was farther than I thought. We might not have found it but for a shepherd we met, who sent his son with us as a guide. We left Cas the secretary there, and rode for Baushpar, passing through Ninyâser only a few days after Santaxma's funeral. Blasphemer some might have named him, but he was also much beloved; mourning cloths hung from nearly every house, and many of the streets were still strewn with flowers and prayer ribbons from the funeral cortege. According to the Palace, his body was too injured to lie openly in state. The corpse the people saw, wrapped in burial cloths, could not possibly have been his—no remains could have been recovered from beneath all that rock. It's said that he was caught in an earthquake while passing through the Dracâriya hills—on his way to Darna to take stock of the unrest in the south, according to some (the official reason given for his journey), and according to others, riding to intercept the man claiming to be the Next Messenger. I suppose it's not surprising that the whole truth is not known, given that any members of Santaxma's retinue who survived the collapse were too far back to see what really happened. As far as I'm aware, the only eyewitnesses were Cas and my men and I.

Of Râvar's approach, the reports we heard were equally conflicting and confused, with opinion evenly divided between those who feared apostasy and those who dismissed those fears as rumor. When we paused at the Âratist complex to reunite with Drolma and the Tapati, I told the administrator the truth and urged him to take his people out of the city. I hope he will obey.

We reached Baushpar five days ago near nightfall. A driving rain was falling; the outlying streets were all but deserted. Beyond the walls, in the old city, the air smelled of wet and charcoal smoke and incense, and from all quarters came the sound of temple bells, ringing evening services—holy Baushpar, as I remember it from so many lifetimes, going about its business as if nothing in the world had changed. As if nothing in the world ever would.

The keeper of the Sunfall Gate nearly fell from his watch post in shock when he saw me, and for the first time (stupidly, I suppose), it occurred to me that my spirit-siblings—to whom I have sent no word all this long time, not even of my desperate flight back to Baushpar, for no courier could have bettered the pace to which I forced my people—might think I had come to harm. Cold and weary as I was, I longed for my own chambers, for a hot bath and the linen of my bed. Instead, I dismissed my Tapati—all but Reanu, who refused to leave me—and hastened to Hysanet's apartments. Her guards were as amazed as the gatekeeper, but better at concealing it. We waited in her anteroom while one of them went to fetch her. She came quickly; when she saw me she checked and clapped her hands over her mouth.

"Do I really look so bad, Hysa?"

She ran to throw her arms around me, even soaking wet as I was. "Oh, Sunni!" She pulled back. "Why didn't you let us know you were coming?"

"Hysa, right now you are the only one who knows I'm here. I need to talk with you."

"Of course."

She led me to one of her inner rooms and left me. After a little while she returned, with dry clothes and a pair of servants carrying a brazier and a tray of food and drink. She dismissed the servants, then drew up a cushion and waited as I stripped off my sodden garments and put on what she had brought me.

"I've been so worried, Sunni," she said as soon as I sat down. "All this time, not knowing for certain where you were or what you were doing—why didn't you send word?"

"Tell me," I said, pulling the tray toward me, "what you know of the events at Dracâriya. Of Santaxma's death."

A strange look came across her face. "You know Vivaniya has returned?"

"I do. And I know what he has told you."

She nodded. "After he spoke to us, Dreamers were assigned to dream the . . . the claimant. They were watching as he approached the hills. They saw the disaster, the hills' collapse."

"Did they see the cause?"

"There is . . . uncertainty." She laced her fingers together on the low table between us. "The interpreters can't agree on the meaning of the symbols. And there are many things we don't understand. It has not officially been said that the King went to meet with the . . . claimant—oh, I don't know what to call him—"

"Call him a pretender. For that is what he is."

Her round, pretty face went still. "You don't agree with Vivaniya, then."

"Did you think I did? Did Vivaniya tell you I did?"

"Not . . . in so many words. He said you were invited to remain as a guest, and that you agreed. We took it—many of us took it to mean you had accepted him."

Ah, Vanyi, I thought.

"We assumed you were traveling with him. Is that not true?"

"No, Hysa. I was with the King."

"The King? But—"

"Hysa, I promise I will tell you. Tomorrow I intend to call a meeting of the council, and relate everything I saw, everything I learned. But right now I need to prepare myself. I need you to tell me all that has happened since Vivaniya returned. From the beginning."

She sighed. "He got back little over two months ago. He did not wait an hour before calling us to council—he said everyone must come, even the spirit-wards, even Magabyras, who was ill and had to be brought on a litter. The moment I saw him, I knew what he would say—he looked . . . transported, like someone burning from the inside. He had with him several of the . . . claimant's followers—"

"What?" I had not known of this. "What followers?"

"Five men with prison scars around their necks. You can imagine Kudrâcari's reaction! They call themselves the First Faithful, and say they were there when the . . . claimant came out of the Burning Land. They stood at Vivaniya's back while he swore that the man in the foothills of the Range of Clouds is the Next Messenger, the true Next Messenger, Ârata's own. Oh, Sunni, there was such an uproar! Everyone was shouting. Kudrâcari and Okhsa cried blasphemy. Ariamnes declared that Vivaniya had gone mad."

"What did Taxmârata do?"

"He let it go on for a time, as he always does. Then he commanded us to silence. Vivaniya continued . . ."

He told them more or less what he had told me in the Awakened City; there is no need to write it out again. Hysanet did not look at me as she spoke, staring instead at the glossy tabletop, on which she traced small circles with her forefinger. I had already guessed she did not believe, but by her tone and actions I saw that neither had she stepped all the way into disbelief. She is an equivocator, my Hysanet; it is too easy for her to see all sides of a debate. In other incarnations it has set us at odds, but not in this one. I trust her above most of my spirit-siblings.

"Vivaniya said he made an oath to this man. That he yielded his authority as guardian of the Way of Ârata. Is it so, Sunni?"

"Yes." At some point during her account I had lost my appetite. I pushed away my rice bowl.

"He says it is a judgment." She was still tracing circles. "He says we failed our duty when we refused to believe the apostate Gyalo Amdo Samchen, and now are no longer fit to rule." She closed her hands into fists and looked up at me. "Sunni, it seems to me he had no right to make such an oath, even to the true Next Messenger. Our father gave us guardianship of the Way. *Forever and for all our lives.* It isn't in our power to cede that trust."

"Nor would the true Messenger demand we do so. Hysa, who accepts Vivaniya's claims?"

"Baushtas and Artavâdhi for certain. They swore their faith at the beginning and have not wavered. Possibly Vimâta and Haminâser. They haven't said so, but that is my feeling."

It was much as I had expected. "And the others?"

"Kudrâcari, Ariamnes, Okhsa, and Martyas have been staunch from the start that Vivaniya allowed himself to be beguiled by an apostate Shaper, who may be either a deliberate blasphemer or a madman, but is certainly an imposter. Dâdar has been almost entirely silent—"

"As well he might be, given the part he has played in this."

"But I have no doubt he stands with Kudrâcari. Taxmârata will not commit himself, nor will Magabyras. Vivaniya is angry—he seems to have expected us all simply to accept his word without debate. We have had council after council, Sunni. We have interrogated Vivaniya's guards, and the men he brought back with him, the First Faithful. We have argued till we are all sick with it. But the lines were drawn at that first council, and have not shifted."

"And you, Hysa. What do you believe?"

She was silent, staring again at her hands, which she had unfisted and laid flat upon the tabletop. "Vivaniya swore that the . . . claimant wears the true Blood."

"Yes. It's so."

"But if that's true, how can—how can—"

"How can I swear he is false? And if he is false, how can he have the true Blood? There's a reason. I promise you'll know it."

"At Dracâriya . . . I told you that there's disagreement among the interpreters as to what their Dreamers saw. Two of them read the symbols as a natural event. But the third swears his Dreamer saw . . . the claimant . . . bring a great shaping on the hills. Most of us have dismissed that interpretation. No one has ever heard of an apostate Shaper with such power, and the Next Messenger . . . why would the Next Messenger do such a thing? But Vivaniya . . . Vivaniya declares that it is punishment, Ârata's punishment for Santaxma's blasphemy in desecrating the Burning Land."

"Ah, the fool!"

Her eyes rose to mine. I saw her doubt as clear as words.

"Hysa, this man *is* an unbound Shaper, just as we first thought. He *did* bring down the hills. And it was Santaxma's own arrogance that wrought his death, so perhaps in that sense it is punishment. But there's no divine purpose in what happened. None. I swear this on my lives."

For a moment she watched me. Then she sighed and nodded. "I trust you, Sunni. If you tell me it is so, I will accept it."

"Where do the Dreamers place the pretender now?"

"South of Ninyâser. There has been . . . unrest. In Abaxtra there seems to have been some sort of riot between his followers and the townsfolk."

I felt a chill pass through me. "Has any thought been given to emptying Baushpar?"

She frowned. "Emptying Baushpar?"

"Hysa, a vastly powerful unbound Shaper with a large train of followers approaches our city. Now that the King is dead, there is no one to oppose him. Whatever you believe about Dracâriya, surely those of you who haven't accepted him must see the danger."

"But Sunni, this is the holy city! Even the Caryaxists honored that. Surely we have nothing to fear?"

Would I, in her place, knowing as little as she knew, have reacted as she did? I don't like to think so, but I cannot be certain. I let it be.

We talked for a little longer. I asked about Utamnos, and decided to leave him with her for another night rather than disturb his sleep. She told me of the conflict in the Lords' Assembly regarding the succession: Many want to crown Hathrida, but the queen is pressing for regency in the name of the little prince, and apparently she has considerable support. Taxmârata has issued a proclamation against the regency, an action I approve—Hathrida is not his brother's equal, but he is the better choice. Arsace must have a strong ruler if it is to remain united. "It is one of the few things," Hysa said, with very un-Hysa-like bitterness, "on which we've been able to agree these past two months."

We made our farewells at last, and I sought my chambers, Reanu like a shadow at my heels. I dreaded the possibility of meeting any of my spirit-siblings, but apart from servants we saw no one. The Evening City is so huge, and so few people inhabit it; even during its busiest hours, silence fills it up like water. That night, perhaps because I was so tired, I seemed less to walk through its great light-filled spaces than to swim.

At my door, I turned to Reanu. "Go to your quarters. Get some rest. Send someone else to guard my rooms."

He stiffened. "Old One—"

I shook my head. "We are home now. There's no need for you to lie across my threshold. Go."

His face was fierce. For a moment I thought he would not obey. Many mortals, having saved the body-life of a Daughter of the Brethren, might pardonably grow proud, but with him it is the opposite. It is as if saving me has burdened him almost beyond bearing, and the only remedy is to watch me every moment.

"Great is Ârata," he said, angrily. "Great is his Way."

"Go in light."

He strode off, upright as a tree. I admit I felt a pang—it has become habit, having him close. More than habit, if I'm honest.

I woke my servants, producing surprise and joy, and got my bath at last. I lay in it for a time, missing Ha-tsun, who would have rubbed the ache from my head and made tea the way I like it. I gave orders that no one be admitted, not even my spirit-siblings, and went to bed.

In the morning I sat down at my writing desk to compose thirteen summonses, one for each of my Brothers and Sisters who sit in council. I sealed them with my seal, then went to my library where Drolma, clean and rested, her scalp freshly shaven, was waiting. I sent her off with the summonses, and she returned an hour later to report that the task was done, the summonses delivered not to aides or servants but directly into the hands of the recipients. Word travels quickly in the Evening City. None of my spirit-siblings expressed surprise to receive a communication from one who, less than a day earlier, they had imagined was half a land away.

I went out half an hour before noon. I was not surprised to find Reanu waiting in my antechamber. He fell to his knees; behind his crossed arms his face was as fierce as it had been the night before, and I knew that if I tried to dismiss him, I would have a battle on my hands. It is not the custom to bring personal guards to a meeting of the council. But at every step of this long journey he has been at my side, and it seemed to me—seems to me—that he had the right to be present.

The vermilion gates to the Courtyard of the Sun stood open when we reached them. The rain had passed in the night; sunlight flooded the vast court, refracting blindingly from the brass seams between the flagstones. Despite the chilly air, the yellow granite of the walkway was warm under the soles of my indoor shoes. The shadows of the colossal Ârata-images, which at morning and evening stretch farther than the width of the court, were inky puddles at the images' feet. I looked up into their great stone faces as I passed, each in turn—World Creator, Primal Warrior, Eon Sleeper, Risen Judge—Ârata in each of his four roles, contemplating eternity as we living creatures scurry underneath.

I left Reanu on the Pavilion's broad porch, and passed between its gilded pillars into the dimness of the council chamber. I was early; only servants were present, lighting lamps and arranging braziers. I took my customary place and waited as my Brothers and Sisters arrived, many with their spirit-wards in tow. All came to greet me, with shows of affection both real and feigned: Baushtas, serene as a well of dark water; Artavâdhi, doing me the honor of heaving her great bulk out of her sedan chair to kiss my cheek, young Gaumârata at her side; Magabyras, clearly not yet recovered from his illness, leaning heavily on Karuva's arm; Dâdar, scowlingly speaking the barest words of courtesy; Okhsa and Kudrâcari, making a better show of it, though Kudrâcari's mouth was tight and Okhsa's black-bead eyes darted everywhere in his effort not to meet mine; Martyas, showing all his snaggle teeth in welcome as he took my hands in his small crooked ones; Ariamnes, pompous as a pigeon, Sonrida trotting at his heels; Hysanet, embracing and kissing me exactly as if we had not met last night; Vimâta, apprehension clear on his handsome face; Haminâser, wiping at the tears that seep always from his blind eyes, his solemn spirit-ward Idrakara at his elbow.

Vivaniya was among the last to arrive. He strode between the pillars with his eyes on the floor. I had wondered what he would do; I was prepared for anything, even an immediate denunciation. But he chose to ignore me—he alone, of all of them—and crossed directly to his chair, misjudging in his awkward way and sitting down too hard. I saw my spirit-siblings take note.

Taxmârata entered from the tiring rooms at the Pavilion's rear. He took his place on the dais and opened the council with the customary phrases, then seated himself in the Bearer's gilded chair and turned toward me. The Blood of Ârata shone on his chest. At his back, the gems and gold of the sun-mural on the chamber's rear wall caught fire from the lamplight.

"Welcome, Sister. It's joy beyond describing to have you among us again."

"I rejoice in my return, Brother."

"We are eager to hear what you have to say to us. And also"—there was an edge in his voice—"to know why we have heard nothing of you for so long."

I rose. Until that moment, I had felt no apprehension. Urgency, yes; but a focused urgency, an urgency of purpose. But as I drew breath to speak, a powerful strangeness seized me. I cannot say why it suddenly seemed to me that I stood not in the Pavilion, but in the hall of my dream of mirrors. For just an instant, I saw the shadows of my spirit-siblings' previous lives pressed close behind them. I felt the weight of the box in my hands.

"Sister?"

Taxmârata's voice seemed to travel across a great distance. The strangeness was gone. But my composure had gone with it. My heart raced. My limbs were cold.

"Brothers and Sisters." I heard the unsteadiness in my voice. "I know what you have learned from our Brother Vivaniya. I know also that many of you have assumed I share his belief."

They watched me—all but Vivaniya, his gaze resolutely turned upon his knees.

"I do *not* share it. The man who claims the title of Next Messenger, who wears around his neck the Blood of Ârata—which is indeed the true Blood, I will confirm that—is an imposter, a pretender. An unbound Shaper, as we originally suspected. Though not, as you think, apostate."

Vivaniya whispered something, too soft to hear. Kudrâcari cast him a sharp look, then turned her gaze on me.

"What other sort of unbound Shaper is there, Sister?"

"The sort who has never been bound at all. His name is Râvar, and he is a Shaper of Refuge. That is why the Blood he wears is real: He got it from the Cavern of the Blood."

Vivaniya's head snapped up. Someone, I could not tell who, cried, "What?" Haminâser turned his blind eyes toward me, tears slipping slowly down his cheeks.

"All of Refuge's Shapers perished, Sister."

"Or so we were informed," said Martyas. "Another falsehood, Sister? Another lie to add to the list?"

"Not an intentional one. No one could have known that Râvar survived.

He closed himself up inside the Cavern when our army came. That's why Dâdar and Vivaniya saw nothing. Had they searched, had they ordered our Shapers to probe the rock, he would have held it closed against them. In falsehood or in truth, our Brothers would have brought back the same tale."

"On what authority do you make this claim, Sister?" Baushtas's smooth brow had creased in the faintest frown.

"Râvar himself told me. And it was confirmed by one who knew him."

"What, more survivors?" Kudrâcari exclaimed.

"A survivor, yes, but not of Refuge."

"Enough of these riddles!" Ariamnes's moon face was swollen with irritation. "Say what you have to say, Sister, and say it plain!"

"She has nothing to say." Vivaniya gripped the arms of his chair. "She is lying."

"I would like to judge that for myself," Kudrâcari snapped. "Though I say now, as I have said before, that I do not admit the existence of this Cavern."

"Come, Brother," said Martyas, with sly malice. "Can't your conviction stand a little testing?"

"All of us have the right to speak in council," Taxmârata said mildly. "All of us have the duty to listen. Sister, continue."

"First I must tell you why my Brother and I did not return together from the Awakened City. He told you that when he departed, I was invited to remain. This is not true. I was forced to remain, held captive by the pretender, who saw that I doubted his claim and did not want me to speak against my Brother in Baushpar. On the night before the start of his long march, he came to me and gave me one last chance to bow down to him. I refused. The next morning, after all his followers had gone, he walled me and my people inside the rock and left us to perish."

Vivaniya shouted: "You lie!"

"No, Brother. It is true. I know you didn't know he meant to kill us. But you did know he kept me against my will. You did know that, Vivaniya."

"But why should he want your body-death, Sister?" Baushtas asked.

"He wants all our body-deaths, in payment for Refuge. That is his desire: vengeance. He told me so before he shut me in, told me the whole of his intent. He marches on Baushpar to disbody us all, and bring Baushpar down upon us."

Vivaniya practically leaped from his chair. "That is a filthy falsehood! The Next Messenger has come in love and joy to guide the world and all in it to perfection! He marches to Baushpar to take his place at the head of the church and reign gloriously in the holy city through the time of Interim! Can you not see what she is doing, Brothers and Sisters? Can you not see how she means to undo my work—"

"Brother, be silent!" Taxmârata's deep voice rang across the Pavilion. "Our Sister will speak, and you will listen. Or I will banish you."

For a moment I thought Vivaniya would not obey. Then he subsided back into his chair. His frustration and his fury spoke in every line of his body. But I had been watching his face when I spoke of Refuge. For just that moment, I think he glimpsed the way it fit.

"You say he intends to destroy the Brethren," said Kudrâcari. "The Brethren cannot be destroyed."

"If all of us are simultaneously disbodied, Sister, who will search out our new incarnations and teach us to recognize ourselves? And our body-deaths are not his only wish. He wants our souls as well. Before we perish, he wants us to bow down to him in faith, and through that blasphemy extinguish any light that may remain in us after all these centuries. It's for that reason he allowed Vivaniya to return—to prepare his way. He believed that on the word of one of us, all of us would believe."

Martyas laughed, drawing angry looks from Kudrâcari and Okhsa. "Clearly he knows us very little."

"If he intended you to perish, Sister," Baushtas said, "how is it you got free?"

"There was another unbound Shaper in the Awakened City—a true apostate. He found us and unmade the stone that confined us. Brothers and Sisters, I know this will seem incredible, but that apostate was Gyalo Amdo Samchen."

Eyes stretched. Mouths dropped open. Dâdar, silent till now, barked an incredulous laugh.

"The man is dead, Sister."

"No, Brother. One of his companions freed him from imprisonment in Faal, making it seem he had fallen from his window. He has been living as a fugitive ever since."

"Ârata!" Kudrâcari's sallow face was flushed with anger. "Did I not warn you all that imprisoning him was not enough? Now see! Free for more than two years to corrupt others with his apostasy, to spread his blasphemous claim of Messengerhood!"

With difficulty I held my patience. "If that were so, don't you think we would have heard of it, just as we heard of Râvar? In fact, he has been spreading nothing. So he said, and I believe him."

"Rather than disputing the past actions of this council," Martyas suggested, "it might be useful to know how he came to be in the Awakened City."

I told them all Gyalo had told me—of Râvar's theft of Gyalo's wife and child, of Gyalo's failed attempt to rescue them, of Râvar's deeds and his enormous power.

"Another Shaper War," said Magabyras, speaking for the first time, his voice husky with his recent sickness.

"This is no Shaper War," Ariamnes declared. "Unbound Shaper he may be, but there's no Shaper army at his back, only a rabble of barefoot followers."

"His power is immense," I said, "as is his skill in wielding it. I bear witness to this. I did not see him bring down the walls of Thuxra City, but I saw him create the disaster at Dracâriya."

"You are mistaken, Sister," Dâdar growled. "The Dreamers affirm that what happened there was natural."

"Their *interpreters* affirm it. And only two of them—the third, I understand, disagrees."

Kudrâcari smiled an insufferably condescending smile. "You know no Shaper has so much strength, Sister, not even one unbound from birth. The third Dreamer is wrong, and so are you."

"There is another question," said Baushtas, with his imperturbable, cool-water calm. "How, Sister, did you come to be at Dracâriya?"

"After we were freed, I traveled with all haste to Santaxma. Only he had the strength to make a stand against Râvar and his army. I brought Gyalo Amdo Samchen with me—"

"You *traveled*? With an *apostate*?" Kudrâcari's voice scaled upward in her horror.

"With a *witness*, Sister, a man who of his own experience could confirm Râvar's identity and the magnitude of his power, and so help me to convince a King who had no wish to heed any word spoken by the Brethren." I told them, as briefly as I could, of our flight to Ninyâser, of our meetings with the King and of Santaxma's flawed plan. They wanted to know why I had not seen fit to inform them of my actions; I gave them the truth, which did not please them, though I saw Martyas nod in understanding. I told them of Dracâriya. In my mind's eye the disaster unfolded again, images whose vividness I will never need to consult my journals to recapture.

"Preposterous," said Ariamnes, who for the last part of my account had been shaking his head with increasing vehemence. "I can believe the King's men mistargeted their assault, or that the blasphemer was able somehow to avoid it, but I am in agreement with Kudrâcari. No single Shaper could accomplish such destruction. There's no historical precedent for such a thing."

"The Next Messenger is not bound by *history*," Vivaniya said, but quietly.

"Can any of us declare with certainty that we would recognize unfettered shaping if we saw it?" Kudrâcari asked. "It has been many incarnations since we have witnessed any shaping beyond the transformations of Communion and Banishing. Sister, you are certainly in error."

Anger sang in my head. "Will you not set aside for one moment your desire to contradict every word I speak, Sister, no matter what it is? Has it entirely escaped your notice that the news I've brought supports your own position? Besides, eight centuries may have passed since *you* saw unfettered shaping, but given the manner of my escape from the caverns, you'll admit it hasn't been quite so long for me."

Kudrâcari looked at me with open loathing. Martyas grinned, enjoying the conflict.

"What of the apostate?" Ariamnes asked. "Where was he in all of this?"

"I don't know," I admitted. "He left us in Ninyâser."

"You *let him go*?" Kudrâcari demanded.

"And how exactly was I to stop him, Sister?"

"The church is not without resources," Ariamnes said. "You know the procedures that are followed in such situations."

"The circumstances were extraordinary. I made the decisions that seemed expedient."

"In other words, you failed your duty to the Doctrine of Baushpar," Kudrâcari said harshly. "Now he is free again, and we have not the slightest idea where he may have gone."

"In the circumstances, Sister, I think we have more pressing concerns," said Hysanet, speaking for the first time, with a sharpness entirely uncharacteristic of her.

"Indeed." All trace of humor was gone from Martyas's face. "Brothers and Sisters, it's clear we face a threat, even if we cannot agree on exactly what manner of threat it is—"

"Enough." Vivaniya surged to his feet, with such force that his chair tipped back and crashed upon the floor. "Can none of you see the truth? Our Sister is afraid, afraid as my Brother and I were afraid when we went up into Refuge—afraid of change, afraid of ending. In her fear she has done what we did—she has invented a lie. She took her lie to the King, who marched upon the Messenger in hatred, but Ârata's glorious will cannot be so easily thwarted, and instead of the destruction she intended, the god's judgment fell on Santaxma. Now she brings her lie to us. I beg you, Brothers and Sisters, do not make this same mistake. Reject her words. Close your ears to her denial of the Messenger." He rounded on me. Ah, there was such loathing in his face! "I'll tell you what part of your tale I do believe, Sister, and that is that he left you to perish in imprisonment. He saw the true shape of your soul. He weighed your faithlessness, and he judged you, he judged you as Ârata will judge you in the time of cleansing. You escaped him, you and your apostate, but you shall not escape the god!"

"Brother!" cried Hysanet, horrified. I stood speechless. As angry as I've been at him for his betrayal—and oh, I have been so angry!—my love for him endures, my Brother, my foster child. I'd hoped it was the same for him—that somehow, at the end of this, we might be reconciled. In that moment I understood that it cannot be so, not in this life. And thus, perhaps, not ever. It turned my heart to stone.

He turned back to the others. "When our father brought the Regent of Ko to Ârata, and members of the Regent's council rose against him in his new faith, the Regent called the councillors and ministers who believed as he did to form a new council, an Assembly of Truth. I call now, as he did. Come with me, those of you who believe. Let us abandon this false council and make another. When the Next Messenger comes we will be waiting. He will know that there are some at least among the Brethren who are worthy."

There was an appalled silence. There's not one of us who has not refused, at one time or another, to answer a summons to the Pavilion of the Sun—sometimes for many months, like Kudrâcari and her faction over the issue of Gyalo's exile. But even in our most terrible disagreements, which splinter us from one another, no one has ever seriously sought to split the council.

"That is enough, Brother." It was Taxmârata, intervening at last. "I have no more patience with your disruption of this council. Be silent, or be gone."

"I will go," Vivaniya said bitterly. "And I will not come back. If I ever had any doubt that the oath he asked of me was necessary, I have none now. Not one of you is fit to guard the Way of Ârata."

He turned and strode from the Pavilion, his head high. For once his clumsiness did not betray him. His steps were firm and true as he passed from shadow into sun, and vanished down the steps.

A terrible hush had fallen. None of my spirit-siblings seemed to wish to break it.

"We must flee," I said. "For our survival, we must abandon Baushpar, as we did when the Caryaxists came. I'm told the pretender is south of Ninyâser, which puts him perhaps a month from our gates. We can be well away by the time he arrives."

"Flee?" Kudrâcari repeated, as if it were a word in an unknown language.

"Where would we go?" Hysanet said.

"One of the remoter monasteries, where our presence can be kept secret. Somewhere in Isar, perhaps. Once we are there, we can decide what to do."

"I will not run from this rabble," Ariamnes declared. "We've subdued apostates before. We can subdue this one also."

"We are hardly defenseless," Kudrâcari said. "There are two thousand Tapati ordinates in the Evening City."

"We tempt the people's anger if we abandon Baushpar again so soon," said Martyas. "A substantial portion of the populace already believes we betrayed our duty by fleeing the Caryaxists. If we flee before this threat also, what faith in our leadership can they ever have?"

Baushtas rose to his feet. His quiet is more commanding than a shout. All voices stilled. All eyes turned to him.

"Our Brother Vivaniya is rash in his passion," he said. "But he is correct in one thing. This debate is misguided. Let us cut through all obscurity. Ârata has risen. No"— he held up his hand—"don't dispute me. There are very few among us who do not now at least suspect that this is so. We've learned much today, some of it ugly, some of it fearful. But I have heard nothing to shake my certainty that the Next Messenger approaches. If anything, I am more certain now than when I walked into this chamber."

"Brother, you are a fool," Kudrâcari said.

"Why, Sister?" Baushtas smiled. His calm is like glass. It's not that it is too deep to be stirred, but that it is too hard. "Because *you* do not believe? When has your voice ever been the one to guide us? Because he locked our Sister Sundit up in stone? But might he not have foreseen the consequences of that act, which allowed him to bring judgment on a faithless King? Because we have learned that this Messenger is a man and not a god? Is this not precisely why we have never taken a firm doctrinal position on the matter—because we knew that Ârata would create his Messenger as he willed, and not as we desired? Our father Marduspida was a man—and not a man of virtue, either, but a man in love with wealth and with the pleasures of the flesh, who six times rejected Ârata's summoning dream. Because this Messenger has cloaked himself in deception? But might this not be a test, a test of our ability to discern the truth? Because this Messenger comes in anger, in vengeance for his lost people? Do we not deserve Ârata's anger—yes, even more than Santaxma deserved it, we who turned from word of the god's rising? And we did not turn from it only once, Brothers and Sisters. Twice we failed our duty. Twice we betrayed our trust—first when the apostate Gyalo Amdo Samchen gave the Blood of Ârata into our hands, and a second time when two of us, and therefore all of us, closed their eyes to the light of Ârata's resting place and decreed the slaughter of those who guarded it—"

"Brother!" cried Kudrâcari. Okhsa and Dâdar were on their feet. Baushtas raised his voice.

"These are the end times. The Next Messenger must come. *Those who sow darkness shall reap ash*, the *Darxasa* says. This is the Next Messenger we deserve, risen in righteous anger from the ashes of our sin. It is our duty to receive him, to accept the fate he brings us. We have sworn a Covenant to do so. Brothers and Sisters, rejoice!" His voice rang with a fierce joy. "Our long travail on this earth is done. With us, the world's transformation will begin. What have we lived for all this long time, if not for that?"

I never really expected him to believe me. But it still horrifies me, how he took my words and twisted them.

"I'll hear no more." Dâdar's pockmarked face was dark with anger. "For weeks we have been pummeled with this talk of punishment, of sin—by the Blood, I've had enough! We've committed no sin. We've done no more than we have ever done for twelve long centuries, which is to guide the Way of Ârata as we see fit. No part of our Covenant says we must sit idle while a madman comes to disbody us all! My vote is for flight."

I was astonished. I had thought he would follow Kudrâcari.

"And mine," said Hysanet.

"Well, mine certainly is not," Kudrâcari snapped.

Taxmârata held up his hands. "No vote has been called," he said, "nor will one be called today. No, Kudrâcari—say no more. This is not a matter to be decided in a few hours. We will take time to rest and consider. We will come together again tomorrow at noon."

He rose from his golden chair and made the sign of Ârata. "In Ârata's name and in the name of our Covenant, I declare this session ended. Great is Ârata. Great is his Way."

"Go in light," we replied, in a unison that utterly belied our divided state.

I returned to my chambers, Reanu at my heels. "How much did you hear?" I asked him before my door.

"Everything. Old One, I stand ready to support you."

I touched his stole-draped arm. "I know you do. And I'm sure you will be called to speak. The others, too."

"Don't send me to my quarters, Old One. I've been at your side day and night since this began. I've shared the risks and the hardship—ash of the Enemy, I've even suffered the companionship of an apostate! For that if nothing else, I have the right to remain."

"I won't send you away, Reanu."

A little later, one of Hysanet's servants brought Utamnos. He came running when he saw me; I caught him up, for an instant forgetting everything but his warm arms around my neck and his sweet child smell. He's heavier than I remember, and taller, too. But then, it has been six months. Six months!

I fed him supper and told him stories, finding a brief and welcome respite in such familiar activities. But when I retired to my bedchamber all my cares returned. I spent most of the night by my window, watching moonlight swim across the court. Colder than the frost-crisp air were my thoughts of Râvar. I thought also of Ha-tsun, who was so ill when we left her. I wonder if she still lives. I thought of Gyalo. *He* lives. In some irreducible part of myself I'm certain of it. *How could it be otherwise?* that part of me asks.

I'll spare myself the drudgery of writing a detailed account of the three days of dispute that followed that initial council. Those who have joined me in my call for flight—Hysa, Dâdar, Magabyras, on the second day, and on the third, with clear reluctance, Martyas—are a minority, and not one that looks likely to change. My guards and Drolma have been called to give testimony; with such a weight of witness Kudrâcari and Ariamnes and Okhsa have been forced to admit that shaping might have been involved at Dracâriya, though they remain adamant that it could not have been wholly responsible and refuse to admit that we should flee. They claim the authority of the historical record. Baushtas has not wavered in his dark belief, and it's clear that Artavâdhi follows him, though she says little. Haminâser also believes, though sometimes I sense doubt. Vimâta vacillates between belief and fear. And Taxmârata, as always, presides in silence, intervening only when the dispute grows too heated. It's impossible to read his thoughts.

As for Vivaniya, he has kept his promise. He is sequestered in his rooms. He is visited there by his supporters, and no one else.

Each day, Râvar draws closer. Yesterday's Dreams seem to indicate some sort of armed confrontation on the Great South Way below Ninyâser, but the interpreters are still working on the symbols, and we won't have a final report until tomorrow.

This morning, unable to bear the thought of another afternoon of fruitless debate, I went to Taxmârata. He was in his library, kneeling at a writing table. He set down his pen when I came in.

"Well, Sister." His gaze was somber. "I've been wondering when you would visit me."

I sat across from him. There was no brazier, for fear of sparks amid all that paper and parchment, and though the window screens were closed, the air was chilly. A pair of standing lamps provided the only light—and the fire of the Blood, flaring on Taxmârata's breast.

"Brother," I said, "if ever you've heeded my counsel, heed it now. Veto these proceedings. Make a ruling, as Haminâser did when he was Blood Bearer and the Caryaxists took Ninyâser. Decree that we must flee."

He shook his head. "There is too much disagreement, Sunni. Such a ruling might be disobeyed. I don't want to set a precedent like that."

"There was disagreement over the Caryaxists, too. In the end we all obeyed."

"That was a different situation."

"Yes, it was different! The danger then was a shadow of the danger now!"

Lamplight touched the broad planes of his face, the heavy muscles of his undraped arm. "You supported flight then, too."

"As did you."

"I was wrong. We should not have fled and lived for eighty years in luxury in Rimpang. We should have cast our lot with the faithful. We should have remained and suffered as they did."

I've suspected before that his thoughts ran in those channels. But he has never said it aloud, to me at least. I felt a premonitory coldness.

"Mâra, you've said almost nothing these past days. I know it's your way to listen first and speak later. But tell me, for my own peace of mind—where do you stand?"

He looked down at his half-finished letter. "*We* stand before a threat."

"So you do see it."

He looked up again. "The threat I see is the possibility that we may choose wrongly."

"As we will if we remain in Baushpar!"

He shook his head. "Sunni, we Brethren are like the beads of a necklace. I, the Blood Bearer, am like the lock that clasps it. It's my task to hold you all, to bear you all, as I bear the Blood of Ârata." One big hand moved to caress the golden lattice that contained the stone. "To do that I must stand apart. I must consider every side. I see the force of your certainty. I also see the force of Vivaniya's faith—"

"Which is born of the force of his guilt! Did you and I not discuss this, the night before my departure? Have I not explained, these past days, how Râvar manipulated him?"

"I see also the force of Baushtas's argument—"

"What, that we have all sinned and therefore deserve disbodiment at Râvar's hands?"

"It is my duty to consider it. As it is my duty to consider the word that you have brought."

I leaned forward. I spoke with care. "If we remain in Baushpar, Brother, Râvar will destroy us. He will obliterate us, just as he obliterated Santaxma. The Way of Ârata will be leaderless, just as Arsace is leaderless. If you think that we have failed in any way, Mâra, imagine what a failure that would be."

His hand had closed fully round the lattice, so that the crystal's fire pulsed below his fist. "Santaxma was a blasphemer."

"And so his death was justified? Don't tell me you believe—"

"This is what I believe, Sunni. Baushtas is correct. Who among us, even Kudrâcari, can now declare with certainty that Ârata has not risen? I certainly cannot. These are the end times. Much as we may fear it, the Next Messenger is coming. We turned from the truth once before. I cannot allow that to occur again."

I said, shocked: "You don't believe in him!"

His hand fell from the necklace, to lie open on the table. "I am . . . uncertain."

"Mâra. Mâra, listen to me." I felt like weeping. I don't think I realized until that moment how much I had counted on his support. "He will kill us all."

He looked at me, a long slow look. "If we are to end," he said, "does it matter how?"

I knew then that I had lost. Perhaps it's really true that he sees all sides and cannot choose—like Hysanet, I would say, but Hysanet *has* chosen. But the deeper truth, I think, is that he has surrendered to the doubt he confessed to me that night in my moon garden. He will not act to stop this fruitless debate, or not soon enough. And action is required. For between those who believe in Râvar, and those who do not believe in him but cannot accept the reality of his power, there will never be consensus.

I got to my feet. "I do not accept that. Do you hear me, Mâra? I don't accept it."

"Great is Ârata," he said. There was sadness in his face, but also resolve. "Great is his Way."

I left him. I've never wept easily, in this body or in any other, but I could not stop my tears. I *did* want his friendship again, the reconciliation he offered six months ago in my moon garden. I know that now. It's a small thing, compared to all else, but sad, so sad.

By the time I reached my apartments, I had composed myself. "Come," I told Reanu. He rose, silent as a dancer, and followed me to my own library.

"We are leaving," I told him. "As soon it can be arranged."

He showed no surprise. "Yes, Old One."

"I don't yet know the exact composition of the party. But I am estimating there will be ten of us, with our servants and aides. We will need conveyances, supplies, an escort—you know what's required. How quickly can you accomplish it?"

"It will take at least a week, Old One, if I am to do it properly."

"Too long. But very well. Also, Baushpar must be warned. I'll write a proclamation and have it copied, and you will see it's posted throughout the city. I want it done tonight, in secret. By the time my spirit-siblings learn of it, it will be too late to take back the knowledge. Also, to that end, I wish to make as public a departure as possible. A grand procession. If the people see the Brethren leaving, perhaps they will be more inclined to follow."

"Rely on me, Old One." He bowed and left me.

I summoned Drolma and dictated the text of the proclamation, instructing her to produce one hundred copies, seal each one with my seal, and convey them to Reanu. "You'll be coming with me," I told her; she nodded. I could see she was afraid.

At the appointed time I went to council, where I claimed the floor as soon as Taxmârata opened the session, and announced my intent before them all. I urged them to accompany me. I begged them at least, if they would not come, to send their spirit-wards. There was, of course, a terrible outcry. I did not stay to argue, but left them in full spate. Hysanet rose and followed me. Martyas came that evening—for him, leaving is only the slightly less terrible of two evil choices, and I sense his deep uncertainty. Magabyras arrived this morning to confirm that he will go; Karuva, however, has refused, and nothing Magabyras can say will change his mind. "He's only a year from taking his place in council," Magabyras told me. "I can't give him orders, for all he is my spirit-ward." Dâdar sent his aide with a note that he and young Ciryas will join us. And to my very great surprise, Vimâta will be coming also, with his little ward Ivaxri. It is a pathetic group, less than half the twenty-four incarnate Brethren. Could I have argued better? Could there have been a different outcome? If so, I am at a loss to know how I could have effected it.

Still, I am tormented by a sense of failure. I should have been able to persuade them all.

But then, that is probably precisely what Vivaniya thinks.

I may know the true Messenger. Often, in the debates of the past days, those words have risen to my lips. I haven't said them—not just because I know none of my spirit-siblings would believe me, but because I don't know if I believe myself. There was a moment, just a moment in Ninyâser, in which I was almost certain . . . but it passed with Gyalo's going, and I cannot now recapture the substance of my certainty, or remember why I was so sure.

I spent the evening deciding what to pack for Utamnos and myself. I will take my journals, although it means I can take little else. Of the riches of my household, only they cannot be replaced. I went to my memory rooms this afternoon, to supervise the packing: four chambers, shelf after shelf of writings, thousands of pages inscribed in as many hands as I have had bodies. My life, in ink and paper. If my memories are destroyed, the greatest part of me goes down into extinction. Perhaps it's vain, perhaps it is foolish, but I cannot bear to imagine it.

I put Utamnos to bed—he knows we are making a trip, and I've done my best to present it as an exciting adventure—then went to my bedchamber and wrote down most of this account. I grew restless before I finished, and left my room. My steps led me, inevitably, to the antechamber where Reanu, having set in motion all the tasks I gave him, knelt on a mat facing the outer door.

"Old One," he said when he saw me, and bowed low. "Great is Ârata. Great is his Way."

"Go in light, Reanu." I sat on one of the benches that stand against the walls. "It's chilly. Shall I have a brazier brought?"

"I'm not cold, Old One. But thank you."

We sat in silence. He was in profile to me, his arms folded beneath his stole. Apart from an occasional slow blink, he was motionless. I could not even see him breathe.

"Do you ever sleep, Reanu?"

He smiled a little; it is a joke between us. "I sleep, Old One. I just do it with my eyes open."

"Sometimes I think you are too perfect to be human."

"Oh, I'm human, Old One. In all ways."

"I've split the council." The way I've come to speak to him is scandalous—many of us are not so frank even with our aides. "In all the history of the Brethren, there has never been a schism like the one I've made."

He turned his head. The light of the wall-lamps sparked in his dark eyes. "They would not flee, Old One. You had no choice."

"I don't even know if there's any purpose to it."

"Survival is its own purpose, Old One."

A warrior's response. On the other hand, it explains everything—everything we have done since Gyalo came out of the Burning Land. All of it, all of it, has centered on survival.

Something had come into Reanu's face. I could see it even behind his tattoos.

"Old One," he said quietly. "Is Ârata risen?"

We have spoken of this before. But I sensed that he was asking for something different this time—not my thought or my belief, not *my* truth, but *the* truth, the true nature of the world. He waited for my answer with complete trust; just so did Utamnos look at me earlier, when he asked if we would be happy in the place where we were going. At least to Reanu I did not have to lie.

"Yes. Ârata is risen."

He nodded, once. "Then all is well."

Perhaps it really is that simple. An immense weariness swept over me. I bowed my head. I did not even know he had risen, cat-silent as he is, until I felt the air move, and looked up to see him sinking to his knees before me. From the inflexible mask of his tattoos his eyes looked into mine, vital and alive. Carefully he reached out and took my hands in his.

"I serve you, Old One," he said softly. "As long as my body has breath, I will be with you. I swear it, by the woken god."

His grip was light, as if I were very fragile. He has touched me before—to assist me, to protect me—but never like this. It is not his place, not the place of any mortal. Still, he reached out, a mortal man, reached past the immortal Daughter to the mortal woman that I also am. It caught me utterly off guard. For the second time this day tears rose in my eyes, spilled down my cheeks.

We sat like that until I mastered myself again. Gently I freed my hands. I admit it: I did not want to let him go.

"Thank you, Reanu."

He nodded, his arms once more folded beneath his stole: the perfect guard, the perfect servant.

I returned to my bedchamber and finished this entry—even, for the sake of the full memory record that may mean nothing now, this last part of it, which perhaps would have been better left unwritten. It's very late, and there will be much to do in the week ahead. I must try to sleep.

All day there has been a tightness in my chest, the breathlessness of some feeling or perception I have not quite been able to identify. I think I recognize it now. It's the pressure of dwindling time, the desire to catch back the moments as they slip away. Time, which was precious when I was mortal and grew cheap when I was transformed into what I am now, has become precious to me again.

That is a strange, perhaps a wondrous, thing.

21

Râvar

H alt."

The four Twentymen who served as bearers lowered Râvar's palanquin to the ground. The palanquin's door slid back. Gray light rolled in, and raw air that smelled of smoke, as if somewhere nearby a fire burned. Ardashir, mantled in his shadowy aura, bowed.

"Beloved One."

Ignoring the First Disciple's extended hand, Râvar gathered up the skirts of his heavy robe—an offering from one of his wealthy followers, lavishly embroidered on the sleeves and hem with gold thread—and climbed from the palanquin without assistance.

They were at the crest of a hill. Below, a long valley cupped a lake, its waters the same leaden color as the sky. On the near bank, amid a patchwork of brown fields, sat a huddle of dwellings—or what had been dwellings, for all were burned, some entirely consumed, others hollowed out, their blackened timbers jutting like snapped bones. The fires were long extinguished, the smoke long dispersed; even so, the odor of char was so thick that Râvar could taste it as well as smell it, acrid at the back of his throat.

He felt a surge of anger so intense it was like being struck in the chest.

"Beloved One," Ardashir said, "I do not know the name of this village, or even if it had one. There is no one now to tell us."

Ardashir had come to him that morning. *There is something I would show you, Beloved One.* When Râvar asked what, and why, the First Disciple put his bandaged hands together and said, in a tone of such intensity that Râvar knew it would be dangerous to refuse: *Beloved One, I entreat you.* And at last they were there, and Râvar knew exactly why, and also why Ardashir had not prepared him.

He looked at the First Disciple, standing by him on the hill. How much courage did it require to stare so fixedly ahead, refusing his gaze? Much, judging by the tension of Ardashir's jaw. Less, probably, than to trick Râvar into coming here.

"Let us take a closer look." Ardashir stepped forward.

Râvar drew his robe around him and followed, as did two of the Twentymen. It was cold; bulky clouds leaned overhead, and Râvar's feet sank into the ground, soft with recent rains. The trees were leafless, as if dead, though they still breathed the light of life—the brightest thing, apart from Râvar's own lifelight and those of his companions, in all the dull landscape. The semblance of deadness was a natural part, in this land, of the turning of the seasons. In Refuge, living plants never dropped all their leaves, and the seasons varied only between hot and less hot, little rain and more rain.

The stench of burned things was growing sickening. Râvar pulled the hanging sleeve of his robe over his hand and pressed it across his nose and mouth. His eyes picked out pattern: the conformations around the settlement that spoke of long use and occupancy, the probable path of the fire, the wood and stone of the houses and other buildings, still recognizable despite the char. In their ugly ruin, the structures were less displeasing to him than they would have been intact. Weeks of close contact had not softened his distaste for the places the people of this world made to live and work in, with their harsh angles and rough materials.

At the foot of the hill a track straggled into being, widening as it neared the first of the houses. It was probably passable enough in summer, but at the moment it was deep with mud. Beside it the first corpses lay, six men sprawled in unnatural poses. Near their hands were weapons: staves and instruments with sharp wooden tines bound to the ends of long handles. The cold had delayed putrefaction, but predators had been at work, enormous black birds with cruel beaks that flapped up as Râvar and the others approached. Râvar felt his stomach lurch. One of the Twentymen made a gagging sound.

"If you're going to be sick," Ardashir said without looking around, "do us the favor of going off to the side."

Enough, Râvar thought. He turned to the two men. "Leave us."

"Beloved One," they said, bowing, and hastened to retrace their steps.

Ardashir had halted by one of the corpses and was gazing down at it, his hands clasped behind his back. In Ninyâser he had indulged his taste for rich clothing, acquiring a wardrobe that filled two leather trunks; he looked like a noble in his elaborate fur-trimmed coat and gold-tooled boots, the neck of his brocade overtunic held with a silver brooch. Even his bandages were fine, soft white linen neatly wrapped and tied at the wrist, though the stains that marked them were the same.

"This one," he said, "is one of your faithful, Beloved One."

Râvar already knew that, for the man's tunic was made of grass cloth. He took careful hold of his anger.

"To what purpose have you brought me here, Ardashir?"

"I wanted you to see, Beloved One. I have been telling you. But I wanted you to see."

"And now I've seen. What would you have me do?"

Ardashir pivoted, and for the first time since they had arrived looked Râvar in the face. "Beloved One, I wanted you to know the darkness that has come to walk beside a journey that began in light. Here, before you in this place, is the thing I warned you of, the consequence of allowing your faithful to spread your word in so violent a way. Rumor of our approach precedes us. The people fear us, and have begun to prepare themselves. In this village, your followers met an armed militia. It drove them off, but they returned in greater numbers, and this is the result. Five of our people killed and fourteen wounded. Ten men of this village dead—or at least, ten who can be counted, since others may have been burned inside their houses. And all the villagers made homeless. I wanted you to see it with your own eyes, Beloved One, for I could never convey to you in words the darkness of what was done here."

"What of the darkness of denying Ârata?"

"We don't know that these people did deny him, Beloved One, only that word of your followers' harsh proselytizing drove them to arm themselves, and so engendered greater violence. Beloved One, this can only grow worse. These things feed upon themselves—believe me, I know. And you will forgive me, but I must speak my mind—it is the coarse element of your following that is responsible, the debased men and women whom you have all along refused to turn away from the Awakened City, and who came to you in such numbers during our sojourn in Ninyâser. These people do not follow you for the joy of Ârata's rising, but because they wish to throw off the rule of law and run mad in the end times—"

"How often, Ardashir, must I answer this argument?"

"Beloved One." On Ardashir's face was the dogged expression that had grown much too familiar these past weeks. "If you will allow such people to come to you, you must accept the necessity of controlling them. I cannot do it for you any longer. The City is grown too scattered, too unruly. There are citizens now who barely know who I am, who refuse to bow to my authority. I have forbidden proselytizing groups like the one that burned this village—

forbidden them in your name! Still they roam. Beloved One, I care nothing for blasphemers, but it should be Ârata's fires that burn them, not ours!"

"Do you forget what *we* have encountered on this march? The betrayals we have suffered? The violence turned toward *us*?"

"It is one thing to destroy armies, to bring judgment on those who oppose you with treachery and the sword. It is another to burn villages and farmsteads, to riot in the towns. The *Darxasa* says—"

"Do not dare to use my father's words to chide me!"

Ardashir's mouth was tight. "Beloved One, I have begun to fear that I have failed my duty to you, for it seems to me sometimes that I have taught you to be *too* human."

Fury flashed like lightning. For a moment the edges of Râvar's vision flickered white. He breathed deeply, summoning control. The moment of confrontation had been approaching for some time. For weeks Ardashir had been reporting incidents, uttering warnings, implying but never quite articulating a course of action Râvar had no intention of following: that he should order the Awakened City to stop ranging out across the countryside, making converts and punishing those who refused. It was time, and past time, that Ardashir understood.

"Ardashir, I know why you brought me to this place, and also why you brought me as you did, without preparing me. You thought I did not understand your warnings. You thought, by showing me the truth, to shock me. You thought by shocking me to move me to forbid my followers to proclaim me in this way."

Ardashir was as rigid as a tree trunk. His face was expressionless, but the heat of his anger showed, just a little, in the flush across his cheekbones.

"I will not forbid them, Ardashir. Shall I tell you why?"

"Yes, Beloved One." Ardashir's lips barely moved.

"It is true that you taught me to be human. But the anger that is in me now I did not learn from you. It was at Dracâriya I learned it, at the hands of the blasphemer King. And in this anger, which you judge too human, I came at last to understand my father's wrath. My father is love and light. But he is also fire and judgment, and when he returns at the end of time that is the face the world will see." Râvar stepped toward the First Disciple, his eyes trained upon Ardashir's unyielding face. "Compassion is the Fifth Foundation of the Way, but it is preceded by Consciousness. I have said it before: My father's word must be given, and it must be given *as it will be understood*. The world and all in it are dark with ash, and there are some who can only understand in punishment." Another step. This time, Ardashir fell back. "So I will not tell my faithful they cannot defend themselves against those who threaten or refuse them." Another step. Again Ardashir fell back. "I will not tell them to turn from treachery and attack." Another step. "I will ask them to speak my father's word with love—but if their love is thrown back into their faces, they have my leave to answer, to show my anger and my father's. For as Dracâriya made clear to me, as the battles since have made clear to me, love is not enough!"

Râvar halted. He had forced Ardashir into the mud of the track. The flush across the First Disciple's cheeks had deepened; his hands were fisted at his sides.

"Do you understand now, Ardashir?"

Ardashir nodded once, stiffly, as if he did not trust himself to speak.

"Don't think," Râvar said more gently, "that I do not grieve for what's happened in this place, or that I do not see your pain. For the sake of the souls that were lost here, and for your sake, because you are my First Disciple, I shall make it clean. I shall take this darkness on myself."

Ardashir's iron composure cracked. An expression of utter consternation came across his face. "Beloved One, I did not intend—"

"Did you not?" Râvar said softly. "But you brought me here. What did you think I would do?"

Their gazes held. Then Ardashir's, slowly, slid away.

"Go back to the others. I'll do this alone."

"Beloved One." Ardashir turned, like a man not entirely in command of his body, and began to climb the hill.

Râvar closed his eyes, gathering himself. He did not want to do this. He did not want to walk among the dead, to forage among the ruins. But he had begun the charade. It must be played out.

He approached the corpses. One by one he stooped beside them and set a bead of light upon each lightless forehead. He half closed his eyes to blur the sight of their wounds and the damage done by the birds, breathing shallowly against the stink of their decay. *I've seen worse*, he told himself. *I've smelled worse*. At least, because of the cold, there were no flies. Still, it was too much, much too much, like the terrible riverbank of his memory.

He entered the village, firming the mud underfoot, unmaking the charred brick and timbers that blocked his way. To those watching from above, it would seem that light traveled before him, that each step created thunder. He went into all the hollow houses. He blessed more sprawled corpses. He blessed the bones he found amid the ash. He blessed even the carcasses of the animals. Ardashir had been right: Many people had died here. Many.

At last he returned to the track. At the bottom of the hill, he faced the village once again. Throwing back his head and spreading wide his arms, he plunged his shaping will into the ground—deep loam and clay, the bedrock far beneath—and altered the patterns of its composition so that it quivered and liquesced. The impact rolled like a wave below his feet; blue-white brilliance lit the sullen afternoon. Softly, the ruins of the village sank and vanished.

He shifted his will, bringing the patterns of the soil back to their proper form. Where the village had been, the ground spread as bare and brown as the winter fields. Apart from those, and the track, there was no trace of what had once existed here.

Slowly Râvar climbed to his followers, waiting at the crest of the hill. The Twentymen's faces showed the familiar awe, but in Ardashir's was something different. As Râvar drew near, he started forward and fell to his knees. He seized the muddy hem of Râvar's robe and bent low, pressing it to his face.

"Beloved One." His voice was muffled. "I am a blackened man. Forgive me."

Râvar looked down at him, feeling the floating weariness that always followed on a large expenditure of power.

"Look at me, Ardashir."

Ardashir obeyed. His expression was naked. Tears stood in his eyes. Râvar dropped to his haunches. He reached out and took the other man's face between his filthy, ash-stained hands.

"You are my First Disciple," he said, too softly for the waiting Twentymen to hear. "I will always forgive you."

He tightened his grip, digging his fingers into Ardashir's temples. Ardashir dragged in his breath. Râvar released him and rose.

"Come," he said. "Let's go back."

The palanquin was comfortable, with padded backrests and fitted cushions. It was the property of one of the nobles who had joined the pilgrimage in Ninyâser, who had been honored to lend it for the purpose of the expedition. Before stepping inside, Râvar had unmade the mud and soot that soiled his hands and boots and the hem of his robe; but somehow he could not quite banish the odor of char. It made him queasy. In his mind's eye he could still see the ruins, the bones, the corpses. As often as he pushed the images away they returned, as if he were still there, still walking.

Ârata, but I'm tired.

It was more than just the physical cost of shaping, more even than the raw exhaustion of his chronic sleeplessness. Since Dracâriya he had felt this way: tired, always tired.

He had lain in his tent for two days, while the Awakened City tended its wounds and buried its dead. On the third day he rose and opened a passage through the fallen hills—an act that demanded less strength than the one that had made the destruction, for unmaking was the easiest of a Shaper's arts, but difficult enough in his depleted state. He took care with it, creating a smooth, level thoroughfare between high rock walls, its curving proportions far more pleasing than the hard-edged road it replaced. The hills' collapse might be ascribed to earthquake or some other natural event, but the thoroughfare could not be dismissed so: Even to those who did not believe in him, it was clearly the work of a great power.

The Awakened City moved on. Below and just above the river Hatane, there had been many other travelers, but after Dracâriya the traffic dwindled, and later, as word of the City's advance spread, it ceased entirely. In some of the towns and villages, Râvar was welcomed—as in the market town of Hâras, whose mayor was waiting to greet him, and stood behind him in the central plaza as he spoke to a large and curious crowd. He took many converts with him when he left. In other places he was shunned. The walled city of Abaxtra barred its gates against him; his angry followers clashed with townsfolk in the suburbs, leaving whole streets burning.

A month after Dracâriya, as the pilgrimage drew near Ninyâser, it came upon a blockade, manned by several companies of Exile cavalry. Ardashir went to parley, and returned with the Exiles' demand: Râvar was to surrender into their hands, and the Awakened City was to be dispersed. Mantling himself in light, Râvar alighted from his coach and approached the commander, who was waiting with several lieutenants. Either the rumors of Râvar's power had not yet reached Ninyâser, or the Exiles had not believed what they heard. Their astonishment as they saw him was almost comical.

"I am the Next Messenger," he declared. "I've come with word of Ârata's rising to the kingdoms of Galea. Stand aside."

The commander controlled his restive horse. "Your arrest has been ordered by the Lords' Assembly of Arsace in the name of King-Elect Hathrida. Submit, or be taken."

"Return to your masters," Râvar said. "Tell them I wish to march across this land in peace. But if I am opposed, I will defend my faithful, as I did in the Dracâriya hills. Remind those you serve of that. Remind them of the judgment I brought on your King."

There was a stir among the Exiles; some of them made the sign of Ârata. The commander said, "You will not surrender?"

"I can surrender to no mortal power. Ârata alone commands me."

"Seize him," the commander ordered.

Two of the lieutenants dismounted, drawing their swords. Râvar allowed them a few steps, then cracked the road in front of them, opening a crevasse. They staggered back, their cries lost in the roar of power. As the men behind them fought their terrified mounts, Râvar called fire on the trees by the roadside, so that one after another they exploded into flame. Those soldiers whose horses did not bolt turned and fled.

"Tell them!" Râvar shouted after them, his voice nearly as thunderous as his shaping. "Tell your masters that I come!"

They did. Ten days later, on the vast agricultural plain that surrounded Ninyâser, Ardashir's scouts returned with word of a large force blocking the way ahead. There were near three thousand men, they reported, foot soldiers and archers and cavalry, and they had with them several long-armed devices that Ardashir called catapults, meant for hurling heavy objects across great distances. Stones, he said. Vessels of manita, Râvar thought.

It made him smile. They thought they knew him. They thought they could accomplish what Santaxma had failed to do.

The City moved on until the army became visible, a dark mass on the table-flat land, haloed in the radiance of its many lives. Râvar called a halt then. Shelling himself in hardened air and bright illusion, he advanced with Ardashir and a phalanx of Twentymen. Before him, the Great South Way ran spear-straight between harvested fields and long rows of trellised vines. At its distant terminus the city floated like a mirage, sunlight gleaming on the golden pinpoints of its domes.

The army was drawn up on either side of the road, following the line of the irrigation ditches, a smaller force on the right, a much larger one on the left. The sun flashed from the bladed weapons of the foot soldiers, from the helms and scale hauberks of the cavalry. From a distance they appeared still, but nearer it was apparent that they were all in restless motion. Horses stamped and tossed their heads. The foot soldiers shifted, the forest of their weapons swaying. He imagined how they must see him—a star drifting slowly toward them, magnificent, inexplicable.

Not quite close enough to make out the faces of the nearest soldiers, he halted. A party of horsemen detached itself from the larger force—four of them, one bearing a golden flag. They gained the road and trotted toward

him. Râvar waited, imagining the catapults, which he knew were ranged somewhere at the back. When he could hear the sound of hoofbeats, he raised his
shining arms and flung forth his shaping will. Behind the parley party, above
the road, a second sun seemed to burst into being. Fire roared from the sky.
Râvar twitched the patterns; the fire screamed like a beast and became a storm
of stone. He shifted focus; and the ground beneath the two halves of the army
thundered into void.

It did not eat them all. As the shuddering echoes died, he saw men stag-
gering beyond the edges of the emptiness he had made. One member of
the parley party lay on the road, thrown by his panicked horse; the rest had
bolted. Râvar turned toward his own men. All were on their knees. Ardashir's
mouth was moving; Râvar, his ears ringing with destruction, read the word he
spoke: *Judgment*.

Râvar rested for the remainder of the day, and for the day after. The following morning he plugged the pit with an enormous plaque of banded sandstone: another testament, another signature, another hidden message. He left
the coach's window covers up and watched Axane's face as they passed over it.
For a moment, understanding swallowed all her careful self-containment, but
when she turned toward him again, her mask was back in place.

By the time the Awakened City reached Ninyâser, half the populace was
gone. The streets were littered with the signs of flight: trampled clothing,
abandoned furnishings, overturned carts. Those who remained lined the
streets as Râvar made a triumphal entry, going on foot before the coach so
that all could see him in his garb of light, his pilgrims shouting and singing
at his back. At his shoulder Ardashir whispered instruction, so that he led the
way as if he knew it, coming at last to a river walled in stone, conducting his
faithful across a bridge painted red and gold, Ârata's colors. Beyond lay the tall
gates of the Âratist religious complex. Most of the monks and nuns had fled;
those who remained fell down before him in adoration.

The City sojourned in Ninyâser for a week. Ardashir claimed for Râvar
the largest residence, a great tile-roofed structure chopped up with walls into
many rooms and hallways, which had belonged to the man who had ruled the
Âratist city-within-a-city. He shut Axane and Parvâti in one of the chambers,
blocking the windows with stiffened air, blocking the door as well, though
there was a device called a lock that supposedly made it fast. In Refuge there
had been no locks, or any doors or windows either. Each evening he chose a
different room, hoping to hate it less than the room he had chosen the night
before, and lay all night listening to the chanting and singing of the faithful,
who kept vigil in the court outside.

He found some relief, ironically enough, in the temple of Ârata. It was made of stacked-up stone rather than hollowed into living rock, but its proportions were familiar in a way most structures of this world were not, for Refuge's Temple had been fashioned according to the same design. He took to spending the afternoons there, sitting crosslegged against the wall of the core, staring at the enormous image of Ârata Creator. Sometimes he watched so fiercely that it almost seemed the image might turn its great face ponderously to his, train on him its marble gaze—a notion that lanced him from throat to groin with a strange thrill of dread and anticipation. Sometimes he considered unmaking it, and all else in the place that spoke of the god or his Way: the wall friezes, the paintings along the inner curve of the gallery. Instead, when the candles that lit the image began to go out (for he had closed the temple to the few remaining vowed Âratists, and there was no one to renew them), he replaced them with sourceless flames, so Ârata's illumination would not diminish.

See, Ârata. I can be generous.

On the last day of the City's stay, a massive induction ceremony was held in the plaza outside the temple. Hundreds of new faithful accepted Râvar's mark and knelt before him to receive his blessing. There were beggars in rags and vowed Âratists in stoles. There were tradesmen and merchants, artists and artisans, pickpockets and whores. There were grandmothers; there were infants. There were even a few nobles, who when the City moved on rode in coaches like Râvar's own and were followed by trains of servants. Râvar sat on an improvised dais, murmuring words of benediction and bestowing points of light until his eyes blurred, his tongue grew as dry as ash, and all the faces became a single face, avid-eyed, openmouthed.

The pilgrimage departed, leaving the Âratist complex, and the surrounding sections of Ninyâser, littered and battered. Many pilgrims chose to remain behind, too ill or exhausted to continue, or perhaps unhappy with the hard edge of anger the progress had acquired since Dracâriya. But the flood of new converts made up those numbers and more. The City was now more than three thousand strong, according to Ardashir, including the train of hangers-on it had acquired, peddlers and minstrels and herbalists and prostitutes who served or exploited the pilgrims according to need and gullibility. For the first time, the majority of the City was composed of newcomers, who had accepted the mark and sworn their faith but had never known the comradeship or the discipline of the caverns. The march, boisterous and unruly and strung over many days of travel, bore little resemblance to the neatly ordered columns that had walked singing out across the steppe. The proselytizing bands roamed at will; at night the pilgrims built bonfires and celebrated until dawn. Though Râvar still provided food and water, many of the faithful took what they needed from the farms and villages they passed, secure in the promise Râvar had made when they took his mark upon their hands: that no further deed they did in the time of Interim could stain them. Ardashir and his loyal Twentymen had largely lost control; the induction ceremony in Ninyâser had been the last event of which Ardashir was indisputably in charge, and even that had devolved into a riot, as new-made citizens surged into the streets to display their wounds and their miraculous blessing-lights to nonbelievers. Pragmatic as always, Ardashir confined himself to supervising the three hundred or so who kept pace with Râvar's coach, a band mainly made up of First Faithful and pilgrims from the caverns, most of whom still accepted his authority.

It would not be fully true to say that the progress was proceeding according to plan. So much of what had happened Râvar had not planned—could not have planned. But it was proceeding according to desire. Everything he had intended he had accomplished. He had loosed his faithful like a plague. Where he passed, he left disorder and destruction. Each day he gathered more faithful, blackened more souls with blasphemy. He had vanquished Arsace's leaders; there was no longer a breath of opposition, and the road to Baushpar lay open and undefended. He had succeeded, in many ways, beyond his wildest dreams. Certainly beyond anything he could have conceived in those sick and helpless days after Thuxra City.

Why, then, did he take so little pleasure in it? He had been so sure that Dracâriya was the turning point, the moment in which he set the seal of his vengeance indelibly upon this world. And it had been—beyond doubt it had been. But the tedium of the journey had not eased. The alienness of the landscapes had not diminished, nor had his distaste for them grown less acute. Occasionally he found the exaltation he craved: in his approach upon the army, as he swept into Ninyâser. Always it dwindled. Always it faded.

Soon, though, he would be in Baushpar. It shimmered before him like a beacon—no more than a week away, even at the City's slow pace. Baushpar, where all but one of the Brethren waited, prepared by the Son Vivaniya. Baushpar, where the heart of his hatred lay. Perhaps that was why the other triumphs had not satisfied him. They were incidental to the true goal, shadows of the true punishment. In Baushpar, he would fill himself with retribution and never again be empty.

The palanquin jolted, canting sharply to the left. Râvar braced his hands against the sides. The burned village thrust into his mind again, vivid as the flash of shaping. For an instant he imagined he could smell decay. Nausea rose into his throat, and also anger. Why should this one dead village affect him so? But though he had killed thousands from a distance, burying them under rock, entombing them in the earth, he was rarely confronted with actual death. The ruins and the corpses had been too close to his nightmares. He had buried the village for effect, a great shaping to fix the moment in the legend of the journey; but at the back of the impulse, though he did not want to admit it, lay a little of what had driven him to do the same for his own people: the desire to make clean.

Would Ardashir, that tireless chronicler, name this deed as he had others? The journey had become a procession of such names, strung together like Communion beads: The Judgment of the Blasphemer. The Sermon in the Hills. The Miracle of Passage. The Testament of Fire. The Testament of Stone. The Sojourn in Ninyâser. Râvar had never seen Ardashir's writings, but he imagined they were far from a literal recounting of events. Perhaps, though, Ardashir would prefer not to memorialize this particular incident.

Ardashir. Râvar felt a wave of weariness. He thought he had dealt effectively with what had happened. Ardashir had certainly seemed repentant. Would it be enough? Clear as Ardashir's distress had been these past weeks, Râvar would not have imagined the First Disciple could do what he had done today. It was not simply that he had resorted to trickery to bring Râvar to the village; it was that he had brought Râvar there at all. Once, he would have exerted every effort to shield the Messenger's tender soul from such a sight. How great must his anger and frustration have become to drive him to such a thing? Râvar was more than familiar with Ardashir's anger, which constantly tested the limits of Ardashir's control. But today was the first time in a long time that he had looked at Ardashir and remembered that this was a man who with his bare hands had killed his wife.

He suspected that Ardashir had guessed about the Daughter Sundit. Ardashir had never said a word to suggest it. But now and then Râvar looked into the First Disciple's face and seemed to see too much understanding looking back. It was an act Ardashir should condone, he who believed the Brethren should be punished. Lately, however, Râvar found he was not so sure.

He did not fear Ardashir's anger. What had he to fear from any ordinary man? But if he lost Ardashir's faith, he would also lose the Awakened City. He could not manage on his own. The very thought was overwhelming.

He rubbed his eyes, smelling on his hands the phantom scent of soot. Profoundly, he longed for sleep. He leaned his head against the cushions, but sleep did not come.

As often as he resolved to abandon her, however, he changed his mind. It would be cruel to separate Parvâti from her mother, he told himself, and he did not wish to be cruel to his daughter. He did not want to explain to Ardashir why he had banished the woman Ârata had supposedly charged him to protect, especially after he had gone to so much trouble to fetch her. Nor was he prepared to deal with the issue of finding one of his followers to tend Parvâti, who, though she was mostly weaned, required care he could not manage with his damaged hands. Those reasons seemed sufficiently compelling; if there were another, he was not prepared to admit it.

Slowly, with time and habit, it grew easier. The task of keeping Parvâti amused during the long hours in the coach gave them a frail expanse of common ground. Also, Axane was so diligent in her efforts to please him, never complaining, obeying all his instructions without hesitation—even when, as he had sometimes amused himself by doing in the beginning, he gave her orders that were cruel or stupid, such as making her sit without a cushion on the coach's hard wooden seat, or hold his water cup all day without drinking herself. As a matter of practicality, he began to accept some of her offers of assistance, in matters that were difficult for him—arranging the bedding, packing up and laying out his clothes, braiding his hair.

He was not foolish. He did not mistake her compliance for a change of heart. He had not forgotten—would never forget—how much she had once kept hidden behind the quiet face she showed the world. *She's not to be trusted,* he reminded himself each morning, each night, each time he allowed her to help him. When he slept and when he left her, he never failed to imprison her.

He returned to the room with the clothes he had removed and dropped them in the chest. He laid the Blood of Ârata atop them, then took the sash Axane offered him and wrapped it around his waist, letting her knot it for him. He went again to sit on the bed.

"Give her to me."

Axane scooped Parvâti up and set her in his lap. She was a year old, too heavy for him to lift with his crooked hands. He wrapped her in his arms and pressed his cheek against her hair, breathing in her warm familiar scent. She did not want to be still today; she wriggled against the confinement of his embrace, babbling nonsense syllables with such conviction that it almost seemed he should understand her, and yanked at his braid, which had fallen forward over his shoulder. He smelled burning again: his hair, which had absorbed the village's charcoal stench.

"Undo this tie for me, would you?"

Axane unfolded herself from the floor, where she had arranged herself neatly on her knees to await his will, and came to unwind the cord that held the plait, leaning close enough that for a moment he was fully enclosed within her lifelight.

"Shall I wash your hair for you?" she asked. "You can dry it by the brazier."

"No," he said, as he usually did when she offered anything that would bring her close to him for an extended time. Yet he felt the temptation, like the pull of sleep—not the sexual temptation that sometimes wracked him when he lay awake at night, but simply the desire to be cared for, to be touched. He recognized the unwisdom of it, even as he drew a breath, and said, "On second thought, yes. That would be good."

"Come, little bird." She came close again to lift Parvâti away. "You must play alone for a little while."

He watched as she settled their daughter among the toys he had made her, rings and sticks and little stone figures. "You never call her Parvâti."

"Yes, I do."

"Do you wish she still had that ugly name?"

"She's always been my little bird." Axane got to her feet. "Ever since she was born. Fill the basin for me, would you?"

He shaped more water, agitating its patterns to warm them. Bracing his hands on the lacquered surface of the stand, he bent low and closed his eyes. She gathered up his hair and dropped it into the basin, scooping water to massage his scalp. Her touch was sure and gentle. He yielded to the pleasure, and in that loosening found a memory: his mother, washing his hair just that way when he was a boy. He could almost smell the odor of the herbs she had used. It was rare that such remembering brought anything but guilt and grief. But today, in the recaptured sense of his mother's tenderness, he found something gentler and more sad—something that for once had no anger in it.

"Lift your head."

He did. She twisted his hair into a rope, wringing it out, then wrapped it in the same cloth he had used to dry his face and hands.

"Shall I comb it for you?"

It seemed quite natural to say yes.

He sat down on the matting. Axane knelt behind him and pulled away the cloth, so that his hair tumbled over his shoulders, its wetness soaking through the fabric of his tunics. He was inside her light again; the air before him shaded meadow green and sky blue, the colors shifting with the fluidity of water. Gently, she began to tease through the tangles, first with her fingers, then with a comb. He yielded to the tugging, his eyes half-closed. Nearby,

Parvâti banged two of her wooden rings together, commenting to herself in her unintelligible baby language.

"Where did you go today?" Axane asked.

He called himself back from the brink of sleep. "A village. One of the proselytizing bands met resistance there and burned it to the ground." From the start he had talked to her freely about such matters. She knew everything he had done and why, even his entombment of the Daughter Sundit. At first it had been to goad her, part of his plan of punishment. Slowly it had become something else. It was more relief than he liked to admit to speak the truth to someone who understood it, even if her understanding carried judgment. He was able also to ask her the questions he did not want to ask Ardashir— elementary, foolish questions about the many things of this world he did not understand or recognize. It was she, in Ninyâser, who had explained locks to him, cooperating in her own imprisonment. "Ardashir wanted me to see it."

"Why?" The comb slipped from crown to waist.

"I've told you why. He wants me to forbid the bands."

"What did you tell him?"

"What he needed to hear."

"You're good at that."

Râvar pulled a little away from her. "What do you mean?"

"You always know what to say. What to do." She reached after him; the comb whispered down his back. "And he believes, they all believe, because they love you. They truly love you, Râvar."

But you don't.

She gathered his hair in her hands and smoothed it, then resumed her combing, stroke after slow stroke. He sank into the rhythm of it. His limbs were warm and heavy. His eyes fell closed.

He came to himself, drifting up from sleep like a swimmer. He was lying on his back. The matting was hard under his body, but he felt profoundly comfortable, warm and cushioned, as if he were swaddled in soft quilts. Distantly, he could hear Parvâti babbling.

He opened his eyes. The ceiling hung above him, the artificial patterns of its construction netting the natural patterns of the pine boards that composed it. He turned his head and saw Axane. She knelt by him, very close; she stared down at him, her lips parted, her face, usually so shuttered, strangely open and uncertain.

His breath caught. Lying by her at night he had imagined forcing her, humbling her, as in the Burning Land. More recently, in the changed atmosphere between them, he had sensed that if he reached for her she would yield. That was no better: A false surrender was hardly different from a coerced one. But at that moment, in the way she looked at him, it seemed to him he saw something different.

Desire seized him. Every fiber of his body, the very blood inside him, seemed to flash into flame. He lifted his hand, meaning to set it against her cheek.

She did not move or pull away. But her expression changed. Infinitesimally; and yet he saw it, and read the message of aversion there. As abruptly as it had taken him, his arousal vanished. He let his hand fall and sat up, pulling away from her.

"Râvar—"

She did not continue. He saw a falling in her face, a kind of acceptance, then a smoothing, like a curtain dropping down. She let out her breath and got to her feet, bending to retrieve the basin, which for some reason was sitting on the floor beside her.

"I was just emptying the water into the pots," she said, and went to put the basin back in its stand.

He got to his feet. He felt angry, and bruisingly stupid. This was what came of letting her touch him—this confusion, this loss of guard. He had actually fallen *asleep!* With the door unbarriered! She could simply have gathered Parvâti up and walked away.

Why didn't she?

He stepped roughly around Parvâti and retrieved his boots, stamping into them barefoot, then took the Blood and seized another of his rich robes and left the room. He turned to block the doorway. Parvâti was crawling after one of her toys; from the stand that held the basin, Axane watched him, her face unreadable. The heat of humiliation rose into his cheeks, burning nearly as hot as his desire had; rage throbbed below his breastbone, though he could scarcely tell if it were for her or for himself.

He laid the shaping across the door. He pulled on the robe, settled the Blood around his neck. Then he went downstairs.

"Ardashir," he called to the First Disciple, sitting with his men in the kitchen. "I will speak to the faithful. Arrange it."

Ardashir sent some of the Twentymen to announce a ceremony. The rest carried Râvar to the town's central plaza. He waited in the palanquin while the faithful gathered. At Ardashir's word he emerged, wrapped in his usual cloak of light. With typical forethought, Ardashir had drawn up a cart so Râvar could stand above the level of the gathering, and arranged wooden boxes and a table into a sort of stairway, so he could ascend with dignity. The faithful shouted when they saw him, a deep, pulsating roar. The eleven Twentymen who had accompanied him—an excessive number, it seemed to Râvar, but Ardashir had insisted—ranged themselves along the cart's front, legs apart, staves braced before them. The plaza was packed from edge to edge; the day's delay had given more of the straggling City time to catch up, and Râvar thought there must be near five hundred pilgrims present. Lifelights shone from every window of the surrounding houses and even on the roofs, where people balanced precariously on the tiles. Many brandished candles or flaring torches. Others held up banners bearing the Messenger's symbols: the open eye surrounded by a circle, the coiled spiral, the hand slashed by a scar, the hexagon centered with a flame.

The shouting went on and on. Râvar had to raise his arms at last to call for quiet. Even then, it was some time before it fell.

He spoke to them of the deeds of the march. Named by the names Ardashir had invented, they did indeed sound glorious. He spoke to them of what was to come: Baushpar, the Brethren's acknowledgment, his investment as the leader of the Ârata's wakened Way. He spoke to them of the wonders of the new primal age, into which he would escort them. For the first time in many weeks the words came to him as they had in the beginning, and he felt the living bond that linked him to his followers: his power, their surrender.

It was near evening when he began; it was full dark when he finished. He shaped trinkets for them and stood watching as they jumped and snatched for them. *Mine.* He felt a rush of fierce emotion. *They are mine.*

He turned, trailing veils of light, and descended from the cart, ignoring Ardashir's upheld hand. "Ready!" Ardashir called to the Twentymen, assuming Râvar meant to get back into the palanquin; it took him a moment to realize that Râvar was moving in the opposite direction.

"Beloved One!" He ran to catch Râvar's arm. "What are you doing?"

Râvar shook him off. "I will go among them. As I always do."

"No, Beloved One! They are not—this is not—"

But Râvar was already amid the crowd. They pressed aside to let him through, falling away from him like leaves; he saw the adoration in their faces, the wonder. Slowly he advanced, as he had during a thousand other ceremonies, holding out his hands so they could view his scars. Behind him, he drew a wake of quiet.

"Light be on you, children." He reached out, touching faces, hands, shoulders, bestowing jewel points of brilliance. "Peace be on you. Holiness be on you."

"Beloved One," they murmured. "Merciful Messenger."

He was deep among them. A young woman in a green dress seized his hand and pressed a hot kiss into his palm. When she released him another, emboldened, imitated her. Behind him, someone touched his hair. Fingers plucked the fabric of his robe, tugged at his sleeves. They were no longer falling away from him so readily. He thrust out his hands to part them; a forest of eager hands reached back. A man seized his fingers and did not release them when he tried to pull away, dragging him off-balance; he staggered and might have fallen had not a dozen pilgrims seized him by the arms and shoulders. Instinctively, he wrenched away. At once his hands were grabbed again, his arms stretched in opposite directions.

"Messenger! Beautiful One! Walker in Light!"

They were not murmuring now, but calling, clamoring for his attention. His shoulder joints cracked; he strained backward against the tension but by then they were gripping not just his hands but his wrists and forearms, and he could not get free. His robe was dragged tight over his chest; he heard the sound of ripping as seams started to give way. Someone seized a handful of his hair and yanked his head back, hard. He felt a searing pain in his scalp.

Animal panic burst within him. He shouted, knowing it only by the tearing in his throat, and flung out his shaping will as another man might have flung out his arms to ward a blow. There was a burst of light, a huge concussion. It hurled the faithful back like chaff.

In the echoing silence, Râvar stood trembling. Around him spread a ring of empty space. Beyond it, pilgrims lay like felled timber. Some were motionless; some struggled dazedly to rise. Those still on their feet were transfixed with shock. The glowing watchers in the windows and at the roofs were still.

Then Ardashir cut through, and the Twentymen, laying about them with their staves, striding across the fallen faithful without heed to whom they trampled. They reached Râvar and closed around him, shoulder to shoulder, a ring of protection.

"See, you fools!" Ardashir shouted at the silent throng, his orator's voice cracking with fury. "See what you have wrought! From this day, he will not come among you again!"

He took Râvar's arm. His grip was like a vise; Râvar, shaking violently, was grateful for the support. "Go," he said, and his men obeyed. Still silent, the crowd fell back to let them through.

Râvar sat shaking through the jolting journey to the house. His mind was strangely blank. At the house, Ardashir pulled back the door of the palanquin and assisted Râvar out, up the steps, inside. He did it all without a word. Once the door was closed, he turned on Râvar like a striking snake.

"What were you thinking of?" he hissed. "What possessed you?"

The stinging aftermath of panic twisted easily into an answering anger. "They could not have harmed me."

"Are you mad? They nearly tore you apart! Look! Look at this!" He snatched at the torn sleeve of Râvar's robe, ripping it entirely off. He tossed it aside. "And this!" He pointed at Râvar's forehead. "They made you bleed! *They made you bleed!*"

Râvar touched his forehead, looked at his fingers. Ardashir was right. His anger vanished; he felt suddenly as if he might faint.

"You are too heedless, Beloved One!" For the second time that day, Ardashir's self-control was in utter disarray. Behind him the Twentymen watched, horrified. "I've told you and told you, those who follow you now are not like the pilgrims in the caverns. You cannot simply go among them any longer. Beloved One, you ignore my counsel in other things, but in this you must heed me! You cannot do this again. Say you will heed me. Say you will heed me!"

"I'll heed you, Ardashir."

Râvar's easy acquiescence seemed to catch Ardashir off guard. He was still fumbling for a response as Râvar turned away. On the first stair, Râvar stumbled; Ardashir leaped forward, but Râvar flung up his arm. "No. Get away."

He managed to get up the stairs without faltering. In the dark front chamber, with its narrow children's beds, reaction overwhelmed him, and he sank shivering to the floor. He experienced the hands again, the avid pulling. There was a throbbing where unseen fingers had yanked his hair. He touched the wetness on his forehead, followed it to the source of the pain: a bloody hollow in his scalp. Whoever it was had not simply pulled his hair, but wrenched out a hank of it at the roots.

He felt the empty echo of his shock. When he stepped among them, it had not seemed any different from the ceremonies in the caverns. He tried, but could not reconstruct the process by which their mood had turned.

I was never in any danger, he told himself. And yet there had been that instant when purely human terror had overwhelmed him, and he had struck out like any ordinary man to defend himself. In memory, he traveled back to the earliest days of his deception, to the first time he had ever gone before his followers and seen how they might tear him into pieces. It had been a long time, very long, since he had thought of that. Since he had had any sense that they could truly touch him.

How many of them had he injured? How seriously? He wondered what the consequences would be. He could compel them to do anything; but could he hurt them and still make them believe he loved them?

He closed his hands into fists. He felt filthy, soiled. He longed for his chambers in the caverns, for the gold-veined pool where he had washed away the residue of so many ceremonies.

He got up at last and pulled off his torn robe, and used the edge of the stair as a lever to remove his boots. In the room beyond, Axane and Parvâti lay on the floor in a tangle of blankets, the child's light shining through her mother's like a jewel seen through water. He opened and remade the barrier, removed the Blood of Ârata, lay down on the bed. It was very quiet in the room, but from outside, muffled, came the clamor of the Awakened City. All night it continued. When dawn grayed the sky beyond the window screens, he could still hear it.

Râvar

A little past noon, as Râvar was amusing Parvâti by calling illusion in various forms, Ardashir brought his horse alongside the moving coach and knocked at the door.

"Beloved One," he said, when Râvar drew aside the canvas window cover, "Baushpar has just come in sight. The emissaries ask permission to ride ahead and inform their masters of your coming."

"Call a stop," Râvar said. "I want to see."

Ardashir gave the order to the driver, then rode back to instruct the Twentymen to halt the pilgrims. Râvar gave Parvâti to Axane and climbed down, pulling his quilted coat tight against the chill. For the past two days they had been mounting into hill country; the coach had halted at the crest of a long slope. Before it the road descended into a shallow valley, at whose bottom ran long fields inexplicably crosshatched with wooden posts, then rose toward an eminence on which a red-walled city crouched amid a tumble of outlying streets and buildings, like a tawny beast with its litter at its feet.

Baushpar.

The clouds had pulled aside the night before. In the crystalline air every detail of the distant scene was clear: the patterns of the terrain bunching toward the hilltop, Baushpar's own patterns wreathing the summit and trailing downward, knotted as a mass of cord. Even with its sprawling suburbs, it was surprisingly small—less than half the size of mighty Ninyâser. The inward-sloping walls were the color of old blood; the thin winter sunlight both lit and shadowed the variously tilted planes of a thousand red- and yellow-tiled roofs. Thrusting above them all, a dozen domes like tight-furled flower buds shone blindingly gold: the domes of the First Temple of Ârata, the oldest temple, so Râvar had been told, in all Galea.

Ardashir, returning, reined in his horse nearby. "Baushpar," he said softly.

Râvar glanced up. The First Disciple was gazing toward the holy city, one hand raised to shade his eyes.

"It was blockaded during the time of the Caryaxists," he said. "Anyone caught trying to get in was arrested and sent to Thuxra. Still, people tried— thousands of them, all through those terrible years. There were guides who'd bring you through, some for faith, some for a fee. It was a sacred thing to say you'd walked Baushpar's streets, that you'd knelt at the First Temple's core, that you'd left offerings at the empty Aspect-shrines. I always hoped to make pilgrimage one day . . ." He paused, then made the sign of Ârata. "And now I am here. Ârata be praised."

Râvar stared at the high red walls, the burning domes. So many times he had imagined this moment, this first sight of the stronghold of the Brethren. Surely he would be filled with triumph to stand before it at last—or with rage, or with righteousness, or with some other great passion. He had even thought he might be overcome, that he might fall to his knees and cry out or weep—actions perfectly appropriate for his faithful to witness, for was he not Ârata's Messenger, looking for the first time on the holy city he would rule? But here he was, and there Baushpar was, and he felt . . . nothing. Or at any rate, little beyond his curiosity as to what sort of stone composed the walls and a certain puzzlement at all those wooden posts.

This is Baushpar, he thought, trying to stir his strange lethargy. *Baushpar! Where I will vanquish my enemies!*

Some sort of gesture seemed advisable, for authenticity's sake. He got down on his knees and bent to kiss the surface of the road. "Holy Baushpar," he proclaimed, rising. "My father's city, in which my City shall dwell."

Behind him, there was an answering murmur from the pilgrims. Ardashir made the god's sign.

"We'll move on now, Ardashir."

"And the emissaries, Beloved One?"

Râvar glanced beyond the First Disciple, to the two tattooed monks who sat their horses just ahead of the coach. They had intercepted the Awakened City three days earlier, and presented him with a message of welcome sealed and signed by the Blood Bearer. It had thrilled Râvar to hold the document in his hands; he had read it many times since, savoring the ornate phrases, the scriptural references written out and annotated in red ink. If not exactly a profession of faith, it was confirmation that the Son Vivaniya had fulfilled his promise. Not, he told himself, that confirmation was needed. Like his arrival, it had been inevitable.

Since then the monks had ridden with the pilgrimage. Their taciturn demeanor spoke neither of belief nor the lack of it. They used Râvar's title and bowed to him with every appearance of respect, and whenever he emerged, as now, their eyes followed him.

"Tell them they can go," he said.

He turned back toward the coach. Behind it, the Twentymen had formed a cordon to restrain the eager pilgrims; since the disaster of the last ceremony, Ardashir had made every effort to keep Râvar and the faithful apart. They cried out to him, straining against the Twentymen's linked arms, reaching past the Twentymen's shoulders. Abruptly, he felt a little of the expected triumph.

"Rejoice, children," he called. "Tonight we sleep in the holy city."

"Praise Ârata!" they cried. "Beloved Messenger! Guardian of Interim!" The Twentymen were starting to have trouble holding them. Râvar turned away and climbed into the coach.

In Axane's lap Parvâti wriggled and held up her arms, but he did not feel like taking her. He sat down by the window, peering through the gap in the cover as the coach lurched and began to move. Over the noise of the wheels he heard something else, soft at first, rising louder. It was a moment before he recognized it, a sound he had not heard since the first days of the journey: the voice of the Awakened City, raised in song.

According to Ardashir's scouts, a good portion of Baushpar's population remained within the walls, in the old districts where the monasteries and nunneries and shrines lay. But as with so many of the towns and villages lately, the suburbs were deserted—the streets vacant, the houses shuttered, the gates of the larger estates chained closed. The packed ash and gravel of the road became a broad, paved avenue, winding through a district of substantial villas with elaborate porches and fanciful roof tiles, each generously embraced by its own walled garden. Here the scouts had claimed a residence for Râvar. The wooden gates already stood open. Preceded by Ardashir and followed by the Twentymen, Râvar's coach turned ponderously aside. The Awakened City marched on into Baushpar, still singing.

The villa was shaped like a double-walled box, with two floors surrounding an open central courtyard. Galleries ran along all four inner walls. The residents had obviously departed in haste; the exquisitely tiled floors were strewn with debris, and many of the chambers still held nearly all their contents. In one of them, a bedchamber on the second floor that smelled faintly of some flowery perfume, Râvar placed Axane and Parvâti. For himself he chose the plainest chamber he could find, an empty room at the front of the house with unmuraled walls and an unornamented plaster ceiling, entirely bare of furnishing—much to the distress of Ardashir, who wanted him to have the luxuriously equipped suite at the villa's rear.

He needed to be magnificent for what was to come, so he swallowed his pride and sought Axane's assistance. He sat stiffly on a stool as she combed oil into his hair, careful of the still-painful scab where his followers had torn his scalp, and pulled it back from his face with intricate knots of cord. She outlined his eyes with kohl and tied the laces of the sumptuous robe he had chosen, whose hanging sleeves nearly brushed the ground. He spoke no word, nor did she. Since the day he had so foolishly let down his guard, they had addressed one another only when it could not be avoided. Across the room, on the wide bed, Parvâti slept.

She finished, and he rose to go. When he was halfway to the door, she spoke.

"Râvar."

He paused. She stood by the stool, her fingers twined together at her waist. "Well?" he said, when she did not continue.

"It's not too late." She drew a breath. "To stop."

It did not surprise him: one last effort, one final attempt to turn him from his course. He watched her a moment; like the city earlier, she seemed very distant and yet very distinct. She returned his gaze in a way that suggested it required all her will. At last he turned and left the room.

He locked the door, and for good measure barred the opening with stiffened air, as he had earlier barred the windows. Then he went to his own chamber and stood looking out across the villa's grounds. There was a paved court just below; beyond it, a broad, graveled thoroughfare led down to the gates. From the surrounding parkland, trees thrust up a lacework of bare branches. He could still hear the sound of his followers' singing; the air, which had been clear when they arrived, now carried the faint tang of smoke. Braziers, he thought. Surely the pilgrims would not set their own holy city to the torch.

He reached up, gently fingering the wound on his scalp. No one had died in his instinctive act of self-defense, but many had been injured. Over the objections of Ardashir, who if he could would have kept Râvar completely sequestered from that moment on, Râvar had gone the next day to visit and pray over them, demonstrating love in the wake of punishment. Ardashir had dubbed the incident the Chastisement of the Greedy, and had done his best to drive home the lesson of that name, at least within the portion of the pilgrimage over which he still exerted tenuous control. Nevertheless, the incident had cost Râvar followers—well over a hundred to date, by Ardashir's estimate. Those who remained seemed to love him with undiminished fervor—proof, if proof were needed, of the invulnerability of his deception.

But he had learned what their love could do. He would never again go among them alone.

Someone knocked. "Enter," he called.

It was Ardashir, shadowy in his shadow light. "Beloved One, there's still no word. Shall I send a message?"

"No. They must come to me." From the start their coming had been important: The Sons and Daughters must approach him, thus soliciting their own doom.

"Beloved One—" Ardashir hesitated. "I beg you to reconsider. Let me assemble a proper escort for you."

Râvar shook his head. "You know my will."

"But you should go to them as a general, with your guard at your back! You should stand before them as a king, mighty in rank and power! You should confront them as a god, with the faith of your followers to bear witness, their voices to cry your glory! Not alone, not unattended, as if—as if—"

He bit off the words. Ardashir had long known the intention he protested, that Râvar meant to go before the Brethren unaccompanied. Of course, this had not prevented him from trying to change Râvar's mind. Perhaps he really believed, as he claimed, that his objections sprang only from his long hatred of the rulers of the church, and from his sense of protocol, his desire that his Messenger always be attended by fitting pomp and ceremony. But Râvar knew that in this as in other things, it was the First Disciple's own desire that most truly spurred him—his driving need to force himself into the crucial moments of his Messenger's life, his inflexible conviction of the privilege due him as the first of Râvar's followers. Ordinarily, confronted with that aspect of Ardashir's character, Râvar felt annoyance or distaste. But, entirely unexpectedly, he was touched by pity.

"I am who I am, Ardashir," he said gently. "What difference does it make who or what surrounds me?"

"Beloved One. I fear for you, alone in that nest of vipers."

Râvar sighed. "I will not change my mind."

Ardashir opened his mouth as if for further protest, then closed it again. Since the burned village, he had been more hesitant to dispute. "Yes, Beloved One."

He bowed and departed. First Axane, Râvar thought, trying in the final moments to change his mind. Now Ardashir. There was a kind of symmetry to it—a necessity, even, like some final preparation that, once completed, need not be thought of again.

He felt a thrill deep in his belly.

He left the room. He paced the galleries as the sun set and darkness fell. In the courtyard below, the Twentymen lit torches; food was prepared and brought up. He paused to eat, then paced on. As earlier, he was aware of no great passion. But it was not the blankness of before. Rather, he was possessed by a deep and powerful calm, similar to the inner stillness he had once found in meditation. The coming confrontation stood before him like the division between night and day, a point of absolute transition beyond which all lay changed. Around him, huge significances breathed. *This is the last sunset I will know before I meet the Brethren. This is the last meal I will eat. The last moonrise I will witness.*

The last night on which Refuge goes unavenged.

He heard the noise first, an outlandish braying underscored by a deeper, pounding rhythm. Louder it grew, closer. The Twentymen left the courtyard. Râvar returned to his chamber, standing to one side of the window so he would not be glimpsed from below. Above the walls that separated the estate from the street he saw the leaping flames of torches, streaming the patterns of their heat.

Two Twentymen pulled wide the gates. Four men marched in, side by side, blowing on enormous instruments that encircled their chests and curved over their shoulders. It was from these that the discordant braying came. A column of tattooed guards followed, each with an upraised torch, then four more guards bearing a magnificent open palanquin, in which sat a shaven-headed figure in red-and-white Âratist garb. By his lifelight, ember-orange and steady as a stone, Râvar recognized the Son Vivaniya. Behind the palanquin walked several men in ordinary clothing—the First Faithful whom Ardashir had sent to guard the Son's conversion. After them came more torch-carrying guards, and finally a band of drummers, hammering out a cadence on shoulder-borne drums: Boom boom *boom* boom. Boom boom *boom* boom.

In front of the villa, the procession split down the middle as neatly as if it had come upon the blade of an invisible knife, the musicians and the guards moving left and right to flank the palanquin. The bearers set their burden down. The Son Vivaniya held up his hands. Instantly, the cacophony ceased.

Ardashir emerged from beneath the entrance portico. Behind him the Twentymen marched in four ranks of five, as disciplined as the tattooed guards. They halted before the palanquin. The Son Vivaniya stood waiting, no doubt for Ardashir to kneel. Ardashir stood like a pillar; he did not even incline his head. The silence drew out. It was the Son, at last, who spoke.

"I have come to greet the Next Messenger." His voice rose clearly from below. "And to conduct him to my Brothers and Sisters in the Evening City, if he wills it."

"He wills it," Ardashir replied, harsh as two stones grinding together.

It's time.

Râvar stepped away from the window. He smoothed his hands across his face, touched the heavy necklace where it dragged upon his neck. The strange calm of the past few hours had vanished; his heart was a hammer in his chest, and heat and chill traveled together across his skin. Closing his eyes, he wove illusion—not his usual coils of white or multicolored light, but fluttering banners of gold and red and twilight blue, like living flame.

He opened his eyes. His chimeric brilliance boiled around him, chased shadow across the floor. He lifted his face to the ceiling, seeing not the patterns of painted plaster but the black, unreadable vault of the sky.

Ârata. Ârata, curse you, look down on me!

Only the thunder of his blood answered.

He left the room. On the stairs he encountered Ardashir, come to fetch him; he passed the First Disciple without a word, illusion leaning out behind him as if he really burned. Into the night he walked, into the sight of the gathering. His men fell to their knees. The vowed Âratists did not kneel, but he saw how their eyes stretched, how their fists tightened on the shafts of their torches, how some of them made the god's sign. A dark joy shook him.

"Child of the First Messenger." His voice rang out, powerful and true. "Have you kept your promise?"

The Son Vivaniya's lips had parted, as if on a word he did not know how to utter. He left the palanquin, stumbling in his haste, and prostrated himself on the paving stones. The others followed—all of them, even the drummers, awkward with the great discs of their instruments.

"I have kept my promise, Beloved One." The Son's voice shook. "To the best of my ability."

"Then all is well. Rise. All of you, rise!"

They obeyed.

"Beloved One, here are your pilgrims who traveled with me." The Son beckoned the men who had walked behind his palanquin. "I've brought them home to you."

"Have they served you faithfully?"

"Most faithfully, Beloved One."

"Come to me, children." The men obeyed and knelt before him, raising their hands so he could see their marks, which as First Faithful they bore on both palms. On each of their foreheads, he set a point of light. "You've done well. You will be rewarded, in this life and the next. Rise and join your fellows."

They did as he commanded. He turned to Ardashir. The First Disciple stood like one of the columns that supported the portico, his arms folded hard across his chest. He held Râvar's eyes, every feature tense. It was not a look of judgment, or thwarted will. Ardashir, Râvar realized, really was afraid.

"Wait for me, my First Disciple," he said, soft. "And be easy. All will be well."

"I cannot be easy, Beloved One," Ardashir replied. "But I will wait."

"Now." Râvar turned once more to the Son. "Bring me to your Brothers and Sisters."

"Beloved One, please." The Son gestured to the palanquin. "I will be honored to follow at your side."

Râvar walked to the palanquin and arranged himself on the cushioned seat, engulfing it in incorporeal flame. The tattooed bearers strained away from him as he passed. Even the Son, coming to stand next to him, was careful to keep clear.

The bearers bent their knees and hoisted. The horns blared again. The drummers took up their throbbing cadence. Slowly, like a fire-scaled snake, the column wound toward the gates.

The street outside was choked with Râvar's followers. They, too, held torches, and candles and lamps and lanterns; between real flame and lifelight, the street seemed to blaze as bright as day. They shouted as he emerged; he saw their faces, wild and ecstatic and greedy, and was glad of the tattooed guards, ranged on either side of the palanquin. The crowd parted to let the procession pass. Some fell to their knees; others ran alongside or danced in front, leaping and whirling to the insistent rhythm of the drums. They sang, their voices rising even above the procession's din: the hymns that had drawn them from the caverns at the journey's beginning and delivered them into Baushpar at its end. They shouted Râvar's titles: "Beloved One! Walker in Light! Opener of the Way!" He raised his hands in benediction, holding them

so his scars could be seen, his ghost-flames billowing. To his right, the Son
Vivaniya walked like a man in a dream.

At the top of the street, a great opening pierced Baushpar's red walls—the
Gate of Summer, Axane had told him it was called, though the actual gates
had been removed after Baushpar was given to the church and nothing had
closed the space in more than a thousand years. Râvar felt the chill of all those
centuries as he passed beneath, a core of cold the seasons could not touch.
Beyond, the same red granite walls enclosed a broad avenue, with fire baskets
blazing all down its length. Here, too, spectators waited, their lifelights gaudy
against the lightless stone. Some wore ordinary clothing, but there were also
many vowed Âratists, in crimson garments and white stoles.

Boom boom *boom* boom. Boom boom *boom* boom. The drumbeat vibrated
in Râvar's bones. His first sight of Baushpar had been nothing like his dreams,
but this mad celebration, this triumphal nighttime march, realized his dreams
so exactly that he felt he had already lived it. In the penultimate moments of
his deception, there was no longer any subterfuge at all. He was simply and
precisely what he claimed to be: a creature more than human, gifted with divine power, possessed by godlike intent. As Baushpar burned before his eyes,
Refuge burned inside his mind—not horrible, as in sleep, not agonizing, as in
memory, but perfect, exquisite, as it had been when it lived. The sky, blue as
turquoise above the red walls of the river cleft. The Plains of Blessing, furred
with silver grass like the flank of a lounging beast. Gâvarti, his teacher, giving
him stern instruction. His mother, her black hair stuck to her forehead with
sweat, pounding grain upon a grinding stone. The great cool spaces of Labyrinth, with its cook fires and its balconies and its constant bustle of life and
work. The dim reaches of the Temple, where he had spent so many hours in
service and in meditation, where he had thought to spend so many more—all
the days of his life. The sense of divine presence he had known there more
strongly than anywhere else—sometimes a whisper and occasionally a shout
but always with him, always with him. A warmth, a weight, a fullness . . . an
immeasurable stirring . . . an awareness, as if far away some colossal intelligence opened a burning eye . . .

Râvar's heart leaped so violently that for a moment he thought the bearers
had stumbled and pitched him to the street. With his entire soul he strained
toward that spark of *presence*. It was there, he knew it, just past the threshold
of perception—hidden again, veiled, but the veil had slipped, it had slipped,
and he had sensed, he had *felt* . . .

He was observed. *Observed.*

For an instant he felt the red pulse of fear—for to be observed was to be known, and to be known meant that each step might be his last. Then triumph seized him and shook away everything but itself. It flung his head back; it dragged laughter from his throat. It swelled into a shout: "Refuge!" The word blazed across the city; it resounded from the walls, the roof tiles, the Temple's golden domes. It tore through the braying of the horns, thundered in the hammering of the drums. It possessed the crowd. "Refuge!" they seemed to howl back at him. "Refuge! Refuge!"

Boom boom *boom* boom. Boom boom *boom* boom. The drums swept the procession into the vast square at Baushpar's heart, past the mountainous bulk of the First Temple of Ârata. They swept it into the Evening City, through halls and courts and gardens unreal in their magnificence. They swept it past a pair of massive vermilion-painted gates, into another immense space where seams of brass ran between the paving stones and a raised walkway bridged the distance to a red-roofed pavilion, its golden columns gleaming in the lamplight that spilled from within. Four great Ârata-images brooded by the walkway, each one taller than the tall walls that enclosed this place. "Refuge," Râvar whispered into the high stone faces as his palanquin passed beneath: a secret only he and the god knew, but soon—soon—the Brethren would know it, too.

At the walkway's end, three tiers of shallow stairs rose up to the pavilion. The hornists and the tattooed guards split apart as they had at the villa, fanning out along the lowest step. The bearers lowered the palanquin. The Son Vivaniya lifted his hands. The instruments fell silent, as if a knife had sliced one note from the next.

"Beloved One." The Son gestured to the pavilion. "My Brothers and Sisters wait."

Râvar stepped from the palanquin. The Son stood aside; the bearers pressed away. The faithful sank to their knees.

"Only the Son may accompany me," Râvar said.

The guards' leader looked toward the Son. Vivaniya gave a small nod.

Râvar gathered the skirts of his robe and began to climb. The embroidered fabric was too heavy for his crippled hands; briefly he regretted he had not chosen something less cumbersome. Then the thought was gone, and the pavilion flooded his awareness, rising before him like the sun. He slowed, spinning out the anticipation. It seemed to him that all of time had drawn down to this instant, all the world contracted to this place. All of life lay in the coming moment—all he was, all he had done, all he would ever do.

Too late, Ârata. Too late to stop me now.

The stairs terminated on a broad landing. Beyond the gilded columns, the pavilion lay open to the night. Its floor and walls and pillars were of some rich dark wood whose patterns Râvar did not recognize, its ceiling lavishly gilded. Light spilled from horn-sided lanterns suspended from brass chains, and also, glinting toward the pavilion's rear, from a cluster of auras. The Brethren.

For an instant, Râvar checked; he could not help himself.

"They wait, Beloved One," Vivaniya murmured.

They were gathered before a dais, on which stood a wide golden chair. Smaller chairs, the same vermilion color as the gates, described an arc on either side. The Brethren did not stir as he approached; they were as still as the columns. Unexpectedly, two were no more than children, clinging to their spirit-siblings' hands.

Seeing this, Râvar saw something else.

Where are the rest of them?

A grave-faced man with a lifelight of intense clear amethyst broke from the others, drawing after him the little boy whose hand he held. He was followed by an immensely fat woman with changeable colors, now silver, now azure; and, after a hesitation, by two teenage boys whose billowing tawny auras were almost exactly the same. The rest remained where they were: an elderly man with a bandage bound across his eyes, leaning on the arm of a third teenager; a younger man whose colors, bright and supple as new-shed blood, lay close along his limbs, his hands resting protectively on the shoulders of the other child. On his broad chest, this man wore a golden necklace more massive than Râvar's, though the flame-hearted crystal that hung from it was half the size. The Blood Bearer. The Brethren's leader.

The five who had come forward knelt, the woman with some difficulty.

"Messenger." The amethyst-auraed man made the sign of Ârata. His expression was serene, his eyes half-closed as if in bliss. The child huddled against him, hiding his face in the folds of the man's stole. "You are glorious, and my heart rejoices. I am the Son Baushtas. This is the Son Yarios." Gently he urged the little boy to look up; the child whimpered, resisting. "Forgive his fear. His soul is old but in most ways he is still a child."

"My soul delights," the woman said, breathless with the effort of moving her great bulk. She wore a look of transcendent joy. "I am the Daughter Artavâdhi. Ârata be praised."

"I am the Son Gaumârata," said the boy beside her; his voice shook with fear. "Ârata . . . Ârata be praised."

"I am the Son Karuva," said the other teenager firmly. "I bless your coming. Ârata be praised."

Râvar barely heard them. His eyes searched the reaches of the pavilion. Shadow masked the farthest walls; elsewhere there was light, pooling beneath the pendant lamps, refracting from the gold and gems of the sun-mosaic that spread across the wall behind the dais. But it was only ordinary light. The light of life he saw nowhere except before him. He felt the press of understanding, trying to take shape. He turned to Vivaniya.

"Where are the others? Where are the rest of the Brethren?"

"Beloved One." Was it fear that flared in Vivaniya's face? "I and these nine are all who remain in Baushpar."

"No." The word was calm. It was not possible. The Son was lying.

"Beloved One, I would rather tear out my own throat than acknowledge it, but many of my Brothers and Sisters proved faithless. They were afraid, Beloved One, afraid of the darkness we have gathered in our lives, afraid of ending, and in that fear they fled—"

"They *fled*? And you allowed it?"

"Beloved One, I could not stop them, their unbelief was like a wall, I spoke and spoke and could not break it down—"

"You are their leader." Râvar looked beyond the Brethren at his feet, to the man with the necklace. "Why did you not command them to stay?"

The man held himself immobile, but his expression flinched. "I have not that power."

"You bear the Blood! You rule them!"

"I *lead* them. And in this room only. Not beyond. We are individual souls, individual wills. It has ever been so."

"Beloved One," said the grave-faced man with the amethyst lifelight, the Son Baushtas. "We who remain are yours. *When you meet the fire*, the *Darxasa* says, *deny not that you know it, for it knows you.* Our spirit-siblings denied, but we do not. We see the fire. We embrace it. We know you, Messenger. We know your name."

"Then why are you not *all* on your knees?" Râvar was trembling, the banners of his illusion shuddering. "*You* do not kneel!" He pointed at the Blood Bearer. "Nor does that one"—he stabbed his hand at the blind man, the child, the youth—"or that one or the other! Are you faithless, like the ones who fled? Or is your faith too weak to bear the sight of me? Do you fear me too much to bend your knees?"

The man with the bandaged eyes slid to the floor. With a shaking hand he made the sign of Ârata. "Messenger, forgive us." His voice broke; he swayed, and if the boy had not stooped to steady him would have fallen. Râvar rounded on Vivaniya.

"You swore an oath. You swore you would bring them to belief—all of them, all of them. You promised you would do it."

"I kept my promise, Beloved One, I kept it to the best of my ability." Vivaniya's face was as pale as stretched parchment. "The others will come to you, they will come when they see your glory, when they see your deeds—we are only the first, Beloved One, they need only time—"

"No!" Râvar shouted. "It was supposed to be all of you. Don't you understand? *It was supposed to be all of you at once!*"

They swayed back, as if his voice were wind. Their faces were alight with fear. Blind rage broke in him, a great red tide. He flung his shaping will like a spear, slamming it into the wall behind the dais. The wall exploded in a thousand fragments. Gem shards, splinters, flakes of gold came pattering down like rain.

"I sent you to secure their hearts!" he shouted over the dying echo of his power. "To win their souls for me, *all* their souls! And instead you give me *nine*—two children barely old enough to walk, a woman who can hardly stand without an arm to lean on, a blind man, three pimple-faced youths, a fool who thinks he knows my name, a leader who cannot lead! What good are they to me, what good are they without the rest? For what else have I come all this long way, endured your foul world, your filthy cities, your ugly customs, the company of blackened men? And you show me these nine, these *nine*, and say you have done your best? Did you think I would be *pleased* there are so few? Did you think I would reward you for failing the task I gave you?"

The Bearer and his companions had fallen prostrate when the mural shattered, the Bearer gathering the child into the shelter of his body. The Son Gaumârata huddled over the small Son Yarios, who, weeping with panic, had squirmed away from his guardian. Vivaniya, too, was on the floor, his arms clasped over his head. But Baushtas and Artavâdhi and Karuva still knelt, their faces ecstatic with dread.

"We deserve your anger, Messenger," Baushtas said. "We who have remained know this. We understand our fault, the betrayal we committed when as a council we turned from news of Ârata's rising. I have long known we would be punished."

Râvar dropped to his haunches, bracing his hands on the floor. "You are a fool," he hissed. "You know nothing. You have no idea what I truly am. Why I have truly come."

The Son did not flinch. "I know you are a human man, Messenger, as our father Marduspida was. I know you have been raised up by Ârata from the calamity we Brethren made, the cruel fate we brought on those who first knew the god awake. I know you come on us in judgment—both your own, for the sake of your lost people, and Ârata's, for the sake of our blindness, our many errors. I *do* know your name." He paused, drew breath. From behind him came the thin sound of Yarios's cries. "It is Râvar."

Râvar crouched motionless. It seemed an age before he could force his tongue to shape words. "How," he said. "How do you know that?"

"Our Sister Sundit came before us and revealed it all. She meant by her words to undo our belief—"

"No." All the air seemed to have left the pavilion. "I locked her. In stone."

"She was freed, by another's hand—"

And Râvar saw it, saw it all. "Gyalo Amdo Samchen," he whispered.

"Yes, Beloved One."

Impossible, impossible. A roaring filled Râvar's ears, as if Thuxra City were falling again, as if the Dracâriya hills were collapsing a second time. Almost, he could smell the dust of those great destructions, feel the earth tremble underfoot.

"You are the god's instrument." Baushtas's head had tipped back; his eyes were half-closed again in that look of rapture. "Do with us as you will."

"Don't mock me." Râvar shook his head. "Do not dare to mock me."

"Messenger, we speak our faith," Artavâdhi panted. "You are the Messenger Ârata made for us when we repudiated his first. You are the Messenger we deserve."

"You cannot believe in me. I am false. *You know that I am false.*"

"You test us, Messenger," Baushtas said. "And it is right, it is holy that you should, for we have failed so many tests. But this one we will not fail, no matter what the pain or the trial. This one we will endure."

"We've lived too long." Reaching out, Artavâdhi took both her Brothers' hands. "It is time for us to end. Let sleep come."

"Let sleep come," Karuva whispered.

"Let sleep come," Baushtas affirmed.

They bowed their heads. Their clasped hands trembled. Râvar felt a mounting horror. This could not be. He had meant them to believe, but only for as long as it took for him to reveal himself. What was important was that they *understand*: that they know themselves deceived, duped, made blasphemers; that they recoil in terror and revulsion from the truth of his nature, from the revelation of his real intent. But in embracing the blasphemy of his deception, the three had twisted it, turned his falsity into a kind of truth. How could that have happened? How could they have accepted such a thing? If he destroyed them now as he had planned, if he called fire on them or plunged them into the earth, they would die not in despair but in joy and resignation, his praises on their lips.

No. It's not what I want. It's not what I want!

"Let sleep come."

The Son Gaumârata was on his knees again behind the others, little Yarios huddled in his arms. He was trembling so hard he could barely speak.

"Let sleep come." It was the blind Son. The boy who had supported him still clung to his arm, his mouth open, his face a perfect mask of terror.

"Let sleep come," Vivaniya whispered. He crawled like a child to the Son Karuva and took his hand.

It was like some awful dream. Was this the answer, at last, to his defiance? When he had taunted the silence, hurling angry words at emptiness, had Ârata been observing—and laughing—all along?

"Curse you!" he shouted, digging his fingers into the tresses of his hair, dragging at the careful cord knots Axane had made. "Curse you, curse you!"

Before him on their knees, they waited for their fate. Of them all only the Bearer, who had risen to his feet when Baushtas began to speak, remained standing, the child Son in his arms, his gaze turned not on Râvar but his spirit-siblings, his broad face still as stone. Directly opposite, Vivaniya stared into Râvar's eyes with the helpless fixity of an animal. A small red bonfire burned in both dark irises—a reflection of Râvar's garment of illusion, of his phantom flames. And all at once a great horror flew out of the night and caught Râvar by the throat, and he knew that these were not his fires at all, that it was not a human man who crouched before him but something else, some *thing* with a flat pale face and ember eyes and behind them a darkness deeper than the void of night. He knew it was indeed as he had believed in childhood and young manhood, the visceral understanding that all his recent experience, all his painfully gathered empirical knowledge, had never quite managed to unseat: This world was a realm of dark illusion, a province of dreams and demons. All this time, insisting to himself it was a true world, he had been wrong.

And then, just as swift, the understanding shifted, and he saw that the illusion—all of it—belonged to him.

A veil seemed to fall across his senses. He rose from where he knelt and left the Brethren behind, passing from the light and shadow of the pavilion into the moon- and starlight of the court. A great shouting greeted him; he threw up his arms in an instinctive gesture of defense. Confused, he saw a field of black below him, and across it a river of varicolored light. His followers. In the pavilion, he had entirely forgotten them, waiting for him to emerge triumphant. Waiting for him to go down to them, so they could bear him away. He felt their love, their awful tearing love.

No. Panic filled him. *I can't.*

He summoned his shaping will. With a dazzle of transformation, a roar of change, he stepped out upon the air. He walked above them, each footstep a new collision of the elements, a solitary storm. They reached toward him, a thousand separate souls howling with a single voice—the beast he had heard at night, breathing beyond his tent. He hastened, wanting only to escape.

Râvar

It had been instinct to take to the air, but beyond the great court it became necessity, for on foot he could never have found his way through the maze of the Brethren's palace, or negotiated the walled avenues of Baushpar—even if he had been able to go unnoticed among the crowds. The city spun below him like an ornament crafted by a mad jeweler, spangled with a thousand hues and strengths of light. What reasons would those below invent, what tales would they tell, of his tumultuous passage overhead? He did not know, or care.

Under ordinary circumstances he would not have been able to pick out the villa from those around it, even from above, for lamps had been lit in many of the formerly vacant dwellings beyond Baushpar's walls. But his followers kept vigil outside his residence, and the clotted brilliance of that crowd guided him. He skimmed above them, glimpsing the upturned faces, the yearning arms. He stepped over the walls, and trod the topmost branches of the winter-bare trees. Before the house he allowed himself to descend. He misjudged his trajectory—something he had never done in the caverns—and staggered as he struck the ground. Ardashir sprang forward from the shadow of the portico, where he had been standing exactly as Râvar had left him.

"Beloved One! I'm here."

Râvar wanted only to be alone. He stumbled past the First Disciple up the steps, his legs shaking with fatigue and the dregs of panic. The Twenty-men on guard before the doors hurried to pull them open. He passed into the lamp-flickering dimness of the hall. Not till that moment did he realize he still wore his flame-illusion. He quenched it like a blown candle. The hall became dimmer still.

"Beloved One." Ardashir spoke from behind, alarm sharp in his voice. "What has happened? Are you hurt?"

Râvar halted. From a great depth he dredged up words. "Don't disturb me."

"Beloved One . . . ?"

"I want . . . not to be disturbed. Until I say."

Ardashir said something, some protest or question, but Râvar had ceased to listen. He trudged down the hall and into the courtyard, where the stair led up to the second floor. He began to climb; when his feet tangled in the trailing skirts of his robe, he wrenched at the laces and shed it like a skin, leaving it where it fell. He gained his room and closed the door and swung the latch into place. He set his shoulders against the wood and allowed himself to slide to the floor. He sat there, knees raised, hands splayed loose at his sides.

Alone. Out of sight, out of reach.

The heavy links of the necklace dragged at his neck. He removed it, let it drop, hearing the clash of metal, the chime as the crystal struck the tiles. He leaned his head back and closed his eyes. His limbs felt loose and light; there was a hollowness at his center, as always after a large release of power. The rage and panic that had taken him in the pavilion were gone, blown out like a violent storm. In their aftermath he did not feel the despair or confusion he might have expected, but rather a high, clear calm, as if his mind, like this empty chamber, had been swept clean. He seemed to stand before himself, before his deeds. Like a man emerging from a forest onto a broad flat plain, he gazed upon his own inner landscape, and knew he had never seen so far before and might never find himself again at such a point of vision.

In the pavilion he had cursed Ârata, certain in that moment that the horrible twisting of his intent was the god's work, that the punishment he had dared and challenged again and again had come on him at last, a most exquisite and subtle retribution. But the great sense of *observation*, the breathless certainty of *attention* that had seized him as the drums bore him into the Evening City was gone, as if it had never been. In the familiar, echoing emptiness he had to ask himself if he had imagined it, created it whole out of the noise and the light and the unbearable anticipation, the jubilation of the crowd, the memories of Refuge that had come to him so vividly. And if Ârata had not been present then, why should he be present in any of it? Why should anything but the emptiness and the silence be the truth? If the god had turned his face away from Râvar's first great blasphemy, the fall of Thuxra, why should he turn toward any of the others?

No godly intervention, anyway, was required to explain how things had gone so wrong. Râvar and Râvar alone had made those disastrous choices. Because he had so wanted Refuge's destroyer to watch as Refuge was avenged, because it had so delighted him to imagine the false Messenger's impotence, his fury, and most of all his *understanding*, he had not decreed Gyalo Amdo Samchen's death but let him go free. Because he who had slain hundreds from a distance had not had the stomach to take a dozen lives face-to-face, he had not killed the Daughter Sundit and her people, but walled them up instead to die. From those two errors had sprung the downfall of his plans. The flight of more than half the Brethren. The premature revelation of his identity, which had somehow sparked the travesty of belief professed by those who remained.

And perhaps even without those errors he would have failed. He had questioned a great deal as he built his legend and planned his journey, but one thing he had never doubted: that all the Brethren would be waiting when he arrived. That assumption had always been in him, unfounded and unquestioned, like a promise he had been given—or a promise he had made himself, as if, godlike, he could bend the world to his desire. He would have assumed it, he thought, even without Vivaniya's conversion, which he had regarded simply as a way of accomplishing in advance some part of the labor of convincing them to acknowledge him. In the preternatural clarity of his present state of mind, that assumption now seemed insane. Even if Sundit had not survived, had not returned to speak against her Brother, was it not certain that at least some would have rejected Vivaniya's words and sought safety beyond Baushpar? They had fled the Caryaxists—why should they not flee him, who had killed their King, who had occupied Ninyâser, whose followers burned villages and massacred unbelievers?

But it wouldn't have had to be all of them. Just most of them. Surely that would have been enough.

But *most of them* was not the vow he had made. And in the pavilion, he had not been able to accomplish even that. They had surrendered, surrendered utterly, and he had not struck them down. He had fled. Like a child, he had turned around and run away.

His eyes sprang open. Someone—Ardashir, no doubt—had brought in a brazier, and a little light rose from the coals, stirring with heat patterns. The tiles were hard under his buttocks, and cold beneath his hands. Outside, he could hear the pilgrims at the gates, their voices rising in the cadences of some hymn.

What if nothing had gone wrong? If he had made no mistakes. If all the Brethren had been gathered as he wished, if they had bowed down in ignorance as he planned, if he had opened their eyes as he intended. If in the moment of their greatest despair he had cast them into the earth, torn down their gilded pavilion and toppled their Ârata-images and laid waste their great brass-netted court, made rubble of the Evening City and walked out to his followers over the debris, triumphant . . . What then? For so long Baushpar had been the pinnacle of his aspiration. As when he crossed the Burning Land with Axane, dreaming of destroying Thuxra City, he had not often thought of what would come after. More marching? More destruction? More harangues by Ardashir, more confrontations with his hungry faithful? More endless hours in the coach with Axane? More sleepless nights in his tent? And for how long? Months? Years? Until they finally found him out? Until he died?

It appalled him.

But it wouldn't have been like that, he thought. He would have been exalted with achieved purpose. He would have been transported with the certainty of retribution, with the *rightness* of having turned Refuge's destroyers into dust. The triumph of it would have filled the emptiness. Surely that would have transformed everything. Surely nothing could have been the same.

Yet had he not felt triumph after he buried Santaxma? After he swept into Ninyâser? Had not those triumphs drained away, like sand through cupped hands, leaving him unchanged?

It felt like betrayal even to frame such thoughts. Not simply to think that avenging his murdered people could bring anything less than lasting triumph, but because it implied that he had pursued vengeance for himself. For his own pain, his own rage. For the hole in him, the desperate need for something to believe in.

Unbidden, Axane's words returned to him, the words she had spoken on the night of her arrival: *Do you think it's what they would have wanted?*

"It is," he said aloud, bowing his face onto his knees, his fingers closing uselessly against the tile. "It wasn't for me. It was never for me."

The unnatural calm had fled. Despair filled him, and awful, burning shame—for his mistakes, for his failure. Memories unfolded behind his eyes, the same memories that had come to him so ecstatically a few hours earlier, unbearable now in their reproach. In the smoky dark, he remembered the fouled riverbank, the scourge of the sun, the madness of the flies. Horror all around him, and in his heart the unanswerable accusation of the slain: *Guilty. Guilty. Guilty.*

He had buried his dead. He had left the riverbank. He had forced himself to go forward: sworn his vow, made his plan, followed his purpose. It was no different now. He could go on. He could return to the Evening City and have the remaining Brethren seized. He could send his people after the rest. Eventually he would find them; there was nowhere for them to go but Galea, and they could not hide forever. It would not be what he had wanted, but it would be vengeance of a kind. He would need explanations, justifications, new doctrine—but he had made up so many tales already. Why not one more? A hundred more? His people would believe him. They always did.

Or . . .

He could say nothing. Do nothing.

He could . . . stop.

Everything in him went still. Glinting like a mirage on the far horizon of his inner self, he seemed to see the possibility of an entirely different path. Not a new idea, not at all—had not Axane spoken it only hours earlier? Had she not spoken it on the night she arrived in the caverns? It had not touched him then, or since. It had not been real. But now . . . *To be finished*, he thought. To let go. To abandon everything, even his vow. To simply . . . make an end.

He did not know how long he sat there, motionless, barely breathing. At last, drawn by an impulse he did not wish to question or to name, he pushed to his feet and left his room. He slipped along the gallery. At Axane's door he banished the barrier and went inside.

She was awake, sitting up in bed, roused perhaps by the small sound of the barrier's unmaking. Parvâti slept undisturbed beside her. A lamp with a pierced cover burned on a table near the bed, its weak wash of yellow light mostly swallowed by the tempest of her colors. Her face as she looked at him was controlled and still; but the coverlets, clutched up in both her fists, told a different story. To reassure her, he did not approach too close, halting well short of the bed.

"What," she whispered, as on the night after he had killed Santaxma. "What did you do?"

He let out his breath. "Nothing." She stared at him. "Really. I didn't do anything. They're still alive, the ones who were there. I didn't touch them."

Her lips parted. "Why?" she said at last.

How could he explain? Shame twisted in him. He shook his head.

"Is it—" She paused. "Is it over?"

"I made so many mistakes, Axane. I've failed everyone. In Refuge . . . now." Grief rose up, a scalding tide. "I only wanted to atone—to make it right—"

She pushed back the covers, swung her legs onto the floor. She wore only a chemise; her arms were bare, and her unbound hair fell heavy on her shoulders and across her breasts.

"I know," she said.

"Do you?"

"They were my people, too."

"How can the world be like this, Axane? How can Ârata—" He lost the words for a moment. "I used to think he was cruel. But now I think . . . he simply isn't watching. How can you . . . how can you even blaspheme against a god who doesn't care?"

"I used to think that." Her great eyes held his. "That he was indifferent. But now . . . Maybe he was here once, and left us long ago. Maybe he never existed at all. But one thing I know, one thing I know for certain—now, today, *there is no god in this world.*" She paused, then said with a kind of wonder: "I've never said that out loud before."

"Doesn't it frighten you?"

"No." And again, as if she had just discovered it: "No."

"Do I frighten you?"

She looked at him, her hands closed on the edge of the mattress. And the same instinct that had brought him to the room rose up again, propelling him toward her, pressing him to his knees, bowing his head into her lap, his cheek turned on her thighs. She made no sound; her whole body jerked rigid. He did not move. Slowly at first, then all at once, her muscles softened. Her hands descended, light as leaves, to rest upon his hair.

He drew a long shuddering breath. She smoothed his hair away from his face. He lay passive, his eyes half-closed, smelling her scent. To be within her light was like entering another world, like stepping sideways into a different stream of time. The pleasure of her touch was exquisite, a bliss that contained nothing carnal. He had not been able to stop himself from wanting her, but he had never permitted himself to long for this—for kindness, for comfort. For just these moments, he let those barriers go.

Through the metamorphic sheen of cobalt and emerald he could see the wall behind the bed, revealed by the low yellow light of the lamp. Its mural of ferns and birds was interrupted by a chest pushed up against it. Dreamily he traced the patterns of the painting—more restful than many of the patterns of this world, for the design was a repeating one—and underneath, the patterns of the plaster: its composition, its thickness, the invisible net of stresses that marked the places where it would one day crack. They clustered especially above the chest, spidering up from behind it as if there had been some impact there.

It came to him all at once what he was seeing. The understanding penetrated his warm trance like a slow flood of cold water. He pulled back, barely noticing as Axane's hands slid away, and got to his feet. He went to stand before the chest.

"Râvar," she said quietly, an admission as good as words.

He set his foot against the chest and shoved it aside, revealing a swath of wall where the plaster had been chipped away, in some places down to the strips of wood that supported it. For a moment he stared at it.

"Where did you put the plaster, Axane?"

She sighed. "In the chest."

"How did you know I wouldn't be in the room you would have come out in?"

"I heard you talking to Ardashir. I knew your room was at the front of the house."

He felt no anger, only a heavy disappointment. At last he was able to admit to himself the hope that had brought him to her room, the same futile hope that had tormented him since he was a boy of fourteen. It would not be so bad to stop, he had thought, if he could stop with her, with Parvâti. If they could become a family, find refuge in this world as their ancestors had found refuge in the Burning Land. What had he been thinking? He knew better than to imagine she would give him such a thing; he needed no hole in the wall to tell him that. And even if that were not so . . . he hated this world. He had no desire to live in it.

Which was, of course, the crux of everything. For that was what came after—after Thuxra. After Baushpar. After whatever else he chose to do: living, surviving in this world.

He turned. She sat very still, her hands once more closed on the mattress.

"Go," he said.

She did not blink. She did not move.

"Go! Go on, get out. Take Parvâti and leave. Right now. Before I change my mind."

Her mouth opened; then it snapped closed. She reached around to lift Parvâti, who woke and whimpered. She slid off the bed and padded swiftly toward the open door, where the glow from the torches in the courtyard below cast a faint illumination across the tiles.

"Wait!"

She went to immobility all in an instant, like an animal. She did not move a muscle as he approached. Parvâti was still whimpering, fretful at the sudden wakening, squirming against her mother's hold. He reached out and set a crooked finger against his daughter's cheek, tracing the soft curve of it. He brushed the rumpled hair from her brow. She quieted and looked up at him with slow-blinking, sleepy eyes, frowning a little. He could always quiet her.

"Little bird," he whispered. She made a sound, then raised her fist and stuffed it in her mouth. He felt as if he had been pierced through the heart. How could he let her go?

But he could not keep her. Of all the souls in the world, hers alone he did not wish to damn by his blasphemy or his downfall.

He laid his palm on her forehead, then stepped back. "Wait a minute," he told Axane.

He returned to the bed. He threw back the covers, dragged off the blanket and spread it on the floor. He tossed onto it items from the big basket in which Axane kept Parvâti's things and her own: gowns, chemises, linens. Axane's shoes. Clumsily, he folded over the ends and rolled it up, then carried it to Axane and helped her grip it under her arm. Her quilted jacket he draped over her shoulders. She watched him all the while, her face very still—her quiet face, her secret face, the face behind which she hid.

"This isn't for you," he said. "I don't care about you. But I want her taken care of properly." Then, when she stood unmoving: "Get out!"

She did not hesitate. He heard her bare feet on the gallery. By the time she reached the stairs, she was running.

He stood where he was, trying to make his mind a void so he would not have to think about what he had done, about how she had been so eager to escape him that she had been ready to dash into the winter night without her shoes, in her chemise. After a while he sat down on the floor, because he no longer had the strength to stand.

A shadow eclipsed the dim light from the doorway. "Beloved One," Ardashir said. "The woman. She—"

"I told her she could go."

"You don't want me to detain her?"

"No. Let her go."

Ardashir turned and spoke briefly to someone standing out of sight. That person departed. Ardashir remained. "Beloved One," he said, soft. "What has happened?"

Râvar said nothing. Ardashir advanced a little way into the room.

"Beloved One, I know something is amiss. Please tell me what it is, so I can help you."

"You can't help me."

"In the Evening City—did the Brethren repudiate you? I told you, Beloved One, I told you they were not to be trusted."

"They bowed down to me. They acknowledged me. They called me by my name."

"Then what—"

"It's too late, Ardashir. There's too much . . . I don't know what comes next."

"Beloved One." Ardashir crouched down in front of him. On his ugly face was a look of mortal dread. "I don't understand. Tell me what to do."

Râvar shook his head. He thought of Parvâti, of Axane running for the stairs. He dropped his face into his ruined hands and began to weep, great tearing sobs that felt as if they damaged something inside him.

There was a frozen pause. Then arms came round him. He felt himself drawn against the warmth of a broad chest. Fingers tangled in his hair, a touch as delicate, as tentative as Axane's.

"Hush," Ardashir murmured, rocking him like a child. "Hush, beloved. Hush."

Râvar leaned into the First Disciple's shoulder and wept, not for himself, not for all the loss and failure, but because at the end of everything he should be left with a man like Ardashir.

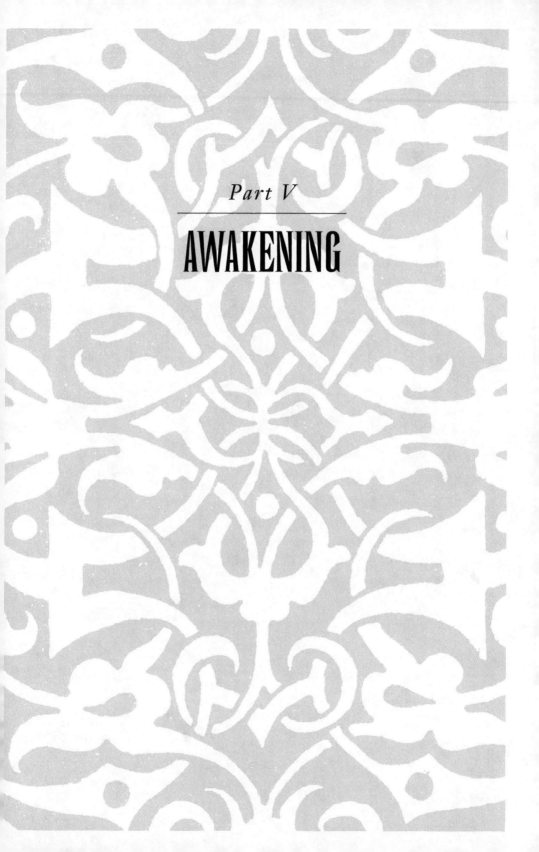

Part V

AWAKENING

24

Gyalo

Gyalo lay in the Burning Land, breathing the parched air of the desert, its dust and grit sharp against his skin. High overhead, the sun raged down. A shadow blocked it: Teispas, tangled hair falling around his face, blood from his lash wounds curling like red ribbon down his arms. He gripped Gyalo's shoulder—the sound shoulder, the one that did not ache. *Wake up*, he said, urgency harsh in his voice. *You've overslept.* Gyalo tried, but could not rise. Teispas tightened his grip and shook him, and said again, *Wake up. Wake up. Wake—*

"—up, Brother. Time to start the day."

"I can't," Gyalo mumbled, realizing even as he did that the desert was a dream, and that the hand on his shoulder belonged to Diasarta.

"Come on, now. You know you'll be angry with me if I let you sleep."

"Sorry." Gyalo rubbed his eyes. "Sorry, Dasa. I was dreaming."

"I've made us breakfast." Diasarta got to his feet.

Gyalo lay a moment, letting the last of the dream slip away. He felt the dull ache in his left shoulder that was always with him now—a pain that carried a sense of invasion, as if the arrow were still embedded in his flesh. The arrowhead had been barbed; Diasarta had had to cut it out, a procedure for which Gyalo thankfully had been unconscious.

Sun slanted into the kitchen of the abandoned farmstead in which they had spread their bedrolls the night before. As with other dwellings they had passed since Ninyâser, it had been abandoned in hope of return, with boards nailed across the door and windows to deter intruders. Unlike many, it had escaped the depredations of Râvar's followers. Diasarta had pried some of the boards loose so they could climb in through a window. It seemed wrong to use the beds of the family that had lived there, so they camped on the floor of the kitchen, building a fire in the clay stove for warmth. Among the many items the farmstead's occupants left behind were cooking implements and a larder full of food. They had eaten well the night before, and would again this morning, judging by the smell of whatever Diasarta was preparing.

Gyalo rose stiffly from his blankets. He folded them and rolled them up and tied them to his pack, simple procedures made awkward by the still-limited use of his left arm. He stamped into his boots and sat down at the table, where Diasarta was setting out their meal: bowls of rice boiled with pickled vegetables and dried meat, cups of strong tea.

"Eat it all," Diasarta ordered.

Gyalo obeyed, though his hunger was satisfied long before the bowl was empty. In the fever that had wracked him after his injury, the very thought of food had made him sick, and his appetite had not yet recovered. He had come close to death. Like the phantom arrow in his shoulder, the sense of that was still with him, a chill beneath his heart, a shadow at the corner of his eye, keeping him always conscious of the understandings he had gained on that dark journey, or perhaps by his return from it—he was not sure.

When they were done, Diasarta cleaned and stowed away the dishes and utensils and doused the fire in the stove. He had already filled their waterskins and packed a bag of supplies. For some time, Gyalo had been strong enough to shape, but Diasarta, ever protective, tried to spare him as much as possible. On his palm Gyalo shaped a lump of gold, and laid it on the table—payment for the shelter and the food. They climbed through the window again. Diasarta pounded the boards back in place, then helped Gyalo don his pack, adjusting the padding that cushioned Gyalo's wounded shoulder. They set off down the track, heading back to the Baushpar road.

They had been journeying steadily for nearly two months, ever since Gyalo, over Diasarta's objections, decided he was well enough to travel. They walked in Râvar's footsteps, witness to his works: the long straight passage he had carved through the fallen hills, the enormous plaque of banded sandstone he had clapped down upon the Plain of Ninyâser like the lid of a crypt. It was impossible not to be awed by those great shapings—an abstract awe, separate from Râvar and the reasons for their making, as might be felt in the aftermath of some hugely destructive natural event. They marked the growing violence of the Awakened City's progress, encountering it first in the city of Abaxtra, where large portions of the suburbs had been vandalized and burned. It was also in Abaxtra, its walls hung with mourning cloths painted with Santaxma's likeness, that they heard the first whispered rumors that the King had not died as the official announcements said—that he had met a horrifying fate in an encounter with a renegade Shaper, or (depending on who was whispering) that he had received judgment at the hands of the Next Messenger.

The words Râvar had spoken in the caverns were often in Gyalo's mind: *I want you to watch as I bring ruin upon your world—you, who brought ruin on mine.* It was as painful a punishment as Râvar could have wished. Though he was often tempted to avoid the empty villages, to pass by the looted houses, to turn away from the marks of Râvar's power, Gyalo forced himself to look, to look and to remember—an affirmation of purpose, a seal on his intent.

He thought often also of Sundit. Did her body lie beside the King's? He hoped not. He hoped she had heeded him and saved herself.

In Ninyâser, littered and battered from the Awakened City's sojourn, the Great South Way ended. Gyalo and Diasarta moved on along the Baushpar road. Except for the Way, engineered for the ages from great slabs of stone, it was the best road in all Arsace, built and maintained by the church. The pilgrimage had undone most of the careful repair work with which the Brethren had remedied the damage of the Caryaxist years; the ash-and-gravel surface was pocked and scarred, the cleared verges strewn with trash and debris. The surrounding countryside was largely empty, homes and villages abandoned; alternatively, people had turned their dwellings into armed encampments. Gyalo and Diasarta, mistaken for Râvar's faithful, were several times chased off with stones and staves. There were also those who for the same reason welcomed them, offering shelter and food—which Diasarta, ever pragmatic, insisted they accept, despite Gyalo's distaste for the pretense such hospitality required. In one town, an entire monastery had converted; claiming shelter on the basis of their pilgrim marks, Gyalo and Diasarta attended a Communion ceremony, which the monastery's Shapers had adapted to reflect their new understanding of Ârata awake. Gyalo, remembering the similarly altered ceremony he had seen in Refuge, was struck yet again by the irony of Râvar's blasphemy—which in perpetuating his false claim of Messengerhood also, strangely, proclaimed the truth. For Ârata *was* risen. The end times *had* come. The world *did* stand upon the cusp of change.

They were close to the holy city: four days' travel, perhaps a little more. Gyalo felt the pull of it all the time, of what waited for him there, a barb hooked into his heart, a thread wound up a little tighter with each mile that fell behind. In his sleep, Teispas harried him. *Make haste,* the captain urged. *Time is short.* And sometimes, as this morning: *Awake! Awake!*

It had been clear at dawn, but by midafternoon the sky was patched with cloud. A chill wind sprang up; Gyalo fastened the ties of his jacket, which he had let hang open in the unexpected warmth of noon, and adjusted his pack, trying to ignore the grinding ache in his shoulder. Some distance ahead, where the road curved out of sight around a hill, he could just see the green glint of a lifelight coming into view from the opposite direction, vivid against the dark surface of the road. In the past few days they had begun to overtake stragglers from the Awakened City, but only rarely had they seen anyone traveling the other way.

"You all right, Brother?" Diasarta asked. "It's near evening. We could find a place to stop."

"I'm well enough."

It was not really true, but he hated the weakness that still troubled him. Diasarta, who had a finely judged sense of when to impose his will and when to keep silent, did not argue.

Gyalo watched the traveler's slowly enlarging lifelight. As always when he glimpsed an emerald aura, his heart had begun to beat uncomfortably fast, a reaction he knew was foolish, given the impossibility of the hope attached to it. He imagined he could make out sapphire as well, and the suggestion of other colors . . . *Don't be ridiculous*, he told his agitated pulse; *you know it can't be her.* Yet it was such a strong light, and so restless. And there *was* blue amid the green, he could definitely see it now . . .

And then he was running, his body understanding what his mind still could not believe. His pack banged on his back; he paused to drag it off and ran on. She was running, too—and he knew it was she, knew beyond any doubt, not just in the great glorious cloud of color she carried with her but by her shape within it, by the way she moved—and then by her face, which he had dreamed of and longed for and imagined so intensely the past eight months that for a moment he felt himself slide out of the world and into another place entirely, and his head spun and he stumbled and might have fallen if she had not reached him just at that moment and caught him beneath the arms and held on to him, weeping and laughing at the same time, saying his name over and over.

"What," he stammered. "How . . . ?"

"He let us go. He let us go."

"But why?"

"I don't know. I don't care."

Axane reached up and pulled his face down to hers and kissed him. His senses spun away again into that other place. It was Chokyi who recalled them, setting up a rising wail from her cocoon on Axane's back. They broke apart; he helped her untie the blanket she had twisted into a makeshift carrier. "Little bird," he said, reaching toward the baby—who was not a baby any longer, but a sturdy little girl—but she only screamed louder, and shrank away from him. Axane lifted her, settled her against her shoulder.

"She doesn't remember me," Gyalo said, feeling a twist of pain within the currents of his joy.

"She will. Give her time."

"She's gotten so big!"

"That's what children do." Axane gave a laugh that turned into a sob. "Oh, Gyalo, Gyalo!"

And he put his arms around her again, around both of them, and they knelt together in the middle of the road and found that place, that place as large, and as small, as the three of them.

At last Gyalo remembered Diasarta. The ex-soldier was standing where Gyalo had left him, obviously waiting to be summoned. Gyalo got to his feet and beckoned. Diasarta limped forward, picking up Gyalo's abandoned pack. Still holding Chokyi, Axane rose and went to meet him, and kissed him full on the mouth.

"Thank you," she said. "Thank you."

Diasarta was speechless. His scarred face burned.

They made camp in a stand of trees a few hundred paces off the road. Diasarta went to gather wood for a fire. "No, no," he said, when Gyalo made to go with him; "you've been apart from them long enough." Then, gripping Gyalo's arm: "I'm happy for you, Brother."

Gyalo untied his bedroll and spread the blankets on the ground so Axane could sit with Chokyi. He crouched before them. From the shelter of Axane's arms, Chokyi regarded him with mistrust.

"Don't you remember me at all, little bird?" he coaxed. "I used to hold you when you cried. I used to carry you on my shoulder. Don't you remember me, Chokyi?"

"She's forgotten her name."

"Her name? Why?"

"He renamed her. *Parvâti*." Axane said it with loathing. "His mother's name. I swore I'd never use it."

"She's beautiful." And she was, with her amber skin and delicate features, Axane's curling hair and Râvar's green eyes.

"Do you hear that, my sweet? You have an admirer."

Chokyi tipped her head back and looked owlishly up into her mother's face. They were both dirty, and Axane's fatigue was palpable, but otherwise they seemed remarkably well. Gyalo could see no sign of neglect or abuse. There were abuses, though, that did not show . . .

"Axane, why did he let you go?"

"I told you. I don't know."

"There has to be a reason."

"Something happened, I think, in the Evening City. He went there the night we reached Baushpar. When he came back he was . . . he seemed to be . . . in despair."

"Did he find the Brethren gone?"

"No. They were there."

So Sundit had not survived to warn them. "He succeeded, then."

She shook her head. "He said he left them living."

Gyalo was incredulous. "Living? Do you think it's true?"

"Yes. Yes, I believed him."

"But why? Did he tell you why?"

"I don't care why. My little bird and I are free, and with you." She gave a laugh that was half a sob. "That's all that matters."

"Oh Axane. Can you ever forgive me?"

She looked at him in surprise. "For what, my love?"

"For leaving you." He could hardly say it. "For being too late at Dracâriya."

"What are you talking about? You were almost killed at Dracâriya! Gyalo, I prayed you wouldn't follow me. I prayed you'd stay in Ninyâser. When I dreamed you coming after me . . . oh, I was so frightened! I used to shout at you in my Dreams to go back. And then . . . when I dreamed you wounded . . . I almost gave myself away that night. I almost did."

Her voice broke. He reached out, gripped her free hand. She closed her fingers tightly around his.

"He had some idea I would be glad he'd stolen me. That I was ready to fall in love with him at last." She did not look at him. Her voice was very soft. "He was so angry when he saw it wasn't so! And when he realized you and I had married—" She caught her breath. "Oh, he fell into such a rage. I think if it had been just me, he would have had his people do away with me, or maybe left me behind in the caverns with the Daughter Sundit. But he wanted Chokyi, and he kept me for her sake. While we were in the caverns, I was prisoned in one of his rooms—he barely let me set a foot outside it. He was careful when we began to travel, too. Whenever he slept or wasn't there to watch us he'd make some sort of . . . transparent cage out of the air. But in the coach he left me free, and also sometimes when he was with us in the tent. If

I'd been on my own I would have watched for a chance to run. With Chokyi, it was too much of a risk. But I began to think that maybe . . . maybe I could find a way to kill him. As I should have done before, in the Burning Land."

Gyalo watched her dark hand, clasped in his light one, his pale aura swallowed by her stormy colors. He had to hear it all; of course he did. But part of him resisted. Part of him said *Stop*. Part of him said *I don't want to know*.

"I waited for the chance. He was always careful, though, and for a long time it didn't come. Then we stopped in a town, and he . . . he fell asleep without locking me up first. There was a basin made of some kind of heavy stone. I thought I could use it to . . . to . . . hit him. I took it . . . I knelt beside him . . . I lifted it up. But I couldn't do it. I could . . . *think* it, I could imagine it, but I couldn't do it. And while I was realizing that, he woke up and looked at me. I thought for certain he'd guess. But—" She paused. "He didn't. He got up and left, and that was that.

"We got to Baushpar. We were in a house, a big house with many rooms. He sealed the door and the windows. But the walls were made of plaster, and it came to me that if I could break through, get into the room on the other side, I could escape that way. He went that night to the Evening City, and I began to make a hole. I had to be careful, because his people were all over the house, and I didn't dare keep at it for very long in case he came back. So I didn't get very far. Then he did come back, and he came into the room . . . I'd forgotten about his patternsense. He saw what I'd done. I'd hidden it, but he saw. I thought he would be enraged." She shook her head. "But he just stood there for a moment, and then he turned around and told me to take the baby and get out. Calmly. Just like that. So I did. I was so afraid he was playing with me—every minute I was looking over my shoulder. I didn't dare travel on the road in case he sent someone after me. In the end I had to, though, because it was where you were."

"You dreamed me."

"Yes. Every night." Her eyes held his. Her grip tightened. She leaned toward him. "Gyalo. He never touched me. Not that way."

"He never—" Gyalo could not complete the sentence.

"No. He never did."

"I imagined—I feared—"

"I know. I know."

He lifted her hand, put it to his cheek. There were no words.

A loud crackling of leaves announced Diasarta's return. He dumped an armful of brush on the ground, then swept a spot clear of twigs and leaf litter and began to build a fire. Chokyi squirmed in her mother's arms, whimpering.

"She's hungry," Axane said. "There's not been much to give her these past few days, and my milk dried up a month ago."

"There'll be food soon." Diasarta rummaged in the supply bag and pulled out a string of dried apple slices. "Here's something she can chew on in the meantime."

"Thanks." Axane favored him with one of her rare smiles. "Come, little bird. This is very good." She held the apple slice to her lips and mimed eating. "See?"

She put the fruit into Chokyi's hands. Chokyi examined it, suspicious, then put it experimentally into her mouth.

"Tell me what happened to you," Axane said to Gyalo. "I've dreamed some of it, and I heard the things you said into my sleep. But there are gaps."

So he did, beginning with his discovery of her absence and his realization of who had taken her. Diasarta kindled the fire, set a ring of stones around it, and began to prepare a meal.

"I shouted at you that night to stay away," she said, when he came to their arrival at the caverns. "Even though I knew you couldn't hear me. I knew you could never get to me. I was so afraid he'd catch you and kill you. And he did catch you, Gyalo. It was a stupid thing you did, going in there after me."

"What else could I have done? Besides, he didn't kill me. It pleased him more to think of me watching and suffering as he laid waste to Arsace. To make me think *you* were dead. For a little while, anyway."

He continued, describing his rescue of Sundit, their journey to Ninyâser, Santaxma's fatal misjudgment.

"I should never have left you," he said. "I should never have gone with her."

"You couldn't know what would happen." She watched Chokyi, now gnawing enthusiastically on her apple slice, her mouth and chin sticky with juice. In the sky some light remained, but among the trees it was night; the two of them shone against the darkness, the ruddy illumination of Diasarta's fire moving on their faces. "You couldn't have done anything if you'd stayed."

"Maybe."

"Tell me how you found him, Dasa." She looked at Diasarta, stirring the iron pot in which their meal was cooking. "After he was wounded. When I dreamed him that night you were already with him."

"It was an accident, really," the ex-soldier said. "He told me he'd come back, and I was watching for him, but I never saw him. And then I was standing by my fire, not thinking of him at all, and he ran right by me. I called, but he didn't hear."

"Actually, I think I did," Gyalo said, "though I didn't realize it at the time."

"He went up the hill on the other side of the road. I went after him. Just before I got to the top there was a sound like . . . thunder, except I knew it wasn't, and the ground shook—"

"The hills." Axane nodded. "I heard it, too."

"It threw me down. Stunned me a bit. I got up to go on, and nearly ran smack into a company of Exile cavalry, waiting at the top of the hill."

"Which I'd already encountered," said Gyalo. "They took me for a pilgrim, and put an arrow in me when I turned to run."

"I ducked behind some bushes and waited for them to move on, or ride down on the pilgrims, or whatever they were going to do. After a while the captain said it had been too long, that the signal should have come by now, that something had gone wrong. They turned and rode north. I got up and began to search. He'd lost a good amount of blood by the time I found him. I patched him up as best I could and made a camp for us up in the hills."

"But the wound got infected," Axane said.

Diasarta nodded. "I didn't have anything to treat him with. So I set out to find help."

"Carrying me over his shoulder. For more than a day."

"I found a crofter's camp. They let us stay and sent for a healer. She did what she could, which wasn't much by that time. I won't pretend I wasn't worried. But I said to myself that Ârata hadn't put me in his path like that just to watch him die. Sure enough, the fever broke. We were at that camp near three weeks. Should've been longer, except as soon as he could walk more than ten steps without falling down he wouldn't hear of staying."

"You're exaggerating, Dasa."

"Not by much." Diasarta took the lid off the cook pot. "Supper's ready."

He dished out bowls of rice and meat. Axane fed Chokyi first, chewing the rice to soften it; only when Chokyi turned her face away from the spoon did she satisfy her own hunger, digging ravenously into the food. Diasarta finished his meal and began to rig a lean-to from the canvas of his and Gyalo's tent. Under it, he laid out blankets.

"Come, little bird," Axane said softly to a dozing Chokyi.

"Wait," Gyalo said. "Let me."

She helped him settle Chokyi against his good shoulder. She whimpered, but then turned her face into his neck, too sleepy to protest for long. She was limp and warm, heavier than his arms remembered, but the rest of her was deeply familiar: the way her head fit the hollow of his shoulder, the softness of her hair under his cheek. He closed his eyes and breathed her in, fancying he could smell her own sweet scent beneath the dirt and soiled linen. He felt a fullness in his chest—a part of him that had been empty for much too long.

He carried her into the shelter of the lean-to and laid her on the blankets, straining a little with his weakened arm. He slipped off his coat and spread it over her, then bent and pressed his lips against her little forehead. Axane knelt by him; her light swallowed his, her shoulder brushed his own. He felt the heat, the tension, which had been building in him since they stopped among the trees, and, suddenly, was unbearable. He reached across the child and caught her hand.

"Come away with me," he whispered.

The heat was in her, too; he saw it in her flushed cheeks, felt it in the quiver of her pulse. "We can't just leave her."

"Diasarta will stay."

The ex-soldier was gathering his bedding. "Thought I'd go off on my own," he said, not looking up. "Give the two of you some privacy."

"No. We'll go. Will you stay with Chokyi?"

"You sure, Brother?"

"Yes."

He took a blanket, and seized Axane's hand again, and drew her away into the blackness among the trees. He heard the quickness of her breath; she had hesitated at first, but when he stopped and threw the blanket on the ground she flung herself at him, and they went down in a clash of knees and elbows, lips and teeth, wrenching at each other's clothing. It was over quickly; they rested, tangled together, then began again, slowly, gripping one another as though drowning. It seemed to Gyalo that he had held her thus only a day ago, yet in the tears on her cheeks, the ache in his throat, the whole void and terror of their separation was contained. She clenched her teeth to keep from crying out; he muffled his own cry in the heavy masses of her hair, which smelled of smoke and moss, and fell across his face like a fathom of black water.

They lay entwined in the leaves. He had drawn her coat over them, and the blanket. The dark trunks of the trees rose all around, stars netted in their bare branches; between the clouds a half-moon peered down, cool and curious. The night was huge and winter-still. Sleep pulled at him, but he did not want to close his eyes, for he was submerged in her light, her beautiful light, and it was a joy almost as great as the feel of her to see the world through that shifting green-blue scrim. Time seemed to have stopped. Perhaps, when it moved on, it would leave the two of them behind, so they might lie forever just like this.

She stirred and pushed herself up against his chest. "I want to take a look at your shoulder."

"It's too dark for you to see anything."

"I can feel it."

She unfastened the breast of his tunic. Her hair trailed across his face again as she leaned over him, reaching around to trace the puckered scar on his back. Gently, she palpated it.

"That hurts."

"Still?"

"Yes, when you probe at it like that."

"And other times?"

"It aches. Sometimes more, sometimes less. The arm is weak. I still can't raise it higher than my shoulder."

"You need to try, even if it hurts. If you don't work the muscles, they'll stiffen permanently, and you'll never get back the full use of it. You should exercise it at least twice a day."

"Yes, mistress healer."

She lay down again. "I dreamed you the night it happened."

"You told me. It must have been terrible."

"I don't ever want to go through that again, Gyalo. You can't imagine what it was like. I didn't want to sleep, because I feared what my Dreams would tell me. But how could I stay awake and not know? Every night I lay down in terror. So many times I woke up crying . . . I always told him I was dreaming of Refuge. He believed me, because he dreamed of it, too." She was silent a moment. "He had terrible dreams. Worse than mine. I'd hear him, thrashing around and gasping. Sometimes he wept. Sometimes . . . he called out names. Dead names, names no one in the world but me would remember."

"You pitied him," Gyalo said, with unwelcome recognition.

"No!" She pushed at his chest, lifting herself away from him. "No, I never did! I hated him. Gyalo, you know I hated him!"

"Yes, love," he said, soothing. He reached to draw her back against him. She resisted.

"Aren't you going to ask what happened between him and me?"

He let his hands fall. "You've already told me everything I need to know."

"No, Gyalo, I haven't. I told you he never touched me. And it's true. But he wanted to, I could see he wanted to, and I began to think perhaps . . . if I could go to *him* . . . it might make a chance for Chokyi and me. I did everything I could to make him think I was . . . willing. I worked to win his trust.

I was obedient. I told him horrible stories about you—oh, Gyalo, I said the most awful things to make him believe I didn't love you! I thought it would be hard. But it wasn't, it wasn't, because I'm a liar, all my life I've been a liar, you are the only person in the world I never lied to. And it worked. The moment came—it came, Gyalo, but when he reached out for me I couldn't, I couldn't do it—"

"Axane!" With an effort Gyalo lowered his voice. "You don't owe me any explanations. Whatever you did—whatever you had to do—you don't need to tell me."

"But I have to know—" Her voice caught. "That you forgive me. How can you forgive me if you don't know what I've done?"

He reached up and took her face between his hands. He had thought it was for her sake that he had sworn never to make her speak of her experience. He understood suddenly that it had been for his. He had imagined what she had just told him, along with a thousand other ugly acts and possibilities. But he had not wanted any of them to be fixed into reality.

"There is nothing to forgive, Axane. Do you hear me? Nothing."

She looked at him, her face drawn with a strange tension. At last, sighing, she lay down against him again. He pulled the blanket up to cover her, tightened his arms around her. He felt her muscles loosen. The stillness of the night reasserted itself. But the languorous serenity, the sense of having passed into some blissful otherplace, had dwindled. He sensed the cold imminence of the ordinary world, the world of jealousy and duty—as close as Diasarta's campfire, which if he turned his head he could just see, glimmering faintly between the trees.

"Well," she said, muffled in his shoulder, "it's over now. We can go home."

It was as if a song had suddenly stopped. The world reached out, closed its fist. Gyalo lay silent.

She raised her head. "Gyalo?"

Still he did not speak. She pushed herself up again. "No," she said, and there was heartbreak in her voice, heartbreak and knowledge. "Oh no."

He sat up also. He was beyond the margin of her colors; he felt the change as harshly as the coldness of his body where she had been against him.

"I have to, Axane. I have to go on."

"Why?" She gathered her dress up from around her waist, covering her breasts. "I'm free. Chokyi's free. What else is there to go on for?"

"You know the answer. I mean to kill him, if I can."

"*What?* Gyalo, you've never even fought another man! You've never used a weapon! And even if you had, you aren't strong enough. No one is strong enough!"

"I've gained knowledge of myself these past months, Axane. There's more power in me than I knew."

"Not like his. When he came back from the Evening City he *walked upon the air!* On the air, do you hear me? I heard the noise of it, I looked out my window, and I saw it. If you go to Baushpar, you'll die. You'll die." She sobbed wildly. "I told you, he was in despair that night. I think he's stopping. I think he's giving up."

"After all he has done? No."

"Is this what you think Ârata wants you to do?" she cried. "Do you think the god wants you to put your life at risk? Ârata doesn't need you! He's a god, he can do his own work!"

"Axane—"

"Or is it for me? For my sake, because he stole me, because of what he did to me before, in the Burning Land? But I don't want you to avenge me! I don't care about that! All I want is for you to come home with me and Chokyi!"

"Axane—I never dreamed he'd let you go—"

"But he did! Why can't you just come home with me and let the rest of it be?"

"Because it isn't over!" he shouted. "Because he's still there! *Because there's only me!*"

She was silent, frozen. She understood. He could see it in her face—the old battle between what she knew about him and what she wanted of him. *No more silence*, he thought. *No more elision.*

"Back in Ninyâser," he said, "before all this began, I told you I hadn't yet decided to go in search of him. It was true. When he kidnapped you and Chokyi, I was still trying to make up my mind. I thought that maybe Ârata was punishing me for my indecision by letting you be taken. Or maybe for the other choice I couldn't make." He drew a breath. "The choice of Messengerhood."

Across from him Axane sat like an image of herself, still clutching the bodice of her dress.

"There was no question I had to go after you. It was a relief, in a way, to have the decision made for me. I told myself all that mattered was getting the two of you back. This was *my* will, and I would follow it, and if the god's will were anywhere in it, I'd discover it, or not, when I came to it. But really that was just cowardice, an excuse to turn away from what I knew had to be done—and perhaps it was just as well, for when I got to the caverns I didn't yet know myself, my power I mean, and if I'd gone in there and tried to challenge him, I certainly would have perished. Then I was drawn away from you, and when I came back I was struck by the Exiles' arrow. When I woke up afterward, I couldn't understand at first that I was actually alive. I'd been absolutely sure that I was dying . . ."

The chill of it swept up in him; he shuddered.

"And there was Dasa, who'd given me back my life, just as he gave me back my freedom when the Brethren imprisoned me in Faal. When he came for me then I saw the god's hand in it, Ârata reaching out to me, giving me a second chance . . . this time it seemed the same. A third chance. Dasa told me what had happened, that the King had been killed and Râvar had moved on. And I saw that just as much as I had to follow you and Chokyi, I had to follow Râvar and his blasphemy. Just as much as I had to save the two of you, I had to try to put an end to him. Not for the Brethren's sake. Not for Baushpar. Not because I want to punish him for what he did to you, though I do, I do! *Because it needs to be done.* Because there may be no one else to do it. I never separated it from you and Chokyi, because I never imagined any possibility you wouldn't be with him when I reached Baushpar. But now you are free. And still I must go on. I must, Axane."

"Do you think," she said out of her frozen face, "that you'll become the Messenger in Baushpar?"

He felt the catch, the involuntary stutter of his breath. Râvar no longer frightened him. But this—this still did. "I don't know. Maybe that's Ârata's will for me. Maybe it isn't. All I know is that I'm tired of asking questions. I'm tired of running away. I'm tired of thinking about it, and I'm tired of trying not to think about it. I'm tired of being afraid. Wherever Ârata's hand lies in these events, I need to make a choice. Whether or not Ârata demands resolution of me, *I demand it of myself.*"

"You are selfish," Axane said. "You and your choices. You and your *duty.*"

Anger flashed in him again. "This is what I am. You've always known it. I'm not capable of changing, any more than you're capable of belief."

"It's true. I don't believe. And you—you set your shaping free. You married me. But you might as well never have left the church."

"No, Axane. There are things I question still, but this I know: The church's time is past. I have most truly left it."

"Still you follow Ârata."

"Ârata and his Way are not the same."

Tears stood in her eyes. "He'll kill you."

"I will do all I can not to let that happen."

"If I asked you not to go." She drew a shuddering breath. "For my sake, for Chokyi's sake. Would you heed me?"

"Axane. Don't force me to that."

Silence. The night flowed between them like a river. He saw her calling up her self-control, drawing down within herself, hiding her true feeling. It was as if she were already leaving him. His heart contracted with the pain of it.

"I understand," she said—quiet, glacially calm.

"Do you?" he answered wearily.

"Oh, I do. Better than you know. You're like *him*. Both of you destroying yourselves for principle—him in hatred, you in duty, but really, what's the difference?" Her voice caught on a sob, like ice cracking. "I won't go with you. I won't wait outside Baushpar while you kill yourself."

"I don't want you to go with me. I want you to be safe. I want you to go home."

"Then there's nothing more to say." She thrust her arms roughly into the sleeves of her dress, and in a rustle of leaves got to her feet. "I'll get Chokyi. We'll be on our way."

"What? Now?"

"Why not? There's no reason to stay."

"Axane, it's the middle of the night. It's cold. There are terrible people on the roads. I can't bear—" He had to stop. "Stay till morning at least. For Chokyi's sake."

She turned her face away. "Very well. Till morning."

She set off toward the faint glow of the campfire. He fastened his disordered clothes, gathered the blanket and the sash and coat she had forgotten, and ran to catch her up. She went straight to the lean-to and lay down by Chokyi. When Gyalo draped the blanket over them both, she did not stir or open her eyes.

He crossed to the fire, where Diasarta sat over the flames. "Get some sleep," he said. "I'll keep watch."

Diasarta looked up at him. "Everything all right, Brother?"

"No." He sat down. "They're leaving. In the morning."

"You and I are going on, then."

"Yes."

Diasarta nodded, unsurprised. He set his hand on Gyalo's shoulder and left it there a moment, then pulled away and got to his feet. "Wake me up at moonset. You need rest, too."

But Gyalo sat by the fire the whole night long, and did not sleep at all.

*　　*　　*

He walked Axane to the road. Overcast dawn was turning to sullen day. Frost crisped the grass and leaves underfoot. She carried the blanket and the bundle of her clothing and the bag of food Diasarta had packed for himself and Gyalo the day before. The two of them would survive by shaping. Gyalo held Chokyi, who, if she did not yet trust him, at least allowed the contact. He thought, with pain, that she would forget him again.

Perhaps forever.

They did not speak as they walked, did not speak as they reached the road, did not speak as he helped Axane fashion the blanket into a carrier for Chokyi. Chokyi gazed at him with round green eyes; when he bent to kiss her, she shrank away. Still silent, he handed Axane the bag and bundle. She slung the bag over her shoulder; the bundle she held to her breast like a shield.

"Here." He pulled a small cloth-wrapped packet out of the pocket of his coat. "This is for your journey."

"What is it?"

"Gold and silver. Some gems." He had shaped them the night before, while the others slept. "I made them small, you shouldn't have trouble trading them."

"Thank you." She took the packet.

"Get well off the road at night. There are bad people about."

"I know."

"I left a key with Ciri. To the house. Some parts of Ninyâser are damaged, but mostly north of the canal. Our area was hardly touched. I checked the house while I was there."

"I don't know," she said, "if that's where I'm going."

It went through him like a knife. "Don't. Don't say that."

"It'll always be this way with you, Gyalo. I knew that when I came to you . . . but I didn't know how hard it would be. I don't know . . . I don't know if I'm strong enough."

"You are." He reached out, put his hands on hers. "You are."

She only stood, her eyes cast down, her face perfectly still. It was an expression he knew well—the mask of composure behind which lived the parts of herself she did not want others to see. The mask she had made for herself in Refuge to hide the secret of her dreaming, with its burden of knowledge and fear and pain. The mask he had thought, when they were first reunited, she would cast aside forever. He thought his heart would break.

"I love you," he said. "I love you both so much."

For an instant her perfect control splintered; she sobbed once, twice. He stepped toward her, but she backed away, out of reach.

"I dreamed last night." Her voice was husky. "Of him. Outside his house a crowd of pilgrims was singing and praying. Inside, he lay in an empty room, curled up on the floor. He's sick. I saw the fever sweat. He was . . . he was whispering the names of the dead."

"Axane, I will keep safe. I will come back. Please, be there when I come back."

Tears spilled down her cheeks. "I'll try not to dream of you."

He watched them go. Except for the hours he had believed her and Chokyi dead, it was the worst pain of his life. He hoped she would pause and look back, but she did not.

Diasarta came up beside him, carrying their packs. "Ready, Brother?"

"She's alone, Dasa." In the distance, Axane and Chokyi were a flash of emerald. "The road is dangerous. What kind of man am I, to let her go like this?"

Diasarta placed a hand on Gyalo's arm. "You do what you have to do, Brother. I understand."

I understand. Axane, too, had said those words. What she understood was not what Diasarta did, yet both believed they knew the truth. And he—what he knew, or thought he knew, was something different still. The world seemed unreal, slippery, a tissue of conjecture. There was nothing solid to hold on to.

The emerald flash was a pinpoint. Gyalo stood, straining after it, till sparks of green whirled across his vision, and he had to close his eyes against a sudden vertigo. When he opened them, the green was gone.

25

Gyalo

That afternoon Gyalo and Diasarta met a party traveling in the opposite direction, the first they had seen in many days apart from Axane and Chokyi: an elderly man, three younger men who looked to be his sons, a woman who was obviously the wife of one of them, and a small girl. They were ragged and grimy, and had a look of shock about them, like survivors of some catastrophe.

"Pilgrims?" the husband called, as Gyalo and Diasarta drew near.

"Yes," Gyalo said, holding up his hand to show his mark. "Heading for the holy city, praise Ârata."

"You might want to change your mind," said the husband. He stopped; the others clustered round him. One side of his face was bruised and swollen, and his arm was tied to his chest. "It's bad there."

"Bad how?"

"The Messenger's in seclusion. Hasn't come out since the night he went to the Brethren. It's said he's talking to the god, taking counsel for the time of Interim. But some are saying he's turned from us—"

"For our sins," the wife said.

"Not *our* sins, Imene. It's not folk like us who've brought darkness on this pilgrimage. Others say he's sick and is like to die. No one knows what's true, or what's to come next. He's stopped providing for us—we had to take what we needed from the city. Got this"—he indicated his face—"yesterday, trying to hold on to a sack of rice."

"It was always going to come to this." The old man leaned heavily on the arm of his youngest son. "I said it. I said it weeks ago."

"Hush, Father," the young man said.

"Anyway, we're going back, if anything's left to go back to. You might think about doing the same."

"Thanks for the warning," Gyalo said. "But we'll go on."

The husband shrugged. "Luck to you, then. Great is Ârata. Great is his wakened Way."

"Go in light."

"He really is sick, then," Diasarta said when they were out of earshot.

"He wanted to destroy Baushpar. Perhaps he means to let his followers do it."

They made an early camp. Gyalo lay staring at the dark, his hand closed around Axane's bracelet, which he had forgotten to give back during their brief reunion. A hundred times that day he had started to turn around. A hundred times he had forced himself to continue. He accepted that his course was set. Still, the questions struggled in him—was he a fool to let them go? Was anything worth their loss?

Did she dream him? For the first time he was not sure, and not only because of her parting words. He was no longer the only soul to whom she was bound, from whom she was separated.

Over the next days they overtook increasing crowds of pilgrim stragglers trudging toward the holy city. They also met growing numbers of people headed for Ninyâser. Many hurried by, their eyes averted. Others called warnings: *There's rioting in Baushpar. Looting and burning. Turn back.* Once the companions passed a long train of Âratist monks led by a group of Shapers in golden stoles, their monastery valuables piled in carts. Apart from these travelers, the countryside was empty—a desertion no different from elsewhere, but somehow, so near Baushpar, more unnerving.

Midway through the morning of the fourth day, they crested a hill and saw Baushpar before them, its red-and-gold magnificence dulled by cloud and drizzle. Even so, the domes of the First Temple shone, drawing to themselves what light there was. Gyalo paused, taken by a memory of the first time he had ever glimpsed the holy city, riding with the returning Brethren after the Caryaxists' fall. The domes had shone that day, too, though their gilding was mostly worn away, stripped by eighty years of neglect. The sight of it had seized him by the throat—holy Baushpar, whose representation he had seen so many times in books and paintings, real at last. It had seemed both larger and smaller, meaner and more magnificent, everything he had expected and nothing like at all. It was the same now, though for a different reason: That first time, he had looked upon a city he had never imagined he would know. This time, he looked upon a city to which he had never thought to return.

The road led between the church's vast manita fields, bare and dark with winter, the gauze that shaded the plants' leathery leaves neatly rolled and tied to the posts that supported it during the growing season. As the companions neared the suburbs, the breeze brought a whiff of burning. Some of what had appeared from a distance to be mist was smoke; Gyalo read the heat patterns, breathing up from several locations outside the city walls.

The packed ash and gravel of the Baushpar road gave way to cobblestones, and the fields to the walled estates of the wealthy. Every gate hung open or had been broken down. Here and there lay the litter of looting—torn clothing, soiled cushions, shards and splinters of porcelain, glass, wood. There was no sign of the vandals: the broad avenue was deserted.

"Hear that, Brother?" Diasarta said.

The sound came and went amid the pattering of the rain: a murmur as of many voices, punctuated by snatches of song. They advanced along the avenue. Around a curve, the light of life came into view—a crowd, gathered before one of the estates, the ragtag mass of it occupying nearly the entire width of the street. Some knelt in attitudes of reverence, heads bowed, wrists crossed before their faces. Some told Communion beads. Some gripped hands or linked arms, swaying to chanted prayers and hymns. All seemed oblivious to the cold and rain.

"This is where he is," Gyalo said.

"What do you want to do, Brother?"

Gyalo stared at the ornamented roof peaks of the mansion, just visible above the wall. Inside, his enemy lay: the rapist of his wife, the thief of his family, the scourge of his adopted land. He had come here to confront this man. Yet with the songs and praises of the pilgrims in his ears, he felt a strange repulsion. Not fear; he was not conscious of fear. Not doubt: It had been a long time since he had suffered any doubt. Something in him simply leaned in a different direction. It was not yet time to enter that house.

"Let's go on."

Diasarta nodded. In ordinary matters—the eating of food, the making of camp—he did not hesitate to impose his will. But true to the pledge he had made when he and Gyalo parted on the steppe, he no longer protested Gyalo's larger decisions.

They skirted the crowd, climbing toward the walls of the old city. The avenue narrowed as it rose; the great villas with their lush parks became tidy tile-roofed cottages with gardens at the back. Many had been boarded up. Others were simply locked and shuttered. Some had been broken into, some not; there seemed no logic in what stood open and looted and what was still intact. One of the fires raged nearby—the flames were not visible, but smoke drifted above the roofs, and the air writhed with heat.

Ahead gaped the great slot of the Summer Gate, and beyond it the red-granite walls of the Avenue of Summer. This enclosed avenue and three others like it were the only means of access to the walled square at Baushpar's heart, where rose the First Temple of Ârata. They were named for the cardinal points at which they originated: Summer, Winter, Dawn, and Sunset. Gyalo had walked the Avenue of Summer daily during his brief residence in Baushpar; that familiarity was still with him, but transformed by the freedom of his Shaper senses, which showed him not just the surfaces of things, but their substance.

Some distance ahead, firelight and lifelight flashed—a bonfire, kindled in the middle of the street. It raged between two of the archways that opened onto the side streets, undiscouraged by the drizzle, smoke pouring off it in fat black coils. The air around it was liquid with heat. People staggered out of the side streets, laden with furniture, fabric, bedding, shutters, anything flammable. A mob of spectators cheered as each new object was heaved onto the pyre.

"Hey, pilgrims!" a woman yelled over the tearing sound of the flames. "Give something to the fire!"

Gyalo held up his hands in a gesture of apology. "Sorry, sister. We've nothing to spare."

"That's easy to fix," a male pilgrim called. "Baushpar's got plenty to spare!"

"Join in, brothers!" cried another. "Make an offering!"

"Not scared of fire, are you, boys?" The woman stepped toward them. "There'll be worse than this when Ârata comes to make the world anew!"

The man beside her laughed madly, grabbed her round the waist. "We're just giving him a bit of help!"

With a roar the center of the bonfire collapsed, belching up a terrific eruption of flames, hurling a veil of sparks higher than the walls. Gyalo saw the heat as it blasted toward him through the substance of the air. It snatched the breath out of his throat; almost, he expected the pilgrims to combust. But they seemed to care as little for roasting as those gathered outside Râvar's house had for freezing. They danced and cheered, shouting the god's name, yelling Râvar's title.

Gyalo and Diasarta retreated along the Avenue, ducking down the first side street they came upon. Only when they were certain no one was following did they pause for breath.

"Bloody ashes," Diasarta said.

"We're on the eastern side of the Avenue of Summer now." Gyalo called on his knowledge of Baushpar—which was slim, for he had lived a bare six months in the holy city before his mission to the Burning Land. "We can cross over to the Avenue of Dawn, and get to Temple Square that way. Assuming it isn't blocked."

"Where are you heading, Brother?"

"I'm not really sure."

They made their way through the dark, rain-shining streets. Gyalo's patternsense kept them moving east amid the maze of branching ways. That quarter of the city was given over mainly to commercial districts, and signs of fire and looting were everywhere. Pilgrim graffiti was scrawled on walls and doors, on paving stones and steps, in charcoal, in chalk, in red and yellow paint: Ârata's sun-symbol, the several sigils of the Waking Road. As in a forest, they heard more signs of life than they saw—cries, shouts, snatches of song, the noise of things breaking—though several times they were forced to jump into doorways or dive down alleys to avoid bands of pilgrims. Once, turning along an east-running avenue lined with the shops of leatherworkers and basketmakers, they were met by a phalanx of staff-carrying men, materializing abruptly from the shadows.

"No entry here," the man in the lead told them, calm but firm.

"We mean you no harm," Gyalo said. "We're just trying to get through to the Avenue of Dawn."

"Well, you'll not use this street. Now move along." The man gestured with his staff. "Try and come back this way, and you'll go nowhere again in this life."

"No problem, friend. We're going."

The Avenue of Dawn was clear all down its length. As they neared its end, the sound of voices rose, harsh and raucous, like the clamor of a marketplace. Passing into Temple Square, they found themselves in a bizarre amalgam of campground and fairground. Makeshift shelters had been constructed along the Square's perimeter, made from scavenged materials, many of them open at the front, their inhabitants going about their lives without a care as to who might be watching. Craftsmen sold wares from portable booths. Vendors in umbrellaed carts hawked nuts and sweets and religious trinkets—at least some of Baushpar's inhabitants, evidently, had found a way to turn invasion into profit. Litter and the discarded spoils of looting lay underfoot, and everywhere was fire: for cooking, for warmth, for trash, ceremonial fires attended by swaying prayer groups, celebratory fires circled by ecstatic dancers, communal fires for the roasting of pigs and goats and something larger that might have been a horse. The high walls and the damp and windless weather trapped the smoke of all these blazes, drowning the Square in a throat-scraping, eye-stinging fog whose acrid stench dominated, but did not entirely conquer, the odors of close-gathered humanity. Above it all, the massive bulk of the First Temple thrust up like a mountain, its domes shining even through the hazy air—the antithesis of the chaos that surrounded it, a perfect harmony of stillness.

"Burn me," Diasarta exclaimed, as they neared a large pavilion with lanterns strung along the outside and a man in gaudy clothing standing by its entrance, "it's a brothel. Can you believe it?"

It seemed to make no less sense than the rest of this seething spectacle.

They skirted the fires and the rubbish, threaded their way between the knots of people. Mostly they were ignored; where they were challenged or urged to join the celebration, their pilgrim scars guaranteed both passage and escape. At last they reached the wall that bounded the western length of the Square—exactly like the other three, built of the same red-granite blocks, topped by the same golden tile. But here, instead of a tall, arched opening onto a ceremonial avenue, there was only a narrow vermilion-painted door. Beyond the deceptively modest entrance, the palace of the Brethren stretched more than five miles square.

The vermilion door was never locked, for all who followed Ârata must have access to the home of those who led his Way; but it was always closed, so those who entered might recognize that they were passing into a separate domain. Now it stood half-ajar. In the courtyard beyond, debris was scattered across the ironstone paving.

"They got in here, too," Diasarta said.

"*He* went in here. They followed."

They crossed the court and entered the stately pavilion that gave access to the Evening City proper. To the left lay the offices and workrooms and conference chambers and libraries and warehouses and artisans' studios of the administrative wing; to the right opened the guest accommodations and the Tapati barracks and the personal quarters of the Brethren. Normally a cadre of Tapati stood guard, but now there was not a soul to be seen. The great red portals of the two entrances, which like the smaller door were normally kept closed, had been thrown back. Each was marked with one of Râvar's sigils: the hexagon with its squiggle of flame.

Gyalo chose the right-hand portal. He had spent most of his time in Baushpar in the administrative wing, and had not often visited the other side;

his patternsense, which oriented itself to naturally occurring patterns and required knowledge of a larger context to read man-made ones, was of little use, and he was quickly lost amid the maze of hallways and galleries and open courts. He let light be his guide: dark corridors he avoided, illuminated ones he ventured down. The signs of looting were here, too—graffiti, breakage, and once a splatter of something that looked like brown paint, but which Gyalo's Shaper senses identified as blood. They saw birds in the courtyards and rats in the halls and once a monkey, someone's pet, which screeched and fled at the sight of them; but no sign of any human inhabitants.

"D'you think the Brethren have fled?" Diasarta asked, stepping over a litter of smashed porcelain.

"They were here when Râvar came. The Evening City is huge. We might wander for the rest of the day and never find them."

In a long hall with alabaster-screened windows all down one side, Gyalo paused in recognition. "This is—this was Utamnos's residence."

"Your old master."

"Yes."

Utamnos's door had been left locked, but someone had kicked it open, splintering the jamb. The rooms within were stripped, though the absence of debris suggested that the damage had not been done by looters. The companions moved from chamber to chamber, until they came to one with a floor of polished spicewood and coral-colored walls muraled with a design of ibises and reeds. Gyalo halted in the doorway.

"This is where Utamnos and I ate supper, the night before I left for the Burning Land."

"Oh yes?" Diasarta came to stand beside him.

"It was a feast. Oysters from the coast. Apricots out of season. He wanted to make a memory for me, something beautiful that I could carry with me." His imagination re-created the room as it had been that night: the low table at which he and Utamnos had sat, the paper lanterns shining like little moons, an ash-fired vase filled with poppies. "He gave me a farewell gift, a book of poetry."

"I remember that book. You used to read in it every night."

"It went across the desert with me and back. They took it away when they imprisoned me . . . I've often wondered what happened to it."

Sadness tightened his throat. How innocent he had been that night, how untested. How strange it was to stand here, remembering that. Like turning a corner, and coming face-to-face with himself.

He turned to Diasarta. "There's one more place I want to go."

They departed the Evening City without difficulty, for they had left a trail that Gyalo's patternsense could read: the traces of their footsteps in the dirt and dust, the lingering disturbance of the air. They emerged into the clamor of Temple Square and made their way toward the Temple. Around its vast circumference lay an area of calm—the only part of the Square that was free of pilgrims and their litter, as if there were some line of demarcation that chaos dared not cross. It was as if the Temple existed on a slightly different plane, a piece of one world somehow set down within another.

It did not seem surprising that the lamps burned as always in the gallery, or that the floor was clean, or that the religious paintings on the inner wall, rich with gems and precious inlay, had not suffered any damage. It did not seem strange that the Temple's core, shadowy and incense-scented, was also untouched, or that the torches and the candle trays around the colossal cast-bronze image of Ârata Eon Sleeper were all alight. A pair of monks worked at Ârata's feet, replacing candles that had burned down, rekindling flames that had gone out. There was even a cluster of worshipers on meditation mats, their lifelights starry in the dimness. It was in truth like stepping into a separate world. There seemed little connection between what was here and what lay outside.

Gyalo and Diasarta approached across the polished expanses of the floor. The god was portrayed as a beautiful naked youth at rest upon his back, the surface under him scored with ripples to represent the ocean of his Blood. Both it and his long hair were gilded. His many wounds wept citrine and topaz and amber.

"Great is Ârata." Gyalo greeted the monks, his voice small in the stone-vaulted silence. "Great is his Way."

"Go in light," one replied. The other watched, wary.

"I'm surprised that anyone is still here."

"The Temple must be cared for," the first monk said.

"You don't fear to stay, with all that's going on outside?"

"Those who have come will depart." Within his soft gray lifelight, the monk's face was tranquil. "The Temple will remain."

They turned back to their labor. Gyalo watched as they moved among the trays, performing their ancient duty. There was courage in their actions—but a futile, pointless courage. Ârata was not here—not in the great shadowed spaces, not in the beautiful image. It was like a cast-off garment, this place—a rich garment, long in the making and in the wearing, but threadbare now, outgrown.

Was that why he had felt such a strong compulsion to come here? To complete the journey of memory, to acknowledge the distance between the man he had become and that innocent self he had encountered in Utamnos's deserted rooms?

Diasarta had paced the length of the image and was gazing up at Ârata's face. Off to the side, the worshipers were getting to their feet. Gyalo had glanced at them as he crossed the core, seeing only a gathering of bodies, a scattering of lifelights. But, as they moved, he looked more closely, aware of something odd . . . too late, he recognized what it was. One man, standing in advance of the others, owned a light that was almost no light at all, the faintest blue flickering around his body.

Ardashir.

Ardashir had seen him. For a moment they stood, eye to eye across the distance, as immobile as sleeping Ârata himself. Then Ardashir said something over his shoulder, and strode forward, leaving his staff-carrying attendants behind.

"You," he said as he reached Gyalo, his voice gravel-harsh. "What are you doing here?"

Gyalo cursed his inattention. But what were the odds, among so many people, that he would meet Ardashir and his men? "That's my business."

"You were told never to approach the Awakened City again."

"This is not the Awakened City. It is Baushpar."

Diasarta, realizing what was occurring, came up behind Gyalo's shoulder. Ardashir's hot gaze jumped to him, then back to Gyalo.

"Have you come to harm him?"

"How could a mortal man harm the Next Messenger?"

"Don't defile his name with your blaspheming tongue."

Gyalo said nothing. Ardashir wore the clothing of a noble: a sumptuous embroidered coat, ornate gold-tooled boots. His chin and cheeks were clean-shaven, his cropped hair faultlessly groomed, and he smelled of scented oil. But he still wore those thick, stained bandages; and above his rich attire his face was shockingly weary, his small eyes bloodshot and rimmed with red.

"Come with me," he said abruptly.

"You have no authority over me."

"You don't understand." Ardashir's expression did not change, but under it some deep emotion seemed to heave, like fire under a rock. "He is sick. Not in his body—in his soul. There is something . . . he will not tell me what. He speaks of you. He speaks your name."

"*My* name?" Gyalo said, disbelieving.

"I don't know how to help him. I've prayed for guidance. Now here you are. It cannot be chance. You must come."

Gyalo felt as if the world had suddenly drawn in its breath. He thought of his hesitation before Râvar's house. He thought of his progress through the ravaged city. He thought of the many steps, the many choices that had brought him precisely here, precisely at this moment.

"I will come."

"Say nothing before my men," Ardashir rasped. "I've told no one of his . . . disability. They believe he is only in seclusion."

"I'll keep your secret."

Ardashir's burning gaze acknowledged no gratitude. He turned and raised a bandaged hand to signal the waiting Twentymen.

"Brother," Diasarta said softly. "Are you sure?"

"This is why we came here, Dasa. This is how it's meant to be."

Diasarta, too, searched Gyalo's face. Then he nodded. When Gyalo stepped forward, he followed without a word.

They returned to Râvar's residence by much the same route Gyalo and Diasarta had taken to Temple Square. The Twentymen walked ahead, their staves held at the ready; for the most part those they encountered yielded easily, but now and then they met pilgrims who questioned or challenged, or to the Twentymen's cry of "Make way for the First Disciple!" responded with jeers.

There were no taunts from the faithful gathered before the gates. They pressed aside, making the sign of Ârata and invoking blessings. Some called questions—when would the Next Messenger return to them? When would he take his place in the palace of the Brethren?—to all of which Ardashir gave the same response: "Be patient, citizens. Be patient."

In the villa's large inner courtyard, Ardashir dismissed his men. "You must leave what you carry," he told Gyalo. "I must also have any weapons you bear. Your companion may wait here."

Diasarta's face was set. "Where he goes I go."

"You have no place above."

"His place is with me," Gyalo said.

Ardashir's eyes flared. But whatever necessity he followed drove him more strongly than his pride. He nodded.

Gyalo and Diasarta unshouldered their packs, and Diasarta pulled the long knife from his sash and the short one from his boot and laid both on the floor. Ardashir searched them, quickly and efficiently. Then he led the way up the stairs.

The clarity, the sense of *rightness* that had seized Gyalo in the Temple was still with him. The world spoke to his senses: the smoky tang of the air, the misty drizzle against his face, the distant drone of chanting from the pilgrims at the gate, and everywhere the stir of pattern: wood and paint and stone and tile, earth and water and the immeasurable currents of the air, all folded within the larger structure of the house, which was itself embraced by the design of its grounds, which was in turn subsumed within the conformations of Baushpar . . . And greater patterns still—the patterns of Arsace, of Galea, of the oceans, of the stars. With each breath, each step, those configurations converged anew, a great weaving of being and possibility contained and re-contained within Gyalo's own singular awareness. In a room above his enemy waited, more powerful than any dream of power. He was not afraid.

The rooms on the second floor were fronted by an open gallery running round all four sides of the courtyard. Ardashir led the way to a closed door. He rapped softly, then took a key from a pocket of his coat and inserted it into the lock.

"You lock him in?" Gyalo said.

"I lock others out. Wait here."

He pushed the door a little and slipped through, closing it behind him. A few moments passed. He reemerged.

"He will see you. I will return in a little while to fetch you." He looked deep into Gyalo's eyes. It was as if he had scraped back a lid over a pan of coals. "Harm him, and apostate or no, I will kill you myself."

He opened the door again, pushing it wide. Gyalo and Diasarta stepped across the threshold, into the dark. The door closed behind them. The key rasped. Then there was silence.

The air stank, an overpowering odor of spoiled food, sweat, and chamber pots. All the window screens were closed. A little daylight filtered through the fretwork, and a brazier gave off a dull red glow, but otherwise the room was unlit. Râvar was near the brazier, lying in a welter of sheets and bolsters, one bare arm hooked over his eyes. But for the piercing gold of his lifelight, Gyalo might not have realized he was there, so still was he.

Diasarta touched Gyalo's arm and gestured to the wall by the door, indicating that he would wait.

Gyalo approached Râvar as he might have approached a dangerous beast, placing his feet with care, breathing shallowly against the smell. His eyes were adjusting to the dimness; he could see that the room was as Axane had described it, with no furnishing but the brazier and Râvar's bedding and, against one wall, an open chest with clothing strewn around it. A tray lay by Râvar's pallet, the food on it untouched. On the other side, the chamber pot sat unpleasantly near.

Râvar, who had given no sign he was aware of Gyalo's presence, suddenly pulled down his arm and turned his head. Gyalo halted. Râvar's tangled hair fell over his face; all Gyalo could see was an eye, a cheek, half a mouth. For what seemed a long time the eye held his, glittering even in the uncertain light. Then Râvar rolled his body in Gyalo's direction, gathering another bolster under his head to prop himself up a little. He appeared to be naked. His knotted hair streamed around him like waterweed. A patchy growth of beard covered his cheeks. His eyes were swollen, as if with weeping, though it might have been from the acrid atmosphere inside the room. Even from a distance Gyalo could smell his unwashed odor.

Râvar's lips stretched in a ghastly smile. "Not quite how you remember me, eh?"

Gyalo was too shocked to speak. Both Axane and Ardashir, in their different ways, had told him Râvar was changed, ill. Yet in his imagination Râvar had remained unaltered: the triumphant enemy who had taunted him in the caverns, the light-wreathed being he had spied on from afar as he followed the Awakened City along the Great South Way. That was the man he had been prepared to face—not this dirty, disheveled specter, burrowed into his sheets and blankets like a sick animal in its nest.

"Don't be fooled." Râvar's voice was hoarse, as if he had not spoken in some time. "My power is as great as it ever was. It's all still there, inside me." He coughed, his bony chest spasming. "Why are you here? Have you come to gloat?" He squinted. "Who's that with you?"

"My companion."

"Is he like you? Unbound?"

"No. He's no Shaper."

"It was stupid of me not to kill you. I should have, when I had the chance. Her, too, the Daughter. I meant to do it. I did. But they were . . . too close. So I sealed her in, thinking she would starve, but all I did was leave her for you. And you set her free, and she carried the truth to Baushpar."

"She reached Baushpar? She's alive?"

"You know she is. You were with her."

"No." Gyalo shook his head. "I've only just arrived."

Râvar stared at him. "So you don't know? What's happened?"

The room was breathlessly hot. Sweat prickled at Gyalo's hairline, pooled under his arms. The transcendent clarity he had felt as he climbed the stairs was gone; the great design, whose edges he had seemed to grasp, had twitched back into the ordinary clutter of existence. Deep in his gut, he was aware of the first stir of dread. His scars had begun to sting.

"No," he said.

"She warned them." Râvar coughed again. "Most of them ran away. When I got here there were only ten of them left. Only ten, less than half. It was supposed to be all of them, all of them! Except her. The ones who stayed . . . they knew the truth about me, but they knelt to me . . . they called me by my name, my real name . . . they declared I was the Messenger. They knew the truth, they knew that I was false, but they believed in me even so." That horrible smile curved his mouth. "Did you know they wanted to be punished? Yes, punished, for turning from news of Ârata's rising when it was first brought to them. They never said anything about Refuge. That was their fault, too, but they never spoke of Refuge at all."

His eyes overflowed suddenly with tears. He showed no sign he was aware of them.

"They said I was the Messenger they deserved. It's time for us to end, they said. Let sleep come. Oh yes, they deserved me—but they weren't supposed to know it! It was the lie they were meant to believe, the blasphemy. And then I would have told them who I was, and they would have known that they were damned, and *then* they were to die. *Then* I would have punished them. But punishment was what they wanted. So I couldn't do it, do you see? I came away. I left them. They're still waiting for me. They think they've done something wrong. They send messengers to beg my forgiveness, to implore me to return. Ardashir turns them all away. He says I'm in seclusion, meditating and purifying myself. Purifying myself!"

He laughed, though the tears still came, sliding into the bolster, dripping from the bridge of his nose.

"Do you pray to Ârata, Gyalo Amdo Samchen?"

Gyalo was still trying to comprehend what Râvar had just told him. "Yes."

"Does the god answer?"

"No."

"He doesn't answer me either. I can't even feel his anger. He is silent. Silent."

Râvar caught his breath. Noticing his tears at last, he put up his ruined hands to scrub them away and kept them there, hiding his face. His nails were ragged, rimmed with black. It came to Gyalo that in that unguarded moment he could act. With his shaping or with his hands, he could do what he had come to do. Yet it was confrontation he had anticipated. Retribution. Self-defense. Not reaching out, coldly and with deliberation, to snuff a life.

In his hesitation, the chance was lost. Râvar lowered his hands. Something in his face had changed, sharpened.

"How did you get here, if you didn't come with the Daughter?" he said.

Gyalo chose to answer literally. "Along the Great South Way."

"So you saw. You saw my works."

"Yes. I saw everything."

"Good. Good." Râvar swiped the heel of his hand under his nose. "Are you here for the same reason, then? Still chasing after *her*?"

Gyalo felt a shock of anger. It was welcome, like cold water. "Have you forgotten that you told me she was dead?"

"No." Râvar grinned his death's-head grin. "It was a lie."

"I know. I knew it then."

"Well." Râvar raised one bare shoulder in a shrug. "It doesn't matter, because they aren't here anymore. I got tired of them. I sent them away."

"I know that, too."

"Would you like to hear what she said to me before I let her go? She said there is no god in this world. Did you know that? Did you know she has no faith?"

"Yes," Gyalo said through clenched teeth. "I know everything about her."

"That's what you think. She has you fooled, the same way she fooled me, the same way she fooled everyone . . . Faithless bitch. If you find her, you can have her. Here's something for you to remember, though—I had her before you did. Before you ever got her, she was mine."

His face contorted as he said it, spiteful as a child's. And all Gyalo's anger left him, collapsing into disgust—for Râvar, who at the end of so much atrocity took refuge in childish taunts and sniveling self-pity; for himself, who had floated into the squalid room on a cloud of exalted intent and discovered he was not, after all, a man who could intentionally kill another. A huge indignation rose in him, and an even greater sorrow.

"All this," he said, feeling the words deep in his chest. "All this destruction. All this misery. For what?"

"For *Refuge*," Râvar spat. "For my *people*."

"No." Gyalo shook his head. "For you. For your anger. For your pain. That's all vengeance ever is—a hole to pour pain into."

Their gazes held. Something seemed to happen in Râvar's face, a kind of falling. For just a moment, everything in him was laid bare.

"I should have killed you," he whispered. "I should have."

With slow effort he rolled onto his back and lay there like one dead.

Gyalo turned. He felt seared, as if he had been standing in a burning room. His hands were on fire.

"Come," he told Diasarta. "We're leaving."

"The door's still locked."

Without thought, Gyalo struck the door with his shaping will. All the metal that was part of it snapped out of existence: lock, tongue, hinges. The sound of it was shocking in the quiet. Unanchored, the door still stood in place. Gyalo put his foot against it and pushed, tipping it with a crash onto the floor of the gallery.

He stepped across it, the winter air shocking his sweaty skin. Diasarta limped after him. Ardashir was nowhere to be seen; no one came to halt them. Behind them, the entrance to Râvar's chamber gaped open, dark and silent.

26

Râvar

The echoes of the crash the door had made, falling, had long died away. But the light framed in the opening, or rather its unremitting presence, produced in Râvar a similar response, a kind of recoil of all his senses. It had been days since he had seen, for any sustained period of time, any light but his own and the red glow of the brazier. Ardashir, entering periodically to bring and take away food, to empty the chamber pot and replenish the brazier's charcoal, to make reports and sometimes to plead for instruction, did not count; even in the dark, he barely gleamed at all.

Why had Ardashir not come to prop the door up again? Anyone might walk by and look into the room. Râvar supposed he could rise and do it himself. But like so much else, it hardly seemed to matter. There was no action he could conceive, however small, that did not founder in the certainty of its own futility. Simply to think of doing a thing was to rob himself of the will to do it.

Faintly, from outside, he could hear the chanting of his faithful. Sometimes he was able to ignore them, but more often the constant droning made him want to jump out of his skin. He had ordered Ardashir to quiet them, but Ardashir either had not obeyed or had not been able to make them obey. What portions of the First Disciple's reports Râvar had actually attended to over the past days suggested that Ardashir had lost control of even that small splinter of the pilgrimage he had commanded when they reached Baushpar. *The Awakened City is rioting in the streets, Beloved One. They are burning houses, looting temples. You must do something. Please, you must control them.* Râvar turned his face away from these requests, as he turned his face away from food, from light, from offers of fresh linen. What did he care if Baushpar burned? What did he care if the Awakened City tore itself apart?

He rolled onto his side, away from the door. The motion released the odor of his unwashed body. His filth repulsed him, yet in a savage way it also pleased him. Like the hot darkness, the sweat-stale sheets, the fetor of the chamber pot, it seemed appropriate. He thought of the shock that had spread across Gyalo Amdo Samchen's face when his enemy first saw him. It had almost made him want to laugh. Almost.

Why had he agreed to receive his enemy? He could not quite recall. Curiosity? Self-torment? The desire to torment the man he hated so? Why then had he allowed him to leave alive? Gyalo Amdo Samchen, standing not ten steps away, looking down with that still face of his, those dark judging eyes . . . How easy it would have been to turn the air around him to crystal and make him slowly suffocate. Or to call fire and burn him alive. But when it came to it, Gyalo Amdo Samchen's life, or death, had not seemed to matter more than anything else. He had not killed the man when he should have killed him. Why kill him now?

The hopelessness, the futility, washed through him like a poison tide. It was beyond anything in his experience, the sickness of spirit that had descended on him. Unlike his other griefs and despairs and disgusts, there was no anger in it. It was as if all his anger had been purged on the night the Brethren knelt to him, the night he let Axane and Parvâti go. Deep in the sickness's grip, nothing else seemed real; it pinned him to his dirty sheets like a hand leaning on his chest and would not let him move. It cast him back to the beginning, lying among strangers he half believed were demons, terrified and injured and alone. He did not miss Axane, faithless traitorous Axane, but he missed Parvâti, an insistent hollow pain as if something in him had been sheared away. He longed to hold her, to set his hand above her heart, to forget everything but the rhythm of her breathing.

Periodically, when the pressure receded a little or he found the strength to claw his thoughts above the flow, he saw that he could not continue this way. Somehow, he must get hold of himself, find the strength to get up and go on. Take control of the Awakened City again. Or abandon it, steal away in secret and lose himself in this hateful world. Something. Soon.

Yet hour by hour, day by day, he huddled in this room and did not rise.

Does it please you, Ârata? Do you like what you see?

Even now, bitterly, he tested the silence. But poison waited there as well, and in recent days he had actually found himself wondering whether Axane could be correct. Was Ârata no longer on the earth? Had he abandoned the world he had made? But if Ârata were gone, what had been the vast warm presence, the deep embracing attention, that Râvar had known for so much of his life? What had been the certainty of love that had transfixed him in ceremony and meditation? A dream? A wish? Himself, mistaken for something greater? The emptiness he had experienced since Refuge's destruction—the emptiness of a god whose face was turned away—was nothing compared to that. Even a hated god, a rejected god, a god who had rejected him, was less terrible than the idea of no god at all.

Râvar heard the sound of footfalls. He rolled over again, feeling under his shoulder the hard lump of the Blood, which he had shoved beneath his bedding so he would not have to look at it. A man-shaped darkness took form within the jangling brightness of the doorway. Ardashir. The First Disciple advanced, becoming visible: the lumpish face, the rich clothes, the shadow-aura, weak as the last breath of a dying flame. Usually he carried something with him—water, a tray of food, charcoal for the brazier—but his bandaged hands were empty.

By Râvar's bedding he knelt, sitting back on his heels. Over the days of Râvar's seclusion his iron self-control had been sorely tested; he was often unable to conceal his fear and his bewilderment. But now he turned on Râvar an expression as composed, as opaque, as stone.

"You said nothing in the caverns," he said, his voice equally calm. "But I could see you knew him."

What was he talking about?

"These past days, you've spoken his name. You've cursed him, called him enemy. I wondered, how can a mortal man be enemy to a Messenger?"

Outside, there was a burst of shouting from the pilgrims. He rolled his head on the bolster. "I told you to quiet them out there. Can't you quiet them?"

"I did not understand," Ardashir said, and for a moment Râvar thought he meant the pilgrims. "But then I saw him in the Temple, unsought, unlooked-for, and it seemed the god's will. So I did not kill him as you ordered me to do if ever I saw him again, but brought him to you, so you could punish him. I thought it might bring you back to us."

"Ardashir, leave me alone. I'm tired."

"You say that so often now." Ardashir still spoke with utter calm. "So often you say it, when I try to speak."

Through the fog of Râvar's self-absorption penetrated the fact that there was something very odd in Ardashir's manner. Râvar attempted to bring his mind to bear, but it was difficult to concentrate.

Ardashir leaned forward. Softly, he said: "What is Refuge?"

Râvar felt the world go away for an instant. *I imagined that. Didn't I?*

He stared at the First Disciple. He realized, suddenly, what the oddness was: Since coming in, Ardashir had not used his title. Apart from the first days, when had that ever been the case? He felt a sluggish stirring of alarm.

"I was listening," Ardashir said. "In the next room. You would not let me care for you, you would not let me help you . . . but I heard you speaking sometimes, and I thought that if I listened, maybe I would discover what to do. So I made a hole in the wall. I went there today. I wanted to know why you hated him. What he had done. And I heard. I heard all you said."

"I was . . . testing him." It was the first response that came to Râvar's mind. He tried for the old authority, the old assurance with which he had made Ardashir and the rest of them accept impossible things. But he was out of practice. Even in his own ears, his voice sounded weak.

"You said . . . the god . . . is silent." Ardashir seemed to have difficulty enunciating the words. "You said . . . that you are—" He stopped, holding himself absolutely still. "False."

"I was testing him," Râvar repeated. "With his own blasphemy. To see if he would renounce it."

"Then why did you not punish him? Why did you let him go?"

"He was not worth my punishment."

"Why? Why was he not worth it? Why is any blasphemer not worth punishment?"

"Ardashir, in time all will be—"

"No!" It was a shout. "Don't tell me it will become clear in time! I need it to be clear now! I have doubted." He caught his breath in a sob. "Ârata forgive me. In Ninyâser, when you would not stop the looting—and later . . . I told myself it was my own weakness, my own failure, that it was not you I should question but myself. I prayed, I did penance. Look!" He wrenched at the bandages that wrapped his hands, exposing his palms, each a mass of open sores and crusted blood. "Look at what I did. But I could not . . . cut the doubt away. And these past days, since you lay down in this room . . . and now . . ." Tears were running freely down his cheeks. "Tell me I am base. Tell me I am blacker than the blackest ash. Tell me I have failed you. But tell me I am wrong. Tell me I am wrong!"

Râvar saw that it had come at last, the thing he had feared so much in the very beginning: the moment when one of them, or all of them, would turn to him and *see*. It was his own fault. He had let himself descend too deep, slip too far away. He had stopped watching the edge on which he danced—had forgotten that there was an edge. He had not even noticed when he began to fall.

Yet it was not too late. He could still reach out and save himself. He saw how it could be done. He would get up on his knees. He would take Ardashir's hands, press his lips to the First Disciple's insane and ugly wounds, as Ardashir had so often given reverence to his own scars. He would beg forgiveness for his inattention, his absence. He would take Ardashir in his arms and call him father—human father, to whom he owed his life, without whom he could not live. In this, which Ardashir most longed for, lay the key to his belief. Râvar would rise then. He would set the Blood around his neck. With Ardashir at his side he would go out to his faithful and never come into this awful room again.

He felt the words upon his tongue, ready to be spoken: *Ardashir, you are wrong.* Yet even as he thought of saying them, other words came into his mind, whispered in a different voice.

Why save it? Why save anything?

It was like the moment in the Pavilion of the Sun, when the world turned upon itself and all his understandings were reversed. Except this time it was not horrifying, but revelatory. He could not help himself: He laughed. He saw the shock of it in Ardashir's face.

"Ardashir. You are *not* wrong."

Ardashir, who had challenged him, now opened his mouth in wordless denial. As he had imagined himself doing, Râvar pushed himself unsteadily to his knees, shaking back the filthy curtain of his hair. He reached toward the ugly man on whom he had come to depend so greatly, and took the wounded hands in his own. Outside, he was aware of the pilgrims' chanting.

"What you heard is the truth. I am no Messenger, just a Shaper, an unbound Shaper like my enemy Gyalo Amdo Samchen—apostate, the people of your world would say. I was born of human parents in a place called Refuge— a far place unknown to you, but a human place. I've come among you to speak blasphemy. To deceive you with false witness. To blacken your souls and my own. My name, my real name, is Râvar."

"No," Ardashir said out of his horrified, denying face. He was trembling; Râvar felt it through their joined grip. "I've seen . . . the wonders you have done. I've seen your miracles."

"Shaping. Only shaping. How should you recognize it, who have spent your life in a land where there were no Shapers?"

"This is . . . a test. You are . . . testing me."

"No, Ardashir!" It was a mad sort of joy, to speak the truth at last. "There are no tests. There have never been any tests. I used you. I needed a man to help me build my blasphemy. I chose you. It wasn't hard—I used your faith, your desire to believe, your guilt about your sin. I didn't even really have to work at it. By the time I woke up after Thuxra, you'd already constructed half the myth yourself."

Ardashir jerked his hands free. His entire body seemed to lean away. His gaze had grown blind. "You used me—to blaspheme—"

"Think of all the absurd things I told you. The time of Interim. You were a priest—when did you ever hear of such a doctrine? The new Way of Ârata. Where is it written that the Next Messenger will make the Way anew? Why should the Next Messenger need to build an army? Why should he be as ignorant of the world as I was—would not Ârata prepare his emissary better? Why should he kidnap a woman and her child and keep them hidden? I know how much you've wondered about the woman and her child, Ardashir—well, here is the truth. The child is mine. I got it on her by rape, in the time before I came to you. Later she became his wife, my enemy's wife, Gyalo Amdo Samchen's wife. I wanted her back, her and the child. So I took them."

"No." The pilgrims' singing seemed to be rising louder—had they broken past the gates? Around the walls, darkness stirred like smoke. "No. It is too base."

"You wanted answers. Now you have them."

"I gave you . . . everything." The words grated like stone on stone. "I built . . . a City for you. You have made . . . a mockery . . . of my work. A mockery . . . of *me*."

Râvar laughed again. "I have made a mockery of your world!"

"Why?" Ardashir's whole body shook. His hands, trailing bandages, clutched the air. "Why?"

The chanting was deafening now. Or perhaps it was only the drumming of Râvar's blood. "For vengeance. For my people, whom your people murdered. For myself. Because I hate your world. *Because I hate you.*"

Ardashir gave a sobbing shout and sprang. His weight bore Râvar back into the tangled bedding. His hands closed around Râvar's throat. His features were contorted into a mask of rage and grief, his eyes once again streaming tears; he was still shouting, a long wailing cry that rose above the pilgrims' singing. Was this what Ardashir's wife had seen before she died? Râvar scrabbled with his crippled hands at the First Disciple's wrists; he reached for his shaping will, to turn the air between them to crystal, to choke Ardashir into unconsciousness as Ardashir was choking him.

And the world turned upon itself again, and the voice spoke once more inside his mind, saying: *Why?*

It seemed the greatest understanding he had ever known. He yielded to it, even as his body struggled involuntarily for survival. Ardashir's face was inches from his own, but it was fading, darkness gathering before his eyes.

Ârata!

A silent cry, no more willed or wanted than the battle for breath. A cry no different from the thousand others he had made—but this time, like a miracle, there was answer. Incandescent *presence* exploded out of the heart of the world, roaring into all the long-empty spaces, stretching them past wanting, past bearing. Râvar's power, which was of the same substance, leaped to meet it. Light seemed to burst inside his chest. Far away, there was a sound of thunder.

Râvar felt, at last, the touch of flame.

Gyalo

Gyalo came gasping out of nightmare. For a moment dream and waking merged, suspending him between two worlds: the cold winter darkness of Baushpar, the heat-shimmering brilliance of the Burning Land. He seemed to see the Awakened City, marching out into the desert—more of them and still more, the whole population of Arsace perhaps, the darkness of damnation breathing up from them like smoke, their passage burying the red soil in soot and ash. Râvar led them, astride a steed as huge and terrible as a thundercloud; Axane rode behind him, and he held Chokyi in his arms. Axane looked back as they went, crying Gyalo's name. Her voice was the last piece of the dream to fade. So distinctly did Gyalo seem to hear her that for an instant he was certain she stood outside his door, come to Baushpar in search of him.

He sat up and drew up his knees, resting his elbows on them and his forehead on his hands, and breathed deeply, allowing his pulse to slow. *She isn't here. She's safe.* He held the thought like an amulet, willing himself to believe it. *They're both safe.*

Nearby, Diasarta snored lightly in his sleep. They were camped in an abandoned villa along the same wide street as the mansion Râvar had commandeered, closer to the city's edge but near enough to hear the monotonous singing of the pilgrims. The house's owners, departing in haste, had left nearly everything behind; the companions could have had their pick of several comfortable bedchambers but had chosen instead a small room on the ground floor, whose door they were able to bar. A pair of braziers, and their own auras, shed a little light. Beneath the tang of smoke that tainted everything in Baushpar, the air smelled of mold.

The events of the day returned to Gyalo, an acid wash of memory. He had gone to his enemy, full of purpose and intent. He had listened to his enemy's confession, condemned his enemy's deeds—and then he had departed, leaving his enemy living. He thought of Axane, scoffing when he told her he meant to end Râvar's life; she had understood him better than he, apparently, understood himself. Yet Râvar had seemed halfway into death already—sick in his soul, as Ardashir had said. But if it were possible that he would cower in his fetid den as the Awakened City tore Baushpar apart, as it tore itself apart and scattered to the winds, it was also possible that he would recall himself, that he would rise to pull his unraveling empire back together. As long as he lived, so did the danger.

I have to return.

The understanding woke no fear, only a profound weariness. Gyalo thought of the transcendent recognition he had seemed to achieve as he climbed the stairs to Râvar's room—the glimpse of vast design, the intimation of a great weaving through which his own life stitched a single, integral thread. The shock of what he had seen and heard inside the room had toppled him from that high perspective, back into his ordinary groundling view. Perhaps that was why he had failed: He had lost the necessary vision. Somehow, he must find his way back to it again.

He rubbed his eyes, sore from smoke and too little sleep. If he had not let Râvar speak, he would not have learned the truth of Râvar's confrontation with the Brethren. How extraordinary, how unfathomably strange that the belief of those who remained should turn on Râvar's true self, that they should willingly embrace the very thing that had been meant to drive them to despair. Who had they been, the ones who begged for retribution, who said *Let sleep come?* Which of them had rejected punishment and fled with Sundit?

When Axane first told him of Râvar's plan of vengeance, Gyalo had wondered whether, as he had been Ârata's test of the Brethren, Râvar might be Ârata's reckoning: a living judgment brought upon them for their cowardice. Later he had dismissed that notion—for Râvar's anger was indiscriminate, and if the Brethren deserved punishment, Arsace and its people did not. But in the strangeness of the Brethren's conversion, Gyalo's thoughts returned to that original path. Judgment. Retribution. All of Râvar's deeds had been in service of his own personal vengeance: the souls he tricked into following him, the dark acts to which he incited them, his own annihilating feats of power. Yet within that ugliness lay deeds of another nature. Thuxra City, built by a godless regime and exploited by a conscienceless one, a blight and a defilement upon the sacred body of the Burning Land—leveled. Santaxma, the ruthless King whose consummate gamesmanship had trapped the weak-willed Brethren into supporting him in blasphemy—executed. Were those not reckonings, reckonings Ârata himself might have decreed? Two great destructions: Thuxra at the birth of Râvar's deception, Santaxma at the midpoint of Râvar's progress through Arsace. Baushpar, at its conclusion, would have been a third.

A beginning, a middle . . . and an end.

It was as if the earth had shifted. Gyalo felt the whole of his understanding turn, all his thoughts falling in an instant into new alignment. Three huge obliterations. Two already accomplished, the third yet undone. That third, not simply of the holy city that was the seat of the Brethren's authority, the heart of the church, but of the Brethren themselves and the institution of their rule. He thought of the insights he had gained since his escape from Faal—the understandings that had distanced him not from faith but from doctrine, not from belief but from the apparatus of its expression. He thought of how, following Râvar along the Great South Way, he had come at last to understand how utterly he had left the church behind. He thought of himself that afternoon, standing amid the dim magnificence of the First Temple of Ârata and comparing it to an outworn garment. *Ârata and his Way are not the same*, he had told Axane just a few nights ago: eight words, the full harvest of his journey toward emancipation. Or so he had believed then. Suddenly, he saw that there was more. If Ârata were no longer contained within the faith that bore his name . . . if the church no longer held the key to truth . . . if in fact it had become the opposite of truth . . . should it not indeed be swept aside?

Was that what it meant to open the way?

Gyalo sat transfixed, his eyes turned blindly on the dark. Râvar, promulgating his blasphemy of Messengerhood, even as he spread true word of Ârata's rising. Râvar, preaching invented doctrines to beguile his followers into heresy—yet was there not indeed a time of Interim, a span of years between the god's rising and his return that was neither the old age nor the new? Should not there be a new faith for that time, a Way of Ârata awake? Râvar, dark and angry, a Messenger consciously false to himself—but to Ârata? Could the god not choose whomever he wished to bear his word, to bring his judgment? Had he not, twelve hundred years ago, chosen Marduspida, a man of no outstanding holiness, so burdened with the universal flaws of human nature that six times he had refused Ârata's summoning dream?

And if Marduspida had refused a seventh time? Would Ârata have looked elsewhere for his Messenger?

I refused. Or at least, refused to choose.

Gyalo clutched his head in both his burning hands. He felt a drowning horror. From the start he had been certain that Râvar was the Brethren's consequence, their own failure turned back against them. But what if Râvar were his failure? His consequence?

From outside, a sudden burst of shouting drowned the pilgrims' chanting. It did not die down, but drew out, rising louder. Diasarta stirred, sat up.

"What's going on out there?"

"I don't know." Gripped by an inexplicable urgency, Gyalo reached for his boots. "I'm going to go look."

They left the house. The night air smote them as they stepped outside, raw and smoky. The rain had stopped, but the sky was overcast, utterly black. The shouting continued; it sounded as if some conflict had broken out. In the direction of the old city, the clouds glowed red.

"Big fire somewhere," Diasarta said.

Gyalo could not have put into words what he suspected. He began to run, down through the villa's parklike grounds, leaving Diasarta behind. The street was a void of darkness bordered on either side by the spectral luster of trees; he raced to the left, toward Râvar's mansion. The shouting intensified. He thought he could hear screaming. He rounded a curve; the crowd of pilgrims came in view, a struggling mass of multicolored brilliance blocking the entire width of the street. The wind gusted, carrying the harsh smell of smoke.

It was Râvar's house that burned. Gyalo could see the flames, leaping toward the sky. The crowd surged against the closed gates, trying to break them down. Pilgrims climbed the walls, shredding clothes and flesh on the sharp ridge of tile meant to discourage such incursion, flinging themselves down on the other side.

A groan, a great noise of splintering. The gates gave way. The pilgrims battled through the opening, shouting, shoving, trampling. Gyalo joined them, fighting to keep his feet. Beyond the bottleneck of the gates the crush expanded; he ran with the others, heedless of lawns and plantings and carefully raked gravel pathways, stumbling, falling, getting up again. Ahead, the house burned with incredible ferocity, the roof already part-collapsed, every window a torch, the door a dragon's mouth. The trees around it were aflame. The roar of combustion drowned even the pilgrims' screams. Smoke hid the sky.

Still some distance from the conflagration, the faithful were halted by a terrific wall of heat. Gyalo, shoving savagely between the packed bodies, felt it on his face like a branding iron; the air, to his Shaper sight, heaved and bubbled like water coming to the boil. As he neared the front he heard a shriek: "No! No! I will follow!" A woman tore from the hands of the man trying to restrain her and hurled herself toward the fire, her hair and clothes blown out behind her by its deadly wind. Up the burning steps she sprinted, through the incandescent door. For an instant she could still be seen, black on red. Then the flames roared up, and she was gone.

The crowd howled. Gyalo shouted with them, horrified. There was another runner, a man, half falling on the steps, picking himself up, diving into the fire's embrace. And then another, and another, a sudden insane flood of them, dashing and stumbling and crawling in pursuit of their Messenger, who had gathered them and led them and still, no matter where he chose to go, must be followed. Something struck Gyalo a blow between his shoulder blades, knocking him to his knees. Another pilgrim thrust past. Gyalo flung himself after the man, grabbing him around the legs, bearing him to the ground. The pilgrim kicked and fought, his face crazed in the red light.

"Let me go!" he screamed. "I will go with him!"

Inside the house something huge crashed down. Sheets of flame erupted from every opening. With an enormous, grinding groan, the rest of the roof collapsed, sending fire towering into the night. The crowd stumbled back from the gale of heat. Gyalo struck the pilgrim away from him and staggered to his feet. He felt his skin crisping, his breath boiling in his chest. Flinging out his arms for balance, he hurled forth his shaping will, seizing the patterns of the inferno, blasting them apart. There was a sound like a giant's footstep. The ground shook. The flames flashed white. Then they were gone—all of them, in an instant.

Silence. Shouting still rose from the street, and there was a crackle of combustion from the burning trees. But in the stunned stillness of the crowd, the hush seemed complete, a clear dome of quiet clapped down over just this place.

Gyalo turned, panting. The light of his power had seared his vision. Phantom shadows swam before his eyes, dimming the pilgrims' brilliance. They knelt or stood or clutched one another in attitudes of shock, staring toward the place where a holocaust had been and now was not. None looked at him. Why should they? They had witnessed Râvar's "miracles," but they knew nothing of free shaping. There was no reason they should understand what they had seen. No reason they should notice him.

"No."

One person *was* looking at him: the pilgrim he had tried to stop. The man had risen to his knees, his face a mask of grief. "No!" he cried again, and launched himself at Gyalo, who by seizing him had deprived him of his chance for immolation. There was no strength behind the attack; Gyalo easily thrust him off. The man fell again, heavily, curling in on himself, weeping.

Gyalo felt a sudden rage rip through him.

"Go home!" he yelled at the pilgrims, his smoke-roughened voice cracking. "Your Messenger is gone. Your pilgrimage is done."

Some had already turned toward him, their attention drawn by the scuffle. Now more did, their ravaged faces uncomprehending.

"The Messenger! Where is the Messenger?"

"Dead!" A woman's voice. "He is dead!"

"The Messenger is dead!"

"Ârata help us! Ârata help us!"

"Your Messenger is gone!" Gyalo shouted. At his feet, the pilgrim sobbed. The burning trees lit up the night like torches. "You've followed him as far as he can be followed. Now Ârata has taken him back. His work is finished, and so is yours. Go home. Go back to Ninyâser, go back to Sardis and Darna and Abaxtra. Go back to your families, to your farms and your trades. Take up your lives again."

"But what will we do until Ârata returns?"

"How will we wait?"

"How will we live?"

"Live in peace. Tell others to do the same. Follow the Foundations. Pray. Ârata is awake. He hears you now."

"Who are you?" Gyalo could see the speaker, a young man with wild black hair and a pale lifelight.

"No one. A witness."

They were all focused on him now, those at the front pushing toward him, those at the back jostling for a better view. He saw that if he remained they would claim him—for they were herd animals, and in their desperation would follow anyone who seemed to offer leadership. Not allowing himself time for thought, he ran at them, diving among them as the runners had dived into the flames. They reached after him, calling, but he did not pause, wrenching free of the hands that tried to hold him. Soon he was past those who had seen and heard him, anonymous again. Their rising lamentations filled his ears; women tore their hair, men rent their clothing. Every face was distorted with terror and with grief.

At the margin of the gathering he slowed. Breathless, he passed through the broken gates. In the street the pilgrims knelt, holding one another, wailing. They chanted broken prayers. They came running from the old city, calling on the god. With the last of his strength, he sought the dark recesses of a neighboring gateway. He sank down on the paving stones, the wet of the recent rain seeping through his clothes. He felt hollow at his center, and drained, as if of blood. His pounding heart refused to slow. His palms and his bad shoulder throbbed, and his face felt like raw meat.

Sometime later—he did not know how long—he saw a familiar green nimbus.

"Dasa," he called, hardly able to get the word past the chattering of his teeth. "Dasa. Over here."

Diasarta came running.

"I've been looking for you." He crouched in front of Gyalo. His voice was unsteady, in the way of someone trying to control overwhelming emotion. "I didn't know what had happened to you."

"I'm sorry."

"Were you in there?"

"Yes."

Diasarta pulled off his own coat and folded it around Gyalo's shoulders. He took Gyalo's freezing hands and chafed them between his own. "Did you see what happened?"

"Yes. It's gone. The house. Everything." Somewhere, a man was chanting the same words, over and over: *Ârata, spare us. Ârata, forgive us. Ârata, spare us. Ârata, forgive us.* "They were throwing themselves into it. Into the fire."

"Ârata!"

"I put it out. I told them to go home."

"Is he dead, then?"

Gyalo looked down the street, where the sky above Râvar's house was still lit by the burning trees. A pall of smoke hung overhead, darker than the cloud-mantled sky. Powerful as he was, Râvar could stand at the center of any conflagration and walk away unscathed. But in Gyalo's mind hung the image that had come to him when he saw the red glare of burning and realized its source: Râvar, nested in his dirty sheets, weeping without noticing his tears.

"Yes. I think he is."

Diasarta nodded once, sharply. "Ârata's will, then."

"Dasa—"

"Yes, Brother?"

"Before this . . . I was thinking. I thought . . . he might really be the Messenger."

"*What?*"

"I thought I saw a pattern . . . I thought perhaps . . . since I had turned away . . . that Ârata chose him instead."

"No." Diasarta shook his head. He looked appalled. "Never. Never, Brother."

Râvar is dead. There was no pattern, just a chance assemblage of events around which Gyalo's overburdened mind had spun a web of significance. He recognized that, or thought he did. Yet the significance, stubbornly, refused to vanish. The arc of deeds, ending in Baushpar. The destruction of the church. Among other things, Gyalo's struggles with the matter of Messengerhood had foundered on one particular mystery: What did it mean to open the way? In Râvar's dark trajectory he thought he had glimpsed an answer, as he never had in the passages of his own life. Though Râvar was gone, the answer remained, lodged in Gyalo's understanding with the unassailable *rightness* reserved only for the most instinctual of truths. He had known that rightness at other times in his life: When, still a child, he had understood that he would vow the Way. When his shaping woke. When he knelt before the Cavern of the Blood. When he recognized his love for Axane—a love he could not follow or accept, but which, even in denial, could not be undone.

"Dasa, I think—" He stopped. Diasarta waited, still chafing Gyalo's hands. Some warmth was returning; his teeth had stopped chattering. "I think I've seen what it means to open the way."

Diasarta's green-lit gaze was steady. "Then you must open it, Brother."

"But you don't know what I've seen."

"You've seen it, Brother. That's enough for me."

The certainty in Diasarta's voice was absolute. And that simply, there it was: the choice. Not abstract, not theoretical, not something for the future. Right in front of him. Right now, this instant.

Terror surged in him, a panic of question. What if he were wrong? What if that soul-deep sense of recognition were illusion? If he were to do it, how must it be done? Did he possess the strength—of will, of faith, of shaping? And afterward . . . if there were an afterward . . . would he know he had chosen rightly? Or was the rightness in the choosing? Must he make the choice to know?

And if he turned away—for he knew he could turn away, as he had turned away before. If he refused to choose . . .

Hours earlier, sitting in the dark, he had imagined with horror that Râvar was the consequence of his refusal, a dark Messenger chosen in his stead. All at once he saw another possibility—that there was no one else, that there had never been and never would be. That if he turned away, the choice would come again—and again, and again, and again, until at last he surrendered, yielded up his dread and his resistance, accepted a destiny that had been decreed for him and yet still must be elected, still must be *willed*. What if Marduspida had refused Árata's dream a seventh time? he had asked himself. Perhaps finally he knew. There would have been an eighth dream. A ninth. A hundredth. As many as were necessary.

The world around him seemed to shudder. He felt a pressure in his chest, as if the god's own hand were closing there.

"Dasa." He gasped. "What if I'm wrong?"

"You're not wrong, Brother." Diasarta dropped Gyalo's hands and gripped Gyalo's shoulders—hard on the uninjured right, gentle on the wounded left. He looked into Gyalo's eyes, his own eyes fierce. "I have no doubt, and never have had. No doubt at all."

From Râvar's house came an earsplitting scream of rending, then a crash—one of the trees, cracking apart. A gust of flame showed briefly above the walls. A tide of sparks swept up, spiraling as the air currents seized them. Among them perhaps danced some of Râvar—turned, like Ârdaxcasa, into ash.

Ârata, Gyalo thought. *Show me your will. Once, just once, let me know what it is you want.*

But Ârata would not answer. That was the point. The choice must be a true one.

He looked into Diasarta's face, and saw his companion's utter certainty. He looked into himself, where understanding shone, defiant of all his doubt and question. One last time his soul rebelled; like the sparks from the ruin of Râvar's house, the *whys* surged up in him, the *whats* and *hows* and *maybes*. Anger roared through him like a wall of flame, white-hot and futile. And then it was gone, burned out. Just that simply, he yielded. Not only in acceptance of the need, in recognition of the inevitability of the burden; but in weariness. He was tired of resisting.

He was still afraid. But it was a different fear. Perhaps that was the most that could be expected of any choice: the exchange of one dread for another.

He felt wetness on his scorched face. The rain had started again, fat drops pattering on the cobbles of the street. He tilted back his head and closed his eyes. The incongruity of it struck him: to make such a momentous decision in such a place, in the rain, in the dark. But Marduspida, too, had chosen Messengerhood in the dark, alone in his bed.

At least I'm not alone.

"Dasa." He opened his eyes. "Come with me."

He had thought he would feel the difference—that there would be some sense of shift, of transformation. But as he and Diasarta climbed the hill to the Summer Gate, there was only himself, aching and profoundly weary, his chest sore from the smoke he had breathed and his skin raw from the heat he had endured, wet to the bone and frightened of what was to come. Would it always be this way? Would he ever feel holy?

Yet he knew exactly where he must go, exactly what he must do. The *rightness* of it was something he could sense, an incorporeal pattern.

Later, he remembered only flashes of that long walk. The terror in the faces of the faithful rushing down the Avenue of Summer, drawn out of the old city by news of the blaze. The darkness of Temple Square, its makeshift habitations deserted, the pilgrims' fires extinguished by the pouring rain. The lamplit arch of the Temple's entrance. The echoing vacancy of the Evening City—where, either by inspiration or some buried memory, he found his way unerringly to the Courtyard of the Sun. In the pitchy corridors, he and Diasarta were their own torches; Diasarta, blind, held Gyalo's good shoulder. That was the most vivid memory of all, the light pressure of Diasarta's hand—his protector, his conscience, his only follower. His friend.

The gates to the Courtyard of the Sun were barred from the inside. Gyalo slipped his will through the hair-thin space where the portals lay together and sliced the bar in two. The crash as the two halves fell was only a little louder than the crack of his shaping. They pushed the gates open and set out across the long tongue of the walkway, the brass-seamed flagstones below gleaming faintly with the rain, the Ârata-images huge shadows against a sky only a little less black. Ahead, the Pavilion of the Sun rose like an obsidian mountain, its gilded pillars the vaguest shimmer across its front.

They mounted the stairs. On the wide landing at the top, Gyalo paused. The rain sluiced down. He was so cold he could not feel his fingers or his feet. Between the dim shafts of the pillars, the Pavilion's interior was as dark as the inside of closed eyelids—except for a single point at the back, where a paper lantern rested on the floor, throwing around itself a soft circle of illumination. Nearby, in the Blood Bearer's golden chair, someone sat—a big man, bulky with muscle, his lifelight crimson as new blood. His shaven head was bowed upon his hand. His face was hidden.

Gyalo had expected to find the Pavilion empty. But he felt the *rightness* of the man's presence, like the sound of a bell only he could hear. He started forward again, Diasarta at his shoulder. The sound of the rain receded.

"Who's there?" The Blood Bearer lifted his head, squinting at the darkness.

Gyalo reached the limit of the lanternlight, stepped into it. For a long moment the Bearer looked at him. The Blood throbbed on his breast. His chair shone, ancient wood under new gilding. At his back, where the jeweled sun-mural should have glittered, was a jagged hole.

"You," he said.

"Yes," Gyalo agreed.

The Bearer's gaze took in Gyalo's burned face and dripping clothes, slipped to Diasarta at his back, returned.

"Perhaps I should be surprised," he said. "I find that I am not."

"Râvar is dead."

The Bearer blinked. "How?"

"He burned."

The Bearer's eyes fell. "Ârata forgive us."

"How many of you are still here?"

"Ten Brethren. Our servants and aides. A few hundred Tapati." His gaze came up again, somber. "Have you come to judge us?"

Gyalo shook his head. "Only Ârata can judge."

"We did not all have the same reasons for staying. Baushtas and Artavâdhi and Vivaniya and Karuva and Gaumârata waited because they believed. Hamināser wanted to believe, and Idrakara stayed because Hamināser did. The two little ones had no choice; it was their guardians' will that kept them. And I—I stayed because I could not find a way to choose. Because I feared to choose wrongly. I thought that if I saw him, I would know. I thought my heart would speak to me." The Bearer paused. "He came to us, clad in light, more beautiful than any human man should be. He was awesome in his glory and his anger. I believed we deserved that anger—that we deserved his judgment. I was prepared to receive it. But I looked at him, and my heart said nothing. Nothing."

"Do the others understand?"

"Idrakara. Hamināser. The rest still wait for his return. They fast, they meditate, they seek to call him with their spirits, as once we summoned Ârata to bless our Covenant." He lifted one big hand, closed it round the cage of golden wire that held the Blood. "Instead you have come. I did not know until this moment that it would be you. But now it's as if I've always known."

"You must leave Baushpar," Gyalo said.

"Leave Baushpar?"

"And never come back. Ârata has risen. His old Way, which was made for the time of his slumber, is no longer the true Way. It is finished, and so is your rule. Travel anywhere you wish, settle anywhere you choose. But not together. The Brethren must disperse. For twelve centuries the Sons and Daughters have never been apart, but you must await the time of Ârata's return alone. The lives you live now must be the last in which you know yourselves."

The Bearer's broad face tightened, as if with pain. "I don't know if I can make my spirit-siblings obey such a decree."

"You must." With part of himself Gyalo stood apart, marveling. To speak such words! To give such orders! Yet the *rightness* was overwhelming, the awareness of design—the same vision he had so briefly achieved on his way to Râvar's room, now fully fledged and present in him.

"What will become of the holy city?" the Bearer asked.

"It will cease to be holy. Perhaps it will fall to ruin. Perhaps it will survive. But it will not hold the Brethren. It will not hold the church. The church's age is done. A new age dawns."

The Bearer caught his breath. "Is there no alternative?"

"None."

"So this is what it means to open the way."

"Yes."

One word. A single syllable. A puff of breath. Yet as Gyalo said it the whole of existence seemed to split, all reality cracking open like an egg, a hot white flash of infinite totality. It was gone at once, too huge to hold, leaving behind only the recognition of profundity and the core-deep ache of perception forced beyond its limits. But Gyalo knew, like a seal upon his soul, that the god, at last, had answered him.

Perhaps the Bearer sensed some echo of this. There was a look of wonder on his face. "We will obey," he said.

"Take the rest of this night and the day to prepare. By sunset the Evening City must be empty. By sunset, you must be gone."

"I understand."

The Bearer got to his feet. He put his hands to his neck, lifted over his head the thick links of his necklace. The Blood swung from it, a tiny captive sun.

"This was my father's," he said. "Three times, across the centuries, it has been mine. Now it is yours, you who come at the end of things."

He stepped from the dais. Gyalo had never stood before him face-to-face; always he had been at a distance, or on his knees, looking up from below. He was surprised to discover that the Bearer, who seemed such a massive man, was no taller than he. The Bearer raised the necklace and slipped it over Gyalo's head, settling it on Gyalo's shoulders. It was heavier than Gyalo expected, warm with the Bearer's body heat. Abruptly and vividly, he recalled the dream that had come to him in Ninyâser, the night Axane first confessed her own Dreams: Teispas, offering him his lost simulacrum, ordering him to take it.

"I pray each day," the Bearer said, "that we may be forgiven for our blindness."

"You must teach your spirit-siblings to do the same. Ârata hears us now. Prayer is possible."

The Bearer nodded. Turning, he moved into the darkness. The supple crimson of his aura shimmered. There was the sound of an opening door; it closed, and he was gone.

Gyalo turned toward Diasarta, feeling the weight of the Blood around his neck. The ex-soldier sank to his knees, his scarred face slack with awe.

"Messenger," he whispered.

Gyalo looked down at him. "You know now what it means to open the way. Are you still willing to follow me?"

"Yes. Yes." Diasarta made the god's sign. "Always, I will follow you."

His face, his voice, held dread and joy.

"Listen, Dasa. The rain has stopped."

Gyalo crossed to the Pavilion's front. The Courtyard shone with water. The clouds had begun to pull apart, revealing pinpoint stars. He was aware of his wet clothes, of the chill in his body—but distantly, as if those sensations did not truly belong to him. At the bottom of his vision the Blood pulsed fire. He lifted the lattice that contained it—examining the crystal's shuddering heart of flame, so like and yet not like the light of life; reading the patterns of the gold, which had been old when it was made into this ancient necklace. For so long he had begged the god in vain for signs; now, at last, they had been given—this necklace. The god's voice, still echoing at the root of perception. He was grateful for these gifts. Part of him, the same part that had marveled at his own stern words, felt an almost suffocating wonder at receiving them. Yet with much more of himself, he was aware that he no longer sought such confirmation. He no longer needed it.

Was this holiness?

"Brother." Diasarta had come to stand beside him. "What will happen at sunset?"

Gyalo set the Blood back on his chest—where by chance it rested exactly above Axane's bracelet, on its cord around his neck. "I'll destroy the Pavilion of the Sun, and pull down the images and the walkway and the walls of the Court. This is the center of the Brethren's power, the heart of the church. No one must be able to return here. And then—"

"Then?"

"Then I shall see."

The destruction of the Courtyard was necessary, but it was not enough. Baushpar itself must be marked—the Evening City, the Temple, the streets and monasteries and shrines. Râvar could have destroyed Baushpar in a moment, in a single act of will. Even if Gyalo had been capable of such a thing, he would not have done it, for the city was still full of people who must be made to leave. How much *was* he capable of? He knew what he had done in the past; beyond that he had no idea. But he would accomplish it. He had no doubt.

"Dasa, I'll rest now. Keep watch."

"Yes, Brother."

Gyalo sat down where he was, between two of the Pavilion's pillars, and began the breathing exercises that would aid his descent into contemplation. He intended simply to meditate for a little while, to clear his thoughts and calm his spirit. Afterward, he would sleep. But as he fell into the familiar state of mindfulness, attuning his awareness to the rhythms of his breath, he felt a deeper pull. Down he sank and down, parting the waters of self as cleanly as a diver, driving toward a different place within him, a place beyond or outside of physical sensation and the surge of time—as if, spinning in the swift currents of a river, he had kicked just a fraction to the right or left and so escaped the flow. In other meditations, he had sometimes touched this place; but he had never been able to hold himself there. This time he stepped easily onto the riverbank and effortlessly remained.

Beyond him, the world rushed on. The rain clouds drew off, and the sky blazed with stars. Dawn came up, eclipsing them. The sun appeared, devouring the long shadows of its rising, stretching them out again as it declined. The air began to dim, the western sky to burn. Each instant was a window on eternity. All of them together passed as swiftly as a breath.

Sunset.

Gyalo reached out, or up, or past: it was not possible to know. He felt the shift as he returned to the flow, the rushing exchange of birth and dissolution, of being and becoming, of essence and existence: all the principles it was a Shaper's gift to know. He let himself rest a moment, adjusting to the change, then got to his feet, feeling the protest of flesh forgotten, of muscles locked for hours.

"Dasa." It was strange to speak, after so profound a silence.

"Here, Brother."

Diasarta emerged from the shadows of the Pavilion, carrying a cup. Water. Gyalo realized how thirsty he was. He drained the water in a series of long swallows, then stooped and set the cup down.

"It's time."

"Brother." Diasarta's face was fearful. "What must I do?"

"Stay by me."

Gyalo led the way down the stairs, to the brass-seamed flagstones of the

Court. In all that great deserted space, his footsteps and Diasarta's were the only sound. The Blood pulled at his neck. He closed his hand around the lattice, as the Bearer had, to ease some of its weight. Beneath the flux of his senses, he was aware that he had not entirely left the riverbank: a little of its stillness was still there inside him, a little of that inhuman disconnection, a hard pebble of quiet that seemed to reside just below the base of his throat.

Halfway to the gates, at a midpoint between the walkway and the western wall, he stopped and turned. The Court swam with twilight, but above the walls the sky was still bright. The last light of the sun burnished the Pavilion's gilded pillars and kindled the red tiles of its roof, embracing the towering Ârata-images to the waist: the World Creator, smiling in ecstasy, the sun cupped between his hands; the Primal Warrior, his face fierce with battle lust, his sword of flame uplifted; the Eon Sleeper, mouth drawn with pain, his body scored with wounds; the Risen Judge, stern of eye and brow, fire rising from his outstretched palms. Patterns of stone, of gold, of brass—and binding them all, blurring them all, the pattern of the Courtyard's immense antiquity.

Gyalo closed his eyes. He had thought to pray. But to speak the god's name seemed enough.

"Ârata."

He opened his eyes. In that brief instant of darkness, something in himself—or outside him—had shifted. He looked upon a world defined by the possibility of destruction. Everywhere was flaw. Everywhere was defect. Just there, for instance, where the structure of the walkway had settled, and a sharp unmaking would cause a whole section to buckle. And there, where the great blocks from which the Ârata-images were carved had separated, and a finger of transformation would send them toppling. And at the walls, where a hundred imperfections spoke of the potential for collapse; and in the Court, where the shifting of the earth had unseated the flagstones and twisted their brass seaming; and at the Pavilion's foundations, where a complex interplay of stress and force revealed exactly how the entire structure could be brought crashing down.

Gyalo had never before seen, or thought to see, in such a way. He knew it for a final sign, a final gift: a gift of vision. He breathed deep, drawing on the stillness, the certainty he had brought back from another place. He pulled all his muscles into alignment. He opened himself to will: not to make, not to change, but to dissolve. To uncreate.

He set it free.

He had planned to strike at the Pavilion's foundations, bringing it down first. But in the moment of release, he changed his mind and directed the whole force of his will upon the flagstones at the foot of the long stairway. Blue-white light shot upward. The Courtyard shuddered like a table hammered by a colossal fist. He struck again, his will arcing from him hot and clean and true. Lightning sizzled across the flagstones; they heaved, grinding together, cracking apart. Again he flung his power forth—more power than he had thought he was capable of releasing, more power than he had ever imagined he possessed. The Pavilion sagged, its pillars splitting, red tiles crashing from its roof. The Ârata-images swayed. The golden sun flew from the hands of the World Creator like a stone from a catapult. The gilded sword of the Primal Warrior broke off at the hilt, smashing down onto the walkway.

Gyalo felt the pulse of ecstasy.

He knew now why he had struck at the stairs: There was a dissonance beneath them, far below the level of the soil—an instability, a flaw deep in the bedrock. Deliriously, drunk on destruction, he reached for that weakness, delving toward it, tearing downward with the greedy fingers of his gift. He was close, very close—it was much bigger than he had realized, much more unstable—

Comprehending all at once what would happen if he touched it, he tried to catch back his will. It was too late. He had released too much, relinquished too much control. He felt his power twisting from his grip—or perhaps he had never gripped it—perhaps he had not seized, but had been seized—

Not me—it isn't me—

A great voice shouted in him, a single cataclysmic word that was not any word he knew or was capable of knowing. He felt his soul tear open. He screamed; fire seemed to leap from his throat.

He touched the flaw.

The earth groaned. His will snapped back into him with a force that stunned him to the bone, toppling him like the Ârata-images. The ground leaped and bucked like an animal under the lash. He felt Diasarta's arms go round him, the other man shielding him with his body as the world came crashing down around them both.

Sundit

In the middle of the morning, when we were by my reckoning no more than two days from Baushpar, Reanu, in the lead of our little group, drew his horse abruptly to a halt, holding up a hand to indicate that we should also stop. In the quiet I could hear what had alerted him: the sound of hooves and harness from ahead, where the road curved out of sight.

"Off the road," he ordered. "Now."

We urged our mounts into the trees, and waited as the party came in view. I saw the tattooed faces of the riders in the lead, the trundling black coach that followed—so precisely what I had hoped to see, all through this backward journey, that for a moment I hardly believed it.

"Thank the god!" I said. "They've decided to flee after all."

We rode down. There was shouting as they saw us. The long snake of the procession lurched to a stop: a phalanx of mounted Tapati, four coaches, more Tapati, a mass of vowed Âratists on foot, and a train of ox-drawn carts, all of it winding out of sight around the bend in the road.

The canvas covering of the first coach's window twitched aside. My Brother Taxmârata stared at me as if I were an apparition.

"Sunni," he said blankly, as I reined in alongside. Reanu and the other three fell back to give us privacy. "What are you doing here? Where are the others?"

"On their way to Faal." In the release of the urgency I had carried for so long, the terrible dread that I would be too late, I felt an urge to weep and laugh at once. "I turned back. I couldn't continue, knowing you and others had remained. I thought to try again to persuade you to flee. Ah, Mâra, Mâra, I am so glad."

He shook his head. In the slanting morning sunlight, he looked aged, his face drawn in lines of weariness and sorrow, but beneath the strain there was something else, something I could not immediately identify. Little Athiya sat on the cushioned bench beside him, watching with large eyes. "We are not all here, Sunni. I did what I could, but not all of them would heed me."

The dread clutched at me again. "Who?"

"Baushtas. Artavâdhi. And Yarios—I begged, but Baushtas would not give him up. I did what I could," he repeated. "They are in Ârata's care."

"I'll go on, then. I'll persuade them—"

"No, Sunni. There's nothing you can do. They believe in him, the false Messenger. Even word of his death was not enough to shake them."

"He is dead?"

"Yes. Burned in a fire. Ârata's hand, perhaps, reaching down in punishment. For the true Messenger has come."

I stared at him. The corners of his wide mouth curved up, and suddenly I understood what lay under his exhaustion: joy.

"I know now, Sunni. He has been among us all along, but in our fear we could not see him."

"Gyalo Amdo Samchen," I whispered.

"Of all of us, I thought perhaps only you would not be surprised."

"How did you—what did he—Brother, tell me what has happened."

"The false Messenger arrived in Baushpar a little over a week ago, with his pilgrim army. Most of the city had already fled. There were terrible reports from Ninyâser after you and the others left. He made—the false Messenger made—some sort of cataclysm that swallowed up the army sent to stop him there, and he and his people swept down upon the city. Even those of us who had determined to receive him were frightened, and Kudrâcari and Okhsa and Ariamnes and Sonrida changed their minds about remaining and fled for Rimpang. So there were only ten of us to greet him in the Pavilion of the Sun. It was exactly as you said, Sunni—he wanted us to bow down to him in blasphemy, in ignorance of his real nature. When he realized we knew the truth, he flew into a rage and left us. The others prayed for his return, but I did not—I knew that you were right, and we had been wrong to wait. And yet we were *not* wrong. Three nights ago the true Messenger arrived in the Evening City. He came to me in the Pavilion of the Sun, as the false Messenger had. I knew him even before he named himself—I looked at him and saw the truth, all of it in an instant. Ah, Sunni, how blind we have been! He told me what I must do. What *we* must do." He reached through the window of the coach, caught my hand. "Our rule is over. We must leave Baushpar forever. The Brethren must disperse, and the church must pass away."

"What?" I snatched my hand from his. "The church cannot pass away! The church is Ârata's!"

"It is a fearful thing, I know. Even as I gave the orders, I questioned. But with each passing hour, my certainty has grown." He smiled again, that smile of bliss, like the expression artists give to images of Ârata Creator. "*The soul knows the soul's truth*, the *Darxasa* says, and it is so. This is what it means to open the way."

"It cannot be." I shook my head. "You did not hear aright. You misunderstood."

"No, Sister. It's as I have said."

"Is he down there, Gyalo Amdo Samchen? Is he still in Baushpar?"

"I left him in the Evening City. Sunni, tell your men to join the rest. Ride with me and Athiya."

"No." There was no question; the intent was absolute, immediate. "No, I will go on."

"Always you must see for yourself, yes, Sunni?" The joy seemed to cloud a little. "I don't know what you will find."

"What do you mean?"

"I spoke with him at night. We left before sunset the next day. I heard nothing, saw nothing in this coach, but those on foot say that as dark fell the earth trembled, and a plume of dust rose above Baushpar."

"Dust? Brother! What has happened?"

"We did not turn back to see. The Messenger ordered me to go, and I obeyed."

I pushed aside my anger and my fear; there would be time for such things later. "Will you follow the others to Faal now, Brother? Whatever it is that we must do, we must first gather to decide."

"Yes." Slowly he nodded. "Faal. Ârata guide you, Sister. Be safe."

"And you." Now at last I noticed something, which perhaps I should have noticed first. "Mâra, where is the Blood?"

"With him. Our father was the first. He is the last. You'll see, Sunni. You'll see."

He leaned from the window and called his driver to move on, then withdrew inside the coach. The driver shouted an order. The procession lurched into motion. I sat my horse as my spirit-siblings passed, leaning out to greet me: Idrakara and blind Haminâser in the third coach, Gaumârata and Karuva in the fourth. In the second coach was Vivaniya, alone; I had seen him when

I first came alongside, peering from his window, but he had drawn the cover down again, and it did not even twitch as his coach went by.

My men and I turned and rode on. It took some time to reach the procession's end: The foot train comprised several hundred people, and there must have been fifty carts bringing up the rear, piled high with furniture and other goods. We rode continuously after that, stopping only to rest and water the horses and once, for a few hours, to sleep. The urgency was sharp in me—the same urgency as before, dread for Baushpar and for my spirit-siblings. I concentrated on it so I would not have to think about what else I might need to dread. *Gyalo Amdo Samchen*, my mind sang, *Gyalo Amdo Samchen*.

Late in the afternoon of the following day, we came over a rise and saw Baushpar below us, laid out in its valley like a child's toy. For an instant my eyes showed me what I wished to see: the long light of the sun burnishing the red and yellow roofs, striking fire from the Temple's lotus domes, kindling the walls of the old city to the color of half-dried blood. But that longed-for image was not the truth. The city I looked down on had been ravaged. Parts of it still seemed intact: the walls, the interior sections immediately adjacent to them, the crowded suburbs. But there were no lotus domes. There was no Temple, no Evening City. The center of Baushpar was gone.

We were transfixed, my men and I. Over the centuries, the region has been shaken by earthquake—seriously enough, on two occasions, to force us to rebuild large portions of Baushpar. But this did not look like any earthquake. It did not look natural at all. It was as if an enormous fist had struck the city, printing a ragged flower of destruction at its heart. In that territory of ruin, I could see nothing standing. I thought of Dracâriya, of Santaxma and his entourage. Somewhere underneath the rubble, my spirit-siblings' flesh-shells lay. And how many others? How many hundreds, how many thousands, of others?

I don't know how long we sat, staring down. Reanu, at last, broke our silence.

"Old One, perhaps we should make camp here for the night."

"My Brother was wrong," I said. My throat was so tight I could hardly speak. "Râvar isn't dead. He did this."

Reanu's grim face told me he agreed.

"I want to see." Blindly I fumbled for the reins, which had slipped from my hands. "I want to go on."

Reanu reached out and gently took my wrist. "Old One, it will be dark soon. You won't be able to see anything in the dark."

Of course he was right. He and the others set up our camp, pitching my little tent, hobbling the horses, making a fire and boiling tea. Commonplace actions, performed without speaking. I could see and feel their shock. They were born in Kanu-Tapa and ordained in Rimpang; the holy city has never truly been their home. Yet I know they grieved, for the sake of the church, for the sake of history. For my sake. I felt very close to them that night—Reanu and Apui and Lopalo and Omarau, the four who had been with me since the beginning, who had seen all I had seen and would see all that was yet to be witnessed. Below, on the black lake of the valley, a little light trembled up from poor ruined Baushpar—signs of life, or maybe only fires kindled by the disaster. Occasionally something flashed blue-white, like lightning.

I slept little. I wondered if Râvar remained in the city, if Gyalo did. I cursed Baushtas for refusing to send little Yarios with Taxmârata, for condemning to body-death a child incapable of choosing for himself. I cursed Artavâdhi for supporting him. I wept, silently, for the three of them, their souls adrift upon the world.

At first light we rose and packed the camp and rode down to Baushpar. We reached the northern perimeter of the suburbs perhaps an hour after sunrise. We were no longer elevated above the level of the walls, and thus not able to see the destruction; as we approached, it was almost possible to believe that nothing was amiss, for the walls were whole and the ground undisturbed, and from a distance the houses seemed undamaged. In the streets, though, signs of vandalism were everywhere—the work, I assumed, of Râvar's pilgrim army. Doors hung open, window screens had been smashed out. Pilgrim sigils defaced nearly every surface. Reanu and the others, tense as drums, closed around me in a diamond formation; I drew down the hood of my coat so my tattoo would not show. The suburbs were deserted. We met cats and dogs and pigs, starlings and sparrows and pigeons, but not a single human being. I began to hope that in the old city it might be the same, that not so many lives had been lost after all.

We passed beneath the heavy lintel of the Winter Gate, and rode down the Avenue of Winter. For half its length, Winter ran intact; beyond that it was choked by rubble, entirely impassable. We retreated, turning east into the maze of side streets, heading for the Avenue of Dawn. The streets and houses were whole, though marked like the suburbs with signs of human violence. Once again we encountered no one. As we drew near Dawn, however, we began to hear the sound of shouting, and now and then a thump or crash, as of falling stone or timber.

Like Winter, Dawn was stopped by the wreckage of its walls, and also by the roof of an adjacent monastery, which had slid nearly intact off the building and landed in the street. A gang of vowed Âratists was digging for survivors, dragging aside great beams, passing tiles and bricks from hand to hand. They were so covered with dirt and dust that they resembled men made out of clay. Their dead were laid out along the Avenue—scores of them, it seemed, though I could not bear to count. The stench of decay was ugly under the pall of dust.

Reanu pulled one of the diggers aside. In a voice so hoarse it hardly sounded human, he told us that he and his fellows had chosen to remain in Baushpar not because they believed the true Messenger approached, but to guard their monastery. He described Râvar's triumphal procession into the city, how his faithful had run wild in the ensuing week. He told us how, four days ago at sunset, the earth had quaked and the center of Baushpar had come roaring down. Reanu asked the questions; I kept my hood low and said nothing. The man must surely have wondered at us, but he showed no sign of suspecting that he spoke to a Daughter of the Brethren.

"We've been digging ever since," he said. "We've pulled some out alive. We can still hear cries."

"What of the false Messenger?" Reanu asked. "Is he still in the city?"

The monk shook his head, impatient to return to his labor. "He took a residence outside the walls. That's all I know."

We released him and moved on. For the rest of the day we circled the perimeter of the ruins, speaking with such citizens of Baushpar as we encountered, who had remained in stubbornness or in belief and were now, like the monks, fighting a doomed battle to rescue any who might still survive beneath the rubble. What did I hope to learn by this painful journey? Even now, I'm not completely sure. Yet it seemed to me that I owed it to Baushpar, my beloved city, to gather as much knowledge as I could. And to myself, I suppose. I've never been content unless I understand.

Our journey, however, produced no understanding. Everyone we met spoke of Râvar's entry into Baushpar and the violence of the pilgrims, but beyond that there was little agreement. Some thought the Brethren had refused Râvar when he went to them, and he (or Ârata) had in anger made an earthquake to destroy a faithless city. Some thought the disaster had come of natural causes, and bore no connection to the Messenger's (or the false Messenger's, depending on who was speaking) advent. Some thought Râvar had left Baushpar to preach his doctrines to the other kingdoms of Galea. Some swore he had been crushed in the collapse. Some were certain he was still present, preparing to raise a new Temple on the foundations of the old. There were even some who claimed that they had seen him, with the Blood around his neck, walking the ruins in the fearful light of his power. I remembered the blue-white flashes I had seen the night before, and drew my hood even farther across my face.

Outside the Summer Gate, we encountered a dusty, draggled group that greeted our questions with a chorus of lamentation. They led us down into the southern suburbs, to a place where a crowd kept vigil by the charred remnants of a house. There, from Râvar's own palm-scarred followers, we heard an entirely different story. The way had been opened; Ârata's return was imminent. The Messenger, his work upon the earth complete, had been reclaimed by his father in a cataclysm of fire. They had been told this by a stranger, a Witness (clearly they considered this some sort of title), who had suddenly appeared before them, then vanished again. I thought of Ardashir, that tireless servant. Yet if Ardashir had been the Witness, surely the people would have recognized him.

Twilight was beginning to fall. I was weary past expression, grieved past telling, sick with what I had seen that day and overwhelmed with question: Was Râvar alive or dead? Was he present in Baushpar, or gone? What of Gyalo Amdo Samchen? We rode beyond the suburbs to make camp, for I could not bear the thought of passing a night in the carcass of Baushpar. None of us could eat much of the meal Lopalo prepared, nor did any of us wish to sleep. We huddled round our fire in the frost-crisp air, listening to the faint singing of the pilgrims at Râvar's burned house. Overhead, the slimmest crescent moon floated amid a glorious array of stars—the world going on as always, beyond the affairs of men and gods.

It looked like a spark at first, dancing on the dark in the direction of the city. I squinted at it, wondering. It enlarged, turning from a spark into an ember, like a cat's eye when torchlight catches it. I thought I could hear something—a shuffling, a rustling.

In the same instant that I recognized the sound of an approaching crowd, Reanu and the others were on their feet, their knives flashing in their hands. I found myself standing also, breathless with dread. For I knew what it was, that glowing cat's eye. I knew who approached me through the deep dark, knew I had been a fool to imagine I could enter Baushpar and remain hidden from his hatred.

But it was not Râvar who stepped into the firelight. It was Gyalo Amdo Samchen.

My men and I stood in silent shock. He looked like someone who had escaped from underground—his clothing filthy and torn, his hair a tangle around his shoulders, his beard-stubbled face raw with scrapes and cuts.

A bandage wrapped his thigh. Around his neck hung my father's necklace, strangely pristine, the pulsing golden ember that had alerted me to his approach. I could just see the mass of people behind him, a suggestion of form at the farthest margin of the firelight. One, a little ahead of the rest, seemed familiar.

"Sundit," Gyalo said. Then, to Reanu: "I don't mean you harm."

"What about them?" Reanu gestured with one of his knives toward the silent crowd.

"They follow me." Gyalo coughed, cleared his throat, coughed again. "I can't stop them. But they are peaceful."

Now I recognized the man waiting like a pillar at his back, the firelight partially illuminating his face: Gyalo's companion when we first met, the ex-soldier Diasarta.

Gyalo sat down, abruptly, as if his knees had given way. I followed suit, and more slowly, my guards.

"How did you find me?" I asked, still trying to comprehend that it was he and not Râvar. I don't know why this should have surprised me so—why, when I saw the Blood shining on the dark, I never thought of him. Perhaps over the course of the day I had grown more afraid than I realized.

"I heard of four Tapati asking questions in the city, with a fifth companion whose face was covered. I thought it must be one of you. I didn't know which one till I saw your lifelight."

There was a strange flatness to the way he spoke, as if he were so exhausted that he could not summon even the energy for emotion.

"Were you caught in the collapse?" I said.

"Yes. Dasa and I. We've been digging. With our hands." He held them up, as battered as the rest of him, several fingers bloody where the nails had torn. "Also with my shaping."

I thought of those blue-white flashes, of the people who had said they saw the Messenger walking in the ruins. A chill went through me. I heard Taxmârata's voice: *I looked at him and understood the truth.* There he sat, just across the fire from me, no farther than in our nighttime conversations on the steppe. I looked at him, and I did not know what I saw.

"What has happened here?" I asked. "Did Râvar do this?"

He shook his head. "Râvar is dead."

"It's certain, then?"

"I saw the fire that consumed him." Again Gyalo coughed, this time as though it pained him. Behind him, Diasarta stood immobile; the crowd was a wall of shadows. "It was I."

"You killed him?"

"The act of shaping that destroyed Baushpar was mine."

"Ârata!" It was Reanu. I could not have spoken.

"I'm not strong enough. Not naturally." He paused, holding himself absolutely still. "The strength was given me."

"But . . ." I struggled to find words. "Why?"

"This is what it means to open the way."

"No." I shook my head. "No."

"Baushpar was built for the Age of Exile. It was built to honor Ârata sleeping. But Ârata is awake, and so Baushpar honors a falsehood. It had to fall."

"But . . . this is Ârata's holy city." My voice was faint. I felt as if I had passed into a nightmare. "Every stone of it speaks his glory."

"The church must also fall." He still spoke in that flat way, terrible phrases uttered without any visible expression. "For it, too, enshrines Ârata sleeping. And it clings to that falsehood, clings tight, like a living creature whose survival is its first concern. It cannot of its own will pass away. It has become not merely a vessel of ignorance but an impediment to the truth. Not until it is gone can Ârata return. To that end, the Brethren must disperse. To that end, Baushpar must lose its holiness. To that end, the Way of Ârata, the sleeping Way, must cease to exist."

Words cannot convey my horror. I'd told myself that Mâra must have misunderstood. But he had not misunderstood. It was exactly as he said. My heart quailed. Was this what I must accept? Was this the man I must call Messenger, this pitiless creature with his glittering eyes and his toneless voice? I looked at him, his face lit by the flames almost to the color of the Blood on his chest. I looked at Diasarta, as still and watchful as my own guards. I looked at the tenebrous crowd behind him, the people who had walked so quietly at his back and now waited so patiently for him to be finished. Followers. Pilgrims.

"This is what Râvar wanted," I said. It was hard to find my breath to speak. "To destroy Baushpar, to murder the Brethren. This is what he meant to do."

"No," Gyalo said, for the first time showing some emotion. "He only wanted vengeance."

"If the church falls, what will hold faith in the hearts of the people? What will keep Shapers to their manita, without the Brethren to oversee the Doctrine of Baushpar?"

"The church is not the author of faith. Faith built the church, not the other way around. As for the Shapers, perhaps they will find a middle way." He drew a breath. "As I did not."

"The church is the house in which faith lives. It is what prevents faith from becoming what Râvar made it! Without the church, the world will become as it was before my father brought the Way to Galea! Ârata! What have you done?"

"What was required."

"It was *required* to bring the city down on living people? On three of my spirit-siblings? No. Ârata would never condone such an act! Do you think he loves us human creatures so little, that our lives count so little to him?"

"Ârata loves us," he said. "It's just that he doesn't love us the way we love each other."

"What—what is that meant to mean?"

"We grieve at death, for our lives are all we have. But what does death mean to Ârata, who will raise us all perfected into the new primal age? What does pain mean to him, who will burn us to make us clean?"

Everything in me recoiled from these words. "What do they mean to you, Gyalo Amdo Samchen?" I cried at him, my voice breaking. "For you are the one who has made them here!"

In a convulsive motion he raised his battered hands and pressed them against his eyes. "I know it," he said. "I know it."

He sat like that a moment. Then he let his hands fall. He was not expressionless now. Emotion was naked in his face.

"I had thought . . . of all of them . . . that you would understand, Sundit. That night in Ninyâser, the night I left—you knew me then. You knew me, before I knew myself."

I shook my head, weak with the memory of that moment. "The man I thought you were that night would never have done what you have done."

He looked at me. The firelight moved on him, bright and dark. "I haven't changed. The truth is what it was that night. I am the Messenger. I always have been."

For the first time there was sound from his followers, a murmur of reverence, rising quickly, dwindling back to silence. I glanced toward my men. Reanu and Omarau stood like the warriors they are, bodies tense, faces hard and alert. Lopalo's and Apui's stances were the same—but in the faces of those two I saw something different, an awe that even their tattoos and the shadows could not disguise. They, too, had known this man who sat beyond the fire. They, too, had witnessed his deeds and perhaps, like me, begun to draw conclusions about his nature. Now those conclusions pulled them away from me. I could almost see them going, slipping across the border of belief.

Somehow, the sight of their surrender brought me to my senses. My mind cleared, an absolute transition, as if a great wind had swept through me. All my doubt fell away.

"No." My tongue embraced the word. Its rightness was tangible to me, like the heat of the flames. "I was wrong that night. I see it now. I repudiate you, Gyalo Amdo Samchen. Whoever the Messenger is, you are not he."

Silence. We sat eye to eye, each fully revealed to the other—enemies at first, then briefly friends, now enemies again. I wonder why, knowing what he is, it never occurred to me to fear him.

At last he drew in his breath, and nodded. "So be it."

He pushed to his feet. It required a perceptible effort; he staggered a little as he came upright, and Diasarta stepped swiftly forward to catch his arm. A ripple went through the crowd, more felt than seen in the darkness.

"You've made your choice," he said to me, "as I've made mine. But I would have you know. It was not my intent to kill your spirit-siblings. It was not my intent . . . to crush living people under the rubble of Baushpar. If I could have made a different choice—" He stopped. He stood a moment, his face and body rigid, and I realized that his expressionlessness was not any lack of feeling, or even the blankness of exhaustion, but the exercise of a terrible control. "I would have spared them all." He raised a bloody hand, pointed a finger at my throat. "I charge you, Sundit. By the life you owe me. When you speak against me to your spirit-siblings, also tell them that."

I felt as if I spoke around a stone. "Ârata will read the truth of it in your soul, if it is true. I cannot."

He looked down at me a moment longer, ragged and—yes, I will admit it—majestic, my father's necklace shining on his chest. Then he turned and walked off into the night, Diasarta still supporting him. The shuffling crowd of believers followed. I could hear the noise they made long after they passed out of sight.

I knew I should remain with my men—comfort them, offer counsel. But I was worn and soiled and hollowed out with anger and with grief, and I needed desperately to be alone. I retired into my tent, where for a third night I lay unsleeping. I heard them talking, their voices rising now and then as if they were arguing; they did not speak Arsacian but their own language. Occasionally, a creak or thud or groan came from inside the city. I thought of Gyalo Amdo Samchen, walking the ruins, employing the power that had wrought so much death in search of those who might survive. As if that could absolve him.

The Tapati fell silent before dawn. As soon as it was light enough to see, I left my tent, and found them all still sitting by the coals of the fire. They conveyed a sense of unity, as if something had been mutually decided.

"Well?" I said.

They exchanged a glance. "Old One," Lopalo said. "Apui and I would beg a favor of you."

I already knew what the favor was. "Speak."

"We wish to remain in Baushpar. To help in the search for survivors."

"And perhaps," I said, "to join this so-called Messenger?"

Their eyes fell. "Whatever you command, Old One," Lopalo said, "we will obey."

"What of you, Omarau?"

"My place is with you, Old One. And my belief," he added, glancing sidelong at his fellows.

I turned to Reanu. He answered without being asked, his face stern behind his tattoos. "I told you once that I would never leave you, Old One. Where you go, I go. Always."

I was almost ashamed of the intensity of my relief.

"You may remain," I told Lopalo and Apui. "But know that your choice is irrevocable. If you change your minds, if you ever realize you are mistaken, you cannot return to me."

"We understand, Old One," Lopalo said. "We're grateful."

Both of them bowed to the ground.

Lopalo built up the fire again, and he and Apui prepared breakfast. They seemed eager to offer me this last service, and I forced myself to eat. We could still hear Râvar's pilgrims, who had not stopped singing all night long. Then the four men together readied the horses and packed up the camp. Lopalo and Apui begged my blessing before they went, and I gave it; perhaps I should not have, but they have been so staunch, and though their defection grieves me, I cannot find it in my heart to be angry at them. They will face enough chastisement in the time to come, when Ârata returns.

Reanu and Omarau and I rode north, circling wide around the city, picking up the road into the hills well beyond the northern suburbs. At the crest of the hill where I first looked down on Baushpar's ruins, I reined in and sat for some time. Reanu and Omarau waited in patient silence. At last I wiped the tears from my cheeks, and we moved on.

I write this entry in my tent. My battered writing desk rests on my knees, a candle flickering in its holder. I am weary down to my bones. Yet I think I will not sleep this night either.

Two false Messengers. Two separate sets of misguided followers. Two heretical doctrines. Gyalo, I think, is worse than Râvar, whose blasphemy was no less, but who at least knew himself as false. Râvar gloried in his deeds, and

Gyalo's pain was clear—yet it may be that very pain that feeds his falsehood, the terror of the consequences of understanding he was wrong. It stops my breath to imagine such self-deception. It stops my heart to think that I allowed myself, even for a moment, to believe in him.

I will not let my grief consume me. I will fix my mind on what I can control. I'll go to Faal. I'll speak against Taxmârata. I will try to hold my spirit-siblings united—yes, even Kudrâcari and her faction. Ages ago, on the steppe, Gyalo spoke of tests. It may be that he is right in that at least: Perhaps all of us are being tested.

I must not fail. Whether Ârata wakes or sleeps, the true Next Messenger is yet to come. When he does, we Brethren must be waiting.

29

Gyalo

They entered Ninyâser from the northwest, along the Baushpar road, and walked together through the city. At the beginning of the Great South Way, just beyond the King's Gate, they reached the agreed-upon point of parting. Diasarta and Apui and Lopalo would head south, then west into Haruko. Gyalo would go home.

The day was bright but chill, with a sharp gusty wind. They stood together at the Way's edge, out of the stream of traffic—four travel-weary men in ragged clothing, their drawn and hollow faces attesting to some recent suffering or trial. The two Tapati no longer wore Âratist garb, and their growing hair and beards obscured the swoops and swirls of their tattoos, but it was still immediately apparent what they were, or had been. In Baushpar, Gyalo's band of followers had accepted the presence of the Brethren's legendary guardians with little curiosity. Here people stared, fascinated or fearful or simply trying to work out why these men were apart from their masters, trudging the roads and sleeping rough like common people.

The companions had not spoken as they walked. In these last moments also they stood silent. Farewells had been made the night before, and Gyalo had forbidden any public displays of reverence. Still, in the imminence of separation, Gyalo felt there was something he should say or do. The way the other three watched him told him that they felt so, too. But he could not think of anything.

At last he simply said: "I'll be on my way."

Diasarta nodded. "Go well, Brother."

"And you. All of you."

"We'll be back." Diasarta looked Gyalo in the eye. "Three years from now, on the day of Baushpar's fall. Don't forget."

It was halfway between a promise and a threat.

Diasarta had laid his plans in secret and sworn the others to secrecy also. Not until the night after the four of them left Baushpar did he reveal what he intended. Gyalo, whose single-minded toil among the ruins had blinded him to nearly everything else, listened in amazement as Diasarta told him of the thirty men and women he had recruited from among Gyalo's followers, of the oath they, and he, and Lopalo and Apui, had sworn: to carry word of the Messenger's coming and Ârata's rising to the kingdoms of Galea, and teach the faith that must be followed in the time before the god's return—a Way of Ârata ungoverned by leaders like the Brethren and uncoupled from the institution of the church, in which the god, awake and aware, overlooked the world and the Five Foundations were joined by a Sixth: Prayer.

"A Sixth Foundation," Gyalo repeated, wonderingly. Such a thing had not occurred to him—might never have occurred to him. Yet the instant Diasarta said it, he felt the same *rightness* he had experienced in the hours immediately following his choice.

"It's no more than what you've said yourself, Brother. Ârata hears us now. People should know that, in the time between."

"The time of Interim," Gyalo said.

"That's *his* name for it."

"Yes, but it's a good name. So much of what he taught was true, in a backward sort of way."

"Interim it is, then, Brother. If you say so."

"This is really what you want, Dasa? This task? This . . . labor?"

"Me and the others. Yes. Though I always thought it'd be you who'd lead us."

It was as close to condemnation as the ex-soldier had come since their conflicts on the steppe.

Gyalo regarded him now: a homely man whose hard-lived life made him look at least a decade older than his thirty-two years, whose sallow skin and close-set eyes suggested dissoluteness. Yet his straight stance spoke of a new-gained authority, and his gaze, clear and calm, conveyed a certainty beyond mere knowledge. Lopalo and Apui had it, too, that certainty. It breathed from the three of them like a collective lifelight. One could see they had some special understanding. Looking at them, one wanted to have it, too.

"I won't forget," Gyalo said.

Diasarta stepped forward. They embraced. The Tapati stood like stones;

such liberty was not for them, for they were only the Messenger's disciples. Yet they were the first, as Diasarta was the first—the first companion, the first protector—and that would count for much in the time to come. So, Gyalo knew, they believed.

He lifted his hand—half farewell, half blessing—and turned away. He could feel their eyes on him all the way to the King's Gate. But when he paused there to look back, they were gone.

In the northern half of the city, above the Year-Canal, the companions had passed through areas that clearly spoke of Râvar's violent sojourn. The battered districts around the Âratist religious complex were still deserted. But the southern city, with its mean squares and alleyways and the cancer of the Nines clinging to its southwest quarter, had largely escaped the pilgrims' depredations, and though the streets were emptier than they should have been, things seemed to be going on much as usual. Gyalo was ragged and unkempt and dirty, but so were many who lived there, and no one gave him a second glance as he made his way through the familiar streets. It was sweet, the anonymity—the first he had had since he and Diasarta climbed out over the ruins of Baushpar. He would miss Diasarta—missed him already, with a sharpness that did not quite seem real, as if he had only to turn his head to find the ex-soldier walking next to him. But he would not miss being known, being recognized, being followed. He would not miss being the Messenger.

His steps slowed as he neared his own street. Across from the roofed passage that gave access to the little square, he paused. The passage thrust a finger of space between two of the dwellings, revealing at its end a sunlit snippet of the court: an expanse of paving stones and the fountain, and beyond it, the green door of his own home. Like Diasarta's absence, it seemed unreal. He could not, for a moment, bring himself to step into it. As always when he stopped moving, he was aware of his fatigue—not the weariness of bone and muscle, which had come to seem a normal state of being, but a stretched, overburdened weakness that he felt sometimes in his bowels, sometimes in his chest, sometimes at the base of his skull, but really in none of those places, for the exhaustion was of his shaping, which lay at the foundation of his being but not in any physical part of him.

And beneath it, deeper even than the roots of power, the pebble of quiet he had brought back from another realm. He felt that, too, and not only when he was still.

At last, his heart beating in his throat, he crossed the street and inserted himself into the darkness of the passage. The court was empty—it was too cold for wives to sit in their open doorways shelling beans, or for the old grandfather in the house next to Gyalo's to occupy his stool in the sun. The green shutters of the house, like the door that matched them, were shut tight. It did not mean anything, he told himself—on such a chilly day, anyone might choose to keep their shutters closed.

The bundle he carried on his arm did not contain a key. The key had been lost in the caverns, along with his pack. Of the possessions with which he had begun the journey, only Axane's bracelet remained, safe on its cord beneath his clothes. Yet even if he had had the key, he would not have brought it out—for he wanted the door to be open, and to approach it with the key in his hand would have denied the possibility of openness.

It required an effort of will to reach for the latch.

It lifted easily. The door swung open.

There was no one in the room. He stood on the threshold, searching for signs of occupancy. The pressure in his chest would not allow him to call out. He crossed to the kitchen: It was empty also. But there was a fire in the stove. He could see its heat, distorting the substance of the air.

Behind him, something changed.

He turned, clumsily, as if he were underwater. Axane stood at the foot of the stairs, cloaked in the glorious turmoil of her colors. Her hands hung at her sides; her face was still.

He could not stir. He could not even say her name.

She walked toward him without haste. She came right up against him, and slid her arms around his waist and laid her cheek on his chest. The world turned green, turned blue, turned green again. He sighed, a long exhalation that felt like the release of more than breath. He let the bundle drop and wrapped his own arms around her, feeling her warmth, smelling the sandal-wood scent of her hair.

They stood that way for a long time, breathing in rhythm, their hearts matching beat for beat. At last he pulled back and took her face between his hands.

"You waited." He hardly recognized his voice.

She looked up at him. "I love you," she said. "Every time I thought of leaving, I came back to that."

He kissed her forehead, her eyes, her mouth. He closed her in his arms again, folded himself around her.

"Where's Chokyi?"

"Upstairs."

She led him to the second floor, where all was as he remembered: his desk, the chests for supplies and clothing, the big bed where Chokyi lay, her thumb in her mouth, flushed and damp with sleep. Gyalo knelt and smoothed the hair from her forehead. The dark crescents of her eyelashes fluttered, but she did not wake. Looking down at her—lost and regained, too young to retain any memory of the terrible events that had swept her up for a time—he felt something in him unravel. Tears filled his eyes, ran down his cheeks.

Axane's arms went around him. He let her hold him for a moment, then wiped his eyes and got to his feet.

"I need to talk to you."

Her face went quiet. He turned from her and led the way downstairs, where the door to the outside still stood open. He closed it, then took off his coat and hung it on the hook and went to sit beside her on a cushion. She looked at him, a look that told him that she did not have to know, that he could keep silent if he chose. She had waited for him; he had come back; they could go on from there. But though he knew it might drive the final wedge between them, he had to speak. Once at least, everything must be told.

He started with the moment she and Chokyi had left him. He told her of his and Diasarta's entry into Baushpar, his encounter with Ardashir, then with Râvar. The fire; Râvar's death. His choice to become the Messenger. His journey to the Courtyard of the Sun; the small destruction he had meant to make, the enormous one that had been made instead, by him and through him. His and Diasarta's survival—not by any forethought on his part, but simply because the spaces of the Court were huge and they had been standing where nothing happened to fall. Their journey out across the wreckage, realizing, horrified, the true scope of the damage. The desperate search for survivors. He had barely noted the passage of night and day during that time, could not remember sleeping or eating or any pause at all apart from the evening he had spoken with Sundit.

"I dreamed that," Axane said. "I saw you talking with her, with Diasarta and all those others behind you." She looked at him. "She repudiated you."

"Yes." The admission was still painful. Of all the Brethren, Sundit's had been the only acknowledgment he really wanted.

He spoke of his followers—near a hundred of them at the end, mostly vowed Âratists and other residents of Baushpar, with a few ex-citizens of the Awakened City. He still did not understand what had held them to him, beyond his shaping and the Bearer's necklace; he had not spoken to them or blessed them or let them praise him, and left it entirely to Diasarta to deal with them. Still they followed, going where he led, digging in the ruins because it was what he did.

He had gone on digging past the point where anyone might reasonably be expected to be found alive, far past the limits of his strength. At last Diasarta and the Tapati had physically overpowered him—he being by that time too weak to resist, either with his hands or with his shaping—and carried him to an empty dwelling outside the walls. He slept for two days, his followers camped nearby. When he woke, he told Diasarta what he meant to do, enduring the ex-soldier's surprise and dismay. A week later, he and Diasarta and Lopalo and Apui slipped out of Baushpar in the middle of the night. At the time he had not cared what his followers would make of his disappearance, but he was grateful, afterward, that Diasarta had prepared them.

He had rehearsed this account often in his mind, and was able to give it without stumbling or pausing or breaking down, though he was not always able to look Axane in the face. Except for that single interruption, she did not speak; no doubt she had seen much of what he told her in her Dreams, but there must also be much she had not seen, and since they parted he had not spoken at all into her sleep. She wore her mask, the quiet face behind which she hid the intensity of her nature, the vulnerability of her heart. He understood, though he wished it were not so. Out of a face like that, rejection might come as easily as acceptance.

At last he was finished. Still without speaking, she got up and went into the kitchen, returning with a cup of water. He drank it down, then sat looking at the cup, reading the structure of the clay and of the glaze, his patternsense drawn with unerring certainty to the flaw at its base where a sharp tap would crack it. It was always what he saw first now: flaw, fault, the possibility of unmaking.

"I was dreaming him," Axane said. "The night of the fire."

"You saw what happened?"

"Yes." She was staring at her hands, clasped on her knees. "They had a confrontation, he and Ardashir. Ardashir accused him of being false. Râvar admitted it—he admitted everything. Ardashir fell into a rage and attacked him. He didn't . . . Râvar didn't even try to defend himself. And then somehow there was fire. I can't be sure, but I think he made it. I think . . . he burned himself."

Gyalo was silent. He had not known this, not exactly. But what she said seemed right.

"I woke up then." A small shudder rippled through her. "I couldn't bear to go back to sleep, so I didn't see . . . you, and what you did. The next night, when I dreamed all the destruction . . . I'd been sure he was dead, but I thought I must have been wrong, that he'd escaped somehow and destroyed Baushpar. But then I saw you and Diasarta. I heard you talking. And I saw the necklace, the Bearer's necklace." She drew in her breath. "I knew then that I'd lost you. That you'd never come back."

"But I did come back. I'm here."

"For how long, Gyalo?" She raised her face, her great dark eyes seeking his. "Is it over? Or is there more?"

"Axane. You know everything now. What I've done. What I am."

"What you believe you are. I've always known that."

"What I *am*, Axane. Whether you accept it or not. And also what it has made me. I am like him now. A murderer."

"You are nothing like him!"

Gyalo set the cup gently on the floor, resisting the rush of feeling that urged him to strike it at its shatterpoint. "I . . . killed . . . thousands . . . of people. Maybe more than he did."

"But you didn't intend for anyone to die. I know you, Gyalo. Even if I hadn't seen you weeping in Diasarta's arms that night, I'd know that. There was a . . . flaw. A fault under the city. You didn't know it was there."

Gyalo remembered the eager hand of his power, delving down into the earth, greedy for dissolution. "My will was used, Axane, but it was still my will. My hand was seized, but it was still my hand. I understand that it was required of me. I know the ash-tainted life we lead in this time before the end of time is just a poor shadow of the perfect life to come. I know our shadow-lives mean little to the god, who loves only the brightness in us . . . But I'm a mortal man, and this is the only life I know, and it was the only life they knew, the people I killed. I can't forget that. I cannot simply say, *It was Ârata's will*, and forget that all those lives came to an end because of me."

"No, you cannot," she said. "And if you could, I'd hate you."

Gyalo sat breathing hard, his face hot and his chest tight. He could not look at her.

"What you've done. I can never understand it, not as you do." She paused, choosing her words. "But I don't mourn Baushpar. And if what's happened really puts an end to the Brethren and the church, I won't mourn them either. And I know—Gyalo, I *know* those deaths were not what you wanted. I know you would give anything to take them back—even your own life. Maybe even mine and Chokyi's. Râvar wanted the death he made. He craved it. It was his triumph. It was his heart. You are nothing like him." She reached out, took hold of his wrist. "Nothing, nothing like him."

He shook his head. "I'm not as I was, Axane. You need to know that."

She said softly, "I'm not afraid of you."

"But can you live with me? I will never renounce the choice I made. I am the Messenger."

"Can *you* live with *me*?" Her fingers tightened on his wrist, so that he had to lift his eyes. "Knowing I will never, never name you so?"

There was no mask. Naked in her face was her fierce unbelief, her absolute repudiation of the truth that lay at the core of his own being. For the first time he understood, really understood, that her lack of faith was not disillusion, or laziness, or a lapse of intelligence or a deficiency of education or any of the causes that lay behind the other atheisms he had encountered, but a willed and deliberate choice not unlike his own. For the first time, he understood that he would never change her. For the first time he realized how much he had hoped, one day, he might.

But she was his heart's desire. For her he had turned from his duty and come home. He had loved her when it was forbidden. Why should he not love her when it was impossible?

"Yes," he said. "I can."

"Are you sure?" Her gaze seemed haunted. "It'll always be between us, you know. Even if we never speak of it again."

"I'm sure. As sure as I've ever been of anything."

"Then I am, too. I love you. I told you before—I always came back to that."

"Axane."

He reached for her, but she put her hand on his chest, holding him away. "There are conditions."

"Conditions?"

"Do you still have the necklace? The Bearer's necklace?"

"Yes."

"You must hide it. Somewhere where I'll never come on it. I never want to see it. Never, do you understand?"

He nodded.

"This one's harder." Her hand was warm against his chest; he could feel the shape of her palm, the pressure of each separate finger. "If you come home, it must be for good. I have to know that, Gyalo. I can live with your belief. But you must swear that the rest of it is over. That it won't come into our lives again."

He saw that to give her any answer but the one she wanted would be to lose her. Though he had meant to tell her the truth—all of it, without exception—he looked into her eyes, and lied.

"It's over, Axane. I swear it."

For a long moment she watched him. Then she sighed and let her hand fall. "That's good, then."

Her touch had reminded him. He reached under his shirt, pulled out the cord from which her bracelet hung.

"My bracelet!"

"I meant to give it to you the night you found me."

He picked at the knot, but it was melded fast with dirt and sweat and at last she had to get a knife to cut it. He took her hand and slid the silver circle onto her wrist, as he had done on their wedding day. She bent her head, looking at it.

"We must make a pact, Gyalo, to forgive each other. Not just now, but always. Every day. We must never grow to hate the differences between us."

He pulled her into his arms. The gratitude he felt was indistinguishable from pain. "I promise."

"We can live now." She clung to him. "We can work and have children. We can grow old. We can do the things that people do. We can be happy."

He closed his eyes on the underwater glory of her colors, and for just that span of time, let himself believe it.

Much later, he uncurled himself from around her and left the warmth of their bed. He pulled on clean clothes, and from beneath his desk retrieved the bundle he had been carrying when he came into the house. From one of his chests he took a length of cord and a square of waxed canvas. He emptied a wooden box of the scrolls it held.

He paused by Chokyi's pallet to draw up the covers she had kicked off, then knelt a moment, looking at her and thinking of the evening just past. Axane had boiled water so he could bathe; she had scrubbed his back and shaved off his unkempt beard and combed and braided his hair. By that time Chokyi was awake, and while Axane prepared a meal he occupied himself with winning back her trust, succeeding well enough that she was willing, once they had eaten, to sit on his lap and allow him to amuse her by calling illusion in various shapes and forms. Her laughter was a lovely thing, almost as lovely as Axane's; he could still feel the happiness their happiness had given him. Yet all the while, a fraction of him stood apart, a small, bright, dispassionate eye watching from the riverbank. Even as Axane and he made love, even as she lay against him afterward with tears drying on her cheeks, even as his own tears flowed, that little eye looked on, unmoved.

I'm not as I was. He had stopped short of telling her how deeply that was so. But she was wise. She would guess.

Fetching his boots, he tiptoed downstairs. In the dark kitchen he took a spade from the cabinet where Axane kept household implements, unlatched the back door, and stepped out into the biting chill of the night. The wind sent clouds scudding across the moon. In the shelter of its walls Axane's garden lay quiet.

On the bench at the garden's midpoint, he laid down the bundle and the canvas and the box. With the spade, he levered up several paving stones and set them aside. He scraped away the gravel beneath, and began to dig down into the cold earth. The light of life was abundant, even in that sleeping season—the thready glint of worms, the nail-head spark of pupating beetles, the pale glow at the crowns of the perennial plants in the garden beds nearby. But all of it was netted in dissolution, in the processes of decay and change; everywhere he looked he saw the patterns of unmaking, of undoing, of destruction. When he first perceived the world that way, in the Courtyard of the Sun, he had thought it a gift—but he had come to hate it, to hate the shift in his Shaper senses. He was not certain whether what he had done had actually transformed his ability, or whether his surrender to destruction had simply brought him to a truer understanding of its nature. Perhaps every Shaper came to that eventually, with enough practice. Perhaps it was how Râvar had seen the world.

Or perhaps only the Messenger must see it so. For to open *was* to undo, to unmake. The Messenger *was* destruction.

When the hole was as deep as his forearm, he set down the spade and sat on the bench to open the bundle. Within were two smaller packages. He teased apart the knots of the first; inside lay the Bearer's necklace, its ancient gold shining in the intermittent moonlight, the bright-hearted crystal shimmering from its cage. The second package was rolled into a dirty Âratist stole. Carefully he unwound the cloth, revealing a second mass of gold: Râvar's necklace, streaked with soot, its links fused into a welted tangle around the fiery fist of the Blood.

He had found it on the night he and Diasarta and Apui and Lopalo slipped out of Baushpar. He had not had any intention of returning to the place where Râvar had died; but as they neared the broken gate he heard the sound of ragged chanting, and was swept by an impulse so powerful he did not dare refuse it. Ignoring Diasarta's objections, he left his companions in the street and walked up to the house. A dwindling cadre of pilgrims still held stubborn vigil there—the very last of the Awakened City, offering up their lives to the memory of their Messenger. Earlier, he had removed the Bearer's necklace and wrapped a stole around his head and face; with his marked palm and dirty, torn clothes, there was nothing to distinguish him from those wretched souls.

He stood among them, his gaze moving on the blackened timbers and the charred brick, his Shaper senses reading how the fire's heat had transformed them. The roof was gone but the walls still stood; beyond the fallen portico, the door gaped like a wound. After a time he began to feel that looking was not enough, so he went round to the back where he would not be seen and climbed inside. His awareness of the pebble of quiet, the little wedge of disconnection between himself and the rush and bustle of the world, was acute that night; he let it guide him, wandering half-tranced through the ruins, followed in the dark by his own illumination.

At the front of the house, gazing up at the stars through a great hole in the second floor, he tripped over a piece of tile, destabilizing some precarious balance and causing an area in front of him, groaning and clattering, to collapse. It was several moments before he dared to move again. As he began to turn away, he caught sight of something glinting. *Lifelight,* he thought, with the reflexive urgency of two weeks spent searching for the faintest flicker of it. But with his rational mind he knew there was nothing alive there. In the next second, he realized what it must be.

Breathless with wonder, he cleared away debris and knelt, looking down at what he had uncovered: the Blood, shining from a bed of ash like a single coal left over from the inferno that had claimed the house. It was pristine, entirely unmarked. What were the odds that he should simply find it like that? Yet it felt right. It was proper that this Blood, too, be given into his keeping.

He pulled the stole from around his face and rolled the heavy mass of gold and crystal into it. He tied it into the bundle that contained the Bearer's necklace and carried both gems past Râvar's faithful, their sad voices dying away behind him. For nearly three weeks the jewels had not left him, borne on his arm by day, at night used for his pillow. At last, he would set them aside. He had made a promise to Axane, and he would keep it.

The quiet in him stirred—almost like a voice, as it could be sometimes, speaking of a different promise. *No,* he told it, as he had before, as he would again, many times perhaps, in the months and years to come.

He had said no to Diasarta also. *But you can't,* Diasarta had cried, shocked and angry, when Gyalo informed the ex-soldier that he intended to go home. *This is only the beginning. There's so much more to do.* Gyalo knew he was right. To become the Messenger was not a choice for a single moment. To open the way was not a single act. It should be he who oversaw the dispersal of the Brethren. It should be he who walked the lands crying word of Ârata's rising. It should be he who taught the new faith with its Foundation of Prayer: generation, in balance with the destruction he had made. Yet in the days after Baushpar's fall he had felt, hardening in him, the determination to walk a different path. It was in Baushpar that he had first said, to the still part of him the god had touched, the part of him that perhaps was the god: *No.* Not in rejection—though he loathed what he had become, the blood upon his hands, the alteration of his Shaper senses. Not in anger—though he had been angry at first, so angry! Yet even as he shouted his rage at the indifferent sky on the first terrible night after the collapse, he understood what had been done and why. Understood, as he had said to Sundit, that a god's purpose did not have to be palatable to mortals, nor was the god constrained to use them kindly. Not even his Messenger.

Not anger, then. Not rejection. Just . . . refusal. He had been called to duty. He would not answer. The Messenger who had opened the way would not pass through.

He whispered it aloud now: "No."

Like a prayer, the word flew off into the night. And as sometimes happened, an answer seemed to come breathing back—not wrathful or impatient, but serene, implacable: *One day.*

His heart twisted. This, too, he knew: the price of refusal. The call had come, and it would not stop coming, no matter how many times he turned from it. One day it would grow too strong—with Diasarta's return, perhaps, or some event out in the world—and he would not be able to prevent himself from answering. He had meant to confess this to Axane. He had meant to tell her that he would try to stay, but did not know if he could, or for how long. Instead, he had lied—because he wanted her so much. Because he, who had given the whole of himself to duty, desired this one thing for himself, if only for a little while.

Perhaps, when the time came, she would forgive him. Perhaps.

He thought of Sundit, to whom he had not lied—who, unlike Axane, would have been capable of understanding all the truth, had she chosen to accept it. He did not grudge her condemnation, which after all was little different from his own. He did not grudge her repudiation either, though he knew she would do all she could to work against the change he had set in motion. She might even be successful. But only briefly. Her struggle, like his refusal, was a hand raised against the inevitable.

He wished her well, in the time to come.

On the bench beside him the crystals shone, the fire at their cores shuddering in counterpoint. He wondered what had happened to the third, the one he had brought out of the Burning Land. Was it with the Brethren? Did it lie beneath the wreckage of Baushpar?

Softly he reached to touch the stones, first Marduspida's in its cage of gold, then Râvar's, careful of the razor facets.

Farewell.

He shrouded them in cloth again. He folded the waxed canvas around the bundle and placed the whole into the wooden box, whose lid he tied closed with cord. Kneeling by the hole, he set the box into it, then took up the spade and began to fill it up again, tamping the soil to make it level. He replaced the gravel and carefully reset the paving stones. With his hands he brushed the surface clean, then stood back to examine his work. No one but a Shaper would see there had been disturbance there. He would know where to dig again, when he had to.

He returned to the kitchen and put away the spade. He dipped water into a bowl and washed his hands, then rinsed the bowl and dried it and set it back where it had been. He stood a moment in the doorway, listening to the silence of the night, watching the shadowed garden, where the Blood lay sleeping in the earth.

"Ârata," he murmured to the god who had claimed him, the god he had refused. The god he knew, as surely as he knew the ground under his feet, he would one day see striding home across the world, the flames of judgment leaping from his hands.

He latched the door and went upstairs, where his wife and child shone upon the darkness. He shed his clothes and slid into bed beside Axane, curving himself around her again. She stirred in protest of his chilled hands and feet, but did not wake. He lay in the green world of her lifelight, breathing her in, feeling in himself the familiar weight of love and change and guilt, and beneath it, hard as crystal, the little piece of him that did not partake of such things, that was not and would never again be of this world. It stirred, that quiet, but not quite as before. For the first time, he thought it whispered of forgiveness.

He closed his eyes, and sank into dreamless sleep.

Epilogue
The Exile

I went to market today with my basket on my arm, like an ordinary village matriarch. I do such things very naturally these days, in this exile of mine. I don't even trouble any longer to conceal my tattoo; here in Isar, where the Way never gained a foothold beyond a scattering of isolated monasteries, many do not recognize it, and those who do care little. I had completed my purchases and was searching among the stalls for a treat to bring to Utamnos, when I heard the sound of voices raised in some sort of dialogue. Not argument or anger; more like a poet's recitation. I followed the voices to the market's edge, where there is a shrine to the Aspect Vahu—or I should say, to the god Vahu, for that is what they believe in Isar. There were four men, standing on the steps. They were clad like paupers, yet they stood like kings. They were speaking of prayer, which they called the Sixth Foundation.

My first impulse was to turn on my heel and go. Yet a kind of awful fascination held me, and I stood listening as they spoke of prayer, of Promises, of Ârata awake. I already knew something of these doctrines, from Reanu's travels—in the past two years such proselytizers have appeared throughout Galea, proclaiming the birth of a new Way of Ârata, defined by this supposed Sixth Foundation. Like Gyalo Amdo Samchen, they declare that Baushpar's destruction was the first act of Ârata's Promise, and marks the opening of the Way. Like Râvar, they call their new faith an act of generation and speak of the ensuing time as an age of Interim. It is such a jumble of principles that even I, who knew both false Messengers, cannot tell from which of them it rises.

The proselytizers' faith was palpable, their passion and their joy (this struck me with great force: their joy). In other kingdoms, many must be moved by such a presentation. But this is Isar. They care nothing for Ârata sleeping here, so why should they care for him awake? The handful of spectators did not display reverence or shock or even distaste, but only the sort of curiosity they might have shown toward a group of jugglers or a band of minstrels. If the joyous speakers noticed this, they gave no sign.

At last I could no longer bear it and set out for home. An uncontrollable flood of memory beset me as I walked, the griefs and regrets that I normally hold prisoned in the darkest parts of me. I found, suddenly, that I needed to commit my thoughts to paper, an impulse I have not felt in a very long time. At home, I did not even pause to empty my basket, but went immediately to the storeroom—a barn once used for sheep shearing, which I have caused to be entirely paneled in cedarwood. I searched out the proper box and pried up its lid, smelling the dry odor of the chalk layered at the bottom to absorb moisture. This journal and my box of writing tools lay atop the rest, ready to my hand. It has been even longer than I remembered since I made an entry; I thought I had recorded something of our journey here, but in fact I set down nothing after that awful day, more than two years ago, when I realized that Taxmârata had won, that my spirit-siblings would yield to Gyalo Amdo Samchen's heretical directives and dissolve the council.

How shall I bridge with words the time that has passed between that entry and this one?

I think I will not write of those final weeks in Faal. The bitterness of the battle I knew was lost, and yet could not help fighting, needs no recounting. Taxmârata had much time while I was absent to win my spirit-siblings to his view, which he did with all the fire and vigor he once employed to raise an army for Santaxma, back when the Caryaxists seemed the greatest threat the church might ever know. Those who would have supported me had already separated themselves—Kudrâcari and Ariamnes and Okhsa and Sonrida, who remained in Rimpang and refused to come to Faal, and Dâdar and Ciryas, who decamped soon after my arrival to join them. The rest, battered by events, haunted by our failures, shocked and shaken by the destruction of Baushpar, were all too eager to embrace self-destruction. Even Martyas, whose wicked cynicism utterly deserted him at the end. Even Hysanet, whom I'd hoped I could at least persuade to come with me into exile.

One day I woke, and knew that I would fight no more. With Reanu and Omarau, who were all I trusted out of the hundreds gathered in Faal, I made plans for a secret departure. It was not easy to arrange, for I was determined to bring with me my journals and Utamnos's—more than three thousand of them in sixty heavy boxes. But Reanu managed with his customary resourcefulness, and in the middle of a starry summer night, I and Utamnos and Ha-tsun and Reanu and Omarau slipped away. No doubt when my spirit-siblings found me gone, they assumed I, too, had headed for Rimpang. Instead we traveled north, toward Isar's remote and rocky coast, and settled in this town whose name I remember from my childhood, not far from the village where, fifty-two years ago, I was born.

With such of my wealth as I was able to carry with me, I purchased a little sheep farm. The barn, as I've said, has been turned into a storeroom, and the house expanded so that all of us can live in comfort and in decency. The people hereabouts find us curious, but I have made donations to Vahu's shrine and to the repair of the public fountains, and we are tolerated, if not accepted. We own a pair of goats and a flock of chickens, and we have a little garden, which Ha-tsun and I tend; I've learned to perform all manner of domestic tasks, and my hands are as rough now as a laborer's, my nails ingrained with dirt. In truth I take pleasure in the simplicity of this labor, which carries no great significance, which requires no great exercise of judgment, which when it is done is simply done and leaves no residue of triumph or regret.

I tried as I could to shield Utamnos from the conflict in Faal, but he could not help but be aware of it, and suffered as children do when they are swept up in affairs beyond their understanding. He was bewildered at first by the changes in the way we live, but with the resilience of the young adapted quickly. He looks like a peasant boy now, brown and sturdy, his feet hard from running barefoot in the summer. He remembers the ceremony and luxury of Baushpar, but only as one might recall a dream.

He is no peasant child, however. I am teaching him to know himself. His memories wait in the storeroom; soon he will be old enough to study them, and to begin his own record. At some point, I suppose I will have to consider going to Rimpang, where Kudrâcari and Dâdar and Ariamnes and Okhsa and Ciryas and young Sonrida have set up a diminished version of the council, and declared Kudrâcari the Blood Bearer. I know that none of them will welcome me. But Utamnos should know his spirit-siblings.

Well. That is not a decision I need to make just yet.

Kudrâcari, by the way, is said to wear a necklace identical to our father's, containing the authentic Blood. It is certainly the third crystal, the one Gyalo Amdo Samchen brought out of the Burning Land, which according to Tax-mârata vanished when she and the others fled Baushpar. Crafty Kudrâ. I'll wager it was not any dread of Râvar that spurred her flight; I think she planned a coup all along, though I don't suppose she imagined any circumstance in which her claim would go uncontested.

Although not quite uncontested. Not content with his victory in Faal, Taxmârata has become a proselytizer of sorts, traveling from monastery to nunnery to temple preaching the dissolution of the church. Reanu saw him in Fantzon, and heard him speak. He goes, apparently, in considerable luxury (having not neglected to bring with him from Baushpar much of his personal wealth), surrounded by a large company of Tapati. With him is little Athiya, who has been given back his birth name and is being raised in ignorance of his nature. Ah, the bitter anger that shakes me as I write of it! As yet, Taxmârata and Kudrâcari challenge only one another's works: She has issued a proclamation denying the coming of the Messenger, and endeavors to counter the spread of dissolution even as he labors to further it. No doubt there will one day be a more open confrontation.

The rest of my spirit-siblings—Karuva and Gaumârata, blind Haminâser and faithful Idrakara, Magabyras, Vimâta and little Ivaxri, my dear malicious Martyas, my beloved Hysanet and young Rukhsane, and cowardly, treacherous Vivaniya—are scattered to the winds. I know not where they are.

What else? In Arsace, Hathrida and his supporters outmaneuvered the queen and hers, and he was crowned King just over a year ago. He is not the ruler his brother was, and has not been able to foster unity within the fractious Lords' Assembly. Already there are signs that Arsace may split along ancient provincial lines, and rumor has it that Chonggye is preparing to reclaim the Sinha region, which Arsace annexed four hundred years ago.

Both false Messengers sought to strip Baushpar of its holiness. But for those who follow the heretical new faith, it is still a place of pilgrimage. Reanu, who has visited it, says that the city itself is deserted, but a transients' town has sprung up in what were once the manita fields, with hostels for pilgrims and a so-called temple of Ârata Awake—cylindrical like the old temples, but open to the sky, with no image of the god inside—and the usual array of brothels and taverns and cookshops and stalls selling overpriced religious trinkets. "It's disgusting," Reanu said, but I only shrugged. Baushpar is dead, beautiful Baushpar with its lotus domes, its shrines and temples, its incense and its bells. What does it matter what people do there now?

As yet there are no rumors of apostasy, or at least none that Reanu has heard. I am certain they will come.

Of Gyalo Amdo Samchen—of any living man calling himself the Messenger—there is no word at all. I don't understand it, and wonder if he met some mishap working in the ruins. Or perhaps he is only biding his time. The rage that fills me when I think of him is as bitter, as consuming, as on the night he spoke to me. Strangely, when I remember that night, it is often

Râvar's face I see looking at me from across the fire. My memory of Râvar, of whom I think far less often, is similarly mutable. But they were united in darkness, and each in a sense gave birth to the other. So perhaps it is not so strange after all.

It's to Reanu that I owe all this knowledge. Along with much else. It was he who got us here, he who taught me the ways of the life we now live. Now he brings the world to me, who can no longer go out into it. I rely on him more than I can say. And yet I feel a good deal of guilt, for though I know that he, and Omarau, too, chose exile gladly, it is a much-diminished life I have forced them to lead.

Recently I steeled myself—for I knew that if they accepted, it would be the first in a series of steps that would lead them away from me forever—I offered to release him and Omarau from their Âratist vows.

"You are still young men," I told him. "You could marry, raise families. You've sacrificed so much. It seems to me that you should have this, if you desire it."

He shook his head. He has let his hair grow out; it hangs now to the middle of his back, black and glossy. Omarau wears a beard to hide his tattoos, but Reanu goes proudly clean-shaven.

"I don't desire it, Old One." Like Ha-tsun, he refuses to stop using my title.

"Reanu." I put down my knife. We were in the kitchen, and I was peeling onions for the evening meal. "At least consider it. This shell of mine won't live forever. I can't bear to think that you will end your life alone."

"I won't be alone. When your spirit leaves the body you wear now, I and the Son Utamnos will seek you out in your new form. Old One, don't ask this of me. Please."

"This is the end." I had never given voice to this before, and it shocked me a little, how easy it was to say. "The false Messenger succeeded. The church is gone. You serve a lost cause."

"I serve Ârata." His eyes were fierce. "And you."

He got up from the table where he was sitting. He came and fell on his knees in front of me, and took my hands, my rough hands pungent with onions, and laid his face in them. I felt his breath on my palms, the flutter of his closed eyelids. I shut my own eyes. I shall not say what it was I felt.

There it is, then. Two years, disposed of in the same number of pages, where once I took twice that to record the events of a single day. It seems there is less to chronicle than I thought.

I know now the meaning of my dream, my dream of mirrors, which has not come to me in all the time since Baushpar fell. I stand apart from my spirit-siblings more fully than I ever imagined I might do. I have scattered the mirrors of my lives most thoroughly. Despite Reanu's promise, who will find me once my spirit leaves this shell?

Still, life goes on. Sometimes at sunset, or in another moment when the beauty of existence overwhelms me, I wonder how it is that so much change has left the world so unaltered. At other times I wonder whether there has been any change at all, beyond the predictable convulsions of human history. Did Ârata rise? Is the Messenger yet to come? Or does the god sleep still? Was all that happened only human folly?

Sometimes I question more than this, questions that strike at the very roots of my being and are too fearful to write down. At such times I feel myself unraveling, as if my life, which always seemed such a solid and seamless thing, were no more than thread wrapped on a spool. I've begun to wonder how much the certainties I cherished owed to the structure of my existence—the rituals, the teaching and the journals, the apparatus of rule, the reinforcement of my Brothers' and Sisters' belief—rather than to what rises from within: real faith, true knowledge.

I even wonder, sometimes, if I will be born again.

If I ever was.

Let that be my final confession.

Utamnos is calling. Soon I will go down and join the flow of life again.

The *Darxasa* says: *Dwell not in dread upon the morrow, for none may say what morning will bring forth. Turn not to yesterday in regret, for none can change the night that has already passed. Abide in the day, and be content.*

It is as good a thought as any, I suppose, on which to end.

Glossary

DRAMATIS PERSONAE

Gyalo Amdo Samchen—A former vowed Âratist, now a free Shaper

Axane—Gyalo's wife, a Dreamer, formerly of Refuge

Chokyi—Axane's daughter by Râvar

Ciri—Gyalo's and Axane's neighbor

Teispas dar Ispindi—Exile captain of the rescue expedition to the Burning Land, in which Gyalo was a participant; now deceased

Diasarta dar Abanish—A former Exile soldier, companion to Gyalo

Râvar—A Shaper, formerly of Refuge—the false Messenger

Ardashir dar Adrax (the First Disciple)—Râvar's second-in-command

Zabrades—One of Râvar's followers

Sariya—One of Râvar's followers

Cina—One of Râvar's followers

Gaubanita—A citizen of Râvar's Awakened City

Obâna—A citizen of Râvar's Awakened City

Narser—A citizen of Râvar's Awakened City

Imene—A citizen of Râvar's Awakened City

Vikrit—A child of Râvar's Awakened City

Santaxma—Present King and liberator of Arsace

Hathrida—His younger brother

Cas—One of his secretaries

Sundit—A Daughter of the Brethren

Utamnos—A Son, her spirit-ward

Ha-tsun—Her servant

Drolma—Her aide, a Shaper

Reanu—An Âratist ordinate from Kanu-Tapa, captain of her guard

Omarau—A Tapati guard

Lopalo—A Tapati guard

Apui—A Tapati guard

Mur—A Tapati guard

Karamsuu—A Tapati guard

Vivaniya—A Son of the Brethren

Amchila—His aide, a Shaper

Yailin—His servant

Taxmârata, also known as the Blood Bearer—A Son, elected leader of the
  Brethren

Athiya—A Son, Taxmârata's spirit-ward

Vimâta—A Son

Ivaxri—A Son, Vimâta's spirit-ward

Artavâdhi—A Daughter

Gaumârata—A Son, Artavâdhi's spirit-ward

Haminâser—A Son

Idrakara—A Son, Haminâser's spirit-ward

Baushtas—A Son

Yarios—A Son, Baushtas's spirit-ward

Ariamnes—A Son

Sonrida—A Son, Ariamnes's spirit-ward

Okhsa—A Son

Hysanet—A Daughter

Rukhsane—A Daughter, Hysanet's spirit-ward

Dâdar—A Son

Ciryas—A Son, Dâdar's spirit-ward

Martyas—A Son

Kudrâcari—A Daughter

Magabyras—A Son

Karuva—A Son, Magabyras's spirit-ward

Historical Characters

Marduspida—Prophet of Ârata, also known as the First Messenger

Fârat—King of Arsace, first royal convert to Âratism

Vantyas—King of Arsace, leader of the Âratist army during the Shaper War

Caryax—Atheistic Arsacian philosopher and social critic executed for treason

Voice of Caryax—Leader of the subsequent rebellion based on Caryax's precepts

Vandapâya IV—Arsacian king deposed by the Caryaxists

GODS AND ASPECTS

Ârata—The sleeping god, principal deity of the Âratist religion

Ârdaxcasa—Ârata's dark brother and foe, also known as the Enemy

Dâdarshi—Aspect of Ârata, patron of luck

Skambys—Aspect of Ârata, patron of war and weather

Hataspa—Aspect of Ârata, patron of fire and weaponry

Tane—Aspect of Ârata, patroness of crops and the moon

Vahu—Aspect of Ârata, patron of healing and childbirth

Jo-Mea—Aspect of Ârata, patron of travelers

Inriku—Aspect of Ârata, patron of wisdom and the arts

PLACE-NAMES

Galea—Continent of the Seven Kingdoms, believed by its inhabitants to be the only landmass in the world

Arsace—Largest and richest of the seven kingdoms, birthplace of the Âratist faith

Baushpar—An Arsacian city, traditional headquarters of the Âratist church

First Temple of Ârata—Ârata's temple in Baushpar, the largest and oldest temple in Galea

Ninyâser—Arsace's capital

Great South Way—A highway built by the Caryaxist regime for transport from Ninyâser to the Burning Land

Fashir—A town along the Great South Way

Darna—A garrison city along the Great South Way

Orimene—A town along the Great South Way

Sardis—A city along the Great South Way

Hâras—A town along the Great South Way

Abaxtra—A city along the Great South Way

Dracâriya Hills—A stretch of barren hill country along the Great South Way

The Hatane—An Arsacian river

Kanu-Tapa—A kingdom of Galea, known for its martial skills

Haruko—Another kingdom of Galea, home to a large population of Arsacian refugees from Caryaxist persecution

Aino—Another kingdom of Galea, home to most Dreamer monasteries and nunneries

Chonggye—Another kingdom of Galea, refuge of the Brethren during the time of Caryaxist rule in Arsace

Rimpang—Chonggye's capital, seat of the Brethren during their Caryaxist exile

Isar—A non-Âratist kingdom of Galea

Faal—A remote Âratist monastery in Isar, in which Gyalo was imprisoned for a time

Yahaz—A non-Âratist kingdom of Galea

The Burning Land—An enormous, unexplored desert occupying the whole of Galea's southern portion, sacred to Ârata, who according to Âratist belief lies sleeping there

Range of Clouds—A vast mountain range that divides the kingdoms of Galea from the Burning Land

Thuxra Notch—The pass through the Range of Clouds that gives access to the Burning Land

Thuxra City—A prison built by the atheistic Caryaxist regime at the edges of the Burning Land, as a deliberate desecration of holy ground

Refuge—Rock-carved settlement of a group of Âratist refugees from Caryaxist persecution, located deep in the Burning Land

Revelation—Refuge's river

Plains of Blessing—The grass steppes beyond Refuge

Labyrinth—Refuge's living quarters

Treasury—A complex housing Refuge's workshops and storehouses

House of Dreams—Abode of Refuge's Dreamers

MISCELLANEOUS TERMS

Âratism (Âratist)—Dominant religion of Galea, followed in all but two of the seven kingdoms

Way of Ârata—Broad term covering the secular and religious practice of Âratism; includes ethical as well as religious precepts

The Five Foundations—The central credos of Âratism: Faith, Affirmation, Increase, Consciousness, and Compassion

Darxasa—Âratism's holy scripture; the word of the god as dictated to Marduspida, the First Messenger

Book of the Messenger—Âratism's second scripture; the life story of the First Messenger

The Next Messenger—Herald of Ârata's awakening

Ârata's Promise—Prophecy of the Next Messenger's coming

The Brethren—The thirty-five Sons and Daughters of the First Messenger, perpetually reincarnated as leaders of the Âratist church. All incarnations born into Arsace during the Caryaxist occupation were lost; only twenty-four incarnations are currently known

The Brethren's Covenant—The pact with Ârata by which the Brethren became immortal

The Blood Bearer—Elected leader of the Brethren

Vowed Âratist—Men and women sworn to Ârata's service

The Sixfold Vow—The vow they take on ordination: to abjure doubt, ignorance, greed, complacency, pride, and fear, the Six Failings that caused the First Messenger six times to reject Ârata's summoning dream

Dreaming (Dreamer)—The power of true dreaming; according to Âratist belief, born into humankind after Ârata lay down to sleep

Shaping (Shaper)—The power to form, unform, and transform inanimate matter; according to Âratist belief, granted to humankind by Ârata at creation

Manita—Plant whose leaves yield a drug that suppresses shaping ability

Doctrine of Baushpar—Seven-point creed formulated after the Shaper War, defining shaping as the property of the church

The Shaper War—Ancient conflict in which pagan Shapers, angry at Âratist attempts to place limits on shaping's practice, attempted to eradicate the Âratist faith from Galea

Caryaxism (Caryaxist)—Modern atheistic political movement that came briefly to power in Arsace

The Awakened City—Râvar's pilgrim army; not a physical city, but a spiritual one